Illustrated Sterling Edition

A STRANGE STORY

BY

EDWARD BULWER LYTTON

WILDSIDE PRESS

www.wildsidepress.com

PREFACE.

Of the many illustrious thinkers whom the schools of France have contributed to the intellectual philosophy of our age, Victor Cousin, the most accomplished, assigns to Maine de Biran the rank of the most original.

In the successive developments of his own mind, Maine de Biran may, indeed, be said to represent the change that has been silently at work throughout the general mind of Europe since the close of the last century. He begins his career of philosopher with blind faith in Condillac and Materialism. As an intellect severely conscientious in the pursuit of truth expands amidst the perplexities it revolves, phenomena which cannot be accounted for by Condillac's sensuous theories open to his eye. To the first rudimentary life of man, the animal life, " characterized by impressions, appetites, movements, organic in their origin and ruled by the Law of Necessity," [1] he is compelled to add, " the second, or human life, from which Free-will and Self-consciousness emerge." He thus arrives at the union of mind and matter; but still a something is wanted, — some key to the marvels which neither of these conditions of vital being suffices to explain. And at last the grand self-completing Thinker attains to the Third Life of Man in Man's Soul.

" There are not," says this philosopher, towards the close of his last and loftiest work, — " there are not only two principles opposed to each other in Man, — there are three. For

---

[1] Œuvres inédites de Maine de Biran, vol. i. See introduction.

there are in him three lives and three orders of faculties.
Though all should be in accord and in harmony between the
sensitive and the active faculties which constitute Man, there
would still be a nature superior, a third life which would not
be satisfied ; which would make felt (*ferait sentir*) the truth
that there is another happiness, another wisdom, another perfection, at once above the greatest human happiness, above the
highest wisdom, or intellectual and moral perfection of which
the human being is susceptible." [1]

Now, as Philosophy and Romance both take their origin
in the Principle of Wonder, so in the " Strange Story " submitted to the Public it will be seen that Romance, through
the freest exercise of its wildest vagaries, conducts its
bewildered hero towards the same goal to which Philosophy
leads its luminous Student, through far grander portents of
Nature, far higher visions of Supernatural Power, than Fable can yield to Fancy. That goal is defined in these
noble words : —

" The relations (*rapports*) which exist between the elements
and the products of the three lives of Man are the subjects of
meditation, the fairest and finest, but also the most difficult.
The Stoic Philosophy shows us all which can be most elevated
in active life ; but it makes abstraction of the animal nature,
and absolutely fails to recognize all which belongs to the life
of the spirit. Its practical morality is beyond the forces of
humanity. Christianity alone embraces the whole Man. It
dissimulates none of the sides of his nature, and avails itself
of his miseries and his weakness in order to conduct him to
his end in showing him all the want that he has of a succor
more exalted." [2]

In the passages thus quoted, I imply one of the objects
for which this tale has been written ; and I cite them, with
a wish to acknowledge one of those priceless obligations

[1] Œuvres inédites de Maine de Biran, vol. iii. p. 546 (Anthropologie).
[2] Œuvres inédites de Maine de Biran, vol. iii. p. 524.

which writings the lightest and most fantastic often incur to reasoners the most serious and profound.

But I here construct a romance which should have, as a romance, some interest for the general reader. I do not elaborate a treatise submitted to the logic of sages. And it is only when " in fairy fiction drest " that Romance gives admission to " truths severe."

I venture to assume that none will question my privilege to avail myself of the marvellous agencies which have ever been at the legitimate command of the fabulist.

To the highest form of romantic narrative, the Epic, crit-ics, indeed, have declared that a supernatural machinery is indispensable. That the Drama has availed itself of the same license as the Epic, it would be unnecessary to say to the countrymen of Shakspeare, or to the generation that is yet studying the enigmas of Goethe's " Faust." Prose Romance has immemorially asserted, no less than the Epic or the Drama, its heritage in the Realm of the Marvellous. The interest which attaches to the supernatural is sought in the earliest Prose Romance which modern times take from the ancient, and which, perhaps, had its origin in the lost Novels of Miletus ;[1] and the right to invoke such in-terest has, ever since, been maintained by Romance through all varieties of form and fancy, — from the majestic epopee of " Télémaque " to the graceful fantasies of " Undine," or the mighty mockeries of " Gulliver's Travels " down to such comparatively commonplace elements of wonder as yet preserve from oblivion " The Castle of Otranto " and " The Old English Baron."

Now, to my mind, the true reason why a supernatural agency is indispensable to the conception of the Epic, is that the Epic is the highest and the completest form in which Art can express either Man or Nature, and that

[1] " The Golden Ass " of Apuleius.

without some gleams of the supernatural, Man is not man, nor Nature, nature.

It is said, by a writer to whom an eminent philosophical critic justly applies the epithets of " pious and profound : " [1]

"Is it unreasonable to confess that we believe in God, not by reason of the Nature which conceals Him, but by reason of the Supernatural in Man which alone reveals and proves Him to exist? . . . . Man reveals God : for Man, by his intelligence, rises above Nature; and in virtue of this intelligence is conscious of himself as a power not only independent of, but opposed to, Nature, and capable of resisting, conquering, and controlling her." [2]

If the meaning involved in the argument, of which I have here made but scanty extracts, be carefully studied, I think that we shall find deeper reasons than the critics who dictated canons of taste to the last century discovered, — why the supernatural is indispensable to the Epic, and why it is allowable to all works of imagination, in which Art looks on Nature with Man's inner sense of a something beyond and above her.

But the Writer who, whether in verse or prose, would avail himself of such sources of pity or terror as flow from the Marvellous, can only attain his object in proportion as the wonders he narrates are of a kind to excite the curiosity of the age he addresses.

In the brains of our time, the faculty of *Causation* is very markedly developed. People nowadays do not delight in the Marvellous according to the old childlike spirit. They say in one breath, " Very extraordinary ! " and in the next breath ask, " How do you account for it ? " If the Author of this work has presumed to borrow from science some elements of interest for Romance, he ventures to hope that

[1] Sir William Hamilton : Lectures on Metaphysics, p. 40.
[2] Jacobi : Von der Göttlichen Dingen ; Werke, p. 424–426.

no thoughtful reader — and certainly no true son of science — will be disposed to reproach him. In fact, such illustrations from the masters of Thought were essential to the completion of the purpose which pervades the work.

That purpose, I trust, will develop itself in proportion as the story approaches the close; and whatever may appear violent or melodramatic in the catastrophe, will, perhaps, be found, by a reader capable of perceiving the various symbolical meanings conveyed in the story, essential to the end in which those meanings converge, and towards which the incidents that give them the character and interest of fiction, have been planned and directed from the commencement.

Of course, according to the most obvious principles of art, the narrator of a fiction must be as thoroughly in earnest as if he were the narrator of facts. One could not tell the most extravagant fairy-tale so as to rouse and sustain the attention of the most infantine listener, if the tale were told as if the tale-teller did not believe in it. But when the reader lays down this "Strange Story," perhaps he will detect, through all the haze of romance, the outlines of these images suggested to his reason: Firstly, the image of sensuous, soulless Nature, such as the Materialist had conceived it; secondly, the image of Intellect, obstinately separating all its inquiries from the belief in the spiritual essence and destiny of man, and incurring all kinds of perplexity and resorting to all kinds of visionary speculation before it settles at last into the simple faith which unites the philosopher and the infant; and thirdly, the image of the erring but pure-thoughted visionary, seeking over-much on this earth to separate soul from mind, till innocence itself is led astray by a phantom, and reason is lost in the space between earth and the stars. Whether in these pictures there be any truth worth the implying, every reader

must judge for himself ; and if he doubt or deny that there
be any such truth, still, in the process of thought which
the doubt or denial enforces, he may chance on a truth
which it pleases himself to discover.

"Most of the Fables of Æsop," — thus says Montaigne in
his charming essay " Of Books " [1] — " have several senses and
meanings, of which the Mythologists choose some one that tal-
lies with the fable.   But for the most part 't is only what presents itself at the first view, and is superficial ; there being
others more lively, essential, and internal, into which they
had not been able to penetrate ; and " — adds Montaigne —
" the case is the very same with me."

[1] Translation, 1776, vol. ii. p. 103.

LIST OF ILLUSTRATIONS.

A STRANGE STORY.

A STRANGE STORY.

CHAPTER I.

In the year 18— I settled as a physician at one of the wealthiest of our great English towns, which I will designate by the initial L——. I was yet young, but I had acquired some reputation by a professional work, which is, I believe, still amongst the received authorities on the subject of which it treats. I had studied at Edinburgh and at Paris, and had borne away from both those illustrious schools of medicine whatever guarantees for future distinction the praise of professors may concede to the ambition of students. On becoming a member of the College of Physicians, I made a tour of the principal cities of Europe, taking letters of introduction to eminent medical men, and gathering from many theories and modes of treatment· hints to enlarge the foundations of unprejudiced and comprehensive practice. I had resolved to fix my ultimate residence in London. But before this preparatory tour was completed, my resolve was changed by one of those unexpected events which determine the fate man in vain would work out for himself. In passing through the Tyro, on my way into the north of Italy, I found in a small inn, remote from medical attendance, an English traveller seized with acute inflammation of the lungs, and in a state of imminent danger. I devoted myself to him night and day; and, perhaps more through careful nursing than active remedies, I had the happiness to effect his complete recovery. The traveller proved to be Julius Faber, a physician of great distinction, contented to reside, where he was born, in the provincial city of L——, but whose reputation as a profound and original pathologist was widely spread, and whose writings had formed no unimportant part of my special studies. It was during a short holiday excursion, from which he was about to return with renovated vigour, that he had been thus stricken down. The patient so accidentally met with became the founder of my professional fortunes. He conceived a warm attachment for me,—perhaps the more affectionate because he was a childless bachelor, and the nephew who would succeed to his wealth evinced no desire to succeed to the toils by which the wealth had been acquired. Thus, having an heir for the one, he had long looked about for an heir to the other, and now resolved on finding that heir in me. So when we parted Dr. Faber made me promise to correspond with him regularly, and it was not long before he disclosed by letter the plans he had formed in my favour. He said that he was growing old; his practice was beyond his strength; he needed a partner; he was not disposed to put up to sale the health of patients whom he had learned to regard as his children: money was no object to him, but it was an object close at his heart that the humanity he had served, and the reputation he had acquired, should suffer no loss in his choice of a successor. In fine, he proposed that I should at once come to L—— as his partner, with the view of succeeding to his entire practice at the end of two years, when it was his intention to retire.

The opening into fortune thus afforded to me was one that rarely presents itself to a young man entering upon an overcrowded profession; and to an aspirant less allured by the desire of fortune than the hope of distinction, the fame of the physician who thus generously offered to me the inestimable benefits of his long experience and his cordial introduction was in itself an assurance that a metropolitan practice is not essential to a national renown.

I went, then, to L——, and before the two years of my partnership had expired, my success justified my kind friend's selection, and far more than realized my own expectations. I was fortunate in effecting some notable cures in the earliest cases submitted to me, and it is everything in the career of a physician when good luck wins betimes for him that confidence which patients rarely accord except to lengthened experience. To the rapid facility with which my way was made, some circumstances apart from professional skill probably contributed. I was saved from the suspicion of a medical adventurer by the accidents of birth and fortune. I belonged to an ancient family (a branch of the once powerful border-clan of the Fenwicks) that had for many generations held a fair estate in the neighbourhood of Windermere. As an only son I had succeeded to that estate on attaining my majority, and had sold it to pay off the debts which had been made by my father, who had the costly tastes of an antiquary and collector. The residue on the sale insured me a modest independence apart from the profits of a profession; and as I had not been legally bound to defray my father's debts, so I obtained that character for disinterestedness and integrity which always in England tends to propitiate the public to the successes achieved by industry or talent. Perhaps, too, any professional ability I might possess was the more readily conceded, because I had cultivated with assiduity the sciences and the scholarship which are collaterally connected with the study of medicine. Thus, in a word, I established a social position which came in aid of my professional repute, and silenced much of that envy which usually embitters and sometimes impedes success.

Dr. Faber retired at the end of the two years agreed upon. He went abroad; and being, though advanced in years, of a frame still robust, and habits of mind still inquiring and eager, he commenced a lengthened course of foreign travel, during which our correspondence, at first frequent, gradually languished, and finally died away.

I succeeded at once to the larger part of the practice which the labours of thirty years had secured to my predecessor. My chief rival was a Dr. Lloyd, a benevolent, fervid man, not without genius, if genius be present where judgment is absent; not without science, if that may be science which fails in precision,— one of those clever desultory men who, in adopting a profession, do not give up to it the whole force and heat of their minds. Men of that kind habitually accept a mechanical routine, because in the exercise of their ostensible calling their imaginative faculties are drawn away to pursuits more alluring. Therefore, in their proper vocation they are seldom bold or inventive,— out of it they are sometimes both to excess. And when they do take up a novelty in their own profession they cherish it with an obstinate tenacity, and an extravagant passion, unknown to those quiet philosophers who take up novelties every day, examine them with the sobriety of practised eyes, to lay down altogether, modify in part, or accept in whole, according as inductive experiment supports or destroys conjecture.

Dr. Lloyd had been esteemed a learned naturalist long before he was admitted to be a tolerable physician. Amidst the privations of his youth he had contrived to form, and with each succeeding year he had perseveringly increased, a zoölogical collection of creatures, not alive, but, happily for the beholder, stuffed or embalmed. From what I have said, it will be truly inferred that Dr. Lloyd's early career as a physician had not been brilliant; but of late years he had gradually rather *aged* than worked himself into that professional authority and station which time confers on a thoroughly respectable man whom no one is disposed to envy, and all are disposed to like.

Now in L—— there were two distinct social circles,— that of the wealthy merchants and traders, and that of a few privileged families inhabiting a part of the town aloof from the marts of commerce, and called the Abbey Hill. These superb Areopagites exercised over the wives and daughters of the inferior citizens to whom all of L——, except the Abbey Hill, owed its prosperity, the same kind of mysterious influence which the fine ladies of May Fair and Belgravia are reported to hold over the female denizens of Bloomsbury and Marylebone.

Abbey Hill was not opulent; but it was powerful by a concentration of its resources in all matters of patronage. Abbey Hill had its own milliner and its own draper, its own confectioner, butcher, baker, and tea-dealer; and the patronage of

Abbey Hill was like the patronage of royalty,—less lucrative
in itself than as a solemn certificate of general merit.   The
shops on which Abbey Hill conferred its custom were certainly not the cheapest, possibly not the best; but they were
undeniably the most imposing.   The proprietors were deco-
rously pompous, the shopmen superciliously polite.   They
could not be more so if they had belonged to the State, and
been paid by a public which they benefited and despised.
The ladies of Low Town (as the city subjacent to the Hill
had been styled from a date remote in the feudal ages) entered those shops with a certain awe, and left them with a
certain pride.   There they had learned what the Hill approved; there they had bought what the Hill had purchased.
It is much in this life to be quite sure that we are in the
right, whatever that conviction may cost us.   Abbey Hill
had been in the habit of appointing, amongst other objects of
patronage, its own physician.   But that habit had fallen into
disuse during the latter years of my predecessor's practice.
His superiority over all other medical men in the town had
become so incontestable, that, though he was emphatically
the doctor of Low Town, the head of its hospitals and infirma-
ries, and by birth related to its principal traders, still as
Abbey Hill was occasionally subject to the physical infirmities of meaner mortals, so on those occasions it deemed it best
not to push the point of honour to the wanton sacrifice of life.
Since Low Town possessed one of the most famous physicians
in England, Abbey Hill magnanimously resolved not to crush
him by a rival.   Abbey Hill let him feel its pulse.

When my predecessor retired, I had presumptuously expected that the Hill would have continued to suspend its normal right to a special physician, and shown to me the same
generous favour it had shown to him, who had declared me
worthy to succeed to his honours.   I had the more excuse for
this presumption because the Hill had already allowed me to
visit a fair proportion of its invalids, had said some very
gracious things to me about the great respectability of the
Fenwick family, and sent me some invitations to dinner, and
a great many invitations to tea.

But my self-conceit received a notable check. Abbey Hill declared that the time had come to reassert its dormant privilege; it must have a doctor of its own choosing,— a doctor who might, indeed, be permitted to visit Low Town from motives of humanity or gain, but who must emphatically assert his special allegiance to Abbey Hill by fixing his home on that venerable promontory. Miss Brabazon, a spinster of uncertain age but undoubted pedigree, with small fortune but high nose, which she would pleasantly observe was a proof of her descent from Humphrey Duke of Gloucester (with whom, indeed, I have no doubt, in spite of chronology, that she very often dined), was commissioned to inquire of me diplomatically, and without committing Abbey Hill too much by the overture, whether I would take a large and antiquated mansion, in which abbots were said to have lived many centuries ago, and which was still popularly styled Abbots' House, situated on the verge of the Hill, as in that case the "Hill" would think of me.

"It is a large house for a single man, I allow," said Miss Brabazon, candidly; and then added, with a sidelong glance of alarming sweetness, "but when Dr. Fenwick has taken his true position (so old a family!) amongst us, he need not long remain single, unless he prefer it."

I replied, with more asperity than the occasion called for, that I had no thought of changing my residence at present, and if the Hill wanted me, the Hill must send for me.

Two days afterwards Dr. Lloyd took Abbots' House, and in less than a week was proclaimed medical adviser to the Hill. The election had been decided by the fiat of a great lady, who reigned supreme on the sacred eminence, under the name and title of Mrs. Colonel Poyntz.

"Dr. Fenwick," said this lady, "is a clever young man and a gentleman, but he gives himself airs,— the Hill does not allow any airs but its own. Besides, he is a new comer: resistance to new comers, and, indeed, to all things new, except caps and novels, is one of the bonds that keep old established societies together. Accordingly, it is by my advice that Dr. Lloyd has taken Abbots' House; the rent would be too high

for his means if the Hill did not feel bound in honour to justify the trust he has placed in its patronage. I told him that
all my friends, when they were in want of a doctor, would
send for him; those who are my friends will do so. What
the Hill does, plenty of common people down *there* will do
also,— so that question is settled!" And it was settled.

Dr. Lloyd, thus taken by the hand, soon extended the range
of his visits beyond the Hill, which was not precisely a
mountain of gold to doctors, and shared with myself, though
in a comparatively small degree, the much more lucrative
practice of Low Town.

I had no cause to grudge his success, nor did I. But to my
theories of medicine his diagnosis was shallow, and his prescriptions obsolete. When we were summoned to a joint
consultation, our views as to the proper course of treatment
seldom agreed. Doubtless he thought I ought to have deferred to his seniority in years; but I held the doctrine which
youth deems a truth and age a paradox,— namely, that in
science the young men are the practical elders, inasmuch as
they are schooled in the latest experiences science has gathered up, while their seniors are cramped by the dogmas they
were schooled to believe when the world was some decades
the younger.

Meanwhile my reputation continued rapidly to advance; it
became more than local; my advice was sought even by patients from the metropolis. That ambition, which, conceived
in early youth, had decided my career and sweetened all its
labours,— the ambition to take a rank and leave a name as
one of the great pathologists to whom humanity accords a
grateful, if calm, renown,— saw before it a level field and a
certain goal.

I know not whether a success far beyond that usually attained at the age I had reached served to increase, but it
seemed to myself to justify, the main characteristic of my
moral organization,— intellectual pride.

Though mild and gentle to the sufferers under my care, as
a necessary element of professional duty, I was intolerant of
contradiction from those who belonged to my calling, or even

from those who, in general opinion, opposed my favourite theories.

I had espoused a school of medical philosophy severely rigid in its inductive logic. My creed was that of stern materialism. I had a contempt for the understanding of men who accepted with credulity what they could not explain by reason. My favourite phrase was "common-sense." At the same time I had no prejudice against bold discovery, and discovery necessitates conjecture, but I dismissed as idle all conjecture that could not be brought to a practical test.

As in medicine I had been the pupil of Broussais, so in metaphysics I was the disciple of Condillac. I believed with that philosopher that "all our knowledge we owe to Nature; that in the beginning we can only instruct ourselves through her lessons; and that the whole art of reasoning consists in continuing as she has compelled us to commence." Keeping natural philosophy apart from the doctrines of revelation, I never assailed the last; but I contended that by the first no accurate reasoner could arrive at the existence of the soul as a third principle of being equally distinct from mind and body. That by a miracle man might live again, was a question of faith and not of understanding. I left faith to religion, and banished it from philosophy. How define with a precision to satisfy the logic of philosophy what was to live again? The body? We know that the body rests in its grave till by the process of decomposition its elemental parts enter into other forms of matter. The mind? But the mind was as clearly the result of the bodily organization as the music of the harpsichord is the result of the instrumental mechanism. The mind shared the decrepitude of the body in extreme old age, and in the full vigour of youth a sudden injury to the brain might forever destroy the intellect of a Plato or a Shakspeare. But the third principle,—the soul,— the something lodged within the body, which yet was to survive it? Where was that soul hidden out of the ken of the anatomist? When philosophers attempted to define it, were they not compelled to confound its nature and its actions with those of the mind? Could they reduce it to the mere moral sense, varying according to education, circumstances, and physical constitution? But even the moral sense in the most virtuous of men may be swept away by a fever. Such at the time I now speak of were the views I held,— views certainly not original nor pleasing; but I cherished them with as fond a tenacity as if they had been consolatory truths of which I was the first discoverer. I was intolerant to those who maintained opposite doctrines,— despised them as irrational, or disliked them as insincere. Certainly if I had fulfilled the career which my ambition predicted,— become the founder of a new school in pathology, and summed up my theories in academical lectures,— I should have added another authority, however feeble, to the sects which circumscribe the interest of man to the life that has its close in his grave.

Possibly that which I have called my intellectual pride was more nourished than I should have been willing to grant by the self-reliance which an unusual degree of physical power is apt to bestow. Nature had blessed me with the thews of an athlete. Among the hardy youths of the Northern Athens I had been pre-eminently distinguished for feats of activity and strength. My mental labours, and the anxiety which is inseparable from the conscientious responsibilities of the medical profession, kept my health below the par of keen enjoyment, but had in no way diminished my rare muscular force. I walked through the crowd with the firm step and lofty crest of the mailed knight of old, who felt himself, in his casement of iron, a match against numbers. Thus the sense of a robust individuality, strong alike in disciplined reason and animal vigour, habituated to aid others, needing no aid for itself, contributed to render me imperious in will and arrogant in opinion. Nor were such defects injurious to me in my profession; on the contrary, aided as they were by a calm manner, and a presence not without that kind of dignity which is the livery of self-esteem, they served to impose respect and to inspire trust.

CHAPTER II.

I HAD been about six years at L—— when I became suddenly involved in a controversy with Dr. Lloyd. Just as this
ill-fated man appeared at the culminating point of his professional fortunes, he had the imprudence to proclaim himself
not only an enthusiastic advocate of mesmerism as a curative
process, but an ardent believer of the reality of somnambular
clairvoyance as an invaluable gift of certain privileged organizations. To these doctrines I sternly opposed myself,
— the more sternly, perhaps, because on these doctrines
Dr. Lloyd founded an argument for the existence of soul,
independent of mind, as of matter, and built thereon a super-
structure of physiological fantasies, which, could it be substantiated, would replace every system of metaphysics on
which recognized philosophy condescends to dispute.

About two years before he became a disciple rather of Puysegur than Mesmer (for Mesmer had little faith in that gift
of clairvoyance of which Puysegur was, I believe, at least in
modern times, the first audacious asserter), Dr. Lloyd had
been afflicted with the loss of a wife many years younger than
himself, and to whom he had been tenderly attached. And
this bereavement, in directing the hopes that consoled him to
a world beyond the grave, had served perhaps to render him
more credulous of the phenomena in which he greeted additional proofs of purely spiritual existence. Certainly, if, in
controverting the notions of another physiologist, I had re-
stricted myself to that fair antagonism which belongs to
scientific disputants anxious only for the truth, I should need
no apology for sincere conviction and honest argument; but
when, with condescending good-nature, as if to a man much
younger than himself, who was ignorant of the phenomena
which he nevertheless denied, Dr. Lloyd invited me to attend
his *séances* and witness his cures, my *amour propre* became

aroused and nettled, and it seemed to me necessary to put
down what I asserted to be too gross an outrage on common-
sense to justify the ceremony of examination. I wrote, therefore, a small pamphlet on the subject, in which I exhausted
all the weapons that irony can lend to contempt. Dr. Lloyd
replied; and as he was no very skilful arguer, his reply injured him perhaps more than my assault. Meanwhile, I had
made some inquiries as to the moral character of his favourite
clairvoyants. I imagined that I had learned enough to justify
me in treating them as flagrant cheats, and himself as their
egregious dupe.

Low Town soon ranged itself, with very few exceptions, on
my side. The Hill at first seemed disposed to rally round its
insulted physician, and to make the dispute a party question,
in which the Hill would have been signally worsted, when
suddenly the same lady paramount, who had secured to Dr.
Lloyd the smile of the Eminence, spoke forth against him,
and the Eminence frowned.

"Dr. Lloyd," said the Queen of the Hill, "is an amiable
creature, but on this subject decidedly cracked. Cracked
poets may be all the better for being cracked, — cracked doctors are dangerous. Besides, in deserting that old-fashioned
routine, his adherence to which made his claim to the Hill's
approbation, and unsettling the mind of the Hill with wild
revolutionary theories, Dr. Lloyd has betrayed the principles
on which the Hill itself rests its social foundations. Of those
principles Dr. Fenwick has made himself champion; and
the Hill is bound to support him. There, the question is
settled!"

And it was settled.

From the moment Mrs. Colonel Poyntz thus issued the
word of command, Dr. Lloyd was demolished. His practice
was gone, as well as his repute. Mortification or anger
brought on a stroke of paralysis which, disabling my opponent, put an end to our controversy. An obscure Dr. Jones,
who had been the special pupil and *protégé* of Dr. Lloyd,
offered himself as a candidate for the Hill's tongues and
pulses. The Hill gave him little encouragement. It once

more suspended its electoral privileges, and, without insist-
ing on calling me up to it, the Hill quietly called me in
whenever its health needed other advice than that of its visiting apothecary. Again it invited me, sometimes to dinner,
often to tea; and again Miss Brabazon assured me by a
sidelong glance that it was no fault of hers if I were still
single.

I had almost forgotten the dispute which had obtained for
me so conspicuous a triumph, when one winter's night I was
roused from sleep by a summons to attend Dr Lloyd, who,
attacked by a second stroke a few hours previously, had, on
recovering sense, expressed a vehement desire to consult the
rival by whom he had suffered so severely. I dressed myself
in haste and hurried to his house.

A February night, sharp and bitter; an iron-gray frost below, a spectral melancholy moon above. I had to ascend the
Abbey Hill by a steep, blind lane between high walls. I
passed through stately gates, which stood wide open, into the
garden ground that surrounded the old Abbots' House. At
the end of a short carriage-drive the dark and gloomy building
cleared itself from leafless skeleton trees, — the moon resting
keen and cold on its abrupt gables and lofty chimney-stacks.
An old woman-servant received me at the door, and, without
saying a word, led me through a long low hall, and up dreary
oak stairs, to a broad landing, at which she paused for a moment, listening. Round and about hall, staircase, and landing
were ranged the dead specimens of the savage world which it
had been the pride of the naturalist's life to collect. Close
where I stood yawned the open jaws of the fell anaconda, its
lower coils hidden, as they rested on the floor below, by the
winding of the massive stairs. Against the dull wainscot
walls were pendent cases stored with grotesque unfamiliar
mummies, seen imperfectly by the moon that shot through
the window-panes, and the candle in the old woman's hand.
And as now she turned towards me, nodding her signal to
follow, and went on up the shadowy passage, rows of gigantic
birds — ibis and vulture, and huge sea glaucus — glared at
me in the false light of their hungry eyes.

So I entered the sick-room, and the first glance told me that my art was powerless there.

The children of the stricken widower were grouped round his bed, the eldest apparently about fifteen, the youngest four; one little girl — the only female child — was clinging to her father's neck, her face pressed to his bosom, and in that room her sobs alone were loud.

As I passed the threshold, Dr. Lloyd lifted his face, which had been bent over the weeping child, and gazed on me with an aspect of strange glee, which I failed to interpret. Then as I stole towards him softly and slowly, he pressed his lips on the long fair tresses that streamed wild over his breast, motioned to a nurse who stood beside his pillow to take the child away, and in a voice clearer than I could have expected in one on whose brow lay the unmistakable hand of death, he bade the nurse and the children quit the room. All went sorrowfully, but silently, save the little girl, who, borne off in the nurse's arms, continued to sob as if her heart were breaking.

I was not prepared for a scene so affecting; it moved me to the quick. My eyes wistfully followed the children so soon to be orphans, as one after one went out into the dark chill shadow, and amidst the bloodless forms of the dumb brute nature, ranged in grisly vista beyond the death-room of man. And when the last infant shape had vanished, and the door closed with a jarring click, my sight wandered loiteringly around the chamber before I could bring myself to ·fix it on the broken form, beside which I now stood in all that glorious vigour of frame which had fostered the pride of my mind. In the moment consumed by my mournful survey, the whole aspect of the place impressed itself ineffaceably on lifelong remembrance. Through the high, deep-sunken casement, across which the thin, faded curtain was but half drawn, the moonlight rushed, and then settled on the floor in one shroud of white glimmer, lost under the gloom of the death-bed. The roof was low, and seemed lower still by heavy intersecting beams, which I might have touched with my lifted hand. And the tall guttering candle by the bed-

side, and the flicker from the fire struggling out through the
fuel but newly heaped on it, threw their reflection on the
ceiling just over my head in a reek of quivering blackness,
like an angry cloud.

Suddenly I felt my arm grasped; with his left hand (the
right side was already lifeless) the dying man drew me
towards him nearer and nearer, till his lips almost touched
my ear, and, in a voice now firm, now splitting into gasp and
hiss, thus he said,—

"I have summoned you to gaze on your own work! You
have stricken down my life at the moment when it was most
needed by my children, and most serviceable to mankind.
Had I lived a few years longer, my children would have entered on manhood, safe from the temptations of want and
undejected by the charity of strangers. Thanks to you, they
will be penniless orphans. Fellow-creatures afflicted by maladies your pharmacopœia had failed to reach came to me for
relief, and they found it. 'The effect of imagination,' you
say. What matters, if I directed the imagination to cure?
Now you have mocked the unhappy ones out of their last
chance of life. They will suffer and perish. Did you believe me in error? Still you knew that my object was research into truth. You employed against your brother in art
venomous drugs and a poisoned probe. Look at me! Are
you satisfied with your work?"

I sought to draw back and pluck my arm from the dying
man's grasp. I could not do so without using a force that
would have been inhuman. His lips drew nearer still to my
ear.

"Vain pretender, do not boast that you brought a genius for
epigram to the service of science. Science is lenient to all
who offer experiment as the test of conjecture. You are of
the stuff of which inquisitors are made. You cry that truth
is profaned when your dogmas are questioned. In your shallow presumption you have meted the dominions of nature,
and where your eye halts its vision, you say, 'There nature
must close;' in the bigotry which adds crime to presumption,
you would stone the discoverer who, in annexing new realms

to her chart, unsettles your arbitrary landmarks. Verily, retribution shall await you! In those spaces which your sight has disdained to explore you shall yourself be a lost and bewildered straggler. Hist! I see them already! The gibbering phantoms are gathering round you!"

The man's voice stopped abruptly; his eye fixed in a glazing stare; his hand relaxed its hold; he fell back on his pillow. I stole from the room; on the landing-place I met the nurse and the old woman-servant. Happily the children were not there. But I heard the wail of the female child from some room not far distant.

I whispered hurriedly to the nurse, "All is over!" passed again under the jaws of the vast anaconda, and on through the blind lane between the dead walls, on through the ghastly streets, under the ghastly moon, went back to my solitary home.

CHAPTER III.

IT was some time before I could shake off the impression made on me by the words and the look of that dying man.

It was not that my conscience upbraided me. What had I done? Denounced that which I held, in common with most men of sense in or out of my profession, to be one of those illusions by which quackery draws profit from the wonder of ignorance. Was I to blame if I refused to treat with the grave respect due to asserted discovery in legitimate science pretensions to powers akin to the fables of wizards? Was I to descend from the Academe of decorous science to examine whether a slumbering sibyl could read from a book placed at her back, or tell me at L—— what at that moment was being done by my friend at the Antipodes?

And what though Dr. Lloyd himself might be a worthy and honest man, and a sincere believer in the extravagances for which he demanded an equal credulity in others, do not honest men every day incur the penalty of ridicule if, from a de-

fect of good sense, they make themselves ridiculous?　Could
I have foreseen that a satire so justly provoked would inflict
so deadly a wound?　Was I inhumanly barbarous because the
antagonist destroyed was morbidly sensitive?　My conscience,
therefore, made me no reproach, and the public was as little
severe as my conscience.　The public had been with me in
our contest; the public knew nothing of my opponent's death-
bed accusations; the public knew only that I had attended
him in his last moments; it saw me walk beside the bier that
bore him to his grave; it admired the respect to his memory
which I evinced in the simple tomb that I placed over his
remains, inscribed with an epitaph that did justice to his unquestionable benevolence and integrity; above all, it praised
the energy with which I set on foot a subscription for his
orphan children, and the generosity with which I headed that
subscription by a sum that was large in proportion to my
means.

To that sum I did not, indeed, limit my contribution.　The
sobs of the poor female child rang still on my heart.　As her
grief had been keener than that of her brothers, so she might
be subjected to sharper trials than they, when the time came
for her to fight her own way through the world; therefore I
secured to her, but with such precautions that the gift could
not be traced to my hand, a sum to accumulate till she was of
marriageable age, and which then might suffice for a small
wedding portion; or if she remained single, for an income
that would place her beyond the temptation of want, or the
bitterness of a servile dependence.

That Dr. Lloyd should have died in poverty was a matter
of surprise at first, for his profits during the last few years
had been considerable, and his mode of life far from extravagant.　But just before the date of our controversy he had
been induced to assist the brother of his lost wife, who was a
junior partner in a London bank, with the loan of his accumulated savings.　This man proved dishonest; he embezzled
that and other sums intrusted to him, and fled the country.
The same sentiment of conjugal affection which had cost Dr.
Lloyd his fortune kept him silent as to the cause of the loss.

LILIAN.

It was reserved for his executors to discover the treachery of the brother-in-law whom he, poor man, would have generously screened from additional disgrace.

The Mayor of L——, a wealthy and public-spirited merchant, purchased the museum, which Dr. Lloyd's passion for natural history had induced him to form; and the sum thus obtained, together with that raised by subscription, sufficed not only to discharge all debts due by the deceased, but to insure to the orphans the benefits of an education that might fit at least the boys to enter fairly armed into that game, more of skill than of chance, in which Fortune is really so little blinded that we see, in each turn of her wheel, wealth and its honours pass away from the lax fingers of ignorance and sloth, to the resolute grasp of labour and knowledge.

Meanwhile a relation in a distant county undertook the charge of the orphans; they disappeared from the scene, and the tides of life in a commercial community soon flowed over the place which the dead man had occupied in the thoughts of his bustling townsfolk.

One person at L——, and only one, appeared to share and inherit the rancour with which the poor physician had denounced me on his death-bed. It was a gentleman named Vigors, distantly related to the deceased, and who had been, in point of station, the most eminent of Dr. Lloyd's partisans in the controversy with myself,—a man of no great scholastic acquirements, but of respectable abilities. He had that kind of power which the world concedes to respectable abilities when accompanied with a temper more than usually stern, and a moral character more than usually austere. His ruling passion was to sit in judgment upon others; and being a magistrate, he was the most active and the most rigid of all the magistrates L—— had ever known.

Mr. Vigors at first spoke of me with great bitterness, as having ruined, and in fact killed, his friend, by the uncharitable and unfair acerbity which he declared I had brought into what ought to have been an unprejudiced examination of simple matter of fact. But finding no sympathy in these charges, he had the discretion to cease from making them,

contenting himself with a solemn shake of his head if he
heard my name mentioned in terms of praise, and an oracular
sentence or two, such as "Time will show," "All 's well that
ends well," etc. Mr. Vigors, however, mixed very little in
the more convivial intercourse of the townspeople. He called
himself domestic; but, in truth, he was ungenial,— a stiff
man, starched with self-esteem. He thought that his dignity
of station was not sufficiently acknowledged by the merchants
of Low Town, and his superiority of intellect not sufficiently
recognized by the exclusives of the Hill. His visits were,
therefore, chiefly confined to the houses of neighbouring
squires, to whom his reputation as a magistrate, conjoined
with his solemn exterior, made him one of those oracles by
which men consent to be awed on condition that the awe is
not often inflicted. And though he opened his house three
times a week, it was only to a select few, whom he first fed
and then biologized. Electro-biology was very naturally the
special entertainment of a man whom no intercourse ever
pleased in which his will was not imposed upon others.
Therefore he only invited to his table persons whom he could
stare into the abnegation of their senses, willing to say that
beef was lamb, or brandy was coffee, according as he willed
them to say. And, no doubt, the persons asked would have
said anything he willed, so long as they had, in substance, as
well as in idea, the beef and the brandy, the lamb and the
coffee. I did not, then, often meet Mr. Vigors at the houses
in which I occasionally spent my evenings. I heard of his
enmity as a man safe in his home hears the sough of a wind
on a common without. If now and then we chanced to pass
in the streets, he looked up at me (he was a small man walking on tiptoe) with a sullen scowl of dislike; and from the
height of my stature, I dropped upon the small man and sullen scowl the affable smile of supreme indifference.

CHAPTER IV.

I HAD now arrived at that age when an ambitious man, satisfied with his progress in the world without, begins to feel in the cravings of unsatisfied affection the void of a solitary hearth. I resolved to marry, and looked out for a wife. I had never hitherto admitted into my life the passion of love. In fact, I had regarded that passion, even in my earlier youth, with a certain superb contempt,— as a malady engendered by an effeminate idleness, and fostered by a sickly imagination.

I wished to find in a wife a rational companion, an affectionate and trustworthy friend. No views of matrimony could be less romantic, more soberly sensible, than those which I conceived. Nor were my requirements mercenary or presumptuous. I cared not for fortune; I asked nothing from connections. My ambition was exclusively professional; it could be served by no titled kindred, accelerated by no wealthy dower. I was no slave to beauty. I did not seek in a wife the accomplishments of a finishing-school teacher.

Having decided that the time had come to select my helpmate, I imagined that I should find no difficulty in a choice that my reason would approve. But day upon day, week upon week, passed away, and though among the families I visited there were many young ladies who possessed more than the qualifications with which I conceived that I should be amply contented, and by whom I might flatter myself that my proposals would not be disdained, I saw not one to whose lifelong companionship I should not infinitely have preferred the solitude I found so irksome.

One evening, in returning home from visiting a poor female patient whom I attended gratuitously, and whose case demanded more thought than that of any other in my list,— for though it had been considered hopeless in the hospital, and

she had come home to die, I felt certain that I could save her,
and she seemed recovering under my care,—one evening—it
was the fifteenth of May—I found myself just before the
gates of the house that had been inhabited by Dr. Lloyd.
Since his death the house had been unoccupied; the rent
asked for it by the proprietor was considered high; and from
the sacred Hill on which it was situated, shyness or pride
banished the wealthier traders. The garden gates stood wide
open, as they had stood on the winter night on which I had
passed through them to the chamber of death. The remembrance of that death-bed came vividly before me, and the dying man's fantastic threat rang again in my startled ears.
An irresistible impulse, which I could not then account for,
and which I cannot account for now,—an impulse the reverse
of that which usually makes us turn away with quickened
step from a spot that recalls associations of pain,—urged me
on through the open gates up the neglected grass-grown road,
urged me to look, under the westering sun of the joyous
spring, at that house which I had never seen but in the gloom
of a winter night, under the melancholy moon. As the
building came in sight, with dark-red bricks, partially overgrown with ivy, I perceived that it was no longer unoccupied.
I saw forms passing athwart the open windows; a van laden
with articles of furniture stood before the door; a servant in
livery was beside it giving directions to the men who were
unloading. Evidently some family was just entering into
possession. I felt somewhat ashamed of my trespass, and
turned round quickly to retrace my steps. I had retreated
but a few yards, when I saw before me, at the entrance gates,
Mr. Vigors, walking beside a lady apparently of middle age;
while, just at hand, a path cut through the shrubs gave view
of a small wicket-gate at the end of the grounds. I felt unwilling not only to meet the lady, whom I guessed to be the
new occupier, and to whom I should have to make a somewhat awkward apology for intrusion, but still more to encounter the scornful look of Mr. Vigors in what appeared to
my pride a false or undignified position. Involuntarily,
therefore, I turned down the path which would favour my

escape unobserved. When about half way between the house
and the wicket-gate, the shrubs that had clothed the path on
either side suddenly opened to the left, bringing into view a
circle of sward, surrounded by irregular fragments of old
brickwork partially covered with ferns, creepers, or rock-
plants, weeds, or wild flowers; and, in the centre of the
circle, a fountain, or rather well, over which was built a
Gothic monastic dome, or canopy, resting on small Norman
columns, time-worn, dilapidated. A large willow overhung
this unmistakable relic of the ancient abbey. There was an
air of antiquity, romance, legend about this spot, so abruptly
disclosed amidst the delicate green of the young shrubberies.
But it was not the ruined wall nor the Gothic well that
chained my footstep and charmed my eye.

It was a solitary human form, seated amidst the mournful
ruins.

The form was so slight, the face so young, that at the first
glance I murmured to myself, " What a lovely child! " But
as my eye lingered it recognized in the upturned thoughtful
brow, in the sweet, serious aspect, in the rounded outlines
of that slender shape, the inexpressible dignity of virgin
woman.

A book was on her lap, at her feet a little basket, half-
filled with violets and blossoms culled from the rock-plants
that nestled amidst the ruins. Behind her, the willow, like
an emerald waterfall, showered down its arching abundant
green, bough after bough, from the tree-top to the sward, descending in wavy verdure, bright towards the summit, in the
smile of the setting sun, and darkening into shadow as it
neared the earth.

She did not notice, she did not see me; her eyes were fixed
upon the horizon, where it sloped farthest into space, above
the tree-tops and the ruins,— fixed so intently that mechanically I turned my own gaze to follow the flight of hers. It
was as if she watched for some expected, familiar sign to
grow out from the depths of heaven; perhaps to greet, before other eyes beheld it, the ray of the earliest star.

The birds dropped from the boughs on the turf around her

so fearlessly that one alighted amidst the flowers in the little basket at her feet. There is a famous German poem, which I had read in my youth, called the Maiden from Abroad, variously supposed to be an allegory of Spring, or of Poetry, according to the choice of commentators: it seemed to me as if the poem had been made for her. Verily, indeed, in her. poet or painter might have seen an image equally true to either of those adornments of the earth; both outwardly a delight to sense, yet both wakening up thoughts within us, not sad, but akin to sadness.

I heard now a step behind me, and a voice which I recognized to be that of Mr. Vigors. I broke from the charm by which I had been so lingeringly spell-bound, hurried on confusedly, gained the wicket-gate, from which a short flight of stairs descended into the common thoroughfare. And there the every-day life lay again before me. On the opposite side, houses, shops, church-spires; a few steps more, and the bustling streets! How immeasurably far from, yet how familiarly near to, the world in which we move and have being is that fairy-land of romance which opens out from the hard earth before us, when Love steals at first to our side, fading back into the hard earth again as Love smiles or sighs its farewell!

CHAPTER V.

AND before that evening I had looked on Mr. Vigors with supreme indifference! What importance he now assumed in my eyes! The lady with whom I had seen him was doubtless the new tenant of that house in which the young creature by whom my heart was so strangely moved evidently had her home. Most probably the relation between the two ladies was that of mother and daughter. Mr. Vigors, the friend of one, might himself be related to both, might prejudice them against me, might — Here, starting up, I snapped the thread of conjecture, for right before my eyes, on the table

beside which I had seated myself on entering my room, lay a
card of invitation: —

MRS. POYNTZ.
At Home,
Wednesday, May 15th.
Early.

. Mrs. Poyntz, — Mrs. Colonel Poyntz, the Queen of the
Hill? There, at her house, I could not fail to learn all
about the new comers, who could never without her sanction
have settled on her domain.

I hastily changed my dress, and, with beating heart, wound
my way up the venerable eminence.

I did not pass through the lane which led direct to Abbots'
House (for that old building stood solitary amidst its grounds
a little apart from the spacious platform on which the society
of the Hill was concentrated), but up the broad causeway,
with vistaed gas-lamps; the gayer shops still-unclosed, the tide
of busy life only slowly ebbing from the still-animated street,
on to a square, in which the four main thoroughfares of the
city converged, and which formed the boundary of Low
Town. A huge dark archway, popularly called Monk's Gate,
at the angle of this square, made the entrance to Abbey Hill.
When the arch was passed, one felt at once that one was in
the town of a former day. The pavement was narrow and
rugged; the shops small, their upper stories projecting, with
here and there plastered fronts, quaintly arabesque. An ascent, short, but steep and tortuous, conducted at once to the
old Abbey Church, nobly situated in a vast quadrangle, round
which were the genteel and gloomy dwellings of the Areopagites of the Hill. More genteel and less gloomy than the
rest — lights at the windows and flowers on the balcony —
stood forth, flanked by a garden wall at either side, the mansion of Mrs. Colonel Poyntz.

As I entered the drawing-room, I heard the voice of the
hostess; it was a voice clear, decided, metallic, bell-like, uttering these words: "Taken Abbots' House? I will tell
you."

CHAPTER VI.

Mrs. Poyntz was seated on the sofa; at her right sat fat Mrs. Bruce, who was a Scotch lord's grand-daughter; at her left thin Miss Brabazon, who was an Irish baronet's niece. Around her — a few seated, many standing — had grouped all the guests, save two old gentlemen, who had remained aloof with Colonel Poyntz near the whist-table, waiting for the fourth old gentleman who was to make up the rubber, but who was at that moment spell-bound in the magic circle which curiosity, that strongest of social demons, had attracted round the hostess.

"Taken Abbots' House? I will tell you. — Ah, Dr. Fenwick, charmed to see you. You know Abbots' House is let at last? Well, Miss Brabazon, dear, you ask who has taken it. I will inform you, — a particular friend of mine."

"Indeed! Dear me!" said Miss Brabazon, looking confused. "I hope I did not say anything to — "

"Wound my feelings. Not in the least. You said your uncle Sir Phelim employed a coachmaker named Ashleigh, that Ashleigh was an uncommon name, though Ashley was a common one; you intimated an appalling suspicion that the Mrs. Ashleigh who had come to the Hill was the coachmaker's widow. I relieve your mind, — she is not; she is the widow of Gilbert Ashleigh, of Kirby Hall."

"Gilbert Ashleigh," said one of the guests, a bachelor, whose parents had reared him for the Church, but who, like poor Goldsmith, did not think himself good enough for it, — a mistake of over-modesty, for he matured into a very harmless creature. "Gilbert Ashleigh? I was at Oxford with him, — a gentleman commoner of Christ Church. Good-looking man, very; *sapped* — "

"Sapped! what 's that? — Oh, studied. That he did all his life. He married young, — Anne Chaloner; she and I

were girls together; married the same year. They settled
at Kirby Hall — nice place, but dull. Poyntz and I spent a
Christmas there. Ashleigh when he talked was charming,
but he talked very little. Anne, when she talked, was commonplace, and she talked very much. Naturally, poor thing,
— she was so happy. Poyntz and I did not spend another
Christmas there. Friendship is long, but life is short. Gilbert Ashleigh's life was short indeed; he died in the seventh
year of his marriage, leaving only one child, a girl. Since
then, though I never spent another Christmas at Kirby Hall,
I have frequently spent a day there, doing my best to cheer
up Anne. She was no longer talkative, poor dear. Wrapped
up in her child, who has now grown into a beautiful girl of
eighteen — such eyes, her father's — the real dark blue —
rare; sweet creature, but delicate; not, I hope, consumptive,
but delicate; quiet, wants life. My girl Jane adores her.
Jane has life enough for two."

"Is Miss Ashleigh the heiress to Kirby Hall?" asked Mrs.
Bruce, who had an unmarried son.

"No. Kirby Hall passed to Ashleigh Sumner, the male
heir, a cousin. And the luckiest of cousins! Gilbert's sister,
showy woman (indeed all show), had contrived to marry her
kinsman, Sir Walter Ashleigh Haughton, the head of the
Ashleigh family, — just the man made to be the reflector of a
showy woman! He died years ago, leaving an only son, Sir
James, who was killed last winter, by a fall from his horse.
And here, again, Ashleigh Sumner proved to be the male
heir-at-law. During the minority of this fortunate youth,
Mrs. Ashleigh had rented Kirby Hall of his guardian. He
is now just coming of age, and that is why she leaves. Lilian
Ashleigh will have, however, a very good fortune, — is what
we genteel paupers call an heiress. Is there anything more
you want to know?"

Said thin Miss Brabazon, who took advantage of her thin-
ness to wedge herself into every one's affairs, "A most interesting account. What a nice place Abbots' House could be
made with a little taste! So aristocratic! Just what I should
like if I could afford it! The drawing-room should be done

up in the Moorish style, with geranium-coloured silk curtains, like dear Lady L——'s boudoir at Twickenham. And Mrs. Ashleigh has taken the house! on lease too, I suppose!" Here Miss Brabazon fluttered her fan angrily, and then exclaimed, "But what on earth brings Mrs. Ashleigh here?"

Answered Mrs. Colonel Poyntz, with the military frankness by which she kept her company in good humour, as well as awe,—

"Why do any of us come here? Can any one tell me?"

There was a blank silence, which the hostess herself was the first to break.

"None of us present can say why we came here. I can tell you why Mrs. Ashleigh came. Our neighbour, Mr. Vigors, is a distant connection of the late Gilbert Ashleigh, one of the executors to his will, and the guardian to the heir-at-law. About ten days ago Mr. Vigors called on me, for the first time since I felt it my duty to express my disapprobation of the strange vagaries so unhappily conceived by our poor dear friend Dr. Lloyd. And when he had taken his chair, just where you now sit, Dr. Fenwick, he said in a sepulchral voice, stretching out two fingers, so,—as if I were one of the what-do-you-call-'ems who go to sleep when he bids them,— 'Marm, you know Mrs. Ashleigh? You correspond with her?' 'Yes, Mr. Vigors; is there any crime in that? You look as if there were.' 'No crime, marm,' said the man, quite seriously. 'Mrs. Ashleigh is a lady of amiable temper, and you are a woman of masculine understanding.'"

Here there was a general titter. Mrs. Colonel Poyntz hushed it with a look of severe surprise. "What is there to laugh at? All women would be men if they could. If my understanding is masculine, so much the better for me. I thanked Mr. Vigors for his very handsome compliment, and he then went on to say that though Mrs. Ashleigh would now have to leave Kirby Hall in a very few weeks, she seemed quite unable to make up her mind where to go; that it had occurred to him that, as Miss Ashleigh was of an age to see a little of the world, she ought not to remain buried in the country; while, being of quiet mind, she recoiled from

the dissipation of London.   Between the seclusion of the one
and the turmoil of the other, the society of L—— was a happy
medium.   He should be glad of my opinion.   He had put off
asking for it, because he owned his belief that I had behaved
unkindly to his lamented friend, Dr. Lloyd; but he now
found himself in rather an awkward position.   His ward,
young Sumner, had prudently resolved on fixing his country
residence at Kirby Hall, rather than at Haughton Park, the
much larger seat which had so suddenly passed to his inheritance, and which he could not occupy without a vast establishment, that to a single man, so young, would be but a
cumbersome and costly trouble.   Mr. Vigors was pledged to
his ward to obtain him possession of Kirby Hall, the precise
day agreed upon, but Mrs. Ashleigh did not seem disposed to
stir,— could not decide where else to go.   Mr. Vigors was
loth to press hard on his old friend's widow and child.   It
was a thousand pities Mrs Ashleigh could not make up her
mind; she had had ample time for preparation.   A word from
me at this moment would be an effective kindness.   Abbots'
House was vacant, with a garden so extensive that the ladies
would not miss the country.   Another party was after it, but
— 'Say no more,' I cried; 'no party but my dear old friend
Anne Ashleigh shall have Abbots' House.   So that question
is settled.'   I dismissed Mr. Vigors, sent for my carriage,—
that is, for Mr. Barker's yellow fly and his best horses,— and
drove that very day to Kirby Hall, which, though not in this
county, is only twenty-five miles distant.   I slept there that
night.   By nine o'clock the next morning I had secured Mrs.
Ashleigh's consent, on the promise to save her all trouble;
came back, sent for the landlord, settled the rent, lease,
agreement; engaged Forbes' vans to remove the furniture
from Kirby Hall; told Forbes to begin with the beds.   When
her own bed came, which was last night, Anne Ashleigh came
too.   I have seen her this morning.   She likes the place, so
does Lilian.   I asked them to meet you all here to-night; but
Mrs. Ashleigh was tired.   The last of the furniture was to
arrive to-day; and though dear Mrs. Ashleigh is an undecided
character, she is not inactive.   But it is not only the plan-

ning where to put tables and chairs that would have tried her
to-day: she has had Mr. Vigors on her hands all the afternoon, and he has been — here's her little note — what are the
words? No doubt 'most overpowering and oppressive;' no,
'most kind and attentive,' — different words, but, as applied
to Mr. Vigors, they mean the same thing.

"And now, next Monday — we must leave them in peace
till then — you will all call on the Ashleighs. The Hill
knows what is due to itself; it cannot delegate to Mr. Vigors,
a respectable man indeed, but who does not belong to its set,
its own proper course of action towards those who would
shelter themselves on its bosom. The Hill cannot be kind
and attentive, overpowering or oppressive by proxy. To
those newborn into its family circle it cannot be an indifferent godmother; it has towards them all the feelings of a
mother, — or of a stepmother, as the case may be. Where it
says 'This can be no child of mine,' it is a stepmother indeed; but in all those whom I have presented to its arms, it
has hitherto, I am proud to say, recognized desirable acquaintances, and to them the Hill has been a mother. And
now, my dear Mr. Sloman, go to your rubber; Poyntz is impatient, though he don't show it. Miss Brabazon, love, we
all long to see you seated at the piano, — you play so di-
vinely! Something gay, if you please; something gay, but
not very noisy, — Mr. Leopold Symthe will turn the leaves
for you. Mrs. Bruce, your own favourite set at vingt-un,
with four new recruits. Dr. Fenwick, you are like me,
don't play cards, and don't care for music; sit here, and talk
or not, as you please, while I knit."

The other guests thus disposed of, some at the card-tables,
some round the piano, I placed myself at Mrs. Poyntz's side,
on a seat niched in the recess of a window which an evening
unusually warm for the month of May permitted to be left
open. I was next to one who had known Lilian as a child,
one from whom I had learned by what sweet name to call the
image which my thoughts had already shrined. How much
that I still longed to know she could tell me! But in what
form of question could I lead to the subject, yet not betray

my absorbing interest in it? Longing to speak, I felt as if
stricken dumb; stealing an unquiet glance towards the face
beside me, and deeply impressed with that truth which the
Hill had long ago reverently acknowledged,— namely, that
Mrs. Colonel Poyntz was a very superior woman, a very powerful creature.

And there she sat knitting, rapidly, firmly; a woman somewhat on the other side of forty, complexion a bronze paleness,
hair a bronze brown, in strong ringlets cropped short behind,
— handsome hair for a man; lips that, when closed, showed
inflexible decision, when speaking, became supple and flexi-
ble with an easy humour and a vigilant finesse; eyes of a red
hazel, quick but steady, — observing, piercing, dauntless eyes;
altogether a fine countenance,— would have been a very fine
countenance in a man; profile sharp, straight, clear-cut, with
an expression, when in repose, like that of a sphinx; a frame
robust, not corpulent; of middle height, but with an air and
carriage that made her appear tall; peculiarly white firm
hands, indicative of vigorous health, not a vein visible on the
surface.

There she sat knitting, knitting, and I by her side, gazing
now on herself, now on her work, with a vague idea that the
threads in the skein of my own web of love or of life were
passing quick through those noiseless fingers. And, indeed,
in every web of romance, the fondest, one of the Parcæ is
sure to be some matter-of-fact She, Social Destiny, as little
akin to romance herself as was this worldly Queen of the
Hill.

CHAPTER VII.

I HAVE given a sketch of the outward woman of Mrs. Colonel Poyntz. The inner woman was a recondite mystery
deep as that of the sphinx, whose features her own resembled.
But between the outward and the inward woman there is ever

a third woman,— the conventional woman,— such as the whole human being appears to the world,— always mantled, sometimes masked.

I am told that the fine people of London do not recognize the title of "Mrs. Colonel." If that be true, the fine people of London must be clearly in the wrong, for no people in the universe could be finer than the fine people of Abbey Hill; and they considered their sovereign had as good a right to the title of Mrs. Colonel as the Queen of England has to that of "our Gracious Lady." But Mrs. Poyntz herself never assumed the title of Mrs. Colonel; it never appeared on her cards,— any more than the title of "Gracious Lady" appears on the cards which convey the invitation that a Lord Steward or Lord Chamberlain is commanded by her Majesty to issue. To titles, indeed, Mrs. Poyntz evinced no superstitious reverence. Two peeresses, related to her, not distantly, were in the habit of paying her a yearly visit which lasted two or three days. The Hill considered these visits an honour to its eminence. Mrs. Poyntz never seemed to esteem them an honour to herself; never boasted of them; never sought to show off her grand relations, nor put herself the least out of the way to receive them. Her mode of life was free from ostentation. She had the advantage of being a few hundreds a year richer than any other inhabitant of the Hill; but she did not devote her superior resources to the invidious exhibition of superior splendour. Like a wise sovereign, the revenues of her exchequer were applied to the benefit of her subjects, and not to the vanity of egotistical parade. As no one else on the Hill kept a carriage, she declined to keep one. Her entertainments were simple, but numerous. Twice a week she received the Hill, and was genuinely at home to it. She contrived to make her parties proverbially agreeable. The refreshments were of the same kind as those which the poorest of her old maids of honour might proffer; but they were better of their kind, the best of their kind,— the best tea, the best lemonade, the best cakes. Her rooms had an air of comfort, which was peculiar to them. They looked like rooms accustomed to receive, and receive in a friendly way;

well warmed, well lighted, card-tables and piano each in the place that made cards and music inviting; on the walls a few old family portraits, and three or four other pictures said to be valuable and certainly pleasing,— two Watteaus, a Canaletti, a Weenix; plenty of easy-chairs and settees covered with a cheerful chintz,— in the arrangement of the furniture generally an indescribable careless elegance. She herself was studiously plain in dress, more conspicuously free from jewelry and trinkets than any married lady on the Hill. But I have heard from those who were authorities on such a subject that she was never seen in a dress of the last year's fashion. She adopted the mode as it came out, just enough to show that she was aware it was out; but with a sober reserve, as much as to say, "I adopt the fashion as far as it suits myself; I do not permit the fashion to adopt me." In short, Mrs. Colonel Poyntz was sometimes rough, sometimes coarse, always masculine, and yet somehow or other masculine in a womanly way; but she was never vulgar because never affected. It was impossible not to allow that she was a thorough gentlewoman, and she could do things that lower other gentlewomen, without any loss of dignity. Thus she was an admirable mimic, certainly in itself the least ladylike condescension of humour. But when she mimicked, it was with so tranquil a gravity, or so royal a good humour, that one could only say, "What talents for society dear Mrs. Colonel has!" As she was a gentlewoman emphatically, so the other colonel, the he-colonel, was emphatically a gentleman; rather shy, but not cold; hating trouble of every kind, pleased to seem a cipher in his own house. If the sole study of Mrs. Colonel had been to make her husband comfortable, she could not have succeeded better than by bringing friends about him and then taking them off his hands. Colonel Poyntz, the he-colonel, had seen, in his youth, actual service; but had retired from his profession many years ago, shortly after his marriage. He was a younger brother of one of the principal squires in the country; inherited the house he lived in, with some other valuable property in and about L——, from an uncle; was considered a good landlord; and popular in Low

Town, though he never interfered in its affairs. He was punctiliously neat in his dress; a thin youthful figure, crowned with a thick youthful wig. He never seemed to read anything but the newspapers and the "Meteorological Journal;" was supposed to be the most weather-wise man in all L——. He had another intellectual predilection,—whist; but in that he had less reputation for wisdom. Perhaps it requires a rarer combination of mental faculties to win an odd trick than to divine a fall in the glass. For the rest, the he-colonel, many years older than his wife, despite the thin youthful figure, was an admirable aid-de-camp to the general in command, Mrs. Colonel; and she could not have found one more obedient, more devoted, or more proud of a distinguished chief.

In giving to Mrs. Colonel Poyntz the appellation of Queen of the Hill, let there be no mistake. She was not a constitutional sovereign; her monarchy was absolute. All her proclamations had the force of laws.

Such ascendancy could not have been attained without considerable talents for acquiring and keeping it. Amidst all her off-hand, brisk, imperious frankness, she had the ineffable discrimination of tact. Whether civil or rude, she was never civil or rude but what she carried public opinion along with her. Her knowledge of general society must have been limited, as must be that of all female sovereigns; but she seemed gifted with an intuitive knowledge of human nature, which she applied to her special ambition of ruling it. I have not a doubt that if she had been suddenly transferred, a perfect stranger, to the world of London, she would have soon forced her way to its selectest circles, and, when once there, held her own against a duchess.

I have said that she was not affected: this might be one cause of her sway over a set in which nearly every other woman was trying rather to seem, than to be, a somebody.

But if Mrs. Colonel Poyntz was not artificial, she was artful,—or perhaps I might more justly say artistic. In all she said and did there were conduct, system, plan. She could be a most serviceable friend, a most damaging enemy; yet I believe she seldom indulged in strong likings or strong hatreds. All was policy,— a policy akin to that of a grand party chief, determined to raise up those whom, for any reason of state, it was prudent to favour, and to put down those whom, for any reason of state, it was expedient to humble or to crush.

Ever since the controversy with Dr. Lloyd, this lady had honoured me with her benignest countenance; and nothing could be more adroit than the manner in which, while imposing me on others as an oracular authority, she sought to subject to her will the oracle itself.

She was in the habit of addressing me in a sort of motherly way, as if she had the deepest interest in my welfare, happiness, and reputation. And thus, in every compliment, in every seeming mark of respect, she maintained the superior dignity of one who takes from responsible station the duty to encourage rising merit; so that, somehow or other, despite all that pride which made me believe that I needed no helping hand to advance or to clear my way through the world, I could not shake off from my mind the impression that I was mysteriously patronized by Mrs. Colonel Poyntz.

We might have sat together five minutes, side by side — in silence as complete as if in the cave of Trophonius — when without looking up from her work, Mrs. Poyntz said abruptly,—

"I am thinking about you, Dr. Fenwick. And you — are thinking about some other woman. Ungrateful man!"

"Unjust accusation! My very silence should prove how intently my thoughts were fixed on you, and on the weird web which springs under your hand in meshes that bewilder the gaze and snare the attention."

Mrs. Poyntz looked up at me for a moment — one rapid glance of the bright red hazel eye — and said,—

"Was I really in your thoughts? Answer truly."

"Truly, I answer, you were."

"That is strange! Who can it be?"

"Who can it be? What do you mean?"

"If you were thinking of me, it was in connection with

3

some other person,— some other person of my own sex. It is certainly not poor dear Miss Brabazon. Who else can it be?"

Again the red eye shot over me, and I felt my cheek redden beneath it.

"Hush!" she said, lowering her voice; "you are in love!"

"In love!— I! Permit me to ask you why you think so?"

"The signs are unmistakable; you are altered in your manner, even in the expression of your face, since I last saw you; your manner is generally quiet and observant,— it is now restless and distracted; your expression of face is generally proud and serene,— it is now humbled and troubled. You have something on your mind! It is not anxiety for your reputation,— that is established; nor for your fortune,— that is made; it is not anxiety for a patient or you would scarcely be here. But anxiety it is,— an anxiety that is remote from your profession, that touches your heart and is new to it!"

I was startled, almost awed; but I tried to cover my confusion with a forced laugh.

"Profound observer! Subtle analyst! You have convinced me that I must be in love, though I did not suspect it before. But when I strive to conjecture the object, I am as much perplexed as yourself; and with you, I ask, who can it be?"

"Whoever it be," said Mrs. Poyntz, who had paused, while I spoke, from her knitting, and now resumed it very slowly and very carefully, as if her mind and her knitting worked in unison together,— "whoever it be, love in you would be serious; and, with or without love, marriage is a serious thing to us all. It is not every pretty girl that would suit Allen Fenwick."

"Alas! is there any pretty girl whom Allen Fenwick would suit?"

"Tut! You should be above the fretful vanity that lays traps for a compliment. Yes; the time has come in your life and your career when you would do well to marry. I give my consent to that," she added with a smile as if in jest, and a slight nod as if in earnest. The knitting here went on more decidedly, more quickly. "But I do not yet see the person.

No! 'T is a pity, Allen Fenwick" (whenever Mrs. Poyntz
called me by my Christian name, she always assumed her
majestic motherly manner),— "a pity that, with your birth,
energies, perseverance, talents, and, let me add, your advantages of manner and person,— a pity that you did not choose
a career that might achieve higher fortunes and louder fame
than the most brilliant success can give to a provincial physician. But in that very choice you interest me. My choice
has been much the same,— a small circle, but the first in it.
Yet, had I been a man, or had my dear Colonel been a man
whom it was in the power of a woman's art to raise one step
higher in that metaphorical ladder which is not the ladder of
the angels, why, then — what then? No matter! I am contented. I transfer my ambition to Jane. Do you not think
her handsome?"

"There can be no doubt of that," said I, carelessly and
naturally.

"I have settled Jane's lot in my own mind," resumed Mrs.
Poyntz, striking firm into another row of knitting. "She
will marry a country gentleman of large estate. He will go
into parliament. She will study his advancement as I study
Poyntz's comfort. If he be clever, she will help to make
him a minister; if he be not clever, his wealth will make her
a personage, and lift him into a personage's husband. And,
now that you see I have no matrimonial designs on you,
Allen Fenwick, think if it will be worth while to confide in
me. Possibly I may be useful — "

".I know not how to thank you; but, as yet, I have nothing
to confide."

While thus saying, I turned my eyes towards the open
window beside which I sat. It was a beautiful soft night,—
the May moon in all her splendour. The town stretched, far
and wide, below with all its numberless lights,— below, but
somewhat distant; an intervening space was covered, here,
by the broad quadrangle (in the midst of which stood, massive and lonely, the grand old church), and, there, by the
gardens and scattered cottages or mansions that clothed the
sides of the hill.

"Is not that house," I said, after a short pause, "yonder, with the three gables, the one in which — in which poor Dr. Lloyd lived — Abbots' House?"

I spoke abruptly, as if to intimate my desire to change the subject of conversation. My hostess stopped her knitting, half rose, looked forth.

"Yes. But what a lovely night! How is it that the moon blends into harmony things of which the sun only marks the contrast? That stately old church tower, gray with its thousand years, those vulgar tile-roofs and chimney-pots raw in the freshness of yesterday,— now, under the moonlight, all melt into one indivisible charm!"

As my hostess thus spoke, she had left her seat, taking her work with her, and passed from the window into the balcony. It was not often that Mrs. Poyntz condescended to admit what is called "sentiment" into the range of her sharp, practical, worldly talk; but she did so at times,— always, when she did, giving me the notion of an intellect much too comprehensive not to allow that sentiment has a place in this life, but keeping it in its proper place, by that mixture of affability and indifference with which some high-born beauty allows the genius, but checks the presumption, of a charming and penniless poet. For a few minutes her eyes roved over the scene in evident enjoyment; then, as they slowly settled upon the three gables of Abbots' House, her face regained that something of hardness which belonged to its decided character; her fingers again mechanically resumed her knitting, and she said, in her clear, unsoftened, metallic chime of voice, "Can you guess why I took so much trouble to oblige Mr. Vigors and locate Mrs. Ashleigh yonder?"

"You favoured us with a full explanation of your reasons."

"Some of my reasons; not the main one. People who undertake the task of governing others, as I do, be their rule ρ kingdom or a hamlet, must adopt a principle of government and adhere to it. The principle that suits best with the Hill is Respect for the Proprieties. We have not much money; *entre nous,* we have no great rank. Our policy is, then, to set up the Proprieties as an influence which money must court and rank is afraid of. I had learned just before Mr. Vigors called on me that Lady Sarah Bellasis entertained the idea of hiring Abbots' House. London has set its face against her; a provincial town would be more charitable. An earl's daughter, with a good income and an awfully bad name, of the best manners and of the worst morals, would have made sad havoc among the Proprieties. How many of our primmest old maids would have deserted tea and Mrs. Poyntz for champagne and her ladyship! The Hill was never in so imminent a danger. Rather than Lady Sarah Bellasis should have had that house, I would have taken it myself, and stocked it with owls.

"Mrs. Ashleigh turned up just in the critical moment. Lady Sarah is foiled, the Proprieties safe, and so that question is settled."

"And it will be pleasant to have your early friend so near you."

Mrs. Poyntz lifted her eyes full upon me.

"Do you know Mrs. Ashleigh?"

"Not in the least."

"She has many virtues and few ideas. She is commonplace weak, as I am commonplace strong. But commonplace weak can be very lovable. Her husband, a man of genius and learning, gave her his whole heart, — a heart worth having; but he was not ambitious, and he despised the world."

"I think you said your daughter was very much attached to Miss Ashleigh? Does her character resemble her mother's?"

I was afraid while I spoke that I should again meet Mrs. Poyntz's searching gaze, but she did not this time look up from her work.

"No; Lilian is anything but commonplace."

"You described her as having delicate health; you implied a hope that she was not consumptive. I trust that there is no serious reason for apprehending a constitutional tendency which at her age would require the most careful watching!"

"I trust not. If she were to die — Dr. Fenwick, what is the matter?"

So terrible had been the picture which this woman's words had brought before me, that I started as if my own life had received a shock.

"I beg pardon," I said falteringly, pressing my hand to my heart; "a sudden spasm here,— it is over now. You were saying that — that — "

"I was about to say — " and here Mrs. Poyntz laid her hand lightly on mine,— "I was about to say that if Lilian Ashleigh were to die, I should mourn for her less than I might for one who valued the things of the earth more. But I believe there is no cause for the alarm my words so inconsiderately excited in you. Her mother is watchful and devoted; and if the least thing ailed Lilian, she would call in medical advice. Mr. Vigors would, I know, recommend Dr. Jones."

Closing our conference with those stinging words, Mrs. Poyntz here turned back into the drawing-room.

I remained some minutes on the balcony, disconcerted, enraged. With what consummate art had this practised diplomatist wound herself into my secret! That she had read my heart better than myself was evident from that Parthian shaft, barbed with Dr. Jones, which she had shot over her shoulder in retreat. That from the first moment in which she had decoyed me to her side, she had detected "the something" on my mind, was perhaps but the ordinary quickness of female penetration. But it was with no ordinary craft that the whole conversation afterwards had been so shaped as to learn the something, and lead me to reveal the some one to whom the something was linked. For what purpose? What was it to her? What motive could she have beyond the mere gratification of curiosity? Perhaps, at first, she thought I had been caught by her daughter's showy beauty, and hence the half-friendly, half-cynical frankness with which she had avowed her ambitious projects for that young lady's matrimonial advancement. Satisfied by my manner that I cherished no presumptuous hopes in that quarter, her scrutiny was doubtless continued from that pleasure in the exercise of a wily intellect which impels schemers and politieians to an activity for which, without that pleasure itself, there would seem no adequate inducement. And besides, the ruling passion of this petty sovereign was power; and if knowledge be power, there is no better instrument of power~over a contumacious subject than that hold on his heart which is gained in the knowledge of its secret.

But "secret"! Had it really come to this? Was it possible that the mere sight of a human face, never beheld before, could disturb the whole tenor of my life,—a stranger of whose mind and character I knew nothing, whose very voice I had never heard? It was only by the intolerable pang of anguish that had rent my heart in the words, carelessly, abruptly spoken, "if she were to die," that I had felt how the world would be changed to me, if indeed that face were seen in it no more! Yes, secret it was no longer to myself,— I loved! And like all on whom love descends, sometimes softly, slowly, with the gradual wing of the cushat settling down into its nest, sometimes with the swoop of the eagle on his unsuspecting quarry, I believed that none ever before loved as I loved; that such love was an abnormal wonder, made solely for me, and I for it. Then my mind insensibly hushed its angrier and more turbulent thoughts, as my gaze rested upon the roof-tops of Lilian's home, and the shimmering silver of the moonlit willow, under which I had seen her gazing into the roseate heavens.

CHAPTER VIII.

WHEN I returned to the drawing-room, the party was evidently about to break up. Those who had grouped round the piano were now assembled round the refreshment-table. The card-players had risen, and were settling or discussing gains and losses. While I was searching for my hat, which I had somewhere mislaid, a poor gentleman, tormented by tic-doloureux, crept timidly up to me,— the proudest and the poorest of all the hidalgos settled on the Hill. He could not afford a fee for a physician's advice; but pain had humbled his pride, and I saw at a glance that he was considering how to take a surreptitious advantage of social intercourse, and obtain the advice without paying the fee. The old man discovered the hat before I did, stooped, took it up, extended it to me with the profound bow of the old school, while the other hand, clenched and quivering, was pressed into the hollow of his cheek, and his eyes met mine with wistful mute entreaty. The instinct of my profession seized me at once. I could never behold suffering without forgetting all else in the desire to relieve it.

"You are in pain," said I, softly. "Sit down and describe the symptoms. Here, it is true, I am no professional doctor, but I am a friend who is fond of doctoring, and knows something about it."

So we sat down a little apart from the other guests, and after a few questions and answers, I was pleased to find that his "tic" did not belong to the less curable kind of that agonizing neuralgia. I was especially successful in my treatment of similar sufferings, for which I had discovered an anodyne that was almost specific. I wrote on a leaf of my pocketbook a prescription which I felt sure would be efficacious, and as I tore it out and placed it in his hand, I chanced to look up, and saw the hazel eyes of my hostess fixed upon me with a kinder and softer expression than they often condescended to admit into their cold and penetrating lustre. At that moment, however, her attention was drawn from me to a servant, who entered with a note, and I heard him say, though in an undertone, "From Mrs. Ashleigh."

She opened the note, read it hastily, ordered the servant to wait without the door, retired to her writing-table, which stood near the place at which I still lingered, rested her face on her hand, and seemed musing. Her meditation was very soon over. She turned her head, and to my surprise, beckoned to me. I approached.

"Sit here," she whispered: "turn your back towards those people, who are no doubt watching us. Read this."

She placed in my hand the note she had just received. It contained but a few words, to this effect: —

DEAR MARGARET, — I am so distressed. Since I wrote to you a few hours ago, Lilian is taken suddenly ill, and I fear seriously. What medical man should I send for? Let my servant have his name and address.   A. A.

I sprang from my seat.

"Stay," said Mrs. Poyntz. "Would you much care if I sent the servant to Dr. Jones?"

"Ah, madam, you are cruel! What have I done that you should become my enemy?"

"Enemy! No. You have just befriended one of my friends. In this world of fools intellect should ally itself with intellect. No; I am not your enemy! But you have not yet asked me to be your friend."

Here she put into my hands a note she had written while thus speaking. "Receive your credentials. If there be any cause for alarm, or if I can be of use, send for me." Resuming the work she had suspended, but with lingering, uncertain fingers, she added, "So far, then, this is settled. Nay, no thanks; it is but little that is settled as yet."

CHAPTER IX.

IN a very few minutes I was once more in the grounds of that old gable house; the servant, who went before me, entered them by the stairs and the wicket-gate of the private entrance; that way was the shortest. So again I passed by the circling glade and the monastic well, — sward, trees, and ruins all suffused in the limpid moonlight.

And now I was in the house; the servant took up-stairs the note with which I was charged, and a minute or two afterwards returned and conducted me to the corridor above, in which Mrs. Ashleigh received me. I was the first to speak.

"Your daughter — is — is — not seriously ill, I hope. What is it?"

"Hush!" she said, under her breath. "Will you step this way for a moment?" She passed through a doorway to the right. I followed her, and as she placed on the table the light she had been holding, I looked round with a chill at the heart, — it was the room in which Dr. Lloyd had died. Impossible to mistake. The furniture indeed was changed, there was no bed in the chamber; but the shape of the room, the position of the high casement, which was now wide open, and through which the moonlight streamed more softly than on that drear winter night, the great square beams intersecting the low ceiling, — all were impressed vividly on my memory. The chair to which Mrs. Ashleigh beckoned me was placed just on the spot where I had stood by the bed-head of the dying man.

I shrank back, — I could not have seated myself there. So I remained leaning against the chimney-piece, while Mrs. Ashleigh told her story.

She said that on their arrival the day before, Lilian had been in more than usually good health and spirits, delighted with the old house, the grounds, and especially the nook by the Monk's Well, at which Mrs. Ashleigh had left her that evening in order to make some purchases in the town, in company with Mr. Vigors. When Mrs. Ashleigh returned, she and Mr. Vigors had sought Lilian in that nook, and Mrs. Ashleigh then detected, with a mother's eye, some change in Lilian which alarmed her. She seemed listless and dejected; and was very pale; but she denied that she felt unwell. On regaining the house she had sat down in the room in which we then were, — "which," said Mrs. Ashleigh, "as it is not required for a sleeping-room, my daughter, who is fond of reading, wished to fit up as her own morning-room, or study. I left her here and went into the drawing-room below with Mr. Vigors. When he quitted me, which he did very soon, I remained for nearly an hour giving directions about the placing of furniture, which had just arrived, from our late residence. I then went up-stairs to join my daughter, and to my terror found her apparently lifeless in her chair. She had fainted away."

I interrupted Mrs. Ashleigh here. "Has Miss Ashleigh been subject to fainting fits?"

"No, never. When she recovered she seemed bewildered, — disinclined to speak. I got her to bed, and as she then fell quietly to sleep, my mind was relieved. I thought it only a passing effect of excitement, in a change of abode; or caused by something like malaria in the atmosphere of that part of the grounds in which I had found her seated."

"Very likely. The hour of sunset at this time of year is trying to delicate constitutions. Go on."

"About three quarters of an hour ago she woke up with a loud cry, and has been ever since in a state of great agitation, weeping violently, and answering none of my questions. Yet she does not seem light-headed, but rather what we call hysterical."

"You will permit me now to see her. Take comfort; in all you tell me I see nothing to warrant serious alarm."

CHAPTER X.

To the true physician there is an inexpressible sanctity in the sick chamber. At its threshold the more human passions quit their hold on his heart. Love there would be profanation; even the grief permitted to others he must put aside. He must enter that room — a calm intelligence. He is disabled for his mission if he suffer aught to obscure the keen quiet glance of his science. Age or youth, beauty or deformity, innocence or guilt, merge their distinctions in one common attribute, — human suffering appealing to human skill.

Woe to the households in which the trusted Healer feels not on his conscience the solemn obligations of his glorious art! Reverently as in a temple, I stood in the virgin's chamber. When her mother placed her hand in mine, and I felt the throb of its pulse, I was aware of no quicker beat of my own heart. I looked with a steady eye on the face more beautiful from the flush that deepened the delicate hues of the young cheek, and the lustre that brightened the dark blue of the wandering eyes. She did not at first heed me, did not seem aware of my presence; but kept murmuring to herself words which I could not distinguish.

At length, when I spoke to her, in that low, soothing tone which we learn at the sick-bed, the expression of her face altered suddenly; she passed the hand I did not hold over her forehead, turned round, looked at me full and long, with unmistakable surprise, yet not as if the surprise displeased her,—less the surprise which recoils from the sight of a stranger than that which seems doubtfully to recognize an unexpected friend. Yet on the surprise there seemed to creep something of apprehension, of fear; her hand trembled, her voice quivered, as she said,—

"Can it be, can it be? Am I awake? Mother, who is this?"

"Only a kind visitor, Dr. Fenwick, sent by Mrs. Poyntz, for I was uneasy about you, darling. How are you now?"

"Better. Strangely better."

She removed her hand gently from mine, and with an involuntary modest shrinking turned towards Mrs. Ashleigh, drawing her mother towards herself, so that she became at once hidden from me.

Satisfied that there was here no delirium, nor even more than the slight and temporary fever which often accompanies a sudden nervous attack in constitutions peculiarly sensitive, I retired noiselessly from the room, and went, not into that which had been occupied by the ill-fated Naturalist, but down-stairs into the drawing-room, to write my prescription. I had already sent the servant off with it to the chemist's before Mrs. Ashleigh joined me.

"She seems recovering surprisingly; her forehead is cooler; she is perfectly self-possessed, only she cannot account for her own seizure,—cannot account either for the fainting or the agitation with which she awoke from sleep."

"I think I can account for both. The first room in which she entered — that in which she fainted — had its window open; the sides of the window are overgrown with rank creeping plants in full blossom. Miss Ashleigh had already predisposed herself to injurious effects from the effluvia by fatigue, excitement, imprudence in sitting out at the fall of a heavy dew. The sleep after the fainting fit was the more disturbed, because Nature, always alert and active in subjects so young, was making its own effort to right itself from an injury. Nature has nearly succeeded. What I have prescribed will a little aid and accelerate that which Nature has yet to do, and in a day or two I do not doubt that your daughter will be perfectly restored. Only let me recommend care to avoid exposure to the open air during the close of the day. Let her avoid also the room in which she was first seized, for it is a strange phenomenon in nervous temperaments that a nervous attack may, without visible cause, be repeated in the same place where it was first experienced. You had better shut up the chamber for at least some weeks, burn fires in it, repaint and paper it, sprinkle chloroform. You are not, perhaps, aware that Dr. Lloyd died in that room after a prolonged illness. Suffer me to wait till your servant returns with the medicine, and let me employ the interval in asking you a few questions. Miss Ashleigh, you say, never had a fainting fit before. I should presume that she is not what we call strong. But has she ever had any illness that alarmed you?"

"Never."

"No great liability to cold and cough, to attacks of the chest or lungs?"

"Certainly not. Still I have feared that she may have a tendency to consumption. Do you think so? Your questions alarm me!"

"I do not think so; but before I pronounce a positive opinion, one question more. You say you have feared a tendency to consumption. Is that disease in her family? She certainly did not inherit it from you. But on her father's side?"

"Her father," said Mrs. Ashleigh, with tears in her eyes, "died young, but of brain fever, which the medical men said was brought on by over study."

"Enough, my dear madam. What you say confirms my belief that your daughter's constitution is the very opposite to that in which the seeds of consumption lurk. It is rather that far nobler constitution, which the keenness of the nervous susceptibility renders delicate but elastic,— as quick to recover as it is to suffer."

"Thank you, thank you, Dr. Fenwick, for what you say. You take a load from my heart; for Mr. Vigors, I know, thinks Lilian consumptive, and Mrs. Poyntz has rather frightened me at times by hints to the same effect. But when you speak of nervous susceptibility, I do not quite understand you. My daughter is not what is commonly called nervous. Her temper is singularly even."

"But if not excitable, should you also say that she is not impressionable? The things which do not disturb her temper may, perhaps, deject her spirits. Do I make myself understood?"

"Yes, I think I understand your distinction; but I am not quite sure if it applies. To most things that affect the spirits she is not more sensitive than other girls, perhaps less so; but she is certainly very impressionable in some things."

"In what?"

"She is more moved than any one I ever knew by objects in external nature, rural scenery, rural sounds, by music, by the books that she reads,— even books that are not works of imagination. Perhaps in all this she takes after her poor father, but in a more marked degree,— at least, I observe it more in her; for he was very silent and reserved. And perhaps also her peculiarities have been fostered by the seclusion in which she has been brought up. It was with a view to make her a little more like girls of her own age that our friend, Mrs. Poyntz, induced me to come here. Lilian was reconciled to this change; but she shrank from the

thoughts of London, which I should have preferred. Her
poor father could not endure London."

"Miss Ashleigh is fond of reading? "

"Yes, she is fond of reading, but more fond of musing.
She will sit by herself for hours without book or work, and
seem as abstracted as if in a dream. She was so even in her
earliest childhood. Then she would tell me what she had
been conjuring up to herself. She would say that she had
seen — positively seen — beautiful lands far away from earth;
flowers and trees not like ours. As she grew older this visionary talk displeased me, and I scolded her, and said that if
others heard her, they would think that she was not only silly
but very untruthful. So of late years she never ventures to
tell me what, in such dreamy moments, she suffers herself to
imagine; but the habit of musing continues still. Do you
not agree with Mrs. Poyntz that the best cure would be a
little cheerful society amongst other young people?"

"Certainly," said I, honestly, though with a jealous pang.
"But here comes the medicine. Will you take it up to her,
and then sit with her half an hour or so? By that time I expect she will be asleep. I will wait here till you return.
Oh, I can amuse myself with the newspapers and books on
your table. Stay! one caution: be sure there are no flowers
in Miss Ashleigh's sleeping-room. I think I saw a treacherous rose-tree in a stand by the window. If so, banish it."

Left alone, I examined the room in which, oh, thought of
joy! I had surely now won the claim to become a privileged
guest. I touched the books Lilian must have touched; in the
articles of furniture, as yet so hastily disposed that the settled look of home was not about them, I still knew that I
was gazing on things which her mind must associate with the
history of her young life. That lute-harp must be surely
hers, and the scarf, with a girl's favourite colours, — pure
white and pale blue, — and the bird-cage, and the childish
ivory work-case, with implements too pretty for use, — all
spoke of her.

It was a blissful, intoxicating revery, which Mrs. Ashleigh's
entrance disturbed.

Lilian was sleeping calmly. I had no excuse to linger there any longer.

"I leave you, I trust, with your mind quite at ease," said I. "You will allow me to call to-morrow, in the afternoon?"

"Oh, yes, gratefully."

Mrs. Ashleigh held out her hand as I made towards the door.

Is there a physician who has not felt at times how that ceremonious fee throws him back from the garden-land of humanity into the market-place of money, — seems to put him out of the pale of equal friendship, and say, "True, you have given health and life. Adieu! there, you are paid for it!" With a poor person there would have been no dilemma, but Mrs. Ashleigh was affluent: to depart from custom here was almost impertinence. But had the penalty of my refusal been the doom of never again beholding Lilian, I could not have taken her mother's gold. So I did not appear to notice the hand held out to me, and passed by with a quickened step.

"But, Dr. Fenwick, stop!"

"No, ma'am, no! Miss Ashleigh would have recovered as soon without me. Whenever my aid is really wanted, then — but Heaven grant that time may never come! We will talk again about her to-morrow."

I was gone, — now in the garden ground, odorous with blossoms; now in the lane, inclosed by the narrow walls; now in the deserted streets, over which the moon shone full as in that winter night when I hurried from the chamber of death. But the streets were not ghastly now, and the moon was no longer Hecate, that dreary goddess of awe and spectres, but the sweet, simple Lady of the Stars, on whose gentle face lovers have gazed ever since (if that guess of astronomers be true) she was parted from earth to rule the tides of its deeps from afar, even as love, from love divided, rules the heart that yearns towards it with mysterious law.

CHAPTER XI.

WITH what increased benignity I listened to the patients who visited me the next morning! The whole human race seemed to be worthier of love, and I longed to diffuse amongst all some rays of the glorious hope that had dawned upon my heart. My first call, when I went forth, was on the poor young woman from whom I had been returning the day before, when an impulse, which seemed like a fate, had lured me into the grounds where I had first seen Lilian. I felt grateful to this poor patient; without her Lilian herself might be yet unknown to me.

The girl's brother, a young man employed in the police, and whose pay supported a widowed mother and the suffering sister, received me at the threshold of the cottage.

"Oh, sir, she is so much better to-day; almost free from pain. Will she live now; can she live?"

"If my treatment has really done the good you say; if she be really better under it, I think her recovery may be pronounced. But I must first see her."

The girl was indeed wonderfully better. I felt that my skill was achieving a signal triumph; but that day even my intellectual pride was forgotten in the luxurious unfolding of that sense of heart which had so newly waked into blossom.

As I recrossed the threshold, I smiled on the brother, who was still lingering there, —

"Your sister is saved, Wady. She needs now chiefly wine, and good though light nourishment; these you will find at my house; call there for them every day."

"God bless you, sir! If ever I can serve you — " His tongue faltered, he could say no more.

Serve me, Allen Fenwick — that poor policeman! Me, whom a king could not serve! What did I ask from earth

4

but Fame and Lilian's heart? Thrones and bread man wins from the aid of others; fame and woman's heart he can only gain through himself.

So I strode gayly up the hill, through the iron gates, into the fairy ground, and stood before Lilian's home.

The man-servant, on opening the door, seemed somewhat confused, and said hastily before I spoke,—

"Not at home, sir; a note for you."

I turned the note mechanically in my hand; I felt stunned.

"Not at home! Miss Ashleigh cannot be out. How is she?"

"Better, sir, thank you."

I still could not open the note; my eyes turned wistfully towards the windows of the house, and there — at the drawing-room window — I encountered the scowl of Mr. Vigors. I coloured with resentment, divined that I was dismissed, and walked away with a proud crest and a firm step.

When I was out of the gates, in the blind lane, I opened the note. It began formally. "Mrs. Ashleigh presents her compliments," and went on to thank me, civilly enough, for my attendance the night before, would not give me the trouble to repeat my visit, and inclosed a fee, double the amount of the fee prescribed by custom. I flung the money, as an asp that had stung me, over the high wall, and tore the note into shreds. Having thus idly vented my rage, a dull gnawing sorrow came heavily down upon all other emotions, stifling and replacing them. At the mouth of the lane I halted. I shrank from the thought of the crowded streets beyond; I shrank yet more from the routine of duties, which stretched before me in the desert into which daily life was so suddenly smitten. I sat down by the roadside, shading my dejected face with a nervous hand. I looked up as the sound of steps reached my ear, and saw Dr. Jones coming briskly along the lane, evidently from Abbots' House. He must have been there at the very time I had called. I was not only dismissed but supplanted. I rose before he reached the spot on which I had seated myself, and went my way into the town, went through my allotted round of professional visits; but my attentions were not so tenderly devoted, my skill so genially quickened by the glow of benevolence, as my poorer patients had found them in the morning. I have said how the physician should enter the sick-room. "A Calm Intelligence!" But if you strike a blow on the heart, the intellect suffers. Little worth, I suspect, was my "calm intelligence" that day. Bichat, in his famous book upon Life and Death, divides life into two classes,—animal and organic. Man's intellect, with the brain for its centre, belongs to life animal; his passions to life organic, centred in the heart, in the viscera. Alas! if the noblest passions through which alone we lift ourselves into the moral realm of the sublime and beautiful really have their centre in the life which the very vegetable, that lives organically, shares with us! And, alas! if it be that life which we share with the vegetable, that can cloud, obstruct, suspend, annul that life centred in the brain, which we share with every being howsoever angelic, in every star howsoever remote, on whom the Creator bestows the faculty of thought!

CHAPTER XII.

BUT suddenly I remembered Mrs. Poyntz. I ought to call on her. So I closed my round of visits at her door. The day was then far advanced, and the servant politely informed me that Mrs. Poyntz was at dinner. I could only leave my card, with a message that I would pay my respects to her the next day. That evening I received from her this note:—

DEAR DR. FENWICK,—I regret much that I cannot have the pleasure of seeing you to-morrow. Poyntz and I are going to visit his brother, at the other end of the county, and we start early. We shall be away some days. Sorry to hear from Mrs. Ashleigh that she has been persuaded by Mr. Vigors to consult Dr. Jones about Lilian. Vigors and Jones both frighten the poor mother, and insist upon consumptive tendencies. Unluckily, you seem to have said there was little

the matter.   Some doctors gain their practice as some preachers fill their churches, — by adroit use of the appeals to terror. You do not want patients, Dr. Jones does.   And, after all, better perhaps as it is.
Yours, etc.
M. POYNTZ.

To my more selfish grief, anxiety for Lilian was now added. I had seen many more patients die from being mistreated for consumption than from consumption itself. And Dr. Jones was a mercenary, cunning, needy man, with much crafty knowledge of human foibles, but very little skill in the treat‧ment of human maladies. My fears were soon confirmed. A few days after I heard from Miss Brabazon that Miss Ashleigh was seriously ill, kept her room. Mrs. Ashleigh made this excuse for not immediately returning the visits which the Hill had showered upon her. Miss Brabazon had seen Dr. Jones, who had shaken his head, said it was a serious case; but that time and care (his time and his care!) might effect wonders.

How stealthily at the dead of the night I would climb the Hill and look towards the windows of the old sombre house, — one window, in which a light burned dim and mournful, the light of a sick-room, — of hers!

At length Mrs. Poyntz came back, and I entered her house, having fully resolved beforehand on the line of policy to be adopted towards the potentate whom I hoped to secure as an ally. It was clear that neither disguise nor half-confidence would baffle the penetration of so keen an intellect, nor propitiate the good will of so imperious and resolute a temper. Perfect frankness here was the wisest prudence; and after all, it was most agreeable to my own nature, and most worthy of my own honour.

Luckily, I found Mrs. Poyntz alone, and taking in both mine the hand she somewhat coldly extended to me, I said, with the earnestness of suppressed emotion, —

"You observed when I last saw you, that I had not yet asked you to be my friend. I ask it now. Listen to me with all the indulgence you can vouchsafe, and let me at least profit by your counsel if you refuse to give me your aid."

Rapidly, briefly, I went on to say how I had first seen Lilian, and how sudden, how strange to myself, had been the impression which that first sight of her had produced.

"You remarked the change that had come over me," said I; "you divined the cause before I divined it myself,— divined it as I sat there beside you, thinking that through you I might see, in the freedom of social intercourse, the face that was then haunting me. You know what has since passed. Miss Ashleigh is ill; her case is, I am convinced, wholly misunderstood. All other feelings are merged in one sense of anxiety,— of alarm. But it has become due to me, due to all, to incur the risk of your ridicule even more than of your reproof, by stating to you thus candidly, plainly, bluntly, the sentiment which renders alarm so poignant, and which, if scarcely admissible to the romance of some wild dreamy boy, may seem an unpardonable folly in a man of my years and my sober calling,— due to me, to you, to Mrs. Ashleigh, because still the dearest thing in life to me is honour. And if you, who know Mrs. Ashleigh so intimately, who must be more or less aware of her plans or wishes for her daughter's future,— if you believe that those plans or wishes lead to a lot far more ambitious than an alliance with me could offer to Miss Ashleigh, then aid Mr. Vigors in excluding me from the house; aid me in suppressing a presumptuous, visionary passion. I cannot enter that house without love and hope at my heart; and the threshold of that house I must not cross if such love and such hope would be a sin and a treachery in the eyes of its owner. I might restore Miss Ashleigh to health; her gratitude might — I cannot continue. This danger must not be to me nor to her, if her mother has views far above such a son-in-law. And I am the more bound to consider all this while it is yet time, because I heard you state that Miss Ashleigh had a fortune,— was what would be here termed an heiress. And the full consciousness that whatever fame one in my profession may live to acquire, does not open those vistas of social power and grandeur which are opened by professions to my eyes less noble in themselves,— that full consciousness, I say, was forced upon me by certain words of your own. For the rest, you know my descent is sufficiently recognized as that amidst well-born gentry to have rendered me no *mésalliance* to families the most proud of their ancestry, if I had kept my hereditary estate and avoided the career that makes me useful to man. But I acknowledge that on entering a profession such as mine — entering any profession except that of arms or the senate — all leave their pedigree at its door, an erased or dead letter. All must come as equals, high-born or low-born, into that arena in which men ask aid from a man as he makes himself; to them his dead forefathers are idle dust. Therefore, to the advantage of birth I cease to have a claim. I am but a provincial physician, whose station would be the same had he been a cobbler's son. But gold retains its grand privilege in all ranks. He who has gold is removed from the suspicion that attaches to the greedy fortune-hunter. My private fortune, swelled by my savings, is sufficient to secure to any one I married a larger settlement than many a wealthy squire can make. I need no fortune with a wife; if she have one, it would be settled on herself. Pardon these vulgar details. Now, have I made myself understood?"

"Fully," answered the Queen of the Hill, who had listened to me quietly, watchfully, and without one interruption,— "fully; and you have done well to confide in me with so generous an unreserve. But before I say further, let me ask, what would be your advice for Lilian, supposing that you ought not to attend her? You have no trust in Dr. Jones; neither have I. And Annie Ashleigh's note received to-day, begging me to call, justifies your alarm. Still you think there is no tendency to consumption?"

"Of that I am certain so far as my slight glimpse of a case that to me, however, seems a simple and not uncommon one, will permit. But in the alternative you put — that my own skill, whatever its worth, is forbidden — my earnest advice is that Mrs. Ashleigh should take her daughter at once to London, and consult there those great authorities to whom I cannot compare my own opinion or experience; and by their counsel abide."

Mrs. Poyntz shaded her eyes with her hand for a few moments, and seemed in deliberation with herself. Then she said, with her peculiar smile, half grave, half ironical,—

"In matters more ordinary you would have won me to your side long ago. That Mr. Vigors should have presumed to cancel my recommendation to a settler on the Hill was an act of rebellion, and involved the honour of my prerogative; but I suppressed my indignation at an affront so unusual, partly out of pique against yourself, but much more, I think, out of regard for you."

"I understand. You detected the secret of my heart; you knew that Mrs. Ashleigh would not wish to see her daughter the wife of a provincial physician."

"Am I sure, or are you sure, that the daughter herself would accept that fate; or if she accepted it, would not repent? "

"Do you not think me the vainest of men when I say this, — that I cannot believe I should be so enthralled by a feeling at war with my reason, unfavoured by anything I can detect in my habits of mind, or even by the dreams of a youth which exalted science and excluded love, unless I was intimately convinced that Miss Ashleigh's heart was free, that I could win, and that I could keep it! Ask me why I am convinced of this, and I can tell you no more why I think that she could love me than I can tell you why I love her! "

"I am of the world, worldly; but I am a woman, womanly, — though I may not care to be thought it. And, therefore, though what you say is, regarded in a worldly point of view, sheer nonsense, regarded in a womanly point of view, it is logically sound. But still you cannot know Lilian as I do. Your nature and hers are in strong contrast. I do not think she is a safe wife for you. The purest, the most innocent creature imaginable, certainly that, but always in the seventh heaven; and you in the seventh heaven just at this moment, but with an irresistible gravitation to the solid earth, which will have its way again when the honeymoon is over — I do not believe you two would harmonize by intercourse. I do not believe Lilian would sympathize with you, and I am sure you could not sympathize with her throughout the long dull course of this workday life. And, therefore, for your sake, as well as hers, I was not displeased to find that Dr. Jones had replaced you; and now, in return for your frankness, I say frankly, do not go again to that house. Conquer this sentiment, fancy, passion, whatever it be. And I will advise Mrs. Ashleigh to take Lilian to town. Shall it be so settled?"

I could not speak. I buried my face in my hands — misery, misery, desolation!

I know not how long I remained thus silent, perhaps many minutes. At length I felt a cold, firm, but not ungentle hand placed upon mine; and a clear, full, but not discouraging voice said to me, —

"Leave me to think well over this conversation, and to ponder well the value of all you have shown that you so deeply feel. The interests of life do not fill both scales of the balance. The heart, which does not always go in the same scale with the interests, still has its weight in the scale opposed to them. I have heard a few wise men say, as many a silly woman says, 'Better be unhappy with one we love, than be happy with one we love not.' Do you say that too?"

"With every thought of my brain, every beat of my pulse, I say it."

"After that answer, all my questionings cease. You shall hear from me to-morrow. By that time, I shall have seen Annie and Lilian. I shall have weighed both scales of the balance, — and the heart here, Allen Fenwick, seems very heavy. Go, now. I hear feet on the stairs, Poyntz bringing up some friendly gossiper; gossipers are spies."

I passed my hand over my eyes, tearless, but how tears would have relieved the anguish that burdened them! and, without a word, went down the stairs, meeting at the landing-place Colonel Poyntz and the old man whose pain my prescription had cured. The old man was whistling a merry tune, perhaps first learned on the playground. He broke from it to thank, almost to embrace me, as I slid by him. I seized his jocund blessing as a good omen, and carried it with me as I passed into the broad sunlight. Solitary — solitary! Should I be so evermore?

CHAPTER XIII.

The next day I had just dismissed the last of my visiting patients, and was about to enter my carriage and commence my round, when I received a twisted note containing but these words: —

Call on me to-day, as soon as you can.

M. POYNTZ.

A few minutes afterwards I was in Mrs. Poyntz's drawing-room.

"Well, Allen Fenwick," said she, "I do not serve friends by halves. No thanks! I but adhere to a principle I have laid down for myself. I spent last evening with the Ashleighs. Lilian is certainly much altered,— very weak, I fear very ill, and I believe very unskilfuly treated by Dr. Jones. I felt that it was my duty to insist on a change of physician; but there was something else to consider before deciding who that physician should be. I was bound, as your *confidante*, to consult your own scruples of honour. Of course I could not say point-blank to Mrs. Ashleigh, 'Dr. Fenwick admires your daughter, would you object to him as a son-in-law?' Of course I could not touch at all on the secret with which you intrusted me; but I have not the less arrived at a conclusion, in agreement with my previous belief, that not being a woman of the world, Annie Ashleigh has none of the ambition which women of the world would conceive for a daughter who has a good fortune and considerable beauty; that her predominant anxiety is for her child's happiness, and her predominant fear is that her child will die. She would never oppose any attachment which Lilian might form; and if that attachment were for one who had preserved her daughter's life, I believe her own heart would gratefully go with her daughter's. So far, then, as honour is concerned, all scruples vanish."

I sprang from my seat, radiant with joy. Mrs. Poyntz dryly continued: "You value yourself on your common-sense, and to that I address a few words of counsel which may not be welcome to your romance. I said that I did not think you and Lilian would suit each other in the long run; reflection confirms me in that supposition. Do not look at me so incredulously and so sadly. Listen, and take heed. Ask yourself what, as a man whose days are devoted to a laborious profession, whose ambition is entwined with its success, whose mind must be absorbed in its pursuits, — ask yourself what kind of a wife you would have sought to win, had not this sudden fancy for a charming face rushed over your better reason, and obliterated all previous plans and resolutions. Surely some one with whom your heart would have been quite at rest; by whom your thoughts would have been undistracted from the channels into which your calling should concentrate their flow; in short, a serene companion in the quiet holiday of a trustful home! Is it not so?"

"You interpret my own thoughts when they have turned towards marriage. But what is there in Lilian Ashleigh that should mar the picture you have drawn?"

"What is there in Lilian Ashleigh which in the least accords with the picture? In the first place, the wife of a young physician should not be his perpetual patient. The more he loves her, and the more worthy she may be of love, the more her case will haunt him wherever he goes. When he returns home, it is not to a holiday; the patient he most cares for, the anxiety that most gnaws him, awaits him there."

"But, good heavens! why should Lilian Ashleigh be a perpetual patient? The sanitary resources of youth are incalculable. And — "

"Let me stop you; I cannot argue against a physician in love! I will give up that point in dispute, remaining convinced that there is something in Lilian's constitution which will perplex, torment, and baffle you. It was so with her father, whom she resembles in face and in character. He showed no symptoms of any grave malady. His outward form was, like Lilian's, a model of symmetry, except in this, that, like hers, it was too exquisitely delicate; but when seemingly in the midst of perfect health, at any slight jar on the nerves he would become alarmingly ill. I was sure that he would die young, and he did so."

"Ay, but Mrs. Ashleigh said that his death was from brain-fever, brought on by over-study. Rarely, indeed, do women so fatigue the brain. No female patient, in the range of my practice, ever died of purely mental exertion."

"Of purely mental exertion, no; but of *heart* emotion, many female patients, perhaps? Oh, you own that! I know nothing about nerves; but I suppose that, whether they act on the brain or the heart, the result to life is much the same if the nerves be too finely strung for life's daily wear and tear. And this is what I mean, when I say you and Lilian will not suit. As yet, she is a mere child; her nature undeveloped, and her affections therefore untried. You might suppose that you had won her heart; she might believe that she gave it to you, and both be deceived. If fairies nowadays condescended to exchange their offspring with those of mortals, and if the popular tradition did not represent a fairy changeling as an ugly peevish creature, with none of the grace of its parents, I should be half inclined to suspect that Lilian was one of the elfin people. She never seems at home on earth; and I do not think she will ever be contented with a prosaic earthly lot. Now I have told you why I do not think she will suit you. I must leave it to yourself to conjecture how far you would suit her. I say this in due season, while you may set a guard upon your impulse; while you may yet watch, and weigh, and meditate; and from this moment on that subject I say no more. I lend advice, but I never throw it away."

She came here to a dead pause, and began putting on her bonnet and scarf, which lay on the table beside her. I was a little chilled by her words, and yet more by the blunt, shrewd, hard look and manner which aided the effect of their delivery; but the chill melted away in the sudden glow of my heart when she again turned towards me and said,—

"Of course you guess, from these preliminary cautions, that you are going into danger? Mrs. Ashleigh wishes to consult you about Lilian, and I propose to take you to her house."

"Oh, my friend, my dear friend, how can I ever repay you?" I caught her hand, the white firm hand, and lifted it to my lips.

She drew it somewhat hastily away, and laying it gently on my shoulder, said, in a soft voice, "Poor Allen, how little the world knows either of us! But how little perhaps we know ourselves! Come, your carriage is here? That is right; we must put down Dr. Jones publicly and in all our state."

In the carriage Mrs. Poyntz told me the purport of that conversation with Mrs. Ashleigh to which I owed my re-introduction to Abbots' House. It seems that Mr. Vigors had called early the morning after my first visit! had evinced much discomposure on hearing that I had been summoned! dwelt much on my injurious treatment of Dr. Lloyd, whom, as distantly related to himself, and he (Mr. Vigors) being distantly connected with the late Gilbert Ashleigh, he endeavoured to fasten upon his listener as one of her husband's family, whose quarrel she was bound in honour to take up. He spoke of me as an infidel "tainted with French doctrines," and as a practitioner rash and presumptuous; proving his own freedom from presumption and rashness by flatly deciding that my opinion must be wrong. Previously to Mrs. Ashleigh's migration to L——, Mr. Vigors had interested her in the pretended phenomena of mesmerism. He had consulted a clairvoyante, much esteemed by poor Dr. Lloyd, as to Lilian's health, and the clairvoyante had declared her to be constitutionally predisposed to consumption. Mr. Vigors persuaded Mrs. Ashleigh to come at once with him and see this clairvoyante herself, armed with a lock of Lilian's hair and a glove she had worn, as the media of mesmerical *rapport*.

The clairvoyante, one of those I had publicly denounced as an impostor, naturally enough denounced me in return. On being asked solemnly by Mr. Vigors "to look at Dr. Fenwick and see if his influence would be beneficial to the subject," the sibyl had become violently agitated, and said that, "when she looked at us together, we were enveloped in a black cloud; that this portended affliction and sinister consequences; that our *rapport* was antagonistic." Mr. Vigors then told her to dismiss my image, and conjure up that of Dr. Jones. Therewith the somnambule became more tranquil, and said: "Dr. Jones would do well if he would be guided by higher lights than his own skill, and consult herself daily as to the proper remedies. The best remedy of all would be mesmerism. But since Dr. Lloyd's death, she did not know of a mesmerist, sufficiently gifted, in affinity with the patient." In fine, she impressed and awed Mrs. Ashleigh, who returned in haste, summoned Dr. Jones, and dismissed myself.

"I could not have conceived Mrs. Ashleigh to be so utterly wanting in common-sense," said I. "She talked rationally enough when I saw her."

"She has common-sense in general, and plenty of the sense most common," answered Mrs. Poyntz; "but she is easily led and easily frightened wherever her affections are concerned, and therefore, just as easily as she had been persuaded by Mr. Vigors and terrified by the somnambule, I persuaded her against the one, and terrified her against the other. I had positive experience on my side, since it was clear that Lilian had been getting rapidly worse under Dr. Jones's care. The main obstacles I had to encounter in inducing Mrs. Ashleigh to consult you again were, first, her reluctance to disoblige Mr. Vigors, as a friend and connection of Lilian's father; and, secondly, her sentiment of shame in re-inviting your opinion after having treated you with so little respect. Both these difficulties I took on myself. I bring you to her house, and, on leaving you, I shall go on to Mr. Vigors, and tell him what is done is my doing, and not to be undone by him; so that matter is settled. Indeed, if you were out of the question, I should not suffer Mr. Vigors to re-introduce all these mummeries of clairvoyance and mesmerism into the precincts of the Hill. I did not demolish a man I really liked in Dr. Lloyd, to set up a Dr. Jones, whom I despise, in his stead. Clairvoyance on Abbey Hill, indeed! I saw enough of it before."

"True; your strong intellect detected at once the absurdity of the whole pretence,— the falsity of mesmerism, the impossibility of clairvoyance."

"No, my strong intellect did nothing of the kind. I do not know whether mesmerism be false or clairvoyance impossible; and I don't wish to know. All I do know is, that I saw the Hill in great danger,— young ladies allowing themselves to be put to sleep by gentlemen, and pretending they had no will of their own against such fascination! Improper and shocking! And Miss Brabazon beginning to prophesy, and Mrs. Leopold Smythe questioning her maid (whom Dr. Lloyd declared to be highly gifted) as to all the secrets of her friends. When I saw this, I said, 'The Hill is becoming demoralized; the Hill is making itself ridiculous; the Hill must be saved!' I remonstrated with Dr. Lloyd as a friend; he remained obdurate. I annihilated him as an enemy, not to me but to the State. I slew my best lover for the good of Rome. Now you know why I took your part,— not because I have any opinion, one way or the other, as to the truth or falsehood of what Dr. Lloyd asserted; but I have a strong opinion that, whether they be true or false, his notions were those which are not to be allowed on the Hill. And so, Allen Fenwick, that matter was settled."

Perhaps at another time I might have felt some little humiliation to learn that I had been honoured with the influence of this great potentate not as a champion of truth, but as an instrument of policy; and I might have owned to some twinge of conscience in having assisted to sacrifice a fellow-seeker after science — misled, no doubt, but preferring his independent belief to his worldly interest — and sacrifice him to those deities with whom science is ever at war,— the Prejudices of a Clique sanctified into the Proprieties of the World. But at that moment the words I heard made no perceptible impression on my mind. The gables of Abbots' House were visible above the evergreens and lilacs; another moment, and the carriage stopped at the door.

CHAPTER XIV.

MRS. ASHLEIGH received us in the dining-room. Her man-ner to me, at first, was a little confused and shy. But my companion soon communicated something of her own happy ease to her gentler friend. After a short conversation we all three went to Lilian, who was in a little room on the ground-floor, fitted up as her study. I was glad to perceive that my interdict of the death-chamber had been respected.

She reclined on a sofa near the window, which was, how-ever, jealously closed; the light of the bright May-day ob-scured by blinds and curtains; a large fire on the hearth; the air of the room that of a hot-house, — the ignorant, senseless, exploded system of nursing into consumption those who are confined on suspicion of it! She did not heed us as we en-tered noiselessly; her eyes were drooped languidly on the floor, and with difficulty I suppressed the exclamation that rose to my lips on seeing her. She seemed within the last few days so changed, and on the aspect of the countenance there was so profound a melancholy! But as she slowly turned at the sound of our footsteps, and her eyes met mine, a quick blush came into the wan cheek, and she half rose, but sank back as if the effort exhausted her. There was a struggle for breath, and a low hollow cough. Was it possible that I had been mistaken, and that in that cough was heard the warning knell of the most insidious enemy to youthful life?

I sat down by her side; I lured her on to talk of indifferent subjects,— the weather, the gardens, the bird in the cage, which was placed on the table near her. Her voice, at first low and feeble, became gradually stronger, and her face lighted up with a child's innocent, playful smile. No, I had not been mistaken! That was no lymphatic, nerveless tem-perament, on which consumption fastens as its lawful prey;

here there was no hectic pulse, no hurried waste of the vital flame. Quietly and gently I made my observations, addressed my questions, applied my stethoscope; and when I turned my face towards her mother's anxious, eager eyes, that face told my opinion; for her mother sprang forward, clasped my hand, and said, through her struggling tears,—

"You smile! You see nothing to fear?"

"Fear! No, indeed! You will soon be again yourself, Miss Ashleigh, will you not?"

"Yes," she said, with her sweet laugh, "I shall be well now very soon. But may I not have the window open; may I not go into the garden? I so long for fresh air."

"No, no, darling," exclaimed Mrs. Ashleigh, "not while the east winds last. Dr. Jones said on no account. On no account, Dr. Fenwick, eh?"

"Will you take my arm, Miss Ashleigh, for a few turns up and down the room?" said I. "We will then see how far we may rebel against Dr. Jones."

She rose with some little effort, but there was no cough. At first her step was languid; it became lighter and more elastic after a few moments.

"Let her come out," said I to Mrs. Ashleigh. "The wind is not in the east, and, while we are out, pray bid your servant lower to the last bar in the grate that fire,— only fit for Christmas."

"But—"

"Ah, no buts! He is a poor doctor who is not a stern despot."

So the straw hat and mantle were sent for. Lilian was wrapped with unnecessary care, and we all went forth into the garden. Involuntarily we took the way to the Monk's Well, and at every step Lilian seemed to revive under the bracing air and temperate sun. We paused by the well.

"You do not feel fatigued, Miss Ashleigh?"

"No."

"But your face seems changed. It is grown sadder."

"Not sadder."

"Sadder than when I first saw it,— saw it when you were

seated here!" I said this in a whisper. I felt her hand tremble as it lay on my arm.

"You saw me seated here!"

"Yes. I will tell you how some day."

Lilian lifted her eyes to mine, and there was in them that same surprise which I had noticed on my first visit,— a surprise that perplexed me, blended with no displeasure, but yet with a something of vague alarm.

We soon returned to the house.

Mrs. Ashleigh made me a sign to follow her into the drawing-room, leaving Mrs. Poyntz with Lilian.

"Well?" said she, tremblingly.

"Permit me to see Dr. Jones's prescriptions. Thank you. Ay, I thought so. My dear madam, the mistake here has been in depressing nature instead of strengthening; in narcotics instead of stimulants. The main stimulants which leave no reaction are air and light. Promise me that I may have my own way for a week,— that all I recommend will be implicitly heeded?"

"I promise. But that cough,— you noticed it?"

"Yes. The nervous system is terribly lowered, and nervous exhaustion is a strange impostor; it imitates all manner of complaints with which it has no connection. The cough will soon disappear! But pardon my question. Mrs. Poyntz tells me that you consulted a clairvoyante about your daughter. Does Miss Ashleigh know that you did so?"

"No; I did not tell her."

"I am glad of that. And pray, for Heaven's sake, guard her against all that may set her thinking on such subjects. Above all, guard her against concentring attention on any malady that your fears erroneously ascribe to her. It is amongst the phenomena of our organization that you cannot closely rivet your consciousness on any part of the frame, however healthy, but it will soon begin to exhibit morbid sensibility. Try to fix all your attention on your little finger for half an hour, and before the half hour is over the little finger will be uneasy, probably even painful. How serious, then, is the danger to a young girl, at the age in which im-

5

agination is most active, most intense, if you force upon her
a belief that she is in danger of a mortal disease! It is a
peculiarity of youth to brood over the thought of early death
much more resignedly, much more complacently, than we do
in maturer years. Impress on a young imaginative girl, as
free from pulmonary tendencies as you and I are, the conviction that she must fade away into the grave, and though she
may not actually die of consumption, you instil slow poison
into her system. Hope is the natural aliment of youth. You
impoverish nourishment where you discourage hope. As soon
as this temporary illness is over, reject for your daughter the
melancholy care which seems to her own mind to mark her out
from others of her age. Rear her for the air, which is the
kindest life-giver; to sleep with open windows: to be out at
sunrise. Nature will do more for her than all our drugs can
do. You have been hitherto fearing Nature; now trust to
her."

Here Mrs. Poyntz joined us, and having, while I had been
speaking, written my prescription and some general injunctions, I closed my advice with an appeal to that powerful
protectress.

"This, my dear madam, is a case in which I need your aid,
and I ask it. Miss Ashleigh should not be left with no other
companion than her mother. A change of faces is often as
salutary as a change of air. If you could devote an hour or
two this very evening to sit with Miss Ashleigh, to talk to
her with your usual cheerfulness, and — "

"Annie," interrupted Mrs. Poyntz, "I will come and drink
tea with you at half-past seven, and bring my knitting; and
perhaps, if you ask him, Dr. Fenwick will come too! He can
be tolerably entertaining when he likes it." .

"It is too great a tax on his kindness, I fear," said Mrs.
Ashleigh. "But," she added cordially, "I should be grateful
indeed if he would spare us an hour of his time."

I murmured an assent which I endeavoured to make not too
joyous.

"So that matter is settled," said Mrs. Poyntz; "and now I
shall go to Mr. Vigors and prevent his further interference."

"Oh, but, Margaret, pray don't offend him,— a connection of my poor dear Gilbert's. And so tetchy! I am sure I do not know how you 'll manage to — "

"To get rid of him? Never fear. As I manage everything and everybody," said Mrs. Poyntz, bluntly. So she kissed her friend on the forehead, gave me a gracious nod, and, declining the offer of my carriage, walked with her usual brisk, decided tread down the short path towards the town.

Mrs. Ashleigh timidly approached me, and again the furtive hand bashfully insinuated the hateful fee.

"Stay," said I; "this is a case which needs the most constant watching. I wish to call so often that I should seem the most greedy of doctors if my visits were to be computed at guineas. Let me be at ease to effect my cure; my pride of science is involved in it. And when amongst all the young ladies of the Hill you can point to none with a fresher bloom, or a fairer promise of healthful life, than the patient you intrust to my care, why, then the fee and the dismissal. Nay, nay; I must refer you to our friend Mrs. Poyntz. It was so settled with her before she brought me here to displace Dr. Jones." Therewith I escaped.

CHAPTER XV.

In less than a week Lilian was convalescent; in less than a fortnight she regained her usual health,— nay, Mrs. Ashleigh declared that she had never known her daughter appear so cheerful and look so well. I had established a familiar intimacy at Abbots' House; most of my evenings were spent there. As horse exercise formed an important part of my advice, Mrs. Ashleigh had purchased a pretty and quiet horse for her daughter; and, except the weather was very unfavourable, Lilian now rode daily with Colonel Poyntz, who was a notable equestrian, and often accompanied by Miss

Jane Poyntz, and other young ladies of the Hill. I was generally relieved from my duties in time to join her as she returned homewards. Thus we made innocent appointments,
openly, frankly, in her mother's presence, she telling me beforehand in what direction excursions had been planned with
Colonel Poyntz, and I promising to fall in with the party —
if my avocations would permit. At my suggestion, Mrs.
Ashleigh now opened her house almost every evening to some
of the neighbouring families; Lilian was thus habituated to
the intercourse of young persons of her own age. Music and
dancing and childlike games made the old house gay. And
the Hill gratefully acknowledged to Mrs. Poyntz, "that the
Ashleighs were indeed a great acquisition."

But my happiness was not uncheckered. In thus unsel-
fishly surrounding Lilian with others, I felt the anguish of
that jealousy which is inseparable from those earlier stages
of love, when the lover as yet has won no right to that self-
confidence which can only spring from the assurance that he
is loved.

In these social reunions I remained aloof from Lilian. I
saw her courted by the gay young admirers whom her beauty
and her fortune drew around her, — her soft face brightening
in the exercise of the dance, which the gravity of my profession rather than my years forbade to join; and her laugh, so
musically subdued, ravishing my ear and fretting my heart
as if the laugh were a mockery on my sombre self and my
presumptuous dreams. But no, suddenly, shyly, her eyes
would steal away from those about her, steal to the corner in
which I sat, as if they missed me, and, meeting my own gaze,
their light softened before they turned away; and the colour
on her cheek would deepen, and to her lip there came a smile
different from the smile that it shed on others. And then —
and then — all jealousy, all sadness vanished, and I felt the
glory which blends with the growing belief that we are
loved.

In that diviner epoch of man's mysterious passion, when
ideas of perfection and purity, vague and fugitive before,
start forth and concentre themselves round one virgin shape,

— that rises out from the sea of creation, welcomed by the Hours and adorned by the Graces,— how the thought that this archetype of sweetness and beauty singles himself from the millions, singles himself for her choice, ennobles and lifts up his being! Though after-experience may rebuke the mortal's illusion, that mistook for a daughter of Heaven a creature of clay like himself, yet for a while the illusion has grandeur. Though it comes from the senses which shall later oppress and profane it, the senses at first shrink into shade, awed and hushed by the presence that charms them. All that is brightest and best in the man has soared up like long-dormant instincts of Heaven, to greet and to hallow what to him seems life's fairest dream of the heavenly! Take the wings from the image of Love, and the god disappears from the form!

Thus, if at moments jealous doubt made my torture, so the moment's relief from it sufficed for my rapture. But I had a cause for disquiet less acute but less varying than jealousy.

Despite Lilian's recovery from the special illness which had more immediately absorbed my care, I remained perplexed as to its cause and true nature. To her mother I gave it the convenient epithet of "nervous;" but the epithet did not explain to myself all the symptoms I classified by it. There was still, at times, when no cause was apparent or conjecturable, a sudden change in the expression of her countenance, in the beat of her pulse; the eye would become fixed, the bloom would vanish, the pulse would sink feebler and feebler till it could be scarcely felt; yet there was no indication of heart disease, of which such sudden lowering of life is in itself sometimes a warning indication. The change would pass away after a few minutes, during which she seemed unconscious, or, at least, never spoke — never appeared to heed what was said to her. But in the expression of her countenance there was no character of suffering or distress; on the contrary, a wondrous serenity, that made her beauty more beauteous, her very youthfulness younger; and when this spurious or partial kind of syncope passed, she recovered at once without effort, without acknowledging that she had

felt faint or unwell, but rather with a sense of recruited vitality, as the weary obtain from a sleep. For the rest her
spirits were more generally light and joyous than I should
have premised from her mother's previous description. She
would enter mirthfully into the mirth of young companions
round her: she had evidently quick perception of the sunny
sides of life; an infantine gratitude for kindness; an infantine joy in the trifles that amuse only those who delight in
tastes pure and simple. But when talk rose into graver and
more contemplative topics, her attention became earnest and
absorbed; and sometimes a rich eloquence, such as I have
never before nor since heard from lips so young, would startle me first into a wondering silence, and soon into a disap-
proving alarm: for the thoughts she then uttered seemed to
me too fantastic, too visionary, too much akin to the vagaries
of a wild though beautiful imagination. And then I would
seek to check, to sober, to distract fancies with which my
reason had no sympathy, and the indulgence of which I regarded as injurious to the normal functions of the brain.

When thus, sometimes with a chilling sentence, sometimes
with a half-sarcastic laugh, I would repress outpourings frank
and musical as the songs of a forest-bird, she would look at
me with a kind of plaintive sorrow, — often sigh and shiver
as she turned away. Only in those modes did she show displeasure; otherwise ever sweet and docile, and ever, if, seeing
that I had pained her, I asked forgiveness, humbling herself
rather to ask mine, and brightening our reconciliation with
her angel smile. As yet I had not dared to speak of love; as
yet I gazed on her as the captive gazes on the flowers and the
stars through the gratings of his cell, murmuring to himself,
" When shall the doors unclose? "

CHAPTER XVI.

It was with a wrath suppressed in the presence of the fair ambassadress, that Mr. Vigors had received from Mrs. Poyntz the intelligence that I had replaced Dr. Jones at Abbots' House not less abruptly than Dr. Jones had previously supplanted me. As Mrs. Poyntz took upon herself the whole responsibility of this change, Mr. Vigors did not venture to condemn it to her face; for the Administrator of Laws was at heart no little in awe of the Autocrat of Proprieties; as Authority, howsoever established, is in awe of Opinion, howsoever capricious.

To the mild Mrs. Ashleigh the magistrate's anger was more decidedly manifested. He ceased his visits; and in answer to a long and deprecatory letter with which she endeavoured to soften his resentment and win him back to the house, he replied by an elaborate combination of homily and satire. He began by excusing himself from accepting her invitations, on the ground that *his* time was valuable, *his* habits domestic; and though ever willing to sacrifice both time and habits where he could do good, he owed it to himself and to mankind to sacrifice neither where his advice was rejected and his opinion contemned. He glanced briefly, but not hastily, at the respect with which her late husband had deferred to his judgment, and the benefits which that deference had enabled him to bestow. He contrasted the husband's deference with the widow's contumely, and hinted at the evils which the contumely would not permit him to prevent. He could not presume to say what women of the world might think due to deceased husbands, but even women of the world generally allowed the claims of living children, and did not act with levity where their interests were concerned, still less where their lives were at stake. As to Dr. Jones, he, Mr. Vigors, had the fullest confidence in his skill. Mrs. Ashleigh must judge for herself whether Mrs. Poyntz was as good an authority upon medical science as he had no doubt she was upon shawls and ribbons. Dr. Jones was a man of caution and modesty; he did not indulge in the hollow boasts by which charlatans decoy their dupes; but Dr. Jones had privately assured him that though the case was one that admitted of no rash experiments, he had no fear of the result if his own prudent system were persevered in. What might be the consequences of any other system, Dr. Jones would not say, because he was too high-minded to express his distrust of the rival who had made use of underhand arts to supplant him. But Mr. Vigors was convinced, from other sources of information (meaning, I presume, the oracular prescience of his clairvoyants), that the time would come when the poor young lady would herself insist on discarding Dr. Fenwick, and when "that person" would appear in a very different light to many who now so fondly admired and so reverentially trusted him. When that time arrived, he, Mr. Vigors, might again be of use; but, meanwhile, though he declined to renew his intimacy at Abbots' House, or to pay unavailing visits of mere ceremony, his interest in the daughter of his old friend remained undiminished, nay, was rather increased by compassion; that he should silently keep his eye upon her; and whenever anything to her advantage suggested itself to him, he should not be deterred by the slight with which Mrs. Ashleigh had treated his judgment from calling on her, and placing before her conscience as a mother his ideas for her child's benefit, leaving to herself then, as now, the entire responsibility of rejecting the advice which he might say, without vanity, was deemed of some value by those who could distinguish between sterling qualities and specious pretences.

Mrs. Ashleigh's was that thoroughly womanly nature which instinctively leans upon others. She was diffident, trustful, meek, affectionate. Not quite justly had Mrs. Poyntz described her as "commonplace weak," for though she might be called weak, it was not because she was commonplace; she had a goodness of heart, a sweetness of disposition, to which that disparaging definition could not apply. She could only

be called commonplace inasmuch as in the ordinary daily
affairs of life she had a great deal of ordinary daily commonplace good-sense. Give her a routine to follow, and no routine could be better adhered to. In the allotted sphere of a
woman's duties she never seemed in fault. No household,
not even Mrs. Poyntz's, was more happily managed. The old
Abbots' House had merged its original antique gloom in the
softer character of pleasing repose. All her servants adored
Mrs. Ashleigh; all found it a pleasure to please her; her
establishment had the harmony of clockwork; comfort diffused itself round her like quiet sunshine round a sheltered
spot. To gaze on her pleasing countenance, to listen to the
simple talk that lapsed from her guileless lips, in even, slow,
and lulling murmur, was in itself a respite from "eating
cares." She was to the mind what the colour of green is to
the eye. She had, therefore, excellent sense in all that
relates to every-day life. There, she needed not to consult
another; there, the wisest might have consulted her with
profit. But the moment anything, however trivial in itself,
jarred on the routine to which her mind had grown wedded,
the moment an incident hurried her out of the beaten track
of woman's daily life, then her confidence forsook her; then
she needed a confidant, an adviser; and by that confidant or
adviser she could be credulously lured or submissively controlled. Therefore, when she lost, in Mr. Vigors, the guide
she had been accustomed to consult whenever she needed
guidance, she turned, helplessly and piteously, first to Mrs.
Poyntz, and then yet more imploringly to me, because a
woman of that character is never quite satisfied without the
advice of a man; and where an intimacy more familiar than
that of his formal visits is once established with a physician,
confidence in him grows fearless and rapid, as the natural
result of sympathy concentrated on an object of anxiety in
common between himself and the home which opens its sacred
recess to his observant but tender eye. Thus Mrs. Ashleigh
had shown me Mr. Vigors's letter, and, forgetting that I
might not be as amiable as herself, besought me to counsel
her how to conciliate and soften her lost husband's friend

and connection. That character clothed him with dignity
and awe in her soft forgiving eyes. So, smothering my own
resentment, less perhaps at the tone of offensive insinuation
against myself than at the arrogance with which this prejudiced intermeddler implied to a mother the necessity of his
guardian watch over a child under her own care, I sketched a
reply which seemed to me both dignified and placatory, ab-
staining from all discussion, and conveying the assurance
that Mrs. Ashleigh would be at all times glad to hear, and
disposed to respect, whatever suggestion so esteemed a friend
of her husband would kindly submit to her for the welfare
of her daughter.

There all communication had stopped for about a month
since the date of my reintroduction to Abbots' House. One
afternoon I unexpectedly met Mr. Vigors at the entrance of
the blind lane, I on my way to Abbots' House, and my first
glance at his face told me that he was coming from it, for the
expression of that face was more than usually sinister; the
sullen scowl was lit into significant menace by a sneer of unmistakable triumph. I felt at once that he had succeeded
in some machination against me, and with ominous misgiv-
ings quickened my steps.

I found Mrs. Ashleigh seated alone in front of the house,
under a large cedar-tree that formed a natural arbour in the
centre of the sunny lawn. She was perceptibly embarrassed
as I took my seat beside her.

"I hope," said I, forcing a smile, "that Mr. Vigors has not
been telling you that I shall kill my patient, or that she looks
much worse than she did under Dr. Jones's care? "

"No," she said. "He owned cheerfully that Lilian had
grown quite strong, and said, without any displeasure, that
he had heard how gay she had been, riding out and even
dancing,— which is very kind in him, for he disapproves of
dancing, on principle."

"But still I can see he has said something to vex or annoy
you; and, to judge by his countenance when I met him in the
lane, I should conjecture that that something was intended to
lower the confidence you so kindly repose in me."

"I assure you not; he did not mention your name, either to me or to Lilian. I never knew him more friendly; quite like old times. He is a good man at heart, very, and was much attached to my poor husband."

"Did Mr. Ashleigh profess a very high opinion of Mr. Vigors?"

"Well, I don't quite know that, because my dear Gilbert never spoke to me much about him. Gilbert was naturally very silent. But he shrank from all trouble — all worldly affairs — and Mr. Vigors managed his estate, and inspected his steward's books, and protected him through a long lawsuit which he had inherited from his father. It killed his father. I don't know what we should have done without Mr. Vigors, and I am so glad he has forgiven me."

"Hem! Where is Miss Ashleigh? Indoors?"

"No; somewhere in the grounds. But, my dear Dr. Fenwick, do not leave me yet; you are so very, very kind, and somehow I have grown to look upon you quite as an old friend. Something has happened which has put me out, — quite put me out."

She said this wearily and feebly, closing her eyes as if she were indeed put out in the sense of extinguished.

"The feeling of friendship you express," said I, with earnestness, "is reciprocal. On my side it is accompanied by a peculiar gratitude. I am a lonely man, by a lonely fireside, — no parents, no near kindred, and in this town, since Dr. Faber left it, without cordial intimacy till I knew you. In admitting me so familiarly to your hearth, you have given me what I have never known before since I came to man's estate, — a glimpse of the happy domestic life; the charm and relief to eye, heart, and spirit which is never known but in households cheered by the face of woman. Thus my sentiment for you and yours is indeed that of an old friend; and in any private confidence you show me, I feel as if I were no longer a lonely man, without kindred, without home."

Mrs. Ashleigh seemed much moved by these words, which my heart had forced from my lips; and, after replying to me with simple unaffected warmth of kindness, she rose, took my arm, and continued thus as we walked slowly to and fro the lawn: "You know, perhaps, that my poor husband left a sister, now a widow like myself, Lady Haughton."

"I remember that Mrs. Poyntz said you had such a sister-in-law, but I never heard you mention Lady Haughton till now. Well!"

"Well, Mr. Vigors has brought me a letter from her, and it is that which has put me out. I dare say you have not heard me speak before of Lady Haughton, for I am ashamed to say I had almost forgotten her existence. She is many years older than my husband was; of a very different character. Only came once to see him after our marriage. Hurt me by ridiculing him as a bookworm; offended him by looking a little down on me, as a nobody without spirit and fashion, which was quite true. And, except by a cold and unfeeling letter of formal condolence after I lost my dear Gilbert, I have never heard from her since I have been a widow, till to-day. But, after all, she is my poor husband's sister, and his eldest sister, and Lilian's aunt; and, as Mr. Vigors says, 'Duty is duty.'"

Had Mrs. Ashleigh said "Duty is torture," she could not have uttered the maxim with more mournful and despondent resignation.

"And what does this lady require of you, which Mr. Vigors deems it your duty to comply with?"

"Dear me! What penetration! You have guessed the exact truth. But I think you will agree with Mr. Vigors. Certainly I have no option; yes, I must do it."

"My penetration is in fault now. Do what? Pray explain."

"Poor Lady Haughton, six months ago, lost her only son, Sir James. Mr. Vigors says he was a very fine young man, of whom any mother would have been proud. I had heard he was wild; Mr. Vigors says, however, that he was just going to reform, and marry a young lady whom his mother chose for him, when, unluckily, he would ride a steeplechase, not being quite sober at the time, and broke his neck. Lady Haughton has been, of course, in great grief. She has retired

to Brighton; and she wrote to me from thence, and Mr.
Vigors brought the letter. He will go back to her to-day."

"Will go back to Lady Haughton? What! Has he been
to her? Is he, then, as intimate with Lady Haughton as he
was with her brother?"

"No; but there has been a long and constant correspondence. She had a settlement on the Kirby Estate, — a sum
which was not paid off during Gilbert's life; and a very
small part of the property went to Sir James, which part Mr.
Ashleigh Sumner, the heir-at-law to the rest of the estate,
wished Mr. Vigors, as his guardian, to buy during his minority, and as it was mixed up with Lady Haughton's settlement her consent was necessary as well as Sir James's. So
there was much negotiation, and, since then, Ashleigh Sumner has come into the Haughton property, on poor Sir James's
decease; so that complicated all affairs between Mr. Vigors
and Lady Haughton, and he has just been to Brighton to see
her. And poor Lady Haughton, in short, wants me and
Lilian to go and visit her. I don't like it at all. But you
said the other day you thought sea air might be good for
Lilian during the heat of the summer, and she seems well
enough now for the change. What do you think?"

"She is well enough, certainly. But Brighton is not the
place I would recommend for the summer; it wants shade,
and is much hotter than L—— "

"Yes; but unluckily Lady Haughton foresaw that objection,
and she has a jointure-house some miles from Brighton, and
near the sea. She says the grounds are well wooded, and the
place is proverbially cool and healthy, not far from St. Leon-
ard's Forest. And, in short, I have written to say we will
come. So we must, unless, indeed, you positively forbid it."

"When do you think of going?"

"Next Monday. Mr. Vigors would make me fix the day. If
you knew how I dislike moving when I am once settled; and
I do so dread Lady Haughton, she is so fine, and so satirical!
But Mr. Vigors says she is very much altered, poor thing! I
should like to show you her letter, but I had just sent it to
Margaret — Mrs. Poyntz — a minute or two before you came.

She knows something of Lady Haughton. Margaret knows everybody. And we shall have to go in mourning for poor Sir James, I suppose; and Margaret will choose it, for I am sure I can't guess to what extent we should be supposed to mourn. I ought to have gone in mourning before — poor Gilbert's nephew — but I am so stupid, and I had never seen him. And — But oh, this *is* kind! Margaret herself, — my dear Margaret!"

We had just turned away from the house, in our up-and-down walk; and Mrs. Poyntz stood immediately fronting us.

"So, Anne, you have actually accepted this invitation — and for Monday next?"

"Yes. Did I do wrong?"

"What does Dr. Fenwick say? Can Lilian go with safety?"

I could not honestly say she might not go with safety, but my heart sank like lead as I answered, —

"Miss Ashleigh does not now need merely medical care; but more than half her cure has depended on keeping her spirits free from depression. She may miss the cheerful companionship of your daughter, and other young ladies of her own age. A very melancholy house, saddened by a recent bereavement, without other guests; a hostess to whom she is a stranger, and whom Mrs. Ashleigh herself appears to deem formidable, — certainly these do not make that change of scene which a physician would recommend. When I spoke of sea air being good for Miss Ashleigh, I thought of our own northern coasts at a later time of the year, when I could escape myself for a few weeks and attend her. The journey to a northern watering-place would be also shorter and less fatiguing; the air there more invigorating."

"No doubt that would be better," said Mrs. Poyntz, dryly; "but so far as your objections to visiting Lady Haughton have been stated, they are groundless. Her house will not be melancholy; she will have other guests, and Lilian will find companions, young like herself, — young ladies — and young gentlemen too!"

There was something ominous, something compassionate,

in the look which Mrs. Poyntz cast upon me, in concluding
her speech, which in itself was calculated to rouse the fears
of a lover. Lilian away from me, in the house of a worldly-
fine lady — such as I judged Lady Haughton to be — surrounded by young gentlemen, as well as young ladies, by admirers, no doubt, of a higher rank and more brilliant fashion
than she had yet known! I closed my eyes, and with strong
effort suppressed a groan.

"My dear Annie, let me satisfy myself that Dr. Fenwick
really *does* consent to this journey. He will say to me what
he may not to you. Pardon me, then, if I take him aside
for a few minutes. Let me find you here again under this
cedar-tree."

Placing her arm in mine, and without waiting for Mrs.
Ashleigh's answer, Mrs. Poyntz drew me into the more sequestered walk that belted the lawn; and when we were out
of Mrs. Ashleigh's sight and hearing, said, —

"From what you have now seen of Lilian Ashleigh, do you
still desire to gain her as your wife? "

"Still? Oh, with an intensity proportioned to the fear
with which I now dread that she is about to pass away from
my eyes — from my life! "

"Does your judgment confirm the choice of your heart?
Reflect before you answer."

"Such selfish judgment as I had before I knew her would
not confirm but oppose it. The nobler judgment that now
expands all my reasonings, approves and seconds my heart.
No, no; do not smile so sarcastically. This is not the voice
of a blind and egotistical passion. Let me explain myself if
I can. I concede to you that Lilian's character is undeveloped; I concede to you, that amidst the childlike freshness
and innocence of her nature, there is at times a strangeness,
a mystery, which I have not yet traced to its cause. But I
am certain that the intellect is organically as sound as the
heart, and that intellect and heart will ultimately — if under
happy auspices — blend in that felicitous union which constitutes the perfection of woman. But it is because she does,
and may for years, may perhaps always, need a more devoted,

thoughtful care than natures less tremulously sensitive, that my judgment sanctions my choice; for whatever is best for her is best for me. And who would watch over her as I should?"

"You have never yet spoken to Lilian as lovers speak?"

"Oh, no, indeed."

"And, nevertheless, you believe that your affection would not be unreturned?"

"I thought so once; I doubt now, — yet, in doubting, hope. But why do you alarm me with these questions? You, too, forebode that in this visit I may lose her forever?"

"If you fear that, tell her so, and perhaps her answer may dispel your fear."

"What! now, already, when she has scarcely known me a month. Might I not risk all if too premature?"

"There is no almanac for love. With many women love is born the moment they know they are beloved. All wisdom tells us that a moment once gone is irrevocable. Were I in your place, I should feel that I approached a moment that I must not lose. I have said enough; now I shall rejoin Mrs. Ashleigh."

"Stay — tell me first what Lady Haughton's letter really contains to prompt the advice with which you so transport, and yet so daunt, me when you proffer it."

"Not now; later, perhaps, — not now. If you wish to see Lilian alone, she is by the Old Monk's Well; I saw her seated there as I passed that way to the house."

"One word more, — only one. Answer this question frankly, for it is one of honour. Do you still believe that my suit to her daughter would not be disapproved of by Mrs. Ashleigh?"

"At this moment I am sure it would not; a week hence I might not. give you the same answer."

So she passed on with her quick but measured tread, back through the shady walk, on to the open lawn, till the last glimpse of her pale gray robe disappeared under the boughs of the cedar-tree. Then, with a start, I broke the irresolute, tremulous suspense in which I had vainly endeavoured to analyze my own mind, solve my own doubts, concentrate my own will, and went the opposite way, skirting the circle of that haunted ground,—as now, on one side its lofty terrace, the houses of the neighbouring city came full and close into view, divided from my fairy-land of life but by the trodden murmurous thoroughfare winding low beneath the ivied parapets; and as now, again, the world of men abruptly vanished behind the screening foliage of luxuriant June.

At last the enchanted glade opened out from the verdure, its borders fragrant with syringa and rose and woodbine; and there, by the gray memorial of the gone Gothic age, my eyes seemed to close their unquiet wanderings, resting spell-bound on that image which had become to me the incarnation of earth's bloom and youth.

She stood amidst the Past, backed by the fragments of walls which man had raised to seclude him from human passion, locking, under those lids so downcast, the secret of the only knowledge I asked from the boundless Future.

Ah! what mockery there is in that grand word, the world's fierce war-cry,— Freedom! Who has not known one period of life, and that so solemn that its shadows may rest over all life hereafter, when one human creature has over him a sovereignty more supreme and absolute than Orient servitude adores in the symbols of diadem and sceptre? What crest so haughty that has not bowed before a hand which could exalt or humble! What heart so dauntless that has not trembled to call forth the voice at whose sound ope the gates of rapture or despair! That life alone is free which rules, and suffices for itself. That life we forfeit when we love!

CHAPTER XVII.

How did I utter it? By what words did my heart make itself known? I remember not. All was as a dream that falls upon a restless, feverish night, and fades away as the eyes unclose on the peace of a cloudless heaven, on the bliss

6

of a golden sun. A new morrow seemed indeed upon the earth when I woke from a life-long yesterday,— her dear hand in mine, her sweet face bowed upon my breast.

And then there was that melodious silence in which there is no sound audible from without; yet within us there is heard a lulling celestial music, as if our whole being, grown harmonious with the universe, joined from its happy deeps in the hymn that unites the stars.

In that silence our two hearts seemed to make each other understood, to be drawing nearer and nearer, blending by mysterious concord into the completeness of a solemn union, never henceforth to be rent asunder.

At length I said softly: "And it was here on this spot that I first saw you,— here that I for the first time knew what power to change our world and to rule our future goes forth from the charm of a human face!"

Then Lilian asked me timidly, and without lifting her eyes, how I had so seen her, reminding me that I promised to tell her, and had never yet done so.

And then I told her of the strange impulse that had led me into the grounds, and by what chance my steps had been diverted down the path that wound to the glade; how suddenly her form had shone upon my eyes, gathering round itself the rose hues of the setting sun, and how wistfully those eyes had followed her own silent gaze into the distant heaven.

As I spoke, her hand pressed mine eagerly, convulsively, and, raising her face from my breast, she looked at me with an intent, anxious earnestness. That look!— twice before it had thrilled and perplexed me.

"What is there in that look, oh, my Lilian, which tells me that there is something that startles you,— something you wish to confide, and yet shrink from explaining? See how, already, I study the fair book from which the seal has been lifted! but as yet you must aid me to construe its language."

"If I shrink from explaining, it is only because I fear that I cannot explain so as to be understood or believed. But you have a right to know the secrets of a life which you would link to your own. Turn your face aside from me; a reprov-

ing look, an incredulous smile, chill— oh, you cannot guess
how they chill me, when I would approach that which to me
is so serious and so solemnly strange."

I turned my face away, and her voice grew firmer as, after
a brief pause, she resumed,—

"As far back as I can remember in my infancy, there have
been moments when there seems to fall a soft hazy veil between my sight and the things around it, thickening and
deepening till it has the likeness of one of those white fleecy
clouds which gather on the verge of the horizon when the air
is yet still, but the winds are about to rise; and then this
vapour or veil will suddenly open, as clouds open, and let in
the blue sky."

"Go on," I said gently, for here she came to a stop.

She continued, speaking somewhat more hurriedly,—

"Then, in that opening, strange appearances present themselves to me, as in a vision. In my childhood these were
chiefly landscapes of wonderful beauty. I could but faintly
describe them then; I could not attempt to describe them
now, for they are almost gone from my memory. My dear
mother chid me for telling her what I saw, so I did not impress it on my mind by repeating it. As I grew up, this kind
of vision — if I may so call it — became much less frequent,
or much less distinct; I still saw the soft veil fall, the pale
cloud form and open, but often what may then have appeared
was entirely forgotten when I recovered myself, waking as
from a sleep. Sometimes, however, the recollection would
be vivid and complete; sometimes I saw the face of my lost
father; sometimes I heard his very voice, as I had seen and
heard him in my early childhood, when he would let me rest
for hours beside him as he mused or studied, happy to be so
quietly near him, for I loved him, oh, so dearly! and I remember him so distinctly, though I was only in my sixth
year when he died. Much more recently — indeed, within
the last few months — the images of things to come are reflected on the space that I gaze into as clearly as in a glass.
Thus, for weeks before I came hither, or knew that such a
place existed, I saw distinctly the old House, yon trees, this

sward, this moss-grown Gothic fount; and, with the sight, an impression was conveyed to me that in the scene before me my old childlike life would pass into some solemn change. So that when I came here, and recognized the picture in my vision, I took an affection for the spot, — an affection not without awe, a powerful, perplexing interest, as one who feels under the influence of a fate of which a prophetic glimpse has been vouchsafed. And in that evening, when you first saw me, seated here — "

"Yes, Lilian, on that evening — "

"I saw you also, but in my vision — yonder, far in the deeps of space, — and — and my heart was stirred as it had never been before; and near where your image grew out from the cloud I saw my father's face, and I heard his voice, not in my ear, but as in my heart, whispering — "

"Yes, Lilian — whispering — what?"

"These words, — only these, — 'Ye will need one another.' But then, suddenly, between my upward eyes and the two forms they had beheld, there rose from the earth, obscuring the skies, a vague, dusky vapour, undulous, and coiling like a vast serpent, — nothing, indeed, of its shape and figure definite, but of its face one abrupt glare; a flash from two dread luminous eyes, and a young head, like the Medusa's, changing, more rapidly than I could have drawn breath, into a grinning skull. Then my terror made me bow my head, and when I raised it again, all that I had seen was vanished. But the terror still remained, even when I felt my mother's arm round me and heard her voice. And then, when I entered the house, and sat down again alone, the recollection of what I had seen — those eyes, that face, that skull — grew on me stronger and stronger till I fainted, and remember no more, until my eyes, opening, saw you by my side, and in my wonder there was not terror. No, a sense of joy, protection, hope, yet still shadowed by a kind of fear or awe, in recognizing the countenance which had gleamed on me from the skies before the dark vapour had risen, and while my father's voice had murmured, 'Ye will need one another.' And now — and now — will you love me less that you know

a secret in my being which I have told to no other,— cannot
construe to myself? Only — only, at least, do not mock me;
do not disbelieve me! Nay, turn from me no longer now:
now I ask to meet your eyes. Now, before our hands can
join again, tell me that you do not despise me as untruthful,
do not pity me as insane."

"Hush, hush!" I said, drawing her to my breast. "Of all
you tell me we will talk hereafter. The scales of our science
have no weights fine enough for the gossamer threads of a
maiden's pure fancies. Enough for me — for us both — if out
from all such illusions start one truth, told to you, lovely
child, from the heavens; told to me, ruder man, on the earth;
repeated by each pulse of this heart that woos you to hear
and to trust,— now and henceforth through life unto death,
'Each has need of the other,' — I of you, I of you! my
Lilian! my Lilian!"

CHAPTER XVIII.

In spite of the previous assurance of Mrs. Poyntz, it was
not without an uneasy apprehension that I approached the
cedar-tree, under which Mrs. Ashleigh still sat, her friend
beside her. I looked on the fair creature whose arm was
linked in mine. So young, so singularly lovely, and with all
the gifts of birth and fortune which bend avarice and ambition the more submissively to youth and beauty, I felt as if I
had wronged what a parent might justly deem her natural lot.

"Oh, if your mother should disapprove!" said I, falteringly.

Lilian leaned on my arm less lightly.. "If I had thought
so," she said with her soft blush, "should I be thus by your
side?"

So we passed under the boughs of the dark tree, and Lilian
left me and kissed Mrs. Ashleigh's cheek; then, seating herself on the turf, laid her head on her mother's lap. I looked
on the Queen of the Hill, whose keen eye shot over me. I

thought there was a momentary expression of pain or displeasure on her countenance; but it passed. Still there
seemed to me something of irony, as well as of triumph or
congratulation, in the half-smile with which she quitted her
seat, and in the tone with which she whispered, as she glided
by me to the open sward, "So, then, it is settled."

She walked lightly and quickly down the lawn. When she
was out of sight I breathed more freely. I took the seat
which she had left, by Mrs. Ashleigh's side, and said, "A
little while ago I spoke of myself as a man without kindred,
without home, and now I come to you and ask for both."

Mrs. Ashleigh looked at me benignly, then raised her
daughter's face from her lap, and whispered, "Lilian;" and
Lilian's lips moved, but I did not hear her answer. Her
mother did. She took Lilian's hand, simply placed it in
mine, and said, "As she chooses, I choose; whom she loves,
I love."

CHAPTER XIX.

From that evening till the day Mrs. Ashleigh and Lilian
went on the dreaded visit, I was always at their house, when
my avocations allowed me to steal to it; and during those few
days, the happiest I had ever known, it seemed to me that
years could not have more deepened my intimacy with Lilian's
exquisite nature, made me more reverential of its purity, or
more enamoured of its sweetness. I could detect in her but
one fault, and I rebuked myself for believing that it was a
fault. We see many who neglect the minor duties of life,
who lack watchful forethought and considerate care for others,
and we recognize the cause of this failing in levity or egotism.
Certainly, neither of those tendencies of character could be
ascribed to Lilian. Yet still in daily trifles there was something of that neglect, some lack of that care and forethought.
She loved her mother with fondness and devotion, yet it never
occurred to her to aid in those petty household cares in which

her mother centred so much of habitual interest. She was full of tenderness and pity to all want and suffering, yet many a young lady on the Hill was more actively beneficent, — visiting the poor in their sickness, or instructing their children in the Infant Schools. I was persuaded that her love for me was deep and truthful; it was clearly void of all ambition; doubtless she would have borne, unflinching and contented, whatever the world considers to be a sacrifice and privation,— yet I should never have expected her to take her share in the troubles of ordinary life. I could never have applied to her the homely but significant name of helpmate. I reproach myself while I write for noticing such defect — if defect it were — in what may be called the practical routine of our positive, trivial, human existence. No doubt it was this that had caused Mrs. Poyntz's harsh judgment against the wisdom of my choice. But such chiller shade upon Lilian's charming nature was reflected from no inert, un-amiable self-love. It was but the consequence of that self-absorption which the habit of revery had fostered. I cautiously abstained from all allusion to those visionary de-ceptions, which she had confided to me as the truthful im-pressions of spirit, if not of sense. To me any approach to what I termed "superstition" was displeasing; any indulgence of fantasies not within the measured and beaten track of healthful imagination more than displeased me in her,— it alarmed. I would not by a word encourage her in persua-sions which I felt it would be at present premature to reason against, and cruel indeed to ridicule. I was convinced that of themselves these mists round her native intelligence, en-gendered by a solitary and musing childhood, would subside in the fuller daylight of wedded life. She seemed pained when she saw how resolutely I shunned a subject dear to her thoughts. She made one or two timid attempts to renew it, but my grave looks sufficed to check her. Once or twice in-deed, on such occasions, she would turn away and leave me, but she soon came back; that gentle heart could not bear one unkindlier shade between itself and what it loved. It was agreed that our engagement should be, for the present, confided only to Mrs. Poyntz. When Mrs. Ashleigh and Lilian returned, which would be in a few weeks at furthest, it should be proclaimed; and our marriage could take place in the autumn, when I should be most free for a brief holiday from professional toils.

So we parted — as lovers part. I felt none of those jealous fears which, before we were affianced, had made me tremble at the thought of separation, and had conjured up irresistible rivals. But it was with a settled, heavy gloom that I saw her depart. From earth was gone a glory; from life a blessing.

———◆———

CHAPTER XX.

DURING the busy years of my professional career, I had snatched leisure for some professional treatises, which had made more or less sensation, and one of them, entitled "The Vital Principle; its Waste and Supply," had gained a wide circulation among the general public. This last treatise contained the results of certain experiments, then new in chemistry, which were adduced in support of a theory I entertained as to the re-invigoration of the human system by principles similar to those which Liebig has applied to the replenishment of an exhausted soil, — namely, the giving back to the frame those essentials to its nutrition, which it has lost by the action or accident of time; or supplying that special pabulum or energy in which the individual organism is constitutionally deficient; and neutralizing or counterbalancing that in which it super-abounds, — a theory upon which some eminent physicians have more recently improved with signal success. But on these essays, slight and suggestive, rather than dogmatic, I set no value. I had been for the last two years engaged on a work of much wider range, endeared to me by a far bolder ambition, — a work upon which I fondly hoped to found an enduring reputation as a severe and original physiologist. It was an Inquiry into Organic Life, similar in comprehensiveness of survey to that by which the illustrious Müller, of Berlin, has enriched the science of our age; however inferior, alas! to that august combination of thought and learning in the judgment which checks presumption, and the genius which adorns speculation. But at that day I was carried away by the ardour of composition, and I admired my performance because I loved my labour. This work had been entirely laid aside for the last agitated month; now that Lilian was gone, I resumed it earnestly, as the sole occupation that had power and charm enough to rouse me from the aching sense of void and loss.

The very night of the day she went, I reopened my manuscript. I had left off at the commencement of a chapter Upon Knowledge as derived from our Senses. As my convictions on this head were founded on the well-known arguments of Locke and Condillac against innate ideas, and on the reasonings by which Hume has resolved the combination of sensations into a general idea to an impulse arising merely out of habit, so I set myself to oppose, as a dangerous concession to the sentimentalities or mysticism of a pseudo-philosophy, the doctrine favoured by most of our recent physiologists, and of which some of the most eminent of German metaphysicians have accepted the substance, though refining into a subtlety its positive form,— I mean the doctrine which Müller himself has expressed in these words: —

"That innate ideas may exist cannot in the slightest degree be denied: it is, indeed, a fact. All the ideas of animals, which are induced by instinct, are innate and immediate : something presented to the mind, a desire to attain which is at the same time given. The new-born lamb and foal have such innate ideas, which lead them to follow their mother and suck the teats. Is it not in some measure the same with the intellectual ideas of man?"[1]

To this question I answered with an indignant "No!" A "Yes" would have shaken my creed of materialism to the dust. I wrote on rapidly, warmly. I defined the properties

[1] Müller's "Elements of Physiology," vol. ii. p. 134. Translated by Dr Baley.

and meted the limits of natural laws, which I would not admit that a Deity himself could alter. I clamped and soldered
dogma to dogma in the links of my tinkered logic, till out
from my page, to my own complacent eye, grew Intellectual
Man, as the pure formation of his material senses; mind, or
what is called soul, born from and nurtured by them alone;
through them to act, and to perish with the machine they
moved. Strange, that at the very time my love for Lilian
might have taught me that there are mysteries in the core of
the feelings which my analysis of ideas could not solve, I
should so stubbornly have opposed as unreal all that could be
referred to the spiritual! Strange, that at the very time
when the thought that I might lose from this life the being
I had known scarce a month had just before so appalled me,
I should thus complacently sit down to prove that, according
to the laws of the nature which my passion obeyed, I must
lose for eternity the blessing I now hoped I had won to my
life! But how distinctly dissimilar is man in his conduct
from man in his systems! See the poet reclined under forest
boughs, conning odes to his mistress; follow him out into the
world; no mistress ever lived for him there![1] See the hard
man of science, so austere in his passionless problems; follow
him now where the brain rests from its toil, where the heart
finds its Sabbath — what child is so tender, so yielding, and
soft?

But I had proved to my own satisfaction that poet and sage
are dust, and no more, when the pulse ceases to beat. And
on that consolatory conclusion my pen stopped.

Suddenly, beside me I distinctly heard a sigh,— a compassionate, mournful sigh. The sound was unmistakable. I
started from my seat, looked round, amazed to discover no
one,— no living thing! The windows were closed, the night
was still. That sigh was not the wail of the wind. But
there, in the darker angle of the room, what was that?
A silvery whiteness, vaguely shaped as a human form, reced-

---

[1] Cowley, who wrote so elaborate a series of amatory poems, is said
"never to have been in love but once, and then he never had resolution to
tell his passion." — Johnson's "Lives of the Poets:" COWLEY.

ing, fading, gone! Why, I know not — for no face was visible, no form, if form it were, more distinct than the colourless outline,— why, I know not, but I cried aloud, "Lilian!
Lilian!" My voice came strangely back to my own ear; I
paused, then smiled and blushed at my folly. "So I, too,
have learned what is superstition," I muttered to myself.
"And here is an anecdote at my own expense (as Müller
frankly tells us anecdotes of the illusions which would haunt
his eyes, shut or open),— an anecdote I may quote when I
come to my chapter on the Cheats of the Senses and Spectral
Phantasms." I went on with my book, and wrote till the
lights waned in the gray of the dawn. And I said then, in
the triumph of my pride, as I laid myself down to rest, "I
have written that which allots with precision man's place in
the region of nature; written that which will found a school,
form disciples; and race after race of those who cultivate truth
through pure reason shall accept my bases if they enlarge my
building." And again I heard the sigh, but this time it
caused no surprise. "Certainly," I murmured, "a very
strange thing is the nervous system!" So I turned on my
pillow, and, wearied out, fell asleep.

CHAPTER XXI.

THE next day, the last of the visiting patients to whom
my forenoons were devoted had just quitted me, when I was
summoned in haste to attend the steward of a Sir Philip
Derval. not residing at his family seat, which was about five
miles from L ——. It was rarely indeed that persons so far
from the town, when of no higher rank than this applicant,
asked my services.

But it was my principle to go wherever I was summoned;
my profession was not gain, it was healing, to which gain
was the incident, not the essential. This case the messenger
reported as urgent. I went on horseback, and rode fast; but

swiftly as I cantered through the village that skirted the approach to Sir Philip Derval's park, the evident care bestowed on the accommodation of the cottagers forcibly struck me. I felt that I was on the lands of a rich, intelligent, and beneficent proprietor. Entering the park, and passing before the manor-house, the contrast between the neglect and the decay of the absentee's stately Hall and the smiling homes of his villagers was disconsolately mournful.

An imposing pile, built apparently by Vanbrugh, with decorated pilasters, pompous portico, and grand perron (or double flight of stairs to the entrance), enriched with urns and statues, but discoloured, mildewed, chipped, half-hidden with unpruned creepers and ivy. Most of the windows were closed with shutters, decaying for want of paint; in some of the casements the panes were broken; the peacock perched on the shattered balustrade, that fenced a garden overgrown with weeds. The sun glared hotly on the place, and made its ruinous condition still more painfully apparent. I was glad when a winding in the park-road shut the house from my sight. Suddenly I emerged through a copse of ancient yew-trees, and before me there gleamed, in abrupt whiteness, a building evidently designed for the family mausoleum,— classical in its outline, with the blind iron door niched into stone walls of massive thickness, and surrounded by a funereal garden of roses and evergreens, fenced with an iron rail, party-gilt.

The suddenness with which this House of the Dead came upon me heightened almost into pain, if not into awe, the dismal impression which the aspect of the deserted home in its neighbourhood had made. I spurred my horse, and soon arrived at the door of my patient, who lived in a fair brick house at the other extremity of the park.

I found my patient, a man somewhat advanced in years, but of a robust conformation, in bed: he had been seized with a fit, which was supposed to be apoplectic, a few hours before; but was already sensible, and out of immediate danger. After I had prescribed a few simple remedies, I took aside the patient's wife, and went with her to the parlour below stairs, to make some inquiry about her husband's ordinary regimen and habits of life. These seemed sufficiently regular; I could discover no apparent cause for the attack, which presented symptoms not familiar to my experience. "Has your husband ever had such fits before?"

"Never!"

"Had he experienced any sudden emotion? Had he heard any unexpected news; or had anything happened to put him out?"

The woman looked much disturbed at these inquiries. I pressed them more urgently. At last she burst into tears, and clasping my hand, said, "Oh, doctor, I ought to tell you — I sent for you on purpose — yet I fear you will not believe me: my good man has seen a ghost!"

"A ghost!" said I, repressing a smile. "Well, tell me all, that I may prevent the ghost coming again."

The woman's story was prolix. Its substance was this: Her husband, habitually an early riser, had left his bed that morning still earlier than usual, to give directions about some cattle that were to be sent for sale to a neighbouring fair. An hour afterwards he had been found by a shepherd, near the mausoleum, apparently lifeless. On being removed to his own house, he had recovered speech, and bidding all except his wife leave the room, he then told her that on walking across the park towards the cattle-sheds, he had seen what appeared to him at first a pale light by the iron door of the mausoleum. On approaching nearer, this light changed into the distinct and visible form of his master, Sir Philip Derval, who was then abroad, — supposed to be in the East, where he had resided for many years. The impression on the steward's mind was so strong, that he called out, "Oh, Sir Philip!" when looking still more intently, he perceived that the face was that of a corpse. As he continued to gaze, the apparition seemed gradually to recede, as if vanishing into the sepulchre itself. He knew no more; he became unconscious. It was the excess of the poor woman's alarm, on hearing this strange tale, that made her resolve to send for me instead of the parish apothecary. She fancied so astound-

ing a cause for her husband's seizure could only be properly
dealt with by some medical man reputed to have more than
ordinary learning; and the steward himself objected to the
apothecary in the immediate neighbourhood, as more likely
to annoy him by gossip than a physician from a comparative
distance.

I took care not to lose the confidence of the good wife by
parading too quickly my disbelief in the phantom her husband declared that he had seen; but as the story itself seemed
at once to decide the nature of the fit to be epileptic, I began
to tell her of similar delusions which, in my experience, had
occurred to those subjected to epilepsy, and finally soothed
her into the conviction that the apparition was clearly reducible to natural causes. Afterwards, I led her on to talk
about Sir Philip Derval, less from any curiosity I felt about
the absent proprietor than from a desire to re-familiarize her
own mind to his image as a living man. The steward had
been in the service of Sir Philip's father, and had known Sir
Philip himself from a child. He was warmly attached to his
master, whom the old woman described as a man of rare benevolence and great eccentricity, which last she imputed to
his studious habits. He had succeeded to the title and estates
as a minor. For the first few years after attaining his majority, he had mixed much in the world. When at Derval
Court his house had been filled with gay companions, and
was the scene of lavish hospitality; but the estate was not in
proportion to the grandeur of the mansion, still less to the
expenditure of the owner. He had become greatly embarrassed; and some love disappointment (so it was rumoured)
occurring simultaneously with his pecuniary difficulties, he
had suddenly changed his way of life, shut himself up from
his old friends, lived in seclusion, taking to books and scientific pursuits, and as the old woman said vaguely and expres-
sively, "to odd ways." He had gradually by an economy
that, towards himself, was penurious, but which did not pre-
clude much judicious generosity to others, cleared off his
debts; and, once more rich, he had suddenly quitted the
country, and taken to a life of travel. He was now about

forty-eight years old, and had been eighteen years abroad. He wrote frequently to his steward, giving him minute and thoughtful instructions in regard to the employment, comforts, and homes of the peasantry, but peremptorily ordering him to spend no money on the grounds and mansion, stating as a reason why the latter might be allowed to fall into decay, his intention to pull it down whenever he returned to England.

I stayed some time longer than my engagements well warranted at my patient's house, not leaving till the sufferer, after a quiet sleep, had removed from his bed to his armchair, taken food, and seemed perfectly recovered from his attack.

Riding homeward, I mused on the difference that education makes, even pathologically, between man and man. Here was a brawny inhabitant of rural fields, leading the healthiest of lives, not conscious of the faculty we call imagination, stricken down almost to Death's door by his fright at an optical illusion, explicable, if examined, by the same simple causes which had impressed me the night before with a moment's belief in a sound and a spectre, — me who, thanks to sublime education, went so quietly to sleep a few minutes after, convinced that no phantom, the ghostliest that ear ever heard or eye ever saw, can be anything else but a nervous phenomenon.

CHAPTER XXII.

THAT evening I went to Mrs. Poyntz's; it was one of her ordinary "reception nights," and I felt that she would naturally expect my attendance as "a proper attention."

I joined a group engaged in general conversation, of which Mrs. Poyntz herself made the centre, knitting as usual, — rapidly while she talked, slowly when she listened.

Without mentioning the visit I had paid that morning, I turned the conversation on the different country places in the neighbourhood, and then incidentally asked, "What sort of a man is Sir Philip Derval? Is it not strange that he should suffer so fine a place to fall into decay?" The answers I received added little to the information I had already obtained. Mrs. Poyntz knew nothing of Sir Philip Derval, except as a man of large estates, whose rental had been greatly increased by a rise in the value of property he possessed in the town of L——, and which lay contiguous to that of her husband. Two or three of the older inhabitants of the Hill had remembered Sir Philip in his early days, when he was gay, high-spirited, hospitable, lavish. One observed that the only person in L—— whom he had admitted to his subsequent seclusion was Dr. Lloyd, who was then without practice, and whom he had employed as an assistant in certain chemical experiments.

Here a gentleman struck into the conversation. He was a stranger to me and to L——, a visitor to one of the dwellers on the Hill, who had asked leave to present him to its queen as a great traveller and an accomplished antiquary.

Said this gentleman: "Sir Philip Derval! I know him. I met him in the East. He was then still, I believe, very fond of chemical science; a clever, odd, philanthropical man; had studied medicine, or at least practised it; was said to have made many marvellous cures. I became acquainted with him in Aleppo. He had come to that town, not much frequented by English travellers, in order to inquire into the murder of two men, of whom one was his friend and the other his countryman."

"This is interesting," said Mrs. Poyntz, dryly. "We who live on this innocent Hill all love stories of crime; murder is the pleasantest subject you could have hit on. Pray give us the details."

"So encouraged," said the traveller, good-humouredly, "I will not hesitate to communicate the little I know. In Aleppo there had lived for some years a man who was held by the natives in great reverence. He had the reputation of extraordinary wisdom, but was difficult of access; the lively imagination of the Orientals invested his character with the fascinations of fable,—in short, Haroun of Aleppo was popularly considered a magician. Wild stories were told of his powers, of his preternatural age, of his hoarded treasures. Apart from such disputable titles to homage, there seemed no question, from all I heard, that his learning was considerable, his charities extensive, his manner of life irreproachably ascetic. He appears to have resembled those Arabian sages of the Gothic age to whom modern science is largely indebted,— a mystic enthusiast, but an earnest scholar. A wealthy and singular Englishman, long resident in another part of the East, afflicted by some languishing disease, took a journey to Aleppo to consult this sage, who, among his other acquirements, was held to have discovered rare secrets in medicine,— his countrymen said in 'charms.' One morning, not long after the Englishman's arrival, Haroun was found dead in his bed, apparently strangled, and the Englishman, who lodged in another part of the town, had disappeared; but some of his clothes, and a crutch on which he habitually supported himself, were found a few miles distant from Aleppo, near the roadside. There appeared no doubt that he, too, had been murdered, but his corpse could not be discovered. Sir Philip Derval had been a loving disciple of this Sage of Aleppo, to whom he assured me he owed not only that knowledge of medicine which, by report, Sir Philip possessed, but the insight into various truths of nature, on the promulgation of which, it was evident, Sir Philip cherished the ambition to found a philosophical celebrity for himself."

"Of what description were those truths of nature?" I asked, somewhat sarcastically.

"Sir, I am unable to tell you, for Sir Philip did not inform me, nor did I much care to ask; for what may be revered as truths in Asia are usually despised as dreams in Europe. To return to my story: Sir Philip had been in Aleppo a little time before the murder; had left the Englishman under the care of Haroun. He returned to Aleppo on hearing the tragic events I have related, and was busy in collecting such evidence as could be gleaned, and instituting inquiries after our missing countryman at the time I myself chanced to arrive in the city. I assisted in his researches, but without avail. The assassins remained undiscovered. I do not myself doubt that they were mere vulgar robbers. Sir Philip had a darker suspicion of which he made no secret to me; but as I confess that I thought the suspicion groundless, you will pardon me if I do not repeat it. Whether since I left the East the Englishman's remains have been discovered, I know not. Very probably; for I understand that his heirs have got hold of what fortune he left,—less than was generally supposed. But it was reported that he had buried great treasures, a rumour, however absurd, not altogether inconsistent with his character."

"What was his character?" asked Mrs. Poyntz.

"One of evil and sinister repute. He was regarded with terror by the attendants who had accompanied him to Aleppo. But he had lived in a very remote part of the East, little known to Europeans, and, from all I could learn, had there established an extraordinary power, strengthened by superstitious awe. He was said to have studied deeply that knowledge which the philosophers of old called 'occult,' not, like the Sage of Aleppo, for benevolent, but for malignant ends. He was accused of conferring with evil spirits, and filling his barbaric court (for he lived in a kind of savage royalty) with charmers and sorcerers. I suspect, after all, that he was only, like myself, an ardent antiquary, and cunningly made use of the fear he inspired in order to secure his authority, and prosecute in safety researches into ancient sepulchres or temples. His great passion was, indeed, in excavating such remains, in his neighbourhood; with what result I know not, never having penetrated so far into regions infested by robbers and pestiferous with malaria. He wore the Eastern dress, and always carried jewels about him. I came to the conclusion that for the sake of these jewels he was murdered, perhaps by some of his own servants (and, indeed, two at least of his suite were missing), who then at once buried his body, and kept their own secret. He was old, very infirm; could never have got far from the town without assistance."

"You have not yet told us his name," said Mrs. Poyntz.

"His name was Grayle."

"Grayle!" exclaimed Mrs. Poyntz, dropping her work. "Louis Grayle?"

"Yes; Louis Grayle. You could not have known him?"

"Known him! No; but I have often heard my father speak of him. Such, then, was the tragic end of that strong dark creature, for whom, as a young girl in the nursery, I used to feel a kind of fearful admiring interest?"

"It is your turn to narrate now," said the traveller.

And we all drew closer round our hostess, who remained silent some moments, her brow thoughtful, her work suspended.

"Well," said she at last, looking round us with a lofty air, which seemed half defying, "force and courage are always fascinating, even when they are quite in the wrong. I go with the world, because the world goes with me; if it did not — " Here she stopped for a moment, clenched the firm white hand, and then scornfully waved it, left the sentence unfinished, and broke into another.

"Going with the world, of course we must march over those who stand against it. But when one man stands single-handed against our march, we do not despise him; it is enough to crush. I am very glad I did not see Louis Grayle when I was a girl of sixteen." Again she paused a moment, and resumed: "Louis Grayle was the only son of a usurer, infamous for the rapacity with which he had acquired enormous wealth. Old Grayle desired to rear his heir as a gentleman; sent him to Eton. Boys are always aristocratic; his birth was soon thrown in his teeth; he was fierce; he struck boys bigger than himself, — fought till he was half killed. My father was at school with him; described him as a tiger-whelp. One day he — still a fag — struck a sixth-form boy. Sixth-form boys do not fight fags; they punish them. Louis Grayle was ordered to hold out his hand to the cane; he received the blow, drew forth his schoolboy knife, and stabbed the punisher. After that, he left Eton. I don't think he was publicly expelled — too mere a child for that honour — but he was taken or sent away; educated with great care under the first masters at home. When he was of age to enter the University, old Grayle was dead. Louis was sent by his guardians to Cam-

bridge, with acquirements far exceeding the average of young
men, and with unlimited command of money. My father was
at the same college, and described him again,— haughty,
quarrelsome, reckless, handsome, aspiring, brave. Does that
kind of creature interest you, my dears?" (appealing to the
ladies).

"La!" said Miss Brabazon; "a horrid usurer's son!"

"Ay, true; the vulgar proverb says it is good to be born
with a silver spoon in one's mouth: so it is when one has
one's own family crest on it; but when it is a spoon on which
people recognize their family crest, and cry out, 'Stolen from
our plate chest,' it is a heritage that outlaws a babe in his
cradle. However, young men at college who want money are
less scrupulous about descent than boys at Eton are. Louis
Grayle found, while at college, plenty of well-born acquaintances willing to recover from him some of the plunder his
father had extorted from theirs. He was too wild to distinguish himself by academical honours, but my father said that
the tutors of the college declared there were not six under-
graduates in the University who knew as much hard and dry
science as wild Louis Grayle. He went into the world, no
doubt, hoping to shine; but his father's name was too notorious to admit the son into good society. The Polite World, it
is true, does not examine a scutcheon with the nice eye of a
herald, nor look upon riches with the stately contempt of a
stoic; still the Polite World has its family pride and its
moral sentiment. It does not like to be cheated,— I mean,
in money matters; and when the son of a man who has
emptied its purse and foreclosed on its acres rides by its club-
windows, hand on haunch, and head in the air, no lion has a
scowl more awful, no hyena a laugh more dread, than that
same easy, good-tempered, tolerant, polite, well-bred World
which is so pleasant an acquaintance, so languid a friend,
and — so remorseless an enemy. In short, Louis Grayle
claimed the right to be courted,— he was shunned; to be admired,— he was loathed. Even his old college acquaintances
were shamed out of knowing him. Perhaps he could have
lived through all this had he sought to glide quietly into posi-

tion; but he wanted the tact of the well-bred, and strove to
storm his way, not to steal it. Reduced for companions to
needy parasites, he braved and he shocked all decorous opinion by that ostentation of excess, which made Richelieus and
Lauzuns the rage. But then Richelieus and Lauzuns were
dukes! He now very naturally took the Polite World into
hate,— gave it scorn for scorn. He would ally himself with
Democracy; his wealth could not get him into a club, but it
would buy him into parliament; he could not be a Lauzun,
nor, perhaps, a Mirabeau, but he might be a Danton. He had
plenty of knowledge and audacity, and with knowledge and
audacity a good hater is sure to be eloquent. Possibly, then,
this poor Louis Grayle might have made a great figure, left
his mark on his age and his name in history; but in contest-
ing the borough, which he was sure to carry, he had to face
an opponent in a real fine gentleman whom his father had
ruined, cool and high-bred, with a tongue like a rapier, a sneer
like an adder. A quarrel of course; Louis Grayle sent a
challenge. The fine gentleman, known to be no coward (fine
gentlemen never are), was at first disposed to refuse with
contempt. But Grayle had made himself the idol of the
mob; and at a word from Grayle, the fine gentleman might
have been ducked at a pump, or tossed in a blanket,— that
would have made him ridiculous; to be shot at is a trifle, to
be laughed at is serious. He therefore condescended to accept the challenge, and my father was his second.

"It was settled, of course, according to English custom,
that both combatants should fire at the same time, and by
signal. The antagonist fired at the right moment; his ball
grazed Louis Grayle's temple. Louis Grayle had not fired.
He now seemed to the seconds to take slow and deliberate
aim. They called out to him not to fire; they were rushing
to prevent him, when the trigger was pulled, and his opponent fell dead on the field. The fight was, therefore, considered unfair; Louis Grayle was tried for his life: he did not
stand the trial in person.[1] He escaped to the Continent;

[1] Mrs. Poyntz here makes a mistake in law which, though very evident, her
listeners do not seem to have noticed. Her mistake will be referred to later.

hurried on to some distant uncivilized lands; could not be
traced; reappeared in England no more. The lawyer who
conducted his defence pleaded skilfully. He argued that the
delay in firing was not intentional, therefore not criminal,—
the effect of the stun which the wound in the temple had occasioned. The judge was a gentleman, and summed up the
evidence so as to direct the jury to a verdict against the low
wretch who had murdered a gentleman; but the jurors were
not gentlemen, and Grayle's advocate had of course excited
their sympathy for a son of the people, whom a gentleman had
wantonly insulted. The verdict was manslaughter; but the
sentence emphatically marked the aggravated nature of
the homicide, — three years' imprisonment. Grayle eluded
the prison, but he was a man disgraced and an exile,— his
ambition blasted, his career an outlaw's, and his age not yet
twenty-three. My father said that he was supposed to have
changed his name; none knew what had become of him. And
so this creature, brilliant and daring, whom if born under
better auspices we might now be all fawning on, cringing to,
—after living to old age, no one knows how, —dies murdered
at Aleppo, no one, you say, knows by whom."

"I saw some account of his death in the papers about three
years ago," said one of the party; "but the name was mis-
spelled, and I had no idea that it was the same man who had
fought the duel which Mrs. Colonel Poyntz has so graphically
described. I have a very vague recollection of the trial; it
took place when I was a boy, more than forty years since.
The affair made a stir at the time, but was soon forgotten."

"Soon forgotten," said Mrs. Poyntz; "ay, what is not?
Leave your place in the world for ten minutes, and when you
come back somebody else has taken it; but when you leave
the world for good, who remembers that you had ever a place
even in the parish register?"

"Nevertheless," said I, "a great poet has said, finely and
truly,—

"'The sun of Homer shines upon us still.'"

"But it does not shine upon Homer; and learned folks tell
me that we know no more who and what Homer was, if there

was ever a single Homer at all, or rather, a whole herd of Homers, than we know about the man in the moon,— if there be one man there, or millions of men. Now, my dear Miss Brabazon, it will be very kind in you to divert our thoughts into channels less gloomy. Some pretty French air — Dr. Fenwick, I have something to say to you." She drew me towards the window. "So Annie Ashleigh writes me word that I am not to mention your engagement. Do you think it quite prudent to keep it a secret?"

"I do not see how prudence is concerned in keeping it se· cret one way or the other,— it is a mere matter of feeling. Most people wish to abridge, as far as they can, the time in which their private arrangements are the topic of public gossip."

"Public gossip is sometimes the best security for the due completion of private arrangements. As long as a girl is not known to be engaged, her betrothed must be prepared for rivals. Announce the engagement, and rivals are warned off."

"I fear no rivals."

"Do you not? Bold man! I suppose you will write to Lilian?"

"Certainly."

"Do so, and constantly. By-the-way, Mrs. Ashleigh, before she went, asked me to send her back Lady Haughton's letter of invitation. What for,— to show to you?"

"Very likely. Have you the letter still? May I see it?"

"Not just at present. When Lilian or Mrs. Ashleigh writes to you, come and tell me how they like their visit, and what other guests form the party."

Therewith she turned away and conversed apart with the traveller.

Her words disquieted me, and I felt that they were meant to do so,— wherefore I could not guess. But there is no language on earth which has more words with a double meaning than that spoken by the Clever Woman, who is never so guarded as when she appears to be frank.

As I walked home thoughtfully, I was accosted by a young

man, the son of one of the wealthiest merchants in the town. I had attended him with success some months before, in a rheumatic fever: he and his family were much attached to me.

"Ah, my dear Fenwick, I am so glad to see you; I owe you an obligation of which you are not aware,— an exceedingly pleasant travelling-companion. I came with him to-day from London, where I have been sight-seeing and holiday-making for the last fortnight."

"I suppose you mean that you kindly bring me a patient?"

"No, only an admirer. I was staying at Fenton's Hotel. It so happened one day that I had left in the coffee-room your last work on the Vital Principle, which, by the by, the bookseller assures me is selling immensely among readers as non-professional as myself. Coming into the coffee-room again, I found a gentleman reading the book. I claimed it politely; he as politely tendered his excuse for taking it. We made acquaintance on the spot. The next day we were intimate. He expressed great interest and curiosity about your theory and your experiments. I told him I knew you. You may guess if I described you as less clever in your practice than you are in your writings; and, in short, he came with me to L——, partly to see our flourishing town, principally on my promise to introduce him to you. My mother, you know, has what she calls a *déjeuner* to-morrow,— *déjeuner* and dance. You will be there?"

"Thank you for reminding me of her invitation. I will avail myself of it if I can. Your new friend will be present? Who and what is he,— a medical student?"

"No, a mere gentleman at ease, but seems to have a good deal of general information. Very young, apparently very rich, wonderfully good-looking. I am sure you will like him; everybody must."

"It is quite enough to prepare me to like him that he is a friend of yours." And so we shook hands and parted.

CHAPTER XXIII.

It was late in the afternoon of the following day before I was able to join the party assembled at the merchant's house; it was a villa about two miles out of the town, pleasantly situated amidst flower-gardens celebrated in the neighbourhood for their beauty. The breakfast had been long over; the company was scattered over the lawn, — some formed into a dance on the smooth lawn; some seated under shady awnings; others gliding amidst parterres, in which all the glow of colour took a glory yet more vivid under the flush of a brilliant sunshine, and the ripple of a soft western breeze. Music, loud and lively, mingled with the laughter of happy children, who formed much the larger number of the party.

Standing at the entrance of an arched trellis, that led from the hardier flowers of the lawn to a rare collection of tropical plants under a lofty glass dome (connecting, as it were, the familiar vegetation of the North with that of the remotest East), was a form that instantaneously caught and fixed my gaze. The entrance of the arcade was covered with parasite creepers, in prodigal luxuriance, of variegated gorgeous tints, — scarlet, golden, purple; and the form, an idealized picture of man's youth fresh from the hand of Nature, stood literally in a frame of blooms.

Never have I seen human face so radiant as that young man's. There was in the aspect an indescribable something that literally dazzled. As one continued to gaze, it was with surprise; one was forced to acknowledge that in the features themselves there was no faultless regularity; nor was the young man's stature imposing, — about the middle height. But the effect of the whole was not less transcendent. Large eyes, unspeakably lustrous; a most harmonious colouring; an expression of contagious animation and joyousness; and the form itself so critically fine, that the welded strength of its sinews was best shown in the lightness and grace of its movements.

He was resting one hand carelessly on the golden locks of a child that had nestled itself against his knees, looking up to his face in that silent loving wonder with which children regard something too strangely beautiful for noisy admiration; he himself was conversing with the host, an old gray-haired, gouty man, propped on his crutched stick, and listening with a look of mournful envy. To the wealth of the old man all the flowers in that garden owed their renewed delight in the summer air and sun. Oh, that his wealth could renew to himself one hour of the youth whose incarnation stood beside him, Lord, indeed, of Creation; its splendour woven into his crown of beauty, its enjoyments subject to his sceptre of hope and gladness.

I was startled by the hearty voice of the merchant's son.

"Ah, my dear Fenwick, I was afraid you would not come, — you are late. There is the new friend of whom I spoke to you last night; let me now make you acquainted with him." He drew my arm in his, and led me up to the young man, where he stood under the arching flowers, and whom he then introduced to me by the name of Margrave.

Nothing could be more frankly cordial than Mr. Margrave's manner. In a few minutes I found myself conversing with him familiarly, as if we had been reared in the same home, and sported together in the same playground. His vein of talk was peculiar, off-hand, careless, shifting from topic to topic with a bright rapidity.

He said that he liked the place; proposed to stay in it some weeks; asked my address, which I gave to him; promised to call soon at an early hour, while my time was yet free from professional visits. I endeavoured, when I went away, to analyze to myself the fascination which this young stranger so notably exercised over all who approached him; and it seemed to me, ever seeking to find material causes for all moral effects, that it rose from the contagious vitality of that rarest of all rare gifts in highly-civilized circles, — perfect health; that health which is in itself the most exquisite

luxury; which, finding happiness in the mere sense of existence, diffuses round it, like an atmosphere, the harmless
hilarity of its bright animal being. Health, to the utmost
perfection, is seldom known after childhood; health to the
utmost cannot be enjoyed by those who overwork the brain,
or admit the sure wear and tear of the passions. The creature I had just seen gave me the notion of youth in the golden
age of the poets,—the youth of the careless Arcadian, before
nymph or shepherdess had vexed his heart with a sigh.

CHAPTER XXIV.

THE house I occupied at L—— was a quaint, old-fashioned
building,—a corner-house. One side, in which was the front
entrance, looked upon a street which, as there were no shops
in it, and it was no direct thoroughfare to the busy centres of
the town, was always quiet, and at some hours of the day almost deserted. The other side of the house fronted a lane;
opposite to it was the long and high wall of the garden to
a Young Ladies' Boarding-school. My stables adjoined the
house, abutting on a row of smaller buildings, with little gardens before them, chiefly occupied by mercantile clerks and
retired tradesmen. By the lane there was a short and ready
access both to the high turnpike-road, and to some pleasant
walks through green meadows and along the banks of a river.

This house I had inhabited since my arrival at L——, and
it had to me so many attractions, in a situation sufficiently
central to be convenient for patients, and yet free from noise,
and favourable to ready outlet into the country for such foot
or horse exercise as my professional avocations would allow
me to carve for myself out of what the Latin poet calls the
"solid day," that I had refused to change it for one better
suited to my increased income; but it was not a house which
Mrs. Ashleigh would have liked for Lilian. The main objec-

tion to it in the eyes of the "genteel" was, that it had formerly belonged to a member of the healing profession who
united the shop of an apothecary to the diploma of a surgeon;
but that shop had given the house a special attraction to me;
for it had been built out on the side of the house which
fronted the lane, occupying the greater portion of a small
gravel court, fenced from the road by a low iron palisade,
and separated from the body of the house itself by a short
and narrow corridor that communicated with the entrance-
hall.   This shop I turned into a rude study for scientific experiments, in which I generally spent some early hours of the
morning, before my visiting patients began to arrive.   I enjoyed the stillness of its separation from the rest of the house;
I enjoyed the glimpse of the great chestnut-trees, which over-
topped the wall of the school-garden; I enjoyed the ease with
which, by opening the glazed sash-door, I could get out, if
disposed for a short walk, into the pleasant fields; and so
completely had I made this sanctuary my own, that not only
my man-servant knew that I was never to be disturbed when
in it, except by the summons of a patient, but even the housemaid was forbidden to enter it with broom or duster, except
upon special invitation.   The last thing at night, before retiring to rest, it was the man-servant's business to see that
the sash-window was closed, and the gate to the iron palisade
locked; but during the daytime I so often went out of the
house by that private way that the gate was then very seldom
locked, nor the sash-door bolted from within.   In the town
of L—— there was little apprehension of house-robberies, —
especially in the daylight, — and certainly in this room, cut
off from the main building, there was nothing to attract a
vulgar cupidity.   A few of the apothecary's shelves and cases
still remained on the walls, with, here and there, a bottle of
some chemical preparation for experiment; two or three worm-
eaten, wooden chairs; two or three shabby old tables; an old
walnut-tree bureau without a lock, into which odds and ends
were confusedly thrust, and sundry ugly-looking inventions
of mechanical science, were, assuredly, not the articles which
a timid proprietor would guard with jealous care from the

chances of robbery. It will be seen later why I have been thus prolix in description. The morning after I had met the young stranger by whom I had been so favourably impressed, I was up as usual, a little before the sun, and long before any of my servants were astir. I went first into the room I have mentioned, and which I shall henceforth designate as my study, opened the window, unlocked the gate, and sauntered for some minutes up and down the silent lane skirting the opposite wall, and overhung by the chestnut-trees rich in the garniture of a glorious summer; then, refreshed for work, I re-entered my study, and was soon absorbed in the examina-.tion of that now well-known machine, which was then, to me at least, a novelty,— invented, if I remember right, by Dubois-Reymond, so distinguished by his researches into the mysteries of organic electricity. It is a wooden cylinder fixed against the edge of a table; on the table two vessels filled with salt and water are so placed that, as you close your hands on the cylinder, the forefinger of each hand can drop into the water; each of the vessels has a metallic plate, and communicates by wires with a galvanometer with its needle. Now the theory is, that if you clutch the cylinder firmly with the right hand, leaving the left perfectly passive, the needle in the galvanometer will move from west to south; if, in like manner, you exert the left arm, leaving the right arm passive, the needle will deflect from west to north. Hence, it is argued that the electric current is induced through the agency of the nervous system, and that, as human Will produces the muscular contraction requisite, so is it human Will that causes the deflection of the needle. I imagine that if this theory were substantiated by experiment, the discovery might lead to some sublime and unconjectured secrets of science. For human Will, thus actively effective on the electric current, and all matter, animate or inanimate, having more or less of electricity, a vast field became opened to conjecture. By what series of patient experimental deduction might not science arrive at the solution of problems which the Newtonian law of gravitation does not suffice to solve; and — But here I halt. At the date which my story has reached, my mind never lost itself long in the Cloudland of Guess.

I was dissatisfied with my experiment. The needle stirred, indeed, but erratically, and not in directions which, according to the theory, should correspond to my movement. I was about to dismiss the trial with some uncharitable contempt of the foreign philosopher's dogmas, when I heard a loud ring at my street-door. While I paused to conjecture whether my servant was yet up to attend to the door, and which of my patients was the most likely to summon me at so unseasonable an hour, a shadow darkened my window. I looked up, and to my astonishment beheld the brilliant face of Mr. Mar-. grave. The sash to the door was already partially opened; he raised it higher, and walked into the room. "Was it you who rang at the street-door, and at this hour?" said I.

"Yes; and observing, after I had rung, that all the shutters were still closed, I felt ashamed of my own rash action; and made off rather than brave the reproachful face of some injured housemaid, robbed of her morning dreams. I turned down that pretty lane,— lured by the green of the chestnut-trees,— caught sight of you through the window, took courage, and here I am! You forgive me?" While thus speaking, he continued to move along the littered floor of the dingy room, with the undulating restlessness of some wild animal in the confines of its den, and he now went on, in short fragmentary sentences, very slightly linked together, but smoothed, as it were, into harmony by a voice musical and fresh as a sky-lark's warble. "Morning dreams, indeed! dreams that waste the life of such a morning. Rosy magnificence of a summer dawn! Do you not pity the fool who prefers to lie a bed, and to dream rather than to live? What! and you, strong man, with those noble limbs, in this den! Do you not long for a rush through the green of the fields, a bath in the blue of the river?"

Here he came to a pause, standing, still in the gray light of the growing day, with eyes whose joyous lustre forestalled the sun's, and lips which seemed to laugh even in repose.

But presently those eyes, as quick as they were bright,

glanced over the walls, the floor, the shelves, the phials, the mechanical inventions, and then rested full on my cylinder fixed to the table. He approached, examined it curiously, asked what it was. I explained. To gratify him I sat down and renewed my experiment, with equally ill success. The needle, which should have moved from west to south, describing an angle of from thirty degrees to forty or even fifty degrees, only made a few troubled, undecided oscillations.

"Tut," cried the young man, "I see what it is; you have a wound in your right hand."

That was true; I had burned my hand a few days before in a chemical experiment, and the sore had not healed.

"Well," said I, "and what does that matter?"

"Everything; the least scratch in the skin of the hand produces chemical actions on the electric current, independently of your will. Let me try."

He took my place, and in a moment the needle in the galvanometer responded to his grasp on the cylinder, exactly as the inventive philosopher had stated to be the due result of the experiment.

I was startled.

"But how came you, Mr. Margrave, to be so well acquainted with a scientific process little known, and but recently discovered?"

"I well acquainted! not so. But I am fond of all experiments that relate to animal life. Electricity, especially, is full of interest."

On that I drew him out (as I thought), and he talked volubly. I was amazed to find this young man, in whose brain I had conceived thought kept one careless holiday, was evidently familiar with the physical sciences, and especially with chemistry, which was my own study by predilection. But never had I met with a student in whom a knowledge so extensive was mixed up with notions so obsolete or so crotchety. In one sentence he showed that he had mastered some late discovery by Faraday or Liebig; in the next sentence he was talking the wild fallacies of Cardan or Van Helmont. I burst out laughing at some paradox about sympathetic powders, which he enounced as if it were a recognized truth.

"Pray tell me," said I, "who was your master in physics; for a cleverer pupil never had a more crack-brained teacher."

"No," he answered, with his merry laugh, "it is not the teacher's fault. I am a mere parrot; just cry out a few scraps of learning picked up here and there. But, however, I am fond of all researches into Nature; all guesses at her riddles. To tell you the truth, one reason why I have taken to you so heartily is not only that your published work caught my fancy in the dip which I took into its contents (pardon me if I say dip, I never do more than dip into any book), but also because young —— tells me that which all whom I have met in this town confirm; namely, that you are one of those few practical chemists who are at once exceedingly cautious and exceedingly bold,— willing to try every new experiment, but submitting experiment to rigid tests. Well, I have an experiment running wild in this giddy head of mine, and I want you, some day when at leisure, to catch it, fix it as you have fixed that cylinder, make something of it. I am sure you can."

"What is it?"

"Something akin to the theories in your work. You would replenish or preserve to each special constitution the special substance that may fail to the equilibrium of its health. But you own that in a large proportion of cases the best cure of disease is less to deal with the disease itself than to support and stimulate the whole system, so as to enable Nature to cure the disease and restore the impaired equilibrium by her own agencies. Thus, if you find that in certain cases of nervous debility a substance like nitric acid is efficacious, it is because the nitric acid has a virtue in locking up, as it were, the nervous energy,— that is, preventing all undue waste. Again, in some cases of what is commonly called feverish cold, stimulants like ammonia assist Nature itself to get rid of the disorder that oppresses its normal action; and, on the same principle, I apprehend, it is contended that a large average of human lives is saved in those hospitals

which have adopted the supporting system of ample nourishment and alcoholic stimulants."

"Your medical learning surprises me," said I, smiling;
"and without pausing to notice where it deals somewhat su-
perficially with disputable points in general, and my own
theory in particular, I ask you for the deduction you draw
from your premises."

"It is simply this: that to all animate bodies, however
various, there must be one principle in common,— the vital
principle itself. What if there be one certain means of recruiting that principle; and what if that secret can be
discovered?"

"Pshaw! The old illusion of the mediæval empirics."

"Not so. But the mediæval empirics were great discov-
erers. You sneer at Van Helmont, who sought, in water, the
principle of all things; but Van Helmont discovered in his
search those invisible bodies called gases. Now the principle of life must be certainly ascribed to a gas.[1] And what-

---

[1] "According to the views we have mentioned, we must ascribe life to a
gas, that is, to an aëriform body."—Liebig: "Organic Chemistry," Playfair's
translation, p. 363. — It is perhaps not less superfluous to add that Liebig does
not support the views "according to which life must be ascribed to a gas,"
than it would be to state, had Dugald Stewart been quoted as writing, "According to the views we have mentioned the mind is but a bundle of impressions," that Dugald Stewart was not supporting, but opposing, the views of
David Hume. The quotation is merely meant to show, in the shortest possible
compass, that there are views entertained by speculative reasoners of our day
which, according to Liebig, would lead to the inference at which Margrave so
boldly arrives. Margrave is, however, no doubt, led to his belief by his
reminiscences of Van Helmont, to whose discovery of gas he is referring.
Van Helmont plainly affirms "that the arterial spirit of our life is of the
nature of a gas;" and in the same chapter (on the fiction of elementary com-
plexions and mixtures) says, "Seeing that the spirit of our life, since it is a
gas, is most mightily and swiftly affected by any other gas," etc. He repeats
the same dogma in his treatise on "Long Life," and indeed very generally
throughout his writings, observing, in his chapter on the Vital Air, that
the spirit of life is a salt, sharp vapour, made of the arterial blood, etc.
Liebig, therefore, in confuting some modern notions as to the nature of con-
tagion by miasma, is leading their reasonings back to that assumption in the
dawn of physiological science by which the discoverer of gas exalted into the
principle of life the substance to which he first gave the name, now so far

8

ever is a gas chemistry should not despair of producing!
But I can argue no longer now,—never can argue long at a
stretch; we are wasting the morning; and, joy! the sun is
up! See! Out! come out! out! and greet the great Life-
giver face to face."

I could not resist the young man's invitation. In a few
minutes we were in the quiet lane under the glinting chestnut-trees. Margrave was chanting, low, a wild tune,—words
in a strange language.

"What words are those,—no European language, I think;
for I know a little of most of the languages which are spoken
in our quarter of the globe, at least by its more civilized
races."

"Civilized race! What is civilization? Those words were
uttered by men who founded empires when Europe itself was
not civilized! Hush, is it not a grand old air?" and lifting
his eyes towards the sun, he gave vent to a voice clear and
deep as a mighty bell! The air was grand; the words had a
sonorous swell that suited it, and they seemed to me jubilant
and yet solemn. He stopped abruptly as a path from the
lane had led us into the fields, already half-bathed in sunlight, dews glittering on the hedgerows.

"Your song," said I, "would go well with the clash of
cymbals or the peal of the organ. I am no judge of melody,
but this strikes me as that of a religious hymn."

"I compliment you on the guess. It is a Persian fire-
worshipper's hymn to the sun. The dialect is very different

---

miliarly known. It is nevertheless just to Van Helmont to add that his
conception of the vital principle was very far from being as purely material-
istic as it would seem to those unacquainted with his writings; for he carefully distinguishes that principle of life which he ascribes to a gas, and by
which he means the sensuous animal life, from the intellectual immortal
principle of soul. Van Helmont, indeed, was a sincere believer of Divine
Revelation. "The Lord Jesus is the way, the truth, and the life," says with
earnest humility this daring genius, in that noble chapter "On the completing of the mind by the 'prayer of silence,' and the loving offering up of the
heart, soul, and strength to the obedience of the Divine will," from which
some of the most eloquent of recent philosophers, arguing against materialism, have borrowed largely in support and in ornament of their lofty cause.

from modern Persian. Cyrus the Great might have chanted
it on his march upon Babylon."

"And where did you learn it? "

"In Persia itself."

"You have travelled much, learned much,—and are so
young and so fresh. Is it an impertinent question if I ask
whether your parents are yet living, or are you wholly lord
of yourself? "

"Thank you for the question,— pray make my answer
known in the town. Parents I have not,— never had."

"Never had parents! "

"Well, I ought rather to say that no parents ever owned
me. I am a natural son, a vagabond, a nobody. When I
came of age I received an anonymous letter, informing me
that a sum — I need not say what, but more than enough for
all I need — was lodged at an English banker's in my name;
that my mother had died in my infancy; that my father was
also dead — but recently; that as I was a child of love, and
he was unwilling that the secret of my birth should ever be
traced, he had provided for me, not by will, but in his life,
by a sum consigned to the trust of the friend who now wrote
to me; I need give myself no trouble to learn more. Faith,
I never did! I am young, healthy, rich,— yes, rich! Now
you know all, and you had better tell it, that I may win no
man's courtesy and no maiden's love upon false pretences.
I have not even a right, you see, to the name I bear. Hist!
let me catch that squirrel."

With what a panther-like bound he sprang! The squirrel
eluded his grasp, and was up the oak-tree; in a moment he
was up the oak-tree too. In amazement I saw him rising
from bough to bough; saw his bright eyes and glittering teeth
through the green leaves. Presently I heard the sharp piteous cry of the squirrel, echoed by the youth's merry laugh;
and down, through that maze of green, Margrave came, dropping on the grass and bounding up, as Mercury might have
bounded with his wings at his heels.

"I have caught him. What pretty brown eyes! "

Suddenly the gay expression of his face changed to that of

a savage; the squirrel had wrenched itself half-loose, and
bitten him. The poor brute! In an instant its neck was
·wrung, its body dashed on the ground; and that fair young
creature, every feature quivering with rage, was stamping
his foot on his victim again and again! It was horrible. I
caught him by the arm indignantly. He turned round on me
like a wild beast disturbed from its prey, — his teeth set, his
hand lifted, his eyes like balls of fire.

"Shame!" said I, calmly; "shame on you!"

He continued to gaze on me a moment or so, his eye
glaring, his breath panting; and then, as if mastering
himself with an involuntary effort, his arm dropped to his
side, and he said quite humbly, "I beg your pardon; indeed
I do. I was beside myself for a moment; I cannot bear
pain;" and he looked in deep compassion for himself at
his wounded hand. "Venomous brute!" And he stamped
again on the body of the squirrel, already crushed out of
shape.

I moved away in disgust, and walked on.

But presently I felt my arm softly drawn aside, and a
voice, dulcet as the coo of a dove, stole its way into my ears.
There was no resisting the charm with which this extraordinary mortal could fascinate even the hard and the cold; nor
them, perhaps, the least. For as you see in extreme old age,
when the heart seems to have shrunk into itself, and to leave
but meagre and nipped affections for the nearest relations if
grown up, the indurated egotism softens at once towards a
playful child; or as you see in middle life, some misanthrope,
whose nature has been soured by wrong and sorrow, shrink
from his own species, yet make friends with inferior races,
and respond to the caress of a dog, — so, for the worldling or
the cynic, there was an attraction in the freshness of this
joyous favourite of Nature, — an attraction like that of a
beautiful child, spoilt and wayward, or of a graceful animal,
half docile, half fierce.

"But," said I, with a smile, as I felt all displeasure gone,
"such indulgence of passion for such a trifle is surely unworthy a student of philosophy!"

"Trifle," he said dolorously. "But I tell you it is pain; pain is no trifle. I suffer. Look!"

I looked at the hand, which I took in mine. The bite no doubt had been sharp; but the hand that lay in my own was that which the Greek sculptor gives to a gladiator; not large (the extremities are never large in persons whose strength comes from the just proportion of all the members, rather than the factitious and partial force which continued muscular exertion will give to one part of the frame, to the comparative weakening of the rest), but with the firm-knit joints, the solid fingers, the finished nails, the massive palm, the supple polished skin, in which we recognize what Nature designs the human hand to be,— the skilled, swift, mighty doer of all those marvels which win Nature herself from the wilderness.

"It is strange," said I, thoughtfully; "but your susceptibility to suffering confirms my opinion, which is different from the popular belief,— namely, that pain is most acutely felt by those in whom the animal organization being perfect, and the sense of vitality exquisitely keen, every injury or lesion finds the whole system rise, as it were, to repel the mischief and communicate the consciousness of it to all those nerves which are the sentinels to the garrison of life. Yet my theory is scarcely borne out by general fact. The Indian savages must have a health as perfect as yours; a nervous system as fine,— witness their marvellous accuracy of ear, of eye, of scent, probably also of touch; yet they are indifferent to physical pain; or must I mortify your pride by saying that they have some moral quality defective in you which enables them to rise superior to it?"

"The Indian savages," said Margrave, sullenly, "have not a health as perfect as mine, and in what you call vitality — the blissful consciousness of life — they are as sticks and stones compared to me."

"How do you know?"

"Because I have lived with them. It is a fallacy to suppose that the savage has a health superior to that of the civilized man,— if the civilized man be but temperate; and even

if not, he has the stamina that can resist for years the effect
of excesses which would destroy the savage in a month. As
to the savage's fine perceptions of sense, such do not come
from exquisite equilibrium of system, but are hereditary attributes transmitted from race to race, and strengthened by
training from infancy. But is a pointer stronger and healthier
than a mastiff, because the pointer through long descent and
early teaching creeps stealthily to his game and stands to it
motionless? I will talk of this later; now I suffer! Pain,
pain! Has life any ill but pain?"

It so happened that I had about me some roots of the white
lily, which I meant, before returning home, to leave with a
patient suffering from one of those acute local inflammations,
in which that simple remedy often affords great relief. I cut
up one of these roots, and bound the cooling leaves to the
wounded hand with my handkerchief.

"There," said I. "Fortunately if you feel pain more sensibly than others, you will recover from it more quickly."

And in a few minutes my companion felt perfectly relieved,
and poured out his gratitude with an extravagance of expression and a beaming delight of countenance which positively
touched me.

"I almost feel," said I, "as I do when I have stilled an
infant's wailing, and restored it smiling to its mother's
breast."

"You have done so. I am an infant, and Nature is my
mother. Oh, to be restored to the full joy of life, the scent
of wild flowers, the song of birds, and this air — summer air
— summer air!"

I know not why it was, but at that moment, looking at him
and hearing him, I rejoiced that Lilian was not at L——.

"But I came out to bathe. Can we not bathe in that
stream?"

"No. You would derange the bandage round your hand;
and for all bodily ills, from the least to the gravest, there is
nothing like leaving Nature at rest the moment we have hit
on the means which assist her own efforts at cure."

"I obey, then; but I so love the water."

"You swim, of course?"

"Ask the fish if it swim. Ask the fish if it can escape me! I delight to dive down — down; to plunge after the startled trout, as an otter does; and then to get amongst those cool, fragrant reeds and bulrushes, or that forest of emerald weed which one sometimes finds waving under clear rivers. Man! man! could you live but an hour of my life you would know how horrible a thing it is to die!"

"Yet the dying do not think so; they pass away calm and smiling, as you will one day."

"I — I! die one day — die!" and he sank on the grass, and buried his face amongst the herbage, sobbing aloud.

Before I could get through half a dozen words I meant to soothe, he had once more bounded up, dashed the tears from his eyes, and was again singing some wild, barbaric chant. Abstracting itself from the appeal to its outward sense by melodies of which the language was unknown, my mind soon grew absorbed in meditative conjectures on the singular nature, so wayward, so impulsive, which had forced intimacy on a man grave and practical as myself.

I was puzzled how to reconcile so passionate a childishness, so undisciplined a want of self-control, with an experience of mankind so extended by travel, with an education desultory and irregular indeed, but which must, at some time or other, have been familiarized to severe reasonings and laborious studies. In Margrave there seemed to be wanting that mysterious something which is needed to keep our faculties, however severally brilliant, harmoniously linked together, — as the string by which a child mechanically binds the wild-flowers it gathers, shaping them at choice into the garland or the chain.

CHAPTER XXV.

My intercourse with Margrave grew habitual and familiar. He came to my house every morning before sunrise; in the evenings we were again brought together: sometimes in the houses to which we were both invited, sometimes at his hotel, sometimes in my own home.

Nothing more perplexed me than his aspect of extreme youthfulness, contrasted with the extent of the travels, which, if he were to be believed, had left little of the known world unexplored. One day I asked him bluntly how old he was.

"How old do I look? How old should you suppose me to be?"

"I should have guessed you to be about twenty, till you spoke of having come of age some years ago."

"Is it a sign of longevity when a man looks much younger than he is?"

"Conjoined with other signs, certainly!"

"Have I the other signs?"

"Yes, a magnificent, perhaps a matchless, constitutional organization. But you have evaded my question as to your age; was it an impertinence to put it?"

"No. I came of age — let me see — three years ago."

"So long since? Is it possible? I wish I had your secret!"

"Secret! What secret?"

"The secret of preserving so much of boyish freshness in the wear and tear of man-like passions and man-like thoughts."

"You are still young yourself, — under forty?"

"Oh, yes! some years under forty."

"And Nature gave you a grander frame and a finer symmetry of feature than she bestowed on me."

"Pooh! pooh! You have the beauty that must charm the eyes of woman, and that beauty in its sunny forenoon of youth. Happy man! if you love and wish to be sure that you are loved again."

"What you call love — the unhealthy sentiment, the feverish folly — I left behind me, I think forever, when — "

" Ay, indeed,— when? "

" I came of age! "

"Hoary cynic! and you despise love! So did I once. Your time may come."

"I think not. Does any animal, except man, love its fellow she-animal as man loves woman? "

" As man loves woman? No, I suppose not."

" And why should the subject animals be wiser than their king? But to return: you would like to have my youth and my careless enjoyment of youth? "

"Can you ask,— who would not? " Margrave looked at me for a moment with unusual seriousness, and then, in the abrupt changes common to his capricious temperament, began to sing softly one of his barbaric chants,— a chant different from any I had heard him sing before, made, either by the modulation of his voice or the nature of the tune, so sweet that, little as music generally affected me, this thrilled to my very heart's core. I drew closer and closer to him, and murmured when he paused,—

" Is not that a love-song? "

" No; " said he, " it is the song by which the serpent-charmer charms the serpent."

CHAPTER XXVI.

INCREASED intimacy with my new acquaintance did not diminish the charm of his society, though it brought to light some startling defects, both in his mental and moral organization. I have before said that his knowledge, though it had

swept over a wide circuit and dipped into curious, unfrequented recesses, was desultory and erratic. It certainly was
not that knowledge, sustained and aspiring, which the poet
assures us is "the wing on which we mount to heaven." So,
in his faculties themselves there were singular inequalities,
or contradictions. His power of memory in some things
seemed prodigious, but when examined it was seldom accurate; it could apprehend, but did not hold together with a
binding grasp what metaphysicians call "complex ideas."
He thus seemed unable to put it to any steadfast purpose in
the sciences of which it retained, vaguely and loosely, many
recondite principles. For the sublime and beautiful in literature he had no taste whatever. A passionate lover of nature, his imagination had no response to the arts by which
nature is expressed or idealized; wholly unaffected by poetry
or painting. Of the fine arts, music alone attracted and
pleased him. His conversation was often eminently suggestive, touching on much, whether in books or mankind,
that set one thinking; but I never remember him to have
uttered any of those lofty or tender sentiments which form
the connecting links between youth and genius; for if poets
sing to the young, and the young hail their own interpreters
in poets, it is because the tendency of both is to idealize the
realities of life,—finding everywhere in the real a something
that is noble or fair, and making the fair yet fairer, and the
noble nobler still.

In Margrave's character there seemed no special vices, no
special virtues; but a wonderful vivacity, joyousness, animal
good-humour. He was singularly temperate, having a dislike to wine, perhaps from that purity of taste which belongs
to health absolutely perfect. No healthful child likes alco-
hol; no animal, except man, prefers wine to water.

But his main moral defect seemed to me in a want of sympathy, even where he professed attachment. He who could
feel so acutely for himself, be unmanned by the bite of a
squirrel, and sob at the thought that he should one day die,
was as callous to the sufferings of another as a deer who de-
serts and butts from him a wounded comrade.

I give an instance of this hardness of heart where I should have least expected to find it in him.

He had met and joined me as I was walking to visit a patient on the outskirts of the town, when we fell in with a group of children, just let loose for an hour or two from their day-school. Some of these children joyously recognized him as having played with them at their homes; they ran up to him, and he seemed as glad as themselves at the meeting.

He suffered them to drag him along with them, and became as merry and sportive as the youngest of the troop.

"Well," said I, laughing, "if you are going to play at leap-frog, pray don't let it be on the high road, or you will be run over by carts and draymen; see that meadow just in front to the left,— off with you there!"

"With all my heart," cried Margrave, "while you pay your visit. Come along, boys."

A little urchin, not above six years old, but who was lame, began to cry; he could not run,— he should be left behind.

Margrave stooped. "Climb on my shoulder, little one, and I'll be your horse."

The child dried its tears, and delightedly obeyed.

"Certainly," said I to myself, "Margrave, after all, must have a nature as gentle as it is simple. What other young man, so courted by all the allurements that steal innocence from pleasure, would stop in the thoroughfares to play with children?"

The thought had scarcely passed through my mind when I heard a scream of agony. Margrave had leaped the railing that divided the meadow from the road, and, in so doing, the poor child, perched on his shoulder, had, perhaps from surprise or fright, loosened its hold and fallen heavily; its cries were piteous. Margrave clapped his hands to his ears, uttered an exclamation of anger, and not even stopping to lift up the boy, or examine what the hurt was, called to the other children to come on, and was soon rolling with them on the grass, and pelting them with daisies. When I came up, only one child remained by the sufferer,— his little brother, a year older than himself. The child had fallen on his arm, which was not broken, but violently contused. The pain must have been intense. I carried the child to his home, and had to remain there some time. I did not see Margrave till the next morning. When he then called, I felt so indignant that I could scarcely speak to him. When at last I rebuked him for his inhumanity, he seemed surprised; with difficulty remembered the circumstance, and then merely said, as if it were the most natural confession in the world,—

"Oh, nothing so discordant as a child's wail. I hate discords. I am pleased with the company of children; but they must be children who laugh and play. Well, why do you look at me so sternly? What have I said to shock you?"

"Shock me! you shock manhood itself! Go; I cannot talk to you now. I am busy."

But he did not go; and his voice was so sweet, and his ways so winning, that disgust insensibly melted into that sort of forgiveness one accords (let me repeat the illustration) to the deer that forsakes its comrade. The poor thing knows no better. And what a graceful beautiful thing *this* was!

The fascination — I can give it no other name — which Margrave exercised, was not confined to me; it was universal,— old, young, high, low, man, woman, child, all felt it. Never in Low Town had stranger, even the most distinguished by fame, met with a reception so cordial, so flattering. His frank confession that he was a natural son, far from being to his injury, served to interest people more in him, and to prevent all those inquiries in regard to his connections and antecedents which would otherwise have been afloat. To be sure, he was evidently rich,— at least he had plenty of money. He lived in the best rooms in the principal hotel; was very hospitable; entertained the families with whom he had grown intimate; made them bring their children,— music and dancing after dinner. Among the houses in which he had established familiar acquaintance was that of the mayor of the town, who had bought Dr. Lloyd's collection of subjects in natural history. To that collection the mayor had added largely by a very recent purchase. He had arranged these various specimens, which his last acquisitions had enriched by the interesting carcasses of an elephant and a hippopotamus, in a large wooden building contiguous to his dwelling, which had been constructed by a former proprietor (a retired fox-hunter) as a riding-house; and being a man who much affected the diffusion of knowledge, he proposed to open this museum to the admiration of the general public, and, at his death, to bequeath it to the Athenæum or Literary Institute of his native town. Margrave, seconded by the influence of the mayor's daughters, had scarcely been three days at L—— before he had persuaded this excellent and public-spirited functionary to inaugurate the opening of his museum by the popular ceremony of a ball. A temporary corridor should unite the drawing-rooms, which were on the ground floor, with the building that contained the collection; and thus the *fête* would be elevated above the frivolous character of a fashionable amusement, and consecrated to the solemnization of an intellectual institute. Dazzled by the brilliancy of this idea, the mayor announced his intention to give a ball that should include the surrounding neighbourhood, and be worthy, in all expensive respects, of the dignity of himself and the occasion. A night had been fixed for the ball,— a night that became memorable indeed to me! The entertainment was anticipated with a lively interest, in which even the Hill condescended to share. The Hill did not much patronize mayors in general; but when a Mayor gave a ball for a purpose so patriotic, and on a scale so splendid, the Hill liberally acknowledged that Commerce was, on the whole, a thing which the Eminence might, now and then, condescend to acknowledge without absolutely derogating from the rank which Providence had assigned to it amongst the High Places of earth. Accordingly, the Hill was permitted by its Queen to honour the first magistrate of Low Town by a promise to attend his ball. Now, as this festivity had originated in the suggestion of Margrave, so, by a natural association of ideas, every one, in talking of the ball, talked also of Margrave.

The Hill had at first affected to ignore a stranger whose *début* had been made in the mercantile circle of Low Town.

But the Queen of the Hill now said, sententiously, "This new man in a few days has become a Celebrity. It is the policy of the Hill to adopt Celebrities, if the Celebrities pay respect to the Proprieties. Dr. Fenwick is requested to procure Mr. Margrave the advantage of being known to the Hill."

I found it somewhat difficult to persuade Margrave to accept the Hill's condescending overture. He seemed to have a dislike to all societies pretending to aristocratic distinction,— a dislike expressed with a fierceness so unwonted, that it made one suppose he had, at some time or other, been subjected to mortification by the supercilious airs that blow upon heights so elevated. However, he yielded to my instances, and accompanied me one evening to Mrs. Poyntz's house. The Hill was encamped there for the occasion. Mrs. Poyntz was exceedingly civil to him, and after a few commonplace speeches, hearing that he was fond of music, consigned him to the caressing care of Miss Brabazon, who was at the head of the musical department in the Queen of the Hill's administration.

Mrs. Poyntz retired to her favourite seat near the window, inviting me to sit beside her; and while she knitted in silence, in silence my eye glanced towards Margrave, in the midst of the group assembled round the piano.

Whether he was in more than usually high spirits, or whether he was actuated by a malign and impish desire to upset the established laws of decorum by which the gayeties of the Hill were habitually subdued into a serene and somewhat pensive pleasantness, I know not; but it was not many minutes before the orderly aspect of the place was grotesquely changed.

Miss Brabazon having come to the close of a complicated and dreary sonata, I heard Margrave abruptly ask her if she could play the Tarantella, that famous Neapolitan air which is founded on the legendary belief that the bite of the tarantula excites an irresistible desire to dance. On that high-bred spinster's confession that she was ignorant of the air, and had not even heard of the legend, Margrave said, "Let

me play it to you, with variations of my own." Miss Brabazon graciously yielded her place at the instrument. Margrave seated himself,—there was great curiosity to hear his
performance. Margrave's fingers rushed over the keys, and
there was a general start, the prelude was so unlike any
known combination of harmonious sounds. Then he began a
chant — song I can scarcely call it — words certainly not in
Italian, perhaps in some uncivilized tongue, perhaps in im-
promptu gibberish. And the torture of the instrument now
commenced in good earnest: it shrieked, it groaned, wilder
and noisier. Beethoven's Storm, roused by the fell touch of
a German pianist, were mild in comparison; and the mighty
voice, dominating the anguish of the cracking keys, had the
full diapason of a chorus. Certainly I am no judge of music,
but to my ear the discord was terrific,— to the ears of better
informed amateurs it seemed ravishing. All were spell-
bound; even Mrs. Poyntz paused from her knitting, as the
Fates paused from their web at the lyre of Orpheus. To this
breathless delight, however, soon succeeded a general desire
for movement. To my amazement, I beheld these formal
matrons and sober fathers of families forming themselves
into a dance, turbulent as a children's ball at Christmas; and
when, suddenly desisting from his music, Margrave started
up, caught the skeleton hand of lean Miss Brabazon, and
whirled her into the centre of the dance, I could have fancied
myself at a witch's sabbat. My eye turned in scandalized
alarm towards Mrs. Poyntz. That great creature seemed as
much astounded as myself. Her eyes were fixed on the scene
in a stare of positive stupor. For the first time, no doubt, in
her life, she was overcome, deposed, dethroned. The awe of
her presence was literally whirled away. The dance ceased
as suddenly as it had begun. Darting from the galvanized
mummy whom he had selected as his partner, Margrave shot
to Mrs. Poyntz's side, and said, "Ten thousand pardons for
quitting you so soon, but the clock warns me that I have an
engagement elsewhere." In another moment he was gone.

The dance halted, people seemed slowly returning to their
senses, looking at each other bashfully and ashamed.

"I could not help it, dear," sighed Miss Brabazon at last, sinking into a chair, and casting her deprecating, fainting eyes upon the hostess.

"It is witchcraft," said fat Mrs. Bruce, wiping her forehead.

"Witchcraft!" echoed Mrs. Poyntz; "it does indeed look like it. An amazing and portentous exhibition of animal spirits, and not to be endured by the Proprieties. Where on earth can that young savage have come from?"

"From savage lands," said I,—"so he says."

"Do not bring him here again," said Mrs. Poyntz. "He would soon turn the Hill topsy-turvy. But how charming! I should like to see more of him," she added, in an under voice, "if he would call on me some morning, and not in the presence of those for whose Proprieties I am responsible. Jane must be out in her ride with the colonel."

Margrave never again attended the patrician festivities of the Hill. Invitations were poured upon him, especially by Miss Brabazon and the other old maids, but in vain.

"Those people," said he, "are too tamed and civilized for me; and so few young persons among them. Even that girl Jane is only young on the surface; inside, as old as the World or her mother. I like youth, real youth,—I am young, I am young!"

And, indeed, I observed he would attach himself to some young person, often to some child, as if with cordial and special favour, yet for not more than an hour or so, never distinguishing them by the same preference when he next met them. I made that remark to him, in rebuke of his fickleness, one evening when he had found me at work on my Ambitious Book, reducing to rule and measure the Laws of Nature.

"It is not fickleness," said he,—"it is necessity."

"Necessity! Explain yourself."

"I seek to find what I have not found," said he; "it is my necessity to seek it, and among the young; and disappointed in one, I turn to the other. Necessity again. But find it at last I must."

"I suppose you mean what the young usually seek in the young; and if, as you said the other day, you have left love behind you, you now wander back to re-find it."

"Tush! If I may judge by the talk of young fools, love may be found every day by him who looks out for it. What I seek is among the rarest of all discoveries. You might aid me to find it, and in so doing aid yourself to a knowledge far beyond all that your formal experiments can bestow."

"Prove your words, and command my services," said I, smiling somewhat disdainfully.

"You told me that you had examined into the alleged phenomena of animal magnetism, and proved some persons who pretend to the gift which the Scotch call second sight to be bungling impostors. You were right. I have seen the clairvoyants who drive their trade in this town; a common gipsy could beat them in their own calling. But your experience must have shown you that there are certain temperaments in which the gift of the Pythoness is stored, unknown to the possessor, undetected by the common observer; but the signs of which should be as apparent to the modern physiologist, as they were to the ancient priest."

"I at least, as a physiologist, am ignorant of the signs: what are they?"

"I should despair of making you comprehend them by mere verbal description. I could guide your observation to distinguish them unerringly were living subjects before us. But not one in a million has the gift to an extent available for the purposes to which the wise would apply it. Many have imperfect glimpses; few, few indeed, the unveiled, lucent sight. They who have but the imperfect glimpses mislead and dupe the minds that consult them, because, being sometimes marvellously right, they excite a credulous belief in their general accuracy; and as they are but translators of dreams in their own brain, their assurances are no more to be trusted than are the dreams of commonplace sleepers. But where the gift exists to perfection, he who knows how to direct and to profit by it should be able to discover all that he desires to know for the guidance and preservation of his own

life. He will be forewarned of every danger, forearmed in
the means by which danger is avoided. For the eye of the
true Pythoness matter has no obstruction, space no confines,
time no measurement."

"My dear Margrave, you may well say that creatures so
gifted are rare; and, for my part, I would as soon search
for a unicorn, as, to use your affected expression, for a
Pythoness."

"Nevertheless, whenever there come across the course of
your practice some young creature to whom all the evil of
the world is as yet unknown, to whom the ordinary cares and
duties of the world are strange and unwelcome; who from the
earliest dawn of reason has loved to sit apart and to muse;
before whose eyes visions pass unsolicited; who converses
with those who are not dwellers on the earth, and beholds in
the space landscapes which the earth does not reflect —"

"Margrave, Margrave! of whom do you speak?"

"Whose frame, though exquisitely sensitive, has still a
health and a soundness in which you recognize no disease;
whose mind has a truthfulness that you know cannot deceive
you, and a simple intelligence too clear to deceive itself; who
is moved to a mysterious degree by all the varying aspects
of external nature, — innocently joyous, or unaccountably sad,
— when, I say, such a being comes across your experience,
inform me; and the chances are that the true Pythoness is
found."

I had listened with vague terror, and with more than one
exclamation of amazement, to descriptions which brought
Lilian Ashleigh before me; and I now sat mute, bewildered,
breathless, gazing upon Margrave, and rejoicing that, at
least, Lilian he had never seen.

He returned my own gaze steadily, searchingly, and then,
breaking into a slight laugh, resumed: —

"You call my word 'Pythoness' affected. I know of no
better. My recollections of classic anecdote and history are
confused and dim; but somewhere I have read or heard that
the priests of Delphi were accustomed to travel chiefly into
Thrace or Thessaly, in search of the virgins who might fitly

administer their oracles, and that the oracles gradually ceased in repute as the priests became unable to discover the organization requisite in the priestesses, and supplied by craft and imposture, or by such imperfect fragmentary developments as belong now to professional clairvoyants, the gifts which Nature failed to afford. Indeed, the demand was one that must have rapidly exhausted so limited a supply. The constant strain upon faculties so wearying to the vital functions in their relentless exercise, under the artful stimulants by which the priests heightened their power, was mortal, and no Pythoness ever retained her life more than three years from the time that her gift was elaborately trained and developed."

"Pooh! I know of no classical authority for the details you so confidently cite. Perhaps some such legends may be found in the Alexandrian Platonists, but those mystics are no authority on such a subject. After all," I added, recovering from my first surprise, or awe, "the Delphic oracles were proverbially ambiguous, and their responses might be read either way,— a proof that the priests dictated the verses, though their arts on the unhappy priestess might throw her into real convulsions, and the real convulsions, not the false gift, might shorten her life. Enough of such idle subjects! Yet no! one question more. If you found your Pythoness, what then?"

"What then? Why, through her aid I might discover the process of an experiment which your practical science would assist me to complete."

"Tell me of what kind is your experiment; and precisely because such little science as I possess is exclusively practical, I may assist you without the help of the Pythoness."

Margrave was silent for some minutes, passing his hand several times across his forehead, which was a frequent gesture of his, and then rising, he answered, in listless accents, —

"I cannot say more now, my brain is fatigued; and you are not yet in the right mood to hear me. By the way, how close and reserved you are with me!"

"How so?"

"You never told me that you were engaged to be married. You leave me, who thought to have won your friendship, to hear what concerns you so intimately from a comparative stranger."

"Who told you?"

"That woman with eyes that pry and lips that scheme, to whose house you took me."

"Mrs. Poyntz! is it possible? When?"

"This afternoon. I met her in the street; she stopped me, and, after some unmeaning talk, asked if I had seen you lately; if I did not find you very absent and distracted: no wonder,—you were in love. The young lady was away on a visit, and wooed by a dangerous rival."

"Wooed by a dangerous rival!"

"Very rich, good-looking, young. Do you fear him? You turn pale."

"I do not fear, except so far as he who loves truly, loves humbly, and fears not that another may be preferred, but that another may be worthier of preference than himself. But that Mrs. Poyntz should tell you all this does amaze me. Did she mention the name of the young lady?"

"Yes; Lilian Ashleigh. Henceforth be more frank with me. Who knows? I may help you. Adieu!"

———◆———

CHAPTER XXVII.

WHEN Margrave had gone, I glanced at the clock,—not yet nine. I resolved to go at once to Mrs. Poyntz. It was not an evening on which she received, but doubtless she would see me. She owed me an explanation. How thus carelessly divulge a secret she had been enjoined to keep; and this rival, of whom I was ignorant? It was no longer a matter of wonder that Margrave should have described Lilian's peculiar idiosyncrasies in his sketch of his fabulous

Pythoness. Doubtless Mrs. Poyntz had, with unpardonable levity of indiscretion, revealed all of which she disapproved in my choice. But for what object? Was this her boasted friendship for me? Was it consistent with the regard she professed for Mrs. Ashleigh and Lilian? Occupied by these perplexed and indignant thoughts, I arrived at Mrs. Poyntz's house, and was admitted to her presence. She was fortunately alone; her daughter and the colonel had gone to some party on the Hill. I would not take the hand she held out to me on entrance; seated myself in stern displeasure, and proceeded at once to inquire if she had really betrayed to Mr. Margrave the secret of my engagement to Lilian.

"Yes, Allen Fenwick; I have this day told, not only Mr. Margrave, but every person I met who is likely to tell it to some one else, the secret of your engagement to Lilian Ashleigh. I never promised to conceal it; on the contrary, I wrote word to Anne Ashleigh that I would therein act as my own judgment counselled me. I think my words to you were that 'public gossip was sometimes the best security for the completion of private engagements.'"

"Do you mean that Mrs. or Miss Ashleigh recoils from the engagement with me, and that I should meanly compel them both to fulfil it by calling in the public to censure them — if — if — Oh, madam, this is worldly artifice indeed!"

"Be good enough to listen to me quietly. I have never yet showed you the letter to Mrs. Ashleigh, written by Lady Haughton, and delivered by Mr. Vigors. That letter I will now show to you; but before doing so I must enter into a preliminary explanation. Lady Haughton is one of those women who love power, and cannot obtain it except through wealth and station,— by her own intellect never obtain it. When her husband died she was reduced from an income of twelve thousand a year to a jointure of twelve hundred, but with the exclusive guardianship of a young son, a minor, and adequate allowances for the charge; she continued, therefore, to preside as mistress over the establishments in town and country; still had the administration of her son's wealth and rank. She stinted his education, in order to maintain her ascendancy over him. He became a brainless prodigal, spend-thrift alike of health and fortune. Alarmed, she saw that, probably, he would die young and a beggar; his only hope of reform was in marriage. She reluctantly resolved to marry him to a penniless, well-born, soft-minded young lady whom she knew she could control; just before this marriage was to take place he was killed by a fall from his horse. The Haughton estate passed to his cousin, the luckiest young man alive,—the same Ashleigh Sumner who had already suc-ceeded, in default of male issue, to poor Gilbert Ashleigh's landed possessions. Over this young man Lady Haughton could expect no influence. She would be a stranger in his house. But she had a niece! Mr. Vigors assured her the niece was beautiful. And if the niece could become Mrs. Ashleigh Sumner, then Lady Haughton would be a less un-important Nobody in the world, because she would still have her nearest relation in a Somebody at Haughton Park. Mr. Vigors has his own pompous reasons for approving an alliance which he might help to accomplish. The first step towards that alliance was obviously to bring into reciprocal attraction the natural charms of the young lady and the acquired merits of the young gentleman. Mr. Vigors could easily induce his ward to pay a visit to Lady Haughton, and Lady Haughton had only to extend her invitations to her niece; hence the letter to Mrs. Ashleigh, of which Mr. Vigors was the bearer, and hence my advice to you, of which you can now under-stand the motive. Since you thought Lilian Ashleigh the only woman you could love, and since I thought there were other women in the world who might do as well for Ashleigh Sumner, it seemed to me fair for all parties that Lilian should not go to Lady Haughton's in ignorance of the sentiments with which she had inspired you. A girl can seldom be sure that she loves until she is sure that she is loved. And now," added Mrs. Poyntz, rising and walking across the room to her bureau, — "now I will show you Lady Haughton's invitation to Mrs. Ashleigh. Here it is!"

I ran my eye over the letter, which she thrust into my hand, resuming her knitting-work while I read.

The letter was short, couched in conventional terms of hollow affection. The writer blamed herself for having so long neglected her brother's widow and child; her heart had been wrapped up too much in the son she had lost; that loss had made her turn to the ties of blood still left to her; she had heard much of Lilian from their common friend, Mr. Vigors; she longed to embrace so charming a niece. Then followed the invitation and the postscript. The postscript ran thus, so far as I can remember: —

"Whatever my own grief at my irreparable bereavement, I am no egotist; I keep my sorrow to myself. You will find some pleasant guests at my house, among others our joint connection, young Ashleigh Sumner."

"Woman's postscripts are proverbial for their significance," said Mrs. Poyntz, when I had concluded the letter and laid it on the table; "and if I did not at once show you this hypocritical effusion, it was simply because at the name Ashleigh Sumner its object became transparent, not perhaps to poor Anne Ashleigh nor to innocent Lilian, but to my knowledge of the parties concerned, as it ought to be to that shrewd intelligence which you derive partly from nature, partly from the insight into life which a true physician cannot fail to acquire. And if I know anything of you, you would have romantically said, had you seen the letter at first, and understood its covert intention, 'Let me not shackle the choice of the woman I love, and to whom an alliance so coveted in the eyes of the world might, if she were left free, be proffered.'"

"I should not have gathered from the postscript all that you see in it; but had its purport been so suggested to me, you are right, I should have so said. Well, and as Mr. Margrave tells me that you informed him that I have a rival, I am now to conclude that the rival is Mr. Ashleigh Sumner?"

"Has not Mrs. Ashleigh or Lilian mentioned him in writing to you?"

"Yes, both; Lilian very slightly, Mrs. Ashleigh with some praise, as a young man of high character, and very courteous to her."

"Yet, though I asked you to come and tell me who were the guests at Lady Haughton's, you never did so."

"Pardon me; but of the guests I thought nothing, and letters addressed to my heart seemed to me too sacred to talk about. And Ashleigh Sumner then courts Lilian! How do you know?"

"I know everything that concerns me; and here, the explanation is simple. My aunt, Lady Delafield, is staying with Lady Haughton. Lady Delafield is one of the women of fashion who shine by their own light; Lady Haughton shines by borrowed light, and borrows every ray she can find."

"And Lady Delafield writes you word — "

"That Ashleigh Sumner is caught by Lilian's beauty."

"And Lilian herself — "

"Women like Lady Delafield do not readily believe that any girl could refuse Ashleigh Sumner; considered in himself, he is steady and good-looking; considered as owner of Kirby Hall and Haughton Park, he has, in the eyes of any sensible mother, the virtues of Cato and the beauty of Antinous."

I pressed my hand to my heart; close to my heart lay a letter from Lilian, and there was no word in that letter which showed that *her* heart was gone from mine. I shook my head gently, and smiled in confiding triumph.

Mrs. Poyntz surveyed me with a bent brow and a compressed lip.

"I understand your smile," she said ironically. "Very likely Lilian may be quite untouched by this young man's admiration, but Anne Ashleigh may be dazzled by so brilliant a prospect for her daughter; and, in short, I thought it desirable to let your engagement be publicly known throughout the town to-day. That information will travel; it will reach Ashleigh Sumner through Mr. Vigors, or others in this neighbourhood, with whom I know that he corresponds. It will bring affairs to a crisis, and before it may be too late. I think it well that Ashleigh Sumner should leave that house; if he leave it for good, so much the better. And, perhaps, the sooner Lilian returns to L—— the lighter your own heart will be."

"And for these reasons you have published the secret of — "

"Your engagement? Yes. Prepare to be congratulated wherever you go. And now if you hear either from mother or daughter that Ashleigh Sumner has proposed, and been, let us say, refused, I do not doubt that, in the pride of your heart, you will come and tell me."

"Rely upon it, I will; but before I take leave, allow me to ask why you described to a young man like Mr. Margrave — whose wild and strange humours you have witnessed and not approved — any of those traits of character in Miss Ashleigh which distinguish her from other girls of her age? "

"I? You mistake. I said nothing to him of her character. I mentioned her name, and said she was beautiful, that was all."

"Nay, you said that she was fond of musing, of solitude; that in her fancies she believed in the reality of visions which might flit before her eyes as they flit before the eyes of all imaginative dreamers."

"Not a word did I say to Mr. Margrave of such peculiarities in Lilian; not a word more than what I have told you, on my honour! "

Still incredulous, but disguising my incredulity with that convenient smile by which we accomplish so much of the polite dissimulation indispensable to the decencies of civilized life, I took my departure, returned home, and wrote to Lilian.

CHAPTER XXVIII.

THE conversation with Mrs. Poyntz left my mind restless and disquieted. I had no doubt, indeed, of Lilian's truth; but could I be sure that the attentions of a young man, with advantages of fortune so brilliant, would not force on her

thoughts the contrast of the humbler lot and the duller walk
of life in which she had accepted as companion a man removed from her romantic youth less by disparity of years
than by gravity of pursuits? And would my suit now be as
welcomed as it had been by a mother even so unworldly as
Mrs. Ashleigh? Why, too, should both mother and daughter
have left me so unprepared to hear that I had a rival; why
not have implied some consoling assurance that such rivalry
need not cause me alarm? Lilian's letters, it is true, touched
but little on any of the persons round her; they were filled
with the outpourings of an ingenuous heart, coloured by the
glow of a golden fancy. They were written as if in the wide
world we two stood apart alone, consecrated from the crowd
by the love that, in linking us together, had hallowed each
to the other. Mrs. Ashleigh's letters were more general and
diffusive, — detailed the habits of the household, sketched the
guests, intimated her continued fear of Lady Haughton, but
had said nothing more of Mr. Ashleigh Sumner than I had
repeated to Mrs. Poyntz. However, in my letter to Lilian I
related the intelligence that had reached me, and impatiently
I awaited her reply.

Three days after the interview with Mrs. Poyntz, and two
days before the long-anticipated event of the mayor's ball, I
was summoned to attend a nobleman who had lately been
added to my list of patients, and whose residence was about
twelve miles from L——. The nearest way was through Sir
Philip Derval's park. I went on horseback, and proposed to
stop on the way to inquire after the steward, whom I had
seen but once since his fit, and that was two days after it,
when he called himself at my house to thank me for my attendance, and to declare that he was quite recovered.

As I rode somewhat fast through the park, I came, however, upon the steward, just in front of the house. I reined
in my horse and accosted him. He looked very cheerful.

"Sir," said he, in a whisper, "I have heard from Sir
Philip; his letter is dated since — since — my good woman
told you what I saw, — well, since then. So that it must
have been all a delusion of mine, as you told her. And yet,

well — well — we will not talk of it, doctor; but I hope you
have kept the secret. Sir Philip would not like to hear of it,
if he comes back."

"Your secret is quite safe with me. But is Sir Philip
likely to come back?"

"I hope so, doctor. His letter is dated Paris, and that's
nearer home than he has been for many years; and — but
bless me! some one is coming out of the house, — a young
gentleman! Who can it be?"

I looked, and to my surprise I saw Margrave descending
the stately stairs that led from the front door. The steward
turned towards him, and I mechanically followed, for I was
curious to know what had brought Margrave to the house of
the long-absent traveller.

It was easily explained. Mr. Margrave had heard at L——
much of the pictures and internal decorations of the mansion.
He had, by dint of coaxing (he said, with his enchanting
laugh), persuaded the old housekeeper to show him the
rooms.

"It is against Sir Philip's positive orders to show the house
to any stranger, sir; and the housekeeper has done very
wrong," said the steward.

"Pray don't scold her. I dare say Sir Philip would not
have refused me a permission he might not give to every idle
sight-seer. Fellow-travellers have a freemasonry with each
other; and I have been much in the same far countries as
himself. I heard of him there, and could tell you more about
him, I dare say, than you know yourself."

"You, sir! pray do then."

"The next time I come," said Margrave, gayly; and, with
a nod to me, he glided off through the trees of the neighbouring grove, along the winding footpath that led to the lodge.

"A very cool gentleman," muttered the steward; "but what
pleasant ways he has! You seem to know him, sir. Who is
he, may I ask?"

"Mr. Margrave, — a visitor at L——, and he has been a
great traveller, as he says; perhaps he met Sir Philip
abroad."

"I must go and hear what he said to Mrs. Gates; excuse me, sir, but I am so anxious about Sir Philip."

"If it be not too great a favour, may I be allowed the same privilege granted to Mr. Margrave? To judge by the outside of the house, the inside must be worth seeing; still, if it be against Sir Philip's positive orders—"

"His orders were, not to let the Court become a show-house,—to admit none without my consent; but I should be ungrateful indeed, doctor, if I refused that consent to you."

I tied my horse to the rusty gate of the terrace-walk, and followed the steward up the broad stairs of the terrace. The great doors were unlocked. We entered a lofty hall with a domed ceiling; at the back of the hall the grand staircase ascended by a double flight. The design was undoubtedly Vanbrugh's,—an architect who, beyond all others, sought the effect of grandeur less in space than in proportion; but Vanbrugh's designs need the relief of costume and movement, and the forms of a more pompous generation, in the bravery of velvets and laces, glancing amid those gilded columns, or descending with stately tread those broad palatial stairs. His halls and chambers are so made for festival and throng, that they become like deserted theatres, inexpressibly desolate, as we miss the glitter of the lamps and the movement of the actors.

The housekeeper had now appeared,—a quiet, timid old woman. She excused herself for admitting Margrave—not very intelligibly. It was plain to see that she had, in truth, been unable to resist what the steward termed his "pleasant ways."

As if to escape from a scolding, she talked volubly all the time, bustling nervously through the rooms, along which I followed her guidance with a hushed footstep. The principal apartments were on the ground-floor, or rather, a floor raised some ten or fifteen feet above the ground; they had not been modernized since the date in which they were built. Hangings of faded silk; tables of rare marble, and mouldered gilding; comfortless chairs at drill against the walls; pictures, of which connoisseurs alone could estimate the value, darkened by dust or blistered by sun and damp, made a general character of discomfort. On not one room, on not one nook, still lingered some old smile of home.

Meanwhile, I gathered from the housekeeper's rambling answers to questions put to her by the steward, as I moved on, glancing at the pictures, that Margrave's visit that day was not his first. He had been to the house twice before,— his ostensible excuse that he was an amateur in pictures (though, as I had before observed, for that department of art he had no taste); but each time he had talked much of Sir Philip. He said that though not personally known to him, he had resided in the same towns abroad, and had friends equally intimate with Sir Philip; but when the steward inquired if the visitor had given any information as to the absentee, it became very clear that Margrave had been rather asking questions than volunteering intelligence.

We had now come to the end of the state apartments, the last of which was a library. "And," said the old woman, "I don't wonder the gentleman knew Sir Philip, for he seemed a scholar, and looked very hard over the books, especially those old ones by the fireplace, which Sir Philip, Heaven bless him, was always poring into."

Mechanically I turned to the shelves by the fireplace, and examined the volumes ranged in that department. I found they contained the works of those writers whom we may class together under the title of mystics,— Iamblichus and Plotinus; Swedenborg and Behmen; Sandivogius, Van Helmont, Paracelsus, Cardan. Works, too, were there, by writers less renowned, on astrology, geomancy, chiromancy, etc. I began to understand among what class of authors Margrave had picked up the strange notions with which he was apt to interpolate the doctrines of practical philosophy.

"I suppose this library was Sir Philip's usual sitting-room?" said I.

"No, sir; he seldom sat here. This was his study;" and the old woman opened a small door, masked by false book-backs. I followed her into a room of moderate size, and evidently of much earlier date than the rest of the house. "It is the only room left of an older mansion," said the steward in answer to my remark. "I have heard it was spared on account of the chimneypiece. But there is a Latin inscription which will tell you all about it. I don't know Latin myself."

The chimneypiece reached to the ceiling. The frieze of the lower part rested on rude stone caryatides; the upper part was formed of oak panels very curiously carved in the geometrical designs favoured by the taste prevalent in the reigns of Elizabeth and James, but different from any I had ever seen in the drawings of old houses,—and I was not quite unlearned in such matters, for my poor father was a passionate antiquary in all that relates to mediæval art. The design in the oak panels was composed of triangles interlaced with varied ingenuity, and enclosed in circular bands inscribed with the signs of the Zodiac.

On the stone frieze supported by the caryatides, immediately under the woodwork, was inserted a metal plate, on which was written, in Latin, a few lines to the effect that "in this room, Simon Forman, the seeker of hidden truth, taking refuge from unjust persecution, made those discoveries in nature which he committed, for the benefit of a wiser age, to the charge of his protector and patron, the worshipful Sir Miles Derval, knight."

Forman! The name was not quite unfamiliar to me; but it was not without an effort that my memory enabled me to assign it to one of the most notorious of those astrologers or soothsayers whom the superstition of an earlier age alternately persecuted and honoured.

The general character of the room was more cheerful than the statelier chambers I had hitherto passed through, for it had still the look of habitation,—the armchair by the fireplace; the knee-hole writing-table beside it; the sofa near the recess of a large bay-window, with book-prop and candlestick screwed to its back; maps, coiled in their cylinders, ranged under the cornice; low strong safes, skirting two sides of the room, and apparently intended to hold papers and title-deeds, seals carefully affixed to their jealous locks. Placed on the top of these old-fashioned receptacles were articles familiar to modern use,— a fowling-piece here, fishing-rods there, two or three simple flower-vases, a pile of music books, a box of crayons. All in this room seemed to speak of residence and ownership,— of the idiosyncrasies of a lone single man, it is true, but of a man of one's own time,— a country gentleman of plain habits but not uncultivated tastes.

I moved to the window; it opened by a sash upon a large balcony, from which a wooden stair wound to a little garden, not visible in front of the house, surrounded by a thick grove of evergreens, through which one broad vista was cut, and that vista was closed by a view of the mausoleum.

I stepped out into the garden,— a patch of sward with a fountain in the centre, and parterres, now more filled with weeds than flowers. At the left corner was a tall wooden summer-house or pavilion,— its door wide open. "Oh, that 's where Sir Philip used to study many a long summer's night," said the steward.

"What! in that damp pavilion?"

"It was a pretty place enough then, sir; but it is very old, — they say as old as the room you have just left."

"Indeed, I must look at it, then."

The walls of this summer-house had once been painted in the arabesques of the Renaissance period; but the figures were now scarcely traceable. The woodwork had started in some places, and the sunbeams stole through the chinks and played on the floor, which was formed from old tiles quaintly tessellated and in triangular patterns, similar to those I had observed in the chimneypiece. The room in the pavilion was large, furnished with old worm-eaten tables and settles.

"It was not only here that Sir Philip studied, but sometimes in the room above," said the steward.

"How do you get to the room above? Oh, I see; a staircase in the angle." I ascended the stairs with some caution, for they were crooked and decayed; and, on entering the room above, comprehended at once why Sir Philip had favoured it.

The cornice of the ceiling rested on pilasters, within which the compartments were formed into open unglazed arches, surrounded by a railed balcony. Through these arches, on three sides of the room, the eye commanded a magnificent extent of prospect. On the fourth side the view was bounded by the mausoleum. In this room was a large telescope; and on stepping into the balcony, I saw that a winding stair mounted thence to a platform on the top of the pavilion,— perhaps once used as an observatory by Forman himself.

"The gentleman who was here to-day was very much pleased with this look-out, sir," said the housekeeper.

"Who would not be? I suppose Sir Philip has a taste for astronomy."

"I dare say, sir," said the steward, looking grave; "he likes most out-of-the-way things."

The position of the sun now warned me that my time pressed, and that I should have to ride fast to reach my new patient at the hour appointed. I therefore hastened back to my horse, and spurred on, wondering whether, in the chain of association which so subtly links our pursuits in manhood to our impressions in childhood, it was the Latin inscription on the chimneypiece that had originally biassed Sir Philip Derval's literary taste towards the mystic jargon of the books at which I had contemptuously glanced.

CHAPTER XXIX.

I DID not see Margrave the following day, but the next morning, a little after sunrise, he walked into my study, according to his ordinary habit.

"So you know something about Sir Philip Derval?" said I. "What sort of a man is he?"

"Hateful!" cried Margrave; and then checking himself, burst out into his merry laugh. "Just like my exaggerations! I am not acquainted with anything to his prejudice. I came across his track once or twice in the East. Travellers are always apt to be jealous of each other."

"You are a strange compound of cynicism and credulity; but I should have fancied that you and Sir Philip would have been congenial spirits, when I found, among his favourite books, Van Helmont and Paracelsus. Perhaps you, too, study Swedenborg, or, worse still, Ptolemy and Lilly?"

"Astrologers? No! They deal with the future! I live for the day; only I wish the day never had a morrow!"

"Have you not, then that vague desire for the *something beyond,*— that not unhappy, but grand discontent with the limits of the immediate Present, from which man takes his passion for improvement and progress, and from which some sentimental philosophers have deduced an argument in favour of his destined immortality?"

"Eh!" said Margrave, with as vacant a stare as that of a peasant whom one has addressed in Hebrew. "What farrago of words is this? I do not comprehend you."

"With your natural abilities," I asked with interest, "do you never feel a desire for fame?"

"Fame? Certainly not. I cannot even understand it!"

"Well, then, would you have no pleasure in the thought that you had rendered a service to humanity?"

Margrave looked bewildered; after a moment's pause, he took from the table a piece of bread that chanced to be there, opened the window, and threw the crumbs into the lane. The sparrows gathered round the crumbs.

"Now," said Margrave, "the sparrows come to that dull pavement for the bread that recruits their lives in this world; do you believe that one sparrow would be silly enough to fly to a house-top for the sake of some benefit to other sparrows, or to be chirruped about after he was dead? I care for science as the sparrow cares for bread,— it may help me to something good for my own life; and as for fame and humanity, I care for them as the sparrow cares for the general interest and posthumous approbation of sparrows!"

"Margrave, there is one thing in you that perplexes me more than all else — human puzzle as you are — in your many eccentricities and self-contradictions."

"What is that one thing in me most perplexing?"

10

"This: that in your enjoyment of Nature you have all the freshness of a child, but when you speak of Man and his objects in the world, you talk in the vein of some worn-out and hoary cynic. At such times, were I to close my eyes, I should say to myself, 'What weary old man is thus venting his spleen against the ambition which has failed, and the love which has forsaken him?' Outwardly the very personation of youth, and revelling like a butterfly in the warmth of the sun and the tints of the herbage, why have you none of the golden passions of the young,—their bright dreams of some impossible love, their sublime enthusiasm for some unattainable glory? The sentiment you have just clothed in the illustration by which you place yourself on a level with the sparrows is too mean and too gloomy to be genuine at your age. Misanthropy is among the dismal fallacies of graybeards. No man, till man's energies leave him, can divorce himself from the bonds of our social kind."

"Our kind! Your kind, possibly; but I—" He swept his hand over his brow, and resumed, in strange, absent, and wistful accents: "I wonder what it is that is wanting here, and of which at moments I have a dim reminiscence." Again he paused, and gazing on me, said with more appearance of friendly interest than I had ever before remarked in his countenance, "You are not looking well. Despite your great physical strength, you suffer like your own sickly patients."

"True! I suffer at this moment, but not from bodily pain."

"You have some cause of mental disquietude?"

"Who in this world has not?"

"I never have."

"Because you own you have never loved. Certainly, you never seem to care for any one but yourself; and in yourself you find an unbroken sunny holiday,—high spirits, youth, health, beauty, wealth. Happy boy!"

At that moment my heart was heavy within me.

Margrave resumed,—

"Among the secrets which your knowledge places at the command of your art, what would you give for one which would enable you to defy and to deride a rival where you place your affections, which could lock to yourself, and imperiously control, the will of the being whom you desire to fascinate, by an influence paramount, transcendent? "

"Love has that secret," said I,— "and love alone."

"A power stronger than love can suspend, can change love itself. But if love be the object or dream of your life, love is the rosy associate of youth and beauty. Beauty soon fades, youth soon departs. What if in nature there were means by which beauty and youth can be fixed into blooming duration,— means that could arrest the course, nay, repair the effects, of time on the elements that make up the human frame? "

"Silly boy! Have the Rosicrucians bequeathed to you a prescription for the elixir of life? "

"If I had the prescription I should not ask your aid to discover its ingredients."

"And is it in the hope of that notable discovery you have studied chemistry, electricity, and magnetism? Again I say, Silly boy! "

Margrave did not heed my reply. His face was overcast, gloomy, troubled.

"That the vital principle is a gas," said he, abruptly, "I am fully convinced. Can that gas be the one which combines caloric with oxygen? "

"Phosoxygen? Sir Humphrey Davy demonstrates that gas not to be, as Lavoisier supposed, caloric, but light, combined with oxygen; and he suggests, not indeed that it is the vital principle itself, but the pabulum of life to organic beings." [1]

"Does he? " said Margrave, his face clearing up. "Possibly, possibly, then, here we approach the great secret of secrets. Look you, Allen Fenwick: I promise to secure to you unfailing security from all the jealous fears that now torture your heart; if you care for that fame which to me is not worth the scent of a flower, the balm of a breeze, I will impart to you a knowledge which, in the hands of ambition,

[1] See Sir Humphrey Davy on Heat, Light, and the Combinations of Light.

would dwarf into commonplace the boasted wonders of recognized science. I will do all this, if, in return, but for one month you will give yourself up to my guidance in whatever experiments I ask, no matter how wild they may seem to you."

"My dear Margrave, I reject your bribes as I would reject the moon and the stars which a child might offer to me in exchange for a toy; but I may give the child its toy for nothing, and I may test your experiments for nothing some day when I have leisure."

I did not hear Margrave's answer, for at that moment my servant entered with letters. Lilian's hand! Tremblingly, breathlessly, I broke the seal. Such a loving, bright, happy letter; so sweet in its gentle chiding of my wrongful fears! It was implied rather than said that Ashleigh Sumner had proposed and been refused. He had now left the house. Lilian and her mother were coming back; in a few days we should meet. In this letter were inclosed a few lines from Mrs. Ashleigh. She was more explicit about my rival than Lilian had been. If no allusion to his attentions had been made to me before, it was from a delicate consideration for myself. Mrs. Ashleigh said that "the young man had heard from L—— of our engagement, and — disbelieved it;" but, as Mrs. Poyntz had so shrewdly predicted, hurried at once to the avowal of his own attachment, and the offer of his own hand. On Lilian's refusal his pride had been deeply mortified. He had gone away manifestly in more anger than sorrow.

"Lady Delafield, dear Margaret Poyntz's aunt, had been most kind iu trying to soothe Lady Haughton's disappointment, which was rudely expressed, — so rudely," added Mrs. Ashleigh, "that it gives us an excuse to leave sooner than had been proposed, — which I am very glad of. Lady Delafield feels much for Mr. Sumner; has invited him to visit her at a place she has near Worthing. She leaves to-morrow in order to receive him; promises to reconcile him to our rejection, which, as he was my poor Gilbert's heir, and was very friendly at first, would be a great relief to my mind. Lilian is well, and so happy at the thoughts of coming back."

When I lifted my eyes from these letters I was as a new man, and the earth seemed a new earth. I felt as if I *had* realized Margrave's idle dreams, — as if youth could never fade, love could never 'grow cold.

"You care for no secrets of mine at this moment," said Margrave, abruptly.

"Secrets!" I murmured; "none now are worth knowing. I am loved! I am loved!"

"I bide my time," said Margrave; and as my eyes met his, I saw there a look I had never seen in those eyes before, — sinister, wrathful, menacing. He turned away, went out through the sash-door of the study; and as he passed towards the fields under the luxuriant chestnut-trees, I heard his musical, barbaric chant, — the song by which the serpent-charmer charms the serpent, — sweet, so sweet, the very birds on the boughs hushed their carol as if to listen.

CHAPTER XXX.

I CALLED that day on Mrs. Poyntz, and communicated to her the purport of the glad news I had received.

She was still at work on the everlasting knitting, her firm fingers linking mesh into mesh as she listened; and when I had done, she laid her skein deliberately down, and said, in her favourite characteristic formula, —

"So at last? — that is settled!"

She rose and paced the room as men are apt to do in reflection, — women rarely need such movement to aid their thoughts; her eyes were fixed on the floor, and one hand was lightly pressed on the palm of the other, — the gesture of a musing reasoner who is approaching the close of a difficult calculation.

At length she paused, fronting me, and said dryly, —

"Accept my congratulations. Life smiles on you now;

guard that smile, and when we meet next, may we be even firmer friends than we are now!"

"When we meet next,— that will be to-night — you surely go to the mayor's great ball? All the Hill descends to Low Town to-night."

"No; we are obliged to leave L—— this afternoon; in less than two hours we shall be gone,— a family engagement. We may be weeks away; you will excuse me, then, if I take leave of you so unceremoniously. Stay, a motherly word of caution. That friend of yours, Mr. Margrave! Moderate your intimacy with him; and especially after you are married. There is in that stranger, of whom so little is known, a something which I cannot comprehend,— a something that captivates and yet revolts. I find him disturbing my thoughts, perplexing my conjectures, haunting my fancies,— I, plain woman of the world! Lilian is imaginative; beware of her imagination, even when sure of her heart. Beware of Margrave. The sooner he quits L—— the better, believe me, for your peace of mind. Adieu! I must prepare for our journey."

"That woman," muttered I, on quitting her house, "seems to have some strange spite against my poor Lilian, ever seeking to rouse my own distrust of that exquisite nature which has just given me such proof of its truth. And yet — and yet — is that woman so wrong here? True! Margrave with his wild notions, his strange beauty! — true — true — he might dangerously encourage that turn for the mystic and visionary which distresses me in Lilian. Lilian should not know him. How induce him to leave L——? Ah, those experiments on which he asks my assistance! I might commence them when he comes again, and then invent some excuse to send him for completer tests to the famous chemists of Paris or Berlin."

CHAPTER XXXI.

It is the night of the mayor's ball! The guests are assembling fast; county families twelve miles round have been invited, as well as the principal families of the town. All, before proceeding to the room set apart for the dance, moved in procession through the museum, — homage to science before pleasure!

The building was brilliantly lighted, and the effect was striking, perhaps because singular and grotesque. There, amidst stands of flowers and evergreens, lit up with coloured lamps, were grouped the dead representatives of races all inferior — some deadly — to man. The fancy of the ladies had been permitted to decorate and arrange these types of the animal world. The tiger glared with glass eyes from amidst artificial reeds and herbage, as from his native jungle; the grisly white bear peered from a mimic iceberg. There, in front, stood the sage elephant, facing a hideous hippopotamus; whilst an anaconda twined its long spire round the stem of some tropical tree in zinc. In glass cases, brought into full light by festooned lamps, were dread specimens of the reptile race, — scorpion and vampire, and cobra capella, with insects of gorgeous hues, not a few of them with venomed stings.

But the chief boast of the collection was in the varieties of the Genus Simia, — baboons and apes, chimpanzees, with their human visage, mockeries of man, from the dwarf monkeys perched on boughs lopped from the mayor's shrubberies, to the formidable ourang-outang, leaning on his huge club.

Every one expressed to the mayor admiration, to each other antipathy, for this unwonted and somewhat ghastly, though instructive, addition to the revels of a ballroom.

Margrave, of course, was there, and seemingly quite at home, gliding from group to group of gayly-dressed ladies, and brilliant with a childish eagerness to play off the show-man. Many of these grim fellow-creatures he declared he had seen, played, or fought with. He had something true or false to say about each. In his high spirits he contrived to make the tiger move, and imitated the hiss of the terrible anaconda. All that he did had its grace, its charm; and the buzz of admiration and the flattering glances of ladies' eyes followed him wherever he moved.

However, there was a general feeling of relief when the mayor led the way from the museum into the ballroom. In provincial parties guests arrive pretty much within the same hour, and so few who had once paid their respects to the apes and serpents, the hippopotamus and the tiger, were disposed to repeat the visit, that long before eleven o'clock the museum was as free from the intrusion of human life as the wilderness in which its dead occupants had been born.

I had gone my round through the rooms, and, little disposed to be social, had crept into the retreat of a window-niche, pleased to think myself screened by its draperies,— not that I was melancholy, far from it; for the letter I had received that morning from Lilian had raised my whole being into a sovereignty of happiness high beyond the reach of the young pleasure-hunters, whose voices and laughter blended with that vulgar music.

To read her letter again I had stolen to my nook, and now, sure that none saw me kiss it, I replaced it in my bosom. I looked through the parted curtain; the room was comparatively empty; but there, through the open folding-doors, I saw the gay crowd gathered round the dancers, and there again, at right angles, a vista along the corridor afforded a glimpse of the great elephant in the deserted museum.

Presently I heard, close beside me, my host's voice.

"Here's a cool corner, a pleasant sofa, you can have it all to yourself. What an honour to receive you under my roof, and on this interesting occasion! Yes, as you say, there are great changes in L—— since you left us. Society has much improved. I must look about and find some persons to introduce to you. Clever! oh, I know your tastes. We have a wonderful man,— a new doctor. Carries all before him; very high character, too; good old family, greatly looked up to, even apart from his profession. Dogmatic a little,— a Sir Oracle,— 'Lets no dog bark;' you remember the quotation, — Shakspeare. Where on earth is he? My dear Sir Philip, I am sure you would enjoy his conversation."

Sir Philip! Could it be Sir Philip Derval to whom the mayor was giving a flattering yet scarcely propitiatory description of myself? Curiosity combined with a sense of propriety in not keeping myself an unsuspected listener; I emerged from the curtain, but silently, and reached the centre of the room before the mayor perceived me. He then came up to me eagerly, linked his arm in mine, and leading me to a gentleman seated on a sofa, close by the window I had quitted, said,—

"Doctor, I must present you to Sir Philip Derval, just re· turned to England, and not six hours in L——. If you would like to see the museum again, Sir Philip, the doctor, I am sure, will accompany you."

"No, I thank you; it is painful to me at present to see, even under your roof, the collection which my poor dear friend, Dr. Lloyd, was so proudly beginning to form when I left these parts."

"Ay, Sir Philip, Dr. Lloyd was a worthy man in his way, but sadly duped in his latter years; took to mesmerism, only think! But our young doctor here showed him up, I can tell you."

Sir Philip, who had acknowledged my first introduction to his acquaintance by the quiet courtesy with which a well-bred man goes through a ceremony that custom enables him to en- dure with equal ease and indifference, now evinced by a slight change of manner how little the mayor's reference to my dis- pute with Dr. Lloyd advanced me in his good opinion. He turned away with a bow more formal than his first one, and said calmly,—

"I regret to hear that a man so simple-minded and so sen- sitive as Dr. Lloyd should have provoked an encounter in which I can well conceive him to have been worsted. With your leave, Mr. Mayor, I will look into your ballroom. I may perhaps find there some old acquantances."

He walked towards the dancers, and the mayor, linking his arm in mine, followed close behind, saying in his loud hearty tones,—

"Come along, you too, Dr. Fenwick, my girls are there; you have not spoken to them yet."

Sir Philip, who was then half way across the room, turned round abruptly, and, looking me full in the face, said,—

"Fenwick, is your name Fenwick,— Allen Fenwick?"

"That is my name, Sir Philip."

"Then permit me to shake you by the hand; you are no stranger, and no mere acquaintance to me. Mr. Mayor, we will look into your ballroom later; do not let us keep you now from your other guests."

The mayor, not in the least offended by being thus summarily dismissed, smiled, walked on, and was soon lost amongst the crowd.

Sir Philip, still retaining my hand, reseated himself on the sofa, and I took my place by his side. The room was still deserted; now and then a straggler from the ballroom looked in for a moment, and then sauntered back to the central place of attraction.

"I am trying to guess," said I, "how my name should be known to you. Possibly you may, in some visit to the Lakes, have known my father?"

"No; I know none of your name but yourself, — if, indeed, as I doubt not, you are the Allen Fenwick to whom I owe no small obligation. You were a medical student at Edinburgh in the year ——? "

"Yes."

"So! At that time there was also at Edinburgh a young man, named Richard Strahan. He lodged in a fourth flat in the Old Town."

"I remember him very well."

"And you remember, also, that a fire broke out at night in the house in which he lodged; that when it was discovered there seemed no hope of saving him. The flames wrapped the lower part of the house; the staircase had given way. A boy, scarcely so old as himself, was the only human being in the crowd who dared to scale the ladder that even 'then scarcely reached the windows from which the smoke rolled in volumes; that boy penetrated into the room, found the inmate almost insensible, rallied, supported, dragged him to the window, got him on the ladder,— saved his life then, and his life later, by nursing with a woman's tenderness, through the fever caused by terror and excitement, the fellow-creature he had rescued by a man's daring. The name of that gallant student was Allen Fenwick, and Richard Strahan is my nearest living relation. Are we friends now? "

I answered confusedly. I had almost forgotten the circumstances referred to. Richard Strahan had not been one of my more intimate companions, and I had never seen nor heard of him since leaving college. I inquired what had become of him.

"He is at the Scotch Bar," said Sir Philip, "and of course without practice. I understand that he has fair average abilities, but no application. If I am rightly informed, he is, however, a thoroughly honourable, upright man, and of an affectionate and grateful disposition."

"I can answer for all you have said in his praise. He had the qualities you name too deeply rooted in youth to have lost them now."

Sir Philip remained for some moments in a musing silence; and I took advantage of that silence to examine him with more minute attention than I had done before, much as the first sight of him had struck me.

He was somewhat below the common height,— so delicately formed that one might call him rather fragile than slight. But in his carriage and air there was remarkable dignity. His countenance was at direct variance with his figure; for as delicacy was the attribute of the last, so power was unmistakably the characteristic of the first. He looked fully the age his steward had ascribed to him,— about forty-eight; at a superficial glance, more, for his hair was prematurely white,— not gray, but white as snow. But his eyebrows were

still jet black, and his eyes, equally dark, were serenely
bright. His forehead was magnificent,— lofty and spacious,
and with only one slight wrinkle between the brows. His
complexion was sunburnt, showing no sign of weak health.
The outline of his lips was that which I have often remarked
in men accustomed to great dangers, and contracting in such
dangers the habit of self-reliance,— firm and quiet, compressed without an effort. And the power of this very noble
countenance was not intimidating, not aggressive; it was
mild, it was benignant. A man oppressed by some formidable tyranny, and despairing to find a protector, would, on
seeing that face, have said, "Here is one who can protect me,
and who will!"

Sir Philip was the first to break the silence.

"I have so many relations scattered over England, that fortunately not one of them can venture to calculate on my
property if I die childless, and therefore not one of them can
feel himself injured when, a few weeks hence, he shall read
in the newspapers that Philip Derval is married. But for
Richard Strahan at least, though I never saw him, I must do
something before the newspapers make that announcement.
His sister was very dear to me."

"Your neighbours, Sir Philip, will rejoice at your marriage, since, I presume, it may induce you to settle amongst
them at Derval Court."

"At Derval Court! No! I shall not settle there." Again
he paused a moment or so, and then went on: "I have long
lived a wandering life, and in it learned much that the wisdom of cities cannot teach. I return to my native land with
a profound conviction that the happiest life is the life most
in common with all. I have gone out of my way to do what
I deemed good, and to avert or mitigate what appeared to me
evil. I pause now and ask myself, whether the most virtuous existence be not that in which virtue flows spontaneously
from the springs of quiet everyday action; when a man does
good without restlessly seeking it, does good unconsciously,
simply because he is good and he lives. Better, perhaps, for
me, if I had thought so long ago! And now I come back to

England with the intention of marrying, late in life though it
be, and with such hopes of happiness as any matter-of-fact
man may form. But my hope will not be at Derval Court.
I shall reside either in London or its immediate neighbourhood, and seek to gather round me minds by which I can correct, if I cannot confide to them, the knowledge I myself have
acquired."

"Nay, if, as I have accidentally heard, you are fond of
scientific pursuits, I cannot wonder, that after so long an absence from England, you should feel interest in learning what
new discoveries have been made, what new ideas are unfolding the germs of discoveries yet to be. But, pardon me, if in
answer to your concluding remark, I venture to say that no
man can hope to correct any error in his own knowledge, unless he has the courage to confide the error to those who can
correct. La Place has said, 'Tout se tient dans le chaine immense des vérités;' and the mistake we make in some science
we have specially cultivated is often only to be seen by the
light of a separate science as specially cultivated by another.
Thus, in the investigation of truth, frank exposition to congenial minds is essential to the earnest seeker."

"I am pleased with what you say," said Sir Philip, "and
I shall be still more pleased to find in you the very confidant
I require. But what was your controversy with my old
friend, Dr. Lloyd? Do I understand our host rightly, that
it related to what in Europe has of late days obtained the
name of mesmerism?"

I had conceived a strong desire to conciliate the good opinion of a man who had treated me with so singular and so
familiar a kindness, and it was sincerely that I expressed my
regret at the acerbity with which I had assailed Dr. Lloyd;
but of his theories and pretensions I could not disguise my
contempt. I enlarged on the extravagant fallacies involved
in a fabulous "clairvoyance," which always failed when put
to plain test by sober-minded examiners. I did not deny
the effects of imagination on certain nervous constitutions.
"Mesmerism could cure nobody; credulity could cure many.
There was the well-known story of the old woman tried as a

witch; she cured agues by a charm. She owned the impeach-
ment, and was ready to endure gibbet or stake for the truth
of her talisman, — more than a mesmerist would for the truth
of his passes! And the charm was a scroll of gibberish sewn
in an old bag and given to the woman in a freak by the judge
himself when a young scamp on the circuit. But the charm
cured? Certainly; just as mesmerism cures. Fools believed
in it. Faith, that moves mountains, may well cure agues."

Thus I ran on, supporting my views with anecdote and
facts, to which Sir Philip listened with placid gravity.

When I had come to an end he said: "Of mesmerism, as
practised in Europe, I know nothing except by report. I can
well understand that medical men may hesitate to admit it
amongst the legitimate resources of orthodox pathology; because, as I gather from what you and others say of its practice, it must, at the best, be far too uncertain in its application
to satisfy the requirements of science. Yet an examination
of its pretensions may enable you to perceive the truth that
lies hid in the powers ascribed to witchcraft; benevolence is
but a weak agency compared to malignity; magnetism perverted to evil may solve half the riddles of sorcery. On this,
however, I say no more at present. But as to that which you
appear to reject as the most preposterous and incredible pretension of the mesmerists, and which you designate by the
word 'clairvoyance,' it is clear to me that you have never
yourself witnessed even those very imperfect exhibitions
which you decide at once to be imposture. I say imperfect,
because it is only a limited number of persons whom the eye
or the passes of the mesmerist can effect; and by such means,
unaided by other means, it is rarely indeed that the magnetic
sleep advances beyond the first vague shadowy twilight-dawn
of that condition to which only in its fuller developments I
would apply the name of 'trance.' But still trance is as essential a condition of being as sleep or as waking, having
privileges peculiar to itself. By means within the range of
the science that explores its nature and its laws, trance, unlike the clairvoyance you describe, is producible in every human being, however unimpressible to mere mesmerism."

"Producible in every human being! Pardon me if I say that I will give any enchanter his own terms who will produce that effect upon me."

"Will you? You consent to have the experiment tried on yourself?"

"Consent most readily."

"I will remember that promise. But to return to the subject. By the word 'trance' I do not mean exclusively the spiritual trance of the Alexandrian Platonists. There is one kind of trance, — that to which all human beings are susceptible, — in which the soul has no share: for of this kind of trance, and it was of this I spoke, some of the inferior animals are susceptible; and, therefore, trance is no more a proof of soul than is the clairvoyance of the mesmerists, or the dream of our ordinary sleep, which last has been called a proof of soul, though any man who has kept a dog must have observed that dogs dream as vividly as we do. But in this trance there is an extraordinary cerebral activity, a projectile force given to the mind, distinct from the soul, by which it sends forth its own emanations to a distance in spite of material obstacles, just as a flower, in an altered condition of atmosphere, sends forth the particles of its aroma. This should not surprise you. Your thought travels over land and sea in your waking state; thought, too, can travel in trance, and in trance may acquire an intensified force. There is, however, another kind of trance which is truly called spiritual, a trance much more rare, and in which the soul entirely supersedes the mere action of the mind."

"Stay!" said I; "you speak of the soul as something distinct from the mind. What the soul may be, I cannot pretend to conjecture; but I cannot separate it from the intelligence!"

"Can you not? A blow on the brain can destroy the intelligence! Do you think it can destroy the soul?

"'From Marlbro's eyes the tears of dotage flow,
And Swift expires, a driveller and a show.'

Towards the close of his life even Kant's giant intellect left him. Do you suppose that in these various archetypes of in-

tellectual man the soul was worn out by the years that loosened the strings, or made tuneless the keys, of the perishing
instrument on which the mind must rely for all notes of its
music? If you cannot distinguish the operations of the mind
from the essence of the soul, I know not by what rational
inductions you arrive at the conclusion that the soul is
imperishable."

I remained silent. Sir Philip fixed on me his dark eyes
quietly and searchingly, and, after a short pause, said,—

"Almost every known body in nature is susceptible of three
several states of existence,— the solid, the liquid, the aëriform. These conditions depend on the quantity of heat they
contain. The same object at one moment may be liquid; at
the next moment solid; at the next aëriform. The water
that flows before your gaze may stop consolidated into ice, or
ascend into air as a vapour. Thus is man susceptible of three
states of existence,— the animal, the mental, the spiritual;
and according as he is brought into relation or affinity with
that occult agency of the whole natural world, which we familiarly call HEAT, and which no science has yet explained,
which no scale can weigh, and no eye discern, one or the
other of these three states of being prevails, or is subjected."

I still continued silent, for I was unwilling discourteously
to say to a stranger so much older than myself, that he seemed
to me to reverse all the maxims of the philosophy to which
he made pretence, in founding speculations audacious and
abstruse upon unanalogous comparisons that would have been
fantastic even in a poet. And Sir Philip, after another pause,
resumed with a half smile,—

"After what I have said, it will perhaps not very much
surprise you when I add that but for my belief in the powers
I ascribe to trance, we should not be known to each other at
this moment."

"How? Pray explain!"

"Certain circumstances, which I trust to relate to you in
detail hereafter, have imposed on me the duty to discover,
and to bring human laws to bear upon, a creature armed with
terrible powers of evil. This monster, for without metaphor,

monster it is, not man like ourselves, has, by arts superior to those of ordinary fugitives, however dexterous in concealment, hitherto for years eluded my research. Through the trance of an Arab child, who, in her waking state, never heard of his existence, I have learned that this being is in England,— is in L——. I am here to encounter him. I expect to do so this very night, and under this very roof."

"Sir Philip!"

"And if you wonder, as you well may, why I have been talking to you with this startling unreserve, know that the same Arab child, on whom I thus implicitly rely, informs me that your life is mixed up with that of the being I seek to unmask and disarm,— to be destroyed by his arts or his agents, or to combine in the causes by which the destroyer himself shall be brought to destruction."

"My life! — your Arab child named me, Allen Fenwick?"

"My Arab child told me that the person in whom I should thus naturally seek an ally was he who had saved the life of the man whom I then meant for my heir, if I died unmarried and childless. She told me that I should not be many hours in this town, which she described minutely, before you would be made known to me. She described this house, with yonder lights, and yon dancers. In her trance she saw us sitting together, as we now sit. I accepted the invitation of our host, when he suddenly accosted me on entering the town, confident that I should meet you here, without even asking whether a person of your name were a resident in the place; and now you know why I have so freely unbosomed myself of much that might well make you, a physician, doubt the soundness of my understanding. The same infant, whose vision has been realized up to this moment, has warned me also that I am here at great peril. What that peril may be I have declined to learn, as I have ever declined to ask from the future what affects only my own life on this earth. That life I regard with supreme indifference, conscious that I have only to discharge, while it lasts, the duties for which it is bestowed on me, to the best of my imperfect power; and aware that minds the strongest and souls the purest may fall

11

into the sloth habitual to predestinarians, if they suffer the action due to the present hour to be awed and paralyzed by some grim shadow on the future! It is only where, irrespectively of aught that can menace myself, a light not struck out of my own reason can guide me to disarm evil or minister to good, that I feel privileged to avail myself of those mirrors on which things, near and far, reflect themselves calm and distinct as the banks and the mountain peak are reflected in the glass of a lake. Here, then, under this roof, and by your side, I shall behold him who— Lo! the moment has come, —I behold him now!"

As he spoke these last words, Sir Philip had risen, and, startled by his action and voice, I involuntarily rose too.

Resting one hand on my shoulder, he pointed with the other towards the threshold of the ballroom. There, the prominent figure of a gay group — the sole male amidst a fluttering circle of silks and lawn, of flowery wreaths, of female loveliness and female frippery — stood the radiant image of Margrave. His eyes were not turned towards us. He was looking down, and his light laugh came soft, yet ringing, through the general murmur.

I turned my astonished gaze back to Sir Philip; yes, unmistakably it was on Margrave that his look was fixed.

Impossible to associate crime with the image of that fair youth! Eccentric notions, fantastic speculations, vivacious egotism, defective benevolence, — yes. But crime! No! impossible!

"Impossible," I said aloud. As I spoke, the group had moved on. Margrave was no longer in sight. At the same moment some other guests came from the ballroom, and seated themselves near us.

Sir Philip looked round, and, observing the deserted museum at the end of the corridor, drew me into it.

When we were alone, he said in a voice quick and low, but decided, —

"It is of importance that I should convince you at once of the nature of that prodigy which is more hostile to mankind than the wolf is to the sheepfold. No words of mine could at present suffice to clear your sight from the deception which cheats it. I must enable you to judge for yourself. It must be now and here. He will learn this night, if he has not learned already, that I am in the town. Dim and confused though his memories of myself may be, they are memories still; and he well knows what cause he has to dread me. I must put another in possession of his secret. Another, and at once! For all his arts will be brought to bear against me, and I cannot foretell their issue. Go, then; enter that giddy crowd, select that seeming young man, bring him hither. Take care only not to mention my name; and when here, turn the key in the door, so as to prevent interruption,— five minutes will suffice."

"Am I sure that I guess whom you mean? The young light-hearted man, known in this place under the name of Margrave? The young man with the radiant eyes, and the curls of a Grecian statue? "

"The same; him whom I pointed out. Quick, bring him hither."

My curiosity was too much roused to disobey. Had I conceived that Margrave, in the heat of youth, had committed some offence which placed him in danger of the law and in the power of Sir Philip Derval, I possessed enough of the old borderer's black-mail loyalty to have given the man whose hand I had familiarly clasped a hint and a help to escape. But all Sir Philip's talk had been so out of the reach of common-sense, that I rather expected to see him confounded by some egregious illusion than Margrave exposed to any well-grounded accusation. All, then, that I felt as I walked into the ballroom and approached Margrave was that curiosity which, I think, any one of my readers will acknowledge that, in my position, he himself would have felt.

Margrave was standing near the dancers, not joining them, but talking with a young couple in the ring. I drew him aside.

"Come with me for a few minutes into the museum; I wish to talk to you." ·

"What about,— an experiment? "

"Yes, an experiment."

"Then I am at your service."

In a minute more, he had followed me into the desolate dead museum. I looked round, but did not see Sir Philip.

CHAPTER XXXII.

MARGRAVE threw himself on a seat just under the great anaconda; I closed and locked the door. When I had done so, my eye fell on the young man's face, and I was surprised to see that it had lost its colour; that it showed great anxiety, great distress; that his hands were visibly trembling.

"What is this?" he said in feeble tones, and raising himself half from his seat as if with great effort. "Help me up! come away! Something in this room is hostile to me,— hostile, overpowering! What can it be?"

"Truth and my presence," answered a stern, low voice; and Sir Philip Derval, whose slight form the huge bulk of the dead elephant had before obscured from my view, came suddenly out from the shadow into the full rays of the lamps which lit up, as if for Man's revel, that mocking catacomb for the playmates of Nature which he enslaves for his service or slays for his sport. As Sir Philip spoke and advanced, Margrave sank back into his seat, shrinking, collapsing, nerveless; terror the most abject expressed in his staring eyes and parted lips. On the other hand, the simple dignity of Sir Philip Derval's bearing, and the mild power of his countenance, were alike inconceivably heightened. A change had come over the whole man, the more impressive because wholly undefinable.

Halting opposite Margrave he uttered some words in a language unknown to me, and stretched one hand over the young man's head. Margrave at once became stiff and rigid, as if turned to stone. Sir Philip said to me,—

"Place one of those lamps on the floor,— there, by his feet."

I took down one of the coloured lamps from the mimic tree round which the huge anaconda coiled its spires, and placed it as I was told.

"Take the seat opposite to him, and watch."

I obeyed.

Meanwhile, Sir Philip had drawn from his breast-pocket a small steel casket, and I observed, as he opened it, that the interior was subdivided into several compartments, each with its separate lid; from one of these he took and sprinkled over the flame of the lamp a few grains of a powder, colourless and sparkling as diamond dust. In a second or so, a delicate perfume, wholly unfamiliar to my sense, rose from the lamp.

"You would test the condition of trance; test it, and in the spirit."

And, as he spoke, his hand rested lightly on my head. Hitherto, amidst a surprise not unmixed with awe, I had preserved a certain defiance, a certain distrust. I had been, as it were, on my guard.

But as those words were spoken, as that hand rested on my head, as that perfume arose from the lamp, all power of will deserted me. My first sensation was that of passive subjugation; but soon I was aware of a strange intoxicating effect from the odour of the lamp, round which there now played a dazzling vapour. The room swam before me. Like a man oppressed by a nightmare, I tried to move, to cry out, feeling that to do so would suffice to burst the thrall that bound me: in vain.

A time that seemed to me inexorably long, but which, as I found afterwards, could only have occupied a few seconds, elapsed in this preliminary state, which, however powerless, was not without a vague luxurious sense of delight. And then suddenly came pain,— pain, that in rapid gradations passed into a rending agony. Every bone, sinew, nerve, fibre of the body, seemed as if wrenched open, and as if some hitherto unconjectured Presence in the vital organization were forcing itself to light with all the pangs of travail. The veins seemed swollen to bursting, the heart labouring to maintain its action by fierce spasms. I feel in this description how language fails me. Enough that the anguish I then endured surpassed all that I have ever experienced of physical pain. This dreadful interval subsided as suddenly as it had commenced. I felt as if a something undefinable by any name had rushed from me, and in that rush that a struggle was over. I was sensible of the passive bliss which attends the release from torture, and then there grew on me a wonderful calm, and, in that calm, a consciousness of some lofty intelligence immeasurably beyond that which human memory gathers from earthly knowledge. I saw before me the still rigid form of Margrave, and my sight seemed, with ease, to penetrate through its covering of flesh, and to survey the mechanism of the whole interior being.

"View that tenement of clay which now seems so fair, as it was when I last beheld it, three years ago, in the house of Haroun of Aleppo! "

I looked, and gradually, and as shade after shade falls on the mountain side, while the clouds gather, and the sun vanishes at last, so the form and face on which I looked changed from exuberant youth into infirm old age,— the discoloured wrinkled skin, the bleared dim eye, the flaccid muscles, the brittle sapless bones. Nor was the change that of age alone; the expression of the countenance had passed into gloomy discontent, and in every furrow a passion or a vice had sown the seeds of grief.

And the brain now opened on my sight, with all its labyrinth of cells. I seemed to have the clew to every winding in the maze.

I saw therein a moral world, charred and ruined, as, in some fable I have read, the world of the moon is described to be; yet withal it was a brain of magnificent formation. The powers abused to evil had been originally of rare order,— imagination, and scope, the energies that dare, the faculties that discover. But the moral part of the brain had failed to dominate the mental,— defective veneration of what is good or great; cynical disdain of what is right and just; in fine, a

great intellect first misguided, then perverted, and now falling with the decay of the body into ghastly but imposing
ruins,— such was the world of that brain as it had been three
years ago. And still continuing to gaze thereon, I observed
three separate emanations of light,— the one of a pale red
hue, the second of a pale azure, the third a silvery spark.

The red light, which grew paler and paler as I looked, un-
dulated from the brain along the arteries, the veins, the
nerves. And I murmured to myself, "Is this the principle
of animal life?"

The azure light equally permeated the frame, crossing and
uniting with the red, but in a separate and distinct ray, exactly as, in the outer world, a ray of light crosses or unites
with a ray of heat, though 'in itself a separate individual
agency. And again I murmured to myself, "Is this the principle of intellectual being, directing or influencing that of
animal life; with it, yet not of it?"

But the silvery spark! What was that? Its centre seemed
the brain; but I could fix it to no single organ. Nay,
wherever I looked through the system, it reflected itself as a
star reflects itself upon water. And I observed that while
the red light was growing feebler and feebler, and the azure
light was confused, irregular,— now obstructed, now hurrying, now almost lost,— the silvery spark was unaltered, undisturbed. So independent was it of all which agitated and
vexed the frame, that I became strangely aware that if the
heart stopped in its action, and the red light died out; if
the brain were paralyzed, that energetic mind smitten into
idiotcy, and the azure light wandering objectless as a meteor
wanders over the morass, — still that silver spark would shine
the same, indestructible by aught that shattered its tabernacle. And I murmured to myself, "Can that starry spark
speak the presence of the soul? Does the silver light shine
within creatures to which no life immortal has been promised
by Divine Revelation?"

Involuntarily I turned my sight towards the dead forms in
the motley collection, and lo, in my trance or my vision, life
returned to them all! — to the elephant and the serpent; to

the tiger, the vulture, the beetle, the moth; to the fish and the polypus, and to yon mockery of man in the giant ape.

I seemed to see each as it lived in its native realm of earth, or of air, or of water; and the red light played more or less warm through the structure of each, and the azure light, though duller of hue, seemed to shoot through the red, and communicate to the creatures an intelligence far inferior indeed to that of man, but sufficing to conduct the current of their will, and influence the cunning of their instincts. But in none, from the elephant to the moth, from the bird in which brain was the largest to the hybrid in which life seemed to live as in plants,— in none was visible the starry silver spark. I turned my eyes from the creatures around, back again to the form cowering under the huge anaconda, and in terror at the animation which the carcasses took in the awful illusions of that marvellous trance; for the tiger moved as if scenting blood, and to the eyes of the serpent the dread fascination seemed slowly returning.

Again I gazed on the starry spark in the form of the man. And I murmured to myself, "But if this be the soul, why is it so undisturbed and undarkened by the sins which have left such trace and such ravage in the world of the brain?" And gazing yet more intently on the spark, I became vaguely aware that it was not the soul, but the halo around the soul, as the star we see in heaven is not the star itself, but its circle of rays; and if the light itself was undisturbed and undarkened, it was because no sins done in the body could annihilate its essence, nor affect the eternity of its duration. The light was clear within the ruins of its lodgment, because it might pass away, but could not be extinguished.

But the soul itself in the heart of the light reflected back on my own soul within me its ineffable trouble, humiliation, and sorrow; for those ghastly wrecks of power placed at its sovereign command it was responsible, and, appalled by its own sublime fate of duration, was about to carry into eternity the account of its mission in time. Yet it seemed that while the soul was still there, though so forlorn and so guilty, even the wrecks around it were majestic. And the

soul, whatever sentence it might merit, was not among the
hopelessly lost; for in its remorse and its shame, it might
still have retained what could serve for redemption. And I
saw that the mind was storming the soul, in some terrible re-
bellious war,— all of thought, of passion, of desire, through
which the azure light poured its restless flow, were surging
up round the starry spark, as in siege. And I could not
comprehend the war, nor guess what it was that the mind
demanded the soul to yield. Only the distinction between
the two was made intelligible by their antagonism. And I
saw that the soul, sorely tempted, looked afar for escape
from the subjects it had ever so ill controlled, and who sought
to reduce to their vassal the power which had lost authority
as their king. I could feel its terror in the sympathy of my
own terror, the keenness of my own supplicating pity. I
knew that it was imploring release from the perils it confessed its want of strength to encounter. And suddenly the
starry spark rose from the ruins and the tumult around it,—
rose into space and vanished; and where my soul had recognized the presence of soul, there was a void. But the red
light burned still, becoming more and more vivid; and as it
thus repaired and recruited its lustre, the whole animal form,
which had been so decrepit, grew restored from decay, grew
into vigour and youth: and I saw Margrave as I had seen
him in the waking world, the radiant image of animal life
in the beauty of its fairest bloom.

And over this rich vitality and this symmetric mechanism
now reigned only, with the animal life, the mind. The starry
light fled and the soul vanished, still was left visible the
mind,— mind, by which sensations convey and cumulate
ideas, and muscles obey volition; mind, as in those animals
that have more than the elementary instincts; mind, as it
might be in men, were men not immortal. As my eyes, in
the Vision, followed the azure light, undulating as before,
through the cells of the brain, and crossing the red amidst
the labyrinth of the nerves, I perceived that the essence of
that azure light had undergone a change: it had lost that
faculty of continuous and concentred power by which man

improves on the works of the past, and weaves schemes to be
developed in the future of remote generations; it had lost all
sympathy in the past, because it had lost all conception of a
future beyond the grave; it had lost conscience, it had lost
remorse; the being it informed was no longer accountable
through eternity for the employment of time. The azure
light was even more vivid in certain organs useful to the conservation of existence, as in those organs I had observed it
more vivid among some of the inferior animals than it is in
man,—secretiveness, destructiveness, and the ready perception of things immediate to the wants of the day; and the
azure light was brilliant in cerebral cells, where before it had
been dark, such as those which harbour mirthfulness and
hope, for there the light was recruited by the exuberant
health of the joyous animal-being. But it was lead-like, or
dim, in the great social organs, through which man subordi-
nates his own interest to that of his species, and utterly lost
in those through which man is reminded of his duties to the
throne of his Maker.

In that marvellous penetration with which the Vision endowed me, I perceived that in this mind, though in energy
far superior to many; though retaining, from memories of
the former existence, the relics of a culture wide and in some
things profound; though sharpened and quickened into formidable, if desultory, force whenever it schemed or aimed at
the animal self-conservation which now made its master-im-
pulse or instinct; and though among the reminiscences of
its state before its change were arts which I could not comprehend, but which I felt were dark and terrible, lending to
a will never checked by remorse arms that no healthful philosophy has placed in the arsenal of disciplined genius;
though the mind in itself had an ally in a body as perfect in
strength and elasticity as man can take from the favour of
nature,—still, I say, I felt that the mind wanted *the something* without which men never could found cities, frame
laws, bind together, beautify, exalt the elements of this
world, by creeds that habitually subject them to a reference
to another. The ant and the bee and the beaver congregate

and construct; but they do not improve. Man improves because the future impels onward that which is not found in
the ant, the bee, and the beaver,— that which was gone from
the being before me.

I shrank appalled into myself, covered my face with my
hands, and groaned aloud: "Have I ever then doubted that
soul is distinct from mind?"

A hand here again touched my forehead, the light in the
lamp was extinguished, I became insensible; and when I recovered I found myself back in the room in which I had first
conversed with Sir Philip Derval, and seated, as before, on
the sofa, by his side.

CHAPTER XXXIII.

My recollections of all which I have just attempted to describe were distinct and vivid; except with respect to time,
it seemed to me as if many hours must have elapsed since I
had entered the museum with Margrave; but the clock on the
mantelpiece met my eyes as I turned them wistfully round
the room; and I was indeed amazed to perceive that five minutes had sufficed for all which it has taken me so long to narrate, and which in their transit had hurried me through ideas
and emotions so remote from anterior experience.

To my astonishment now succeeded shame and indignation,— shame that I, who had scoffed at the possibility of the
comparatively credible influences of mesmeric action, should
have been so helpless a puppet under the hand of the slight
fellow-man beside me, and so morbidly impressed by phan-
tasmagorical illusions; indignation that, by some fumes which
had special potency over the brain, I had thus been, as it
were, conjured out of my senses; and looking full into the
calm face at my side, I said, with a smile to which I sought
to convey disdain,—

"I congratulate you, Sir Philip Derval, on having learned in your travels in the East so expert a familiarity with the tricks of its jugglers."

"The East has a proverb," answered Sir Philip, quietly, "that the juggler may learn much from the dervish, but the dervish can learn nothing from the juggler. You will pardon me, however, for the effect produced on you for a few minutes, whatever the cause of it may be, since it may serve to guard your whole life from calamities, to which it might otherwise have been exposed. And however you may consider that which you have just experienced to be a mere optical illusion, or the figment of a brain super-excited by the fumes of a vapour, look within yourself, and tell me if you do not feel an inward and unanswerable conviction that there is more reason to shun and to fear the creature you left asleep under the dead jaws of the giant serpent, than there would be in the serpent itself, could hunger again move its coils, and venom again arm its fangs."

I was silent, for I could not deny that that conviction had come to me.

"Henceforth, when you recover from the confusion or anger which now disturbs your impressions, you will be prepared to listen to my explanations and my recital in a spirit far different from that with which you would have received them before you were subjected to the experiment, which, allow me to remind you, you invited and defied. You will now, I trust, be fitted to become my confidant and my assistant; you will advise with me how, for the sake of humanity, we should act together against the incarnate lie, the anomalous prodigy which glides through the crowd in the image of joyous beauty. For the present I quit you. I have an engagement, on worldly affairs, in the town this night. I am staying at L——, which I shall leave for Derval Court to-morrow evening. Come to me there the day after to-morrow, at any hour that may suit you the best. Adieu!"

Here Sir Philip Derval rose and left the room. I made no effort to detain him. My mind was too occupied in striving to recompose itself and account for the phenomena that had scared it, and for the strength of the impressions it still retained.

I sought to find natural and accountable causes for effects so abnormal.

Lord Bacon suggests that the ointments with which witches anointed themselves might have had the effect of stopping the pores and congesting the brain, and thus impressing the sleep of the unhappy dupes of their own imagination with dreams so vivid that, on waking, they were firmly convinced that they had been borne through the air to the Sabbat.

I remember also having heard a distinguished French traveller — whose veracity was unquestionable — say, that he had witnessed extraordinary effects produced on the sensorium by certain fumigations used by an African pretender to magic. A person, of however healthy a brain, subjected to the influence of these fumigations, was induced to believe that he saw the most frightful apparitions.

However extraordinary such effects, they were not incredible, — not at variance with our notions of the known laws of nature. And to the vapour or the odours which a powder applied to a lamp had called forth, I was, therefore, prepared to ascribe properties similar to those which Bacon's conjecture ascribed to the witches' ointment, and the French traveller to the fumigations of the African conjuror.

But, as I came to that conclusion, I was seized with an intense curiosity to examine for myself those chemical agencies with which Sir Philip Derval appeared so familiar; to test the contents in that mysterious casket of steel. I also felt a curiosity no less eager, but more, in spite of myself, intermingled with fear, to learn all that Sir Philip had to communicate of the past history of Margrave. I could but suppose that the young man must indeed be a terrible criminal, for a person of years so grave, and station so high, to intimate accusations so vaguely dark, and to use means so extraordinary, in order to enlist my imagination rather than my reason against a youth in whom there appeared none of the signs which suspicion interprets into guilt.

While thus musing, I lifted my eyes and saw Margrave him-

self there at the threshold of the ballroom,— there, where Sir
Philip had first pointed him out as the criminal he had come
to L—— to seek and disarm; and now, as then, Margrave was
the radiant centre of a joyous group. Not the young boy-god
Iacchus, amidst his nymphs, could, in Grecian frieze or picture, have seemed more the type of the sportive, hilarious
vitality of sensuous nature. He must have passed unobserved
by me, in my preoccupation of thought, from the museum
and across the room in which I sat; and now there was as
little trace in that animated countenance of the terror it had
exhibited at Sir Philip's approach, as of the change it had
undergone in my trance or my fantasy.

But he caught sight of me, left his young companions,
came gayly to my side.

"Did you not ask me to go with you into that museum
about half an hour ago, or did I dream that I went with
you?"

"Yes; you went with me into that museum."

"Then pray what dull theme did you select to set me asleep
there?"

I looked hard at him, and made no reply. Somewhat to
my relief, I now heard my host's voice,—

"Why, Fenwick, what has become of Sir Philip Derval?"

"He has left; he had business." And, as I spoke, again I
looked hard on Margrave.

His countenance now showed a change; not surprise, not
dismay, but rather a play of the lip, a flash of the eye, that
indicated complacency,— even triumph.

"So! Sir Philip Derval! He is in L——; he has been
here to-night? So! as I expected."

"Did you expect it?" said our host. "No one else did.
Who could have told you?"

"The movements of men so distinguished need never take
us by surprise. I knew he was in Paris the other day. It is
natural eno' that he should come here. I was prepared for
his coming."

Margrave here turned away towards the window, which he
threw open and looked out.

"There is a storm in the air," said he, as he continued to gaze into the night.

Was it possible that Margrave was so wholly unconscious of what had passed in the museum as to include in oblivion even the remembrance of Sir Philip Derval's presence before he had been rendered insensible, or laid asleep? Was it now only for the first time that he learned of Sir Philip's arrival in L——, and visit to that house? Was there any intimation of menace in his words and his aspect?

I felt that the trouble of my thoughts communicated itself to my countenance and manner; and, longing for solitude and fresh air, I quitted the house. When I found myself in the street I turned round and saw Margrave still standing at the open window, but he did not appear to notice me; his eyes seemed fixed abstractedly on space.

CHAPTER XXXIV.

I WALKED on slowly and with the downcast brow of a man absorbed in meditation. I had gained the broad place in which the main streets of the town converged, when I was overtaken by a violent storm of rain. I sought shelter under the dark archway of that entrance to the district of Abbey Hill which was still called Monk's Gate. The shadow within the arch was so deep that I was not aware that I had a companion till I heard my own name, close at my side. I recognized the voice before I could distinguish the form of Sir Philip Derval.

"The storm will soon be over," said he, quietly. "I saw it coming on in time. I fear you neglected the first warning of those sable clouds, and must be already drenched."

I made no reply, but moved involuntarily away towards the mouth of the arch.

"I see that you cherish a grudge against me!" resumed Sir Philip. "Are you, then, by nature vindictive?"

Somewhat softened by the friendly tone of this reproach, I answered, half in jest, half in earnest,—

"You must own, Sir Philip, that I have some little reason for the uncharitable anger your question imputes to me. But I can forgive you, on one condition."

"What is that?"

"The possession for half an hour of that mysterious steel casket which you carry about with you, and full permission to analyze and test its contents."

"Your analysis of the contents," returned Sir Philip, dryly, "would leave you as ignorant as before of the uses to which they can be applied; but I will own to you frankly, that it is my intention to select some confidant among men of science, to whom I may safely communicate the wonderful properties which certain essences in that casket possess. I invite your acquaintance, nay, your friendship, in the hope that I may find such a confidant in you. But the casket contains other combinations, which, if wasted, could not be resupplied, — at least by any process which the great Master from whom I received them placed within reach of my knowledge. In this they resemble the diamond; when the chemist has found that the diamond affords no other substance by its combustion than pure carbonic-acid gas, and that the only chemical difference between the costliest diamond and a lump of pure charcoal is a proportion of hydrogen less than $\frac{1}{50000}$ part of the weight of the substance, can the chemist make you a diamond?

"These, then, the more potent, but also the more perilous of the casket's contents, shall be explored by no science, submitted to no test. They are the keys to masked doors in the ramparts of Nature, which no mortal can pass through without rousing dread sentries never seen upon this side her wall. The powers they confer are secrets locked in my breast, to be lost in my grave; as the casket which lies on my breast shall not be transferred to the hands of another, till all the rest of my earthly possessions pass away with my last breath in life and my first in eternity."

"Sir Philip Derval," said I, struggling against the appeals

to fancy or to awe, made in words so strange, uttered in a
tone of earnest conviction, and heard amidst the glare of the
lightning, the howl of the winds, and the roll of the thunder,
— "Sir Philip Derval, you accost me in a language which,
but for my experience of the powers at your command, I
should hear with the contempt that is due to the vaunts of a
mountebank, or the pity we give to the morbid beliefs of his
dupe. As it is, I decline the confidence with which you
would favour me, subject to the conditions which it seems
you would impose. My profession abandons to quacks all
drugs which may not be analyzed, all secrets which may not
be fearlessly told. I cannot visit you at Derval Court. I
cannot trust myself, voluntarily, again in the power of a
man, who has arts of which I may not examine the nature,
by which he can impose on my imagination and steal away
my reason."

"Reflect well before you decide," said Sir Philip, with a
solemnity that was stern. "If you refuse to be warned and
to be armed by me, your reason and your imagination will
alike be subjected to influences which I can only explain by
telling you that there is truth in those immemorial legends
which depose to the existence of magic."

"Magic!"

"There is magic of two kinds, — the dark and evil, apper-
taining to witchcraft or necromancy; the pure and beneficent,
which is but philosophy, applied to certain mysteries in Nature remote from the beaten tracks of science, but which deepened the wisdom of ancient sages, and can yet unriddle the
myths of departed races."

"Sir Philip," I said, with impatient and angry interruption, "if you think that a jargon of this kind be worthy a
man of your acquirements and station, it is at least a waste
of time to address it to me. I am led to conclude that you
desire to make use of me for some purpose which I have a
right to suppose honest and blameless, because all you know
of me is, that I rendered to your relation services which cannot lower my character in your eyes. If your object be, as
you have intimated, to aid you in exposing and disabling a

12

man whose antecedents have been those of guilt, and who threatens with danger the society which receives him, you must give me proofs that are not reducible to magic; and you must prepossess me against the person you accuse, not by powders and fumes that disorder the brain, but by substantial statements, such as justify one man in condemning another. And, since you have thought fit to convince me that there are chemical means at your disposal, by which the imagination can be so affected as to accept, temporarily, illusions for re-alities, so I again demand, and now still more decidedly than before, that while you address yourself to my reason, whether to explain your object or to vindicate your charges against a man whom I have admitted to my acquaintance, you will di-vest yourself of all means and agencies to warp my judgment so illicit and fraudulent as those which you own yourself to possess. Let the casket, with all its contents, be transferred to my hands, and pledge me your word that, in giving that casket, you reserve to yourself no other means by which chemistry can be abused to those influences over physical organization, which ignorance or imposture may ascribe to — magic."

"I accept no conditions for my confidence, though I think the better of you for attempting to make them. If I live, you will seek me yourself, and implore my aid. Meanwhile, listen to me, and — "

"No; I prefer the rain and the thunder to the whispers that steal to my ear in the dark from one of whom I have reason to beware."

So saying, I stepped forth, and at that moment the light-ning flashed through the arch, and brought into full view the face of the man beside me. Seen by that glare, it was pale as the face of a corpse, but its expression was compassionate and serene.

I hesitated, for the expression of that hueless countenance touched me; it was not the face which inspires distrust or fear.

"Come," said I, gently; "grant my demand. The casket —"

"It is no scruple of distrust that now makes that demand;

it is a curiosity which in itself is a fearful tempter. Did you now possess what at this moment you desire, how bitterly you would repent! "

"Do you still refuse my demand?"

"I refuse."

"If then you really need me, it is you who will repent."

I passed from the arch into the open space. The rain had passed, the thunder was more distant. I looked back when I had gained the opposite side of the way, at the angle of a street which led to my own house. As I did so, again the skies lightened, but the flash was comparatively slight and evanescent; it did not penetrate the gloom of the arch; it did not bring the form of Sir Philip into view; but, just under the base of the outer buttress to the gateway, I descried the outline of a dark figure, cowering down, huddled up for shelter, the outline so indistinct, and so soon lost to sight as the flash faded, that I could not distinguish if it were man or brute. If it were some chance passer-by, who had sought refuge from the rain, and overheard any part of our strange talk, "the listener," thought I with a half-smile, "must have been mightily perplexed."

CHAPTER XXXV.

On reaching my own home, I found my servant sitting up for me with the information that my attendance was immediately required. The little boy whom Margrave's carelessness had so injured, and for whose injury he had shown so little feeling, had been weakened by the confinement which the nature of the injury required, and for the last few days had been generally ailing. The father had come to my house a few minutes before I reached it, in great distress of mind, saying that his child had been seized with fever, and had become delirious. Hearing that I was at the mayor's house, he had hurried thither in search of me.

I felt as if it were almost a relief to the troubled and haunting thoughts which tormented me, to be summoned to the exercise of a familiar knowledge. I hastened to the bedside of the little sufferer, and soon forgot all else in the anxious struggle for a human life. The struggle promised to be successful; the worst symptoms began to yield to remedies prompt and energetic, if simple. I remained at the house, rather to comfort and support the parents, than because my continued attendance was absolutely needed, till the night was well-nigh gone; and all cause of immediate danger having subsided, I then found myself once more in the streets. An atmosphere palely clear in the gray of dawn had succeeded to the thunder-clouds of the stormy night; the street-lamps, here and there, burned wan and still. I was walking slowly and wearily, so tired out that I was scarcely conscious of my own thoughts, when, in a narrow lane, my feet stopped almost mechanically before a human form stretched at full length in the centre of the road right in my path. The form was dark in the shadow thrown from the neighbouring houses. "Some poor drunkard," thought I, and the humanity inseparable from my calling not allowing me to leave a fellow-creature thus exposed to the risk of being run over by the first drowsy wagoner who might pass along the thoroughfare, I stooped to rouse and to lift the form. What was my horror when my eyes met the rigid stare of a dead man's. I started, looked again; it was the face of Sir Philip Derval! He was lying on his back, the countenance upturned, a dark stream oozing from the breast, — murdered by two ghastly wounds, murdered not long since, the blood was still warm. Stunned and terror-stricken, I stood bending over the body. Suddenly I was touched on the shoulder.

"Hollo! what is this?" said a gruff voice.

"Murder!" I answered in hollow accents, which sounded strangely to my own ear.

"Murder! so it seems." And the policeman who had thus accosted me lifted the body.

"A gentleman by his dress. How did this happen? How did you come here?" and the policeman glanced suspiciously at me.

At this moment, however, there came up another policeman, in whom I recognized the young man whose sister I had
attended and cured.

"Dr. Fenwick," said the last, lifting his hat respectfully,
and at the sound of my name his fellow-policeman changed
his manner and muttered an apology.

I now collected myself sufficiently to state the name and
rank of the murdered man. The policemen bore the body to
their station, to which I accompanied them. I then returned
to my own house, and had scarcely sunk on my bed when
sleep came over me. But what a sleep! Never till then had
I known how awfully distinct dreams can be. The phantasmagoria of the naturalist's collection revived. Life again
awoke in the serpent and the tiger, the scorpion moved, and
the vulture flapped its wings. And there was Margrave, and
there Sir Philip; but their position of power was reversed,
and Margrave's foot was on the breast of the dead man.
Still I slept on till I was roused by the summons to attend
on Mr. Vigors, the magistrate to whom the police had reported the murder.

I dressed hastily and went forth. As I passed through the
street, I found that the dismal news had already spread. I
was accosted on my way to the magistrate by a hundred eager,
tremulous, inquiring tongues.

The scanty evidence I could impart was soon given.

My introduction to Sir Philip at the mayor's house, our accidental meeting under the arch, my discovery of the corpse
some hours afterwards on my return from my patient, my
professional belief that the deed must have been done a very
short time, perhaps but a few minutes, before I chanced upon
its victim. But, in that case, how account for the long interval that had elapsed between the time in which I had left Sir
Philip under the arch and the time in which the murder must
have been committed? Sir Philip could not have been wandering through the streets all those hours. This doubt, however, was easily and speedily cleared up. A Mr. Jeeves, who
was one of the principal solicitors in the town, stated that he
had acted as Sir Philip's legal agent and adviser ever since

Sir Philip came of age, and was charged with the exclusive management of some valuable house-property which the deceased had possessed in L——; that when Sir Philip had arrived in the town late in the afternoon of the previous day, he had sent for Mr. Jeeves; informed him that he, Sir Philip, was engaged to be married; that he wished to have full and minute information as to the details of his house property (which had greatly increased in value since his absence from England), in connection with the settlements his marriage would render necessary; and that this information was also required by him in respect to a codicil he desired to add to his will.

He had, accordingly, requested Mr. Jeeves to have all the books and statements concerning the property ready for his inspection that night, when he would call, after leaving the ball which he had promised the mayor, whom he had accidentally met on entering the town, to attend. Sir Philip had also asked Mr. Jeeves to detain one of his clerks in his office, in order to serve, conjointly with Mr. Jeeves, as a witness to the codicil he desired to add to his will. Sir Philip had accordingly come to Mr. Jeeves's house a little before midnight; had gone carefully through all the statements prepared for him, and had executed the fresh codicil to his testament, which testament he had in their previous interview given to Mr. Jeeves's care, sealed up. Mr. Jeeves stated that Sir Philip, though a man of remarkable talents and great acquirements, was extremely eccentric, and of a very peremptory temper, and that the importance attached to a promptitude for which there seemed no pressing occasion did not surprise him in Sir Philip as it might have done in an ordinary client. Sir Philip said, indeed, that he should devote the next morning to the draft for his wedding settlements, according to the information of his property which he had acquired; and after a visit of very brief duration to Derval Court, should quit the neighbourhood and return to Paris, where his intended bride then was, and in which city it had been settled that the marriage ceremony should take place.

Mr. Jeeves had, however, observed to him, that if he were

so soon to be married, it was better to postpone any revision
of testamentary bequests, since after marriage he would have
to make a new will altogether.

And Sir Philip had simply answered,—

"Life is uncertain; who can be sure of the morrow?"

Sir Philip's visit to Mr. Jeeves's house had lasted some
hours, for the conversation between them had branched off
from actual business to various topics.   Mr. Jeeves had not
noticed the hour when Sir Philip went; he could only say
that as he attended him to the street-door, he observed, rather
to his own surprise, that it was close upon daybreak.

Sir Philip's body had been found not many yards distant
from the hotel at which he had put up, and to which, therefore, he was evidently returning when he left Mr. Jeeves,—
an old-fashioned hotel, which had been the principal one at
L—— when Sir Philip left England, though now outrivalled
by the new and more central establishment in which Margrave
was domiciled.

The primary and natural supposition was that Sir Philip
had been murdered for the sake of plunder; and this supposition was borne out by the fact to which his valet deposed,
namely,—

That Sir Philip had about his person, on going to the
mayor's house, a purse containing notes and sovereigns; and
this purse was now missing.

The valet, who, though an Albanian, spoke English fluently, said that the purse had a gold clasp, on which Sir
Philip's crest and initials were engraved.   Sir Philip's watch
was, however, not taken.

And now, it was not without a quick beat of the heart that
I heard the valet declare that a steel casket, to which Sir
Philip attached extraordinary value, and always carried about
with him, was also missing.

The Albanian described this casket as of ancient Byzantine
workmanship, opening with a peculiar spring, only known to
Sir Philip, in whose possession it had been, so far as the servant knew, about three years: when, after a visit to Aleppo,
in which the servant had not accompanied him, he had first

observed it in his master's hands.   He was asked if this casket contained articles to account for the value Sir Philip set
on it, — such as jewels, bank-notes, letters of credit, etc.   The
man replied that it might possibly do so; he had never been
allowed the opportunity of examining its contents; but that
he was certain the casket held medicines, for he had seen Sir
Philip take from it some small phials, by which he had performed great cures in the East, and especially during a pestilence which had visited Damascus, just after Sir Philip had
arrived at that city on quitting Aleppo.   Almost every European traveller is supposed to be a physician; and Sir Philip
was a man of great benevolence, and the servant firmly believed him also to be of great medical skill.   After this statement, it was very naturally and generally conjectured that
Sir Philip was an amateur disciple of homœopathy, and that
the casket contained the phials or globules in use among
homœopathists.

Whether or not Mr. Vigors enjoyed a vindictive triumph
in making me feel the weight of his authority, or whether his
temper was ruffled in the excitement of so grave a case, I cannot say, but his manner was stern and his tone discourteous
in the questions which he addressed to me.   Nor did the
questions themselves seem very pertinent to the object of
investigation.

"Pray, Dr. Fenwick," said he, knitting his brows, and fixing his eyes on me rudely, "did Sir Philip Derval in his conversation with you mention the steel casket which it seems
he carried about with him? "

I felt my countenance change slightly as I answered,
"Yes."

"Did he tell you what it contained? "

"He said it contained secrets."

"Secrets of what nature, — medicinal or chemical?   Secrets
which a physician might be curious to learn and covetous to
possess? "

This question seemed to me so offensively significant that
it roused my indignation, and I answered haughtily, that "a
physician of any degree of merited reputation did not much

believe in, and still less covet, those secrets in his art which
were the boast of quacks and pretenders."

"My question need not offend you, Dr. Fenwick. I put it
in another shape: Did Sir Philip Derval so boast of the secrets contained in his casket that a quack or pretender might
deem such secrets of use to him?"

"Possibly he might, if he believed in such a boast."

"Humph! — he might if he so believed. I have no more
questions to put to you at present, Dr. Fenwick."

Little of any importance in connection with the deceased
or his murder transpired in the course of that day's examination and inquiries.

The next day, a gentleman distantly related to the young
lady to whom Sir Philip was engaged, and who had been for
some time in correspondence with the deceased, arrived at
L——. He had been sent for at the suggestion of the Albanian servant, who said that Sir Philip had stayed a day at
this gentleman's house in London, on his way to L——, from
Dover.

The new comer, whose name was Danvers, gave a more
touching pathos to the horror which the murder had excited.
It seemed that the motives which had swayed Sir Philip in
the choice of his betrothed were singularly pure and noble.
The young lady's father — an intimate college friend — had
been visited by a sudden reverse of fortune, which had
brought on a fever that proved mortal. He had died some
years ago, leaving his only child penniless, and had bequeathed her to the care and guardianship of Sir Philip.

The orphan received her education at a convent near Paris;
and when Sir Philip, a few weeks since, arrived in that city
from the East, he offered her his hand and fortune.

"I know," said Mr. Danvers, "from the conversation I
held with him when he came to me in London, that he was
induced to this offer by the conscientious desire to discharge
the trust consigned to him by his old friend. Sir Philip was
still of an age that could not permit him to take under his
own roof a female ward of eighteen, without injury to her
good name. He could only get over that difficulty by making

the ward his wife. 'She will be safer and happier with the man she will love and honour for her father's sake,' said the chivalrous gentleman, 'than she will be under any other roof I could find for her.'"

And now there arrived another stranger to L——, sent for by Mr. Jeeves, the lawyer,— a stranger to L——, but not to me; my old Edinburgh acquaintance, Richard Strahan.

The will in Mr. Jeeves's keeping, with its recent codicil, was opened and read. The will itself bore date about six years anterior to the testator's tragic death: it was very short, and, with the exception of a few legacies, of which the most important was £10,000 to his ward, the whole of his property was left to Richard Strahan, on the condition that he took the name and arms of Derval within a year from the date of Sir Philip's decease. The codicil, added to the will the night before his death, increased the legacy to the young lady from £10,000 to £30,000, and bequeathed an annuity of £100 a year to his Albanian servant. Accompanying the will, and within the same envelope, was a sealed letter, addressed to Richard Strahan, and dated at Paris two weeks before Sir Philip's decease. Strahan brought that letter to me. It ran thus : —

" Richard Strahan, I advise you to pull down the house called Derval Court, and to build another on a better site, the plans of which, to be modified according to your own taste and requirements, will be found among my papers. This is a recommendation, not a command. But I strictly enjoin you entirely to demolish the more ancient part, which was chiefly occupied by myself, and to destroy by fire, without perusal, all the books and manuscripts found in the safes in my study. I have appointed you my sole executor, as well as my heir, because I have no personal friends in whom I can confide as I trust I may do in the man I have never seen, simply because he will bear my name and represent my lineage. There will be found in my writing-desk, which always accompanies me in my travels, an autobiographical work, a record of my own life, comprising discoveries, or hints at discovery, in science, through means little cultivated in our age. You will not be surprised that before selecting you as my heir and executor, from a crowd of relations not more distant, I should have made inquiries in order to justify my selection. The result of those inquiries informs me that you have not yourself the peculiar knowledge nor the habits of mind that could enable you to judge of matters which demand the attainments and the practice of science; but that you are of an honest, affectionate nature, and will regard as sacred the last injunctions of a benefactor. I enjoin you, then, to submit the aforesaid manuscript memoir to some man on whose character for humanity and honour you can place confidential reliance, and who is accustomed to the study of the positive sciences, more especially chemistry, in connection with electricity and magnetism. My desire is that he shall edit and arrange this memoir for publication; and that, wherever he feels a conscientious doubt whether any discovery, or hint of discovery, therein contained would not prove more dangerous than useful to mankind, he shall consult with any other three men of science whose names are a guarantee for probity and knowledge, and according to the best of his judgment, after such consultation, suppress or publish the passage of which he has so doubted. I own the ambition which first directed me towards studies of a very unusual character, and which has encouraged me in their pursuit through many years of volun-tary exile, in lands where they could be best facilitated or aided, — the ambition of leaving behind me the renown of a bold discoverer in those recesses of nature which philosophy has hitherto abandoned to supersti-tion. But I feel, at the moment in which I trace these lines, a fear lest, in the absorbing interest of researches which tend to increase to a mar-vellous degree the power of man over all matter, animate or inanimate, I may have blunted my own moral perceptions; and that there may be much in the knowledge which I sought and acquired from the pure desire of investigating hidden truths, that could be more abused to purposes of tremendous evil than be likely to conduce to benignant good. And of this a mind disciplined to severe reasoning, and unin-fluenced by the enthusiasm which has probably obscured my own judg-ment, should be the unprejudiced arbiter. Much as I have coveted and still do covet that fame which makes the memory of one man the com-mon inheritance of all, I would infinitely rather that my name should pass away with my breath, than that I should transmit to my fellow-men any portion of a knowledge which the good might forbear to exer-cise and the bad might unscrupulously pervert. I bear about with me, wherever I wander, a certain steel casket. I received this casket, with its contents, from a man whose memory I hold in profound veneration. Should I live to find a person whom, after minute and intimate trial of his character, I should deem worthy of such confidence, it is my inten-tion to communicate to him the secret how to prepare and how to use such of the powders and essences stored within that casket as I myself have ventured to employ. Others I have never tested, nor do I know how they could be resupplied if lost or wasted. But as the contents of this casket, in the hands of any one not duly instructed as to the mode of applying them, would either be useless, or conduce, through inadvertent and ignorant misapplication, to the most dangerous consequences; so, if I die without having found, and in writing named, such a confidant as I have described above, I command you immediately to empty all the powders and essences found therein into any running stream of water, which will at once harmlessly dissolve them. On no account must they be cast into fire!

" This letter, Richard Strahan, will only come under your eyes in case the plans and the hopes which I have formed for my earthly future should be frustrated by the death on which I do not calculate, but against the chances of which this will and this letter provide. I am about to revisit England, in defiance of a warning that I shall be there subjected to some peril which I refused to have defined, because I am unwilling that any mean apprehension of personal danger should enfeeble my nerves in the discharge of a stern and solemn duty. If I overcome that peril, you will not be my heir; my testament will be remodelled; this letter will be recalled and destroyed. I shall form ties which promise me the happiness I have never hitherto found, though it is common to all men, — the affections of home, the caresses of children, among whom I may find one to whom hereafter I may bequeath, in my knowledge, a far nobler heritage than my lands. In that case, however, my first care would be to assure your own fortunes. And the sum which this codicil assures to my betrothed would be transferred to yourself on my wedding-day. Do you know why, never having seen you, I thus select you for preference to all my other kindred; why my heart, in writing thus, warms to your image? Richard Strahan, your only sister, many years older than yourself — you were then a child — was the object of my first love. We were to have been wedded, for her parents deceived me into the belief that she returned my affection. With a rare and nobler candour, she herself informed me that her heart was given to another, who possessed not my worldly gifts of wealth and station. In resigning my claims to her hand, I succeeded in propitiating her parents to her own choice. I obtained for her husband the living which he held, and I settled on your sister the dower which, at her death, passed to you as the brother to whom she had shown a mother's love, and the interest of which has secured you a modest independence.

" If these lines ever reach you, recognize my title to reverential obe-dience to commands which may seem to you wild, perhaps irrational; and repay, as if a debt due from your own lost sister, the affection I have borne to you for her sake."

While I read this long and strange letter, Strahan sat by my side, covering his face with his hands, and weeping with honest tears for the man whose death had made him powerful and rich.

"You will undertake the trust ordained to me in this letter," said he, struggling to compose himself. "You will read and edit this memoir; you are the very man he himself would have selected. Of your honour and humanity there can be no doubt, and you have studied with success the sciences which he specifies as requisite for the discharge of the task he commands."

At this request, though I could not be wholly unprepared for it, my first impulse was that of a vague terror. It seemed to me as if I were becoming more and more entangled in a mysterious and fatal web. But this impulse soon faded in the eager yearnings of an ardent and irresistible curiosity.

I promised to read the manuscript, and in order that I might fully imbue my mind with the object and wish of the deceased, I asked leave to make a copy of the letter I had just read. To this Strahan readily assented, and that copy I have transcribed in the preceding pages.

I asked Strahan if he had yet found the manuscript. He said, "No, he had not yet had the heart to inspect the papers left by the deceased. He would now do so. He should go in a day or two to Derval Court, and reside there till the murderer was discovered, as doubtless he soon must be through the vigilance of the police. Not till that discovery was made should Sir Philip's remains, though already placed in their coffin, be consigned to the family vault."

Strahan seemed to have some superstitious notion that the murderer might be more secure from justice if his victim were thrust unavenged into the tomb.

CHAPTER XXXVI.

THE belief prevalent in the town ascribed the murder of Sir Philip to the violence of some vulgar robber, probably not an inhabitant of L——. Mr. Vigors did not favour that belief. He intimated an opinion, which seemed extravagant and groundless, that Sir Philip had been murdered, for the sake not of the missing purse, but of the missing casket. It was currently believed that the solemn magistrate had consulted one of his pretended clairvoyants, and that this impostor had gulled him with assurances, to which he attached a credit that perverted into egregiously absurd directions his characteristic activity and zeal.

Be that as it may, the coroner's inquest closed without casting any light on so mysterious a tragedy.

What were my own conjectures I scarcely dared to admit, — I certainly could not venture to utter them; but my suspicions centred upon Margrave. That for some reason or other he had cause to dread Sir Philip's presence in L—— was clear, even to my reason. And how could my reason reject all the influences which had been brought to bear on my imagination, whether by the scene in the museum or my conversation with the deceased? But it was impossible to act on such suspicions,— impossible even to confide them. Could I have told to any man the effect produced on me in the museum, he would have considered me a liar or a madman. And in Sir Philip's accusations against Margrave, there was nothing tangible,— nothing that could bear repetition. Those accusations, if analyzed, vanished into air. What did they imply?— that Margrave was a magician, a monstrous prodigy, a creature exceptional to the ordinary conditions of humanity. Would the most reckless of mortals have ventured to bring against the worst of characters such a charge, on the authority of a deceased witness, and to found on evidence so fantastic

the awful accusation of murder? But of all men, certainly I
— a sober, practical physician — was the last whom the public could excuse for such incredible implications; and certainly, of all men, the last against whom any suspicion of
heinous crime would be readily entertained was that joyous
youth in whose sunny aspect life and conscience alike seemed
to keep careless holiday. But I could not overcome, nor did
I attempt to reason against, the horror akin to detestation,
that had succeeded to the fascinating attraction by which
Margrave had before conciliated a liking founded rather on
admiration than esteem.

In order to avoid his visits I kept away from the study in
which I had habitually spent my mornings, and to which he
had been accustomed to so ready an access; and if he called
at the front door, I directed my servant to tell him that I
was either from home or engaged. He did attempt for the
first few days to visit me as before, but when my intention
to shun him became thus manifest, desisted naturally enough,
as any other man so pointedly repelled would have done.

I abstained from all those houses in which I was likely to
meet him, and went my professional round of visits in a
close carriage, so that I might not be accosted by him in his
walks.

One morning, a very few days after Strahan had shown me
Sir Philip Derval's letter, I received a note from my old college acquaintance, stating that he was going to Derval Court
that afternoon; that he should take with him the memoir
which he had found, and begging me to visit him at his new
home the next day, and commence my inspection of the manuscript. I consented eagerly.

That morning, on going my round, my carriage passed by
another drawn up to the pavement, and I recognized the figure of Margrave standing beside the vehicle, and talking to
some one seated within it. I looked back, as my own carriage whirled rapidly by, and saw with uneasiness and alarm
that it was Richard Strahan to whom Margrave was thus
familiarly addressing himself. How had the two made
acquaintance?

Was it not an outrage on Sir Philip Derval's memory, that the heir he had selected should be thus apparently intimate with the man whom he had so sternly denounced? I became still more impatient to read the memoir: in all probability it would give such explanations with respect to Margrave's antecedents, as, if not sufficing to criminate him of legal offences, would at least effectually terminate any acquaintance between Sir Philip's successor and himself.

All my thoughts were, however, diverted to channels of far deeper interest even than those in which my mind had of late been so tumultuously whirled along, when, on returning home, I found a note from Mrs. Ashleigh. She and Lilian had just come back to L——, sooner than she had led me to anticipate. Lilian had not seemed quite well the last day or two, and had been anxious to return.

----◆----

CHAPTER XXXVII.

LET me recall it — softly, — softly! Let me recall that evening spent with her! — that evening, the last before darkness rose between us like a solid wall.

It was evening, at the close of summer. The sun had set, the twilight was lingering still. We were in the old monastic garden, — garden so quiet, so cool, so fragrant. She was seated on a bench under the one great cedar-tree that rose sombre in the midst of the grassy lawn with its little paradise of flowers. I had thrown myself on the sward at her feet; her hand so confidingly lay in the clasp of mine. I see her still, — how young, how fair, how innocent!

Strange, strange! So inexpressibly English; so thoroughly the creature of our sober, homely life! The pretty delicate white robe that I touch so timorously, and the ribbon-knots of blue that so well become the soft colour of the fair cheek, the wavy silk of the brown hair! She is murmuring low her answer to my trembling question.

As well as when last we parted? Do you love me as well still?"

"There is no 'still' written here," said she, softly pressing her hand to her heart. "Yesterday is as to-morrow in the Forever."

"Ah, Lilian! if I could reply to you in words as akin to poetry as your own!"

"Fie! you who affect not to care for poetry!"

"That was before you went away; before I missed you from my eyes, from my life; before I was quite conscious how precious you were to me, more precious than common words can tell! Yes, there is one period in love when all men are poets, however the penury of their language may belie the luxuriance of their fancies. What would become of me if you ceased to love me?"

"Or of me, if you could cease to love?"

"And somehow it seems to me this evening as if my heart drew nearer to you,— nearer as if for shelter."

"It is sympathy," said she, with tremulous eagerness,— "that sort of mysterious sympathy which I have often heard you deny or deride; for I, too, feel drawn nearer to you, as if there were a storm at hand. I was oppressed by an inde-scribable terror in returning home, and the moment I saw you there came a sense of protection."

Her head sank on my shoulder: we were silent some mo-ments; then we both rose by the same involuntary impulse, and round her slight form I twined my strong arm of man. And now we are winding slow under the lilacs and acacias that belt the lawn. Lilian has not yet heard of the murder, which forms the one topic of the town, for all tales of vio-lence and blood affected her as they affect a fearful child. Mrs. Ashleigh, therefore, had judiciously concealed from her the letters and the journals by which the dismal news had been carried to herself. I need scarcely say that the grim subject was not broached by me. In fact, my own mind escaped from the events which had of late so perplexed and tormented it; the tranquillity of the scene, the bliss of Lilian's presence, had begun to chase away even that

melancholy foreboding which had overshadowed me in the
first moments of our reunion. So we came gradually to converse of the future,—of the day, not far distant, when we
two should be as one. We planned our bridal excursion.
We would visit the scenes endeared to her by song, to me by
childhood,—the banks and waves of my native Windermere,
—our one brief holiday before life returned to labour, and
hearts now so disquieted by hope and joy settled down to the
calm serenity of home.

As we thus talked, the moon, nearly rounded to her full,
rose amidst skies without a cloud. We paused to gaze on
her solemn haunting beauty, as where are the lovers who
have not paused to gaze? We were then on the terrace walk,
which commanded a view of the town below. Before us was
a parapet wall, low on the garden side, but inaccessible on
the outer side, forming part of a straggling irregular street
that made one of the boundaries dividing Abbey Hill from
Low Town. The lamps of the thoroughfares, in many a line
and row beneath us, stretched far away, obscured, here and
there, by intervening roofs and tall church towers. The hum
of the city came to our ears, low and mellowed into a lulling
sound. It was not displeasing to be reminded that there
was a world without, as close and closer we drew each to
each,—worlds to one another! Suddenly there carolled forth
the song of a human voice,—a wild, irregular, half-savage
melody, foreign, uncomprehended words,—air and words not
new to me. I recognized the voice and chant of Margrave.
I started, and uttered an angry exclamation.

"Hush!" whispered Lilian, and I felt her frame shiver
within my encircling arm. "Hush! listen! Yes; I have
heard that voice before — last night — "

"Last night! you were not here; you were more than a
hundred miles away."

"I heard it in a dream! Hush, hush!"

The song rose louder; impossible to describe its effect, in
the midst of the tranquil night, chiming over the serried roof-
tops, and under the solitary moon. It was not like the artful
song of man, for it was defective in the methodical harmony

of tune; it was not like the song of the wild-bird, for it had
no monotony in its sweetness: it was wandering and various
as the sounds from an Æolian harp. But it affected the
senses to a powerful degree, as in remote lands and in vast
solitudes I have since found the note of the mocking-bird,
suddenly heard, affects the listener half with delight, half
with awe, as if some demon creature of the desert were
mimicking man for its own merriment. The chant now had
changed into an air of defying glee, of menacing exultation;
it might have been the triumphant war-song of some antique
barbarian race. The note was sinister; a shadow passed
through me, and Lilian had closed her eyes, and was sighing
heavily; then with a rapid change, sweet as the coo with
which an Arab mother lulls her babe to sleep, the melody
died away. "There, there, look," murmured Lilian, moving
from me, "the same I saw last night in sleep; the same I saw
in the space above, on the evening I first knew you!"

Her eyes were fixed, her hand raised; my look followed
hers, and rested on the face and form of Margrave. The
moon shone full upon him, so full as if concentrating all its
light upon his image. The place on which he stood (a balcony to the upper story of a house about fifty yards distant)
was considerably above the level of the terrace from which
we gazed on him. His arms were folded on his breast, and
he appeared to be looking straight towards us. Even at that
distance, the lustrous youth of his countenance appeared to
me terribly distinct, and the light of his wondrous eye
seemed to rest upon us in one lengthened, steady ray through
the limpid moonshine. Involuntarily I seized Lilian's hand,
and drew her away almost by force, for she was unwilling to
move, and as I led her back, she turned her head to look
round; I, too, turned in jealous rage! I breathed more freely.
Margrave had disappeared!

"How came he there? It is not his hotel. Whose house
is it?" I said aloud, though speaking to myself.

Lilian remained silent, her eyes fixed upon the ground as
if in deep revery. I took her hand; it did not return my
pressure. I felt cut to the heart when she drew coldly from

me that hand, till then so frankly cordial. I stopped short: "Lilian, what is this? you are chilled towards me. Can the mere sound of that man's voice, the mere glimpse of that man's face, have —" I paused; I did not dare to complete my question.

Lilian lifted her eyes to mine, and I saw at once in those eyes a change. Their look was cold; not haughty, but abstracted. "I do not understand you," she said, in a weary, listless accent. "It is growing late; I must go in."

So we walked on moodily, no longer arm in arm, nor hand in hand. Then it occurred to me that, the next day, Lilian would be in that narrow world of society; that there she could scarcely fail to hear of Margrave, to meet, to know him. Jealousy seized me with all its imaginary terrors, and amidst that jealousy, a nobler, purer apprehension for herself. Had I been Lilian's brother instead of her betrothed, I should not have trembled less to foresee the shadow of Margrave's mysterious influence passing over a mind so predisposed to the charm which Mystery itself has for those whose thoughts fuse their outlines in fancies, whose world melts away into Dreamland. Therefore I spoke.

"Lilian, at the risk of offending you — alas! I have never done so before this night — I must address to you a prayer which I implore you not to regard as the dictate of a suspicion unworthy you and myself. The person whom you have just heard and seen is, at present, much courted in the circles of this town. I entreat you not to permit any one to introduce him to you. I entreat you not to know him. I cannot tell you all my reasons for this petition; enough that I pledge you my honour that those reasons are grave. Trust, then, in my truth, as I trust in yours. Be assured that I stretch not the rights which your heart has bestowed upon mine in the promise I ask, as I shall be freed from all fear by a promise which I know will be sacred when once it is given."

"What promise?" asked Lilian, absently, as if she had not heard my words.

"What promise? Why, to refuse all acquaintance with

that man; his name is Margrave. Promise me, dearest, promise me."

"Why is your voice so changed?" said Lilian. "Its tone jars on my ear," she added, with a peevishness so unlike her, that it startled me more than it offended; and without a word further, she quickened her pace, and entered the house.

For the rest of the evening we were both taciturn and distant towards each other. In vain Mrs. Ashleigh kindly sought to break down our mutual reserve. I felt that I had the right to be resentful, and I clung to that right the more because Lilian made no attempt at reconciliation. This, too, was wholly unlike herself, for her temper was ordinarily sweet, — sweet to the extreme of meekness; saddened if the slightest misunderstanding between us had ever vexed me, and yearning to ask forgiveness if a look or a word had pained me. I was in hopes that, before I went away, peace between us would be restored. But long ere her usual hour for retiring to rest, she rose abruptly, and, complaining of fatigue and headache, wished me "good-night," and avoided the hand I sorrowfully held out to her as I opened the door.

"You must have been very unkind to poor Lilian," said Mrs. Ashleigh, between jest and earnest, "for I never saw her so cross to you before. And the first day of her return, too!"

"The fault is not mine," said I, somewhat sullenly; "I did but ask Lilian, and that as a humble prayer, not to make the acquaintance of a stranger in this town against whom I have reasons for distrust and aversion. I know not why that prayer should displease her."

"Nor I. Who is the stranger?"

"A person who calls himself Margrave. Let me at least entreat you to avoid him!"

"Oh, I have no desire to make acquaintance with strangers. But, now Lilian is gone, do tell me all about this dreadful murder. The servants are full of it, and I cannot keep it long concealed from Lilian. I was in hopes that you would have broken it to her."

I rose impatiently; I could not bear to talk thus of an event the tragedy of which was associated in my mind with circumstances so mysterious. I became agitated and even angry when Mrs. Ashleigh persisted in rambling woman-like inquiries,—"Who was suspected of the deed? Who did I think had committed it? What sort of a man was Sir Philip? What was that strange story about a casket?" Breaking from such interrogations, to which I could give but abrupt and evasive answers, I seized my hat and took my departure.

CHAPTER XXXVIII.

LETTER FROM ALLEN FENWICK TO LILIAN ASHLEIGH.

" I HAVE promised to go to Derval Court to-day, and shall not return till to-morrow. I cannot bear the thought that so many hours should pass away with one feeling less kind than usual resting like a cloud upon you and me. Lilian, if I offended you, forgive me! Send me one line to say so! — one line which I can place next to my heart and cover with grateful kisses till we meet again!"

REPLY.

"I scarcely know what you mean, nor do I quite understand my own state of mind at this moment. It cannot be that I love you less — and yet — but I will not write more now. I feel glad that we shall not meet for the next day or so, and then I hope to be quite recovered. I am not well at this moment. Do not ask me to forgive you; but if it is I who am in fault, forgive me, oh, forgive me, Allen!"

And with this unsatisfactory note, not worn next to my heart, not covered with kisses, but thrust crumpled into my desk like a creditor's unwelcome bill, I flung myself on my horse and rode to Derval Court. I am naturally proud; my pride came now to my aid. I felt bitterly indignant against Lilian, so indignant that I resolved on my return to say to her, "If in those words, 'And yet,' you implied a doubt whether you loved me less, I cancel your vows, I give you back your freedom." And I could have passed from her threshold with a firm. foot, though with the certainty that I should never smile again.

Does her note seem to you who may read these pages to justify such resentment? Perhaps not. But there is an atmosphere in the letters of the one we love which we alone — we who love — can feel, and in the atmosphere of that letter I felt the chill of the coming winter.

I reached the park lodge of Derval Court late in the day. I had occasion to visit some patients whose houses lay scat- tered many miles apart, and for that reason, as well as from the desire for some quick bodily exercise which is so natural an effect of irritable perturbation of mind, I had made the journey on horseback instead of using a carriage that I could not have got through the lanes and field-paths by which alone the work set to myself could be accomplished in time.

Just as I entered the park, an uneasy thought seized hold of me with the strength which is ascribed to presentiments. I had passed through my study (which has been so elabo- rately described) to my stables, as I generally did when I wanted my saddle-horse, and, in so doing, had doubtless left open the gate to the iron palisade, and probably the win- dow of the study itself. I had been in this careless habit for several years, without ever once having cause for self- reproach. As I before said, there was nothing in my study to tempt a thief; the study was shut out from the body of the house, and the servant sure at nightfall both to close the win- dow and lock the gate; yet now, for the first time, I felt an impulse, urgent, keen, and disquieting, to ride back to the town, and see those precautions taken. I could not guess why, but something whispered to me that my neglect had ex- posed me to some great danger. I even checked my horse and looked at my watch; too late! — already just on the stroke of Strahan's dinner-hour as fixed in his note; my horse, too, was fatigued and spent: besides, what folly! what bearded man can believe in the warnings of a "pre- sentiment"? I pushed on, and soon halted before the old- fashioned flight of stairs that led up to the Hall. Here I was accosted by the old steward; he had just descended the stairs, and as I dismounted he thrust his arm into mine unceremoniously, and drew me a little aside.

"Doctor, I was right; it *was* his ghost that I saw by the iron door of the mausoleum. I saw it again at the same place last night, but I had no fit then. Justice on his murderer! Blood for blood!"

"Ay!" said I, sternly; for if I suspected Margrave before, I felt convinced now that the inexpiable deed was his. Wherefore convinced? Simply because I now hated him more, and hate is so easily convinced! "Lilian! Lilian!" I murmured to myself that name; the flame of my hate was fed by my jealousy. "Ay!" said I, sternly, "murder will out."

"What are the police about?" said the old man, querulously; "days pass on days, and no nearer the truth. But what does the new owner care? He has the rents and acres; what does he care for the dead? I will never serve another master. I have just told Mr. Strahan so. How do I know whether he did not do the deed? Who else had an interest in it?"

"Hush, hush!" I cried; "you do not know how wildly you are talking."

The old man stared at me, shook his head, released my arm, and strode away.

A labouring man came out of the garden, and having unbuckled the saddle-bags, which contained the few things required for so short a visit, I consigned my horse to his care, and ascended the perron. The old housekeeper met me in the hall, and conducted me up the great staircase, showed me into a bedroom prepared for me, and told me that Mr. Strahan was already waiting dinner for me. I should find him in the study. I hastened to join him. He began apologizing, very unnecessarily, for the state of his establishment. He had as yet engaged no new servants. The housekeeper with the help of a housemaid did all the work.

Richard Strahan at college had been as little distinguishable from other young men as a youth neither rich nor poor, neither clever nor stupid, neither handsome nor ugly, neither audacious sinner nor formal saint, possibly could be.

Yet, to those who understood him well, he was not without some of those moral qualities by which a youth of mediocre intellect often matures into a superior man.

He was, as Sir Philip had been rightly informed, thoroughly honest and upright. But with a strong sense of duty, there was also a certain latent hardness. He was not indulgent. He had outward frankness with acquaintances, but was easily roused to suspicion. He had much of the thriftiness and self-denial of the North countryman, and I have no doubt that he had lived with calm content and systematic economy on an income which made him, as a bachelor, independent of his nominal profession, but would not have sufficed, in itself, for the fitting maintenance of a wife and family. He was, therefore, still single.

It seems to me even during the few minutes in which we conversed before dinner was announced, that his character showed a new phase with his new fortunes. He talked in a grandiose style of the duties of station and the woes of wealth. He seemed to be very much afraid of spending, and still more appalled at the idea of being cheated. His temper, too, was ruffled; the steward had given him notice to quit. Mr. Jeeves, who had spent the morning with him, had said the steward would be a great loss, and a steward at once sharp and honest was not to be easily found.

What trifles can embitter the possession of great goods! Strahan had taken a fancy to the old house; it was conformable to his notions, both of comfort and pomp, and Sir Philip had expressed a desire that the old house should be pulled down. Strahan had inspected the plans for the new mansion to which Sir Philip had referred, and the plans did not please him; on the contrary, they terrified.

"Jeeves says that I could not build such a house under £70,000 or £80,000, and then it will require twice the establishment which will suffice for this. I shall be ruined," cried the man who had just come into possession of at least ten thousand a year.

"Sir Philip did not enjoin you to pull down the old house; he only advised you to do so. Perhaps he thought the site less healthy than that which he proposes for a new building, or was aware of some other drawback to the house, which you may discover later. Wait a little and see before deciding."

"But, at all events, I suppose I must pull down this curious old room,— the nicest part of the old house!"

Strahan, as he spoke, looked wistfully round at the quaint oak chimneypiece; the carved ceiling; the well-built solid walls, with the large mullion casement, opening so pleasantly on the sequestered gardens. He had ensconced himself in Sir Philip's study, the chamber in which the once famous mystic, Forman, had found a refuge.

"So cozey a room for a single man!" sighed Strahan. "Near the stables and dog-kennels, too! But I suppose I must pull it down. I am not bound to do so legally; it is no condition of the will. But in honour and gratitude I ought not to disobey poor Sir Philip's positive injunction."

"Of that," said I, gravely, "there cannot be a doubt."

Here our conversation was interrupted by Mrs. Gates, who informed us that dinner was served in the library. Wine of great age was brought from the long neglected cellars; Strahan filled and re-filled his glass, and, warmed into hilarity, began to talk of bringing old college friends around him in the winter season, and making the roof-tree ring with laughter and song once more.

Time wore away, and night had long set in, when Strahan at last rose from the table, his speech thick and his tongue unsteady. We returned to the study, and I reminded my host of the special object of my visit to him,— namely, the inspection of Sir Philip's manuscript.

"It is tough reading," said Strahan; "better put it off till to-morrow. You will stay here two or three days."

"No; I must return to L—— to-morrow. I cannot absent myself from my patients. And it is the more desirable that no time should be lost before examining the contents of the manuscript, because probably they may give some clew to the detection of the murderer."

"Why do you think that?" cried Strahan, startled from the drowsiness that was creeping over him.

"Because the manuscript may show that Sir Philip had
some enemy, — and who but an enemy could have had a motive for such a crime? Come, bring forth the book. You of
all men are bound to be alert in every research that may
guide the retribution of justice to the assassin of your
benefactor."

"Yes, yes. I will offer a reward of £5,000 for the discovery. Allen, that wretched old steward had the insolence to
tell me that I was the only man in the world who could have
an interest in the death of his master; and he looked at me
as if he thought that I had committed the crime. You are
right; it becomes me, of all men, to be alert. The assassin
must be found. He must hang."

While thus speaking, Strahan had risen, unlocked a desk,
which stood on one of the safes, and drawn forth a thick volume, the contents of which were protected by a clasp and
lock. Strahan proceeded to open this lock by one of a bunch
of keys, which he said had been found on Sir Philip's
person.

"There, Allen, this is the memoir. I need not tell you
what store I place on it, — not, between you and me, that I
expect it will warrant poor Sir Philip's high opinion of his
own scientific discoveries; that part of his letter seems to me
very queer, and very flighty. But he evidently set his heart
on the publication of his work, in part if not in whole; and,
naturally, I must desire to comply with a wish so distinctly
intimated by one to whom I owe so much. I beg you, therefore, not to be too fastidious. Some valuable hints in medicine, I have reason to believe, the manuscript will contain,
and those may help you in your profession, Allen."

"You have reason to believe! Why?"

"Oh, a charming young fellow, who, with most of the
other gentry resident at L——, called on me at my hotel, told
me that he had travelled in the East, and had there heard
much of Sir Philip's knowledge of chemistry, and the cures
it had enabled him to perform."

"You speak of Mr. Margrave. He called on you?"

"Yes."

"You did not, I trust, mention to him the existence of Sir Philip's manuscript."

"Indeed I did; and I said you had promised to examine it. He seemed delighted at that, and spoke most highly of your peculiar fitness for the task."

"Give me the manuscript," said I, abruptly, "and after I have looked at it to-night, I may have something to say to you to-morrow in reference to Mr. Margrave."

"There is the book," said Strahan; "I have just glanced at it, and find much of it written in Latin; and I am ashamed to say that I have so neglected the little Latin I learned in our college days that I could not construe what I looked at."

I sat down and placed the book before me; Strahan fell into a doze, from which he was wakened by the housekeeper, who brought in the tea-things.

"Well," said Strahan, languidly, "do you find much in the book that explains the many puzzling riddles in poor Sir Philip's eccentric life and pursuits?"

"Yes," said I. "Do not interrupt me."

Strahan again began to doze, and the housekeeper asked if we should want anything more that night, and if I thought I could find my way to my bedroom.

I dismissed her impatiently, and continued to read.

Strahan woke up again as the clock struck eleven, and finding me still absorbed in the manuscript, and disinclined to converse, lighted his candle, and telling me to replace the manuscript in the desk when I had done with it, and be sure to lock the desk and take charge of the key, which he took off the bunch and gave me, went upstairs, yawning.

I was alone in the wizard Forman's chamber, and bending over a stranger record than had ever excited my infant wonder, or, in later years, provoked my sceptic smile.

CHAPTER XXXIX.

THE Manuscript was written in a small and peculiar hand-writing, which, though evidently by the same person whose letter to Strahan I had read, was, whether from haste or some imperfection in the ink, much more hard to decipher. Those parts of the Memoir which related to experiments, or alleged secrets in Nature, that the writer intimated a desire to submit exclusively to scholars or men of science, were in Latin, — and Latin which, though grammatically correct, was frequently obscure. But all that detained the eye and attention on the page necessarily served to impress the contents more deeply on remembrance.

The narrative commenced with the writer's sketch of his childhood. Both his parents had died before he attained his seventh year. The orphan had been sent by his guardians to a private school, and his holidays had been passed at Derval Court. Here his earliest reminiscences were those of the quaint old room, in which I now sat, and of his childish wonder at the inscription on the chimneypiece — who and what was the Simon Forman who had there found a refuge from persecution? Of what nature were the studies he had cultivated, and the discoveries he boasted to have made?

When he was about sixteen, Philip Derval had begun to read the many mystic books which the library contained; but without other result on his mind than the sentiment of disappointment and disgust. The impressions produced on the credulous imagination of childhood vanished. He went to the University; was sent abroad to travel: and on his return took that place in the circles of London which is so readily conceded to a young idler of birth and fortune. He passed quickly over that period of his life, as one of extravagance and dissipation, from which he was first drawn by the attachment for his cousin to which his letter to Strahan referred.

Disappointed in the hopes which that affection had conceived, and his fortune impaired, partly by some years of reckless profusion, and partly by the pecuniary sacrifices at which he had effected his cousin's marriage with another, he retired to Derval Court, to live there in solitude and seclusion. On searching for some old title-deeds required for a mortgage, he chanced upon a collection of manuscripts much discoloured, and, in part, eaten away by moth or damp. These, on examination, proved to be the writings of Forman. Some of them were astrological observations and predictions; some were upon the nature of the Cabbala; some upon the invocation of spirits and the magic of the dark ages. All had a certain interest, for they were interspersed with personal remarks, anecdotes of eminent actors in a very stirring time, and were composed as Colloquies, in imitation of Erasmus,— the second person in the dialogue being Sir Miles Derval, the patron and pupil; the first person being Forman, the philosopher and expounder.

But along with these shadowy lucubrations were treatises of a more uncommon and a more startling character,— discussions on various occult laws of nature, and detailed accounts of analytical experiments. These opened a new, and what seemed to Sir Philip a practical, field of inquiry,— a true border-land between natural science and imaginative speculation. Sir Philip had cultivated philosophical science at the University; he resumed the study, and tested himself the truth of various experiments suggested by Forman. Some, to his surprise, proved successful, some wholly failed. These lucubrations first tempted the writer of the memoir towards the studies in which the remainder of his life had been consumed. But he spoke of the lucubrations themselves as valuable only where suggestive of some truths which Forman had accidentally approached, without being aware of their true nature and importance. They were debased by absurd puerilities, and vitiated by the vain and presumptuous ignorance which characterized the astrology of the middle ages. For these reasons the writer intimated his intention (if he lived to return to England) to destroy Forman's manuscripts, together with sundry other books, and a few commentaries of his own upon studies which had for a while misled him,—all now deposited in the safes of the room in which I sat.

After some years passed in the retirement of Derval Court, Sir Philip was seized with the desire to travel, and the taste he had imbibed for occult studies led him towards those Eastern lands in which they took their origin, and still retain their professors.

Several pages of the manuscript were now occupied with minute statements of the writer's earlier disappointment in the objects of his singular research. The so-called magicians, accessible to the curiosity of European travellers, were either but ingenious jugglers, or produced effects that perplexed him by practices they had mechanically learned, but of the *rationale* of which they were as ignorant as himself. It was not till he had resided some considerable time in the East, and acquired a familiar knowledge of its current languages and the social habits of its various populations, that he became acquainted with men in whom he recognized earnest cultivators of the lore which tradition ascribes to the colleges and priesthoods of the ancient world,—men generally living remote from others, and seldom to be bribed by money to exhibit their marvels or divulge their secrets. In his intercourse with these sages, Sir Philip arrived at the conviction that there does exist an art of magic, distinct from the guile of the conjuror, and applying to certain latent powers and affinities in nature,—a philosophy akin to that which we receive in our acknowledged schools, inasmuch as it is equally based on experiment, and produces from definite causes definite results. In support of this startling proposition, Sir Philip now devoted more than half his volume to the details of various experiments, to the process and result of which he pledged his guarantee as the actual operator. As most of these alleged experiments appeared to me wholly incredible, and as all of them were unfamiliar to my practical experience, and could only be verified or falsified by tests that would require no inconsiderable amount of time and care, I passed with little heed over the pages in which they were set forth.

I was impatient to arrive at that part of the manuscript which might throw light on the mystery in which my interest was the keenest. What were the links which connected the existence of Margrave with the history of Sir Philip Derval? Thus hurrying on, page after page, I suddenly, towards the end of the volume, came upon a name that arrested all my attention,— Haroun of Aleppo. He who has read the words addressed to me in my trance may well conceive the thrill that shot through my heart when I came upon that name, and will readily understand how much more vividly my memory retains that part of the manuscript to which I now proceed, than all which had gone before.

" It was," wrote Sir Philip, " in an obscure suburb of Aleppo that I at length met with the wonderful man from whom I have acquired a knowledge immeasurably more profound and occult than that which may be tested in the experiments to which I have devoted so large a share of this memoir. Haroun of Aleppo had, indeed, mastered every secret in nature which the nobler, or theurgic, magic seeks to fathom.

" He had discovered the great Principle of Animal Life, which had hitherto baffled the subtlest anatomist. Provided only that the great organs were not irreparably destroyed, there was no disease that he could not cure; no decrepitude to which he could not restore vigour: yet his science was based on the same theory as that espoused by the best professional practitioner of medicine, — namely, that the true art of healing is to assist nature to throw off the disease; to summon, as it were, the whole system to eject the enemy that has fastened on a part. And thus his processes, though occasionally varying in the means employed, all combined in this, — namely, the re-invigourating and recruiting of the principle of life."

No one knew the birth or origin of Haroun; no one knew his age. In outward appearance he was in the strength and prime of mature manhood; but, according to testimonies in which the writer of the memoir expressed a belief that, I need scarcely say, appeared to me egregiously credulous, Haroun's existence under the same name, and known by the same repute, could be traced back to more than a hundred years. He told Sir Philip that he had thrice renewed his own life, and had resolved to do so no more; he had grown weary of living on. With all his gifts, Haroun owned him-self to be consumed by a profound melancholy. He com-plained that there was nothing new to him under the sun; he said that, while he had at his command unlimited wealth, wealth had ceased to bestow enjoyment, and he preferred living as simply as a peasant; he had tired out all the affec-tions and all the passions of the human heart; he was in the universe as in a solitude. In a word, Haroun would often repeat, with mournful solemnity: "The soul is not meant to inhabit this earth and in fleshy tabernacle for more than the period usually assigned to mortals; and when by art in re-pairing the walls of the body we so retain it, the soul re-pines, becomes inert or dejected. He only," said Haroun, "would feel continued joy in continued existence who could preserve in perfection the sensual part of man, with such mind or reason as may be independent of the spiritual essence, but whom soul itself has quitted! — man, in short, as the grandest of the animals, but without the sublime discontent of earth, which is the peculiar attribute of soul."

One evening Sir Philip was surprised to find at Haroun's house another European. He paused in his narrative to de-scribe this man. He said that for three or four years previ-ously he had heard frequent mention, amongst the cultivators of magic, of an orientalized Englishman engaged in researches similar to his own, and to whom was ascribed a terrible knowledge in those branches of the art which, even in the East, are condemned as instrumental to evil. Sir Philip here distinguished at length, as he had so briefly distinguished in his conversation with me, between the two kinds of magic,—that which he alleged to be as pure from sin as any other species of experimental knowledge, and that by which the agencies of witchcraft are invoked for the purposes of guilt.

The Englishman, to whom the culture of this latter and darker kind of magic was ascribed, Sir Philip Derval had never hitherto come across. He now met him at the house of Haroun; decrepit, emaciated, bowed down with infirmities, and racked with pain. Though little more than sixty, his aspect was that of extreme old age; but still on his face there were seen the ruins of a once singular beauty, and still, in his mind, there was a force that contrasted the decay of the body. Sir Philip had never met with an intellect more pow·erful and more corrupt. The son of a notorious usurer, heir to immense wealth, and endowed with the talents which justify ambition, he had entered upon life burdened with the odium of his father's name. A duel, to which he had been provoked by an ungenerous taunt on his origin, but in which a temperament fiercely vindictive had led him to violate the usages prescribed by the social laws that regulate such encounters, had subjected him to a trial in which he escaped conviction either by a flaw in the technicalities of legal procedure, or by the compassion of the jury; [1] but the moral

---

[1] The reader will here observe a discrepancy between Mrs. Poyntz's account and Sir Philip Derval's narrative. According to the former, Louis Grayle was tried in his absence from England, and sentenced to three years' imprisonment, which his flight enabled him to evade. According to the latter, Louis Grayle stood his trial, and obtained an acquittal. Sir Philip's account must, at least, be nearer the truth than the lady's, because Louis Grayle could not, according to English law, have been tried on a capital charge without being present in court. Mrs. Poyntz tells her story as a woman generally does tell a story, — sure to make a mistake when she touches on a question of law; and — unconsciously perhaps to herself — the Woman of the World warps the facts in her narrative so as to save the personal dignity of the hero, who has captivated her interest, not from the moral odium of a great crime, but the debasing position of a prisoner at the bar. Allen Fenwick, no doubt, purposely omits to notice the discrepancy between these two statements, or to animadvert on the mistake which, in the eyes of a lawyer, would discredit Mrs. Poyntz's. It is consistent with some of the objects for which Allen Fenwick makes public his Strange Story, to invite the reader to draw his own inferences from the contradictions by which, even in the most commonplace matters (and how much more in any tale of wonder!), a fact stated by one person is made to differ from the same fact stated by another. The rapidity with which a truth becomes transformed into fable, when it is once sent on its travels from lip to lip, is illustrated by an amusement at this moment in fashion. The amusement is this: In a party of eight or ten persons, let one whisper to another an account of some supposed transaction, or a piece of invented gossip relating to absent persons, dead or alive; let the person, who thus first hears the story, proceed to whisper it, as exactly as he can remember what he has just heard, to the next; the next does the same to his neighbour, and so on, till the tale has run the round of the party. Each narrator, as soon as he has whispered his version of the tale, writes down what he has

presumptions against him were sufficiently strong to set an indelible brand on his honour, and an insurmountable barrier to the hopes which his early ambition had conceived. After this trial he had quitted his country, to return to it no more. Thenceforth, much of his life had been passed out of sight or conjecture of civilized men in remote regions and amongst barbarous tribes. At intervals, however, he had reappeared in European capitals; shunned by and shunning his equals, surrounded by parasites, amongst whom were always to be found men of considerable learning, whom avarice·or poverty subjected to the influences of his wealth. For the last nine or ten years he had settled in Persia, purchased extensive lands, maintained the retinue, and exercised more than the power of an Oriental prince. Such was the man who, prematurely worn out, and assured by physicians that he had not six weeks of life, had come to Aleppo with the gaudy escort of an Eastern satrap, had caused himself to be borne in his litter to the mud-hut of Haroun the Sage, and now called on the magician, in whose art was his last hope, to reprieve him from the — grave.

　　He turned round to Sir Philip, when the latter entered the room, and exclaimed in English, "I am here because you are. Your intimacy with this man was known to me. I took your character as the guarantee of his own. Tell me that I am no credulous dupe. Tell him that I, Louis Grayle, am no needy petitioner. Tell me of his wisdom; assure him of my wealth."

whispered. And though, in this game, no one has had any interest to misrepresent, but, on the contrary, each for his own credit's sake strives to repeat what he has heard as faithfully as he can, it will be almost invariably found that the story told by the first person has received the most material alterations before it has reached the eighth or the tenth. Sometimes the most important feature of the whole narrative is altogether omitted; sometimes a feature altogether new and preposterously absurd has been added. At the close of the experiment one is tempted to exclaim, " How, after this, can any of those portions of history which the chronicler took from hearsay be believed ? " But, above all, does not every anecdote of scandal which has passed, not through ten lips, but perhaps through ten thousand, before it has reached us, become quite as perplexing to him who would get at the truth, as the marvels he recounts are to the bewildered reason of Fenwick the Sceptic ?

Sir Philip looked inquiringly at Haroun, who remained seated on his carpet in profound silence.

"What is it you ask of Haroun?"

"To live on — to live on! For every year of life he can give me, I will load these floors with gold."

"Gold will not tempt Haroun."

"What will?"

"Ask him yourself; you speak his language."

"I have asked him; he vouchsafes me no answer."

Haroun here suddenly roused himself as from a revery. He drew from under his robe a small phial, from which he let fall a single drop into a cup of water, and said, "Drink this; send to me to-morrow for such medicaments as I may prescribe. Return hither yourself in three days; not before!"

When Grayle was gone, Sir Philip, moved to pity, asked Haroun if, indeed, it were within the compass of his art to preserve life in a frame that appeared so thoroughly exhausted. Haroun answered, "A fever may so waste the lamp of life that one ruder gust of air could extinguish the flame, yet the sick man recovers. This sick man's existence has been one long fever; this sick man can recover."

"You will aid him to do so?"

"Three days hence I will tell you."

On the third day Grayle revisited Haroun, and, at Haroun's request, Sir Philip came also. Grayle declared that he had already derived unspeakable relief from the remedies administered; he was lavish in expressions of gratitude; pressed large gifts on Haroun, and seemed pained when they were refused. This time Haroun conversed freely, drawing forth Grayle's own irregular, perverted, stormy, but powerful intellect.

I can best convey the general nature of Grayle's share in the dialogue between himself, Haroun, and Derval — recorded in the narrative in words which I cannot trust my memory to repeat in detail — by stating the effect it produced on my own mind. It seemed, while I read, as if there passed before me some convulsion of Nature, — a storm, an earthquake, — outcries of rage, of scorn, of despair, a despot's vehemence of will, a rebel's scoff at authority; yet, ever and anon, some swell of lofty thought, some burst of passionate genius, — abrupt variations from the vaunt of superb defiance to the wail of intense remorse.

The whole had in it, I know not what of uncouth but colossal, — like the chant, in the old lyrical tragedy, of one of those mythical giants, who, proud of descent from Night and Chaos, had held sway over the elements, while still crude and conflicting, to be crushed under the rocks, upheaved in their struggle, as Order and Harmony subjected a brightening Creation to the milder influences throned in Olympus. But it was not till the later passages of the dialogue in which my interest was now absorbed, that the language ascribed to this sinister personage lost a gloomy pathos not the less impressive for the awe with which it was mingled. For, till then, it seemed to me as if in that tempestuous nature there were still broken glimpses of starry light; that a character originally lofty, if irregular and fierce, had been embittered by early and continuous war with the social world, and had, in that war, become maimed and distorted; that, under happier circumstances, its fiery strength might have been disciplined to good; that even now, where remorse was so evidently poignant, evil could not be irredeemably confirmed.

At length all the dreary compassion previously inspired vanished in one unqualified abhorrence.

The subjects discussed changed from those which, relating to the common world of men, were within the scope of my reason. Haroun led his wild guest to boast of his own proficiency in magic, and, despite my incredulity, I could not overcome the shudder with which fictions, however extravagant, that deal with that dark Unknown abandoned to the chimeras of poets, will, at night and in solitude, send through the veins of men the least accessible to imaginary terrors.

Grayle spoke of the power he had exercised through the agency of evil spirits, — a power to fascinate and to destroy. He spoke of the aid revealed to him, now too late, which such direful allies could afford, not only to a private revenge, but to a kingly ambition. Had he acquired the knowledge he declared himself to possess before the feebleness of the decaying body made it valueless, how he could have triumphed over that world which had expelled his youth from its pale! He spoke of means by which his influence could work undetected on the minds of others, control agencies that could never betray, and baffle the justice that could never discover. He spoke vaguely of a power by which a spectral reflection of the material body could be cast, like a shadow, to a distance; glide through the walls of a prison, elude the sentinels of a camp, — a power that he asserted to be — when enforced by concentrated will, and acting on the mind, where in each individual temptation found mind the weakest — almost infallible in its effect to seduce or to appall. And he closed these and similar boasts of demoniacal arts, which I remember too obscurely to repeat, with a tumultuous imprecation on their nothingness to avail against the gripe of death. All this lore he would communicate to Haroun, in return for what? A boon shared by the meanest peasant, — life, common life; to breathe yet a while the air, feel yet a while the sun.

Then Haroun replied. He said, with a quiet disdain, that the dark art to which Grayle made such boastful pretence was the meanest of all abuses of knowledge, rightly abandoned, in all ages, to the vilest natures. And then, suddenly changing his tone, he spoke, so far as I can remember the words assigned to him in the manuscript, to this effect, —

"Fallen and unhappy wretch, and you ask me for prolonged life! — a prolonged curse to the world and to yourself. Shall I employ spells to lengthen the term of the Pestilence, or profane the secrets of Nature to restore vigour and youth to the failing energies of Crime?"

Grayle, as if stunned by the rebuke, fell on his knees with despairing entreaties that strangely contrasted his previous arrogance. "And it was," he said, "because his life had been evil that he dreaded death. If life could be renewed he would repent, he would change; he retracted his vaunts, he would forsake the arts he had boasted, he would re-enter the world as its benefactor."

"So ever the wicked man lies to himself when appalled by the shadow of death," answered Haroun. "But know, by the remorse which preys on thy soul, that it is not thy soul that addresses this prayer to me. Couldst thou hear, through the storms of the Mind, the Soul's melancholy whisper, it would dissuade thee from a wish to live on. While I speak, I behold it, that Soul,— sad for the stains on its essence, awed by the account it must render, but dreading, ás the direst calamity, a renewal of years below, darker stains and yet heavier accounts! Whatever the sentence it may now undergo, it has a hope for mercy in the remorse which the mind vainly struggles to quell. But darker its doom if longer retained to earth, yoked to the mind that corrupts it, and enslaved to the senses which thou bidst me restore to their tyrannous forces."

And Grayle bowed his head and covered his face with his hands in silence and in trembling.

Then Sir Philip, seized with compassion, pleaded for him. "At least, could not the soul have longer time on earth for repentance?" And while Sir Philip was so pleading, Grayle fell prostrate in a swoon like that of death. When he recovered, his head was leaning on Haroun's knee, and his opening eyes fixed on the glittering phial which Haroun held, and from which his lips had been moistened.

"Wondrous!" he murmured: "how I feel life flowing back to me. And that, then, is the elixir! it is no fable!"

His hands stretched greedily as to seize the phial, and he cried imploringly, "More, more!" Haroun replaced the vessel in the folds of his robe, and answered,—

"I will not renew thy youth, but I will release thee from bodily suffering: I will leave the mind and the soul free from the pangs of the flesh, to reconcile, if yet possible, their long war. My skill may afford thee months yet for repentance; seek, in that interval, to atone for the evil of sixty years; apply thy wealth where it may most compensate for injury done, most relieve the indigent, and most aid the virtuous. Listen to thy remorse; humble thyself in prayer."

Grayle departed, sighing heavily and muttering to himself.

The next day Haroun summoned Sir Philip Derval, and said to him,—

"Depart to Damascus. In that city the Pestilence has appeared. Go thither thou, to heal and to save. In this casket are stored the surest antidotes to the poison of the plague. Of that essence, undiluted and pure, which tempts to the undue prolongation of soul in the prison of flesh, this casket contains not a drop. I curse not my friend with so mournful a boon. Thou hast learned enough of my art to know by what simples the health of the temperate is easily restored to its balance, and their path to the grave smoothed from pain. Not more should Man covet from Nature for the solace and weal of the body. Nobler gifts far than aught for the body this casket contains. Herein are the essences which quicken the life of those duplicate senses that lie dormant and coiled in their chrysalis web, awaiting the wings of a future development,— the senses by which we can see, though not with the eye, and hear, but not by the ear. Herein are the links between Man's mind and Nature's; herein are secrets more precious even than these,— those extracts of light which enable the Soul to distinguish itself from the Mind, and discriminate the spiritual life, not more from life carnal than life intellectual. Where thou seest some noble intellect, studious of Nature, intent upon Truth, yet ignoring the fact that all animal life has a mind and Man alone on the earth ever asked, and has asked, from the hour his step trod the earth, and his eye sought the Heaven, 'Have I not a soul; can it perish?' — there, such aids to the soul, in the innermost vision vouchsafed to the mind, thou mayst lawfully use. But the treasures contained in this casket are like all which a mortal can win from the mines he explores,— good or ill in their uses as they pass to the hands of the good or the evil. Thou wilt never confide them but to those who will not abuse! and even then, thou art an adept too versed in the mysteries of Nature not to discriminate between the powers that may serve the good to good ends, and the powers that may tempt the good — where less wise than experience has made thee and me — to the ends that are evil; and not even to thy friend the most virtuous — if less proof against passion than thou and I have become — wilt thou confide such contents of the

casket as may work on the fancy, to deafen the conscience
and imperil the soul."

Sir Philip took the casket, and with it directions for use,
which he did not detail. He then spoke to Haroun about
Louis Grayle, who had inspired him with a mingled sentiment of admiration and abhorrence, of pity and terror. And
Haroun answered thus, repeating the words ascribed to him,
so far as I can trust, in regard to them — as to all else in this
marvellous narrative — to a memory habitually tenacious even
in ordinary matters, and strained to the utmost extent of its
power, by the strangeness of the ideas presented to it, and
the intensity of my personal interest in whatever admitted a
ray into that cloud which, gathering fast over my reason,
now threatened storm to my affections, —

"When the mortal deliberately allies himself to the spirits
of evil, he surrenders the citadel of his being to the guard of
its enemies; and those who look from without can only dimly
guess what passes within the precincts abandoned to Powers
whose very nature we shrink to contemplate, lest our mere
gaze should invite them. This man, whom thou pitiest, is
not yet everlastingly consigned to the fiends, because his soul
still struggles against them. His life has been one long war
between his intellect, which is mighty, and his spirit, which
is feeble. The intellect, armed and winged by the passions,
has besieged and oppressed the soul; but the soul has never
ceased to repine and to repent. And at moments it has gained
its inherent ascendancy, persuaded revenge to drop the prey it
had seized, turned the mind astray from hatred and wrath into
unwonted paths of charity and love. In the long desert of guilt,
there have been green spots and fountains of good. The
fiends have occupied the intellect which invoked them, but
they have never yet thoroughly mastered the soul which their
presence appalls. In the struggle that now passes within
that breast, amidst the flickers of waning mortality, only
Allah, whose eye never slumbers, can aid."

Haroun then continued, in words yet more strange and yet
more deeply graved in my memory, —

"There have been men (thou mayst have known such),

who, after an illness in which life itself seemed suspended, have arisen, as out of a sleep, with characters wholly changed. Before, perhaps, gentle and good and truthful, they now become bitter, malignant, and false. To the persons and the things they had before loved, they evince repugnance and loathing. Sometimes this change is so marked and irrational that their kindred ascribe it to madness,— not the madness which affects them in the ordinary business of life, but that which turns into harshness and discord the moral harmony that results from natures whole and complete. But there are dervishes who hold that in that illness, which had for its time the likeness of death, the soul itself has passed away, and an evil genius has fixed itself into the body and the brain, thus left void of their former tenant, and animates them in the unaccountable change from the past to the present existence. Such mysteries have formed no part of my study, and I tell you the conjecture received in the East without hazarding a comment whether of incredulity or belief. But if, in this war between the mind which the fiends have seized, and the soul which implores refuge of Allah; if, while the mind of yon traveller now covets life lengthened on earth for the enjoyments it had perverted its faculties to seek and to find in sin, and covets so eagerly that it would shrink from no crime and revolt from no fiend that could promise the gift, the soul shudderingly implores to be saved from new guilt, and would rather abide by the judgment of Allah on the sins that have darkened it than pass forever irredeemably away to the demons,— if this be so, what if the soul's petition be heard; what if it rise from the ruins around it; what if the ruins be left to the witchcraft that seeks to rebuild them? There, if demons might enter, that which they sought as their prize has escaped them; that which they find would mock them by its own incompleteness even in evil. In vain might animal life the most perfect be given to the machine of the flesh; in vain might the mind, freed from the check of the soul, be left to roam at will through a brain stored with memories of knowledge and skilled in the command of its faculties; in vain, in addition to all that body and brain bestow on the

normal condition of man, might unhallowed reminiscences
gather all the arts and the charms of the sorcery by which
the fiends tempted the soul, before it fled, through the passions of flesh and the cravings of mind: the Thing, thus de-
void of a soul, would be an instrument of evil, doubtless,—
but an instrument that of itself could not design, invent, and
complete. The demons themselves could have no permanent
hold on the perishable materials. They might enter it for
some gloomy end which Allah permits in his inscrutable wisdom; but they could leave it no trace when they pass from
it, because there is no conscience where soul is wanting. The
human animal without soul, but otherwise made felicitously
perfect in its mere vital organization, might ravage and
destroy, as the tiger and the serpent may destroy and ravage,
and, the moment after, would sport in the sunlight harmless
and rejoicing, because, like the serpent and the tiger, it is
incapable of remorse."

"Why startle my wonder," said Derval, "with so fantastic
an image?"

"Because, possibly, the image may come into palpable
form! I know, while I speak to thee, that this miserable
man is calling to his aid the evil sorcery over which he boasts
his control. To gain the end he desires, he must pass
through a crime. Sorcery whispers to him how to pass
through it, secure from the detection of man. The soul re-
sists, but in resisting, is weak against the tyranny of the
mind to which it has submitted so long. Question me no
more. But if I vanish from thine eyes, if thou hear that the
death which, to my sorrow and in my foolishness I have
failed to recognize as the merciful minister of Heaven, has
removed me at last from the earth, believe that the pale Visitant was welcome, and that I humbly accept as a blessed release the lot of our common humanity."

Sir Philip went to Damascus. There he found the pestilence raging, there he devoted himself to the cure of the
afflicted; in no single instance, so at least he declared, did
the antidotes stored in the casket fail in their effect. The
pestilence had passed, his medicaments were exhausted, when

the news reached him that Haroun was no more. The Sage
had been found, one morning, lifeless in his solitary home,
and, according to popular rumour, marks on his throat betrayed the murderous hand of the strangler. Simultaneously,
Louis Grayle had disappeared from the city, and was supposed to have shared the fate of Haroun, and been secretly
buried by the assassins who had deprived him of life. Sir
Philip hastened to Aleppo. There he ascertained that on the
night in which Haroun died, Grayle did not disappear alone;
with him were also missing two of his numerous suite, — the
one, an Arab woman, named Ayesha, who had for some years
been his constant companion, his pupil and associate in the
mystic practices to which his intellect had been debased, and
who was said to have acquired a singular influence over
him, partly by her beauty and partly by the tenderness with
which she had nursed him through his long decline; the
other, an Indian, specially assigned to her service, of whom
all the wild retainers of Grayle spoke with detestation and
terror. He was believed by them to belong to that murderous
sect of fanatics whose existence as a community has only recently been made known to Europe, and who strangle their
unsuspecting victim in the firm belief that they thereby propitiate the favour of the goddess they serve. The current
opinion at Aleppo was, that if those two persons had con-
spired to murder Haroun, perhaps for the sake of the treasures he was said to possess, it was still more certain that
they had made away with their own English lord, whether for
the sake of the jewels he wore about him, or for the sake of
treasures less doubtful than those imputed to Haroun, and of
which the hiding-place would be to them much better known.

"I did not share that opinion," wrote the narrator, "for I assured
myself that Ayesha sincerely loved her awful master; and that love need
excite no wonder, for Louis Grayle was one whom if a woman, and especially a woman of the East, had once loved, before old age and infirmity fell on him, she would love and cherish still more devotedly
when it became her task to protect the being who, in his day of power
and command, had exalted his slave into the rank of his pupil and companion. And the Indian whom Grayle had assigned to her service was

allowed to have that brute kind of fidelity which, though it recoils from no crime for a master, refuses all crime against him.

" I came to the conclusion that Haroun had been murdered by order of Louis Grayle, — for the sake of the elixir of life, — murdered by Juma the Strangler ; and that Grayle himself had been aided in his flight from Aleppo, and tended, through the effects of the life-giving drug thus murderously obtained, by the womanly love of the Arab woman Ayesha. These convictions (since I could not, without being ridiculed as the wildest of dupes, even hint at the vital elixir) I failed to impress on the Eastern officials, or even on a countryman of my own whom I chanced to find at Aleppo. They only arrived at what seemed the common-sense verdict, — namely, that Haroun might have been strangled, or might have died in a fit (the body, little examined, was buried long before I came to Aleppo) ; and that Louis Grayle was murdered by his own treacherous dependents. But all trace of the fugitives was lost.

" And now," wrote Sir Philip, " I will state by what means I discovered that Louis Grayle still lived, — changed from age into youth ; a new form, a new being ; realizing, I verily believe, the image which Haroun's words had raised up, in what then seemed to me the metaphysics of fantasy, — criminal, without consciousness of crime ; the dreadest of the mere animal race ; an incarnation of the blind powers of Nature, — beautiful and joyous, wanton and terrible and destroying ! Such as ancient myths have personified in the idols of Oriental creeds ; such as Nature, of herself, might form man in her moments of favour, if man were wholly the animal, and spirit were no longer the essential distinction between himself and the races to which by superior formation and subtler perceptions he would still be the king.

" But *this* being is yet more dire and portentous than the mere animal man, for in him are not only the fragmentary memories of a pristine intelligence which no mind, unaided by the presence of soul, could have originally compassed, but amidst that intelligence are the secrets of the magic which is learned through the agencies of spirits the most hostile to our race. And who shall say whether the fiends do not enter at their will this void and deserted temple whence the soul has departed, and use as their tools, passive and unconscious, all the faculties which, skilful in sorcery, still place a mind at the control of their malice ?

" It was in the interest excited in me by the strange and terrible fate that befell an Armenian family with which I was slightly acquainted, that I first traced — in the creature I am now about to describe, and whose course I devote myself to watch, and trust to bring to a close — the murderer of Haroun for the sake of the elixir of youth.

"In this Armenian family there were three daughters; one of them —"

I had just read thus far when a dim shadow fell over the page, and a cold air seemed to breathe on me,— cold, so cold, that my blood halted in my veins as if suddenly frozen! Involuntarily I started, and looked up, sure that some ghastly presence was in the room. And then, on the opposite side of the wall, I beheld an unsubstantial likeness of a human form. Shadow I call it, but the word is not strictly correct, for it was luminous, though with a pale shine. In some exhibition in London there is shown a curious instance of optical illusion; at the end of a corridor you see, apparently in strong light, a human skull. You are convinced it is there as you approach; it is, however, only a reflection from a skull at a distance. The image before me was less vivid, less seemingly prominent than is the illusion I speak of. I was not deceived. I felt it was a spectrum, a phantasm; but I felt no less surely that it was a reflection from an animate form,— the form and face of Margrave; it was there, distinct, unmistakable. Conceiving that he himself must be behind me, I sought to rise, to turn round, to examine. I could not move: limb and muscle were overmastered by some incomprehensible spell. Gradually my senses forsook me; I became unconscious as well as motionless. When I recovered, I heard the clock strike three. I must have been nearly two hours insensible! The candles before me were burning low. My eyes rested on the table; the dead man's manuscript was gone!

———◆———

CHAPTER XL.

THE dead man's manuscript was gone. But how? A phantom might delude my eye, a human will, though exerted at a distance, might, if the tales of mesmerism be true, deprive me of movement and of consciousness; but neither phantom nor mesmeric will could surely remove from the

table before me the material substance of the book that had
vanished! Was I to seek explanation in the arts of sorcery
ascribed to Louis Grayle in the narrative? I would not pursue that conjecture. Against it my reason rose up half
alarmed, half disdainful. Some one must have entered the
room, some one have removed the manuscript. I looked
round. The windows were closed, the curtains partly drawn
over the shutters, as they were before my consciousness had
left me: all seemed undisturbed. Snatching up one of the
candles, fast dying out, I went into the adjoining library, the
desolate state-rooms, into the entrance-hall, and examined
the outer door. Barred and locked! The robber had left no
vestige of his stealthy presence.

I resolved to go at once to Strahan's room and tell him of
the loss sustained. A deposit had been confided to me, and
I felt as if there were a slur on my honour every moment in
which I kept its abstraction concealed from him to whom I
was responsible for the trust. I hastily ascended the great
staircase, grim with faded portraits, and found myself in
a long corridor opening on my own bedroom; no doubt also
on Strahan's. Which was his? I knew not. I opened rapidly door after door, peered into empty chambers, went blundering on, when to the right, down a narrow passage, I
recognized the signs of my host's whereabouts,— signs familiarly commonplace and vulgar; signs by which the inmate of any chamber in lodging-house or inn makes himself
known,— a chair before a doorway, clothes negligently thrown
on it, beside it a pair of shoes. And so ludicrous did such
testimony of common every-day life, of the habits which
Strahan would necessarily have contracted in his desultory
unluxurious bachelor's existence,— so ludicrous, I say, did
these homely details seem to me, so grotesquely at variance
with the wonders of which I had been reading, with the wonders yet more incredible of which I myself had been witness
and victim, that as I turned down the passage, I heard my
own unconscious half-hysterical laugh; and, startled by the
sound of that laugh as if it came from some one else, I paused,
my hand on the door, and asked myself: "Do I dream? Am

I awake? And if awake what am I to say to the common-place mortal I am about to rouse? Speak to him of a phantom! Speak to him of some weird spell over this strong frame! Speak to him of a mystic trance in which has been stolen what he confided to me, without my knowledge! What will he say? What should I have said a few days ago to any man who told such a tale to me?" I did not wait to resolve these questions. I entered the room. There was Strahan sound asleep on his bed. I shook him roughly. He started up, rubbed his eyes. "You, Allen,— you! What the deuce? — what's the matter?"

"Strahan, I have been robbed! — robbed of the manuscript you lent me. I could not rest till I had told you."

"Robbed, robbed! Are you serious?"

By this time Strahan had thrown off the bed-clothes, and sat upright, staring at me.

And then those questions which my mind had suggested while I was standing at his door repeated themselves with double force. Tell this man, this unimaginative, hard-headed, raw-boned, sandy-haired North countryman, — tell this man a story which the most credulous school-girl would have rejected as a fable! Impossible!

"I fell asleep," said I, colouring and stammering, for the slightest deviation from truth was painful to me, "and — and — when I awoke — the manuscript was gone. Some one must have entered and committed the theft —"

"Some one entered the house at this hour of the night and then only stolen a manuscript which could be of no value to him! Absurd! If thieves have come in it must be for other objects, — for plate, for money. I will dress; we will see!"

Strahan hurried on his clothes, muttering to himself and avoiding my eye. He was embarrassed. He did not like to say to an old friend what was on his mind; but I saw at once that he suspected I had resolved to deprive him of the manuscript, and had invented a wild tale in order to conceal my own dishonesty.

Nevertheless, he proceeded to search the house. I followed him in silence, oppressed with my own thoughts, and longing

for solitude in my own chamber. We found no one, no trace
of any one, nothing to excite suspicion. There were but two
female servants sleeping in the house,—the old housekeeper,
and a country girl who assisted her. It was not possible to suspect either of these persons; but in the course of our search
we opened the doors of their rooms. We saw that they were
both in bed, both seemingly asleep: it seemed idle to wake and
question them. When the formality of our futile investigation
was concluded, Strahan stopped at the door of my bedroom,
and for the first time fixing his eyes on me steadily, said, —

"Allen Fenwick, I would have given half the fortune I
have come into rather than this had happened. The manuscript, as you know, was bequeathed to me as a sacred trust
by a benefactor whose slightest wish it is my duty to observe re-
ligiously. If it contained aught valuable to a man of your knowledge and profession, why, you were free to use its contents.
Let me hope, Allen, that the book will reappear to-morrow."

He said no more, drew himself away from the hand I involuntarily extended, and walked quickly back towards his
own room.

Alone once more, I sank on a seat, buried my face in my
hands, and strove in vain to collect into some definite shape
my own tumultuous and disordered thoughts. Could I attach
serious credit to the marvellous narrative I had read? Were
there, indeed, such powers given to man, such influences latent
in the calm routine of Nature? I could not believe it; I must
have some morbid affection of the brain; I must be under an
hallucination. Hallucination? The phantom, yes; the trance,
yes. But still, how came the book gone? That, at least, was
not hallucination.

I left my room the next morning with a vague hope that I
should find the manuscript somewhere in the study; that, in
my own trance, I might have secreted it, as sleep-walkers are
said to secrete things, without remembrance of their acts in
their waking state.

I searched minutely in every conceivable place. Strahan
found me still employed in that hopeless task. He had break-
fasted in his own room, and it was past eleven o'clock when

15

he joined me. His manner was now hard, cold, and distant, and his suspicion so bluntly shown that my distress gave way to resentment.

"Is it possible," I cried indignantly, "that you, who have known me so well, can suspect me of an act so base, and so gratuitously base? Purloin, conceal a book confided to me, with full power to copy from it whatever I might desire, use its contents in any way that might seem to me serviceable to science, or useful to me in my own calling!"

"I have not accused you," answered Strahan, sullenly. "But what are we to say to Mr. Jeeves; to all others who know that this manuscript existed? Will they believe what you tell me?"

"Mr. Jeeves," I said, "cannot suspect a fellow-townsman, whose character is as high as mine, of untruth and theft. And to whom else have you communicated the facts connected with a memoir and a request of so extraordinary a nature?"

"To young Margrave; I told you so!"

"True, true. We need not go farther to find the thief. Margrave has been in this house more than once. He knows the position of the rooms. You have named the robber!"

"Tut! what on earth could a gay young fellow like Margrave want with a work of such dry and recondite nature as I presume my poor kinsman's memoir must be?"

I was about to answer, when the door was abruptly opened, and the servant-girl entered, followed by two men, in whom I recognized the superintendent of the L—— police and the same subordinate who had found me by Sir Philip's corpse.

The superintendent came up to me with a grave face, and whispered in my ear. I did not at first comprehend him. "Come with you," I said, "and to Mr. Vigors, the magistrate? I thought my deposition was closed."

The superintendent shook his head. "I have the authority here, Dr. Fenwick."

"Well, I will come, of course. Has anything new transpired?"

The superintendent turned to the servant-girl, who was standing with gaping mouth and staring eyes.

"Show us Dr. Fenwick's room. You had better put up, sir, whatever things you have brought here. I will go upstairs with you," he whispered again. "Come, Dr. Fenwick, I am in the discharge of my duty."

Something in the man's manner was so sinister and menacing that I felt at once that some new and strange calamity had befallen me. I turned towards Strahan. He was at the threshold, speaking in a low voice to the subordinate policeman, and there was an expression of amazement and horror in his countenance. As I came towards him he darted away without a word.

I went up the stairs, entered my bedroom, the superintendent close behind me. As I took up mechanically the few things I had brought with me, the police-officer drew them from me with an abruptness that appeared insolent, and deliberately searched the pockets of the coat which I had worn the evening before, then opened the drawers in the room, and even pried into the bed.

"What do you mean?" I asked haughtily.

"Excuse me, sir. Duty. You are— "

"Well, I am what?"

"My prisoner; here is the warrant."

"Warrant! on what charge?"

"The murder of Sir Philip Derval."

"I — I! Murder!" I could say no more.

I must hurry over this awful passage in my marvellous record. It is torture to dwell on the details; and indeed I have so sought to chase them from my recollection, that they only come back to me in hideous fragments, like the incoherent remains of a horrible dream.

All that I need state is as follows: Early on the very morning on which I had been arrested, a man, a stranger in the town, had privately sought Mr. Vigors, and deposed that on the night of the murder, he had been taking refuge from a sudden storm under shelter of the eaves and buttresses of a wall adjoining an old archway; that he had heard men talking within the archway; had heard one say to the other, "You still bear me a grudge." The other had replied, "I

can forgive you on one condition." That he then lost much
of the conversation that ensued, which was in a lower voice;
but he gathered enough to know that the condition demanded
by the one was the possession of a casket which the other
carried about with him; that there seemed an altercation on
this matter between the two men, which, to judge by the
tones of voice, was angry on the part of the man demanding
the casket; that, finally, this man said in a loud key, "Do
you still refuse?" and on receiving the answer, which the
witness did not overhear, exclaimed threateningly, "It is you
who will repent," and then stepped forth from the arch into
the street. The rain had then ceased, but by a broad flash of
lightning the witness saw distinctly the figure of the person
thus quitting the shelter of the arch,—a man of tall stature,
powerful frame, erect carriage. A little time afterwards,
witness saw a slighter and older man come forth from the
arch, whom he could only examine by the flickering ray of
the gas-lamp near the wall, the lightning having ceased, but
whom he fully believed to be the person he afterwards discovered to be Sir Philip Derval.

He said that he himself had only arrived at the town a few
hours before; a stranger to L——, and indeed to England,
having come from the United States of America, where he
had passed his life from childhood. He had journeyed on
foot to L——, in the hope of finding there some distant rela-
tives. He had put up at a small inn, after which he had
strolled through the town, when the storm had driven him to
seek shelter. He had then failed to find his way back to
the inn, and after wandering about in vain, and seeing no
one at that late hour of night of whom he could ask the way,
he had crept under a portico and slept for two or three hours.
Waking towards the dawn, he had then got up, and again
sought to find his way to the inn, when he saw, in a narrow
street before him, two men, one of whom he recognized as the
taller of the two to whose conversation he had listened under
the arch; the other he did not recognize at the moment. The
taller man seemed angry and agitated, and he heard him say,
"The casket; I will have it." There then seemed to be a

struggle between these two persons, when the taller one struck down the shorter, knelt on his breast, and he caught distinctly the gleam of some steel instrument. That he was so frightened that he could not stir from the place, and that though he cried out, he believed his voice was not heard. He then saw the taller man rise, the other resting on the pavement motionless; and a minute or so afterwards beheld policemen coming to the place, on which he, the witness, walked away. He did not know that a murder had been committed; it might be only an assault; it was no business of his, he was a stranger. He thought it best not to interfere, the police having cognizance of the affair. He found out his inn; for the next few days he was absent from L—— in search of his relations, who had left the town, many years ago, to fix their residence in one of the neighbouring villages.

He was, however, disappointed; none of these relations now survived. He had now returned to L——, heard of the murder, was in doubt what to do, might get himself into trouble if, a mere stranger, he gave an unsupported testimony. But, on the day before the evidence was volunteered, as he was lounging in the streets, he had seen a gentleman pass by on horseback, in whom he immediately recognized the man who, in his belief, was the murderer of Sir Philip Derval. He inquired of a bystander the name of the gentleman; the answer was "Dr. Fenwick." That, the rest of the day, he felt much disturbed in his mind, not liking to volunteer such a charge against a man of apparent respectability and station; but that his conscience would not let him sleep that night, and he had resolved at morning to go to the magistrate and make a clean breast of it.

The story was in itself so improbable that any other magistrate but Mr. Vigors would perhaps have dismissed it in contempt. But Mr. Vigors, already so bitterly prejudiced against me, and not sorry, perhaps, to subject me to the humiliation of so horrible a charge, immediately issued his warrant to search my house. I was absent at Derval Court; the house was searched. In the bureau in my favourite study, which was left unlocked, the steel casket was discovered, and a large case-knife, on the blade of which the stains of blood were still perceptible. On this discovery I was apprehended; and on these evidences, and on the deposition of this vagrant stranger, I was not, indeed, committed to take my trial for murder, but placed in confinement, all bail for my appearance refused, and the examination adjourned to give time for further evidence and inquiries. I had requested the professional aid of Mr. Jeeves. To my surprise and dismay, Mr. Jeeves begged me to excuse him. He said he was pre-engaged by Mr. Strahan to detect and prosecute the murderer of Sir P. Derval, and could not assist one accused of the murder. I gathered from the little he said that Strahan had already been to him that morning and told him of the missing manuscript, that Strahan had ceased to be my friend. I engaged another solicitor, a young man of ability, and who professed personal esteem for me. Mr. Stanton (such was the lawyer's name) believed in my innocence; but he warned me that appearances were grave, he implored me to be perfectly frank with him. Had I held conversation with Sir Philip under the archway as reported by the witness? Had I used such or similar words? Had the deceased said, "I had a grudge against him"? Had I demanded the casket? Had I threatened Sir Philip that he would repent? And of what, — his refusal?

I felt myself grow pale, as I answered, "Yes; I thought such or similar expressions had occurred in my conversation with the deceased."

"What was the reason of the grudge? What was the nature of this casket, that I should so desire its possession?"

There, I became terribly embarrassed. What could I say to a keen, sensible, worldly man of law, — tell him of the powder and the fumes, of the scene in the museum, of Sir Philip's tale, of the implied identity of the youthful Margrave with the aged Grayle, of the elixir of life, and of magic arts? I -- I tell such a romance! I, — the noted adversary of all pretended mysticism; I, — I a sceptical practitioner of medicine! Had that manuscript of Sir Philip's been avail-

able,— a substantial record of marvellous events by a man of
repute for intellect and learning,— I might perhaps have ventured to startle the solicitor of L—— with my revelations.
But the sole proof that all which the solicitor urged me to confide was not a monstrous fiction or an insane delusion had
disappeared; and its disappearance was a part of the terrible
mystery that enveloped the whole.   I answered therefore, as
composedly as I could, that "I could have no serious grudge
against Sir Philip, whom I had never seen before that evening; that the words which applied to my supposed grudge
were lightly said by Sir Philip, in reference to a physiological dispute on matters connected with mesmerical phenomena;
that the deceased had declared his casket, which he had shown
me at the mayor's house, contained drugs of great potency in
medicine; that I had asked permission to test those drugs
myself; and that when I said he would repent of his refusal,
I merely meant that he would repent of his reliance on drugs
not warranted by the experiments of professional science."

My replies seemed to satisfy the lawyer so far, but "how
could I account for the casket and the knife being found in
my room?"

"In no way but this; the window of my study is a door-
window opening on the lane, from which any one might enter
the room.   I was in the habit, not only of going out myself
that way, but of admitting through that door any more familiar private acquaintance."

"Whom, for instance?"

I hesitated a moment, and then said, with a significance I
could not forbear, "Mr. Margrave!   He would know the
locale perfectly; he would know that the door was rarely
bolted from within during the daytime: he could enter at all
hours; he could place, or instruct any one to deposit, the
knife and casket in my bureau, which he knew I never kept
locked; it contained no secrets, no private correspondence,—
chiefly surgical implements, or such things as I might want
for professional experiments."

"Mr. Margrave!   But you cannot suspect him — a lively,
charming young man, against whose character not a whisper

was ever heard — of connivance with such a charge against you, — a connivance that would implicate him in the murder itself; for if you are accused wrongfully, he who accuses you is either the criminal or the criminal's accomplice, his instigator or his tool."

"Mr. Stanton," I said firmly, after a moment's pause, "I do suspect Mr. Margrave of a hand in this crime. Sir Philip, on seeing him at the mayor's house, expressed a strong abhorrence of him, more than hinted at crimes he had committed, appointed me to come to Derval Court the day after that on which the murder was committed. Sir Philip had known something of this Margrave in the East; Margrave might dread exposure, revelations — of what I know not; but, strange as it may seem to you, it is my conviction that this young man, apparently so gay and so thoughtless, is the real criminal, and in some way which I cannot conjecture has employed this lying vagabond in the fabrication of a charge against myself. Reflect: of Mr. Margrave's antecedents we know nothing; of them nothing was known even by the young gentleman who first introduced him to the society of this town. If you would serve and save me, it is to that quarter that you will direct your vigilant and unrelaxing researches."

I had scarcely so said when I repented my candour, for I observed in the face of Mr. Stanton a sudden revulsion of feeling, an utter incredulity of the accusation I had thus hazarded, and for the first time a doubt of my own innocence. The fascination exercised by Margrave was universal; nor was it to be wondered at: for besides the charm of his joyous presence, he seemed so singularly free from even the errors common enough with the young, — so gay and boon a companion, yet a shunner of wine; so dazzling in aspect, so more than beautiful, so courted, so idolized by women, yet no tale of seduction, of profligacy, attached to his name! As to his antecedents, he had so frankly owned himself a natural son, a nobody, a traveller, an idler; his expenses, though lavish, were so unostentatious, so regularly defrayed; he was so wholly the reverse of the character assigned to criminals, that it seemed as absurd to bring a charge of homicide against a butterfly or a goldfinch as against this seemingly innocent and delightful favourite of humanity and nature.

However, Mr. Stanton said little or nothing, and shortly afterwards left me, with a dry expression of hope that my innocence would be cleared in spite of evidence that, he was bound to say, was of the most serious character.

I was exhausted. I fell into a profound sleep early that night; it might be a little after twelve when I woke, and woke as fully, as completely, as much restored to life and consciousness, as it was then my habit to be at the break of day. And so waking, I saw, on the wall opposite my bed, the same luminous phantom I had seen in the wizard's study at Derval Court. I have read in Scandinavian legends of an apparition called the Scin-Læca, or shining corpse. It is supposed in the northern superstition, sometimes to haunt sepulchres, sometimes to foretell doom. It is the spectre of a human body seen in a phosphoric light; and so exactly did this phantom correspond to the description of such an apparition in Scandinavian fable that I knew not how to give it a better name than that of Scin-Læca, — the shining corpse.

There it was before me, corpse-like, yet not dead; there, as in the haunted study of the wizard Forman! — the form and the face of Margrave. Constitutionally, my nerves are strong, and my temper hardy, and now I was resolved to battle against any impression which my senses might receive from my own deluding fancies. Things that witnessed for the first time daunt us witnessed for the second time lose their terror. I rose from my bed with a bold aspect, I approached the phantom with a firm step; but when within two paces of it, and my hand outstretched to touch it, my arm became fixed in air, my feet locked to the ground. I did not experience fear; I felt that my heart beat regularly, but an invincible something opposed itself to me. I stood as if turned to stone. And then from the lips of this phantom there came a voice, but a voice which seemed borne from a great distance, — very low, muffled, and yet distinct; I could not even be sure that my ear heard it, or whether the sound was not conveyed to me by an inner sense.

"I, and I alone, can save and deliver you," said the voice. "I will do so; and the conditions I ask, in return, are simple and easy."

"Fiend or spectre, or mere delusion of my own brain," cried I, "there can be no compact between thee and me. I despise thy malice, I reject thy services; I accept no conditions to escape from the one or to obtain the other."

"You may give a different answer when I ask again."

The Scin-Læca slowly waned, and, fading first into a paler shadow, then vanished. I rejoiced at the reply I had given. Two days elapsed before Mr. Stanton again came to me; in the interval the Scin-Læca did not reappear. I had mustered all my courage, all my common-sense, noted down all the weak points of the false evidence against me, and felt calm and supported by the strength of my innocence.

The first few words of the solicitor dashed all my courage to the ground; for I was anxious to hear news of Lilian, anxious to have some message from her that might cheer and strengthen me, and my first question was this,—

"Mr. Stanton, you are aware that I am engaged in marriage to Miss Ashleigh. Your family are not unacquainted with her. What says, what thinks she of this monstrous charge against her betrothed?"

"I was for two hours at Mrs. Ashleigh's house last evening," replied the lawyer; "she was naturally anxious to see me as employed in your defence. Who do you think was there? Who, eager to defend you, to express his persuasion of your innocence, to declare his conviction that the real criminal would be soon discovered,— who but that same Mr. Margrave, whom, pardon me my frankness, you so rashly and groundlessly suspected."

"Heavens! Do you say that he is received in that house; that he — he is familiarly admitted to her presence?"

"My good sir, why these unjust prepossessions against a true friend? It was as your friend that, as soon as the charge against you amazed and shocked the town of L——, Mr. Margrave called on Mrs. Ashleigh, presented to her by Miss Brabazon, and was so cheering and hopeful that —"

"Enough!" I exclaimed,— "enough!"

I paced the room in a state of excitement and rage, which the lawyer in vain endeavoured to calm, until at length I halted abruptly: "Well, and you saw Miss Ashleigh? What message does she send to me — her betrothed?"

Mr. Stanton looked confused. "Message! Consider, sir, Miss Ashleigh's situation — the delicacy — and — and —"

"I understand, no message, no word, from a young lady so respectable to a man accused of murder."

Mr. Stanton was silent for some moments, and then said quietly, "Let us change this subject; let us think of what more immediately presses. I see you have been making some notes: may I look at them?"

I composed myself and sat down. "This accuser! Have inquiries really been made as to himself, and his statement of his own proceedings? He comes, he says, from America: in what ship? At what port did he land? Is there any evidence to corroborate his story of the relations he tried to discover; of the inn at which he first put up, and to which he could not find his way?"

"Your suggestions are sensible, Dr. Fenwick. I have forestalled them. It is true that the man lodged at a small inn, — the Rising Sun; true that he made inquiries about some relations of the name of Walls, who formerly resided at L——, and afterwards removed to a village ten miles distant,— two brothers, tradesmen of small means but respectable character. He at first refused to say at what sea-port he landed, in what ship he sailed. I suspect that he has now told a falsehood as to these matters. I sent my clerk to Southampton, for it is there he said that he was put on shore; we shall see: the man himself is detained in close custody. I hear that his manner is strange and excitable; but that he preserves silence as much as possible. It is generally believed that he is a bad character, perhaps a returned convict, and that this is the true reason why he so long delayed giving evidence, and has been since so reluctant to account for himself. But even if his testimony should be impugned, should break down, still we should have to account for the fact that the casket and the case-knife were found in your bureau; for, granting that a person could, in your absence, have entered your study and placed the articles in your bureau, it is clear that such a person must have been well acquainted with your house, and this stranger to L—— could not have possessed that knowledge."

"Of course not. Mr. Margrave did possess it!"

"Mr. Margrave again! oh, sir!"

I arose and moved away with an impatient gesture. I could not trust myself to speak. That night I did not sleep; I watched impatiently, gazing on the opposite wall for the gleam of the Scin-Læca. But the night passed away, and the spectre did not appear.

———◆———

CHAPTER XLI.

The lawyer came the next day, and with something like a smile on his lips. He brought me a few lines in pencil from Mrs. Ashleigh; they were kindly expressed, bade me be of good cheer; "she never for a moment believed in my guilt; Lilian bore up wonderfully under so terrible a trial; it was an unspeakable comfort to both to receive the visits of a friend so attached to me, and so confident of a triumphant refutation of the hideous calumny under which I now suffered as Mr. Margrave!"

The lawyer had seen Margrave again,— seen him in that house. Margrave seemed almost domiciled there!

I remained sullen and taciturn during this visit. I longed again for the night. Night came. I heard the distant clock strike twelve, when again the icy wind passed through my hair, and against the wall stood the luminous Shadow.

"Have you considered?" whispered the voice, still as from afar. "I repeat it,— I alone can save you."

"Is it among the conditions which you ask, in return, that I shall resign to you the woman I love?"

"No."

"Is it one of the conditions that I should commit some crime,—a crime perhaps heinous as that of which I am accused?"

"No."

"With such reservations, I accept the conditions you may name, provided I, in my turn, may demand one condition from yourself."

"Name it."

"I ask you to quit this town. I ask you, meanwhile, to cease your visits to the house that holds the woman betrothed to me."

"I will cease those visits. And before many days are over, I will quit this town."

"Now, then, say what you ask from me. I am prepared to concede it. And not from fear for myself, but because I fear for the pure and innocent being who is under the spell of your deadly fascination. This is your power over me. You command me through my love for another. Speak."

"My conditions are simple. You will pledge yourself to desist from all charges of insinuation against myself, of what nature soever. You will not, when you meet me in the flesh, refer to what you have known of my likeness in the Shadow. You will be invited to the house at which I may be also a guest; you will come; you will meet and converse with me as guest speaks with guest in the house of a host."

"Is that all?"

"It is all."

"Then I pledge you my faith; keep your own."

"Fear not; sleep secure in the certainty that you will soon be released from these walls."

The Shadow waned and faded. Darkness settled back, and a sleep, profound and calm, fell over me.

The next day Mr. Stanton again visited me. He had received that morning a note from Mr. Margrave, stating that he had left L—— to pursue, in person, an investigation which he had already commenced through another, affecting the man who had given evidence against me, and that, if his hope should prove well founded, he trusted to establish my innocence, and convict the real murderer of Sir Philip Derval. In the research he thus volunteered, he had asked for, and obtained, the assistance of the policeman Waby, who, grateful to me for saving the life of his sister, had expressed a strong desire to be employed in my service.

Meanwhile, my most cruel assailant was my old college friend, Richard Strahan. For Jeeves had spread abroad Strahan's charge of purloining the memoir which had been entrusted to me; and that accusation had done me great injury in public opinion, because it seemed to give probability to the only motive which ingenuity could ascribe to the foul deed imputed to me. That motive had been first suggested by Mr. Vigors. Cases are on record of men whose life had been previously blameless, who have committed a crime which seemed to belie their nature, in the monomania of some intense desire. In Spain, a scholar reputed of austere morals murdered and robbed a traveller for money in order to purchase books, — books written, too, by Fathers of his Church! He was intent on solving some problem of theological casuistry. In France, an antiquary, esteemed not more for his learning than for amiable and gentle qualities, murdered his most intimate friend for the possession of a medal, without which his own collection was incomplete. These, and similar anecdotes, tending to prove how fatally any vehement desire, morbidly cherished, may suspend the normal operations of reason and conscience, were whispered about by Dr. Lloyd's vindictive partisan; and the inference drawn from them and applied to the assumptions against myself was the more credulously received, because of that over-refining speculation on motive and act which the shallow accept, in their eagerness to show how readily they understand the profound.

I was known to be fond of scientific, especially of chemical experiments; to be eager in testing the truth of any novel invention. Strahan, catching hold of the magistrate's fantastic hypothesis, went about repeating anecdotes of the absorbing passion for analysis and discovery which had characterized

me in youth as a medical student, and to which, indeed, I
owed the precocious reputation I had obtained.

Sir Philip Derval, according not only to report, but to the
direct testimony of his servant, had acquired in the course of
his travels many secrets in natural science, especially as connected with the healing art,— his servant had deposed to the
remarkable cures he had effected by the medicinals stored in
the stolen casket.   Doubtless Sir Philip, in boasting of these
medicinals in the course of our conversation, had excited my
curiosity, inflamed my imagination; and thus when I afterwards suddenly met him in a lone spot, a passionate impulse
had acted on a brain heated into madness by curiosity and
covetous desire.

.All these suppositions, reduced into system, were corrobo-
rated by Strahan's charge that I had made away with the
manuscript supposed to contain the explanations of the medical agencies employed by Sir Philip, and had sought to shelter my theft by a tale so improbable, that a man of my
reputed talent could not have hazarded it if in his sound
senses.   I saw the web that·had thus been spread around me
by hostile prepossessions and ignorant gossip: how could the
arts of Margrave scatter that web to the winds?   I knew not,
but I felt confidence in his promise and his power.   Still, so
great had been my alarm for Lilian, that the hope of clearing
my own innocence was almost lost in my joy that Margrave,
at least, was no longer in her presence, and that I had received his pledge to quit the town in which she lived.

Thus, hours rolled on hours, till, I think, on the third day
from that night in which I had last beheld the mysterious
Shadow, my door was hastily thrown open, a confused crowd
presented itself at the threshold,— the governor of the prison,
the police superintendent, Mr. Stanton, and other familiar
faces shut out from me since my imprisonment.   I knew at
the first glance that I was no longer an outlaw beyond the
pale of human friendship.   And proudly, sternly, as I had
supported myself hitherto in solitude and suspense, when I
felt warm hands clasping mine, heard joyous voices proffering
congratulations, saw in the eyes of all that my innocence had

been cleared, the revulsion of emotion was too strong for me, — the room reeled on my sight, I fainted. I pass, as quickly as I can, over the explanations that crowded on me when I recovered, and that were publicly given in evidence in court next morning. I had owed all to Margrave. It seems that he had construed to my favour the very supposition which had been bruited abroad to my prejudice. "For," said he, "it is conjectured that Fenwick committed the crime of which he is accused in the impulse of a disordered reason. That conjecture is based upon the probability that a madman alone could have committed a crime without adequate motive. But it seems quite clear that the accused is not mad; and I see cause to suspect that the accuser is." Grounding this assumption on the current reports of the witness's manner and bearing since he had been placed under official surveillance, Margrave had commissioned the policeman Waby to make inquiries in the village to which the accuser asserted he had gone in quest of his relations, and Waby had there found persons who remembered to have heard that the two brothers named Walls lived less by the gains of the petty shop which they kept than by the proceeds of some property consigned to them as the nearest of kin to a lunatic who had once been tried for his life. Margrave had then examined the advertisements in the daily newspapers. One of them, warning the public against a dangerous maniac, who had effected his escape from an asylum in the west of England, caught his attention. To that asylum he had repaired.

There he learned that the patient advertised was one whose propensity was homicide, consigned for life to the asylum on account of a murder, for which he had been tried. The description of this person exactly tallied with that of the pretended American. The medical superintendent of the asylum, hearing all particulars from Margrave, expressed a strong persuasion that the witness was his missing patient, and had himself committed the crime of which he had accused another. If so, the superintendent undertook to coax from him the full confession of all the circumstances. Like many other madmen, and not least those whose propensity is to crime, the fugitive maniac was exceedingly cunning, treacherous, secret, and habituated to trick and stratagem,— more subtle than even the astute in possession of all their faculties, whether to achieve his purpose or to conceal it, and fabricate appearances against another. But while, in ordinary conversation, he seemed rational enough to those who were not accustomed to study him, he had one hallucination which, when humoured, led him always, not only to betray himself, but to glory in any crime proposed or committed. He was under the belief that he had made a bargain with Satan, who, in return for implicit obedience, would bear him harmless through all the consequences of such submission, and finally raise him to great power and authority. It is no unfrequent illusion of homicidal maniacs to suppose they are under the influence of the Evil One, or possessed by a Demon. Murderers have assigned as the only reason they themselves could give for their crime, that "the Devil got into them," and urged the deed. But the insane have, perhaps, no attribute more in common than that of superweening self-esteem. The maniac who has been removed from a garret sticks straws in his hair and calls them a crown. So much does inordinate arrogance characterize mental aberration, that, in the course of my own practice, I have detected, in that infirmity, the certain symptom of insanity, long before the brain had made its disease manifest even to the most familiar kindred.

Morbid self-esteem accordingly pervaded the dreadful illusion by which the man I now speak of was possessed. He was proud to be the protected agent of the Fallen Angel. And if that self-esteem were artfully appealed to, he would exult superbly in the evil he held himself ordered to perform, as if a special prerogative, an official rank and privilege; then, he would be led on to boast gleefully of thoughts which the most cynical of criminals in whom intelligence was not ruined would shrink from owning; then, he would reveal himself in all his deformity with as complacent and frank a self-glorying as some vain good man displays in parading his amiable sentiments and his beneficent deeds.

"If," said the superintendent, "this be the patient who has

16

escaped from me, and if his propensity to homicide has been, in some way, directed towards the person who has been murdered, I shall not be with him a quarter of an hour before he will inform me how it happened, and detail the arts he employed in shifting his crime upon another; all will be told as minutely as a child tells the tale of some school-boy exploit, in which he counts on your sympathy, and feels sure of your applause."

Margrave brought this gentleman back to L——, took him to the mayor, who was one of my warmest supporters: the mayor had sufficient influence to dictate and arrange the rest. The superintendent was introduced to the room in which the pretended American was lodged. At his own desire a select number of witnesses were admitted with him. Margrave excused himself; he said candidly that he was too intimate a friend of mine to be an impartial listener to aught that concerned me so nearly.

The superintendent proved right in his suspicions, and verified his promises. My false accuser was his missing patient; the man recognized Dr. —— with no apparent terror, rather with an air of condescension, and in a very few minutes was led to tell his own tale, with a gloating complacency both at the agency by which he deemed himself exalted, and at the dexterous cunning with which he had acquitted himself of the task, that increased the horror of his narrative.

He spoke of the mode of his escape, which was extremely ingenious, but of which the details, long in themselves, did not interest me, and I understood them too imperfectly to repeat. He had encountered a sea-faring traveller on the road, whom he had knocked down with a stone, and robbed of his glazed hat and pea-jacket, as well as of a small sum in coin, which last enabled him to pay his fare in a railway that conveyed him eighty miles away from the asylum. Some trifling remnant of this money still in his pocket, he then travelled on foot along the high-road till he came to a town about twenty miles distant from L——; there he had stayed a day or two, and there he said "that the Devil had told him to buy a case-knife, which he did." "He knew by that order

that the Devil meant him to do something great." "His
Master," as he called the fiend, then directed him the road
he should take. He came to L——, put up, as he had correctly stated before, at a small inn, wandered at night about
the town, was surprised by the sudden storm, took shelter
under the convent arch, overheard somewhat more of my conversation with Sir Philip than he had previously deposed,—
heard enough to excite his curiosity as to the casket: "While
he listened his Master told him he must get possession of that
casket." Sir Philip had quitted the archway almost immediately after I had done so, and he would then have attacked
him if he had not caught sight of a policeman going his
rounds. He had followed Sir Philip to a house (Mr. Jeeves's).
"His Master told him to wait and watch." He did so. . When
Sir Philip came forth, towards the dawn, he followed him,
saw him enter a narrow street, came up to him, seized him
by the arm, demanded all he had about him. Sir Philip tried
to shake him off,—struck at him. What follows I spare the
reader. The deed was done. He robbed the dead man both
of the casket and the purse that he found in the pockets; had
scarcely done so when he heard footsteps. He had just time
to get behind the portico of a detached house at angles with
the street when I came up. He witnessed, from his hiding-
place, the brief conference between myself and the policemen,
and when they moved on, bearing the body, stole unobserved
away. He was going back towards the inn, when it occurred
to him that it would be safer if the casket and purse were not
about his person; that he asked his Master to direct him how
to dispose of them: that his Master guided him to an open
yard (a stone-mason's) at a very little distance from the inn;
that in this yard there stood an old wych-elm tree, from the
gnarled roots of which the earth was worn away, leaving
chinks and hollows, in one of which he placed the casket and
purse, taking from the latter only two sovereigns and some
silver, and then heaping loose mould over the hiding-place.
That he then repaired to his inn, and left it late in the morning, on the pretence of seeking for his relations,— persons,
indeed, who really had been related to him, but of whose

death years ago he was aware. He returned to L—— a few days afterwards, and in the dead of the night went to take up the casket and the money. He found the purse with its contents undisturbed; but the lid of the casket was unclosed. From the hasty glance he had taken of it before burying it, it had seemed to him firmly locked, — he was alarmed lest some one had been to the spot. But his Master whispered to him not to mind, told him that he might now take the casket, and would be guided what to do with it; that he did so, and, opening the lid, found the casket empty; that he took the rest of the money out of the purse, but that he did not take the purse itself, for it had a crest and initials on it, which might lead to the discovery of what had been done; that he therefore left it in the hollow amongst the roots, heaping the mould over it as before; that in the course of the day he heard the people at the inn talk of the murder, and that his own first impulse was to get out of the town immediately, but that his Master "made him too wise for that," and bade him stay; that passing through the streets, he saw me come out of the sash-window door, go to a stable-yard on the other side of the house, mount on horseback and ride away; that he observed the sash-door was left partially open; that he walked by it and saw the room empty; there was only a dead wall opposite; the place was solitary, unobserved; that his Master directed him to lift up the sash gently, enter the room, and deposit the knife and the casket in a large walnut-tree bureau which stood unlocked near the window. All that followed — his visit to Mr. Vigors, his accusation against myself, his whole tale — was, he said, dictated by his Master, who was highly pleased with him, and promised to bring him safely through. And here he turned round with a hideous smile, as if for approbation of his notable cleverness and respect for his high employ.

Mr. Jeeves had the curiosity to request the keeper to inquire how, in what form, or in what manner, the Fiend appeared to the narrator, or conveyed his infernal dictates. The man at first refused to say; but it was gradually drawn from him that the Demon had no certain and invariable form:

sometimes it appeared to him in the form of a rat; sometimes even of a leaf, or a fragment of wood, or a rusty nail;
but that his Master's voice always came to him distinctly,
whatever shape he appeared in; only, he said, with an air of
great importance, his Master, this time, had graciously condescended, ever since he left the asylum, to communicate
with him in a much more pleasing and imposing aspect than
he had ever done before,— in the form of a beautiful youth,
or, rather, like a bright rose-coloured shadow, in which the
features of a young man were visible, and that he had heard
the voice more distinctly than usual, though in a milder tone,
and seeming to come to him from a great distance.

After these revelations the man became suddenly disturbed.
He shook from limb to limb, he seemed convulsed with terror; he cried out that he had betrayed the secret of his Master, who had warned him not to describe his appearance and
mode of communication, or he would surrender his servant to
the tormentors.   Then the maniac's terror gave way to fury;
his more direful propensity made itself declared; he sprang
into the midst of his frightened listeners, seized Mr. Vigors by
the throat, and would have strangled him but for the prompt
rush of the superintendent and his satellites.   Foaming at
the mouth, and horribly raving, he was then manacled, a
strait-waistcoat thrust upon him, and the group so left him
in charge of his captors.   Inquiries were immediately directed
towards such circumstantial evidence as might corroborate
the details he had so minutely set forth.   The purse, recognized as Sir Philip's, by the valet of the deceased, was found
buried under the wych-elm.   A policeman despatched, express, to the town in which the maniac declared the knife to
have been purchased, brought back word that a cutler in the
place remembered perfectly to have sold such a knife to a sea-
faring man, and identified the instrument when it was shown
to him.   From the chink of a door ajar, in the wall opposite
my sash-window, a maid-servant, watching for her sweetheart
(a journeyman carpenter, who habitually passed that way on
going home to dine), had, though unobserved by the murderer, seen him come out of my window at a time that corre

sponded with the dates of his own story, though she had
thought nothing of it at the moment. He might be a patient,
or have called on business; she did not know that I was from
home. The only point of importance not cleared up was
that which related to the opening of the casket,— the disappearance of the contents; the lock had been unquestionably
forced. No one, however, could suppose that some third
person had discovered the hiding-place and forced open the
casket to abstract its contents and then rebury it. The
only probable supposition was that the man himself had
forced it open, and, deeming the contents of no value, had
thrown them away before he had hidden the casket and
purse, and, in the chaos of his reason, had forgotten that he
had so done. Who could expect that every link in a madman's tale would be found integral and perfect? In short,
little importance was attached to this solitary doubt. Crowds
accompanied me to my door, when I was set free, in open
court, stainless; it was a triumphal procession. The popu-
larity I had previously enjoyed, superseded for a moment by
so horrible a charge, came back to me tenfold as with the reaction of generous repentance for a momentary doubt. One
man shared the public favour,— the young man whose acuteness had delivered me from the peril, and cleared the truth
from so awful a mystery; but Margrave had escaped from
congratulation and compliment; he had gone on a visit to
Strahan, at Derval Court.

Alone, at last, in the welcome sanctuary of my own home,
what were my thoughts? Prominent amongst them all was
that assertion of the madman, which had made me shudder
when repeated to me: he had been guided to the murder and
to all the subsequent proceedings by the luminous shadow of
the beautiful youth,— the Scin-Læca to which I had pledged
myself. If Sir Philip Derval could be believed, Margrave
was possessed of powers, derived from fragmentary recollections of a knowledge acquired in a former state of being,
which would render his remorseless intelligence infinitely
dire. and frustrate the endeavours of a reason, unassisted by
similar powers, to thwart his designs or bring the law against

his crimes. Had he then the arts that could thus influence the minds of others to serve his fell purposes, and achieve securely his own evil ends through agencies that could not be traced home to himself?

But for what conceivable purpose had I been subjected as a victim to influences as much beyond my control as the Fate or Demoniac Necessity of a Greek Myth? In the legends of the classic world some august sufferer is oppressed by powers more than mortal, but with an ethical if gloomy vindication of his chastisement, — he pays the penalty of crime committed by his ancestors or himself, or he has braved, by arrogating equality with the gods, the mysterious calamity which the gods alone can inflict. But I, no descendant of Pelops, no Œdipus boastful of a wisdom which could interpret the enigmas of the Sphynx, while ignorant even of his own birth — what had I done to be singled out from the herd of men for trials and visitations from the Shadowland of ghosts and sorcerers? It would be ludicrously absurd to suppose that Dr. Lloyd's dying imprecation could have had a prophetic effect upon my destiny; to believe that the pretences of mesmerizers were specially favoured by Providence, and that to question their assumptions was an offence of profanation to be punished by exposure to preternatural agencies. There was not even that congruity between cause and effect which fable seeks in excuse for its inventions. Of all men living, I, unimaginative disciple of austere science, should be the last to become the sport of that witchcraft which even imagination reluctantly allows to the machinery of poets, and science casts aside into the mouldy lumber-room of obsolete superstition.

Rousing my mind from enigmas impossible to solve, it was with intense and yet most melancholy satisfaction that I turned to the image of Lilian, rejoicing, though with a thrill of awe, that the promise so mysteriously conveyed to my senses had, hereto, been already fulfilled, — Margrave had left the town; Lilian was no longer subjected to his evil fascination. But an instinct told me that that fascination had already produced an effect adverse to all hope of happiness for me. Lilian's love for myself was gone. Impossible otherwise that she — in whose nature I had always admired that generous devotion which is more or less inseparable from the romance of youth — should have never conveyed to me one word of consolation in the hour of my agony and trial; that she, who, till the last evening we had met, had ever been so docile, in the sweetness of a nature femininely submissive to my slightest wish, should have disregarded my solemn injunction, and admitted Margrave to acquaintance, nay, to familiar intimacy, — at the very time, too, when to disobey my injunctions was to embitter my ordeal, and add her own contempt to the degradation imposed upon my honour! No, her heart must be wholly gone from me; her very nature wholly warped. A union between us had become impossible. My love for her remained unshattered; the more tender, perhaps, for a sentiment of compassion. But my pride was shocked, my heart was wounded. My love was not mean and servile. Enough for me to think that she would be at least saved from Margrave. *Her* life associated with his! — contemplation horrible and ghastly! — from that fate she was saved. Later, she would recover the effect of an influence happily so brief. She might form some new attachment, some new tie; but love once withdrawn is never to be restored — and her love was withdrawn from me. I had but to release her, with my own lips, from our engagement, — she would welcome that release. Mournful but firm in these thoughts and these resolutions, I sought Mrs. Ashleigh's house.

CHAPTER XLII.

IT was twilight when I entered, unannounced (as had been my wont in our familiar intercourse), the quiet sitting-room in which I expected to find mother and child. But Lilian was there alone, seated by the open window, her hands crossed and drooping on her knee, her eye fixed upon the darkening summer skies, in which the evening star had just stolen forth, bright and steadfast, near the pale sickle of a half-moon that was dimly visible, but gave us yet no light.

Let any lover imagine the reception he would expect to meet from his betrothed coming into her presence after he had passed triumphant through a terrible peril to life and fame — and conceive what ice froze my blood, what anguish weighed down my heart, when Lilian, turning towards me, rose not, spoke not, gazed at me heedlessly as if at some indifferent stranger — and — and — But no matter. I cannot bear to recall it even now, at the distance of years! I sat down beside her, and took her hand, without pressing it; it rested languidly, passively in mine, one moment; I dropped it then, with a bitter sigh.

"Lilian," I said quietly, "you love me no longer. Is it not so?"

She raised her eyes to mine, looked at me wistfully, and pressed her hand on her forehead; then said, in a strange voice, "Did I ever love you? What do you mean?"

"Lilian, Lilian, rouse yourself; are you not, while you speak, under some spell, some influence which you cannot describe nor account for?"

She paused a moment before she answered, calmly, "No! Again I ask what do you mean?"

"What do I mean? Do you forget that we are betrothed? Do you forget how often, and how recently, our vows of affection and constancy have been exchanged?"

"No, I do not forget; but I must have deceived you and myself — "

"It is true, then, that you love me no more?"

"I suppose so."

"But, oh, Lilian, is it that your heart is only closed to me; or is it — oh, answer truthfully — is it given to another, — to him — to him — against whom I warned you, whom I implored you not to receive? Tell me, at least, that your love is not gone to Margrave — "

"To him! love to him! Oh, no — no — "

"What, then, is your feeling towards him?"

Lilian's face grew visibly paler, even in that dim light. "I know not," she said, almost in a whisper; "but it is partly awe — partly — "

"What?"

"Abhorrence!" she said almost fiercely, and rose to her feet, with a wild defying start.

"If that be so," I said gently, "you would not grieve were you never again to see him — "

"But I shall see him again," she murmured in a tone of weary sadness, and sank back once more into her chair.

"I think not," said I, "and I hope not. And now hear me and heed me, Lilian. It is enough for me, no matter what your feelings towards another, to learn from yourself that the affection you once professed for me is gone. I release you from your troth. If folks ask why we two henceforth separate the lives we had agreed to join, you may say, if you please, that you could not give your hand to a man who had known the taint of a felon's prison, even on a false charge. If that seems to you an ungenerous reason, we will leave it to your mother to find a better. Farewell! For your own sake I can yet feel happiness, — happiness to hear that you do not love the man against whom I warn you still more solemnly than before! Will you not give me your hand in parting — and have I not spoken your own wish?"

She turned away her face, and resigned her hand to me in silence. Silently I held it in mine, and my emotions nearly stifled me. One symptom of regret, of reluctance, on her part, and I should have fallen at her feet, and cried, "Do not let us break a tie which our vows should have made indissoluble; heed not my offers, wrung from a tortured heart! You cannot have ceased to love me!" But no such symptom of relenting showed itself in her, and with a groan I left the room.

CHAPTER XLIII.

I WAS just outside the garden door, when I felt an arm thrown round me, my cheek kissed and wetted with tears. Could it be Lilian? Alas, no! It was her mother's voice, that, between laughing and crying, exclaimed hysterically: "This is joy, to see you again, and on these thresholds. I have just come from your house; I went there on purpose to congratulate you, and to talk to you about Lilian. But you have seen her?"

"Yes; I have but this moment left her. Come this way." I drew Mrs. Ashleigh back into the garden, along the old winding walk, which the shrubs concealed from view of the house. We sat down on a rustic seat where I had often sat with Lilian, midway between the house and the Monks' Well. I told the mother what had passed between me and her daughter; I made no complaint of Lilian's coldness and change; I did not hint at its cause. "Girls of her age will change," said I, "and all that now remains is for us two to agree on such a tale to our curious neighbours as may rest the whole blame on me. Man's name is of robust fibre; it could not push its way to a place in the world, if it could not bear, without sinking, the load idle tongues may lay on it. Not so Woman's Name: what is but gossip against Man, is scandal against Woman."

"Do not be rash, my dear Allen," said Mrs. Ashleigh, in great distress. "I feel for you, I understand you; in your case I might act as you do. I cannot blame you. Lilian is changed,—changed unaccountably. Yet sure I am that the change is only on the surface, that her heart is really yours, as entirely and as faithfully as ever it was; and that later, when she recovers from the strange, dreamy kind of torpor which appears to have come over all her faculties and all her

affections, she would awake with a despair which you cannot
conjecture to the knowledge that you had renounced her."

"I have not renounced her," said I, impatiently; "I did
but restore her freedom of choice. But pass by this now,
and explain to me more fully the change in your daughter,
which I gather from your words is not confined to me."

"I wished to speak of it before you saw her, and for that
reason came to your house. It was on the morning in which
we left her aunt's to return hither that I first noticed something peculiar in her look and manner. She seemed absorbed
and absent, so much so that I asked her several times to tell
me what made her so grave; but I could only get from her that
she had had a confused dream which she could not recall
distinctly enough to relate, but that she was sure it boded
evil. During the journey she became gradually more herself, and began to look forward with delight to the idea of
seeing you again. Well, you came that evening. What
passed between you and her you know best. You complained
that she slighted your request to shun all acquaintance with
Mr. Margrave. I was surprised that, whether your wish
were reasonable or not, she could have hesitated to comply
with it. I spoke to her about it after you had gone, and she
wept bitterly at thinking she had displeased you."

"She wept! You amaze me. Yet the next day what a
note she returned to mine!"

"The next day the change in her became very visible to
me. She told me, in an excited manner, that she was convinced she ought not to marry you. Then came, the following day, the news of your committal. I heard of it, but dared
not break it to her. I went to our friend the mayor, to consult with him what to say, what to do; and to learn more
distinctly than I had done from terrified, incoherent servants,
the rights of so dreadful a story. When I returned, I found,
to my amazement, a young stranger in the drawing-room; it
was Mr. Margrave, — Miss Brabazon had brought him at his
request. Lilian was in the room, too, and my astonishment
was increased, when she said to me with a singular smile,
vague but tranquil: 'I know all about Allen Fenwick; Mr.

Margrave has told me all. He is a friend of Allen's. He says there is no cause for fear.' Mr. Margrave then apologized to me for his intrusion in a caressing, kindly manner, as if one of the family. He said he was so intimate with you that he felt that he could best break to Miss Ashleigh information she might receive elsewhere, for that he was the only man in the town who treated the charge with ridicule. You know the wonderful charm of this young man's manner. I cannot explain to you how it was, but in a few moments I was as much at home with him as if he had been your brother. To be brief, having once come, he came constantly. He had moved, two days before you went to Derval Court, from his hotel to apartments in Mr. ——'s house, just opposite. .We could see him on his balcony from our terrace; he would smile to us and come across. I did wrong in slighting your injunction, and suffering Lilian to do so. I could not help it, he was such a comfort to me,— to her, too — in her tribulation. He alone had no doleful words, wore no long face; he alone was invariably cheerful. 'Everything,' he said, 'would come right in a day or two.' "

"And Lilian could not but admire this young man, he is so beautiful."

"Beautiful? Well, perhaps. But if you have a jealous feeling, you were never more mistaken. Lilian, I am convinced, does more than dislike him; he has inspired her with repugnance, with terror. And much as I own I like him, in his wild, joyous, careless, harmless way, do not think I flatter you if I say that Mr. Margrave is not the man to make any girl untrue to you,— untrue to a lover with infinitely less advantages than you may pretend to. He would be a universal favourite, I grant; but there is something in him, or a something wanting in him, which makes liking and admiration stop short of love. I know not why; perhaps, because, with all his good humour, he is so absorbed in himself, so intensely egotistical, so light; were he less clever, I should say so frivolous. He could not make love, he could not say in the serious tone of a man in earnest, 'I love you.' He owned as much to me, and owned, too, that he knew not even what love was. As to myself, Mr. Margrave appears rich; no whisper against his character or his honour ever reached me. Yet were you out of the question, and were there no stain on his birth, nay, were he as high in rank and wealth as he is favoured by Nature in personal advantages, I confess I could never consent to trust him with my daughter's fate. A voice at my heart would cry, 'No!' It may be an unreasonable prejudice, but I could not bear to see him touch Lilian's hand!"

"Did she never, then — never suffer him even to take her hand?"

"Never. Do not think so meanly of her as to suppose that she could be caught by a fair face, a graceful manner. Reflect: just before she had refused, for your sake, Ashleigh Sumner, whom Lady Haughton said 'no girl in her senses could refuse;' and this change in Lilian really began before we returned to L——, — before she had even seen Mr. Margrave. I am convinced it is something in the reach of your skill as physician, — it is on the nerves, the system. I will give you a proof of what I say, only do not betray me to her. It was during your imprisonment, the night before your release, that I was awakened by her coming to my bedside. She was sobbing as if her heart would break. 'O mother, mother!' she cried, 'pity me, help me! I am so wretched.' 'What is the matter, darling?' 'I have been so cruel to Allen, and I know I shall be so again. I cannot help it. Do not question me; only if we are separated, if he cast me off, or I reject him, tell him some day — perhaps when I am in my grave — not to believe appearances; and that I, in my heart of hearts, never ceased to love him!'"

"She said that! You are not deceiving me?"

"Oh, no! how can you think so?"

"There is hope still," I murmured; and I bowed my head upon my hands, hot tears forcing their way through the clasped fingers.

"One word more," said I; "you tell me that Lilian has a repugnance to this Margrave, and yet that she found comfort in his visits, — a comfort that could not be wholly ascribed to cheering words he might say about myself, since it is all but certain that I was not, at that time, uppermost in her mind. Can you explain this apparent contradiction? "

" I cannot, otherwise than by a conjecture which you would ridicule."

" I can ridicule nothing now. What is your conjecture? "

" I know how much you disbelieve in the stories one hears of animal magnetism and electro-biology, otherwise — "

" You think that Margrave exercises some power of that kind over Lilian? Has he spoken of such a power? "

"Not exactly; but he said that he was sure Lilian possessed a faculty that he called by some hard name, not clairvoyance, but a faculty, which he said, when I asked him to explain, was akin to prevision, — to second sight. Then he talked of the Priestesses who had administered the ancient oracles. Lilian, he said, reminded him of them, with her deep eyes and mysterious smile."

" And Lilian heard him? What said she? "

" Nothing; she seemed in fear while she listened."

" He did not offer to try any of those arts practised by pro fessional mesmerists and other charlatans? "

" I thought he was about to do so, but I forestalled him, saying I never would consent to any experiment of that kind, either on myself or my daughter."

" And he replied — "

" With his gay laugh, 'that I was very foolish; that a person possessed of such a faculty as he attributed to Lilian would, if the faculty were developed, be an invaluable adviser.' He would have said more, but I begged him to desist. Still I fancy at times — do not be angry — that he does somehow or other bewitch her, unconsciously to herself; for she always knows when he is coming. Indeed, I am not sure that he does not bewitch myself, for I by no means justify my conduct in admitting him to an intimacy so familiar, and in spite of your wish; I have reproached myself, resolved to shut my door on him, or to show by my manner that his visits were unwelcome; yet when Lilian has said, in the drowsy lethargic tone which has come into her voice (her voice naturally earnest and impressive, though always low), 'Mother, he will be here in two minutes; I wish to leave the room and cannot,' I, too, have felt as if something constrained me against my will; as if, in short, I were under that influence which Mr. Vigors — whom I will never forgive for his conduct to you — would ascribe to mesmerism. But will you not come in and see Lilian again?"

"No, not to-night; but watch and heed her, and if you see aught to make you honestly believe that she regrets the rupture of the old tie from which I have released her — why, you know, Mrs. Ashleigh, that — that — " My voice failed; I wrung the good woman's hand, and went my way.

I had always till then considered Mrs. Ashleigh — if not as Mrs. Poyntz described her — "commonplace weak" — still of an intelligence somewhat below mediocrity. I now regarded her· with respect as well as grateful tenderness; her plain sense had divined what all my boasted knowledge had failed to detect in my earlier intimacy with Margrave, — namely, that in him there was a something present, or a something wanting, which forbade love and excited fear. Young, beautiful, wealthy, seemingly blameless in life as he was, she would not have given her daughter's hand to him!

CHAPTER XLIV.

THE next day my house was filled with visitors. I had no notion that I had so many friends. Mr. Vigors wrote me a generous and handsome letter, owning his prejudices against me on account of his sympathy with poor Dr. Lloyd, and begging my pardon for what he now felt to have been harshness, if not distorted justice. But what most moved me was the entrance of Strahan, who rushed up to me with the heartiness of old college days. "Oh, my dear Allen, can you ever forgive me; that I should have disbelieved your word,

— should have suspected you of abstracting my poor cousin's memoir?"

"Is it found, then?"

"Oh, yes; you must thank Margrave. He, clever fellow, you know, came to me on a visit yesterday. He put me at once on the right scent. Only guess; but you never can! It was that wretched old housekeeper who purloined the manuscript. You remember she came into the room while you were looking at the memoir. She heard us talk about it; her curiosity was roused; she longed to know the history of her old master, under his own hand; she could not sleep; she heard me go up to bed; she thought you might leave the book on the table when you, too, went to rest. She stole downstairs, peeped through the keyhole of the library, saw you asleep, the book lying before you, entered, took away the book softly, meant to glance at its contents and to return it. You were sleeping so soundly she thought you would not wake for an hour; she carried it into the library, leaving the door open, and there began to pore over it. She stumbled first on one of the passages in Latin; she hoped to find some part in plain English, turned over the leaves, putting her candle close to them, for the old woman's eyes were dim, when she heard you make some sound in your sleep. Alarmed, she looked round; you were moving uneasily in your seat, and muttering to yourself. From watching you she was soon diverted by the consequences of her own confounded curiosity and folly. In moving, she had unconsciously brought the poor manuscript close to the candle; the leaves caught the flame; her own cap and hand burning first made her aware of the mischief done. She threw down the book; her sleeve was in flames; she had first to tear off the sleeve, which was, luckily for her, not sewn to her dress. By the time she recovered presence of mind to attend to the book, half its leaves were reduced to tinder. She did not dare then to replace what was left of the manuscript on your table; returned with it to her room, hid it, and resolved to keep her own secret. I should never have guessed it; I had never even spoken to her of the occurrence; but when I talked over the

17

disappearance of the book to Margrave last night, and expressed my disbelief of your story, he said, in his merry way: 'But do you think that Fenwick is the only person curious about your cousin's odd ways and strange history? Why, every servant in the household would have been equally curious. You have examined your servants, of course?' 'No, I never thought of it.' 'Examine them now, then. Examine especially that old housekeeper. I observe a great change in her manner since I came here, weeks ago, to look over the house. She has something on her mind,—I see it in her eyes.' Then it occurred to me, too, that the woman's manner had altered, and that she seemed always in a tremble and a fidget. I went at once to her room, and charged her with stealing the book. She fell on her knees, and told the whole story as I have told it to you, and as I shall take care to tell it to all to whom I have so foolishly blabbed my yet more foolish suspicions of yourself. But can you forgive me, old friend?"

"Heartily, heartily! And the book is burned?"

"See;" and he produced a mutilated manuscript. Strange, the part burned—reduced, indeed, to tinder—was the concluding part that related to Haroun,—to Grayle: no vestige of that part was left; the earlier portions were scorched and mutilated, though in some places still decipherable; but as my eye hastily ran over those places, I saw only mangled sentences of the experimental problems which the writer had so minutely elaborated.

"Will you keep the manuscript as it is, and as long as you like?" said Strahan.

"No, no; I will have nothing more to do with it. Consult some other man of science. And so this is the old woman's whole story? No accomplice,—none? No one else shared her curiosity and her task?"

"No. Oddly enough, though, she made much the same excuse for her pitiful folly that the madman made for his terrible crime; she said, 'the Devil put it into her head.' Of course he did, as he puts everything wrong into any one's head. That does not mend the matter."

"How! did she, too, say she saw a Shadow and heard a voice?"

"No; not such a liar as that, and not mad enough for such a lie. But she said that when she was in bed, thinking over the book, something irresistible urged her to get up and go down into the study; swore she felt something lead her by the hand; swore, too, that when she first discovered the manuscript was not in English, something whispered in her ear to turn over the leaves and approach them to the candle. But I had no patience to listen to all this rubbish. I sent her out of the house, bag and baggage. But, alas! is this to be the end of all my wise cousin's grand discoveries?"

True, of labours that aspired to bring into the chart of science new worlds, of which even the traditionary rumour was but a voice from the land of fable — nought left but broken vestiges of a daring footstep! The hope of a name imperishable amidst the loftiest hierarchy of Nature's secret temple, with all the pomp of recorded experiment, that applied to the mysteries of Egypt and Chaldæa the inductions of Bacon, the tests of Liebig — was there nothing left of this but what, here and there, some puzzled student might extract, garbled, mutilated, perhaps unintelligible, from shreds of sentences, wrecks of problems! O mind of man, can the works, on which thou wouldst found immortality below, be annulled into smoke and tinder by an inch of candle in the hand of an old woman!

When Strahan left me, I went out, but not yet to visit patients. I stole through by-paths into the fields; I needed solitude to bring my thoughts into shape and order. What was delusion, and what not? Was I right or the Public? Was Margrave really the most innocent and serviceable of human beings, kindly affectionate, employing a wonderful acuteness for benignant ends? Was I, in truth, indebted to him for the greatest boon one man can bestow on another, — for life rescued, for fair name justified? Or had he, by some demoniac sorcery, guided the hand of the murderer against the life of the person who alone could imperil his own? Had he, by the same dark spells, urged the woman to the

act that had destroyed the only record of his monstrous being,— the only evidence that I was not the sport of an illusion in the horror with which he inspired me?

But if the latter supposition could be admissible, did he
use his agents only to betray them afterwards to exposure,
and that, without any possible clew to his own detection as
the instigator? Then, there came over me confused recollections of tales of mediæval witchcraft, which I had read in
boyhood. Were there not on judicial record attestation and
evidence, solemn and circumstantial, of powers analogous to
those now exercised by Margrave,— of sorcerers instigating
to sin through influences ascribed to Demons; making their
apparitions glide through guarded walls, their voices heard
from afar in the solitude of dungeons or monastic cells; sub-
jugating victims to their will, by means which no vigilance
could have detected, if the victims themselves had not confessed the witchcraft that had ensnared, courting a sure and
infamous death in that confession, preferring such death to a
life so haunted? Were stories so gravely set forth in the
pomp of judicial evidence, and in the history of times comparatively recent, indeed to be massed, pell-mell together, as
a *moles indigesta* of senseless superstition,— all the witnesses
to be deemed liars; all the victims and tools of the sorcerers,
lunatics; all the examiners or judges, with their solemn
gradations — lay and clerical — from Commissions of Inquiry
to Courts of Appeal,— to be despised for credulity, loathed
for cruelty; or, amidst records so numerous, so imposingly
attested, were there the fragments of a terrible truth? And
had our ancestors been so unwise in those laws we now deem
so savage, by which the world was rid of scourges more awful
and more potent than the felon with his candid dagger?
Fell instigators of the evil in men's secret hearts, shaping
into action the vague, half-formed desire, and guiding with
agencies impalpable, unseen, their spell-bound instruments
of calamity and death.

Such were the gloomy questions that I — by repute, the
sternest advocate of common-sense against fantastic errors;
by profession, the searcher into flesh and blood, and tissue

and nerve and sinew, for the causes of all that disease the mechanism of the universal human frame; I, self-boasting physician, sceptic, philosopher, materialist — revolved, not amidst gloomy pines, under grim winter skies, but as I paced slow through laughing meadows, and by the banks of merry streams, in the ripeness of the golden August: the hum of insects in the fragrant grass, the flutter of birds amid the delicate green of boughs checkered by playful sunbeams and gentle shadows, and ever in sight of the resorts of busy work-day man, — walls, roof-tops, church-spires rising high; there, white and modern, the handwriting of our race, in this practical nineteenth century, on its square plain masonry and Doric shafts, the Town-Hall, central in the animated market-place. And I — I — prying into long-neglected corners and dust-holes of memory for what my reason had flung there as worthless rubbish; reviving the jargon of French law, in the *procès verbal*, against a Gille de Retz, or an Urbain Grandier, and sifting the equity of sentences on witchcraft!

Bursting the links of this ghastly soliloquy with a laugh at my own folly, I struck into a narrow path that led back towards the city, by a quiet and rural suburb; the path wound on through a wide and solitary churchyard, at the base of the Abbey-hill. Many of the former dwellers on that eminence now slept in the lowly burial-ground at its foot; and the place, mournfully decorated with the tombs which still jealously mark distinctions of rank amidst the levelling democracy of the grave, was kept trim with the care which comes half from piety, and half from pride.

I seated myself on a bench, placed between the clipped yew-trees that bordered the path from the entrance to the church porch, deeming vaguely that my own perplexing thoughts might imbibe a quiet from the quiet of the place.

"And oh," I murmured to myself, "oh that I had one bosom friend to whom I might freely confide all these torturing riddles which I cannot solve, — one who could read my heart, light up its darkness, exorcise its spectres; one in whose wisdom I could welcome a guide through the Nature which now suddenly changes her aspect, opening out from the walls

with which I had fenced and enclosed her as mine own formal
garden; — all her pathways, therein, trimmed to my footstep;
all her blooms grouped and harmonized to my own taste in
colour; all her groves, all her caverns, but the soothing re-
treats of a Muse or a Science; opening out — opening out,
desert on desert, into clewless and measureless space! Gone
is the garden!   Were its confines too narrow for Nature?
Be it so! The Desert replaces the garden, but where ends
the Desert? Reft from my senses are the laws which gave
order and place to their old questionless realm.   I stand lost
and appalled amidst Chaos.   Did my Mind misconstrue the
laws it deemed fixed and immutable? Be it so! But still
Nature cannot be lawless; Creation is not a Chaos. If my
senses deceive me in some things, they are still unerring in
others; if thus, in some things, fallacious, still, in other
things, truthful. Are there within me senses finer than those
I have cultured, or without me vistas of knowledge which
instincts, apart from my senses, divine? So long as I deal
with the Finite alone, my senses suffice me; but when the Infinite is obtruded upon me there, are my senses faithless de-
serters? If so, is there aught else in my royal resources of
Man — whose ambition it is, from the first dawn of his glory
as Thinker, to invade and to subjugate Nature, — is there
aught else to supply the place of those traitors, the senses,
who report to my Reason, their judge and their sovereign, as
truths seen and heard tales which my Reason forfeits her
sceptre if she does not disdain as lies? Oh, for a friend! oh,
for a guide! "

And as I so murmured, my eye fell upon the form of a
kneeling child, — at the farther end of the burial-ground,
beside a grave with its new headstone gleaming white amidst
the older moss-grown tombs, a female child, her head bowed,
her hands clasped. I could see but the outline of her small
form in its sable dress, — an infant beside the dead.

My eye and my thoughts were turned from that silent figure, too absorbed in my own restless tumult of doubt and
dread, for sympathy with the grief or the consolation of a
kneeling child. And yet I should have remembered that

tomb! Again I murmured with a fierce impatience, "Oh, for a friend! oh, for a guide!"

I heard steps on the walk under the yews; and an old man came in sight, slightly bent, with long gray hair, but still with enough of vigour for years to come, in his tread, firm, though slow, in the unshrunken muscle of his limbs and the steady light of his clear blue eye. I started. Was it possible? That countenance, marked, indeed, with the lines of laborious thought, but sweet in the mildness of humanity, and serene in the peace of conscience! I could not be mistaken. Julius Faber was before me,— the profound pathologist, to whom my own proud self-esteem acknowledged inferiority, without humiliation; the generous benefactor to whom I owed my own smooth entrance into the arduous road of fame and fortune. I had longed for a friend, a guide; what I sought stood suddenly at my side.

CHAPTER XLV.

EXPLANATION on Faber's part was short and simple. The nephew whom he designed as the heir to his wealth had largely outstripped the liberal allowance made to him, had incurred heavy debts; and in order to extricate himself from the debts, had plunged into ruinous speculations. Faber had come back to England to save his heir from prison or outlawry, at the expense of more than three-fourths of the destined inheritance. To add to all, the young man had married a young lady without fortune; the uncle only heard of this marriage on arriving in England. The spendthrift was hiding from his creditors in the house of his father-in-law, in one of the western counties. Faber there sought him; and on becoming acquainted with his wife, grew reconciled to the marriage, and formed hopes of his nephew's future redemption. He spoke, indeed, of the young wife with great affec-

tion. She was good and sensible; willing and anxious to
encounter any privation by which her husband might reprieve
the effects of his folly. "So," said Faber, "on consultation
with this excellent creature — for my poor nephew is so
broken down by repentance, that others must think for him
how to exalt repentance into reform — my plans were determined. I shall remove my prodigal from all scenes of temptation. He has youth, strength, plenty of energy, hitherto
misdirected. I shall take him from the Old World into the
New. I have decided on Australia. The fortune still left
to me, small here, will be ample capital there. It is not
enough to maintain us separately, so we must all live together. Besides, I feel that, though I have neither the
strength or the experience which could best serve a young
settler on a strange soil, still, under my eye, my poor boy
will be at once more prudent and more persevering. We sail
next week."

Faber spoke so cheerfully that I knew not how to express
compassion; yet, at his age, after a career of such prolonged
and distinguished labour, to resign the ease and comforts of
the civilized state for the hardships and rudeness of an infant
colony, seemed to me a dreary prospect; and, as delicately,
as tenderly as I could to one whom I loved and honoured as
a father, I placed at his disposal the fortune which, in great
part, I owed to him, — pressing him at least to take from it
enough to secure to himself, in his own country, a home suited
to his years and worthy of his station. He rejected all my
offers, however earnestly urged on him, with his usual modest
and gentle dignity; and assuring me that he looked forward
with great interest to a residence in lands new to his experience, and affording ample scope for the hardy enjoyments
which had always most allured his tastes, he hastened to
change the subject.

"And who, think you, is the admirable helpmate my scape-
grace has had the saving good luck to find? A daughter of
the worthy man who undertook the care of poor Dr. Lloyd's
orphans, — the orphans who owed so much to your generous
exertions to secure a provision for them; and that child, now

just risen from her father's grave, is my pet companion, my darling ewe lamb,— Dr. Lloyd's daughter Amy."

Here the child joined us, quickening her pace as she recognized the old man, and nestling to his side as she glanced wistfully towards myself. A winning, candid, lovable child's face, somewhat melancholy, somewhat more thoughtful than is common to the face of childhood, but calm, intelligent, and ineffably mild. Presently she stole from the old man, and put her hand in mine.

"Are you not the kind gentleman who came to see him that night when he passed away from us, and who, they all say at home, was so good to my brothers and me? Yes, I recollect you now." And she put her pure face to mine, wooing me to kiss it.

I kind! I good! I — I! Alas! she little knew, little guessed, the wrathful imprecation her father had bequeathed to me that fatal night!

I did not dare to kiss Dr. Lloyd's orphan daughter, but my tears fell over her hand. She took them as signs of pity, and, in her infant thankfulness, silently kissed me.

"Oh, my friend!" I murmured to Faber, "I have much that I yearn to say to you — alone — alone! Come to my house with me, be at least my guest as long as you stay in this town."

"Willingly," said Faber, looking at me more intently than he had done before, and with the true eye of the practised Healer, at once soft and penetrating.

He rose, took my arm, and whispering a word in the ear of the little girl, she went on before us, turning her head, as she gained the gate, for another look at her father's grave. As we walked to my house, Julius Faber spoke to me much of this child. Her brothers were all at school; she was greatly attached to his nephew's wife; she had become yet more attached to Faber himself, though on so short an acquaintance; it had been settled that she was to accompany the emigrants to Australia.

"There," said he, "the sum, that some munificent, but unknown friend of her father has settled on her, will provide

her no mean dower for a colonist's wife, when the time comes
for her to bring a blessing to some other hearth than ours."
He went on to say that she had wished to accompany him to
L——, in order to visit her father's grave before crossing the
wide seas; "and she has taken such fond care of me all the
way, that you might fancy I were the child of the two. I
come back to this town, partly to dispose of a few poor houses
in it which still belong to me, principally to bid you farewell
before quitting the Old World, no doubt forever. So, on arriving to-day, I left Amy by herself in the churchyard while
I went to your house, but you were from home. And now I
must congratulate you on the reputation you have so rapidly
acquired, which has even surpassed my predictions."

"You are aware," said I, falteringly, "of the extraordinary
charge from which that part of my reputation dearest to all
men has just emerged!"

He had but seen a short account in a weekly journal, written after my release. He asked details, which I postponed.

Reaching my home, I hastened to provide for the comfort
of my two unexpected guests; strove to rally myself, to be
cheerful. Not till night, when Julius Faber and I were
alone together, did I touch on what was weighing at my
heart. Then, drawing to his side, I told him all,— all of
which the substance is herein written, from the death-scene
in Dr. Lloyd's chamber to the hour in which I had seen Dr.
Lloyd's child at her father's grave. Some of the incidents
and conversations which had most impressed me I had already
committed to writing, in the fear that, otherwise, my fancy
might forge for its own thraldom the links of reminiscence
which my memory might let fall from its chain. Faber listened with a silence only interrupted by short pertinent
questions; and when I had done, he remained thoughtful for
some moments; then the great physician replied thus: —

"I take for granted your conviction of the reality of all you
tell me, even of the Luminous Shadow, of the bodiless Voice;
but, before admitting the reality itself, we must abide by the
old maxim, not to accept as cause to effect those agencies
which belong to the Marvellous, when causes less improbable

for the effect can be rationally conjectured. In this case are there not such causes? Certainly there are —"

"There are?'"

"Listen; you are one of those men who attempt to stifle their own imagination. But in all completed intellect, imagination exists, and will force its way; deny it healthful vents, and it may stray into morbid channels. The death-room of Dr. Lloyd deeply impressed your heart, far more than your pride would own. This is clear from the pains you took to exonerate your conscience, in your generosity to the orphans. As the heart was moved, so was the imagination stirred; and, unaware to yourself, prepared for much that subsequently appealed to it. Your sudden love, conceived in the very grounds of the house so associated with recollections in themselves strange and romantic; the peculiar temperament and nature of the girl to whom your love was attracted; her own visionary beliefs, and the keen anxiety which infused into your love a deeper poetry of sentiment,— all insensibly tended to induce the imagination to dwell on the Wonderful; and, in overstriving to reconcile each rarer phenomenon to the most positive laws of Nature, your very intellect could discover no solution but in the Preternatural.

"You visit a man who tells you he has seen Sir Philip Derval's ghost; on that very evening, you hear a strange story, in which Sir Philip's name is mixed up with a tale of murder, implicating two mysterious pretenders to magic,— Louis Grayle and the Sage of Aleppo. The tale so interests your fancy that even the glaring impossibility of a not unimportant part of it escapes your notice,— namely, the account of a criminal trial in which the circumstantial evidence was more easily attainable than in all the rest of the narrative, but which could not legally have taken place as told. Thus it is whenever the mind begins, unconsciously, to admit the shadow of the Supernatural; the Obvious is lost to the eye that plunges its gaze into the Obscure. Almost immediately afterwards you become acquainted with a young stranger, whose traits of character interest and perplex, attract yet revolt you. All this time you are engaged in a physiological

work which severely tasks the brain, and in which you examine the intricate question of soul distinct from mind.

"And, here, I can conceive a cause deep-hid'amongst what
metaphysicians would call latent associations, for a train of
thought which disposed you to accept the fantastic impressions afterwards made on you by the scene in the Museum
and the visionary talk of Sir Philip Derval. Doubtless,
when at college you first studied metaphysical speculation
you would have glanced over Beattie's 'Essay on Truth' as
one of the works written in opposition to your favourite,
David Hume."

"Yes, I read the book, but I have long since forgotten its
arguments."

"Well, in that essay, Beattie [1] cites the extraordinary instance of Simon Browne, a learned and pious clergyman, who
seriously disbelieved the existence of his own soul; and imagined that, by interposition of Divine power, his soul was
annulled, and nothing left but a principle of animal life,
which he held in common with the brutes! When, years
ago, a thoughtful imaginative student, you came on that
story, probably enough you would have paused, revolved in
your own mind and fancy what kind of a creature a man
might be, if, retaining human life and merely human understanding, he was deprived of the powers and properties which
reasoners have ascribed to the existence of soul. Something
in this young man, unconsciously to yourself, revives that
forgotten train of meditative ideas. His dread of death as
the final cessation of being, his brute-like want of sympathy
with his kind, his incapacity to comprehend the motives
which carry man on to scheme and to build for a future that
extends beyond his grave,— all start up before you at the
very moment your reason is overtasked, your imagination
fevered, in seeking the solution of problems which, to a philosophy based upon your system, must always remain insoluble. The young man's conversation not only thus excites
your fancies,— it disturbs your affections. He speaks not

[1] Beattie's " Essay on Truth," part i. c. ii. 3. The story of Simon Browne
is to be found in " The Adventurer."

only of drugs that renew youth, but of charms that secure
love. You tremble for your Lilian while you hear him
And the brain thus tasked, the imagination thus inflamed,
the heart thus agitated, you are presented to Sir Philip Derval, whose ghost your patient had supposed he saw weeks
ago.

"This person, a seeker after an occult philosophy, which
had possibly acquainted him with some secrets in nature beyond the pale of our conventional experience, though, when
analyzed, they might prove to be quite reconcilable with
sober science, startles you with an undefined mysterious
charge against the young man who had previously seemed to
you different from ordinary mortals. In a room stored with
the dead things of the brute soulless world, your brain becomes intoxicated with the fumes of some vapour which produces effects not uncommon in the superstitious practices of
the East; your brain, thus excited, brings distinctly before
you the vague impressions it had before received. Margrave
becomes identified with the Louis Grayle of whom you had
previously heard an obscure and legendary tale, and all the
anomalies in his character are explained by his being that
which you had contended, in your physiological work, it was
quite possible for man to be,— namely, mind and body without soul! You were startled by the monster which man
would be were your own theory possible; and in order to reconcile the contradictions in this very monster, you account
for knowledge, and for powers that mind without soul could
not have attained, by ascribing to this prodigy broken memories of a former existence, demon attributes from former proficiency in evil magic. My friend, there is nothing here
which your own study of morbid idiosyncracies should not
suffice to solve."

"So, then," said I, "you would reduce all that have affected
my senses as realities into the deceit of illusions? But," I
added, in a whisper, terrified by my own question, "do not
physiologists agree in this: namely, that though illusory
phantasms may haunt the sane as well as the insane, the sane
know that they are only illusions, and the insane do not."

"Such a distinction," answered Faber, "is far too arbitrary and rigid for more than a very general and qualified acceptance. Müller, indeed, who is perhaps the highest authority on such a subject, says, with prudent reserve, 'When a person who is not insane sees spectres and believes them to be real, his intellect must be imperfectly exercised.'[1] He would, indeed, be a bold physician who maintained that every man who believed he had really seen a ghost was of unsound mind. In Dr. Abercrombie's interesting account of spectral illusions, he tells us of a servant-girl who believed she saw, at the foot of her bed, the apparition of Curran, in a sailor's jacket and an immense pair of whiskers.[2] No doubt the spectre was an illusion, and Dr. Abercrombie very ingeniously suggests the association of ideas by which the apparition was conjured up with the grotesque adjuncts of the jacket and the whiskers; but the servant-girl, in believing the reality of the apparition, was certainly not insane. When I read in the American public journals[3] of 'spirit manifestations,' in which large numbers of persons, of at least the average degree of education, declare that they have actually witnessed various phantasms, much more extraordinary than all which you have confided to me, and arrive, at once, at the conclusion that they are thus put into direct communication with departed souls, I must assume that they are under an illusion; but I should be utterly unwarranted in supposing that, because they credited that illusion, they were insane. I should only say with Müller, that in their reasoning on the phenomena presented to them, 'their intellect was imperfectly exercised.' And an impression made on the senses, being in itself sufficiently rare to excite our wonder, may be strengthened till it takes the form of a positive fact, by various coincidences which are accepted as corroborative testimony, yet which are, nevertheless, nothing more than coincidences found

---

[1] Müller's Physiology of the Senses, p. 394.

[2] Abercrombie on the Intellectual Powers, p. 281. (15th edition.)

[3] At the date of Faber's conversation with Allen Fenwick, the (so-called) spirit manifestations had not spread from America over Europe. But if they had, Faber's views would, no doubt, have remained the same.

in every day matters of business, but only emphatically noticed when we can exclaim, 'How astonishing!' In your
case such coincidences have been, indeed, very signal, and
might well aggravate the perplexities into which your reason
was thrown. Sir Philip Derval's murder, the missing casket,
the exciting nature of the manuscript, in which a superstitious
interest is already enlisted by your expectation to find in it
the key to the narrator's boasted powers, and his reasons for
the astounding denunciation of the man whom you suspect to
be his murderer,— in all this there is much to confirm, nay,
to cause, an illusion; and for that very reason, when examined by strict laws of evidence, in all this there is but additional proof that the illusion was — only illusion. Your
affections contribute to strengthen your fancy in its war on your
reason. The girl you so passionately love develops, to your
disquietude and terror, the visionary temperament which, at
her age, is ever liable to fantastic caprices. She hears Margrave's song, which you say has a wildness of charm that
affects and thrills even you. Who does not know the power
of music? and of all music, there is none so potential as that
of the human voice. Thus, in some languages, charm and
song are identical expressions; and even when a critic, in our
own sober newspapers, extols a Malibran or a Grisi, you may
be sure that he will call her 'enchantress.' Well, this lady,
your betrothed, in whom the nervous system is extremely
impressionable, hears a voice which, even to your ear, is
strangely melodious, and sees a form and face which, even
to your eye, are endowed with a singular character of beauty.
Her fancy is impressed by what she thus hears and sees; and
impressed the more because, by a coincidence not very uncommon, a face like that which she beholds has before been
presented to her in a dream or a revery. In the nobleness of
genuine, confiding, reverential love, rather than impute to
your beloved a levity of sentiment that would seem to you a
treason, you accept the chimera of 'magical fascination.' In
this frame of mind you sit down to read the memoir of a
mystical enthusiast. Do you begin now to account for the
Luminous Shadow? A dream! And a dream no less because

your eyes were open and you believed yourself awake. The diseased imagination resembles those mirrors which, being themselves distorted, represent distorted pictures as correct.

"And even this Memoir of Sir Philip Derval's — can you be quite sure that you actually read the part which relates to Haroun and Louis Grayle? You say that, while perusing the manuscript, you saw the Luminous Shadow, and became insensible. The old woman says you were fast asleep. May you not really have fallen into a slumber, and in that slumber have dreamed the parts of the tale that relate to Grayle, — dreamed that you beheld the Shadow? Do you remember what is said so well by Dr. Abercrombie, to authorize the explanation I suggest to you: 'A person under the influence of some strong mental impression falls asleep for a few seconds, perhaps without being sensible of it: some scene or person appears in a dream, and he starts up under the conviction that it was a spectral appearance.' " [1]

"But," said I, "the apparition was seen by me again, and when, certainly, I was not sleeping."

"True; and who should know better than a physician so well read as yourself that a spectral illusion once beheld is *always apt to return again in the same form?* Thus, Goethe

---

[1] Abercrombie on the Intellectual Powers, p. 278. (15th edition.)
This author, not more to be admired for his intelligence than his candour, and who is entitled to praise for a higher degree of original thought than that to which he modestly pretends, relates a curious anecdote illustrating " the analogy between dreaming and spectral illusion, which he received from the gentleman to which it occurred, — an eminent medical friend : " " Having sat up late one evening, under considerable anxiety for one of his children, who was ill, he fell asleep in his chair, and had a frightful dream, in which the prominent figure was an immense baboon. He awoke with the fright, got up instantly, and walked to a table which was in the middle of the room. He was then quite awake, and quite conscious of the articles around him ; but close by the wall in the end of the apartment he distinctly saw the baboon making the same grimaces which he had seen in his dreams ; and this spectre continued visible for about half a minute." Now, a man who saw only a baboon would be quite ready to admit that it was but an optical illusion ; but if, instead of a baboon, he had seen an intimate friend, and that friend, by some coincidence of time, had died about that date, he would be a very strong-minded man if he admitted for the mystery of seeing his friend the same natural solution which he would readily admit for seeing a baboon.

was long haunted by one image,— the phantom of a flower unfolding itself, and developing new flowers.[1] Thus, one of our most distinguished philosophers tells us of a lady known to himself, who would see her husband, hear him move and speak, when he was not even in the house.[2] But instances of the facility with which phantasms, once admitted, repeat themselves to the senses, are numberless. Many are recorded by Hibbert and Abercrombie, and every physician in extensive practice can add largely, from his own experience, to the list. Intense self-concentration is, in itself, a mighty magician. The magicians of the East inculcate the necessity of fast, solitude, and meditation for the due development of their imaginary powers. And I have no doubt with effect; because fast, solitude, and meditation — in other words, thought or fancy intensely concentred — will both raise apparitions and produce the invoker's belief in them. Spinello, striving to conceive the image of Lucifer for his picture of the Fallen Angels, was at last actually haunted by the Shadow of the Fiend. Newton himself has been subjected to a phantom, though to him, Son of Light, the spectre presented was that of the sun! You remember the account that Newton gives to Locke of this visionary appearance. He says that 'though he had looked at the sun with his right eye only, and *not* with the left, yet his fancy began to make an impression upon his left eye as well as his right; for if he shut his right and looked upon the clouds, or a book, or any bright object with his left eye, he could see the sun almost as plain as with the right, if he did but *intend* his fancy a little while on it;' nay, 'for some months after, as often as he began to meditate on the phenomena, the spectrum of the sun began to return, even though he lay in bed at midnight, with his curtains drawn!' Seeing, then, how any vivid impression once made will recur, what wonder that you should behold in your prison the Shining Shadow that had first startled you in a wizard's chamber when poring over the records of a mur-

[1] See Müller's observations on this phenomenon, "Physiology of the Senses," Baley's translation, p. 1395.

[2] Sir David Brewster's Letters on Natural Magic, p. 39.

dered visionary? The more minutely you analyze your own hallucinations — pardon me the word — the more they assume the usual characteristics of a dream; contradictory, illogical, even in the marvels they represent. Can any two persons be more totally unlike each other, not merely as to form and years, but as to all the elements of character, than the Grayle of whom you read, or believe you read, and the Margrave in whom you evidently think that Grayle is existent still? The one represented, you say, as gloomy, saturnine, with vehement passions, but with an original grandeur of thought and will, consumed by an internal remorse; the other you paint to me as a joyous and wayward darling of Nature, acute yet frivolous, free from even the ordinary passions of youth, taking delight in innocent amusements, incapable of continuous study, without a single pang of repentance for the crimes you so fancifully impute to him. And now, when your suspicions, so romantically conceived, are dispelled by positive facts, now, when it is clear that Margrave neither murdered Sir Philip Derval nor abstracted the memoir, you still, unconsciously to yourself, draw on your imagination in order to excuse the suspicion your pride of intellect declines to banish, and suppose that this youthful sorcerer tempted the madman to the murder, the woman to the theft — "

"But you forget the madman said 'that he was led on by the Luminous Shadow of a beautiful youth,' that the woman said also that she was impelled by some mysterious agency."

"I do not forget those coincidences; but how your learning would dismiss them as nugatory were your imagination not disposed to exaggerate them! When you read the authentic histories of any popular illusion, such as the spurious inspirations of the Jansenist Convulsionaries, the apparitions that invaded convents, as deposed in the trial of Urbain Grandier, the confessions of witches and wizards in places the most remote from each other, or, at this day, the tales of 'spirit manifestation' recorded in half the towns and villages of America, — do not all the superstitious impressions of a particular time have a common family likeness? What one sees, another sees, though there has been no communication between the two. I cannot tell you why these phantasms thus partake of the nature of an atmospheric epidemic; the fact remains incontestable. And strange as may be the coincidence between your impressions of a mystic agency and those of some other brains not cognizant of the chimeras of your own, still, is it not simpler philosophy to say, 'They are coincidences of the same nature which made witches in the same epoch all tell much the same story of the broomsticks they rode and the sabbats at which they danced to the fiend's piping,' and there leave the matter, as in science we must leave many of the most elementary and familiar phenomena inexplicable as to their causes,— is not this, I say, more philosophical than to insist upon an explanation which accepts the supernatural rather than leave the extraordinary unaccounted for? "

"As you speak," said I, resting my downcast face upon my hand, "I should speak to any patient who had confided to me the tale I have told to you."

"And yet the explanation does not wholly satisfy you? Very likely: to some phenomena there is, as yet, no explanation. Perhaps Newton himself could not explain quite to his own satisfaction why he was haunted at midnight by the spectrum of a sun; though I have no doubt that some later philosopher whose ingenuity has been stimulated by Newton's account, has, by this time, suggested a rational solution of that enigma.[1] To return to your own case. I have offered

[1] Newton's explanation is as follows : " This story I tell you to let you understand, that in the observation related by Mr. Boyle, the man's fancy probably concurred with the impression made by the sun's light to produce that phantasm of the sun which he constantly saw in bright objects, and so your question about the cause of this phantasm *involves another about the power of the fancy, which I must confess is too hard a knot for me to untie.* To place this effect in a constant motion is hard, because the sun ought then to appear perpetually. It seems rather to consist in a disposition of the sensorium to move the imagination strongly, and to be easily moved both by the imagination and by the light as often as bright objects are looked upon."— *Letter from Sir I. Newton to Locke, Lord King's Life of Locke,* vol. i. pp. 405–408.

Dr Roget (Animal and Vegetable Physiology considered with reference to Natural Theology, " Bridgewater Treatise," pp. 524, 525) thus refers to this phenomenon, which he states " all of us may experience " : —

" When the impressions are very vivid " (Dr. Roget is speaking of visual

such interpretations of the mysteries that confound you as appear to me authorized by physiological science.   Should you adduce other facts which physiological science wants the data to resolve into phenomena always natural, however rare, still

impressions), " another phenomenon often takes place, — namely, *their subsequent recurrence after a certain interval, during which they are not felt, and quite independently of any renewed application of the cause which had originally excited them.*" (I mark by italics the words which more precisely coincide with Julius Faber's explanations.)   " If, for example, we look steadfastly at the sun for a second or two, and then immediately close our eyes, the image, or spectrum, of the sun remains for a long time present to the mind, as if the light were still acting on the retina.   It then gradually fades and disappears ; but if we continue to keep the eyes shut, the *same impression will, after a certain time, recur, and again vanish :* and this phenomenon will be repeated at intervals, the sensation becoming fainter at each renewal.   It is probable that these reappearances of the image, after the light which produced the original impression has been withdrawn, are occasioned by spontaneous affections of the retina itself which are conveyed to the sensorium.   In other cases, where the impressions are less strong, the physical changes producing these changes are perhaps confined to the sensorium."

It may be said that there is this difference between the spectrum of the sun and such a phantom as that which perplexed Allen Fenwick, — namely, that the sun has been actually beheld before its visionary appearance can be reproduced, and that Allen Fenwick only imagines he has seen the apparition which repeats itself to his fancy.   " But there are grounds for the suspicion " (says Dr. Hibbert, " Philosophy of Apparitions," p. 250), " *that when ideas of vision are vivified to the height of sensation, a corresponding affection of the optic nerve accompanies the illusion.*"   Müller (" Physiology of the Senses," p. 1392, Baley's translation) states the same opinion still more strongly ; and Sir David Brewster, quoted by Dr. Hibbert (p. 251) says :   " In examining these mental impressions, I have found that they follow the motions of the eyeball exactly like the spectral impressions of luminous objects, and that they resemble them also in their apparent immobility when the eye is displaced by an external force.   If this result (which I state with much diffidence, from having only my own experience in its favour) shall be found generally true by others, it will follow that *the objects of mental contemplation may be seen as distinctly as external objects, and will occupy the same local position in the axis of vision, as if they had been formed by the agency of light.*"   Hence the impression of an image once conveyed to the senses, no matter how, whether by actual or illusory vision, is liable to renewal, " independently of any renewed application of the cause which had originally excited it," and the image can be seen in that renewal " as distinctly as external objects," for indeed " the revival of the fantastic figure really does affect those points of the retina which had been previously impressed."

hold fast to that simple saying of Goethe: 'Mysteries are not necessarily miracles.' And if all which physiological science comprehends in its experience wholly fails us, I may then hazard certain conjectures in which, by acknowledging ignorance, one is compelled o recognize the Marvellous (for as where knowledge enters, the Marvellous recedes, so where knowledge falters, the Marvellous advances); yet still, even in those conjectures, I will distinguish the Marvellous from the Supernatural. But, for the present, I advise you to accept the guess that may best quiet the fevered imagination which any bolder guess would only more excite."

"You are right," said I, rising proudly to the full height of my stature, my head erect and my heart defying. "And so let this subject be renewed no more between us. I will brood over it no more myself. I regain the unclouded realm of my human intelligence; and, in that intelligence, I mock the sorcerer and disdain the spectre."

CHAPTER XLVI.

JULIUS FABER and Amy Lloyd stayed in my house three days, and in their presence I felt a healthful sense of security and peace. Amy wished to visit her father's house, and I asked Faber, in taking her there, to seize the occasion to see Lilian, that he might communicate to me his impression of a case so peculiar. I prepared Mrs. Ashleigh for this visit by a previous note. When the old man and the child came back, both brought me comfort. Amy was charmed with Lilian, who had received her with the sweetness natural to her real character, and I loved to hear Lilian's praise from those innocent lips.

Faber's report was still more calculated to console me.

"I have seen, I have conversed with her long and familiarly. You were quite right, — there is no tendency to consumption in that exquisite, if delicate, organization; nor do I see cause for the fear to which your statement had pre-inclined me. That head is too nobly formed for any constitutional cerebral infirmity. In its organization, ideality, wonder, veneration, are large, it is true, but they are balanced by other organs, now perhaps almost dormant, but which will come into play as life passes from romance into duty. Something at this moment evidently oppresses her mind. In conversing with her, I observe abstraction, listlessness; but I am so convinced of her truthfulness, that if she has once told you she returned your affection, and pledged to you her faith, I should, in your place, rest perfectly satisfied that whatever be the cloud that now rests on her imagination, and for the time obscures the idea of yourself, it will pass away."

Faber was a believer in the main divisions of phrenology, though he did not accept all the dogmas of Gall and Spurz-heim; while, to my mind, the refutation of phrenology in its fundamental propositions had been triumphantly established by the lucid arguments of Sir W. Hamilton.[1] But when Faber rested on phrenological observations assurances in honour of Lilian, I forgot Sir W. Hamilton, and believed in phrenology. As iron girders and pillars expand and con-tract with the mere variations of temperature, so will the strongest conviction on which the human intellect rests its judgment vary with the changes of the human heart; and the building is only safe where these variations are foreseen and allowed for by a wisdom intent on self-knowledge.[2]

There was much in the affection that had sprung up be-tween Julius Faber and Amy Lloyd which touched my heart and softened all its emotions. This man, unblessed, like my-self, by conjugal and parental ties, had, in his solitary age,

[1] The summary of this distinguished lecturer's objections to phrenology is to be found in the Appendix to vol i. of "Lectures on Metaphysics," p. 404, et seq. Edition 1859.

[2] The change of length of iron girders caused by variation of temperature has not unfrequently brought down the whole edifice into which they were admitted. Good engineers and architects allow for such changes produced by temperature. In the tubular bridge across the Menai Straits, a self-acting record of the daily amount of its contraction and expansion is ingeniously contrived.

turned for solace to the love of a child, as I, in the pride of manhood, had turned to the love of woman. But his love was without fear, without jealousy, without trouble. My ·sunshine came to me in a fitful ray, through clouds that had gathered over my noon; his sunshine covered all his landscape, hallowed and hallowing by the calm of declining day.

And Amy was no common child. She had no exuberant imagination; she was haunted by no whispers from Afar; she was a creature fitted for the earth,— to accept its duties and to gladden its cares. Her tender observation, fine and tranquil, was alive to all the important household trifles by which, at the earliest age, man's allotted soother asserts her privilege to tend and to comfort. It was pleasant to see her moving so noiselessly through the rooms I had devoted to her venerable protector, knowing all his simple wants, and providing for them as if by the mechanism of a heart exquisitely moulded to the loving uses of life. Sometimes when I saw her setting his chair by the window (knowing, as I did, how much he habitually loved to be near the light) and smoothing his papers (in which he was apt to be unmethodical), placing the mark in his book when he ceased to read, divining, almost without his glance, some wish passing through his mind, and then seating herself at his feet, often with her work — which was always destined for him or for one of her absent brothers,— now and then with the one small book that she had carried with her, a selection of Bible stories compiled for·children,— sometimes when I saw her thus, how I wished that Lilian, too, could have seen her, and have compared her own ideal fantasies with those young developments of the natural heavenly Woman!

But was there nothing in that sight from which I, proud of my arid reason even in its perplexities, might have taken lessons for myself?

On the second evening of Faber's visit I brought to him the draft of deeds for the sale of his property. He had never been a man of business out of his profession; he was impatient to sell his property, and disposed to accept an offer at half its value. I insisted on taking on myself the task of

negotiator; perhaps, too, in this office I was egotistically
anxious to prove to the great physician that which he believed to be my "hallucination" had in no way obscured my
common-sense in the daily affairs of life. So I concluded,
and in a few hours, terms for his property that were only
just, but were infinitely more advantageous than had appeared
to himself to be possible. But as I approached him with the
papers, he put his finger to his lips. Amy was standing by
him with her little book in her hand, and his own Bible lay
open on the table. He was reading to her from the Sacred
Volume itself, and impressing on her the force and beauty of
one of the Parables, the adaptation of which had perplexed
her; when he had done, she kissed him, bade him good-night,
and went away to rest. Then said Faber thoughtfully, and
as if to himself more than me, —

"What a lovely bridge between old age and childhood is
religion! How intuitively the child begins with prayer and
worship on entering life, and how intuitively on quitting life
the old man turns back to prayer and worship, putting himself again side by side with the infant!"

I made no answer, but, after a pause, spoke of fines and
freeholds, title-deeds and money; and when the business on
hand was concluded, asked my learned guest if, before he
departed, he would deign to look over the pages of my ambitious Physiological Work. There were parts of it on which
I much desired his opinion, touching on subjects in which his
special studies made him an authority as high as our land
possessed.

He made me bring him the manuscript, and devoted much
of that night and the next day to its perusal.

When he gave it me back, which was not till the morning
of his departure, he commenced with eulogies on the scope of
its design, and the manner of its execution, which flattered
my vanity so much that I could not help exclaiming, "Then,
at least, there is no trace of 'hallucination' here!"

"Alas, my poor Allen! here, perhaps, hallucination, or
self-deception, is more apparent than in all the strange tales
you confided to me. For here is the hallucination of the man

seated on the shores of Nature, and who would say to its measureless sea, 'So far shalt thou go and no farther;' here is the hallucination of the creature, who, not content with exploring the laws of the Creator, ends with submitting to his interpretation of some three or four laws, in the midst of a code of which all the rest are in a language unknown to him, the powers and free-will of the Lawgiver Himself; here is the hallucination by which Nature is left Godless, because Man is left soulless. What would matter all our speculations on a Deity who would cease to exist for us when we are in the grave? Why mete out, like Archytas, the earth and the sea, and number the sands on the shore that divides them, if the end of this wisdom be a handful of dust sprinkled over a skull!

> " ' Nec quidquam tibi prodest
> Aerias tentasse domos, *animoque* rotundum
> Percurrisse polum *morituro.*'

Your book is a proof of the soul that you fail to discover. Without a soul, no man would work for a Future that begins for his fame when the breath is gone from his body. Do you remember how you saw that little child praying at the grave of her father? Shall I tell you that in her simple orisons she prayed for the benefactor,— who had cared for the orphan; who had reared over dust that tomb which, in a Christian burial-ground, is a mute but perceptible memorial of Christian hopes; that the child prayed, haughty man, for you? And you sat by, knowing nought of this; sat by, amongst the graves, troubled and tortured with ghastly doubts, vain of a reason that was sceptical of eternity, and yet shaken like a reed by a moment's marvel. Shall I tell the child to pray for you no more; that you disbelieve in a soul? If you do so, what is the efficacy of prayer? Speak, shall I tell her this? Shall the infant pray for you never more? "

I was silent; I was thrilled.

"Has it never occurred to you, who, in denying all innate perceptions as well as ideas, have passed on to deductions from which poor Locke, humble Christian that he was, would have shrunk in dismay,— has it never occurred to you as a

wonderful fact, that the easiest thing in the world to teach a
child is that which seems to metaphysical schoolmen the ab-
strusest of all problems? Read all those philosophers wrang-
ling about a First Cause, deciding on what *are* miracles, and
then again deciding that such miracles cannot be; and when
one has answered another, and left in the crucible of wisdom
a *caput mortuum* of ignorance, then turn your eyes, and look
at the infant praying to the invisible God at his mother's
knees. This idea, so miraculously abstract, of a Power the
infant has never seen, that cannot be symbolled forth and explained to him by the most erudite sage,— a Power, nevertheless, that watches over him, that hears him, that sees him,
that will carry him across the grave, that will enable him to
live on forever,— this double mystery of a Divinity and of a
Soul, the infant learns with the most facile readiness, at the
first glimpse of his reasoning faculty. Before you can teach
him a rule in addition, before you can venture to drill him
into his horn-book, he leaps, with one intuitive spring of all
his ideas, to the comprehension of the truths which are only
incomprehensible to blundering sages! And you, as you
stand before me, *dare* not say, 'Let the child pray for me no
more!' But will the Creator accept the child's prayer for
the man who refuses prayer for himself? Take my advice,—
pray! And in this counsel I do not overstep my province. I
speak not as a preacher, but as a physician. For health is a
word that comprehends our whole organization, and a just
equilibrium of all faculties and functions is the condition of
health. As in your Lilian the equilibrium is deranged by
the over-indulgence of a spiritual mysticism which withdraws
from the nutriment of duty the essential pabulum of sober
sense, so in you the resolute negation of disciplined spiritual
communion between Thought and Divinity robs imagination
of its noblest and safest vent. Thus, from opposite extremes,
you and your Lilian meet in the same region of mist and
cloud, losing sight of each other and of the true ends of life,
as her eyes only gaze on the stars and yours only bend to the
earth. Were I advising *her*, I should say: 'Your Creator has
placed the scene of your trial below, and not in the stars.'

Advising *you*, I say: 'But in the trial below, man should recognize education for heaven.' In a word, I would draw somewhat more downward her fancy, raise somewhat more upward
your reason. Take my advice then,— Pray. Your mental
system needs the support of prayer in order to preserve its
balance. In the embarrassment and confusion of your senses,
clearness of perception will come with habitual and tranquil
confidence in Him who alike rules the universe and reads the
heart. I only say here what has been said much better before
by a reasoner in whom all Students of Nature recognize a
guide. I see on your table the very volume of Bacon which
contains the passage I commend to your reflection. Here it
is. Listen: 'Take an example of a dog, and mark what a
generosity and courage he will put on when he finds himself
maintained by a man who, to him, is instead of a God, or
melior natura, which courage is manifestly such as that creat·
ure, without that confidence of a better nature than his own,
could never attain. So man, when he resteth and assureth
himself upon Divine protection and favour, gathereth a force
and faith which human nature could not obtain.'[1] You are
silent, but your gesture tells me your doubt,— a doubt which
your heart, so femininely tender, will not speak aloud lest you
should rob the old man of a hope with which your strength of
manhood dispenses,— you doubt the efficacy of prayer! Pause
and reflect, bold but candid inquirer into the laws of that
guide you call Nature. If there were no efficacy in prayer;
if prayer were as mere an illusion of superstitious fantasy
as aught against which your reason now struggles, do you
think that Nature herself would have made it amongst the
most common and facile of all her dictates? Do you believe
that if there really did not exist that tie between Man and
his Maker — that link between life here and life hereafter
which is found in what we call Soul alone — that wherever
you look through the universe, you would behold a child at
prayer? Nature inculcates nothing that is superfluous. Na-

---

[1] Bacon's "Essay on Atheism." This quotation is made with admirable
felicity and force by Dr. Whewell, page 378 of Bridgewater Treatise on Astronomy and General Physics considered with reference to Natural Theology

ture does not impel the leviathan or the lion, the eagle or the moth, to pray; she impels only man. Why? Because man only has soul, and Soul seeks to commune with the Everlasting, as a fountain struggles up to its source. Burn your book. It would found you a reputation for learning and intellect and courage, I allow; but learning and intellect and courage wasted against a truth, like spray against a rock! A truth valuable to the world, the world will never part with. You will not injure the truth, but you will mislead and may destroy many, whose best security is in the truth which you so eruditely insinuate to be a fable. Soul and Hereafter are the heritage of all men; the humblest journeyman in those streets, the pettiest trader behind those counters, have in those beliefs their prerogatives of royalty. You would dethrone and embrute the lords of the earth by your theories. For my part, having given the greater part of my life to the study and analysis of facts, I would rather be the author of the tritest homily, or the baldest poem, that inculcated that imperishable essence of the soul to which I have neither scalpel nor probe, than be the founder of the subtlest school, or the framer of the loftiest verse, that robbed my fellow-men of their faith in a spirit that eludes the dissecting-knife,— in a being that escapes the grave-digger. Burn your book! Accept This Book instead; Read and Pray."

He placed his Bible in my hand, embraced me, and, an hour afterwards, the old man and the child left my hearth solitary once more.

CHAPTER XLVII.

THAT night, as I sat in my study, very thoughtful and very mournful, I resolved all that Julius Faber had said; and the impression his words had produced became gradually weaker and weaker, as my reason, naturally combative, rose up with all the replies which my philosophy suggested. No; if my

imagination had really seduced and betrayed me into monstrous credulities, it was clear that the best remedy to such
morbid tendencies towards the Superstitious was in the severe
exercise of the faculties most opposed to Superstition,— in
the culture of pure reasoning, in the science of absolute fact.
Accordingly, I placed before me the very book which Julius
Faber had advised me to burn; I forced all my powers of
mind to go again over the passages which contained the doctrines that his admonition had censured; and before daybreak, I had stated the substance of his argument, and the
logical reply to it, in an elaborate addition to my chapter on
"Sentimental Philosophers." While thus rejecting the purport of his parting counsels, I embodied in another portion of
my work his views on my own "illusions;" and as here my
common-sense was in concord with his, I disposed of all my
own previous doubts in an addition to my favourite chapter
"On the Cheats of the Imagination." And when the pen
dropped from my hand, and the day-star gleamed through the
window, my heart escaped from the labour of my mind, and
flew back to the image of Lilian. The pride of the philosopher died out of me, the sorrow of the man reigned supreme,
and I shrank from the coming of the sun, despondent.

CHAPTER XLVIII.

NOT till the law had completed its proceedings, and satisfied the public mind as to the murder of Sir Philip Derval,
were the remains of the deceased consigned to the family
mausoleum. The funeral was, as may be supposed, strictly
private, and when it was over, the excitement caused by an
event so tragical and singular subsided. New topics engaged
the public talk, and — in my presence, at least — the delicate
consideration due to one whose name had been so painfully
mixed up in the dismal story forbore a topic which I could
not be expected to hear without distressful emotion. Mrs.

Ashleigh I saw frequently at my own house; she honestly confessed that Lilian had not shown that grief at the cancelling of our engagement which would alone justify Mrs. Ashleigh in asking me again to see her daughter, and retract my conclusions against our union. She said that Lilian was quiet, not uncheerful, never spoke of me nor of Margrave, but seemed absent and pre-occupied as before, taking pleasure in nothing that had been wont to please her; not in music, nor books, nor that tranquil pastime which women call work, and in which they find excuse to meditate, in idleness, their own fancies. She rarely stirred out, even in the garden; when she did, her eyes seemed to avoid the house in which Margrave had lodged, and her steps the old favourite haunt by the Monks' Well. She would remain silent for long hours together, but the silence did not appear melancholy. For the rest, her health was more than usually good. Still Mrs. Ashleigh persisted in her belief that, sooner or later, Lilian would return to her former self, her former sentiments for me; and she entreated me not, as yet, to let the world know that our engagement was broken off. "For if," she said, with good sense, "if it should prove not to be broken off, only suspended, and afterwards happily renewed, there will be two stories to tell when no story be needed. Besides, I should dread the effect on Lilian, if offensive gossips babbled to her on a matter that would excite so much curiosity as the rupture of a union in which our neighbours have taken so general an interest."

I had no reason to refuse acquiescence in Mrs. Ashleigh's request, but I did not share in her hopes; I felt that the fair prospects of my life were blasted; I could never love another, never wed another; I resigned myself to a solitary hearth, rejoiced, at least, that Margrave had not revisited at Mrs. Ashleigh's,—had not, indeed, reappeared in the town. He was still staying with Strahan, who told me that his guest had ensconced himself in Forman's old study, and amused himself with reading — though not for long at a time — the curious old books and manuscripts found in the library, or climbing trees like a schoolboy, and familiarizing himself with the deer and the cattle, which would group round him quite tame, and feed from his hand. Was this the description of a criminal? But if Sir Philip's assertion were really true; if the criminal were man without soul; if without soul, man would have no conscience, never be troubled by repentance, and the vague dread of a future world,—why, then, should not the criminal be gay despite his crimes, as the white bear gambols as friskly after his meal on human flesh? These questions would haunt me, despite my determination to accept as the right solution of all marvels the construction put on my narrative by Julius Faber.

Days passed; I saw and heard nothing of Margrave. I began half to hope that, in the desultory and rapid changes of mood and mind which characterized his restless nature, he had forgotten my existence.

One morning I went out early on my rounds, when I met Strahan unexpectedly.

"I was in search of you," he said, "for more than one person has told me that you are looking ill and jaded. So you are! And the town now is hot and unhealthy. You must come to Derval Court for a week or so. You can ride into town every day to see your patients. Don't refuse. Margrave, who is still with me, sends all kind messages, and bade me say that *he* entreats you to come to the house at which he also is a guest!"

I started. What had the Scin-Læca required of me, and obtained to that condition my promise? "If you are asked to the house at which I also am a guest, you will come; you will meet and converse with me as guest speaks to guest in the house of a host!" Was this one of the coincidences which my reason was bound to accept as coincidences, and nothing more? Tut, tut! Was I returning again to my "hallucinations"? Granting that Faber and common-sense were in the right, what was this Margrave? A man to whose friendship, acuteness, and energy I was under the deepest obligations,—to whom I was indebted for active services that had saved my life from a serious danger, acquitted my honour of a horrible suspicion. "I thank you," I said to Strahan, "I will come; not, indeed, for a week, but, at all events, for a day or two."

"That's right; I will call for you in the carriage at six o'clock. You will have done your day's work by then?"

"Yes; I will so arrange."

On our way to Derval Court that evening, Strahan talked much about Margrave, of whom, nevertheless, he seemed to be growing weary.

"His high spirits are too much for one," said he; "and then so restless,— so incapable of sustained quiet conversation. And, clever though he is, he can't help me in the least about the new house I shall build. He has no notion of construction. I don't think he could build a barn."

"I thought you did not like to demolish the old house, and would content yourself with pulling down the more ancient part of it?"

"True. At first it seemed a pity to destroy so handsome a mansion; but you see, since poor Sir Philip's manuscript, on which he set such store, has been too mutilated, I fear, to allow me to effect his wish with regard to it, I think I ought at least scrupulously to obey his other whims. And, besides, I don't know, there are odd noises about the old house. I don't believe in haunted houses; still there is something dreary in strange sounds at the dead of night, even if made by rats, or winds through decaying rafters. You, I remember at college, had a taste for architecture, and can draw plans. I wish to follow out Sir Philip's design, but on a smaller scale, and with more attention to comfort."

Thus he continued to run on, satisfied to find me a silent and attentive listener. We arrived at the mansion an hour before sunset, the westering light shining full against the many windows cased in mouldering pilasters, and making the general dilapidation of the old place yet more mournfully evident.

It was but a few minutes to the dinner-hour. I went up at once to the room appropriated to me,— not the one I had before occupied. Strahan had already got together a new es-

tablishment. I was glad to find in the servant who attended
me an old acquaintance. He had been in my own employ
when I first settled at L——, and left me to get married.
He and his wife were now both in Strahan's service. He
spoke warmly of his new master and his contentment with
his situation, while he unpacked my carpet-bag and assisted
me to change my dress. But the chief object of his talk and
his praise was Mr. Margrave.

"Such a bright young gentleman, like the first fine day in
May!"

When I entered the drawing-room, Margrave and Strahan
were both there. The former was blithe and genial, as usual,
in his welcome. At dinner, and during the whole evening
till we retired severally to our own rooms, he was the principal talker,— recounting incidents of travel, always very
loosely strung together, jesting, good-humouredly enough, at
Strahan's sudden hobby for building, then putting questions
to me about mutual acquaintances, but never waiting for an
answer; and every now and then, as if at random, startling
us with some brilliant aphorism, or some suggestion drawn
from abstract science or unfamiliar erudition. The whole
effect was sparkling, but I could well understand that, if
long continued, it would become oppressive. The soul has
need of pauses of repose,— intervals of escape, not only from
the flesh, but even from the mind. A man of the loftiest intellect will experience times when mere intellect not only
fatigues him, but amidst its most original conceptions, amidst
its proudest triumphs, has a something trite and commonplace compared with one of those vague intimations of a
spiritual destiny which are not within the ordinary domain
of reason; and, gazing abstractedly into space, will leave
suspended some problem of severest thought, or uncompleted
some golden palace of imperial poetry, to indulge in hazy
reveries, that do not differ from those of an innocent, quiet
child! The soul has a long road to travel — from time
through eternity. It demands its halting hours of contemplation. Contemplation is serene. But with such wants of
an immortal immaterial spirit, Margrave had no fellowship,

19

no sympathy; and for myself, I need scarcely add that the lines I have just traced I should not have written at the date at which my narrative has now arrived.

———◆———

CHAPTER XLIX.

I HAD no case that necessitated my return to L—— the following day. The earlier hours of the forenoon I devoted to Strahan and his building plans. Margrave flitted in and out of the room fitfully as an April sunbeam, sometimes flinging himself on a sofa, and reading for a few minutes one of the volumes of the ancient mystics, in which Sir Philip's library was so rich. I remember it was a volume of Proclus. He read that crabbed and difficult Greek with a fluency that surprised me. "I picked up the ancient Greek," said he, "years ago, in learning the modern." But the book soon tired him; then he would come and disturb us, archly enjoying Strahan's peevishness at interruption; then he would throw open the window and leap down, chanting one of his wild savage airs; and in another moment he was half hid under the drooping boughs of a broad lime-tree, amidst the antlers of deer that gathered fondly round him. In the afternoon my host was called away to attend some visitors of importance, and I found myself on the sward before the house, right in view of the mausoleum and alone with Margrave.

I turned my eyes from that dumb House of Death wherein rested the corpse of the last lord of the soil, so strangely murdered, with a strong desire to speak out to Margrave the doubts respecting himself that tortured me. But — setting aside the promise to the contrary, which I had given, or dreamed I had given, to the Luminous Shadow — to fulfil that desire would have been impossible,— impossible to any one gazing on that radiant youthful face! I think I see him now as I saw him then: a white doe, that even my presence could not scare away from him, clung lovingly to his side, looking up at him with her soft eyes. He stood there like the incarnate principle of mythological sensuous life. I have before applied to him that illustration; let the repetition be pardoned. Impossible, I repeat it, to say to that creature, face to face, "Art thou the master of demoniac arts, and the instigator of secret murder?" As if from redundant happiness within himself, he was humming, or rather cooing, a strain of music, so sweet, so wildly sweet, and so unlike the music one hears from tutored lips in crowded rooms! I passed my hand over my forehead in bewilderment and awe.

"Are there," I said unconsciously, — "are there, indeed, such prodigies in Nature?"

"Nature!" he cried, catching up the word; "talk to me of Nature! Talk of her, the wondrous blissful mother! Mother I may well call her. I am her spoiled child, her darling! But oh, to die, ever to die, ever to lose sight of Nature! — to rot senseless, whether under these turfs or within those dead walls — "

I could not resist the answer, —

"Like yon murdered man! murdered, and by whom?"

"By whom? I thought that was clearly proved."

"The hand was proved; what influence moved the hand?"

"Tush! the poor wretch spoke of a Demon. Who can tell? Nature herself is a grand destroyer. See that pretty bird, in its beak a writhing worm! All Nature's children live to take life; none, indeed, so lavishly as man. What hecatombs slaughtered, not to satisfy the irresistible sting of hunger, but for the wanton ostentation of a feast, which he may scarcely taste, or for the mere sport that he finds in destroying! We speak with dread of the beasts of prey: what beast of prey is so dire a ravager as man, — so cruel and so treacherous? Look at yon flock of sheep, bred and fattened for the shambles; and this hind that I caress, — if I were the park-keeper, and her time for my bullet had come, would you think her life was the safer because, in my own idle whim, I had tamed her to trust to the hand raised to slay her?"

"It is true," said I, — "a grim truth. Nature, on the surface so loving and so gentle, is full of terror in her deeps when our thought descends into their abyss!"

Strahan now joined us with a party of country visitors.

"Margrave is the man to show you the beauties of this park," said he. "Margrave knows every bosk and dingle, twisted old thorn-tree, or opening glade, in its intricate, undulating ground."

Margrave seemed delighted at this proposition; and as he led us through the park, though the way was long, though the sun was fierce, no one seemed fatigued. For the pleasure he felt in pointing out detached beauties which escaped an ordinary eye was contagious. He did not talk as talks the poet or the painter; but at some lovely effect of light amongst the tremulous leaves, some sudden glimpse of a sportive rivulet below, he would halt, point it out to us in silence, and with a kind of childlike ecstasy in his own bright face, that seemed to reflect the life and the bliss of the blithe summer day itself.

Thus seen, all my doubts in his dark secret nature faded away,— all my horror, all my hate; it was impossible to resist the charm that breathed round him, not to feel a tender, affectionate yearning towards him as to some fair happy child. Well might he call himself the Darling of Nature. Was he not the mysterious likeness of that awful Mother, beautiful as Apollo in one aspect, direful as Typhon in another?

CHAPTER L.

"WHAT a strange-looking cane you have, sir!" said a little girl, who was one of the party, and who had entwined her arm round Margrave's. "Let me look at it."

"Yes," said Strahan, "that cane, or rather walking-staff, is worth looking at. Margrave bought it in Egypt, and declares that it is very ancient."

This staff seemed constructed from a reed: looked at, it
seemed light, in the hand it felt heavy; it was of a pale,
faded yellow, wrought with black rings at equal distances,
and graven with half obliterated characters that seemed hiero-
glyphic. I remembered to have seen Margrave with it before,
but I had never noticed it with any attention until now, when
it was passed from hand to hand. At the head of the cane
there was a large unpolished stone of a dark blue.

"Is this a pebble or a jewel?" asked one of the party.

"I cannot tell you its name or nature," said Margrave;
"but it is said to cure the bite of serpents,[1] and has other
supposed virtues,— a talisman, in short."

[1] The following description of a stone at Corfu, celebrated as an antidote
to the venom of the serpent's bite, was given to me by an eminent scholar
and legal functionary in that island : —

DESCRIPTION OF THE BLUESTONE. — This stone is of an oval shape $1\frac{4}{10}$ in.
long, $\frac{7}{10}$ broad, $\frac{3}{10}$ thick, and, having been broken formerly, is now set in gold.

When a person is bitten by a poisonous snake, the bite must be opened
by a cut of a lancet or razor longways, and the stone applied within twenty-
four hours. The stone then attaches itself firmly on the wound, and when
it has done its office falls off; the cure is then complete. The stone
must then be thrown into milk, whereupon it vomits the poison it has absorbed, which remains green on the top of the milk, and the stone is then
again fit for use.

This stone has been from time immemorial in the family of Ventura, of
Corfu, a house of Italian origin, and is notorious, so that peasants immediately apply for its aid. Its virtue has not been impaired by the fracture. Its
nature or composition is unknown.

In a case where two were stung at the same time by serpents, the stone was
applied to one, who recovered ; but the other, for whom it could not be used,
died.

It never failed but once, and then it was applied *after* the twenty-four
hours.

Its colour is so dark as not to be distinguished from black.

                                        P. M. COLQUHOUN.

Corfu, 7th Nov., 1860.

Sir Emerson Tennent, in his popular and excellent work on Ceylon, gives
an account of "snake stones" apparently similar to the one at Corfu, except
that they are "intensely black and highly polished," and which are applied,
in much the same manner, to the wounds inflicted by the cobra-capella.

QUERY. — Might it not be worth while to ascertain the chemical proper

He here placed the staff in my hands, and bade me look at it with care.   Then he changed the conversation and renewed the way, leaving the staff with me, till suddenly I forced it back on him.   I could not have explained why, but its touch, as it warmed in my clasp, seemed to send through my whole frame a singular thrill, and a sensation as if I no longer felt my own weight,— as if I walked on air.

Our rambles came to a close; the visitors went away; I re-entered the house through the sash-window of Forman's study.   Margrave threw his hat and staff on the table, and amused himself with examining minutely the tracery on the mantelpiece.   Strahan and myself left him thus occupied, and, going into the adjoining library, resumed our task of examining the plans for the new house.   I continued to draw outlines and sketches of various alterations, tending to sim-plify and contract Sir Philip's general design.   Margrave soon joined us, and this time took his seat patiently beside our table, watching me use ruler and compass with unwonted attention.

"I wish I could draw," he said; "but I can do nothing useful."

"Rich men like you," said Strahan, peevishly, "can engage others, and are better employed in rewarding good artists than in making bad drawings themselves."

"Yes, I can employ others; and — Fenwick, when you have finished with Strahan I will ask permission to employ you, though without reward; the task I would impose will not take you a minute."

He then threw himself back in his chair, and seemed to fall into a doze.

The dressing-bell rang; Strahan put away the plans,— in-deed, they were now pretty well finished and decided on.

Margrave woke up as our host left the room to dress, and drawing me towards another table in the room, placed before me one of his favourite mystic books, and, pointing to an old woodcut, said,—

ties of these stones, and, if they be efficacious in the extraction of venom con-veyed by a bite, might they not be as successful if applied to the bite of a mad dog as to that of a cobra-capella ?

"I will ask you to copy this for me; it pretends to be a fac-simile of Solomon's famous seal. I have a whimsical desire to have a copy of it. You observe two triangles interlaced and inserted in a circle? — the pentacle, in short. Yes, just so. You need not add the astrological characters: they are the senseless superfluous accessories of the dreamer who wrote the book. But the pentacle itself has an intelligible meaning; it belongs to the only universal language, the language of symbol, in which all races that think — around, and above, and below us — can establish communion of thought. If in the external universe any one constructive principle can be detected, it is the geometrical; and in every part of the world in which magic pretends to a written character, I find that its hieroglyphics are geometrical figures. Is it not laughable that the most positive of all the sciences should thus lend its angles and circles to the use of — what shall I call it ? — the ignorance? — ay, that is the word — the ignorance of dealers in magic? "

He took up the paper, on which I had hastily described the triangles and the circle, and left the room, chanting the serpent-charmer's song.

CHAPTER LI.

WHEN we separated for the night, which we did at eleven o'clock, Margrave said,—

"Good-night and good-by. I must leave you to-morrow, Strahan, and before your usual hour for rising. I took the liberty of requesting one of your men to order me a chaise from L——. Pardon my seeming abruptness, but I always avoid long leave-takings, and I had fixed the date of my departure almost as soon as I accepted your invitation."

"I have no right to complain. The place must be dull indeed to a gay young fellow like you. It is dull even to me. I am meditating flight already. Are you going back to L——? "

"Not even for such things as I left at my lodgings. When I settle somewhere and can give an address, I shall direct them to be sent to me. There are, I hear, beautiful patches of scenery towards the north, only known to pedestrian tourists. I am a good walker; and you know, Fenwick, that I am also a child of Nature. Adieu to you both; and many thanks to you, Strahan, for your hospitality."

He left the room.

"I am not sorry he is going," said Strahan, after a pause, and with a quick breath as if of relief. "Do you not feel that he exhausts one? An excess of oxygen, as you would say in a lecture."

I was alone in my own chamber; I felt indisposed for bed and for sleep; the curious conversation I had held with Margrave weighed on me. In that conversation, we had indirectly touched upon the prodigies which I had not brought myself to speak of with frank courage, and certainly nothing in Margrave's manner had betrayed consciousness of my suspicions; on the contrary, the open frankness with which he evinced his predilection for mystic speculation, or uttered his more unamiable sentiments, rather tended to disarm than encourage belief in gloomy secrets or sinister powers. And as he was about to quit the neighbourhood, he would not again see Lilian, not even enter the town of L——. Was I to ascribe this relief from his presence to the promise of the Shadow; or was I not rather right in battling firmly against any grotesque illusion, and accepting his departure as a simple proof that my jealous fears had been amongst my other chimeras, and that as he had really only visited Lilian out of friendship to me, in my peril, so he might, with his characteristic acuteness, have guessed my jealousy, and ceased his visits from a kindly motive delicately concealed? And might not the same motive now have dictated the words which were intended to assure me that L—— contained no attractions to tempt him to return to it? Thus, gradually soothed and cheered by the course to which my reflections led me, I continued to muse for hours. At length, looking at my watch, I was surprised to find it was the second hour after midnight.

I was just about to rise from my chair to undress, and secure some hours of sleep, when the well-remembered cold wind passed through the room, stirring the roots of my hair; and before me stood, against the wall, the Luminous Shadow.

"Rise and follow me," said the voice, sounding much nearer than it had ever done before.

And at those words I rose mechanically, and like a sleep-walker.

"Take up the light."

I took it. The Scin-Læca glided along the wall towards the threshold, and motioned me to open the door. I did so. The Shadow flitted on through the corridor. I followed, with hushed footsteps, down a small stair into Forman's study. In all my subsequent proceedings, about to be narrated, the Shadow guided me, sometimes by voice, sometimes by sign. I obeyed the guidance, not only unresistingly, but without a desire to resist. I was unconscious either of curiosity or of awe, — only of a calm and passive indifference, neither pleasurable nor painful. In this obedience, from which all will seemed extracted, I took into my hands the staff which I had examined the day before, and which lay on the table, just where Margrave had cast it on re-entering the house. I unclosed the shutter to the casement, lifted the sash, and, with the light in my left hand, the staff in my right, stepped forth into the garden. The night was still; the flame of the candle scarcely trembled in the air; the Shadow moved on before me towards the old pavilion described in an earlier part of this narrative, and of which the mouldering doors stood wide open. I followed the Shadow into the pavilion, up the crazy stair to the room above, with its four great blank unglazed windows, or rather arcades, north, south, east, and west. I halted on the middle of the floor: right before my eyes, through the vista made by breath-less boughs, stood out from the moonlit air the dreary mauso-leum. Then, at the command conveyed to me, I placed the candle on a wooden settle, touched a spring in the handle of the staff; a lid flew back, and I drew from the hollow, first a lump of some dark bituminous substance, next a smaller slender wand of polished steel, of which the point was tipped with a translucent material, which appeared to me like crystal. Bending down, still obedient to the direction conveyed to me, I described on the floor with the lump of bitumen (if I may so call it) the figure of the pentacle with the interlaced triangles, in a circle nine feet in diameter, just as I had drawn it for Margrave the evening before. The material used made the figure perceptible, in a dark colour of mingled black and red. I applied the flame of the candle to the circle, and immediately it became lambent with a low steady splendour that rose about an inch from the floor; and gradually from this light there emanated a soft, gray, transparent mist and a faint but exquisite odour. I stood in the midst of the circle, and within the circle also, close by my side, stood the Scin-Læca, — no longer reflected on the wall, but apart from it, erect, rounded into more integral and distinct form, yet impalpable, and from it there breathed an icy air. Then lifting the wand, the broader end of which rested in the palm of my hand, the two forefingers closing lightly over it in a line parallel with the point, I directed it towards the wide aperture before me, fronting the mausoleum. I repeated aloud some words whispered to me in a language I knew not: those words I would not trace on this paper, could I remember them. As they came to a close, I heard a howl from the watch-dog in the yard, — a dismal, lugubrious howl. Other dogs in the distant village caught up the sound, and bayed in a dirge-like chorus; and the howling went on louder and louder. Again strange words were whispered to me, and I repeated them in mechanical submission; and when they, too, were ended, I felt the ground tremble beneath me, and as my eyes looked straight forward down the vista, that, stretching from the casement, was bounded by the solitary mausoleum, vague formless shadows seemed to pass across the moonlight, — below, along the sward, above, in the air; and then suddenly a terror, not before conceived, came upon me.

And a third time words were whispered; but though I knew no more of their meaning than I did of those that had preceded them, I felt a repugnance to utter them aloud. Mutely

I turned towards the Scin-Læca, and the expression of its face was menacing and terrible; my will became yet more compelled to the control imposed upon it, and my lips commenced the formula again whispered into my ear, when I heard distinctly a voice of warning and of anguish, that murmured "Hold!" I knew the voice; it was Lilian's. I paused; I turned towards the quarter from which the voice had come, and in the space afar I saw the features, the form of Lilian. Her arms were stretched towards me in supplication, her countenance was deadly pale, and anxious with unutterable distress. The whole image seemed in unison with the voice, — the look, the attitude, the gesture of one who sees another in deadly peril, and cries, "Beware!"

This apparition vanished in a moment; but that moment sufficed to free my mind from the constraint which had before enslaved it. I dashed the wand to the ground, sprang from the circle, rushed from the place. How I got into my own room I can remember not, — I know not; I have a vague reminiscence of some intervening wandering, of giant trees, of shroud-like moonlight, of the Shining Shadow and its angry aspect, of the blind walls and the iron door of the House of the Dead, of spectral images, — a confused and dreary phantasmagoria. But all I can recall with distinctness is the sight of my own hueless face in the mirror in my own still room, by the light of the white moon through the window; and, sinking down, I said to myself, "This, at least, is an hallucination or a dream!"

CHAPTER LII.

A HEAVY sleep came over me at daybreak, but I did not undress nor go to bed. The sun was high in the heavens when, on waking, I saw the servant who had attended me bustling about the room.

"I beg your pardon, sir, I am afraid I disturbed you; but I have been three times to see if you were not coming down, and I found you so soundly asleep I did not like to wake you. Mr. Strahan has finished breakfast, and gone out riding; Mr. Margrave has left,— left before six o'clock."

"Ah, he said he was going early."

"Yes, sir; and he seemed so cross when he went. I could never have supposed so pleasant a gentleman could put himself into such a passion!"

"What was the matter?"

"Why, his walking-stick could not be found; it was not in the hall. He said he had left it in the study; we could not find it there. At last he found it himself in the old summer-house, and said — I beg pardon — he said he was sure you had taken it there: that some one, at all events, had been meddling with it. However, I am very glad it was found, since he seems to set such store on it."

"Did Mr. Margrave go himself into the summer-house to look for it?"

"Yes, sir; no one else would have thought of such a place; no one likes to go there, even in the daytime."

"Why?"

"Why, sir, they say it is haunted since poor Sir Philip's death; and, indeed, there are strange noises in every part of the house. I am afraid you had a bad night, sir," continued the servant, with evident curiosity, glancing towards the bed, which I had not pressed, and towards the evening-dress which, while he spoke, I was rapidly changing for that which I habitually wore in the morning. "I hope you did not feel yourself ill?"

"No! but it seems I fell asleep in my chair."

"Did you hear, sir, how the dogs howled about two o'clock in the morning? They woke me. Very frightful!"

"The moon was at her full. Dogs will bay at the moon."

I felt relieved to think that I should not find Strahan in the breakfast-room; and hastening through the ceremony of a meal which I scarcely touched, I went out into the park unobserved, and creeping round the copses and into the neglected gardens, made my way to the pavilion. I mounted the stairs; I looked on the floor of the upper room; yes, there still was the black figure of the pentacle, the circle. So, then, it was not a dream! Till then I had doubted. Or might it not still be so far a dream that I had walked in my sleep, and with an imagination preoccupied by my conversations with Margrave, — by the hieroglyphics on the staff I had handled, by the very figure associated with superstitious practices which I had copied from some weird book at his request, by all the strange impressions previously stamped on my mind, — might I not, in truth, have carried thither in sleep the staff, described the circle, and all the rest been but visionary delusion? Surely, surely, so common-sense, and so Julius Faber would interpret the riddles that perplexed me! Be that as it may, my first thought was to efface the marks on the floor. I found this easier than I had ventured to hope. I rubbed the circle and the pentacle away from the boards with the sole of my foot, leaving but an undistinguishable smudge behind. I know not why, but I felt the more nervously anxious to remove all such evidences of my nocturnal visit to that room, because Margrave had so openly gone thither to seek for the staff, and had so rudely named me to the servant as having meddled with it. Might he not awake some suspicion against me? Suspicion, what of? I knew not, but I feared!

The healthful air of day gradually nerved my spirits and relieved my thoughts. But the place had become hateful to me. I resolved not to wait for Strahan's return, but to walk back to L——, and leave a message for my host. It was sufficient excuse that I could not longer absent myself from my patients; accordingly I gave directions to have the few things which I had brought with me sent to my house by any servant who might be going to L——, and was soon pleased to find myself outside the park-gates and on the high-road.

I had not gone a mile before I met Strahan on horseback. He received my apologies for not waiting his return to bid him farewell without observation, and, dismounting, led his horse and walked beside me on my road. I saw that there was something on his mind; at last he said, looking down,—

"Did you hear the dogs howl last night?"

"Yes! the full moon!"

"You were awake, then, at the time. Did you hear any other sound? Did you see anything?"

"What should I hear or see?"

Strahan was silent for some moments; then he said, with great seriousness,—

"I could not sleep when I went to bed last night; I felt feverish and restless. Somehow or other, Margrave got into my head, mixed up in some strange way with Sir Philip Derval. I heard the dogs howl, and at the same time, or rather a few minutes later, I felt the whole house tremble, as a frail corner-house in London seems to tremble at night when a carriage is driven past it. The howling had then ceased, and ceased as suddenly as it had begun. I felt a vague, superstitious alarm; I got up, and went to my window, which was unclosed (it is my habit to sleep with my windows open); the moon was very bright, and I saw, I declare I saw along the green alley that leads from the old part of the house to the mausoleum — No, I will not say what I saw or believed I saw,— you would ridicule me, and justly. But, whatever it might be, on the earth without or in the fancy within my brain, I was so terrified, that I rushed back to my bed, and buried my face in my pillow. I would have come to you; but I did not dare to stir. I have been riding hard all the morning in order to recover my nerves. But I dread sleeping again under that roof, and now that you and Margrave leave me, I shall go this very day to London. I hope all that I have told you is no bad sign of any coming disease; blood to the head, eh?"

"No; but imagination overstrained can produce wondrous effects. You do right to change the scene. Go to London at once, amuse yourself, and — "

"Not return, till the old house is razed to the ground. That is my resolve. You approve? That's well. All success to you, Fenwick. I will canter back and get my portmanteau ready and the carriage out, in time for the five o'clock train."

So then he, too, had seen — what? I did not dare and I did not desire to ask him. But he, at least, was not walking in his sleep! Did we both dream, or neither?

———◆———

CHAPTER LIII.

THERE is an instance of the absorbing tyranny of every-day life which must have struck all such of my readers as have ever experienced one of those portents which are so at variance with every-day life, that the ordinary epithet bestowed on them is "supernatural."

And be my readers few or many, there will be no small proportion of them to whom once, at least, in the course of their existence, a something strange and *eerie* has occurred, — a something which perplexed and baffled rational conjecture, and struck on those chords which vibrate to superstition. It may have been only a dream unaccountably verified, — an undefinable presentiment or forewarning; but up from such slighter and vaguer tokens of the realm of marvel, up to the portents of ghostly apparitions or haunted chambers, I believe that the greater number of persons arrived at middle age, however instructed the class, however civilized the land, however sceptical the period, to which they belong, have either in themselves experienced, or heard recorded by intimate associates whose veracity they accept as indisputable in all ordinary transactions of life, phenomena which are not to be solved by the wit that mocks them, nor, perhaps, always and entirely, to the contentment of the reason or the philosophy that explains them away. Such phenomena, I say, are infinitely more numerous than would appear from the instances currently quoted and dismissed with a jest; for few of those who have witnessed them are disposed to own it, and they who only hear of them through others, however trustworthy, would not impugn their character for common-sense

by professing a belief to which common-sense is a merciless
persecutor.　But he who reads my assertion in the quiet of
his own room, will perhaps pause, ransack his memory, and
find there, in some dark corner which he excludes from "the
babbling and remorseless day," a pale recollection that proves
the assertion not untrue.

And it is, I say, an instance of the absorbing tyranny of
every-day life, that whenever some such startling incident
disturbs its regular tenor of thought and occupation, that
same every-day life hastens to bury in its sands the object
which has troubled its surface; the more unaccountable, the
more prodigious, has been the phenomenon which has scared
and astounded us, the more, with involuntary effort, the mind
seeks to rid itself of an enigma which might disease the reason that tries to solve it.　We go about our mundane business
with renewed avidity; we feel the necessity of proving to ourselves that we are still sober, practical men, and refuse to be
unfitted for the world which we know, by unsolicited visitations from worlds into which every glimpse is soon lost amid
shadows.　And it amazes us to think how soon such incidents, though not actually forgotten, though they can be
recalled — and recalled too vividly for health — at our will,
are nevertheless thrust, as it were, out of the mind's sight as
we cast into lumber-rooms the crutches and splints that remind us of a broken limb which has recovered its strength
and tone.　It is a felicitous peculiarity in our organization,
which all members of my profession will have noticed, how
soon, when a bodily pain is once passed, it becomes erased
from the recollection, — how soon and how invariably the
mind refuses to linger over and recall it.　No man freed an
hour before from a raging toothache, the rack of a neuralgia,
seats himself in his armchair to recollect and ponder upon
the anguish he has undergone.　It is the same with certain
afflictions of the mind, — not with those that strike on our
affections, or blast our fortunes, overshadowing our whole
future with a sense of loss; but where a trouble or calamity
has been an accident, an episode in our wonted life, where it
affects ourselves alone, where it is attended with a sense of

shame and humiliation, where the pain of recalling it seems idle, and if indulged would almost madden us,— agonies of that kind we do not brood over as we do over the death or falsehood of beloved friends, or the train of events by which we are reduced from wealth to penury. No one, for instance, who has escaped from a shipwreck, from the brink of a precipice, from the jaws of a tiger, spends his days and nights in reviving his terrors past, re-imagining dangers not to occur again, or, if they do occur, from which the experience undergone can suggest no additional safeguards. The current of our life, indeed, like that of the rivers, is most rapid in the midmost channel, where all streams are alike comparatively slow in the depth and along the shores in which each life, as each river, has a character peculiar to itself. And hence, those who would sail *with* the tide of the world, as those who sail with the tide of a river, hasten to take the middle of the stream, as those who sail *against* the tide are found clinging to the shore. I returned to my habitual duties and avocations with renewed energy; I did not suffer my thoughts to dwell on the dreary wonders that had haunted me, from the evening I first met Sir Philip Derval to the morning on which I had quitted the house of his heir; whether realities or hallucinations, no guess of mine could unravel such marvels, and no prudence of mine guard me against their repetition. But I had no fear that they would be repeated, any more than the man who had gone through shipwreck, or the hairbreadth escape from a fall down a glacier, fears again to be found in a similar peril. Margrave had departed, whither I knew not, and, with his departure, ceased all sense of his influence. A certain calm within me, a tranquillizing feeling of relief, seemed to me like a pledge of permanent delivery.

But that which did accompany and haunt me, through all my occupations and pursuits, was the melancholy remembrance of the love I had lost in Lilian. I heard from Mrs. Ashleigh, who still frequently visited me, that her daughter seemed much in the same quiet state of mind,— perfectly reconciled to our separation, seldom mentioning my name; if mentioning it, with indifference; the only thing remarkable in her state was her aversion to all society, and a kind of lethargy that would come over her, often in the daytime. She would suddenly fall into sleep and so remain for hours, but a sleep that seemed very serene and tranquil, and from which she woke of herself. She kept much within her own room, and always retired to it when visitors were announced.

Mrs. Ashleigh began reluctantly to relinquish the persuasion she had so long and so obstinately maintained, that this state of feeling towards myself — and, indeed, this general change in Lilian — was but temporary and abnormal; she began to allow that it was best to drop all thoughts of a renewed engagement, — a future union. I proposed to see Lilian in her presence and in my professional capacity; perhaps some physical cause, especially for this lethargy, might be detected and removed. Mrs. Ashleigh owned to me that the idea had occurred to herself: she had sounded Lilian upon it: but her daughter had so resolutely opposed it, — had said with so quiet a firmness "that all being over between us, a visit from me would be unwelcome and painful,"— that Mrs. Ashleigh felt that an interview thus deprecated would only confirm estrangement. One day, in calling, she asked my advice whether it would not be better to try the effect of change of air and scene, and, in some other place, some other medical opinion might be taken? I approved of this suggestion with unspeakable sadness.

"And," said Mrs. Ashleigh, shedding tears, "if that experiment prove unsuccessful, I will write and let you know; and we must then consider what to say to the world as a reason why the marriage is broken off. I can render this more easy by staying away. I will not return to L—— till the matter has ceased to be the topic of talk, and at a distance any excuse will be less questioned and seem more natural. But still — still — let us hope still."

"Have you one ground for hope?"

"Perhaps so; but you will think it very frail and fallacious."

"Name it, and let me judge."

"One night — in which you were on a visit to Derval Court — "

"Ay, that night."

"Lilian woke me by a loud cry (she sleeps in the next room to me, and the door was left open); I hastened to her bedside in alarm; she was asleep, but appeared extremely agitated and convulsed. She kept calling on your name in a tone of passionate fondness, but as if in great terror. She cried, 'Do not go,. Allen! — do not go! — you know not what you brave! — what you do!' Then she rose in her bed, clasping her hands. Her face was set and rigid; I tried to awake her, but could not. After a little time, she breathed a deep sigh, and murmured, 'Allen, Allen! dear love! did you not hear, did you not see me? What could thus baffle matter and traverse space but love and soul? Can you still doubt me, Allen? — doubt that I love you now, shall love you evermore? —yonder, yonder, as here below?' She then sank back on her pillow, weeping, and then I woke her."

"And what did she say on waking?"

"She did not remember what she had dreamed, except that she had passed through some great terror; but added, with a vague smile, 'It is over, and I feel happy now.' Then she turned round and fell asleep again, but quietly as a child, the tears dried, the smile resting."

"Go, my dear friend, go; take Lilian away from this place as soon as you can; divert her mind with fresh scenes. I hope! — I do hope! Let me know where you fix yourself. I will seize a holiday, — I need one; I will arrange as to my patients; I will come to the same place; she need not know of it, but I must be by to watch, to hear your news of her. Heaven bless you for what you have said! I hope! — I do hope!"

CHAPTER LIV.

SOME days after, I received a few lines from Mrs. Ashleigh. Her arrangements for departure were made. They were to start the next morning. She had fixed on going into the north of Devonshire, and staying some weeks either at Ilfracombe or Lynton, whichever place Lilian preferred. She would write as soon as they were settled.

I was up at my usual early hour the next morning. I resolved to go out towards Mrs. Ashleigh's house, and watch, unnoticed, where I might, perhaps, catch a glimpse of Lilian as the carriage that would convey her to the railway passed my hiding-place.

I was looking impatiently at the clock; it was yet two hours before the train by which Mrs. Ashleigh proposed to leave. A loud ring at my bell! I opened the door. Mrs. Ashleigh rushed in, falling on my breast.

"Lilian! Lilian!"

"Heavens! What has happened?"

"She has left! she is gone,— gone away! Oh, Allen, how? — whither? Advise me. What is to be done?"

"Come in — compose yourself — tell me all,— clearly, quickly. Lilian gone,— gone away? Impossible! She must be hid somewhere in the house,— the garden; she, perhaps, did not like the journey. She may have crept away to some young friend's house. But *I* talk when you should talk: tell me all."

Little enough to tell! Lilian had seemed unusually cheerful the night before, and pleased at the thought of the excursion. Mother and daughter retired to rest early: Mrs. Ashleigh saw Lilian sleeping quietly before she herself went to bed. She woke betimes in the morning, dressed herself, went into the next room to call Lilian — Lilian was not there. No suspicion of flight occurred to her. Perhaps her daughter might be up already, and gone downstairs, remembering something she might wish to pack and take with her on the journey. Mrs. Ashleigh was confirmed in this idea when she noticed that her own room door was left open. She went downstairs, met a maidservant in the hall, who told her, with alarm and surprise, that both the street and garden doors were found unclosed. No one had seen Lilian. Mrs. Ashleigh now became seriously uneasy. On remounting to her daughter's room, she missed Lilian's bonnet and mantle. The house and garden were both searched in vain. There could be no doubt that Lilian had gone,— must have stolen noiselessly at night through her mother's room, and let her-self out of the house and through the garden.

"Do you think she could have received any letter, any message, any visitor unknown to you?"

"I cannot think it. Why do you ask? Oh, Allen, you do not believe there is any accomplice in this disappearance! No, you do not believe it. But my child's honour! What will the world think?"

Not for the world cared I at that moment. I could think only of Lilian, and without one suspicion that imputed blame to her.

"Be quiet, be silent; perhaps she has gone on some visit and will return. Meanwhile, leave inquiry to me."

———◆———

CHAPTER LV.

IT seemed incredible that Lilian could wander far without being observed. I soon ascertained that she had not gone away by the railway — by any public conveyance — had hired no carriage; she must therefore be still in the town, or have left it on foot. The greater part of the day was consumed in unsuccessful inquiries, and faint hopes that she would return; meanwhile the news of her disappearance had spread: how could such news fail to do so?

An acquaintance of mine met me under the archway of Monks' Gate. He wrung my hand and looked at me with great compassion.

"I fear," said he, "that we were all deceived in that young Margrave. He seemed so well conducted, in spite of his lively manners. But — "

"But what?"

"Mrs. Ashleigh was, perhaps, imprudent to admit him into her house so familiarly. He was certainly very handsome. Young ladies will be romantic."

"How dare you, sir!" I cried, choked with rage. "And without any colouring to so calumnious a suggestion! Margrave has not been in the town for many days. No one knows even where he is."

"Oh, yes, it is known where he is. He wrote to order the effects which he had left here to be sent to Penrith."

"When?"

"The letter arrived the day before yesterday. I happened to be calling at the house where he last lodged, when at L——, the house opposite Mrs. Ashleigh's garden. No doubt the servants in both houses gossip with each other. Miss Ashleigh could scarcely fail to hear of Mr. Margrave's address from her maid; and since servants will exchange gossip, they may also convey letters. Pardon me, you know I am your friend."

"Not from the moment you breathe a word against my betrothed wife," said I, fiercely.

I wrenched myself from the clasp of the man's hand, but his words still rang in my ears. I mounted my horse; I rode into the adjoining suburbs, the neighbouring villages; there, however, I learned nothing, till, just at nightfall, in a hamlet about ten miles from L——, a labourer declared he had seen a young lady dressed as I described, who passed by him in a path through the fields a little before noon; that he was surprised to see one so young, so well dressed, and a stranger to the neighbourhood (for he knew by sight the ladies of the few families scattered around) walking alone; that as he stepped out of the path to make way for her, he looked hard into her face, and she did not heed him,— seemed to gaze right before her, into space. If her expression had been less quiet and gentle, he should have thought, he could scarcely say why, that she was not quite right in her mind; there was a strange unconscious stare in her eyes, as if she were walking in her sleep. Her pace was very steady,— neither quick nor slow. He had watched her till she passed out of sight, amidst a wood through which the path wound its way to a village at some distance.

I followed up this clew. I arrived at the village to which my informant directed me, but night had set in. Most of the houses were closed, so I could glean no further information from the cottages or at the inn. But the police superintend- ent of the district lived in the village, and to him I gave in- structions which I had not given, and, indeed, would have been disinclined to give, to the police at L——. He was in- telligent and kindly; he promised to communicate at once with the different police-stations for miles round, and with all delicacy and privacy. It was not probable that Lilian could have wandered in one day much farther than the place at which I then was; it was scarcely to be conceived that she could baffle my pursuit and the practised skill of the police. I rested but a few hours, at a small public-house, and was on horseback again at dawn. A little after sunrise I again heard of the wanderer. At a lonely cottage, by a brick-kiln, in the midst of a wide common, she had stopped the previous even- ing, and asked for a draught of milk. The woman who gave it to her inquired if she had lost her way. She said " No; " and, only tarrying a few minutes, had gone across the com- mon; and the woman supposed she was a visitor at a gentle- man's house which was at the farther end of the waste, for the path she took led to no town, no village. It occurred to me then that Lilian avoided all high-roads, all places, even the humblest, where men congregated together. But where could she have passed the night? Not to fatigue the reader with the fruitless result of frequent inquiries, I will but say that at the end of the second day I had succeeded in ascer- taining that I was still on her track; and though I had ridden to and fro nearly double the distance — coming back again to places I had left behind — it was at the distance of forty miles from L—— that I last heard of her that second day. She had been sitting alone by a little brook only an hour before. I was led to the very spot by a woodman — it was at the hour of twilight when he beheld her; she was leaning her face on her hand, and seemed weary. He spoke to her; she did not answer, but rose and resumed her way along the banks of the streamlet. That night I put up at no inn; I followed the course of the brook for miles, then struck into every path that I could conceive her to have taken, — in vain. Thus I consumed the night on foot, tying my horse to a tree, for he was tired out, and returning to him at sunrise. At noon, the third day, I again heard of her, and in a remote, savage part of the country. The features of the landscape were changed; there was little foliage and little culture, but the ground was broken into moulds and hollows, and covered with patches of heath and stunted brushwood. She had been seen by a shepherd, and he made the same observation as the first who had guided me on her track, — she looked to him "like some one walking in her sleep." An hour or two later, in a dell, amongst the furze-bushes, I chanced on a knot of ribbon. I recognized the colour Lilian habitually wore; I felt certain that the ribbon was hers. Calculating the utmost speed I could ascribe to her, she could not be far off, yet still I failed to discover her. The scene now was as solitary as a desert. I met no one on my way. At length, a little after sunset, I found myself in view of the sea. A small town nestled below the cliffs, on which I was guiding my weary horse. I entered the town, and while my horse was baiting went in search of the resident policeman. The information I had directed to be sent round the country had reached him; he had acted on it, but without result. I was surprised to hear him address me by name, and looking at him more narrowly, I recognized him for the policeman Waby. This young man had always expressed so grateful a sense of my attendance on his sister, and had, indeed, so notably evinced his gratitude in prosecuting with Margrave the inquiries which terminated in the

discovery of Sir Philip Derval's murderer, that I confided to
him the name of the wanderer, of which he had not been previously informed; but which it would be, indeed, impossible
to conceal from him should the search in which his aid was
asked prove successful,— as he knew Miss Ashleigh by sight.
His face immediately became thoughtful. He paused a minute or two, and then said,—

"I think I have it, but I do not like to say; I may pain
you, sir."

"Not by confidence; you pain me by concealment."

The man hesitated still: I encouraged him, and then he
spoke out frankly.

"Sir, did you never think it strange that Mr. Margrave
should move from his handsome rooms in the hotel to a somewhat uncomfortable lodging, from the window of which he
could look down on Mrs. Ashleigh's garden? I have seen
him at night in the balcony of that window, and when I noticed him going so frequently into Mrs. Ashleigh's house
during your unjust detention, I own, sir, I felt for you —"

"Nonsense! Mr. Margrave went to Mrs. Ashleigh's house
as my friend. He has left L—— weeks ago. What has all
this to do with —"

"Patience, sir; hear me out. I was sent from L—— to
this station (on promotion, sir) a fortnight since last Friday,
for there has been a good deal of crime hereabouts; it is a
bad neighbourhood, and full of smugglers. Some days ago, in
watching quietly near a lonely house, of which the owner is
a suspicious character down in my books, I saw, to my amazement, Mr. Margrave come out of that house,— come out of a
private door in it, which belongs to a part of the building not
inhabited by the owner, but which used formerly, when the
house was a sort of inn, to be let to night lodgers of the humblest description. I followed him; he went down to the seashore, walked about, singing to himself; then returned to the
house, and re-entered by the same door. I soon learned that
he lodged in the house,— had lodged there for several days.
The next morning, a fine yacht arrived at a tolerably convenient creek about a mile from the house, and there anchored.

Sailors came ashore, rambling down to this town. The yacht belonged to Mr. Margrave; he had purchased it by commission in London. It is stored for a long voyage. He had directed it to come to him in this out-of-the-way place, where no gentleman's yacht ever put in before, though the creek or bay is handy enough for such craft. Well, sir, is it not strange that a rich young gentleman should come to this unfrequented seashore, put up with accommodation that must be of the rudest kind, in the house of a man known as a desperate smuggler, suspected to be worse; order a yacht to meet him here; is not all this strange? But would it be strange if he were waiting for a young lady? And if a young lady has fled at night from her home, and has come secretly along by-paths, which must have been very fully explained to her beforehand, and is now near that young gentleman's lodging, if not actually in it — if this be so, why, the affair is not so very strange after all. And now do you forgive me, sir?"

"Where is this house? Lead me to it."

"You can hardly get to it except on foot; rough walking, sir, and about seven miles off by the shortest cut."

"Come, and at once; come quickly. We must be there before — before — "

"Before the young lady can get to the place. Well, from what you say of the spot in which she was last seen, I think, on reflection, we may easily do that. I am at your service, sir. But I should warn you that the owners of the house, man and wife, are both of villanous character, — would do anything for money. Mr. Margrave, no doubt, has money enough; and if the young lady chooses to go away with Mr. Margrave, you know I have no power to help it."

"Leave all that to me; all I ask of you is to show me the house."

We were soon out of the town; the night had closed in; it was very dark, in spite of a few stars; the path was rugged and precipitous, sometimes skirting the very brink of perilous cliffs, sometimes delving down to the seashore — there stopped by rock or wave — and painfully rewinding up the ascent.

"It is an ugly path, sir, but it saves four miles; and any·
how the road is a bad one."

We came, at last, to a few wretched fishermen's huts. The
moon had now risen, and revealed the squalor of poverty-
stricken ruinous hovels; a couple of boats moored to the
shore, a moaning, fretful sea; and at a distance a vessel,
with lights on board, lying perfectly still at anchor in a sheltered curve of the bold rude shore. The policeman pointed
to the vessel.

"The yacht, sir; the wind will be in her favour if she sails
to-night."

We quickened our pace as well as the nature of the path
would permit, left the huts behind us, and about a mile farther
on came to a solitary house, larger than, from the policeman's
description of Margrave's lodgement, I should have presup-
posed: a house that in the wilder parts of Scotland might be
almost a laird's; but even in the moonlight it looked very
dilapidated and desolate. Most of the windows were closed,
some with panes broken, stuffed with wisps of straw; there
were the remains of a wall round the house; it was broken in
some parts (only its foundation left). On approaching the
house I observed two doors, — one on the side fronting the sea,
one on the other side, facing a patch of broken ground that
might once have been a garden, and lay waste within the inclosure of the ruined wall, encumbered with various litter;
heaps of rubbish, a ruined shed, the carcass of a worn-out
boat. This latter door stood wide open, — the other was
closed. The house was still and dark, as if either deserted,
or all within it retired to rest.

"I think that open door leads at once to the rooms Mr.
Margrave hires; he can go in and out without disturbing the
other inmates. They used to keep, on the side which they
inhabit, a beer-house, but the magistrates shut it up; still,
it is a resort for bad characters. Now, sir, what shall we
do?"

"Watch separately. You wait within the inclosure of the
wall, hid by those heaps of rubbish, near the door; none can
enter but what you will observe them. If you see her, you

will accost and stop her, and call aloud for me; I shall be in hearing. I will go back to the high part of the ground yonder — it seems to me that she must pass that way; and I would desire, if possible, to save her from the humiliation, the — the shame of coming within the precincts of that man's abode. I feel I may trust you now and hereafter. It is a great thing for the happiness and honour of this poor young lady and her mother, that I may be able to declare that I did not take her from that man, from any man — from that house, from any house. You comprehend me, and will obey? I speak to you as a confidant, — a friend."

"I thank you with my whole heart, sir, for so doing. You saved my sister's life, and the least I can do is to keep secret all that would pain your life if blabbed abroad. I know what mischief folks' tongues can make. I will wait by the door, never fear, and will rather lose my place than not strain all the legal power I possess to keep the young lady back from sorrow."

This dialogue was interchanged in close hurried whisper behind the broken wall, and out of all hearing. Waby now crept through a wide gap into the inclosure, and nestled himself silently amidst the wrecks of the broken boat, not six feet from the open door, and close to the wall of the house itself. I went back some thirty yards up the road, to the rising ground which I had pointed out to him. According to the best calculation I could make — considering the pace at which I had cleared the precipitous pathway, and reckoning from the place and time at which Lilian had been last seen — she could not possibly have yet entered that house. I might presume it would be more than half an hour before she could arrive; I was in hopes that, during the interval, Margrave might show himself, perhaps at the door, or from the windows, or I might even by some light from the latter be guided to the room in which to find him. If, after waiting a reasonable time, Lilian should fail to appear, I had formed my plan of action; but it was important for the success of that plan that I should not lose myself in the strange house, nor bring its owners to Margrave's aid, — that I should surprise him alone and unawares.

Half an hour, three quarters, a whole hour thus passed. No sign of my poor wanderer; but signs there were of the enemy from whom I resolved, at whatever risk, to free and to save her. A window on the ground-floor, to the left of the door, which had long fixed my attention because I had seen light through the chinks of the shutters, slowly unclosed, the shutters fell back, the casement opened, and I beheld Margrave distinctly; he held something in his hand that gleamed in the moonlight, directed not towards the mound on which I stood, nor towards the path I had taken, but towards an open space beyond the ruined wall to the right. Hid by a cluster of stunted shrubs I watched him with a heart that beat with rage, not with terror. He seemed so intent in his own gaze as to be unheeding or unconscious of all else. I stole from my post, and, still under cover, sometimes of the broken wall, sometimes of the shaggy ridges that skirted the path, crept on, on till I reached the side of the house itself; then, there secure from his eyes, should he turn them, I stepped over the ruined wall, scarcely two feet high in that place, on — on towards the door. I passed the spot on which the policeman had shrouded himself; he was seated, his back against the ribs of the broken boat. I put my hand to his mouth that he might not cry out in surprise, and whispered in his ear; he stirred not. I shook him by the arm: still he stirred not. A ray of the moon fell on his face. I saw that he was in a profound slumber. Persuaded that it was no natural sleep, and that he had become useless to me, I passed him by. I was at the threshold of the open door, the light from the window close by falling on the ground; I was in the passage; a glimmer came through the chinks of a door to the left; I turned the handle noiselessly, and, the next moment, Margrave was locked in my grasp.

"Call out," I hissed in his ear, "and I strangle you before any one can come to your help."

He did not call out; his eye, fixed on mine as he writhed round, saw, perhaps, his peril if he did. His countenance betrayed fear, but as I tightened my grasp that expression gave way to one of wrath and fierceness; and as, in turn, I felt the grip of his hand, I knew that the struggle between us would be that of two strong men, each equally bent on the mastery of the other.

I was, as I have said before, endowed with an unusual degree of physical power, disciplined in early youth by athletic exercise and contest. In height and in muscle I had greatly the advantage over my antagonist; but such was the nervous vigour, the elastic energy of his incomparable frame, in which sinews seemed springs of steel, that had our encounter been one in which my strength was less heightened by rage, I believe that I could no more have coped with him than the bison can cope with the boa; but I was animated by that passion which trebles for a time all our forces,— which makes even the weak man a match for the strong. I felt that if I were worsted, disabled, stricken down, Lilian might be lost in losing her sole protector; and on the other hand, Margrave had been taken at the disadvantage of that surprise which will half unnerve the fiercest of the wild beasts; while as we grappled, reeling and rocking to and fro in our struggle, I soon observed that his attention was distracted,— that his eye was turned towards an object which he had dropped involuntarily when I first seized him. He sought to drag me towards that object, and when near it stooped to seize. It was a bright, slender, short wand of steel. I remembered when and where I had seen it, whether in my waking state or in vision; and as his hand stole down to take it from the floor, I set on the wand my strong foot. I cannot tell by what rapid process of thought and association I came to the belief that the possession of a little piece of blunted steel would decide the conflict in favor of the possessor; but the struggle now was concentred on the attainment of that seemingly idle weapon. I was becoming breathless and exhausted, while Margrave seemed every moment to gather up new force, when collecting all my strength for one final effort, I lifted him suddenly high in the air, and hurled him to the farthest end of the cramped arena to which our contest was confined. He fell, and with a force by which most men would have been stunned; but he recovered himself with a quick rebound, and, as he stood facing me, there was something grand as well as terrible in his aspect. His eyes literally flamed, as those of a tiger; his rich hair, flung back from his knitted forehead, seemed to erect itself as an angry mane; his lips, slightly parted, showed the glitter of his set teeth; his whole frame seemed larger in the tension of the muscles, and as, gradually relaxing his first defying and haughty attitude, he crouched as the panther crouches for its deadly spring, I felt as if it were a wild beast, whose rush was coming upon me, — wild beast, but still Man, the king of the animals, fashioned forth from no mixture of humbler races by the slow revolutions of time, but his royalty stamped on his form when the earth became fit for his coming.[1]

At that moment I snatched up the wand, directed it towards him, and advancing with a fearless stride, cried,—

"Down to my feet, miserable sorcerer!"

To my own amaze, the effect was instantaneous. My terrible antagonist dropped to the floor as a dog drops at the word of his master. The muscles of his frowning countenance relaxed, the glare of his wrathful eyes grew dull and rayless; his limbs lay prostrate and unnerved, his head rested against the wall, his arms limp and drooping by his side. I approached him slowly and cautiously; he seemed cast into a profound slumber.

"You are at my mercy now!" said I.

He moved his head as in sign of deprecating submission.

"You hear and understand me? Speak!"

His lips faintly muttered, "Yes."

"I command you to answer truly the questions I shall address to you."

"I must, while yet sensible of the power that has passed to your hand."

"Is it by some occult magnetic property in this wand that

---

[1] And yet, even if we entirely omit the consideration of the soul, that immaterial and immortal principle which is for a time united to his body, and view him only in his merely animal character, man is still the most excellent of animals. — Dr. KIDD, On the Adaptation of External Nature to the Physical Condition of Man (Sect. iii. p. 18).

you have exercised so demoniac an influence over a creature so pure as Lilian Ashleigh?"

"By that wand and by other arts which you could not comprehend."

"And for what infamous object,—her seduction, her dishonour?"

"No! I sought in her the aid of a gift which would cease did she cease to be pure. At first I but cast my influence upon her that through her I might influence yourself. I needed your help to discover a secret. Circumstances steeled your mind against me. I could no longer hope that you would voluntarily lend yourself to my will. Meanwhile, I had found in her the light of a loftier knowledge than that of your science; through that knowledge, duly heeded and cultivated, I hoped to divine what I cannot of myself discover. Therefore I deepened over her mind the spells I command; therefore I have drawn her hither as the loadstone draws the steel, and therefore I would have borne her with me to the shores to which I was about this night to sail. I had cast the inmates of the house and all around it into slumber, in order that none might witness her departure; had I not done so, I should have summoned others to my aid, in spite of your threat."

"And would Lilian Ashleigh have passively accompanied you, to her own irretrievable disgrace?"

"She could not have helped it; she would have been unconscious of her acts; she was, and is, in a trance; nor, had she gone with me, would she have waked from that state while she lived; that would not have been long."

"Wretch! and for what object of unhallowed curiosity do you exert an influence which withers away the life of its victim?"

"Not curiosity, but the instinct of self-preservation. I count on no life beyond the grave. I would defy the grave, and live on."

"And was it to learn, through some ghastly agencies, the secret of renewing existence, that you lured me by the shadow of your own image on the night when we met last?"

The voice of Margrave here became very faint as he answered me, and his countenance began to exhibit the signs of an exhaustion almost mortal.

"Be quick," he murmured, "or I die. The fluid which emanates from that wand, in the hand of one who envenoms that fluid with his own hatred and rage, will prove fatal to my life. Lower the wand from my forehead! low — low, — lower still!"

"What was the nature of that rite in which you constrained me to share?"

"I cannot say. You are killing me. Enough that you were saved from a great danger by the apparition of the protecting image vouchsafed to your eye; otherwise you would — you would — Oh, release me! Away! away!"

The foam gathered to his lips; his limbs became fearfully convulsed.

"One question more: where is Lilian at this moment? Answer that question, and I depart."

He raised his head, made a visible effort to rally his strength, and gasped out,—

"Yonder. Pass through the open space up the cliff, beside a thorn-tree; you will find her there, where she halted when the wand dropped from my hand. But — but — beware! Ha! you will serve me yet, and through her! They said so that night, though you heard them not. THEY said it!" Here his face became death-like; he pressed his hand on his heart, and shrieked out, "Away! away! or you are my murderer!"

I retreated to the other end of the room, turning the wand from him, and when I gained the door, looked back; his convulsions had ceased, but he seemed locked in a profound swoon.

I left the room,— the house,— paused by Waby; he was still sleeping. "Awake!" I said, and touched him with the wand. He started up at once, rubbed his eyes, began stammering out excuses. I checked them, and bade him follow me. I took the way up the open ground towards which Margrave had pointed the wand, and there, motionless, beside a gnarled fantastic thorn-tree, stood Lilian. Her arms were folded across her breast; her face, seen by the moonlight, looked so innocent and so infantine, that I needed no other evidence to tell me how unconscious she was of the peril to which her steps had been drawn. I took her gently by the hand. "Come with me," I said in a whisper, and she obeyed me silently, and with a placid smile.

Rough though the way, she seemed unconscious of fatigue. I placed her arm in mine, but she did not lean on it. We got back to the town. I obtained there an old chaise and a pair of horses. At morning Lilian was under her mother's roof. About the noon of that day fever seized her; she became rapidly worse, and, to all appearance, in imminent danger. Delirium set in; I watched beside her night and day, supported by an inward conviction of her recovery, but tortured by the sight of her sufferings. On the third day a change for the better became visible; her sleep was calm, her breathing regular.

Shortly afterwards she woke out of danger. Her eyes fell at once on me, with all their old ineffable tender sweetness.

"Oh, Allen, beloved, have I not been very ill? But I am almost well now. Do not weep; I shall live for you,— for your sake." And she bent forward, drawing my hand from my streaming eyes, and kissed me with a child's guileless kiss on my burning forehead.

CHAPTER LVI.

LILIAN recovered, but the strange thing was this: all memory of the weeks that had elapsed since her return from visiting her aunt was completely obliterated; she seemed in profound ignorance of the charge on which I had been confined,— perfectly ignorant even of the existence of Margrave. She had, indeed, a very vague reminiscence of her conversa-

tion with me in the garden,— the first conversation which
had ever been embittered by a disagreement,— but that disagreement itself she did not recollect. Her belief was that
she had been ill and light-headed since that evening. From
that evening to the hour of her waking, conscious and revived, all was a blank. Her love for me was restored, as if
its thread had never been broken. Some such instances of
oblivion after bodily illness or mental shock are familiar
enough to the practice of all medical men;[1] and I was therefore enabled to appease the anxiety and wonder of Mrs. Ashleigh, by quoting various examples of loss, or suspension, of
memory. We agreed that it would be necessary to break to
Lilian, though very cautiously, the story of Sir Philip Derval's murder, and the charge to which I had been subjected.
She could not fail to hear of those events from others. How
shall I express her womanly terror, her loving, sympathizing
pity, on hearing the tale, which I softened as well as I
could?

"And to think that I knew nothing of this!" she cried,
clasping my hand; "to think that you were in peril, and that
I was not by your side!"

Her mother spoke of Margrave, as a visitor,— an agreeable,
lively stranger; Lilian could not even recollect his name, but
she seemed shocked to think that any visitor had been ad-

[1] Such instances of suspense of memory are recorded in most physiological
and in some metaphysical works. Dr. Abercrombie notices some, more or
less similar to that related in the text: " A young lady who was present at
a catastrophe in Scotland, in which many people lost their lives by the fall of
the gallery of a church, escaped without any injury, but with the complete
loss of the recollection of any of the circumstances; and this extended not
only to the accident, but to everything that had occurred to her for a certain
time before going to church. A lady whom I attended some years ago in a
protracted illness, in which her memory became much impaired, lost the recollection of a period of about ten or twelve years, but spoke with perfect con-
sistency of things as they stood before that time." Dr. Abercrombie adds:
" As far as I have been able to trace it, the principle in such cases seems to
be, that when the memory is impaired to a certain degree, the loss of it extends backward to some event or some period by which a particularly deep
impression had been made upon the mind." — ABERCROMBIE: *On the Intellectual Powers*, pp. 118, 119 (15th edition).

mitted while I was in circumstances so awful! Need I say
that our engagement was renewed? Renewed! To *her* knowledge and to her heart it had never been interrupted for a moment. But oh! the malignity of the wrong world! Oh, that
strange lust of mangling reputations, which seizes on hearts
the least wantonly cruel! Let two idle tongues utter a tale
against some third person, who never offended the babblers,
and how the tale spreads, like fire, lighted none know how,
in the herbage of an American prairie! Who shall put it
out?

What right have we to pry into the secrets of other men's
hearths? True or false, the tale that is gabbled to us, what
concern of ours can it be? I speak not of cases to which the
law has been summoned, which law has sifted, on which law
has pronounced. But how, when the law is silent, can we
assume its verdicts? How be all judges where there has been
no witness-box, no cross-examination, no jury? Yet, every
day we put on our ermine, and make ourselves judges,—
judges sure to condemn, and on what evidence? That which
no court of law will receive. Somebody has said something
to somebody, which somebody repeats to everybody!

The gossip of L—— had set in full current against Lilian's
fair name. No ladies had called or sent to congratulate Mrs.
Ashleigh on her return, or to inquire after Lilian herself during her struggle between life and death.

How I missed the Queen of the Hill at this critical moment! How I longed for aid to crush the slander, with
which I knew not how to grapple,— aid in her knowledge of
the world and her ascendancy over its judgments! I had
heard from her once since her absence, briefly but kindly
expressing her amazement at the ineffable stupidity which
could for a moment have subjected me to a suspicion of
Sir Philip Derval's strange murder, and congratulating me
heartily on my complete vindication from so monstrous a
charge. To this letter no address was given. I supposed
the omission to be accidental, but on calling at her house to
inquire her direction, I found that the servants did not
know it.

What, then, was my joy when just at this juncture I received a note from Mrs. Poyntz, stating that she had returned the night before, and would be glad to see me.

I hastened to her house. "Ah," thought I, as I sprang lightly up the ascent to the Hill, "how the tattlers will be silenced by a word from her imperial lips!" And only just as I approached her door did it strike me how difficult — nay, how impossible — to explain to her — the hard positive woman, her who had, less ostensibly but more ruthlessly than myself, destroyed Dr. Lloyd for his belief in the comparatively rational pretensions of clairvoyance — all the mystical excuses for Lilian's flight from her home? How speak to her — or, indeed, to any one — about an occult fascination and a magic wand? No matter: surely it would be enough to say that at the time Lilian had been light-headed, under the influence of the fever which had afterwards nearly proved fatal. The early friend of Anne Ashleigh would not be a severe critic on any tale that might right the good name of Anne Ashleigh's daughter. So assured, with a light heart and a cheerful face, I followed the servant into the great lady's pleasant but decorous presence-chamber.

CHAPTER LVII.

MRS. POYNTZ was on her favourite seat by the window, and for a wonder, not knitting — that classic task seemed done; but she was smoothing and folding the completed work with her white comely hand, and smiling over it, as if in complacent approval, when I entered the room. At the fire-side sat the he-colonel inspecting a newly-invented barometer; at another window, in the farthest recess of the room, stood Miss Jane Poyntz, with a young gentleman whom I had never before seen, but who turned his eyes full upon me with a haughty look as the servant announced my name. He was tall, well proportioned, decidedly handsome, but with that expression of cold and concentred self-esteem in his very attitude, as well as his countenance, which makes a man of merit unpopular, a man without merit ridiculous.

The he-colonel, always punctiliously civil, rose from his seat, shook hands with me cordially, and said, "Coldish weather to-day; but we shall have rain to-morrow. Rainy seasons come in cycles. We are about to commence a cycle of them with heavy showers." He sighed, and returned to his barometer.

Miss Jane bowed to me graciously enough, but was evidently a little confused, — a circumstance which might well attract my notice, for I had never before seen that high-bred young lady deviate a hairsbreadth from the even tenor of a manner admirable for a cheerful and courteous ease, which, one felt convinced, would be unaltered to those around her if an earthquake swallowed one up an inch before her feet.

The young gentleman continued to eye me loftily, as the heir-apparent to some celestial planet might eye an inferior creature from a half-formed nebula suddenly dropped upon his sublime and perfected star.

Mrs. Poyntz extended to me two fingers, and said frigidly, "Delighted to see you again! How kind to attend so soon to my note!"

Motioning me to a seat beside her, she here turned to her husband, and said, "Poyntz, since a cycle of rain begins to-morrow, better secure your ride to-day. Take these young people with you. I want to talk with Dr. Fenwick."

The colonel carefully put away his barometer, and saying to his daughter, "Come!" went forth. Jane followed her father; the young gentleman followed Jane.

The reception I had met chilled and disappointed me. I felt that Mrs. Poyntz was changed, and in her change the whole house seemed changed. The very chairs looked civilly unfriendly, as if preparing to turn their backs on me. However, I was not in the false position of an intruder; I had been summoned; it was for Mrs. Poyntz to speak first, and I waited quietly for her to do so.

She finished the careful folding of her work, and then laid it at rest in the drawer of the table at which she sat. Having so done, she turned to me, and said, —

"By the way, I ought to have introduced to you my young guest, Mr. Ashleigh Sumner. You would like him. He has talents, — not showy, but solid. He will succeed in public life."

"So that young man is Mr. Ashleigh Sumner? I do not wonder that Miss Ashleigh rejected him."

I said this, for I was nettled, as well as surprised, at the coolness with which a lady who had professed a friendship for me mentioned that fortunate young gentleman, with so complete an oblivion of all the antecedents that had once made his name painful to my ear.

In turn, my answer seemed to nettle Mrs. Poyntz.

"I am not so sure that she did reject; perhaps she rather misunderstood him; gallant compliments are not always proposals of marriage. However that be, his spirits were not much damped by Miss Ashleigh's disdain, nor his heart deeply smitten by her charms; for he is now very happy, very much attached to another young lady, to whom he proposed three days ago, at Lady Delafield's, and not to make a mystery of what all our little world will know before to-morrow, that young lady is my daughter Jane."

"Were I acquainted with Mr. Sumner, I should offer to *him* my sincere congratulations."

Mrs. Poyntz resumed, without heeding a reply more complimentary to Miss Jane than to the object of her choice, —

"I told you that I meant Jane to marry a rich country gentleman, and Ashleigh Sumner is the very country gentleman I had then in my thoughts. He is cleverer and more ambitious than I could have hoped; he will be a minister some day, in right of his talents, and a peer, if he wishes it, in right of his lands. So that matter is settled."

There was a pause, during which my mind passed rapidly through links of reminiscence and reasoning, which led me to a mingled sentiment of admiration for Mrs. Poyntz as a diplomatist and of distrust for Mrs. Poyntz as a friend. It was now clear why Mrs. Poyntz, before so little disposed to approve my love, had urged me at once to offer my hand to Lilian, in order that she might depart affianced and engaged to the house in which she would meet Mr. Ashleigh Sumner. Hence Mrs. Poyntz's anxiety to obtain all the information I could afford her of the sayings and doings at Lady Haughton's; hence, the publicity she had so suddenly given to my engagement; hence, when Mr. Sumner had gone away a rejected suitor, her own departure from L——; she had seized the very moment when a vain and proud man, piqued by the mortification received from one lady, falls the easier prey to the arts which allure his suit to another. All was so far clear to me. And I — was my self-conceit less egregious and less readily duped than that of yon glided popinjay's! How skilfully this woman had knitted me into her work with the noiseless turn of her white hands! and yet, forsooth, I must vaunt the superior scope of my intellect, and plumb all the fountains of Nature,— I, who could not fathom the little pool of this female schemer's mind!

But that was no time for resentment to her or rebuke to myself. She was now the woman who could best protect and save from slander my innocent, beloved Lilian. But how approach that perplexing subject?

Mrs. Poyntz approached it, and with her usual decision of purpose, which bore so deceitful a likeness to candour of mind.

"But it was not to talk of my affairs that I asked you to call, Allen Fenwick." As she uttered my name, her voice softened, and her manner took that maternal, caressing tenderness which had sometimes amused and sometimes misled me. "No, I do not forget that you asked me to be your friend, and I take without scruple the license of friendship. What are these stories that I have heard already about Lilian Ashleigh, to whom you were once engaged?"

"To whom I am still engaged."

"Is it possible? Oh, then, of course the stories I have heard are all false. Very likely; no fiction in scandal ever surprises me. Poor dear Lilian, then, never ran away from her mother's house?"

I smothered the angry pain which this mode of questioning caused me; I knew how important it was to Lilian to secure to her the countenance and support of this absolute autocrat; I spoke of Lilian's long previous distemper of mind; I accounted for it as any intelligent physician, unacquainted with all that I could not reveal, would account. Heaven forgive me for the venial falsehood, but I spoke of the terrible charge against myself as enough to unhinge for a time the intellect of a girl so acutely sensitive as Lilian; I sought to create that impression as to the origin of all that might otherwise seem strange; and in this state of cerebral excitement she had wandered from home — but alone. I had tracked every step of her way; I had found and restored her to her home. A critical delirium had followed, from which she now rose, cured in health, unsuspicious that there could be a whisper against her name. And then, with all the eloquence I could command, and in words as adapted as I could frame them to soften the heart of a woman, herself a mother, I implored Mrs. Poyntz's aid to silence all the cruelties of calumny, and extend her shield over the child of her own early friend.

When I came to an end, I had taken, with caressing force, Mrs. Poyntz's reluctant hands in mine. There were tears in my voice, tears in my eyes. And the sound of her voice in reply gave me hope, for it was unusually gentle. She was evidently moved. The hope was soon quelled.

"Allen Fenwick," she said, "you have a noble heart; I grieve to see how it abuses your reason. I cannot aid Lilian Ashleigh in the way you ask. Do not start back so indignantly. Listen to me as patiently as I have listened to you. That when you brought back the unfortunate young woman to her poor mother, her mind was disordered, and became yet more dangerously so, I can well believe; that she is now recovered, and thinks with shame, or refuses to think at all, of her imprudent flight, I can believe also; but I do not believe, the World cannot believe, that she did not, knowingly and purposely, quit her mother's roof, and in quest of that young stranger so incautiously, so unfeelingly admitted to her mother's house during the very time you were detained on the most awful of human accusations. Every one in the town knows that Mr. Margrave visited daily at Mrs. Ashleigh's during that painful period; every one in the town knows in what strange out-of-the-way place this young man had niched himself; and that a yacht was bought, and lying in wait there. What for? It is said that the chaise in which you brought Miss Ashleigh back to her home was hired in a village within an easy reach of Mr. Margrave's lodging,— of Mr. Margrave's yacht. I rejoice that you saved the poor girl from ruin; but her good name is tarnished; and if Anne Ashleigh, whom I sincerely pity, asks me my advice, I can but give her this: 'Leave L——, take your daughter abroad; and if she is not to marry Mr. Margrave, marry her as quietly and as quickly as possible to some foreigner.'"

"Madam! madam! this, then, is your friendship to her — to me! Oh, shame on you to insult thus an affianced husband! Shame on me ever to have thought you had a heart!"

"A heart, man!" she exclaimed, almost fiercely, springing up, and startling me with the change in her countenance and voice. "And little you would have valued, and pitilessly have crushed this heart, if I had suffered myself to show it to you! What right have you to reproach me? I felt a warm interest in your career, an unusual attraction in your conversation and society. Do you blame me for that, or should I blame myself? Condemned to live amongst brainless puppets, my dull occupation to pull the strings that moved them, it was a new charm to my life to establish friendship and intercourse with intellect and spirit and courage. Ah! I understand that look, half incredulous, half inquisitive."

"Inquisitive, no; incredulous, yes! You desired my friendship, and how does your harsh judgment of my betrothed wife prove either to me or to her mother, whom you have known from your girlhood, the first duty of a friend, — which is surely not that of leaving a friend's side the moment that he needs countenance in calumny, succour in trouble!"

"It is a better duty to prevent the calumny and avert the trouble. Leave aside Anne Ashleigh, a cipher that I can add or abstract from my sum of life as I please. What is my duty to yourself? It is plain. It is to tell you that your honour commands you to abandon all thoughts of Lilian Ashleigh as your wife. Ungrateful that you are! Do you suppose it was no mortification to my pride of woman and friend, that you never approached me in confidence except to ask my good offices in promoting your courtship to another; no shock to the quiet plans I had formed as to our familiar though harmless intimacy, to hear that you were bent on a marriage in which my friend would be lost to me?"

"Not lost! not lost! On the contrary, the regard I must suppose you had for Lilian would have been a new link be· tween our homes."

"Pooh! Between me and that dreamy girl there could have been no sympathy, there could have grown up no regard. You would have been chained to your fireside, and — and — but no matter. I stifled my disappointment as soon as I felt it, — stifled it, as all my life I have stifled that which either destiny or duty — duty to myself as to others — forbids me to indulge. Ah, do not fancy me one of the weak criminals who can suffer a worthy liking to grow into a debasing love! I was not in love with you, Allen Fenwick."

"Do you think I was ever so presumptuous a coxcomb as to fancy it?"

"No," she said, more softly; "I was not so false to my household ties and to my own nature. But there are some friendships which are as jealous as love. I could have cheerfully aided you in any choice which my sense could have approved for you as wise; I should have been pleased to have found in such a wife my most intimate companion. But that silly child! — absurd! Nevertheless, the freshness and enthusiasm of your love touched me; you asked my aid, and I gave it. Perhaps I did believe that when you saw more of Lilian Ashleigh you would be cured of a fancy conceived by the eye — I should have known better what dupes the wisest men can be to the witcheries of a fair face and eighteen! When I found your illusion obstinate, I wrenched myself away from a vain regret, turned to my own schemes and my

own ambition, and smiled bitterly to think that, in pressing
you to propose so hastily to Lilian, I made your blind passion
an agent in my own plans. Enough of this. I speak thus
openly and boldly to you now, because now I have not a sentiment that can interfere with the dispassionate soundness of
my counsels. I repeat, you cannot now marry Lilian Ashleigh;
I cannot take my daughter to visit her; I cannot destroy the
social laws that I myself have set in my petty kingdom."

"Be it as you will. I have pleaded for her while she is
still Lilian Ashleigh. I plead for no one to whom I have
once given my name. Before the woman whom I have taken
from the altar, I can place, as a shield sufficient, my strong
breast of man. Who has so deep an interest in Lilian's
purity as I have? Who is so fitted to know the exact truth
of every whisper against her? Yet when I, whom you admit
to have some reputation for shrewd intelligence,— I, who
tracked her way,— I, who restored her to her home,— when
I, Allen Fenwick, am so assured of her inviolable innocence
in thought as in deed, that I trust my honour to her keeping,
—surely, surely, I confute the scandal which you yourself do
not believe, though you refuse to reject and to annul it?"

"Do not deceive yourself, Allen Fenwick," said she, still
standing beside me, her countenance now hard and stern.
"Look where I stand, I am the WORLD! The World, not as
satirists depreciate, or as optimists extol its immutable properties, its all-persuasive authority. I am the World! And
my voice is the World's voice when it thus warns you.
Should you make this marriage, your dignity of character
and position would be gone! If you look only to lucre and
professional success, possibly *they* may not ultimately suffer.
You have skill, which men need; their need may still draw
patients to your door and pour guineas into your purse. But
you have the pride, as well as the birth of a gentleman, and
the wounds to that pride will be hourly chafed and never
healed. Your strong breast of man has no shelter to the
frail name of woman. The World, in its health, will look
down on your wife, though its sick may look up to you. This
is not all. The World, in its gentlest mood of indulgence,

will say compassionately, 'Poor man! how weak, and how deceived! What an unfortunate marriage!' But the World is not often indulgent, — it looks most to the motives most seen on the surface. And the World will more frequently say, 'No; much too clever a man to be duped! Miss Ashleigh had money. A good match to the man who liked gold better than honour.'"

I sprang to my feet, with difficulty suppressing my rage; and, remembering it was a woman who spoke to me, "Farewell, madam," said I, through my grinded teeth. "Were you, indeed, the Personation of The World, whose mean notions you mouth so calmly, I could not disdain you more." I turned to the door, and left her still standing erect and menacing, the hard sneer on her resolute lip, the red glitter in her remorseless eye.

CHAPTER LVIII.

If ever my heart vowed itself to Lilian, the vow was now the most trustful and the most sacred. I had relinquished our engagement before; but then her affection seemed, no matter from what cause, so estranged from me, that though I might be miserable to lose her, I deemed that she would be unhappy in our union. Then, too, she was the gem and darling of the little world in which she lived; no whisper assailed her: now I knew that she loved me; I knew that her estrangement had been involuntary; I knew that appearances wronged her, and that they never could be explained. I was in the true position of man to woman: I was the shield, the bulwark, the fearless confiding protector! Resign her now because the world babbled, because my career might be impeded, because my good name might be impeached, — resign her, and, in that resignation, confirm all that was said against her! Could I do so, I should be the most craven of gentlemen, the meanest of men!

I went to Mrs. Ashleigh, and entreated her to hasten my union with her daughter, and fix the marriage-day.

I found the poor lady dejected and distressed. She was now sufficiently relieved from the absorbing anxiety for Lilian to be aware of the change on the face of that World which the woman I had just quitted personified and concentred; she had learned the cause from the bloodless lips of Miss Brabazon.

"My child! my poor child!" murmured the mother. "And she so guileless,—so sensitive! Could she know what is said, it would kill her. She would never marry you, Allen, —she would never bring shame to you!"

"She never need learn the barbarous calumny. Give her to me, and at once; patients, fortune, fame, are not found only at L——. Give her to me at once. But let me name a condition: I have a patrimonial independence, I have amassed large savings, I have my profession and my repute. I cannot touch her fortune — I cannot,— never can! Take it while you live; when you die, leave it to accumulate for her children, if children she have; not to me; not to her — unless I am dead or ruined!"

"Oh, Allen, what a heart! what a heart! No, not heart, Allen,—that bird in its cage has a heart: *soul* — what a soul!"

CHAPTER LIX.

How innocent was Lilian's virgin blush when I knelt to her, and prayed that she would forestall the date that had been fixed for our union, and be my bride before the breath of the autumn had withered the pomp of the woodland and silenced the song of the birds! Meanwhile, I was so fearfully anxious that she should risk no danger of hearing, even of surmising, the cruel slander against her — should meet no cold contemptuous looks, above all, should be safe from the

barbed talk of Mrs. Poyntz — that I insisted on the necessity
of immediate change of air and scene. I proposed that we
should all three depart, the next day, for the banks of my
own beloved and native Windermere. By that pure mountain
air, Lilian's health would be soon re-established; in the
church hallowed to me by the graves of my fathers our vows
should be plighted. No calumny had ever cast a shadow over
those graves. I felt as if my bride would be safer in the
neighbourhood of my mother's tomb.

I carried my point: it was so arranged. Mrs. Ashleigh,
however, was reluctant to leave before she had seen her dear
friend, Margaret Poyntz. I had not the courage to tell her what
she might expect to hear from that dear friend, but, as delicately as I could, I informed her that I had already seen the
Queen of the Hill, and contradicted the gossip that had
reached her; but that as yet, like other absolute sovereigns,
the Queen of the Hill thought it politic to go with the popular stream, reserving all check on its direction till the rush
of its torrent might slacken; and that it would be infinitely
wiser in Mrs. Ashleigh to postpone conversation with Mrs.
Poyntz until Lilian's return to L—— as my wife. Slander
by that time would have wearied itself out, and Mrs. Poyntz
(assuming her friendship to Mrs. Ashleigh to be sincere)
would then be enabled to say with authority to her subjects,
"Dr. Fenwick alone knows the facts of the story, and his
marriage with Miss Ashleigh refutes all the gossip to her
prejudice."

I made that evening arrangements with a young and rising
practitioner to secure attendance on my patients during my
absence. I passed the greater part of the night in drawing
up memoranda to guide my proxy in each case, however humble the sufferer. This task finished, I chanced, in searching
for a small microscope, the wonders of which I thought might
interest and amuse Lilian, to open a drawer in which I kept
the manuscript of my cherished Physiological Work, and, in
so doing, my eye fell upon the wand which I had taken from
Margrave. I had thrown it into that drawer on my return
home, after restoring Lilian to her mother's house, and, in

the anxiety which had subsequently preyed upon my mind, had almost forgotten the strange possession I had as strangely acquired.   There it now lay, the instrument of agencies over the mechanism of nature which no doctrine admitted by my philosophy could accept, side by side with the presumptuous work which had analyzed the springs by which Nature is moved, and decided the principles by which reason metes out, from the inch of its knowledge, the plan of the Infinite Unknown.

I took up the wand and examined it curiously.   It was evidently the work of an age far remote from our own, scored over with half-obliterated characters in some Eastern tongue, perhaps no longer extant.   I found that it was hollow within. A more accurate observation showed, in the centre of this hollow, an exceedingly fine thread-like wire, the unattached end of which would slightly touch the palm when the wand was taken into the hand.   Was it possible that there might be a natural and even a simple cause for the effects which this instrument produced?   Could it serve to collect, from that great focus of animal heat and nervous energy which is placed in the palm of the human hand, some such latent fluid as that which Reichenbach calls the "odic," and which, according to him, "rushes through and pervades universal Nature"?   After all, why not?   For how many centuries lay unknown all the virtues of the loadstone and the amber?   It is but as yesterday that the forces of vapour have become to men genii more powerful than those conjured up by Aladdin; that light, at a touch, springs forth from invisible air; that thought finds a messenger swifter than the wings of the fabled Afrite.   As, thus musing, my hand closed over the wand, I felt a wild thrill through my frame.   I recoiled; I was alarmed lest (according to the plain common-sense theory of Julius Faber) I might be preparing my imagination to form and to credit its own illusions.   Hastily I laid down the wand.   But then it occurred to me that whatever its properties, it had so served the purposes of the dread Fascinator from whom it had been taken, that he might probably seek to repossess himself of it; he might contrive to enter my house in my absence; more prudent to guard in my own watchful keeping the incomprehensible instrument of incomprehensible arts. I resolved, therefore, to take the wand with me, and placed it in my travelling-trunk, with such effects as I selected for use in the excursion that was to commence with the morrow. I now lay down to rest, but I could not sleep. The recollections of the painful interview with Mrs. Poyntz became vivid and haunting. It was clear that the sentiment she had conceived for me was that of no simple friendship,—something more or something less, but certainly something else; and this conviction brought before me that proud hard face, disturbed by a pang wrestled against but not subdued, and that clear metallic voice, troubled by the quiver of an emotion which, perhaps, she had never analyzed to herself. I did not need her own assurance to know that this sentiment was not to be confounded with a love which she would have despised as a weakness and repelled as a crime; it was an inclination of the intellect, not a passion of the heart. But still it admitted a jealousy little less keen than that which has love for its cause,— so true it is that jealousy is never absent where self-love is always present. Certainly, it was no susceptibility of sober friendship which had made the stern arbitress of a coterie ascribe to her interest in me her pitiless judgment of Lilian. Strangely enough, with the image of this archetype of conventional usages and the trite social life, came that of the mysterious Margrave, surrounded by all the attributes with which superstition clothes the being of the shadowy border-land that lies beyond the chart of our visual world itself. By what link were creatures so dissimilar riveted together in the metaphysical chain of association? Both had entered into the record of my life when my life admitted its own first romance of love. Through the aid of this cynical schemer I had been made known to Lilian. At her house I had heard the dark story of that Louis Grayle, with whom, in mocking spite of my reason, conjectures, which that very reason must depose itself before it could resolve into distempered fancies, identified the enigmatical Margrave. And now both she, the representative of the formal world most opposed to visionary creeds, and he, who gathered round

22

him all the terrors which haunt the realm of fable, stood
united against me,—foes with whom the intellect I had so
haughtily cultured knew not how to cope. Whatever assault
I might expect from either, I was unable to assail again.
Alike, then, in this, are the Slander and the Phantom,—that
which appalls us most in their power over us is our impotence
against them.

But up rose the sun, chasing the shadows from the earth,
and brightening insensibly the thoughts of man. After all,
Margrave had been baffled and defeated, whatever the arts he
had practised and the secrets he possessed. It was, at least,
doubtful whether his evil machinations would be renewed.
He had seemed so incapable of long-sustained fixity of purpose, that it was probable he was already in pursuit of some
new agent or victim; and as to this commonplace and conventional spectre, the so-called World, if it is everywhere to him
whom it awes, it is nowhere to him who despises it. What
was the good or bad word of a Mrs. Poyntz to me? Ay, but
to Lilian? There, indeed, I trembled; but still, even in
trembling, it was sweet to think that my home would be her
shelter,—my choice her vindication. Ah! how unutterably
tender and reverential Love becomes when it assumes the
duties of the guardian, and hallows its own heart into a
sanctuary of refuge for the beloved!

CHAPTER LX.

THE beautiful lake! We two are on its grassy margin, —
twilight melting into night; the stars stealing forth, one after
one. What a wonderful change is made within us when
we come from our callings amongst men, chafed, wearied,
wounded; gnawed by our cares, perplexed by the doubts of
our very wisdom, stung by the adder that dwells in cities,—
Slander; nay, even if renowned, fatigued with the burden of
the very names that we have won! What a change is made

within us when suddenly we find ourselves transported into
the calm solitudes of Nature,— into scenes familiar to our
happy dreaming childhood; back, back from the dusty thoroughfares of our toil-worn manhood to the golden fountain of
our youth! Blessed is the change, even when we have no
companion beside us to whom the heart can whisper its sense
of relief and joy. But if the one in whom all our future is
garnered up be with us there, instead of that weary World
which has so magically vanished away from the eye and the
thought, then does the change make one of those rare epochs
of life in which the charm is the stillness. In the pause
from all by which our own turbulent struggles for happiness
trouble existence, we feel with a rapt amazement how calm a
thing it is to be happy. And so as the night, in deepening,
brightened, Lilian and I wandered by the starry lake. Conscious of no evil in ourselves, how secure we felt from evil!
A few days more — a few days more, and we two should be as
one! And that thought we uttered in many forms of words,
brooding over it in the long intervals of enamoured silence.

And when we turned back to the quiet inn at which we had
taken up our abode, and her mother, with her soft face, advanced to meet us, I said to Lilian,—

"Would that in these scenes we could fix our home for life,
away and afar from the dull town we have left behind us,
with the fret of its wearying cares and the jar of its idle
babble! "

"And why not, Allen? Why not? But no, you would not
be happy."

"Not be happy, and with you? Sceptic, by what reasoning
do you arrive at that ungracious conclusion? "

"The heart loves repose and the soul contemplation, but
the mind needs action. Is it not so? "

"Where learned you that aphorism, out of place on such
rosy lips? "

"I learned it in studying you," murmured Lilian, tenderly.

Here Mrs. Ashleigh joined us. For the first time I slept
under the same roof as Lilian. And I forgot that the universe contained an enigma to solve or an enemy to fear.

CHAPTER LXI.

TWENTY days — the happiest my life had ever known —
thus glided on. Apart from the charm which love bestows
on the beloved, there was that in Lilian's conversation which
made her a delightful companion.   Whether it was that, in this
pause from the toils of my career, my mind could more pliantly
supple itself to her graceful imagination, or that her imagination was less vague and dreamy amidst those rural scenes, which
realized in their loveliness and grandeur its long-conceived
ideals, than it had been in the petty garden-ground neigh-
boured by the stir and hubbub of the busy town, — in much
that I had once slighted or contemned as the vagaries of undisciplined fancy, I now recognized the sparkle and play of
an intuitive genius, lighting up many a depth obscure to instructed thought.   It is with some characters as with the
subtler and more ethereal order of poets, — to appreciate them
we must suspend the course of artificial life; in the city
we call them dreamers, on the mountain-top we find them
interpreters.
     In Lilian, the sympathy with Nature was not, as in Mar-
grave, from the joyous sense of Nature's lavish vitality; it
was refined into exquisite perception of the diviner spirit by
which that vitality is informed.   Thus, like the artist, from
outward forms of beauty she drew forth the covert types,
lending to things the most familiar exquisite meanings un-
conceived before.   For it is truly said by a wise critic of old,
that "the attribute of Art is to suggest infinitely more than
it expresses;" and such suggestions, passing from the artist's
innermost thought into the mind that receives them, open on
and on into the Infinite of Ideas, as a moonlit wave struck by
a passing oar impels wave upon wave along one track of
light.

So the days glided by, and brought the eve of our bridal morn. It had been settled that, after the ceremony (which was to be performed by license in the village church, at no great distance, which adjoined my paternal home, now passed away to strangers), we should make a short excursion into Scotland, leaving Mrs. Ashleigh to await our return at the little inn.

I had retired to my own room to answer some letters from anxious patients, and having finished these I looked into my trunk for a Guide-Book to the North, which I had brought with me. My hand came upon Margrave's wand, and remembering that strange thrill which had passed through me when I last handled it, I drew it forth, resolved to examine calmly if I could detect the cause of the sensation. It was not now the time of night in which the imagination is most liable to credulous impressions, nor was I now in the anxious and jaded state of mind in which such impressions may be the more readily conceived. The sun was slowly setting over the delicious landscape; the air cool and serene; my thoughts collected, — heart and conscience alike at peace. I took, then, the wand, and adjusted it to the palm of the hand as I had done before. I felt the slight touch of the delicate wire within, and again the thrill! I did not this time recoil; I continued to grasp the wand, and sought deliberately to analyze my own sensations in the contact. There came over me an increased consciousness of vital power; a certain exhilaration, elasticity, vigour, such as a strong cordial may produce on a fainting man. All the forces of my frame seemed refreshed, redoubled; and as such effects on the physical system are ordinarily accompanied by correspondent effects on the mind, so I was sensible of a proud elation of spirits, — a kind of defying, superb self-glorying. All fear seemed blotted out from my thought, as a weakness impossible to the grandeur and might which belong to Intellectual Man; I felt as if it were a royal delight to scorn Earth and its opinions, brave Hades and its spectres. Rapidly this new-born arrogance enlarged itself into desires vague but daring. My mind reverted to the wild phenomena associated with its memories of Margrave. I said half-aloud, "If a creature so beneath myself in constancy of will and completion of thought can wrest from Nature favours so marvellous, what could not be won from her by me, her patient persevering seeker? What if there be spirits around and about, invisible to the common eye, but whom we can submit to our control; and what if this rod be charged with some occult fluid, that runs through all creation, and can be so disciplined as to establish communication wherever life and thought can reach to beings that live and think? So would the mystics of old explain what perplexes me. Am I sure that the mystics of old duped themselves or their pupils? This, then, this slight wand, light as a reed in my grasp, this, then, was the instrument by which Margrave sent his irresistible will through air and space, and by which I smote himself, in the midst of his tiger-like wrath, into the helplessness of a sick man's swoon! Can the instrument at this distance still control him; if now meditating evil, disarm and disable his purpose?" Involuntarily, as I revolved these ideas, I stretched forth the wand, with a concentred energy of desire that its influence should reach Margrave and command him. And since I knew not his whereabout, yet was vaguely aware that, according to any conceivable theory by which the wand could be supposed to carry its imagined virtues to definite goals in distant space, it should be pointed in the direction of the object it was intended to affect, so I slowly moved the wand as if describing a circle, and thus, in some point of the circle — east, west, north, or south — the direction could not fail to be true. Before I had performed half the circle, the wand of itself stopped, resisting palpably the movement of my hand to impel it onward. Had it, then, found the point to which my will was guiding it, obeying my will by some magnetic sympathy never yet comprehended by any recognized science? I know not; but I had not held it thus fixed for many seconds, before a cold air, well remembered, passed by me, stirring the roots of my hair; and, reflected against the opposite wall, stood the hateful Scin-Læca. The Shadow was dimmer in its light than when before beheld, and the outline of the features was less distinct; still it was the unmistakable *lemur*, or image, of Margrave.

And a voice was conveyed to my senses, saying, as from a great distance, and in weary yet angry accents,—

" You have summoned me? Wherefore? "

I overcame the startled shudder with which, at first, I beheld the Shadow and heard the Voice.

"I summoned you not," said I; "I sought but to impose upon you my will, that you should persecute, with your ghastly influences, me and mine no more. And now, by whatever authority this wand bestows on me, I so abjure and command you! "

I thought there was a sneer of disdain on the lip through which the answer seemed to come,—

" Vain and ignorant, it is but a shadow you command. My body you have cast into a sleep, and it knows not that the shadow is here; nor, when it wakes, will the brain be aware of one reminiscence of the words that you utter or the words that you hear."

" What, then, is this shadow that simulates the body? Is it that which in popular language is called the soul? "

" It is not: soul is no shadow."

" What then? "

" Ask not me. Use the wand to invoke Intelligences higher than mine."

" And how? "

" I will tell you not. Of yourself you may learn, if you guide the wand by your own pride of will and desire; but in the hands of him who has learned not the art, the wand has its dangers. Again I say you have summoned me! Wherefore? "

" Lying shade, I summoned thee not."

" So wouldst thou say to the demons, did they come in their terrible wrath, when the bungler, who knows not the springs that he moves, calls them up unawares, and can neither control nor dispel. Less revengeful than they, I leave thee unharmed, and depart."

" Stay. If, as thou sayest, no command I address to thee — to thee, who art only the image or shadow — can have effect on the body and mind of the being whose likeness thou art, still thou canst tell me what passes now in his brain. Does it now harbour schemes against me through the woman I love? Answer truly."

"I reply for the sleeper, of whom I am more than a likeness, though only the shadow. His thought speaks thus: 'I know, Allen Fenwick, that in thee is the agent I need for achieving the end that I seek. Through the woman thou lovest, I hope to subject thee. A grief that will harrow thy heart is at hand; when that grief shall befall, thou wilt welcome my coming. In me alone thy hope will be placed; through me alone wilt thou seek a path out of thy sorrow. I shall ask my conditions: they will make thee my tool and my slave!'"

The shadow waned,—it was gone. I did not seek to detain it, nor, had I sought, could I have known by what process. But a new idea now possessed me. This shadow, then, that had once so appalled and controlled me, was, by its own confession, nothing more than a shadow! It had spoken of higher Intelligences; from them I might learn what the Shadow could not reveal. As I still held the wand firmer and firmer in my grasp, my thoughts grew haughtier and bolder. Could the wand, then, bring those loftier beings thus darkly referred to before me? With that thought, intense and engrossing, I guided the wand towards the space, opening boundless and blue from the casement that let in the skies. The wand no longer resisted my hand.

In a few moments I felt the floors of the room vibrate; the air was darkened; a vaporous, hazy cloud seemed to rise from the ground without the casement; an awe, infinitely more deep and solemn than that which the Scin-Læca had caused in its earliest apparition, curdled through my veins, and stilled the very beat of my heart.

At that moment I heard, without, the voice of Lilian, singing a simple, sacred song which I had learned at my mother's knees, and taught to her the day before: singing low, and as with a warning angel's voice. By an irresistible impulse I dashed the wand to the ground, and bowed my head as I had bowed it when my infant mind comprehended, without an

effort, mysteries more solemn than those which perplexed me
now. Slowly I raised my eyes, and looked round; the vaporous, hazy cloud had passed away, or melted into the ambient
rose-tints amidst which the sun had sunk.

Then, by one of those common reactions from a period of
overstrained excitement, there succeeded to that sentiment of
arrogance and daring with which these wild, half-conscious
invocations had been fostered and sustained, a profound humility, a warning fear.

"What!" said I, inly, "have all those sound resolutions,
which my reason founded on the wise talk of Julius Faber,
melted away in the wrack of haggard, dissolving fancies! Is
this my boasted intellect, my vaunted science! I — I, Allen
Fenwick, not only the credulous believer, but the blundering
practitioner, of an evil magic! Grant what may be possible,
however uncomprehended, — grant that in this accursed instrument of antique superstition there be some real powers —
chemical, magnetic, no matter what — by which the imagination can be aroused, inflamed, deluded, so that it shapes the
things I have seen, speaks in the tones I have heard, — grant
this, shall I keep ever ready, at the caprice of will, a constant tempter to steal away my reason and fool my senses?
Or if, on the other hand, I force my sense to admit what all
sober men must reject; if I unschool myself to believe that
in what I have just experienced there is no mental illusion;
that sorcery is a fact, and a demon world has gates which
open to a key that a mortal can forge, — who but a saint
would not shrink from the practice of powers by which each
passing thought of ill might find in a fiend its abettor? In
either case — in any case — while I keep this direful relic of
obsolete arts, I am haunted, — cheated out of my senses, unfitted for the uses of life. If, as my ear or my fancy informs
me, grief — human grief — is about to befall me, shall I, in
the sting of impatient sorrow, have recourse to an aid which,
the same voice declares, will reduce me to a tool and a slave,
— tool and slave to a being I dread as a foe? Out on these
nightmares! and away with the thing that bewitches the brain
to conceive them!"

I rose; I took up the wand, holding it so that its hollow should not rest on the palm of the hand. I stole from the house by the back way, in order to avoid Lilian, whose voice I still heard, singing low, on the lawn in front. I came to a creek, to the bank of which a boat was moored, undid its chain, rowed on to a deep part of the lake, and dropped the wand into its waves. It sank at once; scarcely a ripple furrowed the surface, not a bubble arose from the deep. And, as the boat glided on, the star mirrored itself on the spot where the placid waters had closed over the tempter to evil.

Light at heart, I sprang again on the shore, and hastening to Lilian, where she stood on the silvered, shining sward, clasped her to my breast.

"Spirit of my life!" I murmured, "no enchantments for me but thine! Thine are the spells by which creation is beautified, and, in that beauty, hallowed. What though we can see not into the measureless future from the verge of the moment; what though sorrow may smite us while we are dreaming of bliss, let the future not rob me of thee, and a balm will be found for each wound! Love me ever as now, oh, my Lilian; troth to troth, side by side, till the grave!"

"And beyond the grave," answered Lilian, softly.

CHAPTER LXII.

OUR vows are exchanged at the altar, the rite which made Lilian my wife is performed; we are returned from the church amongst the hills, in which my fathers had worshipped; the joy-bells that had pealed for my birth had rung for my marriage. Lilian has gone to her room to prepare for our bridal excursion; while the carriage we have hired is waiting at the door. I am detaining her mother on the lawn, seeking to cheer and compose her spirits, painfully affected by that sense of change in the relations of child and parent which makes itself suddenly felt by the parent's heart on the day that secures to the child another heart on which to lean.

But Mrs. Ashleigh's was one of those gentle womanly natures which, if easily afflicted, are easily consoled. And, already smiling through her tears, she was about to quit me and join her daughter, when one of the inn-servants came to me with some letters, which had just been delivered by the postman. As I took them from the servant, Mrs. Ashleigh asked if there were any for her. She expected one from her housekeeper at L——, who had been taken ill in her absence, and about whom the kind mistress felt anxious. The servant replied that there was no letter for her, but one directed to Miss Ashleigh, which he had just sent up to the young lady.

Mrs. Ashleigh did not doubt that her housekeeper had written to Lilian, whom she had known from the cradle and to whom she was tenderly attached, instead of to her mistress; and, saying something to me to that effect, quickened her steps towards the house.

I was glancing over my own letters, chiefly from patients, with a rapid eye, when a cry of agony, a cry as if of one suddenly stricken to the heart, pierced my ear,— a cry from within the house. "Heavens! was that Lilian's voice?" The same doubt struck Mrs. Ashleigh, who had already gained the door. She rushed on, disappearing within the threshold and calling to me to follow. I bounded forward, passed her on the stairs, was in Lilian's room before her.

My bride was on the floor prostrate, insensible: so still, so colourless, that my first dreadful thought was that life had gone. In her hand was a letter, crushed as with a convulsive sudden grasp.

It was long before the colour came back to her cheek, before the breath was perceptible on her lip. She woke, but not to health, not to sense. Hours were passed in violent convulsions, in which I momentarily feared her death. To these succeeded stupor, lethargy, not benignant sleep. That night, my bridal night, I passed as in some chamber to which I had been summoned to save youth from the grave. At length — at length — life was rescued, was assured! Life came back, but the mind was gone. She knew me not, nor her mother. She spoke little and faintly; in the words she uttered there was no reason.

I pass hurriedly on; my experience here was in fault, my skill ineffectual. Day followed day, and no ray came back to the darkened brain. We bore her, by gentle stages, to London. I was sanguine of good result from skill more consummate than mine, and more especially devoted to diseases of the mind. I summoned the first advisers. In vain! in vain!

CHAPTER LXIII.

AND the cause of this direful shock? Not this time could it be traced to some evil spell, some phantasmal influence. The cause was clear, and might have produced effects as sinister on nerves of stronger fibre if accompanied by a heart as delicately sensitive, an honour as exquisitely pure.

The letter found in her hand was without name; it was dated from L——, and bore the postmark of that town. It conveyed to Lilian, in the biting words which female malice can make so sharp, the tale we had sought sedulously to guard from her ear, — her flight, the construction that scandal put upon it. It affected for my blind infatuation a contemptuous pity; it asked her to pause before she brought on the name I offered to her an indelible disgrace. If she so decided, she was warned not to return to L——, or to prepare there for the sentence that would exclude her from the society of her own sex. I cannot repeat more, I cannot minute down all that the letter expressed or implied, to wither the orange blossoms in a bride's wreath. The heart that took in the venom cast its poison on the brain, and the mind fled before the presence of a thought so deadly to all the ideas which its innocence had heretofore conceived.

I knew not whom to suspect of the malignity of this mean and miserable outrage, nor did I much care to know. The handwriting, though evidently disguised, was that of a woman, and, therefore, had I discovered the author, my manhood would have forbidden me the idle solace of revenge. Mrs. Poyntz, however resolute and pitiless her hostility when once aroused, was not without a certain largeness of nature irreconcilable with the most dastardly of all the weapons that envy or hatred can supply to the vile. She had too lofty a self-esteem and too decorous a regard for the moral sentiment of the world that she typified, to do, or connive at, an act which degrades the gentlewoman. Putting her aside, what other female enemy had Lilian provoked? No matter! What other woman at L—— was worth the condescension of a conjecture?

After listen'ng to all that the ablest of my professional brethren in the metropolis could suggest to guide me, and trying in vain their remedies, I brought back my charge to L——. Retaining my former residence for the visits of patients, I engaged, for the privacy of my home, a house two miles from the town, secluded in its own grounds, and guarded by high walls.

Lilian's mother removed to my mournful dwelling-place. Abbot's House, in the centre of that tattling coterie, had become distasteful to her, and to me it was associated with thoughts of anguish and of terror. I could not, without a shudder, have entered its grounds,— could not, without a stab at the heart, have seen again the old fairy-land round the Monks' Well, nor the dark cedar-tree under which Lilian's hand had been placed in mine; and a superstitious remembrance, banished while Lilian's angel face had brightened the fatal precincts, now revived in full force. The dying man's curse — had it not been fulfilled?

A new occupant for the old house was found within a week after Mrs. Ashleigh had written from London to a house-agent at L——, intimating her desire to dispose of the lease. Shortly before we had gone to Windermere, Miss Brabazon had become enriched by a liberal life-annuity bequeathed to

her by her uncle, Sir Phelim. Her means thus enabled her
to move from the comparatively humble lodging she had
hitherto occupied to Abbot's House; but just as she had
there commenced a series of ostentatious entertainments, implying an ambitious desire to dispute with Mrs. Poyntz the
sovereignty of the Hill, she was attacked by some severe
malady which appeared complicated with spinal disease, and
after my return to L—— I sometimes met her, on the spacious platform of the Hill, drawn along slowly in a Bath
chair, her livid face peering forth from piles of Indian shawls
and Siberian furs, and the gaunt figure of Dr. Jones stalking
by her side, taciturn and gloomy as some sincere mourner
who conducts to the grave the patron on whose life he himself had conveniently lived. It was in the dismal month of
February that I returned to L——, and I took possession of
my plighted nuptial home on the anniversary of the very day
in which I had passed through the dead dumb world from
the naturalist's gloomy death-room.

CHAPTER LXIV.

LILIAN's wondrous gentleness of nature did not desert her
in the suspension of her reason. She was habitually calm,—
very silent; when she spoke it was rarely on earthly things,
on things familiar to her past, things one could comprehend.
Her thought seemed to have quitted the earth, seeking refuge
in some imaginary heaven. She spoke of wanderings with
her father as if he were living still; she did not seem to understand the meaning we attach to the word "Death." She
would sit for hours murmuring to herself: when one sought
to catch the words, they seemed in converse with invisible
spirits. We found it cruel to disturb her at such times, for
if left unmolested, her face was serene,— more serenely beautiful than I had seen it even in our happiest hours; but when

we called her back to the wrecks of her real life, her eye became troubled, restless, anxious, and she would sigh — oh, so heavily! At times, if we did not seem to observe her, she would quietly resume her once favourite accomplishments, — drawing, music. And in these her young excellence was still apparent, only the drawings were strange and fantastic: they had a resemblance to those with which the painter Blake, himself a visionary, illustrated the Poems of the "Night Thoughts" and "The Grave," — faces of exquisite loveliness, forms of aërial grace, coming forth from the bells of flowers, or floating upwards amidst the spray of fountains, their outlines melting away in fountain or in flower. So with her music: her mother could not recognize the airs she played, for a while so sweetly and with so ineffable a pathos, that one could scarcely hear her without weeping; and then would come, as if involuntarily, an abrupt discord, and, starting, she would cease and look around, disquieted, aghast.

And still she did not recognize Mrs. Ashleigh nor myself as her mother, her husband; but she had by degrees learned to distinguish us both from others. To her mother she gave no name, seemed pleased to see her, but not sensibly to miss her when away; me she called her brother: if longer absent than usual, me she missed. When, after the toils of the day, I came to join her, even if she spoke not, her sweet face brightened. When she sang, she beckoned me to come near to her, and looked at me fixedly, with eyes ever tender, often tearful; when she drew she would pause and glance over her shoulder to see that I was watching her, and point to the drawings with a smile of strange significance, as if they conveyed in some covert allegory messages meant for me; so, at least, I interpreted her smile, and taught myself to say, "Yes, Lilian, I understand!"

And more than once, when I had so answered, she rose, and kissed my forehead. I thought my heart would have broken when I felt that spirit-like melancholy kiss.

And yet how marvellously the human mind teaches itself to extract consolations from its sorrows. The least wretched of my hours were those that I had passed in that saddened room,

seeking how to establish fragments of intercourse, invent
signs, by which each might interpret each, between the intellect I had so laboriously cultured, so arrogantly vaunted, and
the fancies wandering through the dark, deprived of their
guide in reason. It was something even of joy to feel myself
needed for her guardianship, endeared and yearned for still
by some unshattered instinct of her heart; and when, parting
from her for the night, I stole the moment in which on her
soft face seemed resting least of shadow, to ask, in a trembling whisper, "Lilian, are the angels watching over you?"
and she would answer "Yes," sometimes in words, sometimes
with a mysterious happy smile — then — then I went to my
lonely room, comforted and thankful.

———◆———

CHAPTER LXV.

THE blow that had fallen on my hearth effectually, inevitably killed all the slander that might have troubled me in
joy. Before the awe of a great calamity the small passions
of a mean malignity slink abashed. I had requested Mrs.
Ashleigh not to mention the vile letter which Lilian had received. I would not give a triumph to the unknown calum-
niator, nor wring forth her vain remorse, by the pain of
acknowledging an indignity to my darling's honour; yet,
somehow or other, the true cause of Lilian's affliction had
crept out, — perhaps through the talk of servants, — and the
public shock was universal. By one of those instincts of
justice that lie deep in human hearts, though in ordinary
moments overlaid by many a worldly layer, all felt (all
mothers felt especially) that innocence alone could have
been so unprepared for reproach. The explanation I had
previously given, discredited then, was now accepted without
a question. Lilian's present state accounted for all that ill-
nature had before misconstrued. Her good name was restored

to its maiden whiteness, by the fate that had severed the ties of the bride. The formal dwellers on the Hill vied with the franker, warmer-hearted households of Low Town in the nameless attentions by which sympathy and respect are rather delicately indicated than noisily proclaimed. Could Lilian have then recovered and been sensible of its repentant homage, how reverently that petty world would have thronged around her! And, ah! could fortune and man's esteem have atoned for the blight of hopes that had been planted and cherished on ground beyond their reach, ambition and pride might have been well contented with the largeness of the exchange that courted their acceptance. Patients on patients crowded on me. Sympathy with my sorrow seemed to create and endear a more trustful belief in my skill. But the profession I had once so enthusiastically loved became to me wearisome, insipid, distasteful; the kindness heaped on me gave no comfort, — it but brought before me more vividly the conviction that it came too late to avail me: it could not restóre to me the mind, the love, the life of my life, which lay dark and shattered in the brain of my guileless Lilian. Secretly I felt a sullen resentment. I knew that to the crowd the resentment was unjust. The world itself is but an appearance; who can blame it if appearances guide its laws? But to those who had been detached from the crowd by the professions of friendship, — those who, when the slander was yet new, and might have been awed into silence had they stood by my side, — to the pressure of *their* hands, *now*, I had no response.

Against Mrs. Poyntz, above all others, I bore a remembrance of unrelaxed, unmitigable indignation. Her schemes for her daughter's marriage had triumphed: Jane was Mrs. Ashleigh Sumner. Her mind was, perhaps, softened now that the object which had sharpened its worldly faculties was accomplished: but in vain, on first hearing of my affliction, had this she-Machiavel owned a humane remorse, and, with all her keen comprehension of each facility that circumstances gave to her will, availed herself of the general compassion to strengthen the popular reaction in favour of Lilian's assaulted

23

honour; in vain had she written to me with a gentleness of sympathy foreign to her habitual characteristics; in vain besought me to call on her; in vain waylaid and accosted me with a humility that almost implored forgiveness. I vouchsafed no reproach, but I could imply no pardon. I put between her and my great sorrow the impenetrable wall of my freezing silence.

One word of hers at the time that I had so pathetically besought her aid, and the parrot-flock that repeated her very whisper in noisy shrillness would have been as loud to defend as it had been to defame; that vile letter might never have been written. Whoever its writer, it surely was one of the babblers who took their malice itself from the jest or the nod of their female despot; and the writer might have justified herself in saying she did but coarsely proclaim what the oracle of worldly opinion, and the early friend of Lilian's own mother, had authorized her to believe.

By degrees, the bitterness at my heart diffused itself to the circumference of the circle in which my life went its cheerless mechanical round. That cordial brotherhood with his patients, which is the true physician's happiest gift and humanest duty, forsook my breast. The warning words of Mrs. Poyntz had come true. A patient that monopolized my thought awaited me at my own hearth! My conscience became troubled; I felt that my skill was lessened. I said to myself, "The physician who, on entering the sick-room, feels, while there, something that distracts the finest powers of his intellect from the sufferer's case is unfit for his calling." A year had scarcely passed since my fatal wedding-day, before I had formed a resolution to quit L—— and abandon my profession; and my resolution was confirmed, and my goal determined, by a letter I received from Julius Faber.

I had written at length to him, not many days after the blow that had fallen on me, stating all circumstances as calmly and clearly as my grief would allow; for I held his skill at a higher estimate than that of any living brother of my art, and I was not without hope in the efficacy of his

advice. The letter I now received from him had been begun,
and continued at some length, before my communication
reached him; and this earlier portion contained animated
and cheerful descriptions of his Australian life and home,
which contrasted with the sorrowful tone of the supplement
written in reply to the tidings with which I had wrung his
friendly and tender heart. In this, the latter part of his letter, he suggested that if time had wrought no material change
for the better, it might be advisable to try the effect of foreign travel. Scenes entirely new might stimulate observation, and the observation of things external withdraw the
sense from that brooding over images delusively formed
within, which characterized the kind of mental alienation I
had described. "Let any intellect create for itself a visionary world, and all reasonings built on it are fallacious: the
visionary world vanishes in proportion as we can arouse a
predominant interest in the actual."

This grand authority, who owed half his consummate skill
as a practitioner to the scope of his knowledge as a philosopher, then proceeded to give me a hope which I had not dared
of myself to form. He said: —

"I distinguish the case you so minutely detail from that insanity
which is reason lost; here it seems rather to be reason held in suspense.
Where there is hereditary predisposition, where there is organic change
of structure in the brain, — nay, where there is that kind of insanity
which takes the epithet of moral, whereby the whole character becomes
so transformed that the prime element of sound understanding, conscience itself, is either erased or warped into the sanction of what in a
healthful state it would most disapprove, — it is only charlatans who
promise effectual cure. But here I assume that there is no hereditary
taint; here I am convinced, from my own observation, that the nobility
of the organs, all fresh as yet in the vigour of youth, would rather submit to death than to the permenent overthrow of their equilibrium in
reason; here, where you tell me the character preserves all its moral
attributes of gentleness and purity, and but over-indulges its own early
habit of estranged contemplation; here, without deceiving you in false
kindness, I give you the guarantee of my experience when I bid you
'hope!' I am persuaded that, sooner or later, the mind, thus for a
time affected, will right itself; because here, in the cause of the malady,

we do but deal with the nervous system. And *that*, once righted, and the mind once disciplined in those practical duties which conjugal life necessitates, the malady itself will never return ; never be transmitted to the children on whom your wife's restoration to health may permit you to count hereafter. If the course of travel I recommend and the prescriptions I conjoin with that course fail you, let me know ; and though I would fain close my days in this land, I will come to you. I love you as my son. I will tend your wife as my daughter."

Foreign travel! The idea smiled on me. Julius Faber's companionship, sympathy, matchless skill! The very thought seemed as a raft to a drowning mariner. I now read more attentively the earlier portions of his letter. They described, in glowing colours, the wondrous country in which he had fixed his home; the joyous elasticity of its atmosphere; the freshness of its primitive, pastoral life; the strangeness of its scenery, with a Flora and a Fauna which have no similitudes in the ransacked quarters of the Old World. And the strong impulse seized me to transfer to the solitudes of that blithesome and hardy Nature a spirit no longer at home in the civilized haunts of men, and household gods that shrank from all social eyes, and would fain have found a wilderness for the desolate hearth, on which they had ceased to be sacred if unveiled. As if to give practical excuse and reason for the idea that seized me, Julius Faber mentioned, incidentally, that the house and property of a wealthy speculator in his immediate neighbourhood were on sale at a price which seemed to me alluringly trivial, and, according to his judgment, far below the value they would soon reach in the hands of a more patient capitalist. He wrote at the period of the agricultural panic in the colony which preceded the discovery of its earliest gold-fields. But his geological science had convinced him that strata within and around the property now for sale were auriferous, and his intelligence enabled him to predict how inevitably man would be attracted towards the gold, and how surely the gold would fertilize the soil and enrich its owners. He described the house thus to be sold — in case I might know of a purchaser. It had been built at a cost unusual in those early times, and by one who clung to

English tastes amidst Australian wilds, so that in this purchase a settler would escape the hardships he had then ordinarily to encounter; it was, in short, a home to which a man more luxurious than I might bear a bride with wants less simple than those which now sufficed for my darling Lilian.

This communication dwelt on my mind through the avocations of the day on which I received it, and in the evening I read all, except the supplement, aloud to Mrs. Ashleigh in her daughter's presence. I desired to see if Faber's descriptions of the country and its life, which in themselves were extremely spirited and striking, would arouse Lilian's interest. At first she did not seem to heed me while I read; but when I came to Faber's loving account of little Amy, Lilian turned her eyes towards me, and evidently listened with attention. He wrote how the child had already become the most useful person in the simple household. How watchful the quickness of the heart had made the service of the eye; all their associations of comfort had grown round her active, noiseless movements; it was she who had contrived to monopolize the management, or supervision, of all that added to Home the nameless, interior charm. Under her eyes the rude furniture of the log-house grew inviting with English neatness; she took charge of the dairy; she had made the garden gay with flowers selected from the wild, and suggested the trellised walk, already covered with hardy vine. She was their confidant in every plan of improvement, their comforter in every anxious doubt, their nurse in every passing ailment, her very smile a refreshment in the weariness of daily toil. "How all that is best in womanhood," wrote the old man, with the enthusiasm which no time had reft from his hearty, healthful genius, — "how all that is best in womanhood is here opening fast into flower from the bud of the infant's soul! The atmosphere seems to suit it,— the child-woman in the child-world! "

I heard Lilian sigh; I looked towards her furtively; tears stood in her softened eyes; her lip was quivering. Presently, she began to rub her right hand over the left — over the wedding-ring — at first slowly; then with quicker movement.

"It is not here," she said impatiently; "it is *not* here!"

"What is not here?" asked Mrs. Ashleigh, hanging over her.

Lilian leaned back her head on her mother's bosom, and answered faintly,—

"The stain! Some one said there was a stain on this hand. I do not see it, do you?"

"There is no stain, never was," said I; "the hand is white as your own innocence, or the lily from which you take your name."

"Hush! you do not know my name. I will whisper it. Soft! — my name is Nightshade! Do you want to know where the lily is now, brother? I will tell you. There, in that letter. You call her Amy,— she is the lily; take her to your breast, hide her. Hist! what are those bells? Marriage-bells. Do not let her hear them; for there is a cruel wind that whispers the bells, and the bells ring out what it whispers, louder and louder,—

> " ' Stain on lily
> Shame on lily,
> Wither lily.'

If she hears what the wind whispers to the bells, she will creep away into the dark, and then she, too, will turn to Nightshade."

"Lilian, look up, awake! You have been in a long, long dream: it is passing away. Lilian, my beloved, my blessed Lilian!"

Never till then had I heard from her even so vague an allusion to the fatal calumny and its dreadful effect, and while her words now pierced my heart, it beat, amongst its pangs, with a thrilling hope.

But, alas! the idea that had gleamed upon her had vanished already. She murmured something about Circles of Fire, and a Veiled Woman in black garments; became restless, agitated, and unconscious of our presence, and finally sank into a heavy sleep.

That night (my room was next to hers with the intervening

door open) I heard her cry out. I hastened to her side. She was still asleep, but there was an anxious labouring expression on her young face, and yet not an expression wholly of pain — for her lips were parted with a smile, — that glad yet troubled smile with which one who has been revolving some subject of perplexity or fear greets a sudden thought that seems to solve the riddle, or prompt the escape from danger; and as I softly took her hand she returned my gentle pressure, and inclining towards me, said, still in sleep, —

"Let us go."

"Whither?" I answered, under my breath, so as not to awake her; "is it to see the child of whom I read, and the land that is blooming out of the earth's childhood?"

"Out of the dark into the light; where the leaves do not change; where the night is our day, and the winter our summer. Let us go! let us go!"

"We will go. Dream on undisturbed, my bride. Oh, that the dream could tell you that my love has not changed in our sorrow, holier and deeper than on the day in which our vows were exchanged! In you still all my hopes fold their wings; where you are, there still I myself have my dreamland!"

The sweet face grew bright as I spoke; all trouble left the smile; softly she drew her hand from my clasp, and rested it for a moment on my bended head, as if in blessing.

I rose; stole back to my own room, closing the door, lest the sob I could not stifle should mar her sleep.

CHAPTER LXVI.

I UNFOLDED my new prospects to Mrs. Ashleigh. She was more easily reconciled to them than I could have supposed, judging by her habits, which were naturally indolent, and averse to all that disturbed their even tenor. But the great grief which had befallen her had roused up that strength of devotion which lies dormant in all hearts that are capable of loving another more than self. With her full consent I wrote to Faber, communicating my intentions, instructing him to purchase the property he had so commended, and inclosing my banker's order for the amount, on an Australian firm. I now announced my intention to retire from my profession; made prompt arrangements with a successor to my practice; disposed of my two houses at L——; fixed the day of my departure. Vanity was dead within me, or I might have been gratified by the sensation which the news of my design created. My faults became at once forgotten; such good qualities as I might possess were exaggerated. The public regret vented and consoled itself in a costly testimonial, to which even the poorest of my patients insisted on the privilege to contribute, graced with an inscription flattering enough to have served for the epitaph on some great man's tomb. No one who has served an art and striven for a name is a stoic to the esteem of others; and sweet indeed would such honours have been to me had not publicity itself seemed a wrong to the sanctity of that affliction which set Lilian apart from the movement and the glories of the world.

The two persons most active in "getting up" this testimonial were, nominally, Colonel Poyntz — in truth, his wife — and my old disparager, Mr. Vigors! It is long since my narrative has referred to Mr. Vigors. It is due to him now to state that, in his capacity of magistrate, and in his own way, he had been both active and delicate in the inquiries set on foot for Lilian during the unhappy time in which she had wandered, spellbound, from her home. He, alone, of all the more influential magnates of the town, had upheld her innocence·against the gossips that aspersed it; and during the last trying year of my residence at L——, he had sought me, with frank and manly confessions of his regret for his former prejudice against me, and assurances of the respect in which he had held me ever since my marriage — marriage but in rite — with Lilian. He had then, strong in his ruling passion, besought me to consult his clairvoyants as to her case. I declined this invitation so as not to affront him, — declined it, not as I should once have done, but with no word nor look of incredulous disdain. The fact was, that I had conceived a solemn terror of all practices and theories out of the beaten track of sense and science. Perhaps in my refusal I did wrong. I know not. I was afraid of my own imagination. He continued not less friendly in spite of my refusal. And, such are the vicissitudes in human feeling, I parted from him whom I had regarded as my most bigoted foe 'with a warmer sentiment of kindness than for any of those on whom I had counted on friendship. *He* had not deserted Lilian. It was not so with Mrs. Poyntz. I would have paid tenfold the value of the testimonial to have erased, from the list of those who subscribed to it, her husband's name.

The day before I quitted L——, and some weeks after I had, in fact, renounced my practice, I received an urgent entreaty from Miss Brabazon to call on her. She wrote in lines so blurred that I could with difficulty decipher them, that she was very ill, given over by Dr. Jones, who had been attending her. She implored my opinion.

CHAPTER LXVII.

On reaching the house, a formal man-servant, with indifferent face, transferred me to the guidance of a hired nurse, who led me up the stairs, and, before I was well aware of it, into the room in which Dr. Lloyd had died. Widely different, indeed, the aspect of the walls, the character of the furniture! The dingy paper-hangings were replaced by airy muslins, showing a rose-coloured ground through their fanciful openwork; luxurious *fauteuils*, gilded wardrobes, full-length mirrors, a toilet-table tricked out with lace and ribbons, and glittering with an array of silver gewgaws and jewelled trinkets,— all transformed the sick chamber of the simple man of science to a boudoir of death for the vain coquette. But the room itself, in its high lattice and heavy ceiling, was the same — as the coffin itself has the same confines, whether it be rich in velvets and bright with blazoning, or rude as a pauper's shell.

And the bed, with its silken coverlet, and its pillows edged with the thread-work of Louvain, stood in the same sharp angle as that over which had flickered the frowning smoke-reek above the dying, resentful foe. As I approached, a man, who was seated beside the sufferer, turned round his face, and gave me a silent kindly nod of recognition. He was Mr. C——, one of the clergy of the town, the one with whom I had the most frequently come into contact wherever the physician resigns to the priest the language that bids man hope. Mr. C——, as a preacher, was renowned for his touching eloquence; as a pastor, revered for his benignant piety; as friend and neighbour, beloved for a sweetness of nature which seemed to regulate all the movements of a mind eminently masculine by the beat of a heart tender as the gentlest woman's.

This good man, then whispering something to the sufferer which I did not overhear, stole towards me, took me by the hand, and said, also in a whisper, "Be merciful as Christians are." He led me to the bedside, there left me, went out, and closed the door.

"Do you think I am really dying, Dr. Fenwick?" said a feeble voice. "I fear Dr. Jones has misunderstood my case. I wish I had called you in at the first, but — but I could not — I could not! Will you feel my pulse? Don't you think you could do me good?"

I had no need to feel the pulse in that skeleton wrist; the aspect of the face sufficed to tell me that death was drawing near.

Mechanically, however, I went through the hackneyed formulæ of professional questions. This vain ceremony done, as gently and delicately as I could, I implied the expediency of concluding, if not yet settled, those affairs which relate to this world.

"This duty," I said, "in relieving the mind from care for

others to whom we owe the forethought of affection, often
relieves the body also of many a gnawing pain, and sometimes, to the surprise of the most experienced physician, prolongs life itself."

"Ah," said the old maid, peevishly, "I understand! But
it is not my will that troubles me. I should not be left to a
nurse from a hospital if my relations did not know that my
annuity dies with me; and I forestalled it in furnishing this
house, Dr. Fenwick, and all these pretty things will be sold
to pay those horrid tradesmen! — very hard! — so hard! —
just as I got things about me in the way I always said I
would have them if I could ever afford it! I always said I
would have my bedroom hung with muslin, like dear Lady
L——'s ; and the drawing-room in geranium-coloured silk:
so pretty. You have not seen it: you would not know the
house, Dr. Fenwick. And just when all is finished, to be
taken away and thrust into the grave. It is so cruel!" And
she began to weep. Her emotion brought on a violent parox-
ysm, which, when she recovered from it, had produced one of
those startling changes of mind that are sometimes witnessed
before death, — changes whereby the whole character of a life
seems to undergo solemn transformation. The hard will becomes gentle, the proud meek, the frivolous earnest. That
awful moment when the things of earth pass away like dissolving scenes, leaving death visible on the background by the
glare that shoots up in the last flicker of life's lamp.

And when she lifted her haggard face from my shoulder,
and heard my pitying, soothing voice, it was not the grief of
a trifler at the loss of fondled toys that spoke in the fallen
lines of her lip, in the woe of her pleading eyes.

"So this is death," she said. "I feel it hurrying on. I
must speak. I promised Mr. C—— that I would. Forgive
me, can you — can you? That letter — that letter to Lilian
Ashleigh, I wrote it! Oh, do not look at me so terribly; I
never thought it could do such evil! And am I not punished
enough? I truly believed when I wrote that Miss Ashleigh
was deceiving you, and once I was silly enough to fancy that
you might have liked me. But I had another motive; I had

been so poor all my life — I had become rich unexpectedly; 1
set my heart on this house — I had always fancied it — and
I thought if I could prevent Miss Ashleigh marrying you,
and scare her and her mother from coming back to L——, I
could get the house. And I did get it. What for? — to die.
I had not been here a week before I got the hurt that is killing me — a fall down the stairs, — coming out of this very
room; the stairs had been polished. If I had stayed in my
old lodging, it would not have happened. Oh, say you forgive me! Say, say it, even if you do not feel you can! Say
it!" And the miserable woman grasped me by the arm as
Dr. Lloyd had grasped me.

I shaded my averted face with my hands; my heart heaved
with the agony of my suppressed passion. A wrong, however
deep, only to myself, I could have pardoned without effort;
such a wrong to Lilian, — no! I could not say "I forgive."

The dying wretch was perhaps more appalled by my silence
than she would have been by my reproach. Her voice grew
shrill in her despair.

"You will not pardon me! I shall die with your curse on
my head! Mercy! mercy! That good man, Mr. C——, assured me you would be merciful. Have *you* never wronged
another? Has the Evil One never tempted *you?*"

Then I spoke in broken accents: "Me! Oh, had it been I
whom you defamed — but a young creature so harmless, so
unoffending, and for so miserable a motive!"

"But I tell you, I swear to you, I never dreamed I could
cause such sorrow; and that young man, that Margrave, put
it into my head!"

"Margrave! He had left L—— long before that letter was
written!"

"But he came back for a day just before I wrote: it was
the very day. I met him in the lane yonder. He asked after
you, — after Miss Ashleigh; and when he spoke he laughed,
and I said, 'Miss Ashleigh had been ill, and was gone away;'
and he laughed again. And I thought he knew more than he
would tell me, so I asked him if he supposed Mrs. Ashleigh
would come back, and said how much I should like to take

this house if she did not; and again he laughed, and said, 'Birds never stay in the nest after the young ones are hurt,' and went away singing. When I got home, his laugh and his song haunted me. I thought I saw him still in my room, prompting me to write, and I sat down and wrote. Oh, pardon, pardon me! I have been a foolish poor creature, but never meant to do such harm. The Evil One tempted me! There he is, near me now! I see him yonder! there, at the doorway. He comes to claim me! As you hope for mercy yourself, free me from him! Forgive me!"

I made an effort over myself. In naming Margrave as her tempter, the woman had suggested an excuse, echoed from that innermost cell of my mind, which I recoiled from gazing into, for there I should behold his image. Inexpiable though the injury she had wrought against me and mine, still the woman was human — fellow-creature — like myself; — but HE?

I took the pale hand that still pressed my arm, and said, with firm voice, —

"Be comforted. In the name of Lilian, my wife, I forgive you for her and for me as freely and as fully as we are enjoined by Him, against whose precepts the best of us daily sin, to forgive — we children of wrath — to forgive one another!"

"Heaven bless you! — oh, bless you!" she murmured, sinking back upon her pillow.

"Ah!" thought I, "what if the pardon I grant for a wrong far deeper than I inflicted on him whose imprecation smote me in this chamber, should indeed be received as atonement, and this blessing on the lips of the dying annul the dark curse that the dead has left on my path through the Valley of the Shadow!"

I left my patient sleeping quietly, — the sleep that precedes the last. As I went down the stairs into the hall, I saw Mrs. Poyntz standing at the threshold, speaking to the man-servant and the nurse.

I would have passed her with a formal bow, but she stopped me.

"I came to inquire after poor Miss Brabazon," said she.

"You can tell me more than the servants can: is there no hope?"

"Let the nurse go up and watch beside her. She may pass away in the sleep into which she has fallen."

"Allen Fenwick, I must speak with you — nay, but for a few minutes. I hear that you leave L—— to-morrow. It is scarcely among the chances of life that we should meet again." While thus saying, she drew me along the lawn down the path that led towards her own home. "I wish," said she, earnestly, "that you could part with a kindlier feeling towards me; but I can scarcely expect it. Could I put myself in your place, and be moved by your feelings, I know that I should be implacable; but I —"

"But you, madam, are The World! and the World governs itself, and dictates to others, by laws which seem harsh to those who ask from its favour the services which the World cannot tender, for the World admits favourites, but ignores friends. You did but act to me as the World ever acts to those who mistake its favour for its friendship."

"It is true," said Mrs. Poyntz, with blunt candour; and we continued to walk on silently. At length she said abruptly, "But do you not rashly deprive yourself of your only consolation in sorrow? When the heart suffers, does your skill admit any remedy like occupation to the mind? Yet you abandon that occupation to which your mind is most accustomed; you desert your career; you turn aside, in the midst of the race, from the fame which awaits at the goal; you go back from civilization itself, and dream that all your intellectual cravings can find content in the life of a herdsman, amidst the monotony of a wild! No, you will repent, for you are untrue to your mind!"

"I am sick of the word 'mind'!" said I, bitterly. And therewith I relapsed into musing.

The enigmas which had foiled my intelligence in the unravelled Sibyl Book of Nature were mysteries strange to every man's normal practice of thought, even if reducible to the fraudulent impressions of outward sense; for illusions in a brain otherwise healthy suggest problems in our human organization which the colleges that record them rather guess at than solve. But the blow which had shattered my life had been dealt by the hand of a fool. Here, there were no mystic enchantments. Motives the most commonplace and paltry, suggested to a brain as trivial and shallow as ever made the frivolity of woman a theme for the satire of poets, had sufficed, in devastating the field of my affections, to blast the uses for which I had cultured my mind; and had my intellect been as great as heaven ever gave to man, it would have been as vain a shield as mine against the shaft that had lodged in my heart. While I had, indeed, been preparing my reason and my fortitude to meet such perils, weird and marvellous, as those by which tales round the winter fireside scare the credulous child, a contrivance — so vulgar and hackneyed that not a day passes but what some hearth is vexed by an anonymous libel — had wrought a calamity more dread than aught which my dark guess into the Shadow-Land unpierced by Philosophy could trace to the prompting of malig·· nant witchcraft. So, ever this truth runs through all legends of ghost and demon — through the uniform records of what wonder accredits and science rejects as the supernatural — lo! the dread machinery whose wheels roll through Hades! What need such awful engines for such mean results? The first blockhead we meet in our walk to our grocer's can tell us more than the ghost tells us; the poorest envy we ever aroused hurts us more than the demon. How true an interpreter is Genius to Hell as to Earth! The Fiend comes to Faust, the tired seeker of knowledge; Heaven and Hell stake their cause in the Mortal's temptation. And what does the Fiend to astonish the Mortal? Turn wine into fire, turn love into crime. We need no Mephistopheles to accomplish these marvels every day!

Thus silently thinking, I walked by the side of the world-wise woman; and when she next spoke, I looked up, and saw that we were at the Monks' Well, where I had first seen Lilian gazing into heaven!

Mrs. Poyntz had, as we walked, placed her hand on my arm; and, turning abruptly from the path into the glade, I

found myself standing by her side in the scene where a new
sense of being had first disclosed to my sight the hues with
which Love, the passionate beautifier, turns into purple and
gold the gray of the common air. Thus, when romance has
ended in sorrow, and the Beautiful fades from the landscape,
the trite and positive forms of life, banished for a time, reappear, and deepen our mournful remembrance of the glories
they replace. And the Woman of the World, finding how
little I was induced to respond to her when she had talked of
myself, began to speak, in her habitual clear, ringing accents,
of her own social schemes and devices, —

"I shall miss you when you are gone, Allen Fenwick; for
though, during the last year or so, all actual intercourse between us has ceased, yet my interest in you gave some occupation to my thoughts when I sat alone, — having lost my
main object of ambition in settling my daughter, and having
no longer any one in the house with whom I could talk of the
future, or for whom I could form a project. It is so wearisome to count the changes which pass within us, that we take
interest in the changes that pass without. Poyntz still has
his weather-glass; I have no longer my Jane."

"I cannot linger with you on this spot," said I, impatiently turning back into the path; she followed, treading
over fallen leaves. And unheeding my interruption, she thus
continued her hard talk, —

"But I am not sick of my mind, as you seem to be of
yours; I am only somewhat tired of the little cage in which,
since it has been alone, it ruffles its plumes against the flimsy
wires that confine it from wider space. I shall take up my
home for a time with the new-married couple: they want me.
Ashleigh Sumner has come into parliament. He means to
attend regularly and work hard, but he does not like Jane to
go into the world by herself, and he wishes her to go into the
world, because he wants a wife to display his wealth for the
improvement of his position. In Ashleigh Sumner's house I
shall have ample scope for my energies, such as they are. I
have a curiosity to see the few that perch on the wheels of
the State and say, 'It is we who move the wheels!' It will

"LILIAN LOVED TO SIT ON THE DECK WHEN THE NIGHTS WERE FAIR."

amuse me to learn if I can maintain in a capital the authority I have won in a country town; if not, I can but return to my small principality. Wherever I live I must sway, not serve. If I succeed — as I ought, for in Jane's beauty and Ashleigh's fortune I have materials for the woof of ambition, wanting which here, I fall asleep over my knitting — if I succeed, there will be enough to occupy the rest of my life. Ashleigh Sumner must be a power; the power will be represented and enjoyed by my child, and created and maintained by me! Allen Fenwick, do as I do. Be world with the world, and it will only be in moments of spleen and chagrin that you will sigh to think that the heart may be void when the mind is full. Confess you envy me while you listen."

"Not so; all that to you seems so great appears to me so small! Nature alone is always grand, in her terrors as well as her charms. The World for you, Nature for me. Farewell!"

"Nature!" said Mrs. Poyntz, compassionately. "Poor Allen Fenwick! Nature indeed,— intellectual suicide! Nay, shake hands, then, if for the last time."

So we shook hands and parted, where the wicket-gate and the stone stairs separated my blighted fairy-land from the common thoroughfare.

CHAPTER LXVIII.

THAT night as I was employed in collecting the books and manuscripts which I proposed to take with me, including my long-suspended physiological work, and such standard authorities as I might want to consult or refer to in the portions yet incompleted, my servant entered to inform me, in answer to the inquiries I had sent him to make, that Miss Brabazon had peacefully breathed her last an hour before. Well! my pardon had perhaps soothed her last moments; but how unavailing her death-bed repentance to undo the wrong she had done!

I turned from that thought, and, glancing at the work into which I had thrown all my learning, methodized into system with all my art, I recalled the pity which Mrs. Poyntz had expressed for my meditated waste of mind. The tone of superiority which this incarnation of common-sense accompanied by uncommon will assumed over all that was too deep or too high for her comprehension had sometimes amused me; thinking over it now, it piqued. I said to myself, "After all, I shall bear with me such solace as intellectual occupation can afford. I shall have leisure to complete this labour; and a record that I have lived and thought may outlast all the honours which worldly ambition may bestow upon Ashleigh Sumner!" And, as I so murmured, my hand, mechanically selecting the books I needed, fell on the Bible that Julius Faber had given to me.

It opened at the Second Book of Esdras, which our Church places amongst the Apocrypha, and is generally considered by scholars to have been written in the first or second century of the Christian era,[1] — but in which the questions raised by man in the remotest ages, to which we can trace back his desire "to comprehend the ways of the Most High," are invested with a grandeur of thought and sublimity of word to which I know of no parallel in writers we call profane.

My eye fell on this passage in the lofty argument between the Angel whose name was Uriel, and the Prophet, perplexed by his own cravings for knowledge: —

" He [the Angel] answered me, and said, I went into a forest, into a plain, and the trees took counsel,

" And said, Come, let us go and make war against the sea, that it may depart away before us, and that we may make us more woods.

" The floods of the sea also in like manner took counsel, and said, Come, let us go up and subdue the woods of the plain, that there also we may make us another country.

[1] Such is the supposition of Jahn. Dr. Lee, however, is of opinion that the author was contemporary, and, indeed, identical, with the author of the Book of Enoch.

" The thought of the wood was in vain, for the fire came and consumed it.

" The thought of the floods of the sea came likewise to nought, for
the sand stood up and stopped them.

" If thou wert judge now betwixt these two, whom wouldst thou
begin to justify; or whom wouldst thou condemn ?

" I answered and said, Verily it is a foolish thought that they both
have devised; for the ground is given unto the wood, and the sea also
hath his place to bear his floods.

" Then answered he me, and said, Thou hast given a right judgment;
but why judgest thou not thyself also ?

" For like as the ground is given unto the wood, and the sea to his
floods, even so they that dwell upon the earth may understand nothing
but that which is upon the earth; and He that dwelleth above the
heavens may only understand the things that are above the height of
the heavens."

I paused at those words, and, closing the Sacred Volume,
fell into deep, unquiet thought.

CHAPTER LXIX.

I HAD hoped that the voyage would produce some beneficial
effect upon Lilian; but no effect, good or bad, was perceptible, except, perhaps, a deeper silence, a gentler calm. She
loved to sit on the deck when the nights were fair, and the
stars mirrored on the deep. And once thus, as I stood beside
her, bending over the rail of the vessel, and gazing on the
long wake of light which the moon made amidst the darkness
of an ocean to which no shore could be seen, I said to myself,
"Where is my track of light through the measureless future?
Would that I could believe as I did when a child! Woe is
me, that all the reasonings I take from my knowledge should
lead me away from the comfort which the peasant who mourns
finds in faith! Why should riddles so dark have been thrust
upon me,— me, no fond child of fancy; me, sober pupil of

schools the severest? Yet what marvel — the strangest my
senses have witnessed or feigned in the fraud they have
palmed on me — is greater than that by which a simple affection, that all men profess to have known, has. changed the
courses of life pre-arranged by my hopes and confirmed by
my judgment? How calmly before I knew love I have anato-
mized its mechanism, as the tyro who dissects the web-work
of tissues and nerves in the dead! Lo! it lives, lives in me;
and, in living, escapes from my scalpel, and mocks all my
knowledge. Can love be reduced to the realm of the senses?
No; what nun is more barred by her grate from the realm of
the senses than my bride by her solemn affliction? Is love,
then, the union of kindred, harmonious minds? No, my beloved one sits by my side, and I guess not her thoughts, and
my mind is to her a sealed fountain. Yet I love her more —
oh, ineffably more! — for the doom which destroys the two
causes philosophy assigns to love — in the form, in the mind!
How can I now, in my vain physiology, say what is love,
what is not? Is it love which must tell me that man has a
soul, and that in soul will be found the solution of problems
never to be solved in body or mind alone?"

My self-questionings halted here as Lilian's hand touched
my shoulder. She had risen from her seat, and had come
to me.

"Are not the stars very far from earth?" she said.

"Very far."

"Are they seen for the first time to-night?"

"They were seen, I presume, as we see them, by the fathers
of all human races!"

"Yet close below us they shine reflected in the waters; and
yet, see, wave flows on wave before we can count it!"

"Lilian, by what sympathy do you read and answer my
thought?"

Her reply was incoherent and meaningless. If a gleam of
intelligence had mysteriously lighted my heart to her view,
it was gone. But drawing her nearer towards me, my eye
long followed wistfully the path of light, dividing the darkness on either hand, till it closed in the sloping horizon.

CHAPTER LXX.

THE voyage is over. At the seaport at which we landed I
found a letter from Faber. My instructions had reached him
in time to effect the purchase on which his descriptions had
fixed my desire. The stock, the implements of husbandry,
the furniture of the house, were included in the purchase.
All was prepared for my arrival, and I hastened from the
then miserable village, which may some day rise into one
of the mightiest capitals of the world, to my lodge in the
wilderness.

It was the burst of the Australian spring, which commences
in our autumn month of October. The air was loaded with
the perfume of the acacias. Amidst the glades of the open
forest land, or climbing the craggy banks of winding silvery
creeks,[1] creepers and flowers of dazzling hue contrasted the
olive-green of the surrounding foliage. The exhilarating effect of the climate in that season heightens the charm of the
strange scenery. In the brilliancy of the sky, in the lightness of the atmosphere, the sense of life is wondrously quickened. With the very breath the Adventurer draws in from
the racy air, he feels as if inhaling hope.

We have reached our home, we are settled in it; the early
unfamiliar impressions are worn away. We have learned to
dispense with much that we at first missed, and are reconciled
to much that at first disappointed or displeased.

The house is built but of logs; the late proprietor had commenced, upon a rising ground, a mile distant, a more imposing edifice of stone, but it is not half finished.

This log-house is commodious, and much has been done,
within and without, to conceal or adorn its primitive rudeness. It is of irregular, picturesque form, with verandas

---

[1] Creek is the name given by Australian colonists to precarious water-
courses and tributary streams.

round three sides of it, to which the grape-vine has been trained, with glossy leaves that clamber up to the gable roof. There is a large garden in front, in which many English fruit-trees have been set, and grow fast amongst the plants of the tropics and the orange-trees of Southern Europe. Beyond stretch undulous pastures, studded not only with sheep, but with herds of cattle, which my speculative predecessor had bred from parents of famous stock, and imported from England at mighty cost; but as yet the herds had been of little profit, and they range their luxuriant expanse of pasture with as little heed. To the left soar up, in long range, the many-coloured hills; to the right meanders a creek, belted by feathery trees; and on its opposite bank a forest opens, through frequent breaks, into park-like glades and alleys. The territory, of which I so suddenly find myself the lord, is vast, even for a colonial capitalist.

It had been originally purchased as "a special survey," comprising twenty thousand acres, with the privilege of pasture over forty thousand more. In very little of this land, though it includes some of the most fertile districts in the known world, has cultivation been even commenced. At the time I entered into possession, even sheep were barely profitable; labour was scarce and costly. Regarded as a speculation, I could not wonder that my predecessor fled in fear from his domain. Had I invested the bulk of my capital in this lordly purchase, I should have deemed myself a ruined man; but a villa near London, with a hundred acres, would have cost me as much to buy, and thrice as much to keep up. I could afford the investment I had made. I found a Scotch bailiff already on the estate, and I was contented to escape from rural occupations, to which I brought no experience, by making it worth his while to serve me with zeal. Two domestics of my own, and two who had been for many years with Mrs. Ashleigh, had accompanied us: they remained faithful and seemed contented. So the clockwork of our mere household arrangements went on much the same as in our native home. Lilian was not subjected to the ordinary privations and discomforts that await the wife even of the wealthy emigrant. Alas! would she have heeded them if she had been?

The change of scene wrought a decided change for the better in her health and spirits, but not such as implied a dawn of reviving reason. But her countenance was now more rarely overcast. Its usual aspect was glad with a soft mysterious smile. She would murmur snatches of songs, that were partly borrowed from English poets, and partly glided away into what seemed spontaneous additions of her own, — wanting intelligible meaning, but never melody nor rhyme. Strange, that memory and imitation — the two earliest parents of all inventive knowledge — should still be so active, and judgment — the after faculty, that combines the rest into purpose and method — be annulled!

Julius Faber I see continually, though his residence is a few miles distant. He is sanguine as to Lilian's ultimate recovery; and, to my amazement and to my envy, he has contrived, by some art which I cannot attain, to establish between her and himself intelligible communion. She comprehends his questions, when mine, though the simplest, seem to her in unknown language; and he construes into sense her words, that to me are meaningless riddles.

"I was right," he said to me one day, leaving her seated in the garden beside her quiet, patient mother, and joining me where I lay — listless yet fretful — under the shadeless gum-trees, gazing not on the flocks and fields that I could call my own, but on the far mountain range, from which the arch of the horizon seemed to spring, — "I was right," said the great physician; "this is reason suspended, not reason lost. Your wife will recover; but — "

"But what?"

"Give me your arm as I walk homeward, and I will tell you the conclusion to which I have come."

I rose, the old man leaned on me, and we went down the valley along the craggy ridges of the winding creek. The woodland on the opposite bank was vocal with the chirp and croak and chatter of Australian birds, — all mirthful, all songless, save that sweetest of warblers, which some early irreverent emigrant degraded to the name of magpie, but whose note is sweeter than the nightingale's, and trills through the lucent air with a distinct ecstatic melody of joy that dominates all the discords, so ravishing the sense, that, while it sings, the ear scarcely heeds the scream of the parrots.

CHAPTER LXXI.

"You may remember," said Julius Faber, "Sir Humphry Davy's eloquent description of the effect produced on him by the inhalation of nitrous oxide. He states that he began to lose the perception of external things; trains of vivid visible images rapidly passed through his mind, and were connected with words in such a manner as to produce perceptions perfectly novel. 'I existed,' he said, 'in a world of newly-connected and newly-modified ideas.' When he recovered, he exclaimed: 'Nothing exists but thoughts; the universe is composed of impressions, ideas, pleasures, and pains!'

"Now observe, that thus a cultivator of positive science, endowed with one of the healthiest of human brains, is, by the inhalation of a gas, abstracted from all external life, — enters into a new world, which consists of images he himself creates and ,animates so vividly that, on waking, he resolves the universe itself into thoughts."

"Well," said I, "but what inference do you draw from that voluntary experiment, applicable to the malady of which you bid me hope the cure?"

"Simply this: that the effect produced on a healthful brain by the nitrous oxide may be produced also by moral causes operating on the blood, or on the nerves. There is a degree of mental excitement in which ideas are more vivid than sensations, and then the world of external things gives way to the world within the brain.[1] But this, though a suspension

[1] See, on the theory elaborated from this principle, Dr. Hibbert's interesting and valuable work on the " Philosophy of Apparitions."

of that reason which comprehends accuracy of judgment, is no more a permanent aberration of reason than were Sir Humphry Davy's visionary ecstasies under the influence of the gas. The difference between the two states of suspension is that of time, and it is but an affair of time with our beloved patient. Yet prepare yourself. I fear that the mind will not recover without some critical malady of the body!"

"Critical! but not dangerous? — say not dangerous! I can endure the pause of her reason; I could not endure the void in the universe if her life were to fade from the earth."

"Poor friend! would not you yourself rather lose life than reason?"

"I — yes! But we men are taught to set cheap value on our own lives; we do not estimate at the same rate the lives of those we love. Did we do so, Humanity would lose its virtues."

"What, then! Love teaches that there is something of nobler value than mere mind? Yet surely it cannot be the mere body? What is it, if not that continuance of being which your philosophy declines to acknowledge,— namely, SOUL? If you fear so painfully that your Lilian should die, is it not that you fear to lose her forever?"

"Oh, cease, cease!" I cried impatiently. "I cannot now argue on metaphysics. What is it that you anticipate of harm to her life? Her health has been stronger ever since her affliction. She never seems to know ailment now. Do you not perceive that her cheek has a more hardy bloom, her frame a more rounded symmetry, than when you saw her in England?"

"Unquestionably. Her physical forces have been silently recruiting themselves in the dreams which half lull, half amuse her imagination. IMAGINATION! that faculty, the most glorious which is bestowed on the human mind, because it is the faculty which enables thought to create, is of all others the most exhausting to life when unduly stimulated and consciously reasoning on its own creations. I think it probable that had this sorrow not befallen you, you would

have known a sorrow yet graver,— you would have long survived your Lilian. As it is now, when she recovers, her
whole organization, physical and mental, will have undergone a beneficent change. But, I repeat my prediction,—
some severe malady of the body will precede the restoration
of the mind; and it is my hope that the present suspense or
aberration of the more wearing powers of the mind may fit
the body to endure and surmount the physical crisis. I remember a case, within my own professional experience, in
many respects similar to this, but in other respects it was
less hopeful. I was consulted by a young student of a very
delicate physical frame, of great mental energies, and consumed by an intense ambition. He was reading for university honours. He would not listen to me when I entreated
him to rest his mind. I thought that he was certain to
obtain the distinction for which he toiled, and equally certain
to die a few months after obtaining it. He falsified both my
prognostics. He so overworked himself that, on the day of
examination, his nerves were agitated, his memory failed
him; he passed, not without a certain credit, but fell far
short of the rank amongst his fellow competitors to which he
aspired. Here, then, the irritated mind acted on the disappointed heart, and raised a new train of emotions. He was
first visited by spectral illusions; then he sank into a state
in which the external world seemed quite blotted out. He
heeded nothing that was said to him; seemed to see nothing
that was placed before his eyes,— in a word, sensations became dormant, ideas preconceived usurped their place, and
those ideas gave him pleasure. He believed that his genius
was recognized, and lived amongst its supposed creations enjoying an imaginary fame. So it went on for two years,
during which suspense of his reason, his frail form became
robust and vigorous. At the end of that time he was seized
with a fever, which would have swept him in three days to
the grave had it occurred when I was first called in to attend
him. He conquered the fever, and, in recovering, acquired
the full possession of the intellectual faculties so long suspended. When I last saw him, many years afterwards, he

was in perfect health, and the object of his young ambition was realized; the body had supported the mind,— he had achieved distinction. Now what had so, for a time, laid this strong intellect into visionary sleep? The most agonizing of human emotions in a noble spirit,— shame! What has so stricken down your Lilian? You have told me the story: shame! — the shame of a nature pre-eminently pure. But observe that, in his case as in hers, the shock inflicted does not produce a succession of painful illusions: on the contrary, in both, the illusions are generally pleasing. Had the illusions been painful, the body would have suffered, the patient died. Why did a painful shock produce pleasing illusions? Because, no matter how a shock on the nerves may originate, if it affects the reason, it does but make more vivid than impressions from actual external objects the ideas previously most cherished. Such ideas in the young student were ideas of earthly fame; such ideas in the young maiden are ideas of angel comforters and heavenly Edens. You miss her mind on the earth, and, while we speak, it is in paradise."

"Much that you say, my friend, is authorized by the speculations of great writers, with whom I am not unfamiliar; but in none of those writers, nor in your encouraging words, do I find a solution for much that has no precedents in my experience,— much, indeed, that has analogies in my reading, but analogies which I have hitherto despised as old wives' fables. I have bared to your searching eye the weird mysteries of my life. How do you account for facts which you cannot resolve into illusions,— for the influence which that strange being, Margrave, exercised over Lilian's mind or fancy, so that for a time her love for me was as dormant as is her reason now; so that he could draw her — her whose nature you admit to be singularly pure and modest — from her mother's home? The magic wand; the trance into which that wand threw Margrave himself; the apparition which it conjured up in my own quiet chamber when my mind was without a care and my health without a flaw,— how account for all this: as you endeavoured, and perhaps successfully, to account for all my impressions of the Vision in the Museum, of the luminous, haunting shadow in its earlier apparitions, when my fancy was heated, my heart tormented, and, it might be, even the physical forces of this strong frame disordered? "

"Allen," said the old pathologist, "here we approach a ground which few physicians have dared to examine. Honour to those who, like our bold contemporary, Elliotson, have braved scoff and sacrificed dross in seeking to extract what is practical in uses, what can be tested by experiment, from those exceptional phenomena on which magic sought to found a philosophy, and to which philosophy tracks the origin of magic."

"What! do I understand you? Is it you, Julius Faber, who attach faith to the wonders attributed to animal magnetism and electro-biology, or subscribe to the doctrines which their practitioners teach? "

"I have not examined into those doctrines, nor seen with my own eyes the wonders recorded, upon evidence too respectable, nevertheless, to permit me peremptorily to deny what I have not witnessed.[1] But wherever I look through the

---

[1] What Faber here says is expressed with more authority by one of the most accomplished metaphysicians of our time (Sir W. Hamilton) : —

" Somnambulism is a phenomenon still more astonishing [than dreaming]. In this singular state a person performs a regular series of rational actions, and those frequently of the most difficult and delicate nature ; and what is still more marvellous, with a talent to which he could make no pretension when awake. (Cr. Ancillon, *Essais Philos.* ii. 161.)   His memory and reminiscence supply him with recollections of words and things which, perhaps, never were at his disposal in the ordinary state, — he speaks more fluently a more refined language. And if we are to credit what the evidence on which it rests hardly allows us to disbelieve, he has not only perception of things through other channels than the common organs of sense, but the sphere of his cognition is amplified to an extent far beyond the limits to which sensible perception is confined. This subject is one of the most perplexing in the whole compass of philosophy ; for, on the one hand, the phenomena are so remarkable that they cannot be believed, and yet, on the other, they are of so unambiguous and palpable a character, and the witnesses to their reality are so numerous, so intelligent, and so high above every suspicion of deceit, that it is equally impossible to deny credit to what is attested by such ample and un-

History of Mankind in all ages and all races, I find a concurrence in certain beliefs which seem to countenance the theory
that there is in some peculiar and rare temperaments a power
over forms of animated organization, with which they establish some unaccountable affinity; and even, though much
more rarely, a power over inanimate matter. You are familiar with the theory of Descartes, 'that those particles of
the blood which penetrate to the brain do not only serve to
nourish and sustain its substance, but to produce there a certain very subtle Aura, or rather a flame very vivid and pure,
that obtains the name of the Animal Spirits;'[1] and at the
close of his great fragment upon Man, he asserts that 'this
flame is of no other nature than all the fires which are in
inanimate bodies.'[2] This notion does but forestall the more
recent doctrine that electricity is more or less in all, or nearly
all, known matter. Now, whether in the electric fluid or some

exceptionable evidence." — Sir W. HAMILTON: *Lectures on Metaphysics and
Logic*, vol. ii. p. 274.

This perplexity, in which the distinguished philosopher leaves the judgment so equally balanced that it finds it impossible to believe, and yet impossible to disbelieve, forms the right state of mind in which a candid thinker
should come to the examination of those more extraordinary phenomena
which he has not himself yet witnessed, but the fair inquiry into which may
be tendered to him by persons above the imputation of quackery and fraud.
Müller, who is not the least determined, as he is certainly one of the most
distinguished, disbelievers of mesmeric phenomena, does not appear to have
witnessed, or at least to have carefully examined, them, or he would, perhaps,
have seen that even the more extraordinary of those phenomena confirm,
rather than contradict, his own general theories, and may be explained by
the sympathies one sense has with another, — " the laws of reflection through
the medium of the brain." (Physiology of the Senses, p. 1311.) And again
by the maxim " that the mental principle, or cause of the mental phenomena,
cannot be confined to the brain, but that it exists in a latent state in every
part of the organism." (*Ibid.*, p. 1355.) The " nerve power," contended for
by Mr. Bain, also may suggest a rational solution of much that has seemed
incredible to those physiologists who have not condescended to sift the genuine phenomena of mesmerism from the imposture to which, in all ages, the
phenomena exhibited by what may be called the ecstatic temperament have
been applied.

[1] Descartes, L'Homme, vol. iv. p. 345. Cousin's Edition.
[2] *Ibid.*, p. 428.

other fluid akin to it of which we know still less, thus equally
pervading all matter, there may be a certain magnetic property more active, more operative upon sympathy in some
human constitutions than in others, and which can account
for the mysterious power I have spoken of, is a query I might
suggest, but not an opinion I would hazard.   For an opinion
I must have that basis of experience or authority which I do
not need when I submit a query to the experience and authority of others.   Still, the supposition conveyed in the query is
so far worthy of notice, that the ecstatic temperament (in
which phrase I comprehend all constitutional mystics) is peculiarly sensitive to electric atmospheric influences.   This is
a fact which most medical observers will have remarked in
the range of their practice.   Accordingly, I was prepared to
find Mr. Hare Townshend, in his interesting work,[1] state that
he himself was of 'the electric temperament,' sparks flying
from his hair when combed in the dark, etc.   That accomplished writer, whose veracity no one would impugn, affirms
that 'between this electrical endowment and whatever mesmeric properties he might possess, there is a remarkable rela-
tionship and parallelism.   Whatever state of the atmosphere
tends to accumulate and insulate electricity in the body, pro-
motes equally ' (says Mr. Townshend) 'the power and facility
with which I influence others mesmerically.'   What Mr.
Townshend thus observes in himself, American physicians
and professors of chemistry depose to have observed in those
modern magicians, the mediums of (so-called) 'spirit manifestation.'   They state that all such mediums are of the
electric temperament, thus everywhere found allied with the
ecstatic, and their power varies in proportion as the state of
the atmosphere serves to depress or augment the electricity
stored in themselves.   Here, then, in the midst of vagrant
phenomena, either too hastily dismissed as altogether the
tricks of fraudful imposture, or too credulously accepted as
supernatural portents — here, at least, in one generalized
fact, we may, perhaps, find a starting point, from which
inductive experiment may arrive, soon or late, at a rational

[1] Facts in Mesmerism.

theory. But however the power of which we are speaking (a power accorded to special physical temperament) may or may not be accounted for by some patient student of nature, I am persuaded that it is in that power we are to seek for whatever is not wholly imposture, in the attributes assigned to magic or witchcraft. It is well said, by a writer who has gone into the depth of these subjects with the research of a scholar and the science of a pathologist, 'that if magic had exclusively reposed on credulity and falsehood, its reign would never have endured so long; but that its art took its origin in singular phenomena, proper to certain affections of the nerves, or manifested in the conditions of sleep. These phenomena, the principle of which was at first unknown, served to root faith in magic, and often abused even enlightened minds. The enchanters and magicians arrived, by divers practices, at the faculty of provoking in other brains a determined order of dreams, of engendering hallucinations of all kinds, of inducing fits of hypnotism, trance, mania, during which the persons so affected imagined that they saw, heard, touched, supernatural beings, conversed with them, proved their influences, assisted at prodigies of which magic proclaimed itself to possess the secret. The public, the enchanters, and the enchanted were equally dupes.' [1] Accepting this explanation, unintelligible to no physician of a practice so lengthened as mine has been, I draw from it the corollary, that as these phenomena are exhibited only by certain special affections, to which only certain special constitutions are susceptible, so not in any superior faculties of intellect, or of spiritual endowment, but in peculiar physical temperaments, often strangely disordered, the power of the sorcerer in affecting the imagination of others is to be sought. In the native tribes of Australasia the elders are instructed in the arts of this so-called sorcery, but only in a very few constitutions does instruction avail to produce effects in which the savages recognize the powers of a sorcerer: it is so with the Obi of the negroes. The fascination of Obi is an unques-

[1] La Magie et l'Astrologie dans l'Antiquité et au Moyen-Age. Par L. F. Alfred Maury, Membre de l'Institut. P. 225.

tionable fact, but the Obi man cannot be trained by formal lessons; he is born a fascinator, as a poet is born a poet. It is so with the Laplanders, of whom Tornæus reports that of those instructed in the magical art 'only a few are capable of it.' 'Some,' he says, 'are naturally magicians.' And this fact is emphatically insisted upon by the mystics of our own middle ages, who state that a man must be *born* a magician; in other words, that the gift is constitutional, though developed by practice and art. Now, that this gift and its practice should principally obtain in imperfect states of civilization, and fade into insignificance in the busy social enlightenment of cities, may be accounted for by reference to the known influences of imagination. In the cruder states of social life not only is imagination more frequently predominant over all other faculties, but it has not the healthful vents which the intellectual competition of cities and civilization affords. The man who in a savage tribe, or in the dark feudal ages, would be a magician, is in our century a poet, an orator, a daring speculator, an inventive philosopher. In other words, his imagination is drawn to pursuits congenial to those amongst whom it works. It is the tendency of all intellect to follow the directions of the public opinion amidst which it is trained. Where a magician is held in reverence or awe, there will be more practitioners of magic than where a magician is despised as an impostor or shut up as a lunatic. In Scandinavia, before the introduction of Christianity, all tradition records the wonderful powers of the Vala, or witch, who was then held in reverence and honour. Christianity was introduced, and the early Church denounced the Vala as the instrument of Satan, and from that moment down dropped the majestic prophetess into a miserable and execrated old hag!"

"The ideas you broach," said I, musingly, "have at moments crossed me, though I have shrunk from reducing them to a theory which is but one of pure hypothesis. But this magic, after all, then, you would place in the imagination of the operator, acting on the imagination of those whom it affects? Here, at least, I can follow you, to a certain extent, for here we get back into the legitimate realm of physiology."

"And possibly," said Faber, "we may find hints to guide us to useful examination, if not to complete solution of problems that, once demonstrated, may lead to discoveries of infinite value,— hints, I say, in two writers of widely opposite genius, Van Helmont and Bacon. Van Helmont, of all the mediæval mystics, is, in spite of his many extravagant whims, the one whose intellect is the most suggestive to the disciplined reasoners of our day. He supposed that the faculty which he calls Fantasy, and which we familiarly call Imagination, is invested with the power of creating for itself ideas independent of the senses, each idea clothed in a form fabricated by the imagination, and becoming an operative entity. This notion is so far favoured by modern physiologists, that Lincke reports a case where the eye itself was extirpated; yet the extirpation was followed by the appearance of luminous figures before the orbit. And again, a woman, stone-blind, complained of 'luminous images, with pale colours, before her eyes.' Abercrombie mentions the case 'of a lady quite blind, her eyes being also disorganized and sunk, who never walked out without seeing a little old woman in a red cloak, who seemed to walk before her.'[1] Your favourite authority, the illustrious Müller, who was himself in the habit of 'seeing different images in the field of vision when he lay quietly down to sleep, asserts that these images are not merely presented to the fancy, but that even the images of dreams *are really seen*,' and that 'any one may satisfy himself of this by accustoming himself regularly to open his eyes when waking after a dream,— the images seen in the dream are then sometimes visible, and can be observed to disappear gradually.' He confirms this statement not only by the result of his own experience, but by the observations made by Spinoza, and the yet higher authority of Aristotle, who accounts for spectral appearance as *the internal action of the*

[1] " She had no illusions when within doors." — ABERCROMBIE, *On the Intellectual Powers,* p 277. (15th Edition.)

25

sense of vision.[1]   And this opinion is favoured by Sir David
Brewster, whose experience leads him to suggest 'that the
objects of mental contemplation may be seen as distinctly as
external objects, and will occupy the same local position in
the axis of vision as if they had been formed by the agency
of light.'   Be this as it may, one fact remains,— that images
can be seen even by the blind as distinctly and vividly as you
and I now see the stream below our feet and the opossums
at play upon yonder boughs.   Let us come next to some remarkable suggestions of Lord Bacon.   In his Natural History, treating of the force of the imagination, and the help
it receives 'by one man working by another,' he cites an instance he had witnessed of a kind of juggler, who could tell
a person what card he thought of.   He mentioned this 'to a
pretended learned man, curious in such things,' and this sage
said to him, 'It is not the knowledge of the man's thought,
for that is proper to God, but the enforcing of a thought upon
him, and binding his imagination by a stronger, so that he
could think of no other card.'   You see this sage anticipated
our modern electro-biologists!   And the learned man then
shrewdly asked Lord Bacon, 'Did the juggler tell the card to
the man himself who had thought of it, or bid another tell
it?'   'He bade another tell it,' answered Lord Bacon.   'I
thought so,' returned his learned acquaintance, 'for the juggler himself could not have put on so strong an imagination;
but by telling the card to the other, who believed the juggler
was some strange man who could do strange things, that
other man caught a strong imagination.'[2]   The whole story

[1] Müller, Physiology of the Senses, Baley's translation, pp. 1068 — 1395,
and elsewhere.   Mr. Bain, in his thoughtful and suggestive work on the
"Senses and Intellect," makes very powerful use of these statements in support of his proposition, which Faber advances in other words, namely, "the
return of the nervous currents exactly on their old track in revived
sensations."

[2] Perhaps it is for the reason suggested in the text, namely, that the
magician requires the interposition of a third imagination between his own
and that of the consulting believer, that any learned adept in (so-called)
magic will invariably refuse to exhibit without the presence of a third person.
Hence the author of "Dogme et Rituel de la Haute Magie," printed at Paris,

is worth reading, because Lord Bacon evidently thinks it conveys a guess worth examining. And Lord Bacon, were he now living, would be the man to solve the mysteries that branch out of mesmerism or (so-called) spiritual manifestation, for he would not pretend to despise their phenomena for fear of hurting his reputation for good sense. Bacon then goes on to state that there are three ways to fortify the imagination. 'First, authority derived from belief in an art and in the man who exercises it; secondly, means to quicken and corroborate the imagination; thirdly, means to repeat and refresh it.' For the second and the third he refers to the practices of magic, and proceeds afterwards to state on what things imagination has most force, — 'upon things that have the lightest and easiest motions, and, therefore, above all, upon the spirits of men, and, in them, on such affections as move lightest, — in love, in fear, in irresolution. And,' adds Bacon, earnestly, in a very different spirit from that which dictates to the sages of our time the philosophy of rejecting without trial that which belongs to the Marvellous, — 'and whatsoever is of this kind, should be *thoroughly inquired into.*' And this great founder or renovator of the sober inductive system of investigation even so far leaves it a matter of speculative inquiry, whether imagination may not be so powerful that it can actually operate upon a plant, that he says: 'This likewise should be made upon plants, and that diligently, as if you should tell a man that such a tree would die this year, and *will* him, at these and these times, to go unto it and see how it thriveth.' I presume that no philosopher has followed such recommendations: had some great philosopher done so, possibly we should by this time know all the secrets of what is popularly called witchcraft."

And as Faber here paused, there came a strange laugh from the fantastic she-oak-tree overhanging the stream, — a wild, impish laugh.

1852-53 — a book less remarkable for its learning than for the earnest belief of a scholar of our own day in the reality of the art of which he records the history — insists much on the necessity of rigidly observing Le Ternaire, in the number of persons who assist in an enchanter's experiments.

"Pooh! it is but the great kingfisher, the laughing-bird of the Australian bush," said Julius Faber, amused at my start of superstitious alarm.

We walked on for some minutes in musing silence, and the rude log-hut in which my wise companion had his home came in view,— the flocks grazing on undulous pastures, the kine drinking at a watercourse fringed by the slender gum-trees, and a few fields, laboriously won from the luxuriant grass-land, rippling with the wave of corn.

I halted, and said, "Rest here for a few moments, till I gather up the conclusions to which your speculative reasoning seems to invite me."

We sat down on a rocky crag, half mantled by luxuriant creepers with vermilion buds.

"From the guesses," said I, "which you have drawn from the erudition of others and your own ingenious and reflective inductions, I collect this solution of the mysteries, by which the experience I gain from my senses confounds all the dogmas approved by my judgment. To the rational conjectures by which, when we first conversed on the marvels that perplexed me, you ascribe to my imagination, predisposed by mental excitement, physical fatigue or derangement, and a concurrence of singular events tending to strengthen such predisposition, the phantasmal impressions produced on my senses,— to these conjectures you now add a new one, more startling and less admitted by sober physiologists. You conceive it possible that persons endowed with a rare and peculiar temperament can so operate on imagination, and, through the imagination, on the senses of others, as to exceed even the powers ascribed to the practitioners of mesmerism and electro-biology, and give a certain foundation of truth to the old tales of magic and witchcraft. You imply that Margrave may be a person thus gifted, and hence the influence he unquestionably exercised over Lilian, and over, perhaps, less innocent agents, charmed or impelled by his will. And not discarding, as I own I should have been originally induced to do, the queries or suggestions adventured by Bacon in his discursive speculations on Nature, to wit, 'that there be many things, some of them inanimate, that operate upon the spirits of men by secret sympathy and antipathy,' and to which Bacon gave the quaint name of 'imaginants,' so even that wand, of which I have described to you the magic-like effects, may have had properties communicated to it by which it performs the work of the magician, as mesmerists pretend that some substance mesmerized by them can act on the patient as sensibly as if it were the mesmerizer himself. Do I state your suppositions correctly?"

"Yes; always remembering that they are only suppositions, and volunteered with the utmost diffidence. But since, thus seated in the early wilderness, we permit ourselves the indulgence of childlike guess, may it not be possible, apart from the doubtful question whether a man can communicate to an inanimate material substance a power to act upon the mind or imagination of another man — may it not, I say, be possible that such a substance may contain in itself such a virtue or property potent over certain constitutions, though not over all. For instance, it is in my experience that the common hazel-wood will strongly affect some nervous temperaments, though wholly without effect on others. I remember a young girl, who having taken up a hazel-stick freshly cut, could not relax her hold of it; and when it was wrenched away from her by force, was irresistibly attracted towards it, repossessed herself of it, and, after holding it a few minutes, was cast into a kind of trance, in which she beheld phantasmal visions. Mentioning this curious case, which I supposed unique, to a learned brother of our profession, he told me that he had known other instances of the effect of the hazel upon nervous temperaments in persons of both sexes. Possibly it was some such peculiar property in the hazel that made it the wood selected for the old divining-rod. Again, we know that the bay-tree, or laurel, was dedicated to the oracular Pythian Apollo. Now wherever, in the old world, we find that the learning of the priests enabled them to exhibit exceptional phenomena, which imposed upon popular credulity, there was a something or other which is worth a philosopher's while to explore; and, accordingly, I always

suspected that there was in the laurel some property favoura
ble to ecstatic vision in highly impressionable temperaments.
My suspicion, a few years ago, was justified by the experience
of a German physician, who had under his care a cataleptic
or ecstatic patient, and who assured me that he found nothing
in this patient so stimulated the state of 'sleep-waking,' or so
disposed that state to indulge in the hallucinations of prevision, as the berry of the laurel.[1] Well, we do not know
what this wand that produced a seemingly magical effect
upon you was really composed of. You did not notice the
metal employed in the wire, which you say communicated a
thrill to the sensitive nerves in the palm of the hand. You
cannot tell how far it might have been the vehicle of some
fluid force in nature. Or still more probably, whether the
pores of your hand insensibly imbibed, and communicated to
the brain, some of those powerful narcotics from which the
Buddhists and the Arabs make unguents that induce visionary
hallucinations, and in which substances undetected in the
hollow of the wand, or the handle of the wand itself, might
be steeped.[2] One thing we do know, namely, that amongst
the ancients, and especially in the East, the construction of
wands for magical purposes was no commonplace mechanical
craft, but a special and secret art appropriated to men who
cultivated with assiduity all that was then known of natural
science in order to extract from it agencies that might appear
supernatural. Possibly, then, the rods or wands of the East,
of which Scripture makes mention, were framed upon some
principles of which we in our day are very naturally ignorant, since we do not ransack science for the same secrets;
and thus, in the selection or preparation of the material employed, mainly consisted whatever may be referrible to natural
philosophical causes in the antique science of Rhabdomancy,
or divination and enchantment by wands. The staff, or wand,

[1] I may add that Dr. Kerner instances the effect of laurel-berries on the
Seeress of Prevorst, corresponding with that asserted by Julius Faber in the
text.

[2] See for these unguents the work of M. Maury, before quoted, "La
Magie et l'Astrologie," etc., p. 417.

of which you tell me, was, you say, made of iron or steel and tipped with crystal. Possibly iron and crystal do really contain some properties not hitherto scientifically analyzed, and only, indeed, potential over exceptional temperaments, which may account for the fact that iron and crystal have been favourites with all professed mystics, ancient and modern. The Delphic Pythoness had her iron tripod, Mesmer his iron bed; and many persons, indisputably honest, cannot gaze long upon a ball of crystal but what they begin to see visions. I suspect that a philosophical cause for such seemingly preternatural effects of crystal and iron will be found in connection with the extreme impressionability to changes in temperatures which is the characteristic both of crystal and iron. But if these materials do contain certain powers over exceptional constitutions, we do not arrive at a supernatural but at a natural phenomenon."

"Still," said I, "even granting that your explanatory hypotheses hit or approach the truth,— still what a terrible power you would assign to man's will over men's reason and deeds! "

"Man's will," answered Faber, "has over men's deeds and reason, habitual and daily, power infinitely greater and, when uncounterbalanced, infinitely more dangerous than that which superstition exaggerates in magic. Man's will moves a war that decimates a race, and leaves behind it calamities little less dire than slaughter. Man's will frames, but it also corrupts laws; exalts, but also demoralizes opinion; sets the world mad with fanaticism, as often as it curbs the heart's fierce instincts by the wisdom of brother-like mercy. You revolt at the exceptional, limited sway over some two or three individuals which the arts of a sorcerer (if sorcerer there be) can effect; and yet, at the very moment in which you were perplexed and appalled by such sway, or by your reluctant belief in it, your will was devising an engine to unsettle the reason and wither the hopes of millions! "

"My will! What engine? "

" A book conceived by your intellect, adorned by your learning, and directed by your will, to steal from the minds of other men their persuasion of the soul's everlasting Hereafter."

I bowed my head, and felt myself grow pale.

"And if we accept Bacon's theory of 'secret sympathy,' or the plainer physiological maxim that there must be in the imagination, morbidly impressed by the will of another, some trains of idea in affinity with such influence and preinclined to receive it, no magician could warp you to evil, except through thoughts that themselves went astray. Grant that the Margrave who still haunts your mind did really, by some occult, sinister magnetism, guide the madman to murder, did influence the servant-woman's vulgar desire to pry into the secrets of her ill-fated master, or the old maid's covetous wish and envious malignity: what could this awful magician do more than any commonplace guilty adviser, to a mind predisposed to accept the advice?"

"You forget one example which destroys your argument,— the spell which this mysterious fascinator could cast upon a creature so pure from all guilt as Lilian!"

"Will you forgive me if I answer frankly?"

"Speak."

"Your Lilian is spotless and pure as you deem her, and the fascination, therefore, attempts no lure through a sinful desire; it blends with its attraction no sentiment of affection untrue to yourself. Nay, it is justice to your Lilian, and may be melancholy comfort to you, to state my conviction, based on the answers my questions have drawn from her, that you were never more cherished by her love than when that love seemed to forsake you. Her imagination impressed her with the illusion that through your love for her you were threatened with a great peril. What seemed the levity of her desertion was the devotion of self-sacrifice. And, in her strange, dream-led wanderings, do not think that she was conscious of the fascination you impute to this mysterious Margrave: in her belief it was your own guardian angel that guided her steps, and her pilgrimage was ordained to disarm the foe that menaced you, and dissolve the spell that divided her life from yours! But had she not, long before this, willingly prepared herself to be so deceived? Had not her fancies been deliberately encouraged to dwell remote from the duties we are placed on the earth to perform? The loftiest faculties in our nature are those that demand the finest poise, not to fall from their height and crush all the walls that they crown. With exquisite beauty of illustration, Hume says of the dreamers of 'bright fancies,' 'that they may be compared to those angels whom the Scriptures represent as covering their eyes with their wings.' Had you been, like my nephew, a wrestler for bread with the wilderness, what helpmate would your Lilian have been to you? How often would you have cried out in justifiable anger, 'I, son of Adam, am on earth, not in Paradise! Oh, that my Eve were at home on my hearth, and not in the skies with the seraphs!' No Margrave, I venture to say, could have suspended the healthful affections, or charmed into danger the wide-awake soul of my Amy. When she rocks in its cradle the babe the young parents intrust to her heed; when she calls the kine to the milking, the chicks to their corn; when she but flits through my room to renew the flowers on the stand, or range in neat order the books that I read, no spell on her fancy could lead her a step from the range of her provident cares! At day she is contented to be on the commonplace earth; at evening she and I knock together at the one door of heaven, which opes to thanksgiving and prayer; and thanksgiving and prayer send us back, calm and hopeful, to the task that each morrow renews."

I looked up as the old man paused, and in the limpid clearness of the Australian atmosphere, I saw the child he thus praised standing by the garden-gate, looking towards us, and though still distant she seemed near. I felt wroth with her. My heart so cherished my harmless, defenceless Lilian, that I was jealous of the praise taken from her to be bestowed on another.

"Each of us," said I, coldly, "has his or her own nature, and the uses harmonious to that nature's idiosyncrasy. The world, I grant, would get on very ill if women were not more or less actively useful and quietly good, like your Amy. But the world would lose standards that exalt and refine, if no woman were permitted to gain, through the indulgence of fancy, thoughts exquisite as those which my Lilian conceived, while thought, alas! flowed out of fancy. I do not wound you by citing your Amy as a type of the mediocre; I do not claim for Lilian the rank we accord to the type of genius. But both are alike to such types in this: namely, that the uses of mediocrity are for every-day life, and the uses of genius, amidst a thousand mistakes which mediocrity never commits, are to suggest and perpetuate ideas which raise the standard of the mediocre to a nobler level. There would be fewer Amys in life if there were no Lilian! as there would be far fewer good men of sense if there were no erring dreamer of genius! "

"You say well, Allen Fenwick. And who should be so indulgent to the vagaries of the imagination as the philosophers who taught your youth to doubt everything in the Maker's plan of creation which could not be mathematically proved? 'The human mind,' said Luther, 'is like a drunkard on horseback; prop it on one side, and it falls on the other.' So the man who is much too enlightened to believe in a peasant's religion, is always sure to set up some insane superstition of his own. Open biographical volumes wherever you please, and the man who has no faith in religion is a man who has faith in a nightmare. See that type of the elegant sceptics, — Lord Herbert of Cherbury. He is writing a book against Revelation; he asks a sign from heaven to tell him if his book is approved by his Maker, and the man who cannot believe in the miracles performed by his Saviour gravely tells us of a miracle vouchsafed to himself. Take the hardest and strongest intellect which the hardest and strongest race of mankind ever schooled and accomplished. See the greatest of great men, the great Julius Cæsar! Publicly he asserts in the Senate that the immortality of the soul is a vain chimera. He professes the creed which Roman voluptuaries deduced from Epicurus, and denies all Divine interference in the affairs of the earth. A great authority for the Materialists — they have none greater! They can show on their side no intellect equal to Cæsar's! And yet this magnificent freethinker, rejecting a soul and a Deity, habitually entered his chariot muttering a charm; crawled on his knees up the steps of a temple to propitiate the abstraction called 'Nemesis;' and did not cross the Rubicon till he had consulted the omens. What does all this prove? — a very simple truth. Man has some instincts with the brutes; for instance, hunger and sexual love. Man has one instinct peculiar to himself, found universally (or with alleged exceptions in savage States so rare, that they do not affect the general law [1]), — an instinct of an invisible power without this earth, and of a life beyond the grave, which that power vouchsafes to his spirit. But the best of us cannot violate an instinct with impunity. Resist hunger as long as you can, and, rather than die of starvation, your instinct will make you a cannibal; resist love when youth and nature impel to it, and what pathologist does not track one broad path into madness or crime? So with the noblest instinct of all. Reject the internal conviction by which the grandest thinkers have sanctioned the hope of the humblest Christian, and you are servile at once to some faith inconceivably more hard to believe. The imagination will not be withheld from its yearnings for vistas beyond the walls of the flesh, and the span of the present hour. Philosophy itself, in rejecting the healthful creeds by which man finds his safeguards in sober prayer and his guide through the wilderness of visionary doubt, invents systems compared to which the mysteries of theology are simple.

---

[1] It seems extremely doubtful whether the very few instances in which it has been asserted that a savage race has been found without recognition of a Deity and a future state would bear searching examination. It is set forth, for example, in most of the popular works on Australia, that the Australian savages have no notion of a Deity or a Hereafter, that they only worship a devil, or evil spirit. This assumption, though made more peremptorily, and by a greater number of writers than any similar one regarding other savages, is altogether erroneous, and has no other foundation than the ignorance of the writers. The Australian savages recognize a Deity, but He is too august for a name in their own language; in English they call Him the Great Master, — an expression synonymous with "The Great Lord." They believe in a hereafter of eternal joy, and place it amongst the stars. — See Strzelecki's Physical Description of New South Wales.

Suppose any man of strong, plain understanding had never heard of a Deity like Him whom we Christians adore, then ask this man which he can the better comprehend in his mind, and accept as a natural faith,— namely, the simple Christianity of his shepherd or the Pantheism of Spinoza? Place before an accomplished critic (who comes with a perfectly unprejudiced mind to either inquiry), first, the arguments of David Hume against the gospel miracles, and then the metaphysical crotchets of David Hume himself. This subtle philosopher, not content, with Berkeley, to get rid of matter,— not content, with Condillac, to get rid of spirit or mind,— proceeds to a miracle greater than any his Maker has yet vouchsafed to reveal. He, being then alive and in the act of writing, gets rid of himself altogether. Nay, he confesses he cannot reason with any one who is stupid enough to think he has a self. His words are: 'What we call a mind is nothing but a heap or collection of different perceptions or objects united together by certain relations, and supposed, though falsely, to be endowed with perfect simplicity and identity. If any one, upon serious and candid reflection, thinks he has a different notion of himself, I must confess I can reason with him no longer.' Certainly I would rather believe all the ghost stories upon record than believe that I am not even a ghost, distinct and apart from the perceptions conveyed to me, no matter how,— just as I am distinct and apart from the furniture in my room, no matter whether I found it there or whether I bought it. If some old cosmogonist asked you to believe that the primitive cause of the solar system was not to be traced to a Divine Intelligence, but to a nebulosity, originally so diffused that its existence can with difficulty be conceived, and that the origin of the present system of organized beings equally dispensed with the agency of a creative mind, and could be referred to molecules formed in the water by the power of attraction, till by modifications of cellular tissue in the gradual lapse of ages, one monad became an oyster and another a Man,— would you not say this cosmogony could scarce have misled the human understanding even in the earliest dawn of speculative inquiry?

Yet such are the hypotheses to which the desire to philoso-
phize away that simple proposition of a Divine First Cause,
which every child can comprehend, led two of the greatest
geniuses and profoundest reasoners of modern times,— La
Place and La Marck.[1] Certainly, the more you examine
those arch phantasmagorists, the philosophers who would
leave nothing in the universe but their own delusions, the
more your intellectual pride may be humbled. The wildest phenomena which have startled you are not more extravagant than the grave explanations which intellectual presumption adventures on the elements of our own organism and
the relations between the world of matter and the world of
ideas."

Here our conversation stopped, for Amy had now joined us,
and, looking up to reply, I saw the child's innocent face between me and the furrowed brow of the old man.

CHAPTER LXXII.

I TURNED back alone. The sun was reddening the summits
of the distant mountain-range, but dark clouds, that portended rain, were gathering behind my way and deepening
the shadows in many a chasm and hollow which volcanic fires
had wrought on the surface of uplands undulating like dilu-
vian billows fixed into stone in the midst of their stormy
swell. I wandered on and away from the beaten track, absorbed in thought. Could I acknowledge in Julius Faber's
conjectures any basis for logical ratiocination; or were they
not the ingenious fancies of that empirical Philosophy of
Sentiment by which the aged, in the decline of severer faculties, sometimes assimilate their theories to the hazy romance
of youth? I can well conceive that the story I tell will be

---

[1] See the observations on La Place and La Marck in the Introduction to
Kirby's "Bridgewater Treatise."

regarded by most as a wild and fantastic fable; that by some
it may be considered a vehicle for guesses at various riddles
of Nature, without or within us, which are free to the license
of romance, though forbidden to the caution of science. But,
I — I — know unmistakably my own identity, my own positive place in a substantial universe. And beyond that knowledge, what do I know? Yet had Faber no ground for his
startling parallels between the chimeras of superstition and
the alternatives to faith volunteered by the metaphysical
speculations of knowledge? On the theorems of Condillac,
I, in common with numberless contemporaneous students
(for, in my youth, Condillac held sway in the schools, as
now, driven forth from the schools, his opinions float loose
through the talk and the scribble of men of the world, who
perhaps never opened his page), — on the theorems of Condillac I had built up a system of thought designed to immure
the swathed form of material philosophy from all rays and
all sounds of a world not material, as the walls of some blind
mausoleum shut out, from the mummy within, the whisper
of winds and the gleaming of stars.

And did not those very theorems, when carried out to their
strict and completing results by the close reasonings of
Hume, resolve my own living identity, the one conscious indivisible ME, into a bundle of memories derived from the
senses which had bubbled and duped my experience, and reduce into a phantom, as spectral as that of the Luminous
Shadow, the whole solid frame of creation?

While pondering these questions, the storm whose fore-
warnings I had neglected to heed burst forth with all the
suddenness peculiar to the Australian climes. The rains
descended like the rushing of floods. In the beds of water-
courses, which, at noon, seemed dried up and exhausted, the
torrents began to swell and to rave; the gray crags around
them were animated into living waterfalls. I looked round,
and the landscape was as changed as a scene that replaces a
scene on the player's stage. I was aware that I had wandered far from my home, and I knew not what direction I
should take to regain it. Close at hand, and raised above

the torrents that now rushed in many a gully and tributary creek, around and before me, the mouth of a deep cave, overgrown with bushes and creeping flowers tossed wildly to and fro between the rain from above and the spray of cascades below, offered a shelter from the storm. I entered,—scaring innumerable flocks of bats striking against me, blinded by the glare of the lightning that followed me into the cavern, and hastening to resettle themselves on the pendants of stalactites, or the jagged buttresses of primæval wall.

From time to time the lightning darted into the gloom and lingered amongst its shadows; and I saw, by the flash, that the floors on which I stood were strewed with strange bones, some amongst them the fossilized relics of races destroyed by the Deluge. The rain continued for more than two hours with unabated violence; then it ceased almost as suddenly as it had come on, and the lustrous moon of Australia burst from the clouds shining bright as an English dawn, into the hollows of the cave. And then simultaneously arose all the choral songs of the wilderness,—creatures whose voices are heard at night,—the loud whir of the locusts, the musical boom of the bullfrog, the cuckoo note of the morepork, and, mournful amidst all those merrier sounds, the hoot of the owl, through the wizard she-oaks and the pale green of the gum-trees.

I stepped forth into the open air and gazed, first instinctively on the heavens, next, with more heedful eye, upon the earth. The nature of the soil bore the evidence of volcanic fires long since extinguished. Just before my feet, the rays fell full upon a bright yellow streak in the block of quartz half imbedded in the soft moist soil. In the midst of all the solemn thoughts and the intense sorrows which weighed upon heart and mind, that yellow gleam startled the mind into a direction remote from philosophy, quickened the heart to a beat that chimed with no household affections. Involuntarily I stooped; impulsively I struck the block with the hatchet, or tomahawk, I carried habitually about me, for the purpose of marking the trees that I wished to clear from the waste of my broad domain. The quartz was shattered by the stroke,

and left disburied its glittering treasure. **My first glance**
had not deceived me. I, vain seeker after knowledge, had,
at least, discovered gold. I took up the bright metal — gold!
I paused; I looked round; the land that just before had
seemed to me so worthless took the value of Ophir. Its features had before been as unknown to me as the Mountains of
the Moon, and now my memory became wonderfully quickened. I recalled the rough map of my possessions, the first
careless ride round their boundaries. Yes, the land on which
I stood — for miles, to the spur of those farther mountains —
the land was mine, and, beneath its surface, there was gold!
I closed my eyes; for some moments visions of boundless
wealth, and of the royal power which such wealth could command, swept athwart my brain. But my heart rapidly settled
back to its real treasure. "What matters," I sighed, "all
this dross? Could Ophir itself buy back to my Lilian's smile
one ray of the light which gave 'glory to the grass and splendour to the flower'?"

So muttering, I flung the gold into the torrent that raged
below, and went on through the moonlight, sorrowing silently,— only thankful for the discovery that had quickened
my reminiscence of the landmarks by which to steer my way
through the wilderness.

The night was half gone, for even when I had gained **the**
familiar track through the pastures, the swell of the **many**
winding creeks that now intersected the way obliged me often
to retrace my steps; to find, sometimes, the bridge of a felled
tree which had been providently left unremoved over the now
foaming torrent, and, more than once, to swim across the current, in which swimmers less strong or less practised would
have been dashed down the falls, where loose logs and torn
trees went clattering and whirling: for I was in danger of life.
A band of the savage natives were stealthily creeping on my
track,— the natives in those parts were not then so much
awed by the white man as now. A boomerang [1] had whirred
by me, burying itself amongst the herbage close before my
feet. I had turned, sought to find and to face these dastardly

[1] A missile weapon peculiar to the Australian savages.

foes; they contrived to elude me. But when I moved on, my ear, sharpened by danger, heard them moving, too, in my rear. Once only three hideous forms suddenly faced me, springing up from a thicket, all tangled with honeysuckles and creepers of blue and vermilion. I walked steadily up to them. They halted a moment or so in suspense; but perhaps they were scared by my stature or awed by my aspect; and the Unfamiliar, though Human, had terror for them, as the Unfamiliar, although but a Shadow, had had terror for me. They vanished, and as quickly as if they had crept into the earth.

At length the air brought me the soft perfume of my well-known acacias, and my house stood before me, amidst English flowers and English fruit-trees, under the effulgent Australian moon. Just as I was opening the little gate which gave access from the pasture-land into the garden, a figure in white rose up from under light, feathery boughs, and a hand was laid on my arm. I started; but my surprise was changed into fear when I saw the pale face and sweet eyes of Lilian.

"Heavens! you here! you! at this hour! Lilian, what is this?"

"Hush!" she whispered, clinging to me; "hush! do not tell: no one knows. I missed you when the storm came on; I have missed you ever since. Others went in search of you and came back. I could not sleep, but the rest are sleeping, so I stole down to watch for you. Brother, brother, if any harm chanced to you, even the angels could not comfort me; all would be dark, dark! But you are safe, safe, safe!" And she clung to me yet closer.

"Ah, Lilian, Lilian, your vision in the hour I first beheld you was indeed prophetic, — 'each has need of the other.' Do you remember?"

"Softly, softly," she said, "let me think!" She stood quietly by my side, looking up into the sky, with all its numberless stars, and its solitary moon now sinking slow behind the verge of the forest. "It comes back to me," she murmured softly, — "the Long ago, — the sweet Long ago!"

I held my breath to listen.

26

"There, there!" she resumed, pointing to the heavens "do you see? You are there, and my father, and — and — Oh! that terrible face, those serpent eyes, the dead man's skull! Save me! save me!"

She bowed her head upon my bosom, and I led her gently back towards the house. As we gained the door which she had left open, the starlight shining across the shadowy gloom within, she lifted her face from my breast, and cast a hurried fearful look round the shining garden, then into the dim recess beyond the threshold.

"It is there — there! — the Shadow that lured me on, whispering that if I followed it I should join my beloved. False, dreadful Shadow! it will fade soon, — fade into the grinning horrible skull. Brother, brother, where is my Allen? Is he dead — dead — or is it I who am dead to him?"

I could but clasp her again to my breast, and seek to mantle her shivering form with my dripping garments, all the while my eyes — following the direction which hers had taken — dwelt on the walls of the nook within the threshold, half lost in darkness, half white in starlight. And there I, too, beheld the haunting Luminous Shadow, the spectral effigies of the mysterious being, whose very existence in the flesh was a riddle unsolved by my reason. Distinctly I saw the Shadow, but its light was far paler, its outline far more vague, than when I had beheld it before. I took courage, as I felt Lilian's heart beating against my own. I advanced, I crossed the threshold, — the Shadow was gone.

"There is no Shadow here, — no phantom to daunt thee, my life's life," said I, bending over Lilian.

"It has touched me in passing; I feel it — cold, cold, cold!" she answered faintly.

I bore her to her room, placed her on her bed, struck a light, watched over her. At dawn there was a change in her face, and from that time health gradually left her; strength slowly, slowly, yet to me perceptibly, ebbed from her life away.

CHAPTER LXXIII.

MONTHS upon months have rolled on since the night in which Lilian had watched for my coming amidst the chilling airs under the haunting moon. I have said that from the date of that night her health began gradually to fail, but in her mind there was evidently at work some slow revolution. Her visionary abstractions were less frequent; when they occurred, less prolonged. There was no longer in her soft face that celestial serenity which spoke her content in her dreams, but often a look of anxiety and trouble. She was even more silent than before; but when she did speak, there were now evident some struggling gleams of memory. She startled us, at times, by a distinct allusion to the events and scenes of her early childhood. More than once she spoke of commonplace incidents and mere acquaintances at L——. At last she seemed to recognize Mrs. Ashleigh as her mother; but me, as Allen Fenwick, her betrothed, her bridegroom, no! Once or twice she spoke to me of her beloved as of a stranger to myself, and asked me not to deceive her — should she ever see him again? There was one change in this new phase of her state that wounded me to the quick. She had always previously seemed to welcome my presence; now there were hours, sometimes days together, in which my presence was evidently painful to her. She would become agitated when I stole into her room, make signs to me to leave her, grow yet more disturbed if I did not immediately obey, and become calm again when I was gone.

Faber sought constantly to sustain my courage and administer to my hopes by reminding me of the prediction he had hazarded,—namely, that through some malady to the frame the reason would be ultimately restored.

He said, "Observe! her mind was first roused from its slumber by the affectionate, unconquered impulse of her

heart. You were absent; the storm alarmed her, she missed
you,—feared for you. The love within her, not alienated,
though latent, drew her thoughts into definite human tracks.
And thus, the words that you tell me she uttered when you
appeared before her were words of love, stricken, though as
yet irregularly, as the winds strike the harp-strings from
chords of awakened memory. The same unwonted excitement, together with lengthened exposure to the cold night-
air, will account for the shock to her physical system, and
the languor and waste of strength by which it has been
succeeded."

"Ay, and the Shadow that we *both* saw within the threshold. What of that?"

"Are there no records on evidence, which most physicians
of very extended practice will perhaps allow that their experience more or less tend to confirm — no records of the singular coincidences between individual impressions which are
produced by sympathy? Now, whether you or your Lilian
were first haunted by this Shadow I know not. Perhaps before it appeared to you in the wizard's chamber it had appeared to her by the Monks' Well. Perhaps, as it came to
you in the prison, so it lured her through the solitudes, asso-
ciating its illusory guidance with dreams of you. And again,
when she saw it within your threshold, your fantasy, so abruptly invoked, made you see with the eyes of your Lilian!
Does this doctrine of sympathy, though by that very mystery
you two loved each other at first,— though, without it, love
at first sight were in itself an incredible miracle,— does, I
say, this doctrine of sympathy seem to you inadmissible?
Then nothing is left for us but to revolve the conjecture I
before threw out. Have certain organizations like that of
Margrave the power to impress, through space, the imagina-
tions of those over whom they have forced a control? I know
not. But if they have, it is not supernatural; it is but one
of those operations in Nature so rare and exceptional, and of
which testimony and evidence are so imperfect and so liable
to superstitious illusions, that they have not yet been traced
—as, if truthful, no doubt they can be, by the patient genius

of science — to one of those secondary causes by which the Creator ordains that Nature shall act on Man."

By degrees I became dissatisfied with my conversations with Faber. I yearned for explanations; all guesses but bewildered me more. In his family, with one exception, I found no congenial association. His nephew seemed to me an ordinary specimen of a very trite human nature, — a young man of limited ideas, fair moral tendencies, going mechanically right where not tempted to wrong. The same desire of gain which had urged him to gamble and speculate when thrown in societies rife with such example, led him, now in the Bush, to healthful, industrious, persevering labour. "Spes fovet agricolas," says the poet; the same Hope which entices the fish to the hook impels the plough of the husbandman. The young farmer's young wife was somewhat superior to him; she had more refinement of taste, more culture of mind, but, living in his life, she was inevitably levelled to his ends and pursuits; and, next to the babe in the cradle, no object seemed to her so important as that of guarding the sheep from the scab and the dingoes. I was amazed to see how quietly a man whose mind was so stored by life and by books as that of Julius Faber — a man who had loved the clash of conflicting intellects, and acquired the rewards of fame — could accommodate himself to the cabined range of his kinsfolks' half-civilized existence, take interest in their trivial talk, find varying excitement in the monotonous household of a peasant-like farmer. I could not help saying as much to him once. "My friend," replied the old man, "believe me that the happiest art of intellect, however lofty, is that which enables it to be cheerfully at home with the Real!"

The only one of the family in which Faber was domesticated in whom I found an interest, to whose talk I could listen without fatigue, was the child Amy. Simple though she was in language, patient of labour as the most laborious, I recognized in her a quiet nobleness of sentiment, which exalted above the commonplace the acts of her commonplace life. She had no precocious intellect, no enthusiastic fancies, but she had an exquisite activity of heart. It was her heart that animated her sense of duty, and made duty a sweetness and a joy. She felt to the core the kindness of those around her; exaggerated, with the warmth of her gratitude, the claims which that kindness imposed. Even for the blessing of life, which she shared with all creation, she felt as if singled out by the undeserved favour of the Creator, and thus was filled with religion, because she was filled with love.

My interest in this child was increased and deepened by my saddened and not wholly unremorseful remembrance of the night on which her sobs had pierced my ear,—the night from which I secretly dated the mysterious agencies that had wrenched from their proper field and career both my mind and my life. But a gentler interest endeared her to my thoughts in the pleasure that Lilian felt in her visits, in the affectionate intercourse that sprang up between the afflicted sufferer and the harmless infant. Often when we failed to comprehend some meaning which Lilian evidently wished to convey to us — we, her mother and her husband — she was understood with as much ease by Amy, the unlettered child, as by Faber, the gray-haired thinker.

"How is it,—how is it?" I asked, impatiently and jealously, of Faber. "Love is said to interpret where wisdom fails, and you yourself talk of the marvels which sympathy may effect between lover and beloved; yet when, for days together, I cannot succeed in unravelling Lilian's wish or her thought — and her own mother is equally in fault — you or Amy, closeted alone with her for five minutes, comprehend and are comprehended "

"Allen," answered Faber, "Amy and I believe in spirit; and she, in whom mind is dormant but spirit awake, feels in such belief a sympathy which she has not, in that respect, with yourself, nor even with her mother. You seek only through your mind to conjecture hers. Her mother has sense clear enough where habitual experience can guide it, but that sense is confused, and forsakes her when forced from the regular pathway in which it has been accustomed to tread. Amy and I through soul guess at soul, and though mostly contented with earth, we can both rise at times into heaven. We pray."

"Alas!" said I, half mournfully, half angrily, "when you thus speak of Mind as distinct from Soul, it was only in that Vision which you bid me regard as the illusion of a fancy stimulated by chemical vapours, producing on the brain an effect similar to that of opium or the inhalation of the oxide gas, that I have ever seen the silver spark of the Soul distinct from the light of the Mind. And holding, as I do, that all intellectual ideas are derived from the experiences of the body, whether I accept the theory of Locke, or that of Condillac, or that into which their propositions reach their final development in the wonderful subtlety of Hume, I cannot detect the immaterial spirit in the material substance,— much less follow its escape from the organic matter in which the principle of thought ceases with the principle of life. When the metaphysician, contending for the immortality of the thinking faculty, analyzes Mind, his analysis comprehends the mind of the brute, nay, of the insect, as well as that of man. Take Reid's definition of Mind, as the most comprehensive which I can at the moment remember: 'By the mind of a man we understand that in him which thinks, remembers, reasons, and wills.' But this definition only distinguishes the mind of man from that of the brute by superiority in the same attributes, and not by attributes denied to the brute. An animal, even an insect, thinks, remembers, reasons, and wills.[1] Few naturalists will now

---

[1] " Are intelligence and instinct, thus differing in their relative proportion in man as compared with all other animals, yet the same in kind and manner of operation in both ? To this question we must give at once an affirmative answer. The expression of Cuvier, regarding the faculty of reasoning in lower animals, ' Leur intelligence exécute des opérations du même genre,' is true in its full sense. We can in no manner define reason so as to exclude acts which are at every moment present to our observation, and which we find in many instances to contravene the natural instincts of the species. The demeanour and acts of the dog in reference to his master, or the various uses to which he is put by man, are as strictly logical as those we witness in the ordinary transactions of life." — Sir HENRY HOLLAND, chapters on " Mental Physiology," p. 220.

The whole of the chapter on Instincts and Habits in this work should be

support the doctrine that all the mental operations of brute
or insect are to be exclusively referred to instincts; and, even
if they do, the word 'instinct' is a very vague word,— loose
and large enough to cover an abyss which our knowledge has
not sounded. And, indeed, in proportion as an animal like
the dog becomes cultivated by intercourse, his instincts grow
weaker, and his ideas formed by experience (namely, his
mind), more developed, often to the conquest of the instincts
themselves. Hence, with his usual candour, Dr. Abercrombie
— in contending 'that everything mental ceases to exist after
death, when we know that everything corporeal continues to
exist, is a gratuitous assumption contrary to every rule of
philosophical inquiry' — feels compelled, by his reasoning,
to admit the probability of a future life even to the lower
animals. His words are: 'To this mode of reasoning it has
been objected that it would go to establish an immaterial
principle in the lower animals which in them exhibits many
of the phenomena of mind. I have only to answer, Be it so.
There are in the lower animals many of the phenomena of
mind, and with regard to these, we also contend that they
are entirely distinct from anything we know of the properties of matter, which is all that we mean, or can mean, by
being immaterial.'[1] Am I then driven to admit that if man's
mind is immaterial and imperishable, so also is that of the
ape and the ant?"

"I own," said Faber, with his peculiar smile, arch and
genial, "that if I were compelled to make that admission, it
would not shock my pride. I do not presume to set any limit
to the goodness of the Creator; and should be as humbly
pleased as the Indian, if in —

> "'yonder sky,
> My faithful dog should bear me company.'

You are too familiar with the works of that Titan in wisdom
and error, Descartes, not to recollect the interesting corre-

read in connection with the passage just quoted. The work itself, at once
cautious and suggestive, is not one of the least obligations which philosophy
and religion alike owe to the lucubrations of English medical men.

[1] Abercrombie's Intellectual Powers, p. 26. (15th Edition.)

spondence between the urbane philosopher and our combative countryman, Henry More,[1] on this very subject; in which certainly More has the best of it when Descartes insists on reducing what he calls the soul (*l'âme*) of brutes into the same kind of machines as man constructs from inorganized matter. The learning, indeed, lavished on the insoluble question involved in the psychology of the inferior animals is a proof at least of the all-inquisitive, redundant spirit of man.[2] We have almost a literature in itself devoted to endeavours to interpret the language of brutes.[3] Dupont de Nemours has discovered that dogs talk in vowels, using only two consonants, G, Z, when they are angry. He asserts that cats employ the same vowels as dogs; but their language is more affluent in consonants, including M, N, B, R, V, F. How many laborious efforts have been made to define and to construe the song of the nightingale! One version of that song, by Beckstein, the naturalist, published in 1840, I remember to have seen. And I heard a lady, gifted with a singularly charming voice, chant the mysterious vowels with so exquisite a pathos, that one could not refuse to believe her when she declared that she fully comprehended the bird's meaning, and gave to the nightingale's warble the tender interpretation of her own woman's heart.

"But leaving all such discussions to their proper place amongst the Curiosities of Literature, I come in earnest to the question you have so earnestly raised; and to me the distinction between man and the lower animals in reference to a spiritual nature designed for a future existence, and the mental operations whose uses are bounded to an existence on earth, seems ineffaceably clear. Whether ideas or even perceptions be innate or all formed by experience is a specula-

---

[1] Œuvres de Descartes, vol. x. p. 178, et seq. (Cousin's Edition.)

[2] M. Tissot the distinguished Professor of Philosophy at Dijon, in his recent work, "La Vie dans l'Homme," p. 255, gives a long and illustrious list of philosophers who assign a rational soul (*âme*) to the inferior animals, though he truly adds, "that they have not always the courage of their opinion."

[3] Some idea of the extent of research and imagination bestowed on this subject may be gleaned from the sprightly work of Pierquin de Gemblouz, "Idiomologie des Animaux," published at Paris, 1844.

tion for metaphysicians, which, so far as it affects the question
of an immaterial principle, I am quite willing to lay aside.
I can well understand that a materialist may admit innate
ideas in Man, as he must admit them in the instinct of brutes,
tracing them to hereditary predispositions. On the other
hand, we know that the most devout believers in our spiritual
nature have insisted, with Locke, in denying any idea, even
of the Deity, to be innate.

"But here comes my argument. I care not how ideas are
formed,— the material point is, how are the *capacities to receive ideas formed?* The ideas may all come from experience,
but the capacity to receive the ideas must be inherent. I take
the word 'capacity' as a good plain English word, rather than
the more technical word 'receptivity,' employed by Kant.
And by capacity I mean the passive power [1] to receive ideas,
whether in man or in any living thing by which ideas are received. A man and an elephant is each formed with capacities to receive ideas suited to the several places in the universe
held by each.

"The more I look through Nature the more I find that on
all varieties of organized life is carefully bestowed the *capacity* to receive the impressions, be they called perceptions or
ideas, which are adapted to the uses each creature is intended
to derive from them. I find, then, that Man alone is endowed
with the capacity to receive the ideas of a God, of Soul, of
Worship, of a Hereafter. I see no trace of such a capacity
in the inferior races; nor, however their intelligence may
be refined by culture, is such capacity ever apparent in
them.

"But wherever capacities to receive impressions are sufficiently general in any given species of creature to be called
universal to that species, and yet not given to another species, then, from all analogy throughout Nature, those capacities are surely designed by Providence for the distinct use
and conservation of the species to which they are given.

"It is no answer to me to say that the inherent capacities

---

[1] "Faculty is active power: capacity is passive power."—Sir W. HAMIL-
TON: *Lectures on Metaphysics and Logic*, vol. i. p. 178.

thus bestowed on Man do not suffice in themselves to make
him form right notions of a Deity or a Hereafter; because it is
plainly the design of Providence that Man must learn to correct and improve all his notions by his own study and observation.   He must build a hut before he can build a Parthenon;
he must believe with the savage or the heathen before he can
believe with the philosopher or Christian.   In a word, in all
his capacities, Man has only given to him, not the immediate
knowledge of the Perfect, but the means to strive towards the
Perfect.   And thus one of the most accomplished of modern
reasoners, to whose lectures you must have listened with delight, in your college days, says well: —

" ' Accordingly the sciences always studied with keenest interest are
those in a state of progress and uncertainty; absolute certainty and absolute completion would be the paralysis of any study, and the last
worst calamity that could befall Man, as he is at present constituted,
would be that full and final possession of speculative truth which
he now vainly anticipates as the consummation of his intellectual
happiness.' [1]

"Well, then, in all those capacities for the reception of
impressions from external Nature which are given to Man
and not to the brutes, I see the evidence of Man's Soul.   I
can understand why the inferior animal has no capacity to
receive the idea of a Deity and of Worship — simply because
the inferior animal, even if graciously admitted to a future
life, may not therein preserve the sense of its identity.   I
can understand even why that sympathy with each other
which we men possess and which constitutes the great virtue
we emphatically call Humanity, is not possessed by the lesser
animals (or, at least, in a very rare and exceptional degree)
even where they live in communities, like beavers, or bees,
or ants; because men are destined to meet, to know, and to
love each other in the life to come, and the bond between the
brute ceases here.

"Now the more, then, we examine the inherent capacities
bestowed distinctly and solely on Man, the more they seem

[1] Sir W. Hamilton's " Lectures," vol. i. p. 10.

to distinguish him from the other races by their comprehension of objects beyond his life upon this earth.

" ' Man alone,' says Müller, ' can conceive abstract notions ; and it is in abstract notions — such as time, space, matter, spirit, light, form, quantity, essence — that man grounds, not only all philosophy, all science, but all that practically improves one generation for the benefit of the next.'

And why? Because all these abstract notions unconsciously lead the mind away from the material into the immaterial,— from the present into the future. But if Man ceases to exist when he disappears in the grave, you must be compelled to affirm that he is the only creature in existence whom Nature or Providence has condescended to deceive and cheat by capacities for which there are no available objects. How nobly and how truly has Chalmers said : —

" ' What inference shall we draw from this remarkable law in Nature that there is nothing waste and nothing meaningless in the feelings and faculties wherewith living creatures are endowed ? For each desire there is a counterpart object ; for each faculty there is room and opportunity for exercise either in the present or the coming futurity. Now, but for the doctrine of immortality, Man would be an exception to this law, — he would stand forth as an anomaly in Nature, with aspirations in his heart for which the universe had no antitype to offer, with capacities of understanding and thought that never were to be followed by objects of corresponding greatness through the whole history of his being !

.   .   .   .

" ' With the inferior animals there is a certain squareness of adjustment, if we may so term it, between each desire and its correspondent gratification. The one is evenly met by the other, and there is a fulness and definiteness of enjoyment up to the capacity of enjoyment. Not so with Man, who, both from the vastness of his propensities and the vastness of his powers, feels himself chained and beset in a field too narrow for him. He alone labours under the discomfort of an incongruity between his circumstances and his powers ; and unless there be new circumstances awaiting him in a more advanced state of being, he, the noblest of Nature's products here, would turn out to be the greatest of her failures.' [1]

[1] Chalmers, " Bridgewater Treatise," vol. ii. pp. 28, 30. Perhaps I should observe, that here and elsewhere in the dialogues between Faber and Fen-

This, then, I take to be the proof of Soul in Man, not that he has a mind — because, as you justly say, inferior animals have that, though in a lesser degree — but because he has the capacities to comprehend, as soon as he is capable of any abstract ideas whatsoever, the very truths not needed for self-conservation on earth, and therefore not given to yonder ox and opossum, — namely, the nature of Deity, Soul, Hereafter. And in the recognition of these truths, the Human society, that excels the society of beavers, bees, and ants, by perpetual and progressive improvement on the notions inherited from its progenitors, rests its basis. Thus, in fact, this world is benefited for men by their belief in the next, while the society of brutes remains age after age the same. Neither the bee nor the beaver has, in all probability, improved since the Deluge.

"But inseparable from the conviction of these truths is the impulse of prayer and worship. It does not touch my argument when a philosopher of the school of Bolingbroke or Lucretius says, 'that the origin of prayer is in Man's ignorance of the phenomena of Nature.' That it is fear or ignorance which, 'when rocked the mountains or when groaned the ground, taught the weak to bend, the proud to pray.' My answer is, the brutes are much more forcibly impressed by natural phenomena than Man is; the bird and the beast know before you and I do when the mountain will rock and the ground groan, and their instinct leads them to shelter; but it does not lead them to prayer. If my theory be right that Soul is to be sought not in the question whether mental ideas be innate or formed by experience, by the sense, by association or habit, but in the *inherent capacity* to receive ideas, then, the capacity bestowed on Man alone, to be impressed by Nature herself with the idea of a Power superior to Nature, with which Power he can establish commune, is a proof that to Man alone the Maker has made Nature itself proclaim His existence, — that to Man alone the

wick, it has generally been thought better to substitute the words of the author quoted for the mere outline or purport of the quotation which memory afforded to the interlocutor.

Deity vouchsafes the communion with Himself which comes from prayer."

"Even were this so," said I, "is not the Creator omniscient? If all-wise, all-foreseeing? If all-foreseeing, all-pre-ordaining? Can the prayer of His creature alter the ways of His will?"

"For the answer to a question," returned Faber, "which is not unfrequently asked by the clever men of the world, I ought to refer you to the skilled theologians who have so triumphantly carried the reasoner over that ford of doubt which is crossed every day by the infant. But as we have not their books in the wilderness, I am contented to draw my reply as a necessary and logical sequence from the propositions I have sought to ground on the plain observation of Nature. I can only guess at the Deity's Omniscience, or His modes of enforcing His power by the observation of His general laws; and of all His laws, I know of none more general than the impulse which bids men pray,— which makes Nature so act, that all the phenomena of Nature we can conceive, however startling and inexperienced, do not make the brute pray, but there is not a trouble that can happen to Man, but what his impulse is to pray,— always provided, indeed, that he is not a philosopher. I say not this in scorn of the philosopher, to whose wildest guess our obligations are infinite, but simply because for all which is impulsive to Man, there is a reason in Nature which no philosophy can explain away. I do not, then, bewilder myself by seeking to bind and limit the Omniscience of the Deity to my finite ideas. I content myself with supposing that somehow or other, He has made it quite compatible with His Omniscience that Man should obey the impulse which leads him to believe that, in addressing a Deity, he is addressing a tender, compassionate, benignant Father, and in that obedience shall obtain beneficial results. If that impulse be an illusion, then we must say that Heaven governs the earth by a lie; and that is impossible, because, reasoning by analogy, all Nature is truthful,— that is, Nature gives to no species instincts or impulses which are not of service to it. Should I not be a

shallow physician if, where I find in the human organization
a principle or a property so general that I must believe it
normal to the healthful conditions of that organization, I
should refuse to admit that Nature intended it for use?
Reasoning by all analogy, must I not say the habitual neglect
of its use must more or less injure the harmonious well-being
of the whole human system? I could have much to add upon
the point in dispute by which the creed implied in your question would enthrall the Divine mercy by the necessities of its
Divine wisdom, and substitute for a benignant Deity a relentless Fate. But here I should exceed my province. I am no
theologian. Enough for me that in all my afflictions, all my
perplexities, an impulse, that I obey as an instinct, moves me
at once to prayer. Do I find by experience that the prayer is
heard, that the affliction is removed, the doubt is solved?
That, indeed, would be presumptuous to say. But it is not
presumptuous to think that by the efficacy of prayer my heart
becomes more fortified against the sorrow, and my reason
more serene amidst the doubt."

I listened, and ceased to argue. I felt as if in that solitude, and in the pause of my wonted mental occupations, my
intellect was growing languid, and its old weapons rusting in
disuse. My pride took alarm. I had so from my boyhood
cherished the idea of fame, and so glorified the search after
knowledge, that I recoiled in dismay from the thought that I
had relinquished knowledge, and cut myself off from fame.
I resolved to resume my once favourite philosophical pursuits, re-examine and complete the Work to which I had once
committed my hopes of renown; and, simultaneously, a restless desire seized me to commundiate, though but at brief
intervals, with other minds than those immediately within
my reach, — minds fresh from the old world, and reviving the
memories of its vivid civilization. Emigrants frequently
passed my doors, but I had hitherto shrunk from tendering
the hospitalities so universally accorded in the colony. I
could not endure to expose to such rough strangers my Lilian's
mournful affliction, and that thought was not less intolerable
to Mrs. Ashleigh. I now hastily constructed a log-building

a few hundred yards from the house, and near the main track taken by travellers through the spacious pastures. I transported to this building my books and scientific instruments. In an upper story I placed my telescopes and lenses, my crucibles and retorts. I renewed my chemical experiments; I sought to invigorate my mind by other branches of science which I had hitherto less cultured,— meditated new theories on Light and Colour, collected specimens in Natural History, subjected animalcules to my microscope, geological fossils to my hammer. With all these quickened occupations of thought, I strove to distract myself from sorrow, and strengthen my reason against the illusion of my fantasy. The Luminous Shadow was not seen again on my wall, and the thought of Margrave himself was banished.

In this building I passed many hours of each day; more and more earnestly plunging my thoughts into depths of abstract study, as Lilian's unaccountable dislike to my presence became more and more decided. When I thus ceased to think that my life cheered and comforted hers, my heart's occupation was gone. I had annexed to the apartment reserved for myself in the log-hut a couple of spare rooms, in which I could accommodate passing strangers. I learned to look forward to their coming with interest, and to see them depart with regret; yet, for the most part, they were of the ordinary class of colonial adventurers,— bankrupt tradesmen, unlucky farmers, forlorn mechanics, hordes of unskilled labourers, now and then a briefless barrister, or a sporting collegian who had lost his all on the Derby. One day, however, a young man of education and manners that unmistakably proclaimed the cultured gentleman of Europe, stopped at my door. He was a cadet of a noble Prussian family, which for some political reasons had settled itself in Paris; there he had become intimate with young French nobles, and living the life of a young French noble had soon scandalized his German parents, forestalled his slender inheritance, and been compelled to fly his father's frown and his tailor's bills. All this he told me with a lively frankness which proved how much the wit of a German can be quickened in the atmosphere of Paris. An old college friend, of birth inferior to his own, had been as unfortunate in seeking to make money as this young prodigal had been an adept in spending it. The friend, a few years previously, had accompanied other Germans in a migration to Australia, and was already thriving; the spendthrift noble was on his way to join the bankrupt trader, at a German settlement fifty miles distant from my house. This young man was unlike any German I ever met. He had all the exquisite levity by which the well-bred Frenchman gives to the doctrines of the Cynic the grace of the Epicurean. He owned himself to be good for nothing with an elegance of candour which not only disarmed censure, but seemed to challenge admiration; and, withal, the happy spendthrift was so inebriate with hope,— sure that he should be rich before he was thirty. How and wherefore rich, he could have no more explained than I can square the circle. When the grand serious German nature does Frenchify itself, it can become so extravagantly French!

I listened, almost enviously, to this light-hearted profligate's babble, as we sat by my rude fireside,— I, sombre man of science and sorrow, he, smiling child of idleness and pleasure, so much one of Nature's courtier-like nobles, that there, as he smoked his villanous pipe, in his dust-soiled shabby garments, and with his ruffianly revolver stuck into his belt, I would defy the daintiest Aristarch who ever presided as critic over the holiday world not to have said, "There smiles the genius beyond my laws, the born darling of the Graces, who in every circumstance, in every age, like Aristippus, would have socially charmed; would have been welcome to the orgies of a Cæsar or a Clodius, to the boudoirs of a Montespan or a Pompadour; have lounged through the Mulberry Gardens with a Rochester and a Buckingham, or smiled from the death-cart, with a Richelieu and a Lauzun, a gentleman's disdain of a mob! "

I was so thinking as we sat, his light talk frothing up from his careless lips, when suddenly from the spray and the sparkle of that light talk was flung forth the name of Margrave.

"Margrave!" I exclaimed. "Pardon me. What of him?"

"What of him! I asked if, by chance, you knew the only Englishman I ever had the meanness to envy?"

"Perhaps you speak of one person, and I thought of another."

"*Pardieu,* my dear host, there can scarcely be two Margraves! The one of whom I speak flashed like a meteor upon Paris, bought from a prince of the Bourse a palace that might have lodged a prince of the blood-royal, eclipsed our Jew bankers in splendour, our *jeunesse dorée* in good looks and hair-brain adventures, and, strangest of all, filled his *salons* with philosophers and charlatans, chemists and spirit-rappers; insulting the gravest dons of the schools by bringing them face to face with the most impudent quacks, the most ridiculous dreamers,— and yet, withal, himself so racy and charming, so *bon prince,* so *bon enfant!* For six months he was the rage at Paris: perhaps he might have continued to be the rage there for six years, but all at once the meteor vanished as suddenly as it had flashed. Is this the Margrave whom you know?"

"I should not have thought the Margrave whom I knew could have reconciled his tastes to the life of cities."

"Nor could this man: cities were too tame for him. He has gone to some far-remote wilds in the East,— some say in search of the Philosopher's Stone; for he actually maintained in his house a Sicilian adventurer, who, when at work on that famous discovery, was stifled by the fumes of his own crucible. After that misfortune, Margrave took Paris in disgust, and we lost him."

"So this is the only Englishman whom you envy! Envy him? Why?"

"Because he is the only Englishman I ever met who contrived to be rich and yet free from the spleen; I envied him because one had only to look at his face and see how thoroughly he enjoyed the life of which your countrymen seem to be so heartily tired. But now that I have satisfied your curiosity, pray satisfy mine. Who and what is this Englishman?"

"Who and what was he supposed at Paris to be?"

"Conjectures were numberless. One of your countrymen suggested that which was the most generally favoured. This gentleman, whose name I forget, but who was one of those old *roués* who fancy themselves young because they live with the young, no sooner set eyes upon Margrave, than he exclaimed, 'Louis Grayle come to life again, as I saw him forty-four years ago! But no — still younger, still handsomer — it must be his son!'"

"Louis Grayle, who was said to be murdered at Aleppo?"

"The same. That strange old man was enormously rich; but it seems that he hated his lawful heirs, and left behind him a fortune so far below that which he was known to possess that he must certainly have disposed of it secretly before his death. Why so dispose of it, if not to enrich some natural son, whom, for private reasons, he might not have wished to acknowledge, or point out to the world by the signal bequest of his will? All that Margrave ever said of himself and the source of his wealth confirmed this belief. He frankly proclaimed himself a natural son, enriched by a father whose name he knew not nor cared to know."

"It is true. And Margrave quitted Paris for the East. When?"

"I can tell you the date within a day or two, for his flight preceded mine by a week; and, happily, all Paris was so busy in talking of it, that I slipped away without notice."

And the Prussian then named a date which it thrilled me to hear, for it was in that very month, and about that very day, that the Luminous Shadow had stood within my threshold.

The young count now struck off into other subjects of talk: nothing more was said of Margrave. An hour or two afterwards he went on his way, and I remained long gazing musingly on the embers of the dying glow on my hearth.

CHAPTER LXXIV.

My Work, my Philosophical Work — the ambitious hope
of my intellectual life — how eagerly I returned to it again!
Far away from my household grief, far away from my haggard perplexities — neither a Lilian nor a Margrave there!

As I went over what I had before written, each link in its
chain of reasoning seemed so serried, that to alter one were
to derange all; and the whole reasoning was so opposed to
the possibility of the wonders I myself had experienced, so
hostile to the subtle hypotheses of a Faber, or the childlike
belief of an Amy, that I must have destroyed the entire work
if I had admitted such contradictions to its design!

But the work was I myself! — I, in my solid, sober, health-
ful mind, before the brain had been perplexed by a phantom.
Were phantoms to be allowed as testimonies against science?
No; in returning to my Book, I returned to my former Me!

How strange is that contradiction between our being as
man and our being as Author! Take any writer enamoured
of a system: a thousand things may happen to him every day
which might shake his faith in that system; and while he
moves about as mere man, his faith *is* shaken. But when he
settles himself back into the phase of his being as author, the
mere act of taking pen in hand and smoothing the paper before him restores his speculations to their ancient mechanical
train. The system, the beloved system, re-asserts its tyran-
nic sway, and he either ignores, or moulds into fresh proofs
of his theory as author, all which, an hour before, had given
his theory the lie in his living perceptions as man.

I adhered to my system, — I continued my work. Here, in
the barbarous desert, was a link between me and the Cities of
Europe. All else might break down under me. The love I
had dreamed of was blotted out from the world, and might
never be restored; my heart might be lonely, my life be an

exile's. My reason might, at last, give way before the spectres which awed my senses, or the sorrow which stormed my heart. But here at least was a monument of my rational thoughtful Me,— of my individualized identity in multiform creation. And my mind, in the noon of its force, would shed its light on the earth when my form was resolved to its elements. Alas! in this very yearning for the Hereafter, though but the Hereafter of a Name, could I see only the craving of Mind, and hear not the whisper of Soul!

The avocation of a colonist, usually so active, had little interest for me. This vast territorial lordship, in which, could I have endeared its possession by the hopes that animate a Founder, I should have felt all the zest and the pride of ownership, was but the run of a common to the passing emigrant, who would leave no son to inherit the tardy products of his labour. I was not goaded to industry by the stimulus of need. I could only be ruined if I risked all my capital in the attempt to improve. I lived, therefore, amongst my fertile pastures, as careless of culture as the English occupant of the Highland moor, which he rents for the range of its solitudes.

I knew, indeed, that if ever I became avaricious, I might swell my modest affluence into absolute wealth. I had revisited the spot in which I had discovered the nugget of gold, and had found the precious metal in rich abundance just under the first coverings of the alluvial soil. I concealed my discovery from all. I knew that, did I proclaim it, the charm of my bush-life would be gone. My fields would be infested by all the wild adventurers who gather to gold as the vultures of prey round a carcass; my servants would desert me, my very flocks would be shepherdless!

Months again rolled on months. I had just approached the close of my beloved Work, when it was again suspended, and by an anguish keener than all which I had previously known.

Lilian became alarmingly ill. Her state of health, long gradually declining, had hitherto admitted checkered intervals of improvement, and exhibited no symptoms of actual danger. But now she was seized with a kind of chronic fever, attended with absolute privation of sleep, an aversion to even the lightest nourishment, and an acute nervous susceptibility to all the outward impressions of which she had long seemed so unconscious; morbidly alive to the faintest sound, shrinking from the light as from a torture. Her previous impatience at my entrance into her room became aggravated into vehement emotions, convulsive paroxysms of distress; so that Faber banished me from her chamber, and, with a heart bleeding at every fibre, I submitted to the cruel sentence.

Faber had taken up his abode in my house and brought Amy with him; one or the other never left Lilian, night or day. The great physician spoke doubtfully of the case, but not despairingly.

"Remember," he said, "that in spite of the want of sleep, the abstinence from food, the form has not wasted as it would do were this fever inevitably mortal. It is upon that phenomenon I build a hope that I have not been mistaken in the opinion I hazarded from the first. We are now in the midst of the critical struggle between life and reason; if she preserve the one, my conviction is that she will regain the other. That seeming antipathy to yourself is a good omen. You are inseparably associated with her intellectual world; in proportion as she revives to it, must become vivid and powerful the reminiscences of the shock that annulled, for a time, that world to her. So I welcome, rather than fear, the over-susceptibility of the awakening senses to external sights and sounds. A few days will decide if I am right. In this climate the progress of acute maladies is swift, but the recovery from them is yet more startlingly rapid. Wait, endure, be prepared to submit to the will of Heaven; but do not despond of its mercy."

I rushed away from the consoler, — away into the thick of the forests, the heart of the solitude. All around me, there, was joyous with life; the locust sang amidst the herbage; the cranes gambolled on the banks of the creek; the squirrel-like opossums frolicked on the feathery boughs. "And what," said I to myself, — "what if that which seems so fabulous in the distant being whose existence has bewitched my own, be

substantially true? What if to some potent medicament Margrave owes his glorious vitality, his radiant youth? Oh, that
I had not so disdainfully turned away from his hinted so-
licitations — to what? — to nothing guiltier than lawful experiment. Had I been less devoted a bigot to this vain
schoolcraft, which we call the Medical Art, and which, alone
in this age of science, has made no perceptible progress since
the days of its earliest teachers — had I said, in the true humility of genuine knowledge, 'these alchemists were men of
genius and thought; we owe to them nearly all the grand
hints of our chemical science, — is it likely that they would
have been wholly drivellers and idiots in the one faith they
clung to the most?' — had I said that, I might now have no
fear of losing my Lilian. Why, after all, should there not
be in Nature one primary essence, one master substance, in
which is stored the specific nutriment of life?"

Thus incoherently muttering to the woods what my pride
of reason would not have suffered me gravely to say to my
fellow-men, I fatigued my tormented spirits into a gloomy
calm, and mechanically retraced my steps at the decline of
day. I seated myself at the door of my solitary log-hut, leaning my cheek upon my hand, and musing. Wearily I looked
up, roused by a discord of clattering hoofs and lumbering
wheels on the hollow-sounding grass-track. A crazy groan-
ing vehicle, drawn by four horses, emerged from the copse of
gum-trees, — fast, fast along the road, which no such pompous
vehicle had traversed since that which had borne me — luxurious satrap for an early colonist — to my lodge in the wilderness. What emigrant rich enough to squander in the hire
of such an equipage more than its cost in England, could
thus be entering on my waste domain? An ominous thrill
shot through me.

The driver — perhaps some broken-down son of luxury in
the Old World, fit for nothing in the New World but to ply,
for hire, the task that might have led to his ruin when plied
in sport — stopped at the door of my hut, and called out,
"Friend, is not this the great Fenwick Section, and is not
yonder long pile of building the Master's house?"

Before I could answer I heard a faint voice, within the
vehicle, speaking to the driver; the last nodded, descended
from his seat, opened the carriage-door, and offered his arm
to a man, who, waving aside the proffered aid, descended
slowly and feebly; paused a moment as if for breath, and
then, leaning on his staff, walked from the road, across the
sward rank with luxuriant herbage, through the little gate in
the new-set fragrant wattle-fence, wearily, languidly, halting
often, till he stood facing me, leaning both wan and emaciated
hands upon his staff, and his meagre form shrinking deep
within the folds of a cloak lined thick with costly sables.
His face was sharp, his complexion of a livid yellow, his eyes
shone out from their hollow orbits, unnaturally enlarged and
fatally bright. Thus, in ghastly contrast to his former splendour of youth and opulence of life, Margrave stood before
me.

"I come to you," said Margrave, in accents hoarse and
broken, "from the shores of the East. Give me shelter and
rest. I have that to say which will more than repay you."

Whatever, till that moment, my hate and my fear of this
unexpected visitant, hate would have been inhumanity, fear a
meanness, conceived for a creature so awfully stricken down.

Silently, involuntarily, I led him into the house. There he
rested a few minutes, with closed eyes and painful gasps for
breath. Meanwhile, the driver brought from the carriage a
travelling-bag and a small wooden chest or coffer, strongly
banded with iron clamps. Margrave, looking up as the man
drew near, exclaimed fiercely, "Who told you to touch that
chest? How dare you? Take it from that man, Fenwick!
Place it here,— here by my side!"

I took the chest from the driver, whose rising anger at being so imperiously rated in the land of democratic equality
was appeased by the gold which Margrave lavishly flung to
him.

"Take care of the poor gentleman, squire," he whispered
to me, in the spontaneous impulse of gratitude, "I fear he
will not trouble you long. He must be monstrous rich. Arrived in a vessel hired all to himself, and a train of outland-

ish attendants, whom he has left behind in the town yonder. May I bait my horses in your stables? They have come a long way."

I pointed to the neighbouring stables, and the man nodded his thanks, remounted his box, and drove off.

I returned to Margrave. A faint smile came to his lips as I placed the chest beside him.

"Ay, ay," he muttered. "Safe! safe! I shall soon be well again,—very soon! And now I can sleep in peace!"

I led him into an inner room, in which there was a bed. He threw himself on it with a loud sigh of relief. Soon, half raising himself on his elbow, he exclaimed, "The chest —bring it hither! I need it always beside me! There, there! Now for a few hours of sleep; and then, if I can take food, or some such restoring cordial as your skill may suggest, I shall be strong enough to talk. We will talk! we will talk!"

His eyes closed heavily as his voice fell into a drowsy mutter: a moment more and he was asleep.

I watched beside him, in mingled wonder and compassion. Looking into that face, so altered yet still so young, I could not sternly question what had been the evil of that mystic life, which seemed now oozing away through the last sands in the hour-glass. I placed my hand softly on his pulse: it scarcely beat. I put my ear to his breast, and involuntarily sighed, as I distinguished in its fluttering heave that dull, dumb sound, in which the heart seems knelling itself to the greedy grave!

Was this, indeed, the potent magician whom I had so feared! — this the guide to the Rosicrucian's secret of life's renewal, in whom, but an hour or two ago, my fancies gulled my credulous trust!

But suddenly, even while thus chiding my wild superstitions, a fear, that to most would seem scarcely less superstitious, shot across me. Could Lilian be affected by the near neighbourhood of one to whose magnetic influence she had once been so strangely subjected? I left Margrave still sleeping, closed and locked the door of the hut, went back to my dwelling, and met Amy at the threshold. Her smile was so cheering that I felt at once relieved.

"Hush!" said the child, putting her finger to her lips, "she is so quiet! I was coming in search of you, with a message from her."

"From Lilian to me — what! to me!"

"Hush! About an hour ago, she beckoned me to draw near to her, and then said, very softly: 'Tell Allen that light is coming back to me, and it all settles on him — on him. Tell him that I'pray to be spared to walk by his side on earth, hand-in-hand to that heaven which is no dream, Amy. Tell him that, — no dream!'"

While the child spoke my tears gushed, and the strong hands in which I veiled my face quivered like the leaf of the aspen. And when I could command my voice, I said plaintively, —

"May I not, then, see her? — only for a moment, and answer her message though but by a look?"

"No, no!"

"No! Where is Faber?"

"Gone into the forest, in search of some herbs, but he gave me this note for you."

I wiped the blinding tears from my eyes, and read these lines: —

"I have, though with hesitation, permitted Amy to tell you the cheering words, by which our beloved patient confirms my belief that reason is coming back to her, — slowly, labouringly, but if she survive, for permanent restoration. On no account attempt to precipitate or disturb the work of nature. As dangerous as a sudden glare of light to eyes long blind and newly regaining vision in the friendly and soothing dark would be the agitation that your presence at this crisis would cause. Confide in me."

I remained brooding over these lines and over Lilian's message long and silently, while Amy's soothing whispers stole into my ear, soft as the murmurs of a rill heard in the gloom of forests. Rousing myself at length, my thoughts returned to Margrave. Doubtless he would soon awake. I bade Amy bring me such slight nutriment as I thought best suited to his enfeebled state, telling her it was for a sick traveller, resting himself in my hut. When Amy returned, I took from her the little basket with which she was charged, and having, meanwhile, made a careful selection from the contents of my medicine-chest, went back to the hut. I had not long resumed my place beside Margrave's pillow before he awoke.

"What o'clock is it?" he asked, with an anxious voice.

"About seven."

"Not later? That is well; my time is precious."

"Compose yourself, and eat."

I placed the food before him, and he partook of it, though sparingly, and as if with effort. He then dozed for a short time, again woke up, and impatiently demanded the cordial, which I had prepared in the mean while. Its effect was greater and more immediate than I could have anticipated, proving, perhaps, how much of youth there was still left in his system, however undermined and ravaged by disease. Colour came back to his cheek, his voice grew perceptibly stronger. And as I lighted the lamp on the table near us — for it was growing dark — he gathered himself up, and spoke thus,—

"You remember that I once pressed on you certain experiments. My object then was to discover the materials from which is extracted the specific that enables the organs of life to expel disease and regain vigour. In that hope I sought your intimacy,— an intimacy you gave, but withdrew."

"Dare you complain? Who and what was the being from whose intimacy I shrank appalled?"

"Ask what questions you please," cried Margrave, impatiently, "later — if I have strength left to answer them; but do not interrupt me, while I husband my force to say what alone is important to me and to you. Disappointed in the hopes I had placed in you, I resolved to repair to Paris,— that great furnace of all bold ideas. I questioned learned formalists; I listened to audacious empirics. The first, with all their boasted knowledge, were too timid to concede my premises; the second, with all their speculative daring, too knavish to let me trust to their conclusions. I found but one man, a Sicilian, who comprehended the secrets that are called occult, and had the courage to meet Nature and all her agencies face to face. He believed, and sincerely, that he was approaching the grand result, at the very moment when he perished from want of the common precautions which a tyro in chemistry would have taken. At his death the gaudy city became hateful; all its pretended pleasures only served to exhaust life the faster. The true joys of youth are those of the wild bird and wild brute, in the healthful enjoyment of Nature. In cities, youth is but old age with a varnish. I fled to the East; I passed through the tents of the Arabs; I was guided — no matter by whom or by what — to the house of a Dervish, who had had for his teacher the most erudite master of secrets occult, whom I knew years ago at Aleppo — Why that exclamation? "

"Proceed. What I have to say will come — later."

"From this Dervish I half forced and half purchased the secret I sought to obtain. I now know from what peculiar substance the so-called elixir of life is extracted; I know also the steps of the process through which that task is accomplished. You smile incredulously. What is your doubt? State it while I rest for a moment. My breath labours; give me more of the cordial."

"Need I tell you my doubt? You have, you say, at your command the elixir of life of which Cagliostro did not leave his disciples the recipe; and you stretch out your hand for a vulgar cordial which any village chemist could give you! "

"I can explain this apparent contradiction. The process by which the elixir is extracted from the material which hoards its essence is one that requires a hardihood of courage which few possess. This Dervish, who had passed through that process once, was deaf to all prayer, and unmoved by all bribes, to attempt it again. He was poor; for the secret by which metals may be transmuted is not, as the old alchemists seem to imply, identical with that by which the elixir of life is extracted. He had only been enabled to discover, in the niggard strata of the lands within range of his travel, a few scanty morsels of the glorious substance. From these he had extracted scarcely enough of the elixir to fill a third of that little glass which I have just drained. He guarded every drop for himself. Who that holds healthful life as the one boon above all price to the living, would waste upon others what prolongs and recruits his own being? Therefore, though he sold me his secret, he would not sell me his treasure."

"Any quack may sell you the information how to make not only an elixir, but a sun and a moon, and then scare you from the experiment by tales of the danger of trying it! How do you know that this essence which the Dervish possessed was the elixir of life, since, it seems, you have not tried on yourself what effect its precious drops could produce? Poor wretch, who once seemed to me so awfully potent! do you come to the Antipodes in search of a drug that only exists in the fables by which a child is amused?"

"The elixir of life is no fable," cried Margrave, with a kindling of eye, a power of voice, a dilatation of form, that startled me in one just before so feeble. "That elixir was bright in my veins when we last met. From that golden draught of the life-spring of joy I took all that can gladden creation. What sage would not have exchanged his wearisome knowledge for my lusty revels with Nature? What monarch would not have bartered his crown, with its brainache of care, for the radiance that circled my brows, flashing out from the light that was in me? Oh again, oh again! to enjoy the freedom of air with the bird, and the glow of the sun with the lizard; to sport through the blooms of the earth, Nature's playmate and darling; to face, in the forest and desert, the pard and the lion, — Nature's bravest and fiercest, — her first-born, the heir of her realm, with the rest of her children for slaves!"

As these words burst from his lips, there was a wild grandeur in the aspect of this enigmatical being which I had never beheld in the former time of his affluent, dazzling youth. And, indeed, in his language, and in the thoughts it clothed, there was an earnestness, a concentration, a directness, a purpose, which had seemed wanting to his desultory talk in the

earlier days I expected that reaction of languor and exhaustion would follow his vehement outbreak of passion; but,
after a short pause, he went on with steady accents. His will
was sustaining his strength. He was determined to force his
convictions on me, and the vitality, once so rich, rallied all
its lingering forces to the aid of its intense desire.

"I tell you, then," he resumed, with deliberate calmness,
"that, years ago, I tested in my own person that essence
which is the sovereign medicament. In me, as you saw me
at L——, you beheld the proof of its virtues. Feeble and ill
as I am now, my state was incalculably more hopeless when
formerly restored by the elixir. He from whom I then took
the sublime restorative died without revealing the secret of
its composition. What I obtained was only just sufficient to
recruit the lamp of my life, then dying down — and no drop
was left for renewing the light which wastes its own rays
in the air that it gilds. Though the Dervish would not
sell me his treasure, he permitted me to see it. The appearance and odour of this essence are strangely peculiar,—
unmistakable by one who has once beheld and partaken of
it. In short, I recognized in the hands of the Dervish the
bright life-renewer, as I had borne it away from the corpse
of the Sage of Aleppo."

"Hold! Are you then, in truth, the murderer of Haroun,
and is your true name Louis Grayle?"

"I am no murderer, and Louis Grayle did not leave me his
name. I again adjure you to postpone, for this night at least,
the questions you wish to address to me.

"Seeing that this obstinate pauper possessed that for which
the pale owners of millions, at the first touch of palsy or
gout, would consent to be paupers, of course I coveted the
possession of the essence even more than the knowledge of
the substance from which it is extracted. I had no coward
fear of the experiment, which this timid driveller had not
the nerve to renew. But still the experiment might fail. I
must traverse land and sea to find the fit place for it, while,
in the rags of the Dervish, the unfailing result of the experiment was at hand. The Dervish suspected my design, he

dreaded my power. He fled on the very night in which I
had meant to seize what he refused to sell me. After all, I
should have done him no great wrong; for I should have left
him wealth enough to transport himself to any soil in which
the material for the elixir may be most abundant; and the
desire of life would have given his shrinking nerves the courage to replenish its ravished store. I had Arabs in my pay,
who obeyed me as hounds their master. I chased the fugitive. I came on his track, reached a house in a miserable
village, in which, I was told, he had entered but an hour before. The day was declining, the light in the room imperfect. I saw in a corner what seemed to me the form of the
Dervish,— stooped to seize it, and my hand closed on an asp.
The artful Dervish had so piled his rags that they took the
shape of the form they had clothed, and he had left, as a substitute for the giver of life, the venomous reptile of death.

"The strength of my system enabled me to survive the effect of the poison; but during the torpor that numbed me, my
Arabs, alarmed, gave no chase to my quarry. At last, though
enfeebled and languid, I was again on my horse. Again the
pursuit, again the track! I learned — but this time by a
knowledge surer than man's — that the Dervish had taken
his refuge in a hamlet that had sprung up over the site of a
city once famed through Assyria. The same voice that informed me of his whereabouts warned me not to pursue. I
rejected the warning. In my eager impatience I sprang on
to the chase; in my fearless resolve I felt sure of the prey.
I arrived at the hamlet wearied out, for my forces were no
longer the same since the bite of the asp. The Dervish
eluded me still; he had left the floor, on which I sank exhausted, but a few minutes before my horse stopped at the
door. The carpet, on which he had rested, still lay on the
ground. I dismissed the youngest and keenest of my troop
in search of the fugitive. Sure that this time he would not
escape, my eyes closed in sleep.

"How long I slept I know not,— a long dream of solitude,
fever, and anguish. Was it the curse of the Dervish's carpet? Was it a taint in the walls of the house, or of the air,

which broods sickly and rank over places where cities lie buried? I know not; but the Pest of the East had seized me in slumber. When my senses recovered I found myself alone, plundered of my arms, despoiled of such gold as I had carried about me. All had deserted and left me, as the living leave the dead whom the Plague has claimed for its own. As soon as I could stand I crawled from the threshold. The moment my voice was heard, my face seen, the whole squalid populace rose as on a wild beast,—a mad dog. I was driven from the place with imprecations and stones, as a miscreant whom the Plague had overtaken while plotting the death of a holy man. Bruised and bleeding, but still defying, I turned in wrath on that dastardly rabble; they slunk away from my path. I knew the land for miles around. I had been in that land years, long years ago. I came at last to the road which the caravans take on their way to Damascus. There I was found, speechless and seemingly lifeless, by some European travellers. Conveyed to Damascus, I languished for weeks between life and death. But for the virtue of that essence, which lingered yet in my veins, I could not have survived — even thus feeble and shattered. I need not say that I now abandoned all thought of discovering the Dervish. I had at least his secret, if I had failed of the paltry supply he had drawn from its uses. Such appliances as he had told me were needful are procured in the East with more ease than in Europe. To sum up, I am here, instructed in all the knowledge, and supplied with all the aids, which warrant me in saying, 'Do you care for new life in its richest enjoyments, if not for yourself, for one whom you love and would reprieve from the grave? Then, share with me in a task that a single night will accomplish, and ravish a prize by which the life that you value the most will be saved from the dust and the worm, to live on, ever young, ever blooming, when each infant, new-born while I speak, shall have passed to the grave. Nay, where is the limit to life, while the earth hides the substance by which life is renewed?"

I give as faithfully as I can recall them the words in which Margrave addressed me. But who can guess by cold words transcribed, even were they artfully ranged by a master of language, the effect words produce when warm from the breath of the speaker? Ask one of an audience which some orator held enthralled, why his words do not quicken a beat in the reader's pulse, and the answer of one who had listened will be, "The words took their charm from the voice and the eye, the aspect, the manner, the man!" So it was with the incomprehensible being before me. Though his youth was faded, though his beauty was dimmed, though my fancies clothed him with memories of abhorrent dread, though my reason opposed his audacious beliefs and assumptions, still he charmed and spell-bound me; still he was the mystical fascinator; still, if the legends of magic had truth for their basis, he was the *born magician*,— as genius, in what calling soever, *is* born with the gift to enchant and subdue us.

Constraining myself to answer calmly, I said, "You have told me your story; you have defined the object of the experiment in which you ask me to aid. You do right to bid me postpone my replies or my questions. Seek to recruit by sleep the strength you have so sorely tasked. To-morrow —"

"To-morrow, ere night, you will decide whether the man whom out of all earth I have selected to aid me shall be the foe to condemn me to perish! I tell you plainly I need your aid, and your prompt aid. Three days from this, and all aid will be too late!"

I had already gained the door of the room, when he called to me to come back.

"You do not live in this hut, but with your family yonder. Do not tell them that I am here; let no one but yourself see me as I now am. Lock the door of the hut when you quit it. I should not close my eyes if I were not secure from intruders." .

"There is but one in my house, or in these parts, whom I would except from the interdict you impose. You are aware of your own imminent danger; the life, which you believe the discovery of a Dervish will indefinitely prolong, seems to my eye of physician to hang on a thread. I have already formed my own conjecture as to the nature of the disease that

28

enfeebles you. But I would fain compare that conjecture with the weightier opinion of one whose experience and skill are superior to mine. Permit me, then, when I return to you to-morrow, to bring with me the great physician to whom I refer. His name will not, perhaps, be unknown to you: I speak of Julius Faber."

"A physician of the schools! I can guess well enough how learnedly he would prate, and how little he could do. But I will not object to his visit, if it satisfies you that, since I should die under the hands of the doctors, I may be permitted to indulge my own whim in placing my hopes in a Dervish. Yet stay. You have, doubtless, spoken of me to this Julius Faber, your fellow-physician and friend? Promise me, if you bring him here, that you will not name me,— that you will not repeat to him the tale I have told you, or the hope which has led me to these shores. What I have told you, no matter whether, at this moment, you consider me the dupe of a chimera, is still under the seal of the confidence which a patient reposes in the physician he himself selects for his confidant. I select you, and not Julius Faber!"

"Be it as you will," said I, after a moment's reflection. "The moment you make yourself my patient, I am bound to consider what is best for you. And you may more respect, and profit by, an opinion based upon your purely physical condition than by one in which you might suppose the advice was directed rather to the disease of the mind than to that of the body."

"How amazed and indignant your brother-physician will be if he ever see me a second time! How learnedly he will prove that, according to all correct principles of science and nature, I ought to be dead!"

He uttered this jest with a faint weary echo of his old merry, melodious laugh, then turned his face to the wall; and so I left him to repose.

CHAPTER LXXV.

I FOUND Mrs. Ashleigh waiting for me in our usual sitting-room. She was in tears. She had begun to despond of Lilian's recovery, and she infected me with her own alarm. However, I disguised my participation in her fears, soothed and sustained her as I best could, and persuaded her to retire to rest. I saw Faber for a few minutes before I sought my own chamber. He assured me that there was no perceptible change for the worse in Lilian's physical state since he had last seen me, and that her mind, even within the last few hours, had become decidedly more clear. He thought that, within the next twenty-four hours, the reason would make a strong and successful effort for complete recovery; but he declined to hazard more than a hope that the effort would not exhaust the enfeebled powers of the frame. He himself was so in need of a few hours of rest that I ceased to harass him with questions which he could not answer, and fears which he could not appease. Before leaving him for the night, I told him briefly that there was a traveller in my hut smitten by a disease which seemed to me so grave that I would ask his opinion of the case, if he could accompany me to the hut the next morning.

My own thoughts that night were not such as would suffer me to sleep.

Before Margrave's melancholy state much of my former fear and abhorrence faded away. This being, so exceptional that fancy might well invest him with preternatural attributes, was now reduced by human suffering to human sympathy and comprehension; yet his utter want of conscience was still as apparent as in his day of joyous animal spirits. With what hideous candour he had related his perfidy and ingratitude to the man to whom, in his belief, he owed an inestimable obligation, and with what insensibility to the signal retribution which in most natures would have awakened remorse!

And by what dark hints and confessions did he seem to confirm the incredible memoir of Sir Philip Derval! He owned that he had borne from the corpse of Haroun the medicament to which he ascribed his recovery from a state yet more hopeless than that under which he now laboured! He had alluded, rapidly, obscurely, to some knowledge at his command "surer than man's." And now, even now the mere wreck of his former existence — by what strange charm did he still control and confuse my reason? And how was it that I felt myself murmuring, again and again, "But what, after all, if his hope be no chimera, and if Nature do hide a secret by which I could save the life of my beloved Lilian?"

And again and again, as that thought would force itself on me, I rose and crept to Lilian's threshold, listening to catch the faintest sound of her breathing. All still, all dark! In that sufferer recognized science detects no mortal disease, yet dares not bid me rely on its amplest resources of skill to turn aside from her slumber the stealthy advance of death; while in yon log-hut one whose malady recognized science could not doubt to be mortal has composed himself to sleep, confident of life! Recognized science?—recognized ignorance! The science of to-day is the ignorance of to-morrow! Every year some bold guess lights up a truth to which, but the year before, the schoolmen of science were as blinded as moles.

"What, then," my lips kept repeating, — "what if Nature do hide a secret by which the life of my life can be saved? What do we know of the secrets of Nature? What said Newton himself of his knowledge? 'I am like a child picking up pebbles and shells on the sand, while the great ocean of Truth lies all undiscovered around me!' And did Newton himself, in the ripest growth of his matchless intellect, hold the creed of the alchemists in scorn? Had he not given to one object of their research, in the transmutation of metals, his days and his nights? Is there proof that he ever convinced himself that the research was the dream, which we,

who are not Newtons, call it?[1]   And that other great sage,
inferior only to Newton — the calculating doubt-weigher,
Descartes — had he not believed in the yet nobler hope of
the alchemists, — believed in some occult nostrum or process by which human life could attain to the age of the
Patriarchs?"[2]

[1] "Besides the three great subjects of Newton's labours — the fluxional cal-
culus, physical astronomy, and optics — a very large portion of his time, while
resident in his college, was devoted to researches of which scarcely a trace
remains. Alchemy, which had fascinated so many eager and ambitious
minds, seems to have tempted Newton with an overwhelming force. What
theories he formed, what experiments he tried, in that laboratory where, it is
said, the fire was scarcely extinguished for weeks together, will never be
known. It is certain that no success attended his labours; and Newton was
not a man — like Kepler — to detail to the world all the hopes and disap-
pointments, all the crude and mystical fancies, which mixed themselves up
with his career of philosophy. . . . Many years later we find Newton in correspondence with Locke, with reference to a mysterious red earth by which
Boyle, who was then recently dead, had asserted that he could effect the
grand desideratum of multiplying gold. By this time, however, Newton's
faith had become somewhat shaken by the unsatisfactory communications
which he had himself received from Boyle on the subject of the golden recipe, though he did not abandon the idea of giving the experiment a further trial as soon as the weather should become suitable for furnace experiments."— *Quarterly Review*, No. 220, pp. 125, 126.

[2] Southey, in his "Doctor," vol. vi. p. 2, reports the conversation of Sir
Kenelm Digby with Descartes, in which the great geometrician said, "That
as for rendering man immortal, it was what he could not venture to promise,
but that he was very sure he could prolong his life to the standard of the
patriarchs." And Southey adds, "that St. Evremond, to whom Digby repeated this, says that this opinion of Descartes was well known both to his
friends in Holland and in France." By the stress Southey lays on this hearsay evidence, it is clear that he was not acquainted with the works and
biography of Descartes, or he would have gone to the fountain-head for authority on Descartes's opinions, — namely, Descartes himself. It is to be
wished that Southey had done so, for no one more than he would have ap-
preciated the exquisitely candid and lovable nature of the illustrious Frenchman, and the sincerity with which he cherished in his heart whatever doctrine
he conceived in his understanding. Descartes, whose knowledge of anatomy
was considerable, had that passion for the art of medicine which is almost inseparable from the pursuit of natural philosophy. At the age of twenty-four
he had sought (in Germany) to obtain initiation into the brotherhood of the
Rosicrucians, but unluckily could not discover any member of the society to
introduce him. "He desired," says Cousin, "to assure the health of man,

In thoughts like these the night wore away, the moonbeams that streamed through my window lighting up the spacious solitudes beyond,— mead and creek, forest-land, mountain-top,— and the silence without broken by the wild cry of the night hawk and the sibilant melancholy dirge of the shining chrysococyx,[1] — bird that never sings but at night, and obsti-

diminish his ills, extend his existence. He was terrified by the rapid and almost momentary passage of man upon earth. He believed it was not, perhaps, impossible to prolong its duration." There is a hidden recess of grandeur in this idea, and the means proposed by Descartes for the execution of his project were not less grand. In his "Discourse on Method," Descartes says, "If it is possible to find some means to render generally men more wise and more able than they have been till now, it is, I believe, in medicine that those means must be sought. . . . I am sure that there is no one, even in the medical profession, who will not avow that all which one knows of the medical art is almost nothing in comparison to that which remains to learn, and that one could be exempted from an infinity of maladies, both of body and mind, and even, perhaps, from the decrepitude of old age, if one had sufficient lore of their causes and of all the remedies which nature provides for them. Therefore, having *design to employ all my life in the research of a science so necessary, and having discovered a path which appears to me such that one ought infallibly, in following, to find it,* if one is not hindered prematurely by the brevity of life or by the defects of experience, I consider that there is no better remedy against those two hindrances than to communicate faithfully to the public the little I have found," etc. ("Discours de la Méthode," vol. i. Œuvres de Descartes, Cousin's Edition.' And again, in his "Correspondence" (vol. ix. p. 341), he says: "The conservation of health has been always the principal object of my studies, and I have no doubt that there is a means of acquiring much knowledge touching medicine which, up to this time, is ignored." He then refers to his meditated Treatise on Animals as only an entrance upon that knowledge. But whatever secrets Descartes may have thought to discover, they are not made known to the public according to his promise. And in a letter to M. Chanut, written in 1646 (four years before he died), he says ingenuously : "I will tell you in confidence that the notion, such as it is, which I have endeavoured to acquire in physical philosophy, had greatly assisted me to establish certain foundations for moral philosophy ; and that I am more easily satisfied upon this point than I am on many others touching medicine, to which I have, nevertheless, devoted much more time. So that" (adds the grand thinker, with a pathetic nobleness)—"so that, *instead of finding the means to preserve life, I have found another good, more easy and more sure, which is — not to fear death."*

[1] Chrysococyx lucidus, — namely, the bird popularly called the shining or bronzed cuckoo. "Its note is an exceedingly melancholy whistle, heard at night, when it is very annoying to any sick or nervous person who may be

nately haunts the roofs of the sick and dying, ominous of woe and death.

But up sprang the sun, and, chasing these gloomy sounds, out burst the wonderful chorus of Australian groves, the great kingfisher opening the jocund melodious babble with the glee of his social laugh.

And now I heard Faber's step in Lilian's room,— heard through the door her soft voice, though I could not distinguish the words. It was not long before I saw the kind physician standing at the threshold of my chamber. He pressed his finger to his lip, and made me a sign to follow him. I obeyed, with noiseless tread and stifled breathing. He awaited me in the garden under the flowering acacias, passed his arm in mine, and drew me into the open pasture-land.

"Compose yourself," he then said; "I bring you tidings both of gladness and of fear. Your Lilian's mind is restored: even the memories which had been swept away by the fever that followed her return to her home in L—— are returning, though as yet indistinct. She yearns to see you, to bless you for all your noble devotion, your generous, great-hearted love; but I forbid such interview now. If, in a few hours, she become either decidedly stronger or decidedly more enfeebled, you shall be summoned to her side. Even if you are condemned to a loss for which the sole consolation must be placed in the life hereafter, you shall have, at least, the last mortal commune of soul with soul. Courage! courage! You are man! Bear as man what you have so often bid other men submit to endure."

I had flung myself on the ground,— writhing worm that had no home but on earth! Man, indeed! Man! All, at that moment, I took from manhood was its acute sensibility to love and to anguish!

But after all such paroxysms of mortal pain, there comes a

inclined to sleep. I have known many instances where the bird has been perched on a tree in the vicinity of the room of an invalid, uttering its mournful notes, and it was only with the greatest difficulty that it could be dislodged from its position." — Dr. BENNETT: *Gatherings of a Naturalist in Australasia.*

strange lull. Thought itself halts, like the still hush of water between two descending torrents. I rose in a calm, which Faber might well mistake for fortitude.

"Well," I said quietly, "fulfil your promise. If Lilian is to pass away from me, I shall see her, at least, again; no wall, you tell me, between our minds; mind to mind once more,— once more!"

"Allen," said Faber, mournfully and softly, "why do you shun to repeat my words — soul to soul?"

"Ay, ay,— I understand. Those words mean that you have resigned all hope that Lilian's life will linger here, when her mind comes back in full consciousness; I know well that last lightning flash and the darkness which swallows it up!"

"You exaggerate my fears. I have not resigned the hope that Lilian will survive the struggle through which she is passing, but it will be cruel to deceive you — my hope is weaker than it was."

"Ay, ay. Again, I understand! Your science is in fault, — it desponds. Its last trust is in the wonderful resources of Nature, the vitality stored in the young!"

"You have said,— those resources of Nature *are* wondrous. The vitality of youth is a fountain springing up from the deeps out of sight, when, a moment before, we had measured the drops oozing out from the sands, and thought that the well was exhausted."

"Come with me,— come. I told you of another sufferer yonder. I want your opinion of his case. But can you be spared a few minutes from Lilian's side?"

"Yes; I left her asleep. What is the case that perplexes your eye of physician, which is usually keener than mine, despite all the length of my practice?"

"The sufferer is young, his organization rare in its vigour. He has gone through and survived assaults upon life that are commonly fatal. His system has been poisoned by the fangs of a venomous asp, and shattered by the blast of the plague. These alone, I believe, would not suffice to destroy him. But he is one who has a strong dread of death; and while the heart was thus languid and feeble, it has been gnawed by emotions of hope or of fear. I suspect that he is dying, not from the bite of the reptile, not from the taint of the pestilence, but from the hope and the fear that have overtasked the heart's functions. Judge for yourself."

We were now at the door of the hut. I unlocked it: we entered. Margrave had quitted his bed, and was pacing the room slowly. His step was less feeble, his countenance less haggard than on the previous evening.

He submitted himself to Faber's questioning with a quiet indifference, and evidently cared nothing for any opinion which the great physician might found on his replies.

When Faber had learned all he could, he said, with a grave smile: "I see that my advice will have little weight with you; such as it is, at least reflect on it. The conclusions to which your host arrived in his view of your case, and which he confided to me, are, in my humble judgment, correct. I have no doubt that the great organ of the heart is involved in the cause of your sufferings; but the heart is a noble and much-enduring organ. I have known men in whom it has been more severely and unequivocally affected with disease than it is in you, live on for many years, and ultimately die of some other disorder. But then life was held, as yours must be held, upon one condition,— repose. I enjoin you to abstain from all violent action, to shun all excitements that cause moral disturbance. You are young: would you live on, you must live as the old. More than this,— it is my duty to warn you that your tenure on earth is very precarious; you may attain to many years; you may be suddenly called hence to-morrow. The best mode to regard this uncertainty with the calm in which is your only chance of long life, is so to arrange all your worldly affairs, and so to discipline all your human anxieties, as to feel always prepared for the summons that may come without warning. For the rest, quit this climate as soon as you can, — it is the climate in which the blood courses too quickly for one who should shun all excitement. Seek the most equable atmosphere, choose the most tranquil pursuits; and Fenwick himself, in his magnificent pride of

stature and strength, may be nearer the grave than you
are."

"Your opinion coincides with that I have just heard?"
asked Margrave, turning to me.

"In much — yes."

"It is more favourable than I should have supposed. I am
far from disdaining the advice so kindly offered. Permit me,
in turn, two or three questions, Dr. Faber. Do you prescribe
to me no drugs from your pharmacopœia?"

"Drugs may palliate many sufferings incidental to organic
disease, but drugs cannot reach organic disease itself."

"Do you believe that, even where disease is plainly organic, Nature herself has no alternative and reparative powers,
by which the organ assailed may recover itself?"

"A few exceptional instances of such forces in Nature are upon
record; but we must go by general laws, and not by exceptions."

"Have you never known instances — do you not at this
moment know one — in which a patient whose malady baffles
the doctor's skill, imagines or dreams of a remedy? Call it
a whim if you please, learned sir; do you not listen to the
whim, and, in despair of your own prescriptions, comply with
those of the patient?"

Faber changed countenance, and even started. Margrave
watched him and laughed.

"You grant that there are such cases, in which the patient
gives the law to the physician. Now, apply your experience
to my case. Suppose some strange fancy had seized upon my
imagination — that is the doctor's cant word for all phenomena which we call exceptional — some strange fancy that
I had thought of a cure for this disease for which you have
no drugs; and suppose this fancy of mine to be so strong, so
vivid, that to deny me its gratification would produce the
very emotion from which you warn me as fatal, — storm the
heart, that you would soothe to repose, by the passions of
rage and despair, — would you, as my trusted physician, concede or deny me my whim?"

"Can you ask? I should grant it at once, if I had no reason to know that the thing that you fancied was harmful."

"Good man and wise doctor! I have no other question to ask. I thank you."

Faber looked hard on the young, wan face, over which played a smile of triumph and irony; then turned away with an expression of doubt and trouble on his own noble countenance. I followed him silently into the open air.

"Who and what is this visitor of yours?" he asked abruptly.

"Who and what? I cannot tell you."

Faber remained some moments musing, and muttering slowly to himself, "Tut! but a chance coincidence, — a haphazard allusion to a fact which he could not have known!"

"Faber," said I, abruptly, "can it be that Lilian is the patient in whose self-suggested remedies you confide more than in the various learning at command of your practised skill?"

"I cannot deny it," replied Faber, reluctantly. "In the intervals of that suspense from waking sense, which in her is not sleep, nor yet altogether catalepsy, she has, for the last few days, stated accurately the precise moment in which the trance — if I may so call it — would pass away, and prescribed for herself the remedies that should be then administered. In every instance, the remedies so self-prescribed, though certainly not those which would have occurred to my mind, have proved efficacious. Her rapid progress to reason I ascribe to the treatment she herself ordained in her trance, without remembrance of her own suggestions when she awoke. I had meant to defer communicating these phenomena in the idiosyncrasy of her case until our minds could more calmly inquire into the process by which ideas — not apparently derived, as your metaphysical school would derive all ideas, from preconceived experiences — will thus sometimes act like an instinct on the human sufferer for self-preservation, as the bird is directed to the herb or the berry which heals or assuages its ailments. We know how the mesmerists would account for this phenomenon of hygienic introvision and clairvoyance. But here, there is no mesmerizer, unless the patient can be supposed to mesmerize herself. Long, however, before mesmerism was heard of, medical history attests examples in which patients who baffled the skill of the ablest physicians have fixed their fancies on some remedy that physicians would call inoperative for good or for harm, and have recovered by the remedies thus singularly self-suggested. And Hippocrates himself, if I construe his meaning rightly, recognizes the powers for self-cure which the condition of trance will sometimes bestow on the sufferer, 'where' (says the father of our art) 'the sight being closed to the external, the soul more truthfully perceives the affections of the body.' In short — I own it — in this instance, the skill of the physician has been a compliant obedience to the instinct called forth in the patient; and the hopes I have hitherto permitted myself to give you were founded on my experience that her own hopes, conceived in trance, had never been fallacious or exaggerated. The simples that I gathered for her yesterday she had described; they are not in our herbal. But as they are sometimes used by the natives, I had the curiosity to analyze their chemical properties shortly after I came to the colony, and they seemed to me as innocent as lime-blossoms. They are rare in this part of Australia, but she told me where I should find them, — a remote spot, which she has certainly never visited. Last night, when you saw me disturbed, dejected, it was because, for the first time, the docility with which she had hitherto, in her waking state, obeyed her own injunctions in the state of trance, forsook her. She could not be induced to taste the decoction I had made from the herbs; and if you found me this morning with weaker hopes than before, this is the real cause, — namely, that when I visited her at sunrise, she was not in sleep but in trance, and in that trance she told me that she had nothing more to suggest or reveal; that on the complete restoration of her senses, which was at hand, the abnormal faculties vouchsafed to trance would be withdrawn. 'As for my life,' she said quietly, as if unconscious of our temporary joy or woe in the term of its tenure here, — 'as for my life, your aid is now idle; my own vision obscure; on my life a dark and cold shadow is resting. I cannot foresee if it will pass away. When I strive to look around, I see but my Allen — '"

"And so," said I, mastering my emotions, "in bidding me
hope, you did not rely on your own resources of science, but
on the whisper of Nature in the brain of your patient?"

"It is so."

We both remained silent some moments, and then, as he
disappeared within my house, I murmured,—

"And when she strives to look beyond the shadow, she sees
only me! Is there some prophet-hint of Nature there also,
directing me not to scorn the secret which a wanderer, so
suddenly dropped on my solitude, assures me that Nature will
sometimes reveal to her seeker? And oh! that dark wanderer — has Nature a marvel more weird than himself?"

———◆———

CHAPTER LXXVI.

I STRAYED through the forest till noon, in debate with myself, and strove to shape my wild doubts into purpose, before
I could nerve and compose myself again to face Margrave
alone.

I re-entered the hut. To my surprise, Margrave was not
in the room in which I had left him, nor in that which adjoined it. I ascended the stairs to the kind of loft in which
I had been accustomed to pursue my studies, but in which I
had not set foot since my alarm for Lilian had suspended my
labours. There I saw Margrave quietly seated before the
manuscript of my Ambitious Work, which lay open on the
rude table, just as I had left it, in the midst of its concluding
summary.

"I have taken the license of former days, you see," said
Margrave, smiling, "and have hit by chance on a passage I
can understand without effort. But why such a waste of argument to prove a fact so simple? In man, as in brute, life
once lost is lost forever; and that is why life is so precious
to man."

I took the book from his hand, and flung it aside in wrath. His approval revolted me more with my own theories than all the argumentative rebukes of Faber.

"And now," I said, sternly, "the time has come for the explanation you promised. Before I can aid you in any experiment that may serve to prolong your life, I must know how far that life has been a baleful and destroying influence?"

"I have some faint recollection of having saved *your* life from an imminent danger, and if gratitude were the attribute of man, as it is of the dog, I should claim your aid to serve mine as a right. Ask me what you will. You must have seen enough of me to know that I do not affect either the virtues or vices of others. I regard both with so supreme an indifference, that I believe I am vicious or virtuous unawares. I know not if I can explain what seems to have perplexed you, but if I cannot explain I have no intention to lie. Speak — I listen! We have time enough now before us."

So saying, he reclined back in the chair, stretching out his limbs wearily. All round this spoilt darling of Material Nature were the aids and appliances of Intellectual Science, — books and telescopes and crucibles, with the light of day coming through a small circular aperture in the boarded casement, as I had constructed the opening for my experimental observation of the prismal rays.

While I write, his image is as visible before my remembrance as if before the actual eye, — beautiful even in its decay, awful even in its weakness, mysterious as is Nature herself amidst all the mechanism by which our fancied knowledge attempts to measure her laws and analyze her light.

But at that moment no such subtle reflections delayed my inquisitive eager mind from its immediate purpose, — who and what was this creature boasting of a secret through which I might rescue from death the life of her who was my all upon the earth?

I gathered rapidly and succinctly together all that I knew and all that I guessed of Margrave's existence and arts. I commenced from my vision in that mimic Golgotha of creatures inferior to man, close by the scene of man's most trivial and meaningless pastime. I went on, — Derval's murder; the missing contents of the casket; the apparition seen by the maniac assassin guiding him to the horrid deed; the luminous haunting shadow; the positive charge in the murdered man's memoir connecting Margrave with Louis Grayle, and accusing him of the murder of Haroun; the night in the moonlit pavilion at Derval Court; the baneful influence on Lilian; the struggle between me and himself in the house by the seashore, — the strange All that is told in this Strange Story.

But warming as I spoke, and in a kind of fierce joy to be enabled thus to free my own heart of the doubts that had burdened it, now that I was fairly face to face with the being by whom my reason had been so perplexed and my life so tortured, I was restrained by none of the fears lest my own fancy deceived me, with which in his absence I had striven to reduce to natural causes the portents of terror and wonder. I stated plainly, directly, the beliefs, the impressions which I had never dared even to myself to own without seeking to explain them away. And coming at last to a close, I said: "Such are the evidences that seem to me to justify abhorrence of the life that you ask me to aid in prolonging. Your own tale of last night but confirms them. And why to me — to me — do you come with wild entreaties to lengthen the life that has blighted my own? How did you even learn the home in which I sought unavailing refuge? How — as your hint to Faber clearly revealed — were you aware that, in yon house, where the sorrow is veiled, where the groan is suppressed, where the foot-tread falls ghostlike, there struggles now between life and death my heart's twin, my world's sunshine? Ah! through my terror for her, is it a demon that tells you how to bribe my abhorrence into submission, and supple my reason into use to your ends?"

Margrave had listened to me throughout with a fixed attention, at times with a bewildered stare, at times with exclamations of surprise, but not of denial. And when I had done, he remained for some moments silent, seemingly stupefied, passing his hand repeatedly over his brow, in the gesture so familiar to him in former days.

At length he said quietly, without evincing any sign either of resentment or humiliation, —

"In much that you tell me I recognize myself; in much I am as lost in amazement as you in wild doubt or fierce wrath. Of the effect that you say Philip Derval produced on me I have no recollection. Of himself I have only this, — that he was my foe, that he came to England intent on schemes to shorten my life or destroy its enjoyments. All my faculties tend to self-preservation; there, they converge as rays in a focus; in that focus they illume and — they burn. I willed to destroy my intended destroyer. Did my will enforce itself on the agent to which it was guided? Likely enough. Be it so. Would you blame me for slaying the tiger or serpent — not by the naked hand, but by weapons that arm it? But what could tiger and serpent do more against me than the man who would rob me of life? He had his arts for assault, I had mine for self-defence. He was to me as the tiger that creeps through the jungle, or the serpent uncoiling his folds for the spring. Death to those whose life is destruction to mine, be they serpent or tiger or man! Derval perished. Yes! the spot in which the maniac had buried the casket *was* revealed to me — no matter how; the contents of the casket passed into my hands. I coveted that possession because I believed that Derval had learned from Haroun of Aleppo the secret by which the elixir of life is prepared, and I supposed that some stores of the essence would be found in his casket. I was deceived — not a drop! What I there found I knew not how to use or apply, nor did I care to learn. What I sought was not there. You see a luminous shadow of myself; it haunts, it accosts, it compels you. Of this I know nothing. Was it the emanation of my intense will really producing this spectre of myself, or was it the thing of your own imagination, — an imagination which my will impressed and subjugated? I know not. At the hours when my shadow, real or supposed, was with you, my senses would have been locked in sleep. It is true, however, that I intensely desire to learn from races always near to man, but concealed from his every-day vision, the secret that I believed Philip Derval had carried with him to the tomb; and from some cause or another I cannot now of myself alone, as I could years ago, subject those races to my command,— I must, in that, act through or with the mind of another. It is true that I sought to impress upon your waking thoughts the images of the circle, the powers of the wand, which, in your trance or sleep-walking, made you the involuntary agent of my will. I knew by a dream — for by dreams, more or less vivid, are the results of my waking will sometimes divulged to myself — that the spell had been broken, the discovery I sought not effected. All my hopes were then transferred from yourself, the dull votary of science, to the girl whom I charmed to my thraldom through her love for you and through her dreams of a realm which the science of schools never enters. In her, imagination was all pure and all potent; and tell me, O practical reasoner, if reason has ever advanced one step into knowledge except through that imaginative faculty which is strongest in the wisdom of ignorance, and weakest in the ignorance of the wise. Ponder this, and those marvels that perplex you will cease to be marvellous. I pass on to the riddle that puzzles you most. By Philip Derval's account I am, in truth, Louis Grayle restored to youth by the elixir, and while yet infirm, decrepit, murdered Haroun,— a man of a frame as athletic as yours! By accepting this notion you seem to yourself alone to unravel the mysteries you ascribe to my life and my powers. O wise philosopher! O profound logician! you accept that notion, yet hold my belief in the Dervish's tale a chimera! I am Grayle made young by the elixir, and yet the elixir itself is a fable! ''

He paused and laughed, but the laugh was no longer even an echo of its former merriment or playfulness,— a sinister and terrible laugh, mocking, threatening, malignant.

Again he swept his hand over his brow, and resumed,—

"Is it not easier to so accomplished a sage as you to believe that the idlers of Paris have guessed the true solution of that problem, my place on this earth? May I not be the love-son of Louis Grayle? And when Haroun refused the elixir to

him, or he found that his frame was too far exhausted for
even the elixir to repair organic lesions of structure in the
worn frame of old age, may he not have indulged the common
illusion of fathers, and soothed his death-pangs with the
thought that he should live again in his son? Haroun is
found dead on his carpet — rumour said strangled. What
proof of the truth of that rumour? Might he not have passed
away in a fit? Will it lessen your perplexity if I state recollections? They are vague, — they often perplex myself; but
so far from a wish to deceive you, my desire is to relate
them so truthfully that you may aid me to reduce them into
more definite form."

His face now became very troubled, the tone of his voice
very irresolute, — the face and the voice of a man who is
either blundering his way through an intricate falsehood, or
through obscure reminiscences.

"This Louis Grayle! this Louis Grayle! I remember him
well, as one remembers a nightmare. Whenever I look back,
before the illness of which I will presently speak, the image
of Louis Grayle returns to me. I see myself with him in
African wilds, commanding the fierce Abyssinians. I see
myself with him in the fair Persian valley, — lofty, snow-
covered mountains encircling the garden of roses. I see myself with him in the hush of the golden noon, reclined by the
spray of cool fountains, — now listening to cymbals and lutes,
now arguing with graybeards on secrets bequeathed by the
Chaldees, — with him, with him in moonlit nights, stealing
into the sepulchres of mythical kings. I see myself with him
in the aisles of dark caverns, surrounded by awful shapes,
which have no likeness amongst the creatures of earth.
Louis Grayle! Louis Grayle! all my earlier memories go
back to Louis Grayle! All my arts and powers, all that
I have learned of the languages spoken in Europe, of the
sciences taught in her schools, I owe to Louis Grayle. But
am I one and the same with him? No — I am but a pale
reflection of his giant intellect. I have not even a reflection of his childlike agonies of sorrow. Louis Grayle! He
stands apart from me, as a rock from the tree that grows

out from its chasms. Yes, the gossip was right; I must be his son."

He leaned his face on both hands, rocking himself to and fro. At length, with a sigh, he resumed, —

"I remember, too, a long and oppressive illness, attended with racking pains, a dismal journey in a wearisome litter, the light hand of the woman Ayesha, so sad and so stately, smoothing my pillow or fanning my brows. I remember the evening on which my nurse drew the folds of the litter aside, and said, 'See Aleppo! and the star of thy birth shining over its walls!'

"I remember a face inexpressibly solemn and mournful. I remember the chill that the calm of its ominous eye sent through my veins, — the face of Haroun, the Sage of Aleppo. I remember the vessel of crystal he bore in his hand, and the blessed relief from my pains that a drop from the essence which flashed through the crystal bestowed! And then — and then — I remember no more till the night on which Ayesha came to my couch and said, 'Rise.'

"And I rose, leaning on her, supported by her. We went through dim narrow streets, faintly lit by wan stars, disturbing the prowl of the dogs, that slunk from the look of that woman. We came to a solitary house, small and low, and my nurse said, 'Wait.'

"She opened the door and went in; I seated myself on the threshold. And after a time she came out from the house, and led me, still leaning on her, into her chamber.

"A man lay, as in sleep, on the carpet, and beside him stood another man, whom I recognized as Ayesha's special attendant, — an Indian. 'Haroun is dead,' said Ayesha. 'Search for that which will give thee new life. Thou hast seen, and wilt know it, not I.'

"And I put my hand on the breast of Haroun — for the dead man was he — and drew from it the vessel of crystal.

"Having done so, the frown of his marble brow appalled me. I staggered back, and swooned away.

"I came to my senses, recovering and rejoicing, miles afar from the city, the dawn red on its distant wall. Ayesha had tended me; the elixir had already restored me.

"My first thought, when full consciousness came back to me, rested on Louis Grayle, for he also had been at Aleppo; I was but one of his numerous train. He, too, was enfeebled and suffering; he had sought the known skill of Haroun for himself as for me; and this woman loved and had tended him as she had loved and tended me. And my nurse told me that he was dead, and forbade me henceforth to breathe his name.

"We travelled on,—she and I, and the Indian her servant,—my strength still renewed by the wondrous elixir. No longer supported by her, what gazelle ever roved through its pasture with a bound more elastic than mine?

"We came to a town, and my nurse placed before me a mirror. I did not recognize myself. In this town we rested, obscure, till the letter there reached me by which I learned that I was the offspring of love, and enriched by the care of a father recently dead. Is it not clear that Louis Grayle was this father?"

"If so, was the woman Ayesha your mother?"

"The letter said that 'my mother had died in my infancy.' Nevertheless, the care with which Ayesha had tended me induced a suspicion that made me ask her the very question you put. She wept when I asked her, and said, 'No, only my nurse. And now I needed a nurse no more.' The day after I received the letter which announced an inheritance that allowed me to vie with the nobles of Europe, this woman left me, and went back to her tribe."

"Have you never seen her since?"

Margrave hesitated a moment, and then answered, though with seeming reluctance, "Yes, at Damascus. Not many days after I was borne to that city by the strangers who found me half-dead on their road, I woke one morning to find her by my side. And she said, 'In joy and in health you did not need me. I am needed now.'"

"Did you then deprive yourself of one so devoted? You have not made this long voyage—from Eygpt to Australia—alone,—you, to whom wealth gave no excuse for privation?"

"The woman came with me; and some chosen attendants. I engaged to ourselves the vessel we sailed in."

" Where have you left your companions? "

" By this hour," answered Margrave, "they are in reach of my summons; and when you and I have achieved the discovery — in the results of which we shall share — I will exact no more from your aid. I trust all that rests for my cure to my nurse and her swarthy attendants. You will aid me now, as a matter of course; the physician whose counsel you needed to guide your own skill enjoins you to obey my whim — if whim you still call it; you will obey it, for on that whim rests your own sole hope of happiness, — you, who can love — I love nothing but life. Has my frank narrative solved all the doubts that stood between you and me, in the great meeting-grounds of an interest in common? "

" Solved all the doubts! Your wild story but makes some the darker, leaving others untouched: the occult powers of which you boast, and some of which I have witnessed, — your very insight into my own household sorrows, into the interests I have, with yourself, in the truth of a faith so repugnant to reason — "

" Pardon me," interrupted Margrave, with that slight curve of the lip which is half smile and half sneer, "if, in my account of myself, I omitted what I cannot explain, and you cannot conceive: let me first ask how many of the commonest actions of the commonest men are purely involuntary and wholly inexplicable. When, for instance, you open your lips and utter a sentence, you have not the faintest idea beforehand what word will follow another. When you move a muscle can you tell me the thought that prompts to the movement? And, wholly unable thus to account for your own simple sympathies between impulse and act, do you believe that there exists a man upon earth who can read all the riddles in the heart and brain of another? Is it not true that not one drop of water, one atom of matter, ever really touches another? Between each and each there is always a space, however infinitesimally small. How, then, could the world go on, if every man asked another to make his whole

history and being as lucid as daylight before he would buy
and sell with him? All interchange and alliance rest but on
this,—an interest in common. You and I have established
that interest: all else, all you ask more, is superfluous. Could
I answer each doubt you would raise, still, whether the answer should please or revolt you, your reason would come
back to the same starting-point,—namely, In one definite
proposal have we two an interest in common?"

And again Margrave laughed, not in mirth, but in mockery.
The laugh and the words that preceded it were not the laugh
and the words of the young. Could it be possible that Louis
Grayle had indeed revived to false youth in the person of
Margrave, such might have been his laugh and such his words.
The whole mind of Margrave seemed to have undergone change
since I last saw him; more rich in idea, more crafty even in
candour, more powerful, more concentred. As we see in our
ordinary experience, that some infirmity, threatening disso-
lution, brings forth more vividly the reminiscences of early
years, when impressions were vigorously stamped, so I might
have thought that as Margrave neared the tomb, the memories he had retained from his former existence, in a being
more amply endowed, more formidably potent, struggled back
to the brain; and the mind that had lived in Louis Grayle
moved the lips of the dying Margrave.

"For the powers and the arts that it equally puzzles your
reason to assign or deny to me," resumed my terrible guest,
"I will say briefly but this: they come from faculties stored
within myself, and doubtless conduce to my self-preservation,—faculties more or less, perhaps (so Van Helmont asserts), given to all men, though dormant in most; vivid and
active in me because in me self-preservation has been and yet
is the strong master-passion, or instinct; and because I have
been taught how to use and direct such faculties by disciplined teachers,—some by Louis Grayle, the enchanter; some
by my nurse, the singer of charmed songs. But in much
that I will to have done, I know no more than yourself how
the agency acts. Enough for me to will what I wish, and
sink calmly into slumber, sure that the will would work

somehow its way. But when I have willed to know what, when known, should shape my own courses, I could see, without aid from your pitiful telescopes, all objects howsoever far. What wonder in that? Have you no learned puzzle-brained metaphysicians who tell you that space is but an idea, all this palpable universe an idea in the mind, and no more? Why am I an enigma as dark as the Sibyls, and your metaphysicians as plain as a hornbook?" Again the sardonic laugh. "Enough: let what I have said obscure or enlighten your guesses, we come back to the same link of union, which binds man to man, bids States arise from the desert, and foeman embrace as brothers. I need you and you need me; without your aid my life is doomed; without my secret the breath will have gone from the lips of your Lilian before the sun of to-morrow is red on the hill-tops."

"Fiend or juggler," I cried in rage, "you shall not so enslave and enthrall me by this mystic farrago and jargon. Make your fantastic experiment on yourself if you will: trust to your arts and your powers. My Lilian's life shall not hang on your fiat. I trust it — to — "

"To what — to man's skill? Hear what the sage of the college shall tell you, before I ask you again for your aid. Do you trust to God's saving mercy? Ah, of course you believe in a God? Who, except a philosopher, can reason a Maker away? But that the Maker will alter His courses to hear you; that, whether or not you trust in Him, or in your doctor, it will change by a hairbreadth the thing that must be — do you believe *this*, Allen Fenwick?"

And there sat this reader of hearts! a boy in his aspect, mocking me and the graybeards of schools.

I could listen no more; I turned to the door and fled down the stairs, and heard, as I fled, a low chant: feeble and faint, it was still the old barbaric chant, by which the serpent is drawn from its hole by the charmer.

CHAPTER LXXVII.

To those of my readers who may seek with Julius Faber to explore, through intelligible causes, solutions of the marvels I narrate, Margrave's confession may serve to explain away much that my own superstitious beliefs had obscured. To them Margrave is evidently the son of Louis Grayle. The elixir of life is reduced to some simple restorative, owing much of its effect to the faith of a credulous patient: youth is so soon restored to its joy in the sun, with or without an elixir. To them Margrave's arts of enchantment are reduced to those idiosyncrasies of temperament on which the disciples of Mesmer build up their theories,—exaggerated, in much, by my own superstitions; aided, in part, by such natural, purely physical magic as, explored by the ancient priest-crafts, is despised by the modern philosophies, and only remains occult because Science delights no more in the slides of the lantern which fascinated her childhood with simulated phantoms. To them Margrave is, perhaps, an enthusiast, but, because an enthusiast, not less an impostor. "L'Homme se pique," says Charron. Man cogs the dice for himself ere he rattles the box for his dupes. Was there ever successful impostor who did not commence by a fraud on his own understanding? Cradled in Orient Fableland, what though Margrave believes in its legends; in a wand, an elixir; in sorcerers or Afrites? That belief in itself makes him keen to detect, and skilful to profit by, the latent but kindred credulities of others. In all illustrations of Duper and Duped through the records of superstition—from the guile of a Cromwell, a Mahomet, down to the cheats of a gypsy—professional visionaries are amongst the astutest observers. The knowledge that Margrave had gained of my abode, of my affliction, or of the innermost thoughts in my mind, it surely demanded no preternatural aids to acquire.

An Old Bailey attorney could have got at the one, and any quick student of human hearts have readily mastered the other. In fine, Margrave, thus rationally criticised, is no other prodigy (save in degree and concurrence of attributes simple, though not very common) than may be found in each alley that harbours a fortune-teller who has just faith enough in the stars or the cards to bubble himself while he swindles his victims; earnest, indeed, in the self-conviction that he is really a seer, but reading the looks of his listeners, divining the thoughts that induce them to listen, and acquiring by practice a startling ability to judge what the listeners will deem it most seer-like to read in the cards or divine from the stars.

I leave this interpretation unassailed. It is that which is the most probable; it is clearly that which, in a case not my own, I should have accepted; and yet I revolved and dismissed it. The moment we deal with things beyond our comprehension, and in which our own senses are appealed to and baffled, we revolt from the Probable, as it seems to the senses of those who have not experienced what we have. And the same principle of Wonder that led our philosophy up from inert ignorance into restless knowledge, now winding back into shadow land, reverses its rule by the way, and, at last, leaves us lost in the maze, our knowledge inert, and our ignorance restless.

And putting aside all other reasons for hesitating to believe that Margrave was the son of Louis Grayle,— reasons which his own narrative might suggest,— was it not strange that Sir Philip Derval, who had instituted inquiries so minute, and reported them in his memoir with so faithful a care, should not have discovered that a youth, attended by the same woman who had attended Grayle, had disappeared from the town on the same night as Grayle himself disappeared? But Derval had related truthfully, according to Margrave's account, the flight of Ayesha and her Indian servant, yet not alluded to the flight, not even to the existence of the boy, who must have been of no mean importance in the suite of Louis Grayle, if he were, indeed, the son whom Grayle had

458   A STRANGE STORY.

made his constant companion, and constituted his principal
heir.

Not many minutes did I give myself up to the cloud of reflections through which no sunbeam of light forced its way.
One thought overmastered all; Margrave had threatened death
to my Lilian, and warned me of what I should learn from the
lips of Faber, "the sage of the college." I stood, shuddering,
at the door of my home; I did not dare to enter.

"Allen," said a voice, in which my ear detected the unwonted tremulous faltering, "be firm, — be calm. I keep my
promise. The hour is come in which you may again see the
Lilian of old, mind to mind, soul to soul."

Faber's hand took mine, and led me into the house.

"You do, then, fear that this interview will be too much
for her strength?" said I, whisperingly.

"I cannot say; but she demands the interview, and I dare
not refuse it."

———◆———

CHAPTER LXXVIII.

I LEFT Faber on the stairs, and paused at the door of
Lilian's room. The door opened suddenly, noiselessly, and
her mother came out with one hand before her face, and the
other locked in Amy's, who was leading her as a child leads
the blind. Mrs. Ashleigh looked up, as I touched her, with
a vacant, dreary stare. She was not weeping, as was her
womanly wont in every pettier grief, but Amy was. No
word was exchanged between us. I entered, and closed the
door; my eyes turned mechanically to the corner in which
was placed the small virgin bed, with its curtains white as
a shroud. Lilian was not there. I looked around, and saw
her half reclined on a couch near the window. She was
dressed, and with care. Was not that her bridal robe?

"Allen! Allen!" she murmured. "Again, again my Allen
— again, again your Lilian!" And, striving in vain to rise,

she stretched out her arms in the yearning of reunited love. And as I knelt beside her, those arms closed round me for the first time in the frank, chaste, holy tenderness of a wife's embrace.

"Ah!" she said, in her low voice (her voice, like Cordelia's, was ever low), "all has come back to me,— all that I owe to your protecting, noble, trustful, guardian love!"

"Hush! hush! the gratitude rests with me; it is so sweet to love, to trust, to guard! my own, my beautiful — still my beautiful! Suffering has not dimmed the light of those dear eyes to me! Put your lips to my ear. Whisper but these words: 'I love you, and for your sake I wish to live.'"

"For your sake, I pray — with my whole weak human heart — I pray to live! Listen. Some day hereafter, if I am spared, under the purple blossoms of yonder waving trees I shall tell you all, as I see it now; all that darkened or shone on me in my long dream, and before the dream closed around me, like a night in which cloud and star chase each other! Some day hereafter, some quiet, sunlit, happy, happy day! But now, all I would say is this: Before that dreadful morning —" Here she paused, shuddered, and passionately burst forth, "Allen, Allen! you did not believe that slanderous letter! God bless you! God bless you! Great-hearted, high-souled — God bless you, my darling! my husband! And He will! Pray to Him humbly as I do, and He will bless you." She stooped and kissed away my tears; then she resumed, feebly, meekly, sorrowfully,—

"Before that morning I was not worthy of such a heart, such a love as yours. No, no; hear me. Not that a thought of love for another ever crossed me! Never, while conscious and reasoning, was I untrue to you, even in fancy. But I was a child,— wayward as the child who pines for what earth cannot give, and covets the moon for a toy. Heaven had been so kind to my lot on earth, and yet with my lot on earth I was secretly discontented. When I felt that you loved me, and my heart told me that I loved again, I said to myself, 'Now the void that my soul finds on earth will be filled.' I longed for your coming, and yet when you went I murmured,

'But is this the ideal of which I have dreamed?' I asked for
an impossible sympathy. Sympathy with what? Nay, smile
on me, dearest! — sympathy with what? I could not have
said. Ah, Allen, then, then, I was not worthy of you! Infant that I was, I asked you to understand me: now I know
that I am a woman, and my task is to study you. Do I make
myself clear? Do you forgive me? I was not untrue to you;
I was untrue to my own duties in life. I believed, in my
vain conceit, that a mortal's dim vision of heaven raised me
above the earth; I did not perceive the truth that earth is a
part of the same universe as heaven! Now, perhaps, in the
awful affliction that darkened my reason, my soul has been
made more clear. As if to chastise but to teach me, my soul
has been permitted to indulge its own presumptuous desire;
it has wandered forth from the trammels of mortal duties and
destinies; it comes back, alarmed by the dangers of its own
rash and presumptuous escape from the tasks which it should
desire upon earth to perform. Allen, Allen, I am less unworthy of you now! Perhaps in my darkness one rapid
glimpse of the true world of spirit has been vouchsafed to
me. If so, how unlike to the visions my childhood indulged
as divine! Now, while I know still more deeply that there
is a world for the angels, I know, also, that the mortal must
pass through probation in the world of mortals. Oh, may I
pass through it with you, grieving in your griefs, rejoicing in
your joy!"

Here language failed her. Again the dear arms embraced
me, and the dear face, eloquent with love, hid itself on my
human breast.

--------◆--------

CHAPTER LXXIX.

THAT interview is over! Again I am banished from Lilian's
room; the agitation, the joy of that meeting has overstrained
her enfeebled nerves. Convulsive tremblings of the whole

frame, accompanied with vehement sobs, succeeded our brief interchange of sweet and bitter thoughts. Faber, in tearing me from her side, imperiously and sternly warned me that the sole chance yet left of preserving her life was in the merciful suspense of the emotions that my presence excited. He and Amy resumed their place in her chamber. Even her mother shared my sentence of banishment. So Mrs. Ashleigh and I sat facing each other in the room below; over me a leaden stupor had fallen, and I heard, as a voice from afar or in a dream, the mother's murmured wailings,—

"She will die! she will die! Her eyes have the same heavenly look as my Gilbert's on the day on which his closed forever. Her very words are his last words,— 'Forgive me all my faults to you.' She will die! she will die!"

Hours thus passed away. At length Faber entered the room; he spoke first to Mrs. Ashleigh,— meaningless soothings, familiar to the lips of all who pass from the chamber of the dying to the presence of mourners, and know that it is a falsehood to say "hope," and a mockery as yet, to say, "endure."

But he led her away to her own room, docile as a wearied child led to sleep, stayed with her some time, and then returned to me, pressing me to his breast father-like.

"No hope! no hope!" said I, recoiling from his embrace. "You are silent. Speak! speak! Let me know the worst."

"I have a hope, yet I scarcely dare to bid you share it; for it grows rather out of my heart as man than my experience as physician. I cannot think that her soul would be now so reconciled to earth, so fondly, so earnestly, cling to this mortal life, if it were about to be summoned away. You know how commonly even the sufferers who have dreaded death the most become calmly resigned to its coming, when death visibly reveals itself out from the shadows in which its shape has been guessed and not seen. As it is a bad sign for life when the patient has lost all will to live on, so there is hope while the patient, yet young and with no perceptible breach in the great centres of life (however violently their forts may be stormed), has still intense faith in recovery, perhaps drawn (who can say?) from the whispers conveyed from above to the soul.

"I cannot bring myself to think that all the uses for which a reason, always so lovely even in its errors, has been restored, are yet fulfilled. It seems to me as if your union, as yet so imperfect, has still for its end that holy life on earth by which two mortal beings strengthen each other for a sphere of existence to which this is the spiritual ladder. Through yourself I have hope yet for her. Gifted with powers that rank you high in the manifold orders of man, — thoughtful, laborious, and brave; with a heart that makes intellect vibrate to every fine touch of humanity; in error itself, conscientious; in delusion, still eager for truth; in anger, forgiving; in wrong, seeking how to repair; and, best of all, strong in a love which the mean would have shrunk to defend from the fangs of the slanderer, — a love, raising passion itself out of the realm of the senses, made sublime by the sorrows that tried its devotion, — with all these noble proofs in yourself of a being not meant to end here, your life has stopped short in its uses, your mind itself has been drifted, a bark without rudder or pilot, over seas without shore, under skies without stars. And wherefore? Because the mind you so haughtily vaunted has refused its companion and teacher in Soul.

"And therefore, through you, I hope that she will be spared yet to live on; she, in whom soul has been led dimly astray, by unheeding the checks and the definite goals which the mind is ordained to prescribe to its wanderings while here; the mind taking thoughts from the actual and visible world, and the soul but vague glimpses and hints from the instinct of its ultimate heritage. Each of you two seems to me as yet incomplete, and your destinies yet uncompleted. Through the bonds of the heart, through the trials of time, ye have both to consummate your marriage. I do not — believe me — I do not say this in the fanciful wisdom of allegory and type, save that, wherever deeply examined, allegory and type run through all the most commonplace phases of outward and material life. I hope, then, that she may yet be spared to you; hope it, not from my skill as physician, but my inward belief as a Christian. To perfect your own being and end, ' *Ye will need one another!* ' "

I started — the very words that Lilian had heard in her vision!

"But," resumed Faber, "how can I presume to trace the numberless links of effect up to the First Cause, far off — oh; far off — out of the scope of my reason. I leave that to philosophers, who would laugh my meek hope to scorn. Possibly, probably, where I, whose calling has been but to save flesh from the worm, deem that the life of your Lilian is needed yet, to develop and train your own convictions of soul, Heaven in its wisdom may see that her death would instruct you far more than her life. I have said, Be prepared for either, — wisdom through joy, or wisdom through grief. Enough that, looking only through the mechanism by which this moral world is impelled and improved, you know that cruelty is impossible to wisdom. Even a man, or man's law, is never wise but when merciful. But mercy has general conditions; and that which is mercy to the myriads may seem hard to the one, and that which seems hard to the one in the pang of a moment may be mercy when viewed by the eye that looks on through eternity."

And from all this discourse — of which I now, at calm distance of time, recall every word — my human, loving heart bore away for the moment but this sentence, " Ye will need one another; " so that I cried out, "Life, life, life! Is there no hope for her life? Have you no hope as physician? I am a physician, too; I will see her. I will judge. I will not be banished from my post."

" Judge, then, as physician, and let the responsibility rest with you. At this moment, all convulsion, all struggle, has ceased; the frame is at rest. Look on her, and perhaps only the physician's eye could distinguish her state from death. It is not sleep, it is not trance, it is not the dooming coma from which there is no awaking. Shall I call it by the name received in our schools? Is it the catalepsy in which life is suspended, but consciousness acute? She is motionless, rigid;

it is but with a strain of my own sense that I know that the breath still breathes, and the heart still beats. But I am convinced that though she can neither speak, nor stir, nor give sign, she is fully, sensitively conscious of all that passes around her. She is like those who have seen the very coffin carried into their chamber, and been unable to cry out, 'Do not bury me alive!' Judge then for yourself, with this intense consciousness and this impotence to evince it, what might be the effect of your presence,— first an agony of despair, and then the complete extinction of life!"

"I have known but one such case,— a mother whose heart was wrapped up in a suffering infant. She had lain for two days and two nights, still, as if in her shroud. All save myself said, 'Life is gone.' I said, 'Life still is there.' They brought in the infant, to try what effect its presence would produce; then her lips moved, and the hands crossed upon her bosom trembled."

"And the result?" exclaimed Faber, eagerly. "If the result of your experience sanction your presence, come; the sight of the babe rekindled life?"

"No; extinguished its last spark! I will not enter Lilian's room. I will go away,— away from the house itself. That acute consciousness! I know it well! She may even hear me move in the room below, hear me speak at this moment. Go back to her, go back! But if hers be the state which I have known in another, which may be yet more familiar to persons of far ampler experience than mine, there is no immediate danger of death. The state will last through to-day, through to-night, perhaps for days to come. Is it so?"

"I believe that for at least twelve hours there will be no change in her state. I believe also that if she recover from it, calm and refreshed, as from a sleep, the danger of death will have passed away."

"And for twelve hours my presence would be hurtful?"

"Rather say fatal, if my diagnosis be right."

I wrung my friend's hand, and we parted.

Oh, to lose her now!— now that her love and her reason had both returned, each more vivid than before! Futile, indeed, might be Margrave's boasted secret; but at least in that secret was hope. In recognized science I saw only despair.

And at that thought all dread of this mysterious visitor vanished, — all anxiety to question more of his attributes or his history. His life itself became to me dear and precious. What if it should fail me in the steps of the process, whatever that was, by which the life of my Lilian might be saved!

The shades of evening were now closing in. I remembered that I had left Margrave without even food for many hours. I stole round to the back of the house, filled a basket with elements more generous than those of the former day; extracted fresh drugs from my stores, and, thus laden, hurried back to the hut. I found Margrave in the room below, seated on his mysterious coffer, leaning his face on his hand. When I entered, he looked up, and said, —

"You have neglected me. My strength is waning. Give me more of the cordial, for we have work before us to-night, and I need support."

He took for granted my assent to his wild experiment; and he was right.

I administered the cordial. I placed food before him, and this time he did not eat with repugnance. I poured out wine, and he drank it sparingly, but with ready compliance, saying, "In perfect health, I looked upon wine as poison; now it is like a foretaste of the glorious elixir."

After he had thus recruited himself, he seemed to acquire an energy that startlingly contrasted his languor the day before; the effort of breathing was scarcely perceptible; the colour came back to his cheeks; his bended frame rose elastic and erect.

"If I understood you rightly," said I, "the experiment you ask me to aid can be accomplished in a single night?"

"In a single night, — this night."

"Command me. Why not begin at once? What apparatus or chemical agencies do you need?"

"Ah!" said Margrave, "formerly, how I was misled!
30

Formerly, how my conjectures blundered! I thought, when I asked you to give a month to the experiment I wish to make, that I should need the subtlest skill of the chemist. I then believed, with Van Helmont, that the principle of life is a gas, and that the secret was but in the mode by which the gas might be rightly administered. But now all that I need is contained in this coffer, save one very simple material,—fuel sufficient for a steady fire for six hours. I see even that is at hand, piled up in your outhouse. And now for the substance itself,—to that you must guide me."

"Explain."

"Near this very spot is there not gold — in mines yet undiscovered? — and gold of the purest metal?"

"There is. What then? Do you, with the alchemists, blend in one discovery gold and life?"

"No. But it is only where the chemistry of earth or of man produces gold, that the substance from which the great pabulum of life is extracted by ferment can be found. Possibly, in the attempts at that transmutation of metals, which I think your own great chemist, Sir Humphry Davy, allowed might be possible, but held not to be worth the cost of the process,— possibly, in those attempts, some scanty grains of this substance were found by the alchemists, in the crucible, with grains of the metal as niggardly yielded by pitiful mimicry of Nature's stupendous laboratory; and from such grains enough of the essence might, perhaps, have been drawn forth, to add a few years of existence to some feeble graybeard,— granting, what rests on no proofs, that some of the alchemists reached an age rarely given to man. But it is not in the miserly crucible, it is in the matrix of Nature herself, that we must seek in prolific abundance Nature's grand principle,— life. As the loadstone is rife with the magnetic virtue, as amber contains the electric, so in this substance, to which we yet want a name, is found the bright life-giving fluid. In the old gold-mines of Asia and Europe the substance exists, but can rarely be met with. The soil for its nutriment may there be well-nigh exhausted. It is here, where Nature herself is all vital with youth, that the nutriment of youth must be sought. Near this spot is gold; guide me to it."

"You cannot come with me. The place which I know as auriferous is some miles distant, the way rugged. You cannot walk to it. It is true I have horses, but — "

"Do you think I have come this distance and not foreseen and forestalled all that I want for my object? Trouble yourself not with conjectures how I can arrive at the place. I have provided the means to arrive at and leave it. My litter and its bearers are in reach of my call. Give me your arm to the rising ground, fifty yards from your door."

I obeyed mechanically, stifling all surprise. I had made my resolve, and admitted no thought that could shake it.

When we reached the summit of the grassy hillock, which sloped from the road that led to the seaport, Margrave, after pausing to recover breath, lifted up his voice, in a key, not loud, but shrill and slow and prolonged, half cry and half chant, like the night-hawk's. Through the air — so limpid and still, bringing near far objects, far sounds — the voice pierced its way, artfully pausing, till wave after wave of the atmosphere bore and transmitted it on.

In a few minutes the call seemed re-echoed, so exactly, so cheerily, that for the moment I thought that the note was the mimicry of the shy mocking Lyre-Bird, which mimics so merrily all that it hears in its coverts, from the whir of the locust to the howl of the wild dog.

"What king," said the mystical charmer, and as he spoke he carelessly rested his hand on my shoulder, so that I trembled to feel that this dread son of Nature, Godless and soulless, who had been — and, my heart whispered, who still could be — my bane and mind-darkener, leaned upon me for support, as the spoilt younger-born on his brother, — "what king," said this cynical mocker, with his beautiful boyish face, — "what king in your civilized Europe has the sway of a chief of the East? What link is so strong between mortal and mortal, as that between lord and slave? I transport yon poor fools from the land of their birth; they preserve here their old habits, — obedience and awe. They would wait till they starved in the solitude,— wait to hearken and answer my call. And I, who thus rule them, or charm them — I use and despise them. They know that, and yet serve me! Between you and me, my philosopher, there is but one thing worth living for,— life for oneself."

Is it age, is it youth, that thus shocks all my sense, in my solemn completeness of man? Perhaps, in great capitals, young men of pleasure will answer, "It is youth; and we think what he says!" Young friends, I do not believe you.

———◆———

CHAPTER LXXX.

ALONG the grass-track I saw now, under the moon, just risen, a strange procession, never seen before in Australian pastures. It moved on, noiselessly but quickly. We descended the hillock, and met it on the way,— a sable litter, borne by four men, in unfamiliar Eastern garments; two other servitors, more bravely dressed, with yataghans and silver-hilted pistols in their belts, preceded this sombre equipage. Perhaps Margrave divined the disdainful thought that passed through my mind, vaguely and half-unconsciously; for he said, with a hollow, bitter laugh that had replaced the lively peal of his once melodious mirth,—

"A little leisure and a little gold, and your raw colonist, too, will have the tastes of a pacha."

I made no answer. I had ceased to care who and what was my tempter. To me his whole being was resolved into one problem: Had he a secret by which death could be turned from Lilian?

But now, as the litter halted, from the long dark shadow which it cast upon the turf the figure of a woman emerged and stood before us. The outlines of her shape were lost in the loose folds of a black mantle, and the features of her face were hidden by a black veil, except only the dark, bright, solemn eyes. Her stature was lofty, her bearing majestic, whether in movement or repose.

Margrave accosted her in some language unknown to me. She replied in what seemed to me the same tongue. The tones of her voice were sweet, but inexpressibly mournful. The words that they uttered appeared intended to warn, or deprecate, or dissuade; but they called to Margrave's brow a lowering frown, and drew from his lips a burst of unmistakable anger. The woman rejoined, in the same melancholy music of voice. And Margrave then, leaning his arm upon her shoulder, as he had leaned it on mine, drew her away from the group into a neighbouring copse of the flowering eucalypti,— mystic trees, never changing the hues of their pale-green leaves, ever shifting the tints of their ash-gray, shedding bark. For some moments I gazed on the two human forms, dimly seen by the glinting moonlight through the gaps in the foliage. Then turning away my eyes, I saw, standing close at my side, a man whom I had not noticed before. His footstep, as it stole to me, had fallen on the sward without sound. His dress, though Oriental, differed from that of his companions, both in shape and colour; fitting close to the breast, leaving the arms bare to the elbow, and of a uniform ghastly white, as are the cerements of the grave. His visage was even darker than those of the Syrians or Arabs behind him, and his features were those of a bird of prey,— the beak of the eagle, but the eye of the vulture. His cheeks were hollow; the arms, crossed on his breast, were long and fleshless. Yet in that skeleton form there was a something which conveyed the idea of a serpent's suppleness and strength; and as the hungry, watchful eyes met my own startled gaze, I recoiled impulsively with that inward warning of danger which is conveyed to man, as to inferior animals, in the very aspect of the creatures that sting or devour. At my movement the man inclined his head in the submissive Eastern salutation, and spoke in his foreign tongue, softly, humbly, fawningly, to judge by his tone and his gesture.

I moved yet farther away from him with loathing, and now the human thought flashed upon me: was I, in truth, exposed to no danger in trusting myself to the mercy of the weird and remorseless master of those hirelings from the East,— seven men in number, two at least of them formidably armed, and docile as bloodhounds to the hunter, who has only to show them their prey? But fear of man like myself is not my weakness; where fear found its way to my heart, it was through the doubts or the fancies in which man like myself disappeared in the attributes, dark and unknown, which we give to a fiend or a spectre. And, perhaps, if I could have paused to analyze my own sensations, the very presence of this escort — creatures of flesh and blood — lessened the dread of my incomprehensible tempter. Rather, a hundred times, front and defy those seven Eastern slaves — I, haughty son of the Anglo-Saxon who conquers all races because he fears no odds — than have seen again on the walls of my threshold the luminous, bodiless Shadow! Besides: Lilian! Lilian! for one chance of saving her life, however wild and chimerical that chance might be, I would have shrunk not a foot from the march of an army.

Thus reassured and thus resolved, I advanced, with a smile of disdain, to meet Margrave and his veiled companion, as they now came from the moonlit copse.

"Well," I said to him, with an irony that unconsciously mimicked his own, "have you taken advice with your nurse? I assume that the dark form by your side is that of Ayesha."

The woman looked at me from her sable veil, with her steadfast solemn eyes, and said, in English, though with a foreign accent: "The nurse born in Asia is but wise through her love; the pale son of Europe is wise through his art. The nurse says, 'Forbear!' Do you say, 'Adventure'?"

"Peace!" exclaimed Margrave, stamping his foot on the ground. "I take no counsel from either; it is for me to resolve, for you to obey, and for him to aid. Night is come, and we waste it; move on."

The woman made no reply, nor did I. He took my arm and walked back to the hut. The barbaric escort followed. When we reached the door of the building, Margrave said a few words to the woman and to the litter-bearers. They en-

tered the hut with us. Margrave pointed out to the woman
his coffer, to the men the fuel stowed in the outhouse. Both
were borne away and placed within the litter. Meanwhile,
I took from the table, on which it was carelessly thrown,
the light hatchet that I habitually carried with me in my
rambles.

"Do you think that you need that idle weapon?" said
Margrave. "Do you fear the good faith of my swarthy
attendants?"

"Nay, take the hatchet yourself; its use is to sever the
gold from the quartz in which we may find it embedded, or to
clear, as this shovel, which will also be needed, from the
slight soil above it, the ore that the mine in the mountain
flings forth, as the sea casts its waifs on the sands."

"Give me your hand, fellow-labourer!" said Margrave,
joyfully. "Ah, there is no faltering terror in this pulse! I
was not mistaken in the Man. What rests, but the Place and
the Hour? I shall live! I shall live!"

CHAPTER LXXXI.

MARGRAVE now entered the litter, and the Veiled Woman
drew the black curtains round him. I walked on, as the
guide, some yards in advance. The air was still, heavy, and
parched with the breath of the Australasian sirocco.

We passed through the meadow-lands, studded with slumbering flocks; we followed the branch of the creek, which was
linked to its source in the mountains by many a trickling
waterfall; we threaded the gloom of stunted, misshapen trees,
gnarled with the stringy bark which makes one of the signs
of the strata that nourish gold; and at length the moon, now
in all her pomp of light, mid-heaven amongst her subject
stars, gleamed through the fissures of the cave, on whose
floor lay the relics of antediluvian races, and rested in one

flood of silvery splendour upon the hollows of the extinct volcano, with tufts of dank herbage, and wide spaces of paler sward, covering the gold below,— Gold, the dumb symbol of organized Matter's great mystery, storing in itself, according as Mind, the informer of Matter, can distinguish its uses, evil and good, bane and blessing.

Hitherto the Veiled Woman had remained in the rear, with the white-robed, skeleton-like image that had crept to my side unawares with its noiseless step. Thus in each winding turn of the difficult path at which the convoy following behind me came into sight, I had seen, first, the two gayly-dressed, armed men, next the black bier-like litter, and last the Black-veiled Woman and the White-robed Skeleton.

But now, as I halted on the tableland, backed by the mountain and fronting the valley, the woman left her companion, passed by the litter and the armed men, and paused by my side, at the mouth of the moonlit cavern.

There for a moment she stood, silent, the procession below mounting upward laboriously and slow; then she turned to me, and her veil was withdrawn.

The face on which I gazed was wondrously beautiful, and severely awful. There was neither youth nor age, but beauty, mature and majestic as that of a marble Demeter.

"Do you believe in that which you seek?" she asked, in her foreign, melodious, melancholy accents.

"I have no belief," was my answer. "True science has none. True science questions all things, takes nothing upon credit. It knows but three states of the mind,— Denial, Conviction, and that vast interval between the two, which is not belief, but suspense of judgment."

The woman let fall her veil, moved from me, and seated herself on a crag above that cleft between mountain and creek, to which, when I had first discovered the gold that the land nourished, the rain from the clouds had given the rushing life of the cataract; but which now, in the drought and the hush of the skies, was but a dead pile of stones.

The litter now ascended the height: its bearers halted; a lean hand tore the curtains aside, and Margrave descended, leaning, this time, not on the Black-veiled Woman, but on the White-robed Skeleton.

There, as he stood, the moon shone full on his wasted form; on his face, resolute, cheerful, and proud, despite its hollowed outlines and sicklied hues. He raised his head, spoke in the language unknown to me, and the armed men and the litter-bearers grouped round him, bending low, their eyes fixed on the ground. The Veiled Woman rose slowly and came to his side, motioning away, with a mute sign, the ghastly form on which he leaned, and passing round him silently, instead, her own sustaining arm. Margrave spoke again a few sentences, of which I could not even guess the meaning. When he had concluded, the armed men and the litter-bearers came nearer to his feet, knelt down, and kissed his hand. They then rose, and took from the bier-like vehicle the coffer and the fuel. This done, they lifted again the litter, and again, preceded by the armed men, the procession descended down the sloping hillside, down into the valley below.

Margrave now whispered, for some moments, into the ear of the hideous creature who had made way for the Veiled Woman. The grim skeleton bowed his head submissively, and strode noiselessly away through the long grasses,— the slender stems, trampled under his stealthy feet, relifting themselves, as after a passing wind. And thus he, too, sank out of sight down into the valley below. On the tableland of the hill remained only we three,— Margrave, myself, and the Veiled Woman.

She had reseated herself apart, on the gray crag above the dried torrent. He stood at the entrance of the cavern, round the sides of which clustered parasital plants, with flowers of all colours, some amongst them opening their petals and exhaling their fragrance only in the hours of night; so that, as his form filled up the jaws of the dull arch, obscuring the moonbeam that strove to pierce the shadows that slept within, it stood now — wan and blighted — as I had seen it first, radiant and joyous, literally "framed in blooms."

CHAPTER LXXXII.

"So," said Margrave, turning to me, "under the soil that
spreads around us lies the gold which to you and to me is at
this moment of no value, except as a guide to its twin-born,
— the regenerator of life!"

"You have not yet described to me the nature of the substance which we are to explore, nor of the process by which
the virtues you impute to it are to be extracted."

"Let us first find the gold, and instead of describing the
life-amber, so let me call it, I will point it out to your own
eyes. As to the process, your share in it is so simple, that
you will ask me why I seek aid from a chemist. The life-
amber, when found, has but to be subjected to heat and fer-
mentation for six hours; it will be placed, in a small caldron
which that coffer contains, over the fire which that fuel will
feed. To give effect to the process, certain alkalies and other
ingredients are required; but these are prepared, and mine is
the task to commingle them. From your science as chemist
I need and ask nought. In you I have sought only the aid of
a man."

"If that be so, why, indeed, seek me at all? Why not confide in those swarthy attendants, who doubtless are slaves to
your orders?"

"Confide in slaves! when the first task enjoined to them
would be to discover, and refrain from purloining gold!
Seven such unscrupulous knaves, or even one such, and I,
thus defenceless and feeble! Such is not the work that wise
masters confide to fierce slaves. But that is the least of the
reasons which exclude them from my choice, and fix my
choice of assistant on you. Do you forget what I told you
of the danger which the Dervish declared no bribe I could
offer could tempt him a second time to brave?"

"I remember now; those words had passed away from my
mind."

"And because they had passed away from your mind, I chose you for my comrade. I need a man by whom danger is scorned."

"But in the process of which you tell me I see no possible danger unless the ingredients you mix in your caldron have poisonous fumes."

"It is not that. The ingredients I use are not poisons."

"What other danger, except you dread your own Eastern slaves? But, if so, why lead them to these solitudes; and, if so, why not bid me be armed?"

"The Eastern slaves, fulfilling my commands, wait for my summons where their eyes cannot see what we do. The danger is of a kind in which the boldest son of the East would be more craven, perhaps, than the daintiest Sybarite of Europe, who would shrink from a panther and laugh at a ghost. In the creed of the Dervish, and of all who adventure into that realm of nature which is closed to philosophy and open to magic, there are races in the magnitude of space unseen as animalcules in the world of a drop. For the tribes of the drop, science has its microscope. Of the host of yon azure Infinite magic gains sight, and through them gains command over fluid conductors that link all the parts of creation. Of these races, some are wholly indifferent to man, some benign to him, and some dreadly hostile. In all the regular and prescribed conditions of mortal being, this magic realm seems as blank and tenantless as yon vacant air. But when a seeker of powers beyond the rude functions by which man plies the clockwork that measures his hours, and stops when its chain reaches the end of its coil, strives to pass over those boundaries at which philosophy says, 'Knowledge ends,' — then he is like all other travellers in regions unknown; he must propitiate or brave the tribes that are hostile, — must depend for his life on the tribes that are friendly. Though your science discredits the alchemist's dogmas, your learning informs you that all alchemists were not ignorant impostors; yet those whose discoveries prove them to have been the nearest allies to your practical knowledge, ever hint in their mystical works at the reality of that realm which is open to magic,

— ever hint that some means less familiar than furnace and bellows are essential to him who explores the elixir of life. He who once quaffs that elixir, obtains in his very veins the bright fluid by which he transmits the force of his will to agencies dormant in nature, to giants unseen in the space. And here, as he passes the boundary which divides his allotted and normal mortality from the regions and races that magic alone can explore, so, here, he breaks down the safeguard between himself and the tribes that are hostile. Is it not ever thus between man and man? Let a race the most gentle and timid and civilized dwell on one side a river or mountain, and another have home in the region beyond, each, if it pass not the intervening barrier, may with each live in peace. But if ambitious adventurers scale the mountain, or cross the river, with design to subdue and enslave the population they boldly invade, then all the invaded arise in wrath and defiance, — the neighbours are changed into foes. And therefore this process — by which a simple though rare material of nature is made to yield to a mortal the boon of a life which brings, with its glorious resistance to Time, desires and faculties to subject to its service beings that dwell in the earth and the air and the deep — has ever been one of the same peril which an invader must brave when he crosses the bounds of his nation. By this key alone you unlock all the cells of the alchemist's lore; by this alone understand how a labour, which a chemist's crudest apprentice could perform, has baffled the giant fathers of all your dwarfed children of science. Nature, that stores this priceless boon, seems to shrink from conceding it to man; the invisible tribes that abhor him, oppose themselves to the gain that might give them a master. The duller of those who were the life-seekers of old would have told you how some chance, trivial, unlooked-for, foiled their grand hope at the very point of fruition, — some doltish mistake, some improvident oversight, a defect in the sulphur, a wild overflow in the quicksilver, or a flaw in the bellows, or a pupil who failed to replenish the fuel, by falling asleep by the furnace. The invisible foes seldom vouchsafe to make themselves visible where they can frustrate the bungler, as they mock at his toils from their ambush. But the mightier adventurers, equally foiled in despite of their patience and skill, would have said, 'Not with us rests the fault; we neglected no caution, we failed from no oversight. But out from the caldron dread faces arose, and the spectres or demons dismayed and baffled us.' Such, then, is the danger which seems so appalling to a son of the East, as it seemed to a seer in the dark age of Europe. But we can deride all its threats, you and I. For myself, I own frankly I take all the safety that the charms and resources of magic bestow. You, for your safety, have the cultured and disciplined reason which reduces all fantasies to nervous impressions; and I rely on the courage of one who has questioned, unquailing, the Luminous Shadow, and wrested from the hand of the magician himself the wand which concentred the wonders of will!"

To this strange and long discourse I listened without interruption, and now quietly answered,—

"I do not merit the trust you affect in my courage; but I am now on my guard against the cheats of the fancy, and the fumes of a vapour can scarcely bewilder the brain in the open air of this mountain-land. I believe in no races like those which you tell me lie viewless in space, as do gases. I believe not in magic; I ask not its aids, and I dread not its terrors. For the rest, I am confident of one mournful courage,—the courage that comes from despair. I submit to your guidance, whatever it be, as a sufferer whom colleges doom to the grave submits to the quack who says, 'Take my specific and live!' My life is nought in itself; my life lives in another. You and I are both brave from despair; you would turn death from yourself, I would turn death from one I love more than myself. Both know how little aid we can win from the colleges, and both, therefore, turn to the promises most audaciously cheering. Dervish or magician, alchemist or phantom, what care you and I? And if they fail us, what then? They cannot fail us more than the colleges do!"

CHAPTER LXXXIII.

The gold has been gained with an easy labour. I knew where to seek for it, whether under the turf or in the bed of the creek. But Margrave's eyes, hungrily gazing round every spot from which the ore was disburied, could not detect the substance of which he alone knew the outward appearance. I had begun to believe that, even in the description given to him of this material, he had been credulously duped, and that no such material existed, when, coming back from the bed of the watercourse, I saw a faint yellow gleam amidst the roots of a giant parasite plant, the leaves and blossoms of which climbed up the sides of the cave with its antediluvian relics. The gleam was the gleam of gold, and on removing the loose earth round the roots of the plant, we came on — No, I will not, I dare not, describe it. The gold-digger would cast it aside, the naturalist would pause not to heed it; and did I describe it, and chemistry deign to subject it to analysis, could chemistry alone detach or discover its boasted virtues?

Its particles, indeed, are very minute, not seeming readily to crystallize with each other; each in itself of uniform shape and size, spherical as the egg which contains the germ of life, and small as the egg from which the life of an insect may quicken.

But Margrave's keen eye caught sight of the atoms upcast by the light of the moon. He exclaimed to me, "Found! I shall live!" And then, as he gathered up the grains with tremulous hands, he called out to the Veiled Woman, hitherto still seated motionless on the crag. At his word she rose and went to the place hard by, where the fuel was piled, busying herself there. I had no leisure to heed her. I continued my search in the soft and yielding soil that time and the decay of vegetable life had accumulated over the Pre-Adamite strata on which the arch of the cave rested its mighty keystone.

When we had collected of these particles about thrice as much as a man might hold in his hand, we seemed to have exhausted their bed. We continued still to find gold, but no more of the delicate substance, to which, in our sight, gold was as dross.

"Enough," then said Margrave, reluctantly desisting. "What we have gained already will suffice for a life thrice as long as legend attributes to Haroun. I shall live,— I shall live through the centuries."

"Forget not that I claim my share."

"Your share — yours! True — your half of my life! It is true." He paused with a low, ironical, malignant laugh; and then added, as he rose and turned away, "But the work is yet to be done."

CHAPTER LXXXIV.

WHILE we had thus laboured and found, Ayesha had placed the fuel where the moonlight fell fullest on the sward of the tableland,— a part of it already piled as for a fire, the rest of it heaped confusedly close at hand; and by the pile she had placed the coffer. And there she stood, her arms folded under her mantle, her dark image seeming darker still as the moonlight whitened all the ground from which the image rose motionless. Margrave opened his coffer, the Veiled Woman did not aid him, and I watched in silence, while he as silently made his weird and wizard-like preparations.

CHAPTER LXXXV.

ON the ground a wide circle was traced by a small rod, tipped apparently with sponge saturated with some combustible naphtha-like fluid, so that a pale lambent flame followed

the course of the rod as Margrave guided it, burning up the
herbage over which it played, and leaving a distinct ring, like
that which, in our lovely native fable-talk, we call the "Fairy's
Ring," but yet more visible because marked in phosphores-
cent light. On the ring thus formed were placed twelve
small lamps, fed with the fluid from the same vessel, and
lighted by the same rod. The light emitted by the lamps
was more vivid and brilliant than that which circled round
the ring.

Within the circumference, and immediately round the wood-
pile, Margrave traced certain geometrical figures, in which —
not without a shudder, that I overcame at once by a strong
effort of will in murmuring to myself the name of "Lilian"
— I recognized the interlaced triangles which my own hand,
in the spell enforced on a sleep-walker, had described on the
floor of the wizard's pavilion. The figures were traced, like
the circle, in flame, and at the point of each triangle (four in
number) was placed a lamp, brilliant as those on the ring.
This task performed, the caldron, based on an iron tripod,
was placed on the wood-pile. And then the woman, before,
inactive and unheeding, slowly advanced, knelt by the
pile, and lighted it. The dry wood crackled and the flame
burst forth, licking the rims of the caldron with tongues of
fire.

Margrave flung into the caldron the particles we had collected, poured over them first a liquid, colourless as water,
from the largest of the vessels drawn from his coffer, and
then, more sparingly, drops from small crystal phials, like
the phials I had seen in the hand of Philip Derval.

Having surmounted my first impulse of awe, I watched
these proceedings, curious yet disdainful, as one who watches
the mummeries of an enchanter on the stage.

"If," thought I, "these are but artful devices to inebriate
and fool my own imagination, my imagination is on its guard,
and reason shall not, this time, sleep at her post!"

"And now," said Margrave, "I consign to you the easy
task by which you are to merit your share of the elixir. It
is my task to feed and replenish the caldron; it is Ayesha's

Margrave, Dr. Fenwick, and Ayesha preparing the Elixir
of Life.

to heed the fire, which must not for a moment relax in its measured and steady heat. Your task is the lightest of all: it is but to renew from this vessel the fluid that burns in the lamps, and on the ring. Observe, the contents of the vessel must be thriftily husbanded; there is enough, but not more than enough, to sustain the light in the lamps, on the lines traced round the caldron, and on the farther ring, for six hours. The compounds dissolved in this fluid are scarce,— only obtainable in the East, and even in the East months might have passed before I could have increased my supply. I had no months to waste. Replenish, then, the light only when it begins to flicker or fade. Take heed, above all, that no part of the outer ring — no, not an inch — and no lamp of the twelve, that are to its zodiac like stars, fade for one moment in darkness."

I took the crystal vessel from his hand.

"The vessel is small," said I, "and what is yet left of its contents is but scanty; whether its drops suffice to replenish the lights I cannot guess,— I can but obey your instructions. But, more important by far than the light to the lamps and the circle, which in Asia or Africa might scare away the wild beasts unknown to this land — more important than light to a lamp, is the strength to your frame, weak magician! What will support you through six weary hours of night-watch?"

"Hope," answered Margrave, with a ray of his old dazzling style. "Hope! I shall live,— I shall live through the centuries!"

CHAPTER LXXXVI.

ONE hour passed away; the fagots under the caldron burned clear in the sullen sultry air. The materials within began to seethe, and their colour, at first dull and turbid, changed into a pale-rose hue; from time to time the Veiled Woman replenished the fire, after she had done so reseating herself close by

31

the pyre, with her head bowed over her knees, and her face
hid under her veil.

The lights in the lamps and along the ring and the triangles
now began to pale. I resupplied their nutriment from the
crystal vessel. As yet nothing strange startled my eye or
my ear beyond the rim of the circle, — nothing audible, save,
at a distance, the musical wheel-like click of the locusts, and,
farther still, in the forest, the howl of the wild dogs, that
never bark; nothing visible, but the trees and the mountain-
range girding the plains silvered by the moon, and the arch
of the cavern, the flush of wild blooms on its sides, and the
gleam of dry bones on its floor, where the moonlight shot into
the gloom.

The second hour passed like the first. I had taken my
stand by the side of Margrave, watching with him the process
at work in the caldron, when I felt the ground slightly vibrate beneath my feet, and, looking up, it seemed as if all
the plains beyond the circle were heaving like the swell of
the sea, and as if in the air itself there was a perceptible
tremor.

I placed my hand on Margrave's shoulder and whispered,
"To me earth and air seem to vibrate. Do they seem to vibrate to you?"

"I know not, I care not," he answered impetuously. "The
essence is bursting the shell that confined it. Here are my
air and my earth! Trouble me not. Look to the circle! feed
the lamps if they fail."

I passed by the Veiled Woman as I walked towards a place
in the ring in which the flame was waning dim; and I whispered to her the same question which I had whispered to
Margrave. She looked slowly around, and answered, "So is
it before the Invisible make themselves visible! Did I not
bid him forbear?" Her head again drooped on her breast,
and her watch was again fixed on the fire.

I advanced to the circle and stooped to replenish the light
where it waned. As I did so, on my arm, which stretched
somewhat beyond the line of the ring, I felt a shock like that
of electricity. The arm fell to my side numbed and nerve-

less, and from my hand dropped, but within the ring, the vessel that contained the fluid. Recovering my surprise or my stun, hastily with the other hand I caught up the vessel, but some of the scanty liquid was already spilled on the sward; and I saw with a thrill of dismay, that contrasted indeed the tranquil indifference with which I had first undertaken my charge, how small a supply was now left.

I went back to Margrave, and told him of the shock, and of its consequence in the waste of the liquid.

"Beware," said he, "that not a motion of the arm, not an inch of the foot, pass the verge of the ring; and if the fluid be thus unhappily stinted, reserve all that is left for the protecting circle and the twelve outer lamps! See how the Grand Work advances! how the hues in the caldron are glowing blood-red through the film on the surface!"

And now four hours of the six were gone; my arm had gradually recovered its strength. Neither the ring nor the lamps had again required replenishing; perhaps their light was exhausted less quickly, as it was no longer to be exposed to the rays of the intense Australian moon. Clouds had gathered over the sky, and though the moon gleamed at times in the gaps that they left in blue air, her beam was more hazy and dulled. The locusts no longer were heard in the grass, nor the howl of the dogs in the forest. Out of the circle, the stillness was profound.

And about this time I saw distinctly in the distance a vast Eye! It drew nearer and nearer, seeming to move from the ground at the height of some lofty giant. Its gaze riveted mine; my blood curdled in the blaze from its angry ball; and now as it advanced larger and larger, other Eyes, as if of giants in its train, grew out from the space in its rear; numbers on numbers, like the spear-heads of some Eastern army, seen afar by pale warders of battlements doomed to the dust. My voice long refused an utterance to my awe; at length it burst forth shrill and loud,—

"Look! look! Those terrible Eyes! Legions on legions! And hark! that tramp of numberless feet; *they* are not seen, but the hollows of earth echo the sound of their march!"

Margrave, more than ever intent on the caldron, in which, from time to time, he kept dropping powders or essences drawn forth from his coffer, looked up, defyingly, fiercely. —

"Ye come," he said, in a low mutter, his once mighty voice sounding hollow and labouring, but fearless and firm, — "ye come, — not to conquer, vain rebels! — ye whose dark chief I struck down at my feet in the tomb where my spell had raised up the ghost of your first human master, the Chaldee! Earth and air have their armies still faithful to me, and still I remember the war-song that summons them up to confront you! Ayesha! Ayesha! recall the wild troth that we pledged amongst roses; recall the dread bond by which we united our sway over hosts that yet own thee as queen, though my sceptre is broken, my diadem reft from my brows!"

The Veiled Woman rose at this adjuration. Her veil now was withdrawn, and the blaze of the fire between Margrave and herself flushed, as with the rosy bloom of youth, the grand beauty of her softened face. It was seen, detached as it were, from her dark-mantled form; seen through the mist of the vapours which rose from the caldron, framing it round like the clouds that are yieldingly pierced by the light of the evening star.

Through the haze of the vapour came her voice, more musical, more plaintive than I had heard it before, but far softer, more tender; still in her foreign tongue; the words unknown to me, and yet their sense, perhaps, made intelligible by the love, which has one common language and one common look to all who have loved, — the love unmistakably heard in the loving tone, unmistakably seen in the loving face.

A moment or so more, and she had come round from the opposite side of the fire-pile, and bending over Margrave's upturned brow, kissed it quietly, solemnly; and then her countenance grew fierce, her crest rose erect; it was the lioness protecting her young. She stretched forth her arm from the black mantle, athwart the pale front that now again bent over the caldron, — stretched it towards the haunted and hollow-sounding space beyond, in the gesture of one whose right hand has the sway of the sceptre. And then her voice stole on the air in the music of a chant, not loud, yet far-reaching; so thrilling, so sweet, and yet so solemn, that I could at once comprehend how legend united of old the spell of enchantment with the power of song. All that I recalled of the effects which, in the former time, Margrave's strange chants had produced on the ear that they ravished and the thoughts they confused, was but as the wild bird's imitative carol, compared to the depth and the art and the soul of the singer, whose voice seemed endowed with a charm to en-thrall all the tribes of creation, though the language it used for that charm might to them, as to me, be unknown. As the song ceased, I heard, from behind, sounds like those I had heard in the spaces before me,— the tramp of invisible feet, the whir of invisible wings, as if armies were marching to aid against armies in march to destroy.

"Look not in front nor around," said Ayesha. "Look, like him, on the caldron below. The circle and the lamps are yet bright; I will tell you when the light again fails."

I dropped my eyes on the caldron.

"See," whispered Margrave, "the sparkles at last begin to arise, and the rose-hues to deepen,— signs that we near the last process."

CHAPTER LXXXVII.

The fifth hour had passed away, when Ayesha said to me, "Lo! the circle is fading; the lamps grow dim. Look now without fear on the space beyond; the eyes that appalled thee are again lost in air, as lightnings that fleet back into cloud."

I looked up, and the spectres had vanished. The sky was tinged with sulphurous hues, the red and the black inter-mixed. I replenished the lamps and the ring in front, thriftily, heedfully; but when I came to the sixth lamp, not a drop in the vessel that fed them was left. In a vague dis-may, I now looked round the half of the wide circle in rear of the two bended figures intent on the caldron. All along that disk the light was already broken, here and there flickering up, here and there dying down; the six lamps in that half of the circle still twinkled, but faintly, as stars shrinking fast from the dawn of day. But it was not the fading shine in that half of the magical ring which daunted my eye and quickened with terror the pulse of my heart; the Bushland beyond was on fire. From the background of the forest rose the flame and the smoke,— the smoke, there, still half smothering the flame. But along the width of the grasses and herbage, between the verge of the forest and the bed of the water-creek just below the raised platform from which I beheld the dread conflagration, the fire was advancing,— wave upon wave, clear and red against the columns of rock behind,—as the rush of a flood through the mists of some Alp crowned with lightnings.

Roused from my stun at the first sight of a danger not foreseen by the mind I had steeled against far rarer portents of Nature, I cared no more for the lamps and the circle. Hurrying back to Ayesha, I exclaimed: "The phantoms have gone from the spaces in front; but what incantation or spell can arrest the red march of the foe, speeding on in the rear! While we gazed on the caldron of life, behind us, unheeded, behold the Destroyer!"

Ayesha looked, and made no reply; but, as by involuntary instinct, bowed her majestic head, then rearing it erect, placed herself yet more immediately before the wasted form of the young magician (he still bending over the caldron, and hearing me not in the absorption and hope of his watch),— placed herself before him, as the bird whose first care is her fledgling.

As we two there stood, fronting the deluge of fire, we heard Margrave behind us, murmuring low, "See the bubbles of light, how they sparkle and dance! I shall live, I shall live!" And his words scarcely died in our ears before, crash upon crash, came the fall of the age-long trees in the forest; and nearer, all near us, through the blazing grasses, the hiss of the serpents, the scream of the birds, and the bellow and

tramp of the herds plunging wild through the billowy red of
their pastures.

Ayesha now wound her arms around Margrave, and wrenched
him, reluctant and struggling, from his watch over the seeth-
ing caldron. In rebuke of his angry exclamations, she pointed
to the march of the fire, spoke in sorrowful tones a few words
in her own language, and then, appealing to me in English,
said,—

"I tell him that here the Spirits who oppose us have summoned a foe that is deaf to my voice, and — "

"And," exclaimed Margrave, no longer with gasp and effort, but with the swell of a voice which drowned all the discords of terror and of agony sent forth from the Phlegethon
burning below,— "and this witch, whom I trusted, is a vile
slave and impostor, more desiring my death than my life.
She thinks that in life I should scorn and forsake her, that in
death I should die in her arms! Sorceress, avaunt! Art
thou useless and powerless now when I need thee most? Go!
Let the world be one funeral pyre! What to *me* is the world?
My world is my life! Thou knowest that my last hope is
here,— that all the strength left me this night will die down,
like the lamps in the circle, unless the elixir restore it. Bold
friend, spurn that sorceress away. Hours yet ere those flames
can assail us! A few minutes more, and life to your Lilian
and me!"

Thus having said, Margrave turned from us, and cast into
the caldron the last essence yet left in his empty coffer.

Ayesha silently drew her black veil over her face; and
turned, with the being she loved, from the terror he scorned,
to share in the hope that he cherished.

Thus left alone, with my reason disenthralled, disenchanted,
I surveyed more calmly the extent of the actual peril with
which we were threatened, and the peril seemed less, so
surveyed.

It is true all the Bush-land behind, almost up to the bed of
the creek, was on fire; but the grasses, through which the
flame spread so rapidly, ceased at the opposite marge of the
creek. Watery pools were still, at intervals, left in the bed

of the creek, shining tremulous, like waves of fire, in the
glare reflected from the burning land; and even where the
water failed, the stony course of the exhausted rivulet was a
barrier against the march of the conflagration. Thus, unless
the wind, now still, should rise, and waft some sparks to the
parched combustible herbage immediately around us, we were
saved from the fire, and our work might yet be achieved.

I whispered to Ayesha the conclusion to which I came.

"Thinkest thou," she answered, without raising her mournful head, "that the Agencies of Nature are the movements of
chance? The Spirits I invoked to his aid are leagued with
the hosts that assail. A mightier than I am has doomed
him!"

Scarcely had she uttered these words before Margrave exclaimed, "Behold how the Rose of the alchemist's dream en-
larges its blooms from the folds of its petals! I shall live,
I shall live!"

I looked, and the liquid which glowed in the caldron had
now taken a splendour that mocked all comparisons borrowed
from the lustre of gems. In its prevalent colour it had, indeed, the dazzle and flash of the ruby; but out from the mass
of the molten red, broke coruscations of all prismal hues,
shooting, shifting, in a play that made the wavelets themselves seem living things, sensible of their joy. No longer
was there scum or film upon the surface; only ever and anon
a light rosy vapour floating up, and quick lost in the haggard, heavy, sulphurous air, hot with the conflagration rushing towards us from behind. And these coruscations formed,
on the surface of the molten ruby, literally the shape of a
Rose, its leaves made distinct in their outlines by sparks of
emerald and diamond and sapphire.

Even while gazing on this animated liquid lustre, a buoyant
delight seemed infused into my senses; all terrors conceived
before were annulled; the phantoms, whose armies had filled
the wide spaces in front, were forgotten; the crash of the
forest behind was unheard. In the reflection of that glory,
Margrave's wan cheek seemed already restored to the radiance
it wore when I saw it first in the framework of blooms.

As I gazed, thus enchanted, a cold hand touched my own.

"Hush!" whispered Ayesha, from the black veil, against which the rays of the caldron fell blunt, and absorbed into Dark. "Behind us, the light of the circle is extinct, but there we are guarded from all save the brutal and soulless destroyers. But before! — but before! — see, two of the lamps have died out! — see the blank of the gap in the ring! Guard that breach, — there the demons will enter."

"Not a drop is there left in his vessel by which to :.plenish the lamps on the ring."

"Advance, then; thou hast still the light of the soul, and the demons may recoil before a soul that is dauntless and guiltless. If not, Three are lost! — as it is, One is doomed."

Thus adjured, silently, involuntarily, I passed from the Veiled Woman's side, over the sere lines on the turf which had been traced by the triangles of light long since extinguished, and towards the verge of the circle. As I advanced, overhead rushed a dark cloud of wings, — birds dislodged from the forest on fire, and screaming, in dissonant terror, as they flew towards the farthermost mountains; close by my feet hissed and glided the snakes, driven forth from their blazing coverts, and glancing through the ring, unscared by its waning lamps; all undulating by me, bright-eyed and hissing, all made innocuous by fear, — even the terrible Death-adder, which I trampled on as I halted at the verge of the circle, did not turn to bite, but crept harmless away. I halted at the gap between the two dead lamps, and bowed my head to look again into the crystal vessel. Were there, indeed, no lingering drops yet left, if but to recruit the lamps for some priceless minutes more? As I thus stood, right into the gap between the two dead lamps strode a gigantic Foot. All the rest of the form was unseen; only, as volume after volume of smoke poured on from the burning land behind, it seemed as if one great column of vapour, eddying round, settled itself aloft from the circle, and that out from that column strode the giant Foot. And, as strode the Foot, so with it came, like the sound of its tread, a roll of muttered thunder.

I recoiled, with a cry that rang loud through the lurid air.

"Courage!" said the voice of Ayesha. "Trembling soul, yield not an inch to the demon!"

At the charm, the wonderful charm, in the tone of the Veiled Woman's voice, my will seemed to take a force more sublime than its own. I folded my arms on my breast, and stood as if rooted to the spot, confronting the column of smoke and the stride of the giant Foot. And the Foot halted, mute.

Again, in the momentary hush of that suspense, I heard a voice,— it was Margrave's.

"The last hour expires, the work is accomplished! Come! come! Aid me to take the caldron from the fire; and quick! —or a drop may be wasted in vapour — the Elixir of Life from the caldron!"

At that cry I receded, and the Foot advanced.

And at that moment, suddenly, unawares, from behind, I was stricken down. Over me, as I lay, swept a whirlwind of trampling hoofs and glancing horns. The herds, in their flight from the burning pastures, had rushed over the bed of the watercourse, scaled the slopes of the banks. Snorting and bellowing, they plunged their blind way to the mountains. One cry alone, more wild than their own savage blare, pierced the reek through which the Brute Hurricane swept. At that cry of wrath and despair I struggled to rise, again dashed to earth by the hoofs and the horns. But was it the dream-like deceit of my reeling senses, or did I see that giant Foot stride past through the close-serried ranks of the maddening herds? Did I hear, distinct through all the huge uproar of animal terror, the roll of low thunder which followed the stride of that Foot?

CHAPTER LXXXVIII.

WHEN my sense had recovered its shock, and my eyes looked dizzily round, the charge of the beasts had swept by; and of all the wild tribes which had invaded the magical circle, the only lingerer was the brown Death-adder, coiled close by the spot where my head had rested. Beside the extinguished lamps which the hoofs had confusedly scattered, the fire, arrested by the watercourse, had consumed the grasses that fed it, and there the plains stretched, black and desert as the Phlegræan Field of the Poet's Hell. But the fire still raged in the forest beyond,— white flames, soaring up from the trunks of the tallest trees, and forming, through the sullen dark of the smoke-reek, innumerable pillars of fire, like the halls in the City of fiends.

Gathering myself up, I turned my eyes from the terrible pomp of the lurid forest, and looked fearfully down on the hoof-trampled sward for my two companions.

I saw the dark image of Ayesha still seated, still bending, as I had seen it last. I saw a pale hand feebly grasping the rim of the magical caldron, which lay, hurled down from its tripod by the rush of the beasts, yards away from the dim fading embers of the scattered wood-pyre. I saw the faint writhings of a frail wasted frame, over which the Veiled Woman was bending. I saw, as I moved with bruised limbs to the place, close by the lips of the dying magician, the flash of the ruby-like essence spilled on the sward, and, meteorlike, sparkling up from the torn tufts of herbage.

I now reached Margrave's side. Bending over him as the Veiled Woman bent, and as I sought gently to raise him, he turned his face, fiercely faltering out, "Touch me not, rob me not! *You* share with me! Never! never! These glorious drops are all mine! Die all else! I will live! I will live!" Writhing himself from my pitying arms, he plunged his face amidst the beautiful, playful flame of the essence, as if to lap the elixir with lips scorched away from its intolerable burning. Suddenly, with a low shriek, he fell back, his face upturned to mine, and on that face unmistakably reigned Death!

Then Ayesha tenderly, silently, drew the young head to her lap, and it vanished from my sight behind her black veil.

I knelt beside her, murmuring some trite words of comfort; but she heeded me not, rocking herself to and fro as the mother who cradles a child to sleep. Soon the fast-flickering sparkles of the lost elixir died out on the grass; and with their last sportive diamond-like tremble of light, up, in all the suddenness of Australian day, rose the sun, lifting himself royally above the mountain-tops, and fronting the meaner blaze of the forest as a young king fronts his rebels. And as there, where the bush-fires had ravaged, all was a desert, so there, where their fury had not spread, all was a garden. Afar, at the foot of the mountains, the fugitive herds were grazing; the cranes, flocking back to the pools, renewed the strange grace of their gambols; and the great kingfisher, whose laugh, half in mirth, half in mockery, leads the choir that welcome the morn, — which in Europe is night, — alighted bold on the roof of the cavern, whose floors were still white with the bones of races, extinct before — so helpless through instincts, so royal through Soul — rose MAN!

But there, on the ground where the dazzling elixir had wasted its virtues, — there the herbage already had a freshness of verdure which, amid the duller sward round it, was like an oasis of green in a desert. And there wild-flowers, whose chill hues the eye would have scarcely distinguished the day before, now glittered forth in blooms of unfamiliar beauty. Towards that spot were attracted myriads of happy insects, whose hum of intense joy was musically loud. But the form of the life-seeking sorcerer lay rigid and stark; blind to the bloom of the wild-flowers, deaf to the glee of the insects, — one hand still resting heavily on the rim of the emptied caldron, and the face still hid behind the Black Veil. What! the wondrous elixir, sought with such hope and well-nigh achieved through such dread, fleeting back to the earth from which its material was drawn, to give bloom, indeed,—but to herbs: joy indeed,— but to insects!

And now, in the flash of the sun, slowly wound up the slopes that led to the circle the same barbaric procession which had sunk into the valley under the ray of the moon. The armed men came first, stalwart and tall, their vests brave with crimson and golden lace, their weapons gayly gleaming with holiday silver. After them, the Black Litter. As they came to the place, Ayesha, not raising her head, spoke to them in her own Eastern tongue. A wail was her answer. The armed men bounded forward, and the bearers left the litter.

All gathered round the dead form with the face concealed under the black veil; all knelt, and all wept. Far in the distance, at the foot of the blue mountains, a crowd of the savage natives had risen up as if from the earth; they stood motionless, leaning on their clubs and spears, and looking towards the spot on which we were,— strangely thus brought into the landscape, as if they too, the wild dwellers on the verge which Humanity guards from the Brute, were among the mourners for the mysterious Child of mysterious Nature! And still, in the herbage, hummed the small insects, and still, from the cavern, laughed the great kingfisher. I said to Ayesha, "Farewell! your love mourns the dead, mine calls me to the living. You are now with your own people, they may console you; say if I can assist."

"There is no consolation for me! What mourner can be consoled if the dead die forever? Nothing for him is left but a grave; that grave shall be in the land where the song of Ayesha first lulled him to sleep. Thou assist ME,— thou, the wise man of Europe! From me ask assistance. What road wilt thou take to thy home?"

"There is but one road known to me through the maze of the solitude,— that which we took to this upland."

"On that road Death lurks, and awaits thee! Blind dupe, couldst thou think that if the grand secret of life had been won, he whose head rests on my lap would have yielded thee one petty drop of the essence which had filched from his store of life but a moment? Me, who so loved and so cherished him,— me he would have doomed to the pitiless cord of my servant, the Strangler, if my death could have lengthened a hair-breadth the span of his being. But what matters to me his crime or his madness? I loved him! I loved him!"

She bowed her veiled head lower and lower; perhaps, under the veil, her lips kissed the lips of the dead. Then she said whisperingly,—

"Juma the Strangler, whose word never failed to his master, whose prey never slipped from his snare, waits thy step on the road to thy home! But thy death cannot now profit the dead, the beloved. And thou hast had pity for him who took but thine aid to design thy destruction. His life is lost, thine is saved."

She spoke no more in the tongue that I could interpret. She spoke, in the language unknown, a few murmured words to her swarthy attendants; then the armed men, still weeping, rose, and made a dumb sign to me to go with them. I understood by the sign that Ayesha had told them to guard me on my way; but she gave no reply to my parting thanks.

———◆———

CHAPTER LXXXIX.

I DESCENDED into the valley; the armed men followed. The path, on that side of the watercourse not reached by the flames, wound through meadows still green, or amidst groves still unscathed. As a turning in the way brought in front of my sight the place I had left behind, I beheld the black litter creeping down the descent, with its curtains closed, and the Veiled Woman walking by its side. But soon the funeral procession was lost to my eyes, and the thoughts that it roused were erased. The waves in man's brain are like those of the sea, rushing on, rushing over the wrecks of the vessels that rode on their surface, to sink, after storm, in their deeps.

One thought cast forth into the future now mastered all in the past: "Was Lilian living still?" Absorbed in the gloom of that thought, hurried on by the goad that my heart, in its tortured impatience, gave to my footstep, I outstripped the slow stride of the armed men, and, midway between the place I had left and the home which I sped to, came, far in advance of my guards, into the thicket in which the bushmen had started up in my path on the night that Lilian had watched for my coming. The earth at my feet was rife with creeping plants and many-coloured flowers, the sky overhead was half-hid by motionless pines. Suddenly, whether crawling out from the herbage, or dropping down from the trees, by my side stood the white-robed and skeleton form,— Ayesha's attendant, the Strangler.

I sprang from him shuddering, then halted and faced him. The hideous creature crept towards me, cringing and fawning, making signs of humble good-will and servile obeisance. Again I recoiled,— wrathfully, loathingly; turned my face homeward, and fled on. I thought I had baffled his chase, when, just at the mouth of the thicket, he dropped from a bough in my path close behind me. Before I could turn, some dark muffling substance fell between my sight and the sun, and I felt a fierce strain at my throat. But the words of Ayesha had warned me; with one rapid hand I seized the noose before it could tighten too closely, with the other I tore the bandage away from my eyes, and, wheeling round on the dastardly foe, struck him down with one spurn of my foot. His hand, as he fell, relaxed its hold on the noose; I freed my throat from the knot, and sprang from the copse into the broad sunlit plain. I saw no more of the armed men or the Strangler. Panting and breathless, I paused at last before the fence, fragrant with blossoms, that divided my home from the solitude.

The windows of Lilian's room were darkened; all within the house seemed still.

Darkened and silenced Home! with the light and sounds of the jocund day all around it. Was there yet hope in the Universe for me? All to which I had trusted Hope had broken down!   The anchors I had forged for her hold in the beds of the ocean, her stay from the drifts of the storm, had snapped like the reeds which pierce the side that leans on the barb of their points, and confides in the strength of their stems.   No hope in the baffled resources of recognized knowledge!   No hope in the daring adventures of Mind into regions unknown; vain alike the calm lore of the practised physician, and the magical arts of the fated Enchanter!   I had fled from the commonplace teachings of Nature, to explore in her Shadow-land marvels at variance with reason.   Made brave by the grandeur of love, I had opposed without quailing the stride of the Demon, and by hope, when fruition seemed nearest, had been trodden into dust by the hoofs of the beast!   And yet, all the while, I had scorned, as a dream more wild than the word of a sorcerer, the hope that the old man and the child, the wise and the ignorant, took from their souls as inborn.   Man and fiend had alike failed a mind, not ignoble, not skilless, not abjectly craven; alike failed a heart not feeble and selfish, not dead to the hero's devotion, willing to shed every drop of its blood for a something more dear than an animal's life for itself!   What remained — what remained for man's hope? — man's mind and man's heart thus exhausting their all with no other result but despair!   What remained but the mystery of mysteries, so clear to the sunrise of childhood, the sunset of age, only dimmed by the clouds which collect round the noon of our manhood?   Where yet was Hope found?   In the soul; in its every-day impulse to supplicate comfort and light, from the Giver of soul, wherever the heart is afflicted, the mind is obscured.

Then the words of Ayesha rushed over me: "What mourner can be consoled, if the Dead die forever?"   Through every pulse of my frame throbbed that dread question.   All Nature around seemed to murmur it.   And suddenly, as by a flash from heaven, the grand truth in Faber's grand reasoning shone on me, and lighted up all, within and without.   Man alone, of all earthly creatures, asks, "Can the Dead die forever?" and the instinct that urges the question is God's answer to man!   No instinct is given in vain.

And born with the instinct of soul is the instinct that leads the soul from the seen to the unseen, from time to eternity, from the torrent that foams towards the Ocean of Death, to the source of its stream, far aloft from the Ocean.

"Know thyself," said the Pythian of old. "That precept descended from Heaven." Know thyself! Is that maxim wise? If so, know thy soul. But never yet did man come to the thorough conviction of soul but what he acknowledged the sovereign necessity of prayer. In my awe, in my rapture, all my thoughts seemed enlarged and illumined and exalted. I prayed,— all my soul seemed one prayer. All my past, with its pride and presumption and folly, grew distinct as the form of a penitent, kneeling for pardon before setting forth on the pilgrimage vowed to a shrine. And, sure now, in the deeps of a soul first revealed to myself, that the Dead do not die forever, my human love soared beyond its brief trial of terror and sorrow. Daring not to ask from Heaven's wisdom that Lilian, for my sake, might not yet pass away from the earth, I prayed that my soul might be fitted to bear with submission whatever my Maker might ordain. And if surviving her — without whom no beam from yon material sun could ever warm into joy a morrow in human life — so to guide my steps that they might rejoin her at last, and, in rejoining, regain forever!

How trivial now became the weird riddle that, a little while before, had been clothed in so solemn an awe! What mattered it to the vast interests involved in the clear recognition of Soul and Hereafter, whether or not my bodily sense, for a moment, obscured the face of the Nature I should one day behold as a spirit? Doubtless the sights and the sounds which had haunted the last gloomy night, the calm reason of Faber would strip of their magical seemings; the Eyes in the space and the Foot in the circle might be those of no terrible Demons, but of the wild's savage children whom I had seen, halting, curious and mute, in the light of the morning. The tremor of the ground (if not, as heretofore, explicable by the illusory impression of my own treacherous senses) might be but the natural effect of elements struggling yet under a soil unmistakably charred by volcanoes. The luminous atoms dissolved in the caldron might as little be fraught with a vital elixir as are the splendours of naphtha or phosphor. As it was, the weird rite had no magic result. The magician was not rent limb from limb by the fiends. By causes as natural as ever extinguished life's spark in the frail lamp of clay, he had died out of sight — under the black veil.

What mattered henceforth to Faith, in its far grander questions and answers, whether Reason, in Faber, or Fancy, in me, supplied the more probable guess at a hieroglyph which, if construed aright, was but a word of small mark in the mystical language of Nature? If all the arts of enchantment recorded by Fable were attested by facts which Sages were forced to acknowledge, Sages would sooner or later find some cause for such portents — not supernatural. But what Sage, without cause supernatural, both without and within him, can guess at the wonders he views in the growth of a blade of grass, or the tints on an insect's wing? Whatever art Man can achieve in his progress through time, Man's reason, in time, can suffice to explain. But the wonders of God? These belong to the Infinite; and these, O Immortal! will but develop new wonder on wonder, though thy sight be a spirit's, and thy leisure to track and to solve an eternity.

As I raised my face from my clasped hands, my eyes fell full upon a form standing in the open doorway. There, where on the night in which Lilian's long struggle for reason and life had begun, the Luminous Shadow had been beheld in the doubtful light of a dying moon and a yet hazy dawn; there, on the threshold, gathering round her bright locks the aureole of the glorious sun, stood Amy, the blessed child! And as I gazed, drawing nearer and nearer to the silenced house, and that Image of Peace on its threshold, I felt that Hope met me at the door, — Hope in the child's steadfast eyes, Hope in the child's welcoming smile!

"I was at watch for you," whispered Amy. "All is well."

"She lives still — she lives! Thank God! thank God!"

"She lives, — she will recover!" said another voice, as my head sunk on Faber's shoulder. "For some hours in the night her sleep was disturbed, convulsed. I feared, then, the worst. Suddenly, just before the dawn, she called out aloud, still in sleep,—

"'The cold and dark shadow has passed away from me and from Allen,— passed away from us both forever!'

"And from that moment the fever left her; the breathing became soft, the pulse steady, and the colour stole gradually back to her cheek. The crisis is past. Nature's benign Disposer has permitted Nature to restore your life's gentle partner, heart to heart, mind to mind — "

"And soul to soul," I cried, in my solemn joy. "Above as below, soul to soul!" Then, at a sign from Faber, the child took me by the hand and led me up the stairs into Lilian's room.

Again those dear arms closed around me in wife-like and holy love, and those true lips kissed away my tears,— even as now, at the distance of years from that happy morn, while I write the last words of this Strange Story, the same faithful arms close around me, the same tender lips kiss away my tears.

THE END.

www.ingramcontent.com/pod-product-compliance
Lightning Source LLC
Chambersburg PA
CBHW031211050726
47495CB00017B/177